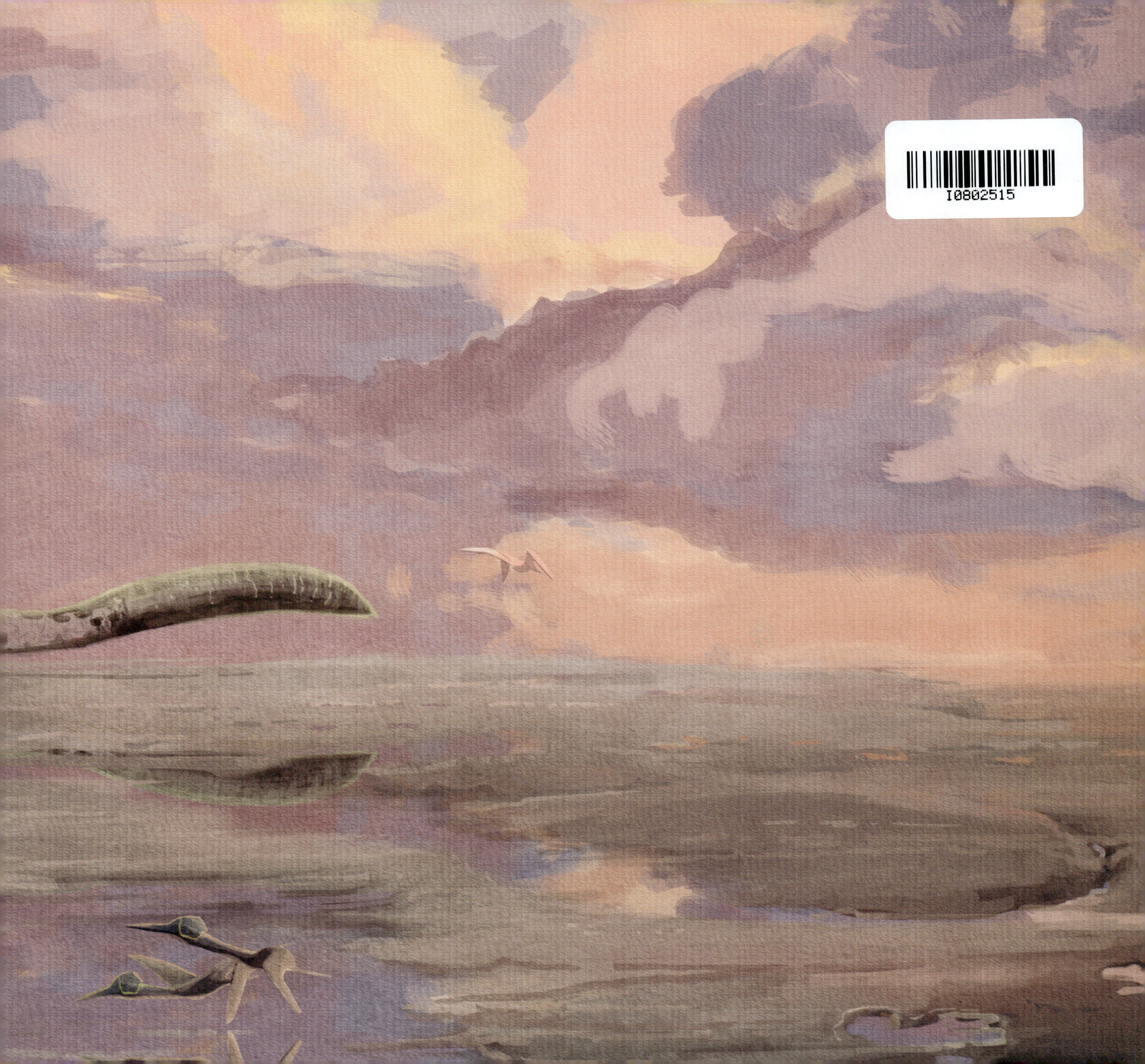

I0802515

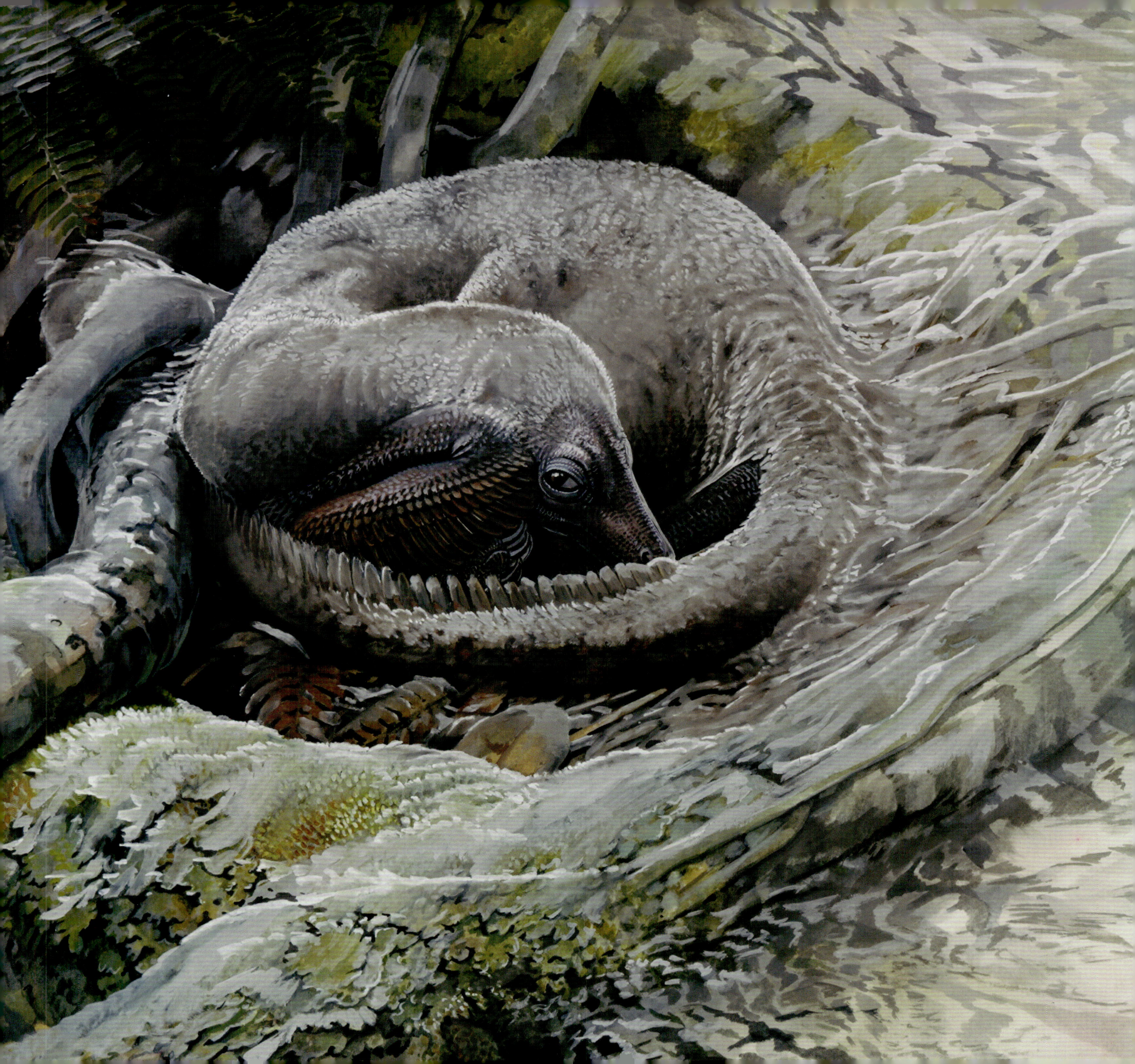

(Front endpaper)
Short-Limbed Spinosaurine and Pterosaurs
Mark Witton
Digital, 2016

(Previous page)
Mei long
Peter Schouten
Watercolor, Gouache, 2005

(Below)
***Eoabelisaurus* sketch**
Andrey Atuchin
Pencils, Digital Sketch, 2012

(Title page)
Dromaeosaur Pair
Emily Willoughby
Pencils, 2015

(Foreword)
Yearling *Allosaurus*
Mark Witton
Digital, 2015

(Back endpaper)
Sinornithosaurus millenii
Peter Schouten
Watercolor, Gouache, 2006

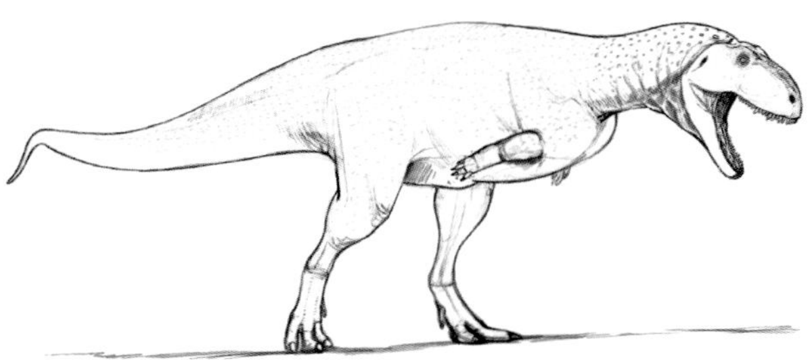

DINOSAUR ART II
ISBN 9781785653988

Published by
Titan Books
A division of Titan Publishing Group Ltd.
144 Southwark St.
London
SE1 0UP

First edition: October 2017
10 9 8 7 6 5 4 3 2 1

Scientific Consultant
Dr. Darren Naish

Featured animal text written by Steve White

ACKNOWLEDGEMENTS
First and foremost, I'd like to thank the all the artists who took time out of their hectic schedules to gather their artwork and answer my questions (special thanks to those to whom English wasn't their first language!). I must also and once again thank Darren Naish for all his invaluable help and insights; Mike Ryan and Bob Nicholls for their valued contributions; Team Titan – Jo Boylett, Tim Scrivens and especially designer Natalie Clay – who fashioned such a wonderful book; and finally, thanks to Jess Woo, whose excellent copy-editing skills should not go unacknowledged, and who offered support and encouragement throughout this book's long but thoroughly enjoyable labor.

Titan Books would like to thank everyone involved for their hard work in assembling volume II of this series. Special thanks to Steve White for bringing together another 10 leading lights of the paleoart world, and to Darren Naish for once more lending his expertise. Thanks also to Brian Switek for the Foreword and Robert Nicholls for the fascinating Introduction. Most importantly, deepest thanks to the 10 artists featured herein for sharing their beautiful art and unique perspectives.

All artwork is copyright © 2017 the respective artist: Robert Nicholls, Sergey Krasovskiy, Emily Willoughby, Peter Schouten, Andrey Atuchin, Jason Brougham, Vitali Klatt, Tom Björklund, Mark Witton, Julio Lacerda, Velizar Simeonovski.

Did you enjoy this book? We love to hear from our readers. Please e-mail us at: readerfeedback@titanemail.com or write to Reader Feedback at the above address.

To receive advance information, news, competitions, and exclusive offers online, please sign up for the Titan newsletter on our website: **www.titanbooks.com**

No part of this publication may be reproduced, stored in a retrieval system, or transmitted, in any form or by any means without the prior written permission of the publisher, nor be otherwise circulated in any form of binding or cover other than that in which it is published and without a similar condition being imposed on the subsequent purchaser.

A CIP catalogue record for this title is available from the British Library.

Printed and bound in China.

DINOSAUR ART II

THE CUTTING EDGE OF PALEOART

EDITED BY STEVE WHITE

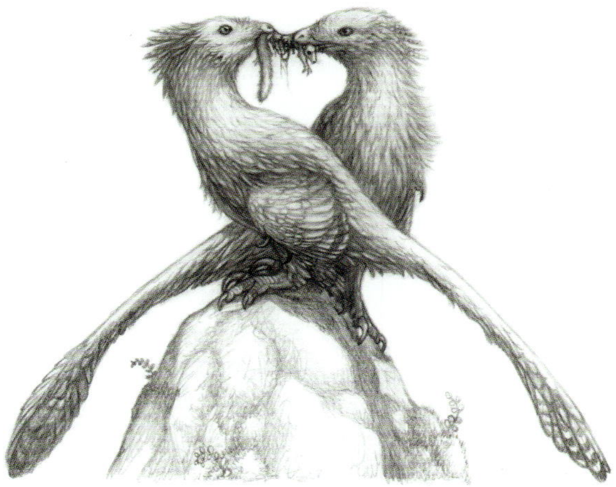

TITAN BOOKS

CONTENTS

FOREWORD

Paleontology cannot exist without art. It's as much a part of a paleontologist's toolkit as a rock hammer or microscope, and has been from the very beginning.

Decades before anyone even thought of mounting a reconstructed dinosaur skeleton, or there was even enough fossil material to do it, artists were bringing dinosaurs to life. They were the chief interpreters of lost worlds, bringing skills from the humanities to visualize the cutting edge of scientific discovery. John Martin's apocalyptic watercolor *The Country of the Iguanodon* [1837], Benjamin Waterhouse Hawkins' gnarly Crystal Palace sculptures [unveiled in 1854], Charles R. Knight's *Leaping Laelaps* [1896], and Rudolph Zallinger's *Age of Reptiles* fresco secco [1943-1947] would easily be as cozy displayed in any fine art museum as a museum hall filled to the brim with fossil bones.

Yet the innovation and skill of paleoart is often forgotten, pushed to the side as kitsch because of the subject matter. And even among scientifically minded aficionados, the relationship between paleontology and paleoart is often expressed as one of cause and effect. An intrepid paleontologist ventures into the field, finds something new, reconstructs that lost species in the lab, and the artist is then brought in to put flesh on old bones and create a vivid image to express the science and dazzle the public.

This chain of events isn't necessarily wrong, but it downplays paleoart into a product of science rather than an essential part of paleontology's ultimate endeavor – to envision what extinct species were like when alive. There are questions of musculature, skin, scales, fuzz, color, behavior, ecology, and more, requiring that paleoartists develop technical expertise that surely give them claim to the title of honorary paleontologist, at the least. At its heart, paleoart is the effort to breathe life into something dead, catching something of the spark that rests in ancient remains. The same motives drive art as well as science.

This connection goes deeper still, cycling back into the science itself. The explosive imagery of the late 20th century's Dinosaur Renaissance – which lifted dragging tails, moved swamp monsters onto land, and gave dinosaurs a supercharged metabolism – wouldn't have been possible if paleoart of previous decades hadn't been dominated by images of dinosaurs as stupid, sluggish lizards.

The paleoart feedback loop continues to this day. Whether to feather a dinosaur or not, for example, is now a standard question in restoring ancient life, phylogenetics and evolutionary hypotheses coming into play with aesthetics and the image of dinosaurs as we currently understand them. Given that science is ongoing and self-correcting, future paleontologists are likely to look at images made today and point out all the things we got wrong or didn't know. That's a feature, not a fault, underscoring the importance of art not only in expressing science but providing fodder for debate over how our knowledge has changed.

We live in a very special time for paleoart. Not only are there a greater number of illustrators than ever before – their work showing up everywhere from museum exhibits to Instagram and DeviantArt – but there's been a groundswell of pieces that aim to challenge tropes and the status quo. Traditional depictions of snarling sabercats and roaring tyrannosaurs are not enough anymore. Efforts such as the "All Yesterdays" movement are pushing to explore the full range of prehistoric behaviors and anatomical possibilities that go beyond the hidebound depictions that marked much of the last century. Some of this art will turn out to be off the mark or maybe even create new tropes that will be later overturned, but it's nonetheless refreshing to see paleoart enter its experimental phase.

What you hold in your hands, then, is a nested time capsule. At the most obvious level, this book is a passport to lost worlds that we will never get to see with our own eyes. They are vignettes drawn and reassembled from what's left of real, fantastic creatures that fire our imaginations like nothing else. But it is also an anthology of paleoart at the dawn of the 21st century, when fluffy dinosaurs pop with color. This is how we see the past from where we stand today, and what a wonderful view it is.

BRIAN SWITEK
Author of *Written in Stone, My Beloved Brontosaurus,* and *Prehistoric Predators*

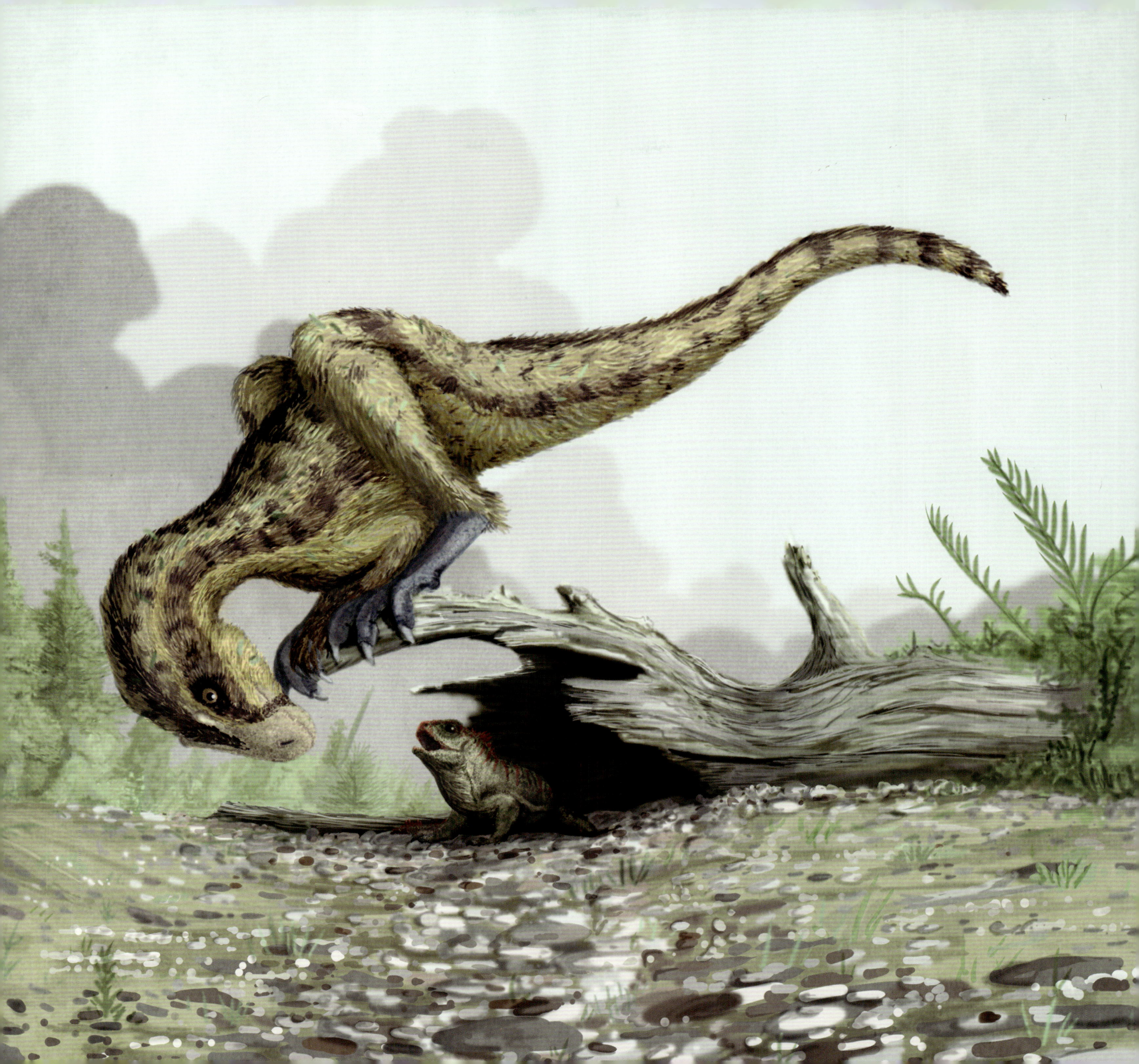

"THE WORLD'S MOST ACCURATE DINOSAUR RECONSTRUCTION"
PALEOART FROM THE INSIDE OUT

BY ROBERT NICHOLLS

When I was a boy, a weekend or school holiday was judged successful if it was spent drawing dinosaurs without experiencing the necessity to change out of my pyjamas. I am now in my forties and, although I don't own He-Man pyjamas anymore, I must admit that this spare-time evaluation criterion hasn't entirely changed. Other interests and hobbies have come and gone, but my thirst for recreating distant worlds with art tools and materials is as strong as ever. If this sounds familiar to you, you might fantasise about making a living from paleoart. If you do, then welcome to the club, my friend! And I have some good and bad news for you.

First, the bad news; there are no jobs in paleoart. But the good news is that you can make a living for yourself as a freelance artist. This is what I did, and if I can do it, so can you. I'm a dyslexic country boy who had zero paleontology education and zero experience of self-employment, but I achieved my goal by attending paleontology conferences and by working ridiculously hard. It is difficult enough making a living as a generalist illustrator, so limiting oneself to the subject of paleontology is like a greengrocer deciding to sell only organic turnips. And thoroughly researched paleoartwork is like an organic turnip; not everyone is interested in paying for the finest quality. Clients usually want artwork cheap and fast. However, at the risk of sounding like a luminous-toothed motivational speaker, if you want it enough, you can do it.

The primary thing that separates a good paleoartist from the average Joe or Jane is the reconstruction process. Without a reconstruction process, paleo-themed artworks can only be science fiction, a meme (a stereotypical regurgitation of an artistic theme), or blatant plagiarism. Science fiction is fine so long as the artist is honest about the degree of speculation. Not all memes are bad or inaccurate either, but most of them are clichés and/or red herrings. Plagiarism is more serious and it is rife in paleoart, perhaps more than any other field of natural history art. I suspect plagiarism and paleoart memes are common because it is standard practice for artists to source picture references in books and on the internet. For most subjects this would be photographs of existing animals and objects, and that's fine, but for paleontological subjects the reference images will often be one or

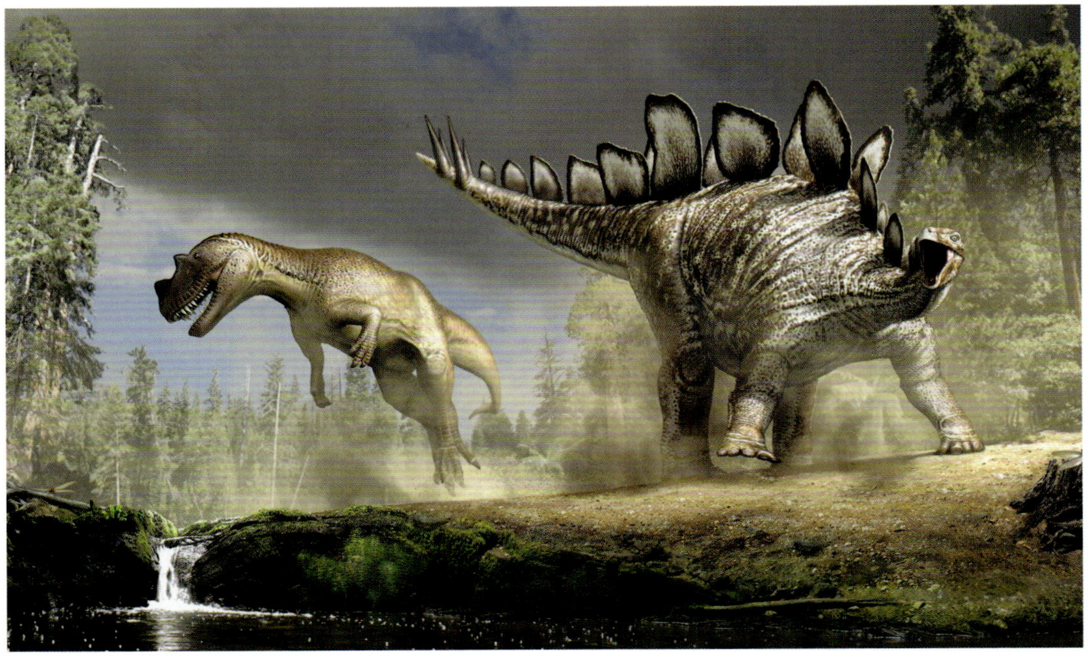

A Lesson Learned
Robert Nicholls
Digital/Photographic Composite, 2014
The London Natural History Museum's *Stegosaurus* "Sophie" defending herself against a predatory *Ceratosaurus*. The *Ceratosaurus* was rendered using a variety of fossil references and a Scott Hartman skeletal drawing.

two fossil photos to accompany a bunch of other artists' work. Copying another artist's work is fine when you are producing paleoart for fun, but if you want to be paid for your art you can't pass off other people's work as your own.

To overcome the time demands and complexities of paleo-reconstruction, many paleoartists rely on skeletal reconstructions by brilliant experts, such as Gregory S. Paul and Scott Hartman. I have, and I bet you have, too! In fact, I suspect Paul and Hartman are two of the most influential paleoartists of all time.Personally, I think it is long overdue for everyone to agree that whenever someone else's skeletal reconstruction has been used as a foundation for our work, the skeletal reconstruction artist should be credited. It is the very least we can do; they have saved us hundreds of hours of work and considerable expense not having to travel long distances to photograph and measure fossils. Having said this, over the past few years I have become increasingly uncomfortable using other artists' skeletal drawings as my primary reference. Doing so makes me feel a bit of a cheat and I want my paleoart to be 100% my own. No two artists will ever interpret fossils into a skeleton in precisely the same way, so it is now standard practice for me to attempt my own skeletal reconstructions. My skeletal drawings rarely take the form of a finished piece, like those of Paul and Hartman, but they are always meticulously proportioned. Most often they are simple pencil drawings, but they form an essential step in a rigorous inside-out reconstruction process.

To illustrate the complete inside-out paleo-reconstruction process I am going to talk through the production of a life-size *Psittacosaurus* model. I built this model for the research paper *3D Camouflage in an Ornithischian Dinosaur*, by Vinther *et al.*, published by *Current Biology* in 2016. It is not just a 3D reconstruction of a generic *Psittacosaurus*; it is a reconstruction of a specific individual *Psittacosaurus* on exhibit in the Naturmuseum Senckenberg in Frankfurt, Germany. It is currently unclear what species of *Psittacosaurus* this specimen is. It might be P. *lujiatunensis*, but it is probably not P. *mongoliensis*, as it is labelled in the museum. The fossil's code is SMF R 4970, but this is rather a mouthful, so from here on I will call the Senckenberg *Psittacosaurus* "Senck-Psittaco."

The Senck-Psittaco was fossilized in the sediment at the bottom of a freshwater lake. It is exposed belly up in the fossil, laid on its back with its feet in the air and showing us the underside of its "chin." The preservation is so good that the fossil possesses bones, teeth, tail "bristles" (or "keratinous epidermal appendages"), gastroliths, *and* fossilized melanosomes. In addition to allowing me to reconstruct its anatomy with great precision, the melanosomes enabled me to reconstruct the dinosaur's color patterns too. Therefore, my co-authors and I have enjoyed referring to the model as "the world's most accurate dinosaur reconstruction," but we are aware that it is impossible to know to what extent this statement is true. Without seeing a live Senck-Psittaco we cannot be certain of the model's accuracy, so we should probably say "world's most credible" or "most plausible." Nevertheless, the fossil possesses such an extraordinary amount of information about the anatomy and integument, I would argue that the model really must be a contender for most accurate non-avian dinosaur reconstruction ever created. You might not be convinced, so let me explain how it was built.

The first step in building the Senck-Psittaco was to gather reliable information and reference material. This is the same for all paleo-reconstructions, two- and three-dimensional. It is an irony that much of the art in paleoart is the skill of eliminating any gaps in our knowledge that will later need to be filled in with conjecture and, subsequently, self-expression (it is for this reason that some artists quite understandably consider paleoart a form of illustration and not art at all). So, I flew out to Frankfurt and

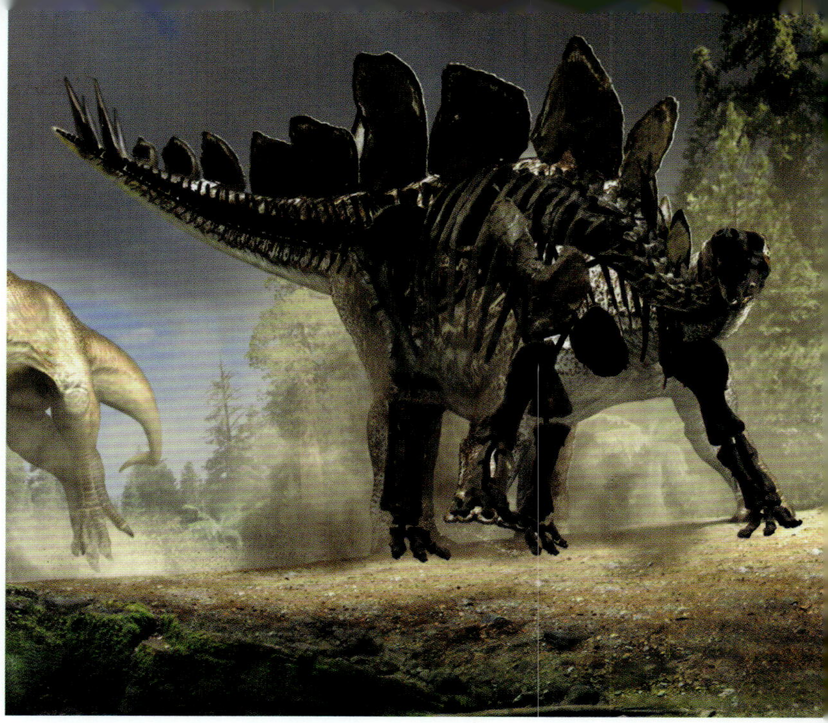

Getting It Accurate
The posture and anatomy of the *Stegosaurus* was determined by the skeletal mount exhibited in the London Natural History Museum. To capture the correct perspective, I laid on the floor under a desk to take the photo of the skeleton. I then reconstructed the *Stegosaurus* from the inside out by overlaying the soft tissues and eventually the integument. When the original photograph is placed over the final illustration (as above) you can see how closely I kept to the skeleton's proportions. This level of accuracy is only achievable by using an inside-out reconstruction process.

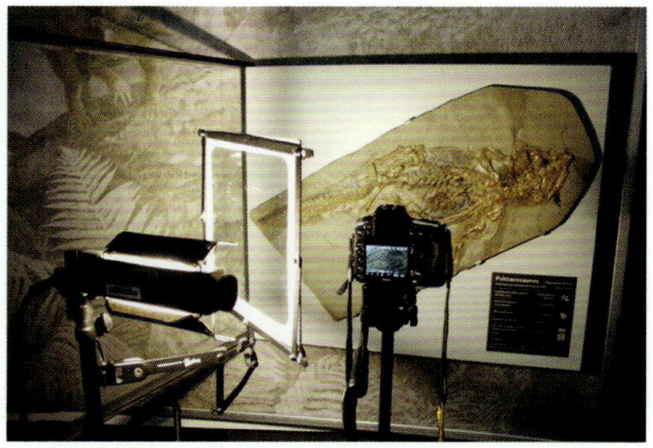

Cross Polarized Photography
The 800W tungsten light source was shone through a linear polarizing gel onto the fossil. The camera, a Nikon D800, enabled me to set the white balance to 3200K and take nice big TIFF photographs (5520 x 3680 pixels). The polarizing filter on the 60mm macro lens was rotated to exclude the subjective maximum (polarized) glare from the fossil's surface.

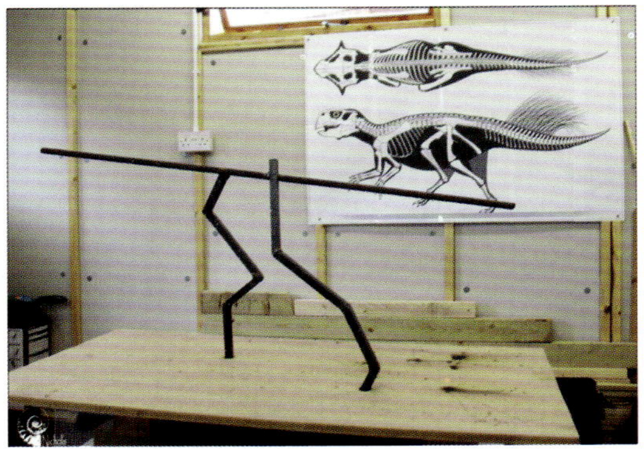

The Armature
The first stage of building a model is the armature. The armature is the sculpture's skeleton and it provides a strong and rigid foundation for the subsequent processes.

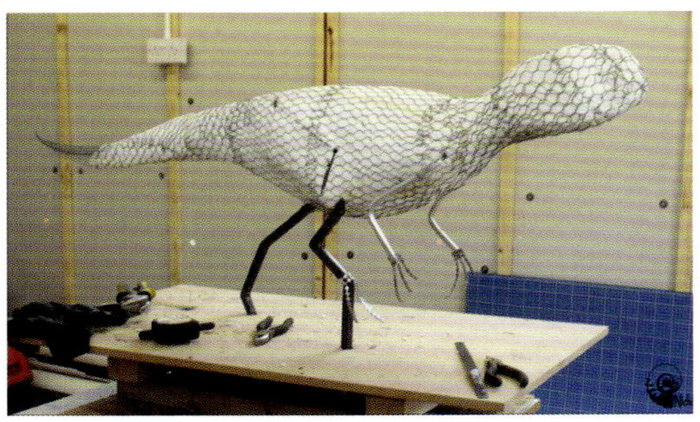

Bulking Out the Sculpture
The model is bulked out with polystyrene to speed up the sculpting process and reduce the quantity of heavy clay being supported by the armature. Wire mesh is wrapped around the polystyrene to provide a good texture for the clay to bond to.

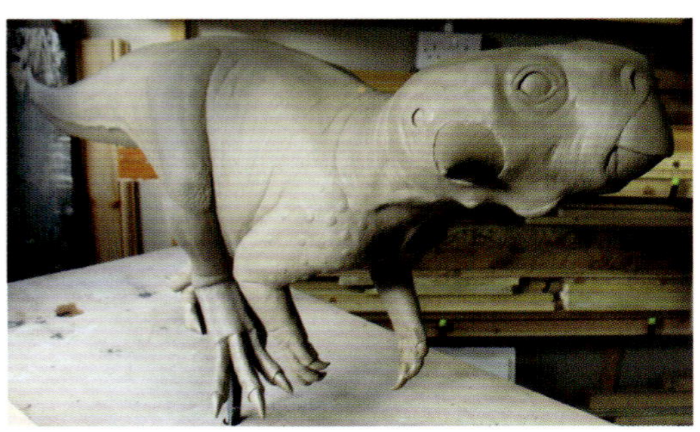

The Clay Sculpture
Sculptures come to life when the clay is added. It required weeks of painstaking sculpting to copy all the textures preserved in the fossil onto the model.

spent three days examining, measuring and photographing the Senck-Psittaco. I returned to Bristol, England, with a wealth of information, including two types of photograph; some were taken with a direct light source and the others were taken using cross polarized photography. The cross polarized photographs were perfect for capturing the preserved color patterns because the technique removes the reflected light. The regular photographs, meanwhile, were ideal for illustrating the fossil's relief, especially the shape of the bones. However, I didn't rely on the photographs for the Senck-Psittaco's proportions because even a basic 60mm macro lens can cause distortion. Instead, I relied on measurements taken directly from the fossil.

The first artwork I produced using my photos and measurements was a detailed drawing of the skeleton, in dorsal and lateral views. This drawing revealed a variety of important and surprising features that would greatly affected the appearance of the eventual sculpture. I love it when a reconstruction surprises me because it is confirmation that I have followed the evidence rather than any preconceived ideas I might have in my head. On this occasion the most pleasing skeletal characteristics included robust limbs, the ability to stand and move bipedally, and a proportionally large skull. To assist with reconstructing the flattened skull in three dimensions, Stephan Lautenschlager (University of Bristol) supplied me with a 3D print of a juvenile *Psittacosaurus lujiatunensis* skull and jaw (BSPG 2007 I 63). Stephan CT-scanned the juvenile skull and jaw then retro-deformed and mirrored it sagittally (divided it into left and right) to remove preservation artefacts. It was extremely useful and I only had to alter the dimensions very slightly to match those preserved in the Senck-Psittaco, which is an adult, not a juvenile. The most obvious of these slight alterations was the well-preserved keratinous horn on the specimen's left cheek. It is 4.9cm long but incomplete, so I calculated an approximate total length of 6cm by following the preserved curvature of the horn's margins. Also worth noting are the dorsoventrally deep but laterally narrow tail; and the ossified tendons along the dorsal vertebrae, which imply the barrel-like torso was not highly flexible. Finally, great care was taken to accurately represent the curvature of the ribs because they have a considerable effect on the shape of the body.

The tail brush is an integumentary feature but it is conspicuous in the skeletal drawing, so I guess now would be a good time to say a few things about it. The keratinous bristles on the tail, approximately 99 in total (I keep counting between 97 and 102), vary in length and taper to points at their distal ends. They all have a similar 2mm diameter near the roots, where they are overlaid by tail skin, and they appear to have grown from soft tissues directly above the neural spines. The bristles grow from the tail to create a brush with clear anterior and posterior edges, but the latter is a little obscured by the downward and backward curve of the bristles. I must admit that I had always been sceptical about these clear anterior and posterior edges. When I flew out to Frankfurt, I expected to find evidence that the brush continued further down the tail or towards the hip, but there was nothing in the Senck-Psittaco to suggest this was the case. So, for now at least, this species of *Psittacosaurus* must keep its wonderfully weird tail brush.

The second illustration I produced was of the soft tissues. Fortunately, there is some information regarding the volume of muscle preserved around the skeleton. However, because of the Senck-Psittaco's belly-up position, the picture is far from complete. Observable muscular characteristics include strong hind- and forelimbs, while the base of the tail is broad and powerful, supporting the theory that this dinosaur could walk bipedally. Much of the respiratory and digestive systems would be contained within the ribcage, but considerable volume was added to the abdomen to accommodate the capacious

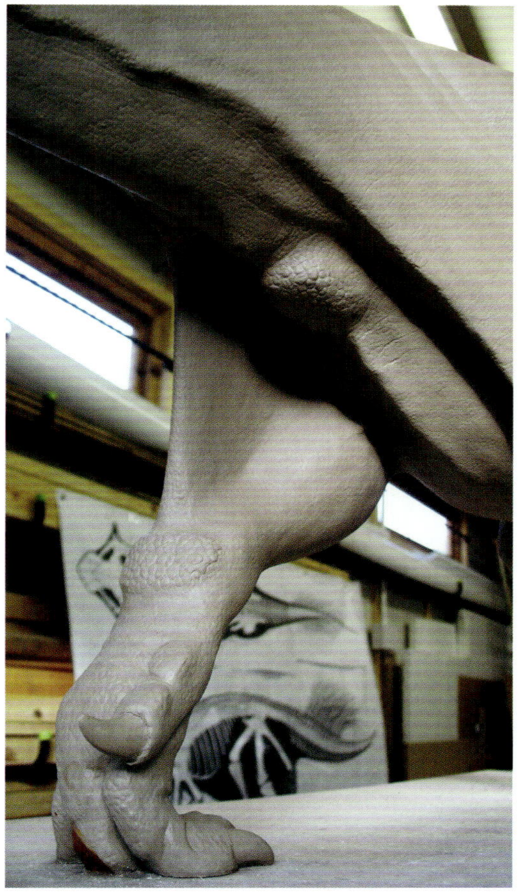

stomach and intestines of a herbivore. Volume was also added to the neck to accommodate the oesophagus and trachea. Information regarding the nervous and circulatory systems is not preserved and, because these soft tissues have little influence on the external form of extant animals, they were amalgamated into the Senck-Psittaco's musculature. The sensory organs – ears, eyes and nostrils – would be made conspicuous later during the sculpting process.

A particularly unique soft tissue feature is a patagium (skin flap) along the back of each hind limb, running from ankle to tail (*see above*). It is the feature that has caused the most excitement. No doubt some of you reading this will question whether the patagium exists at all and might suggest that the width of soft tissue visible behind the left hind limb is an artefact of distortion during fossilisation. However, studies have shown (Briggs and Williams, 1981) that compression fossils do not show any lateral distortion or widening during the process of flattening. So, the Senck-Psittaco can be interpreted as a 2D compression of a 3D view with a good degree of certainty. It is not impossible that some expansion distortion occurred in one location behind the left leg, but this is less likely than the existence of a patagium. Plus, the color patterns on this proposed patagium are particularly contrasted and ornate, perhaps suggesting some sort of display function. And, the fourth trochanter (a bony protuberance) on the posterior side of the femur is hooked down towards the ankle, which suggests the presence of the "tendon of Sutton." If present, this tendon could have acted as a support for a soft tissue structure, such as a patagium. So, do I know for sure that this dinosaur had a patagium on its hind legs? No, but to reconstruct the Senck-Psittaco without them would require me to ignore considerable evidence. So, until equal amounts of contrary evidence are found, I will argue that this species of *Psittacosaurus* should be illustrated with a soft tissue structure behind the hind limbs. It might have been an inflatable air sack – I've seen a good-sized air sack behind the knee of a dissected ostrich – or a pouch for storing fat, but I chose to play it safe with a skin flap. Yes, I think including a simple patagium is the *conservative* option!

The full extent of the patagium is somewhat obscured by matrix and the overlay of abdominal soft tissue. However, I decided upon the illustrated size and shape by following the curvature of the exposed posterior margin. I estimated that the patagium would connect to the tail approximately 10cm behind the ilium along the contour where the bulge of the *caudofemoralis* muscle extends to the fourth trochanter. Since the research paper was published I have seen several alternative reconstructions of the Senck-Psittaco with reduced patagiums, presumably because the artists are uneasy about such a radical structure. The only problem I have with this is that they tend to illustrate the reduced patagium running from the tail to the knee, instead of to the ankle. But the only evidence for the patagium existing at all is the visible section running from ankle to abdomen. Therefore, if it is to be included at all, it must begin at the ankle and the reduction must come from the attachment point to the tail or thigh. And on this, I am open to alternative interpretations.

Now we come to the integument: skin, hair, scales, feathers, claws, etc. Integumentary features preserved in the fossil are scales of varying sizes, callosities, skin folds, the tail brush, and color patterns. The rounded clusters of highly pigmented scales on the shoulders are particularly interesting. These might appear to be large scales or scutes, but they are actually clusters of regularly sized scales that appear to be fused together (perhaps by the melanin). They might have helped to protect the shoulders from attack, or from wear and tear as the dinosaur pushed through vegetation, but they might also have been for display. However, the well-preserved callosities were almost certainly to protect against wear and tear. The callosities located at the distal end of the ischium (ischial callosity), the knee, ankle, and the elbow, have large scales; those on the callosities on the underside of the pes (foot) and manus (hand) have small scales. The presence of protective pads on the dinosaur's left manus suggest the Senck-Psittaco spent at least some of its time walking or standing quadrupedally. However, the alternative option of a bipedal posture – which is backed up with anatomical evidence, previous studies (Zhao *et al.*, 2013), and a relatively more pigmented chest – was chosen for a more active pose. At last, after several weeks of preliminary work, I was ready to start building.

All models, large and small, begin with a supportive armature. In the case of the Senck-Psittaco, it was a welded steel frame connected to the plinth below the right pes and where the left pes would touch the ground. The skeletal

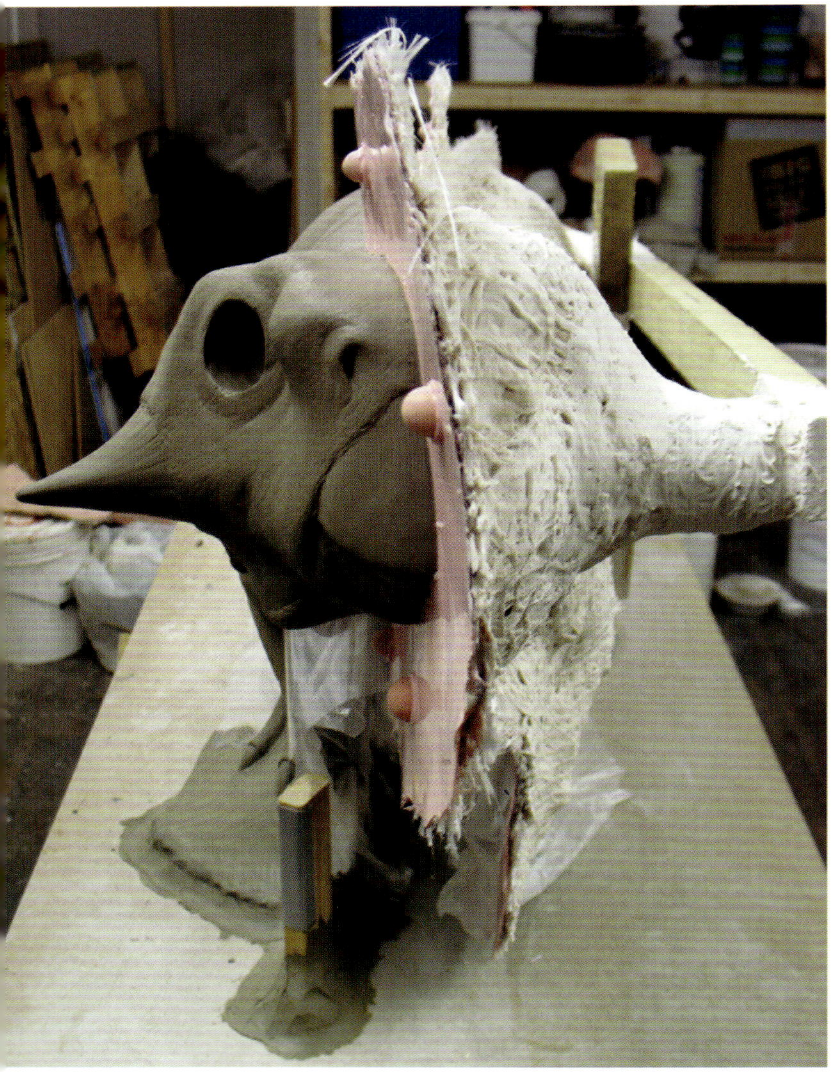

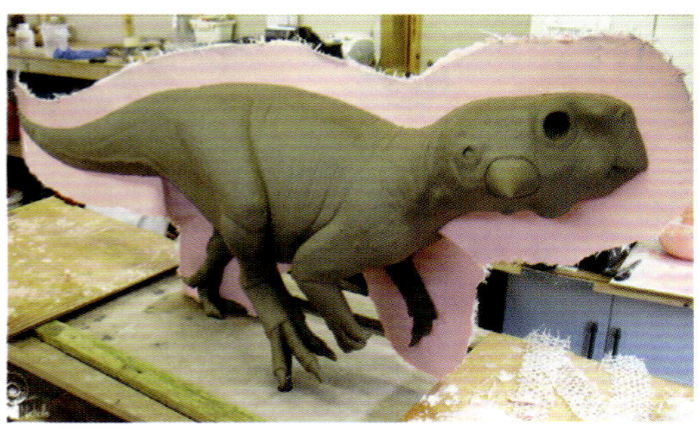

Building a Mold
Once the clay sculpture has been completed a mold needs to be built around it. The clay will dry out and crack but, once the mold has been built, multiple identical copies can be produced.

and soft tissue drawings were printed on paper at life-size and used as reference throughout the sculpting process. This would enable me to keep the dimensions and proportions as true to the fossil as possible. First, blocks of polystyrene were cut and fixed to the armature, using expanding foam. Then, the polystyrene was sculpted into a form 20-50mm smaller than that depicted by the preliminary drawings, as if the Senck-Psittaco had been deflated; the sculpture was later "inflated" to the actual size when the clay was added. Next, flexible wire was inserted into the polystyrene to create an armature of the forelimbs. Then, wire mesh was tightly wrapped around the whole structure. The mesh creates a good surface for the clay to bond to.

The clay added to the structure was 20-50mm thick. It was adjusted until the proportions precisely matched the preliminary drawings. A life-size, high-resolution photograph of the whole fossil also enabled me to accurately copy the varying skin folds, scale sizes, and callosities. Compression wrinkles not present in the fossil were added to the right side of the torso, where the skin is compressed between the limbs during stride, and to the dorsal side of the neck. A subtle margin between the hypaxial and epaxial muscle groups (those muscles surrounding the trunk and tail of a vertebrate animal) was also added to the center portion of the tail. A bulge of tissue was added to the cloaca, posterior to the ischium (indicated in the fossil by the dense patch of pigment), to simulate the equivalent anatomy in extant birds. Next, the sensory organs were added to the head. The orbit of the Senck-Psittaco is extremely large, but the reconstructed sclerotic ring and soft tissues suggested an eyeball approximately 40mm in diameter, with an iris of approximately 28mm in diameter. The eyeball was sculpted in the center of the orbit, but this was cut away prior to molding to create a cavity to house the final glass eye, which would be 28mm in diameter to match the iris. Once the eyelids were sculpted the visible eye was about 20mm in diameter. The nostrils were located at the anterior edge of the external nares and the bird-like external ear drum was positioned below the otic notch, between the back of the skull and the *depressor mandibulae* (a muscle that contracts to open the mouth). By the way, the *depressor mandibulae* is an important muscle for paleoartists to know about. It would have bulged at the back of the jaw and skull where many artists create a cavity to illustrate a separation between the head and neck – a result of 'shrink wrapping', a style of paleoart where the skin is reconstructed tightly around the skeleton. It's a meme that needs to be abandoned.

The head posed a considerable problem during sculpting because almost all the skin texture and color pattern information has either been worn off or prepared away (I shudder to think about the many other fossils that might have been unwittingly over-prepared and the integument lost forever!). This was overcome by examining the fossil up close and identifying fragments of scales and pigment across the whole head then filling the gaps with corresponding details. For example, there is very little soft tissue information preserved around the mouth, but there is some evidence of cheeks due to the presence of highly pigmented integument extending across the lower jaw. Therefore, tissue was sculpted around the beak, which would have enabled the mouth to open and prevented food from falling out. Later, this would also be darkly painted to represent the heavy pigmentation. In contrast, there is no observable pigmentation on or around the beak. This might be because the beak was light in color or it might be because the integument has been removed. If the integument has been removed then it is possible that the beak's keratin was heavily pigmented, like the horns and most of the face. This lack of information also meant I couldn't be completely sure of the size and shape of the beak, so I just played it safe and added what seemed most

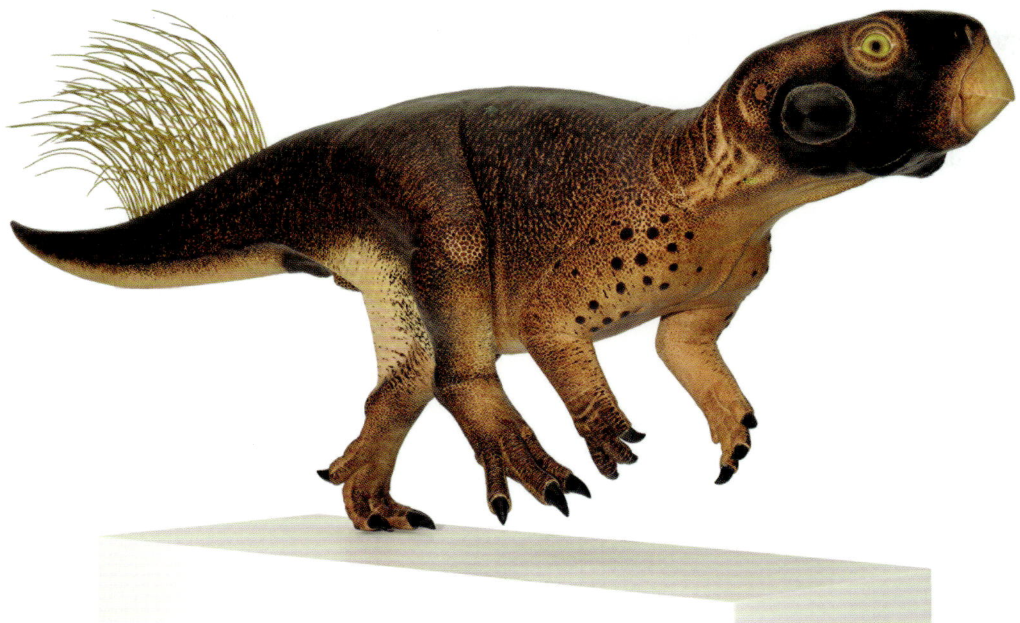

The Final Model
Two weeks of painting were required to apply the fossilized color patterns to the model. A variety of utensils were used to apply the paint.

functionally useful. I had a similar issue with the unguals (claws), because there are no pigmented keratin sheaths remaining on the pes or manus. The extent of the keratinous sheaths was estimated to be approximately 20% longer than the well-preserved unguals, but they might have been a little longer or shorter either way.

What should be obvious by now is that some parts of the Senck-Psittaco's anatomy are well represented and can be reconstructed with confidence, whereas other parts are not so clear and require a judgment call. These gaps in our knowledge are where the artist's own decision-making can create the greatest differences between reconstructions of the same species. For example, you might have decided that the beak of the Senck-Psittaco was darkly colored like the rest of the face, or estimated that the keratinous sheaths over the unguals were longer. Both of these alternatives are plausible and could be argued with sound reasoning. This is why copying another artist's work is such a big risk in palaeoart; you might be copying anatomical features you would disagree with if you had taken the time to reconstruct the subject for yourself. Undertaking your own reconstruction process is the best way to avoid this potential pitfall, and it will allow you to create unique, personal, and exciting paleoart.

The whole process of applying the information preserved in the Senck-Psittaco fossil onto the clay sculpture required about five weeks of painstaking work. But I was still only half way through the build. Over time the clay sculpture would dry out and crumble to pieces, so I needed to mold it and cast a durable fiberglass and resin copy. The molding begins by determining where the sections of the mold will separate and lock together using plastic shim walls. This can be tricky, because if you get it wrong, your mold will be jammed together, or against the model, and it won't come apart. Only once I am certain the mold will separate do I insert the plastic shim into the clay all around the sculpture. The first mold layer to be applied to the clay sculpture and shim walls is silicone rubber. It is applied as a liquid and it captures all the fine details in the clay. I strengthen the silicone layer with silicone-soaked matting, which also makes it more capable of holding its form. However, the silicone rubber layer is still very flexible, so a ridged casing, made of acrylic resin and matting, is built around it. When all the mold sections have been built this way, I drill holes through the mold walls so the whole mold can be taken apart and reassembled in precisely the same positions. The mold-making process is time consuming and messy, but if it is done correctly, it will enable the artist to make multiple identical copies of the clay sculpture.

A fiberglass and resin cast was taken from the mold and repaired where necessary with resin putty. Resin putty was also used to sculpt the eyelids over the glass eyes, which were inserted into holes through the middle of what would be the orbit. A bird-like eye with a round pupil was chosen because a vertical or horizontal slit eye would be suggestive of a predatory and/or nocturnal animal. A horizontal rectangular pupil was also rejected because the Lower Cretaceous environment in north-eastern China was not open grassland equivalent. Finally, the replica bristles were fixed into the tail and bent into curves that mimic those preserved in the Senck-Psittaco fossil. The cast was then complete and ready to be painted.

The color patterns were applied to the cast, using a combination of sponges, brushes and an airbrush to achieve the required effects. Every square centimeter of the cast's surface was carefully considered and the patterns preserved in the Senck-Psittaco fossil were applied to the precise corresponding locations. This meant that many scales had to be individually half or even quarter painted with dark pigment. This was a laborious process that took about two weeks to complete, including several alterations to the chest, legs, feet, and hind limb patagiums. Such alterations meant I was eradicating previous paintwork that represented many hours of labor, but this is an unavoidable task when you are attempting to achieve perfection. The complication that made

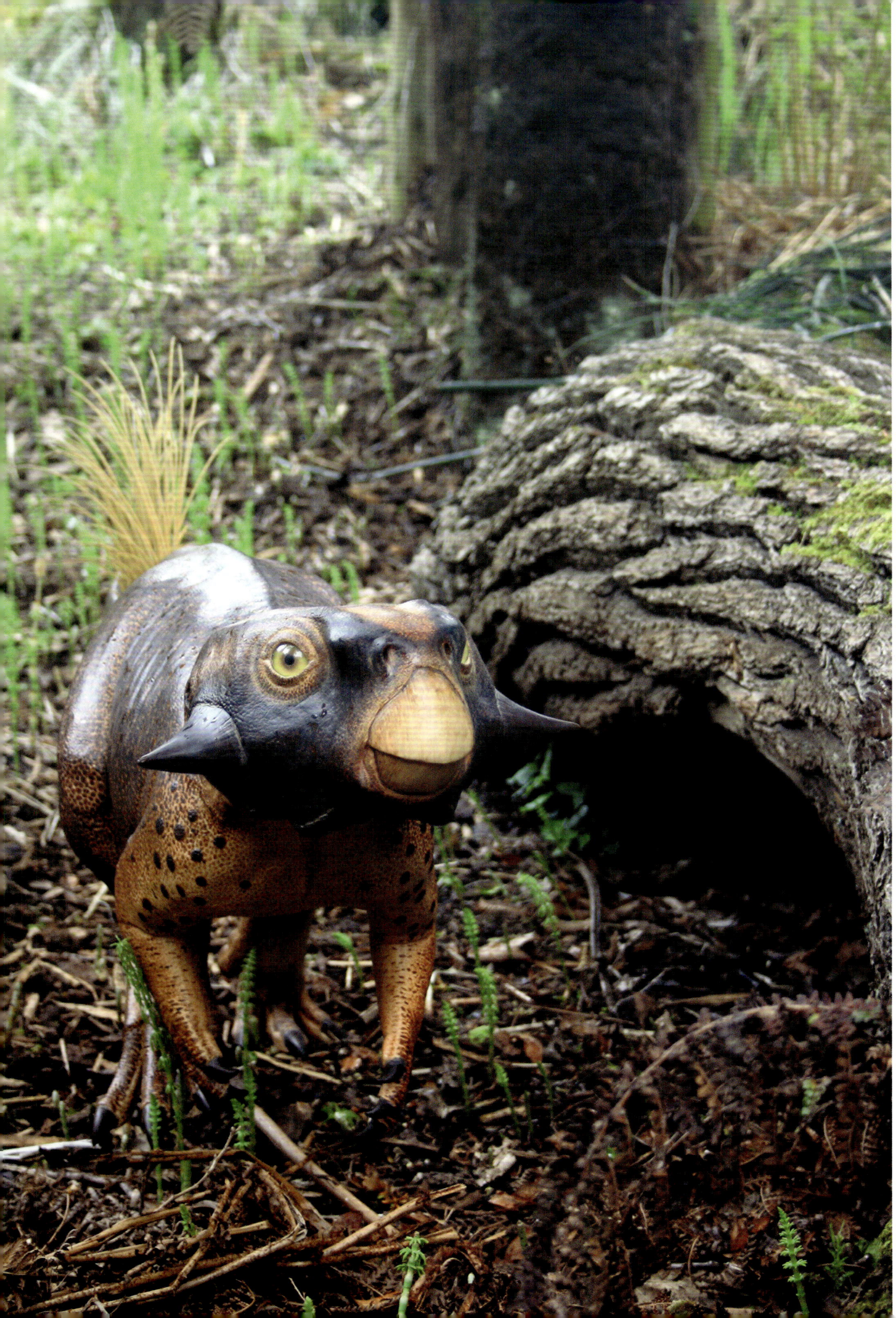

some of the alterations necessary was that parts of the fossil represent multiple color patterns overlaying each other. For example, some internal organs contain melanin and at first glance they make the belly of the Senck-Psittaco appear darker than the integument really was. Separating these superimposed patterns was problematic but possible because of two very different techniques. The first was laser-stimulated florescence imaging, which uses a violet laser to illuminate the fossil while a time exposure photograph is taken. This method made it obvious that the skin covering the belly was lighter than the organic material in the stomach. The second, much lower-tech, technique was to simply observe where the color patterns continued over or beneath the bones. The best example of this was the left hind limb, where the pattern on the outside of the leg (a combination of intricate patterns of contrasting values and gradients from light to heavily pigmented areas) is superimposed by the inside leg pattern (spots amalgamated into stripes). Fortunately, the patterns could be separated because the inside leg pattern can be observed on the tibia and the outside leg pattern cannot.

Now, ever wondered why the model is painted brown when the fossilized patterns are almost black? Well, here's where it gets technical. Animals derive their colors from pigments in their tissues and the most common of these pigments is melanin. Melanin exists in the animal's cells in the form of organelles, called melanosomes. Recent studies have shown that fossilized color patterns are due to the original distribution of melanosomes. Also, the preserved color intensities are correlated with melanosome densities, so fossilized color patterns are a reliable proxy for the original color pattern. Melanosomes are found in fossils as either microbodies or impressions of microbodies. The microbodies in the Senck-Psittaco are ovoid in shape (approximately 400 nanometers in length and 250nm wide), which suggest a melanosome rich in pheomelanin, a pigment with a pink to red hue, depending on its concentration. It could therefore be predicted that, in this case, the original color would be a reddish brown, not black. However, this isn't the end of the story. Animals also use a variety of other pigments to create color patterns, such as carotenoids, porphyrins, psittacofulvins, pterins and purine; they are often combined. For example, birds combine layers of melanin with reflective microstructures in their skin and feathers to create blue and iridescence. So, although the melanin pigmentation must have resembled what has been applied to my model, in life, the Senck-Psittaco might have possessed some color variations due to other types of currently undetectable pigments (only melanin is currently detectable). However, the purpose of my model was to illustrate the fossil evidence as closely as possible, so on this occasion I simply could not manufacture speculative coloration.

If you want to create your own interpretation of the Senck-Psittaco, be sure to comply with the reddish brown pheomelanin patterns and, if you add additional colors, be ready and able to explain your decision-making. I see a lot of beautifully colored dinosaurs in paleoart these days, but the patterns often conflict with what we see in the natural world today. There are coloration trends throughout the animal kingdom that we paleoartists need to learn about so we can improve our reconstructions. For example, did you know that animals that live in open and closed environments have predictably different counter coloration? Animals that live in open environments, such as savannahs, have abrupt transitions from dark dorsal coloration to light ventral colors. This transition is usually high on the body to counter the strong shadows cast by direct sunlight overhead, which has the effect of flattening the animal's form and hiding it in the landscape. However, animals that live in closed environments, such as woodlands, have a much more gradual transition from dark to light. This more gradual transition is usually much lower on the body to counteract the weak shadows caused by the diffused light. From this information, you should be able to tell that the Senck-Psittaco lived in a closed woodland environment, which was confirmed by experiments by Dr Jakob Vinther and Dr Innes Cuthill, at the University of Bristol. So, to credibly reconstruct an extinct animal, one must always learn about the type of environment that animal lived in, and where they might have fitted into the ecosystem. Ask yourself how they might have needed to use color in their day-to-day activities. Might they have used counter shading or another color strategy, like crypsis or disruptive patterns? We should also never forget that most birds can see more colors than we can (they are violet and ultraviolet sensitive) and therefore some dinosaurs probably could too. These issues and many more should be considered before adding color patterns to your reconstruction.

Knowing when to stop working on an artwork is not an exact science and the cut-off point varies greatly depending on the individual artist's personal view. As old Leo da Vinci once said, "art is never finished, only abandoned." For artists seeking realism, I think it is usually the end when our knowledge of how to improve an artwork is exhausted. However, the primary reason for me declaring the Senck-Psittaco reconstruction finished was I reached the point where additional details would be unnoticed and unappreciated by the viewer. So, after about 12 weeks of work, my Senck-Psittaco was done. Or so I thought. A problem with being a professional paleoartist is that, if you are good at your job, your artworks will constantly become out of date. As we become more and more informed about our subjects, we become better able to scrutinise past artwork. And sure enough, after a year or so of continued study of the Senck-Psittaco fossil, there are now numerous alterations I plan to make to my model. But we paleoartists shouldn't consider the outdating of our work as a failing. It is a positive sign that we are succeeding at upping our game. I will update the Senck-Psittaco model at some point in the near future, but I do not update all my artwork. Paleoart is a visual history of our developing understanding of the evolution of life, so I don't think we should be embarrassed to preserve artwork that contributes to that magnificent story.

So there you are: that is how I turned the Naturmuseum Senckenberg's *Psittacosaurus* fossil into a credible life-size 3D reconstruction. I know that it will not always be possible to reconstruct an extinct species with the same rigor as I've just explained. I know few people will ever get the chance to photograph their subject while it's illuminated by a laser, but most of the process I have outlined will be possible. And don't let other pressures divert you from the direction the evidence is pointing you in. For example, during the process of sculpting the clay, it became clear to me that my Senck-Psittaco was going to look cute and for a brief moment I considered making the face rather more ferocious. This would have given the media what they expected and it would have pleased the many people who want dinosaurs to remain scary, scaly monsters. But I quickly corrected myself and decided my model would look however the fossilized anatomy dictated it should – inference from evidence! Paleoart is about discovering what dinosaurs (and other prehistoric animals) really looked like, not perpetuating stereotypes, memes or nostalgia. No doubt some dinosaurs would have been fierce or scary, but they would also have been beautiful, ugly, downright weird, and, yes, even cute sometimes. If you reconstruct your subject from the inside out, you will no doubt come up with some surprising results. Subsequently, you will occasionally encounter some "it doesn't look how I want it to look" criticisms. But your reconstruction process will have armed you with all the logic you need to invalidate that criticism. And, more importantly, your artwork might just represent what the extinct animal really looked like.

SERGEY KRASOVSKIY

UKRAINE

A chance meeting on a Russian-language dinosaur forum, Dinoweb, put Sergey in touch with Andrey Atuchin and it was his advice and guidance that led Sergey to become a professional paleoartist. Since then his work has appeared in numerous books and exhibitions, most recently a series of pictures for the Primorsky Oceanarium. His artwork has been exhibited in numerous international paleoart competitions, where they have been awarded several prizes, including a first place in 2015. He and Andrey are currently working on a new prehistoric encyclopedia together.

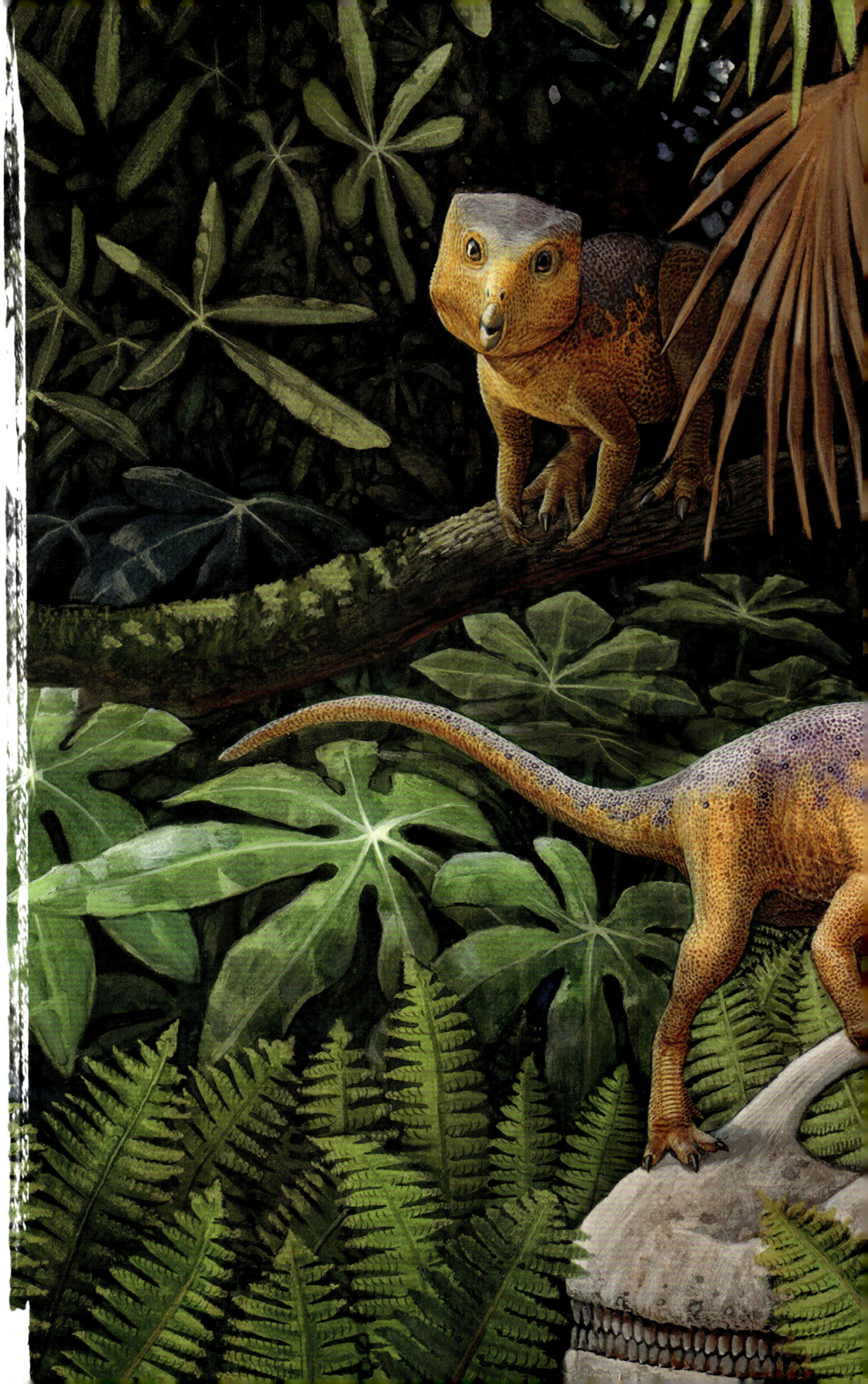

Yinlong downsi
Gouache, 2014
Found in 2004, *Yinlong* is from the Shishugou Formation of Xinjiang, China, dated from the Oxfordian Stage of the Late Jurassic. Its name means 'hidden dragon' in Mandarin Chinese, a reference to the movie *Crouching Tiger, Hidden Dragon*, scenes of which were filmed in the province of Xinjiang.

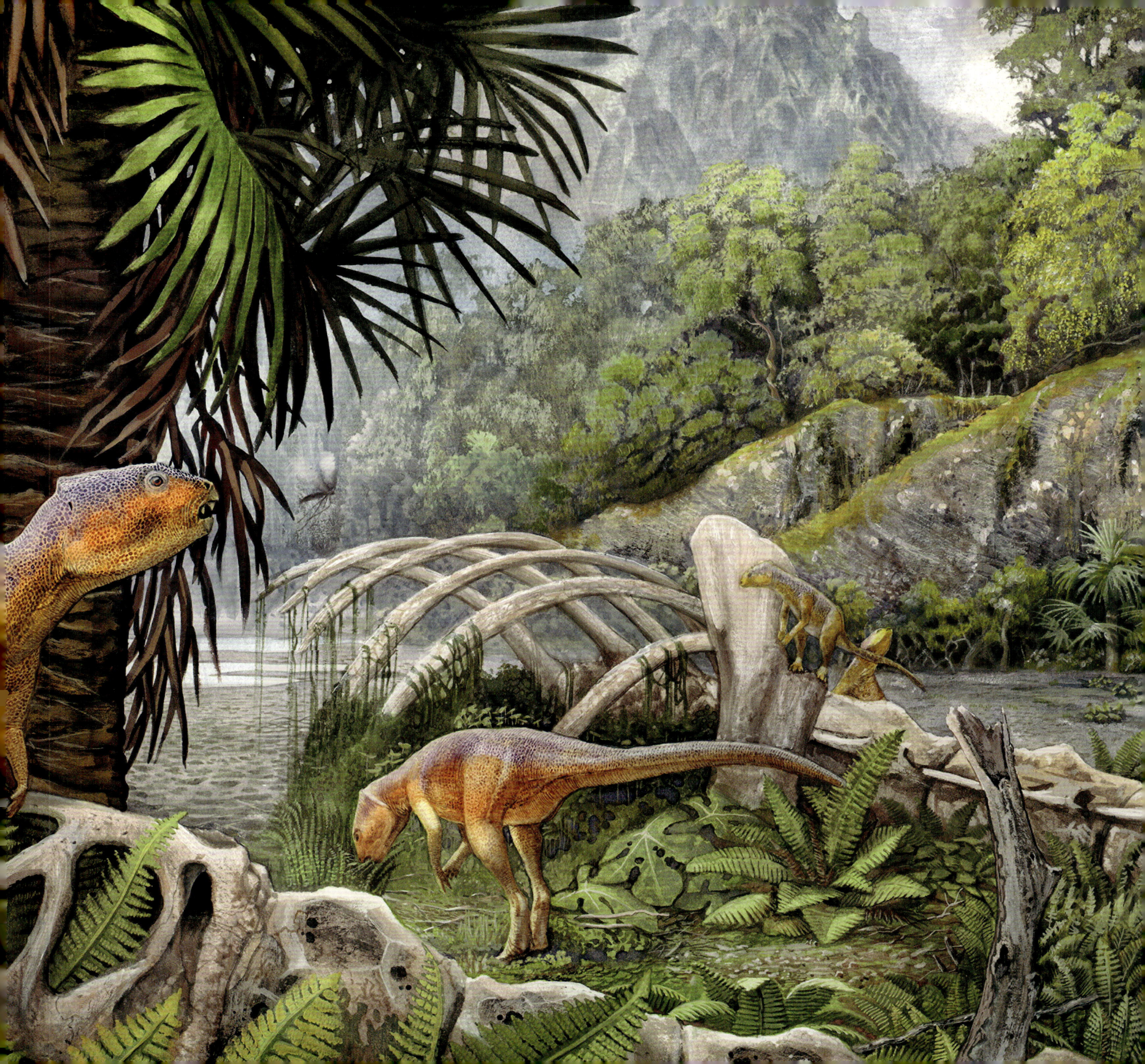

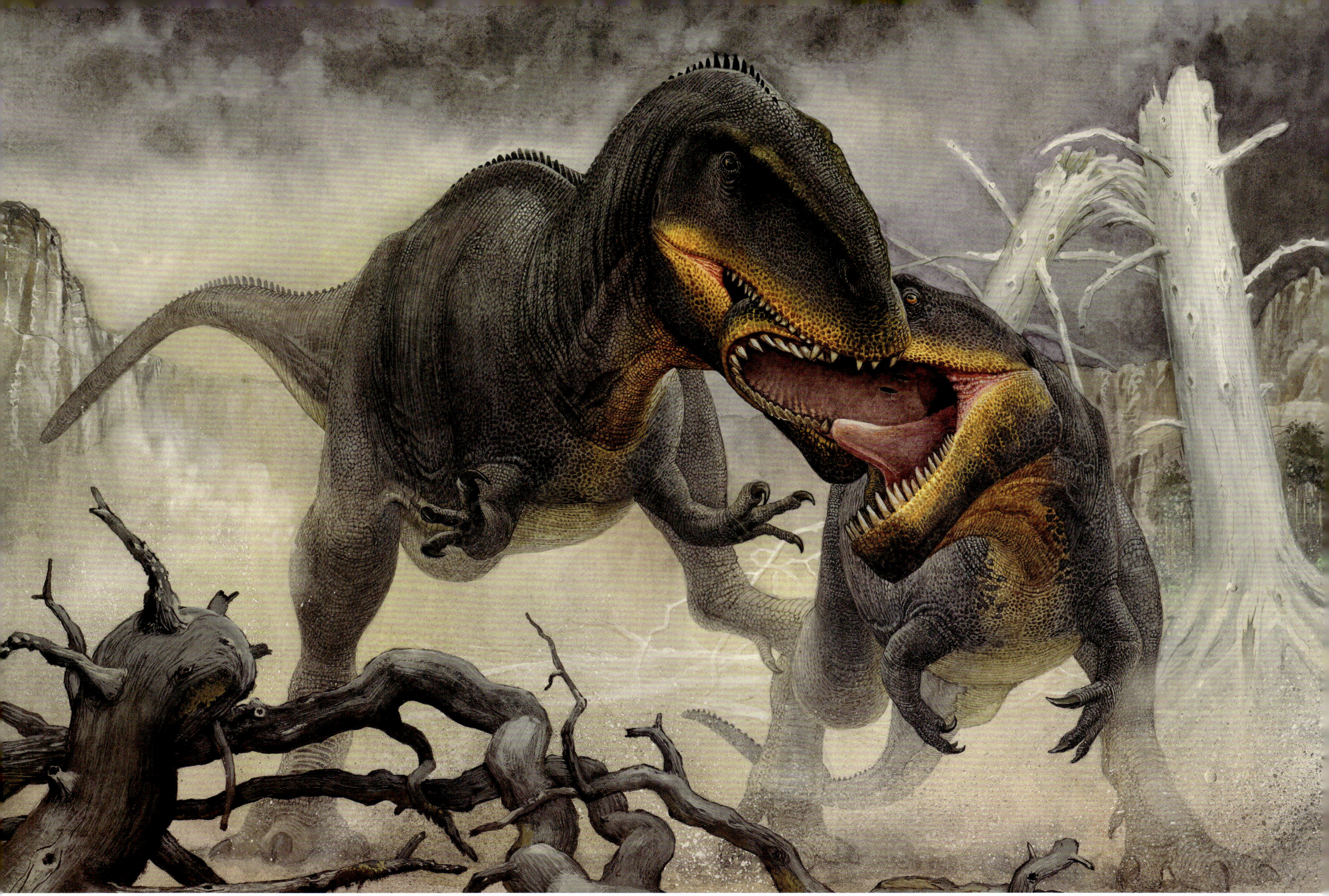

Were you one of those children who always drew dinosaurs?
Yes, I became acquainted with dinosaurs in 1982, at the age of seven – I was drawn to their wild beauty. I started out by copying pictures from books, notably those illustrated by [Soviet] artists such as Zdeněk Burian, Konstantin Flerov and Ruben Varshamov. In the end, I enjoyed drawing so much that I decided to follow art as a profession, and went on to train at Lugansk Art College. It's fair to say that my love of dinosaurs was the reason I became an artist.
How difficult was it to keep track of changes in dinosaur paleontology in the Ukraine?
It was hard getting access to the necessary literature in the Soviet Union. My parents did encourage my interest by taking me around to various libraries, and my aunt was actually a librarian and was often able to help source books for me. In the 90s, translated foreign books started to become available, at which point I first saw the

Tyrannotitan chubutensis
Gouache, 2014
A large carcharodontosaurid theropod known from fragmentary remains found in the Cerro Barcino formation of Argentina. Aptian Stage, Early Cretaceous, 112-121mya.

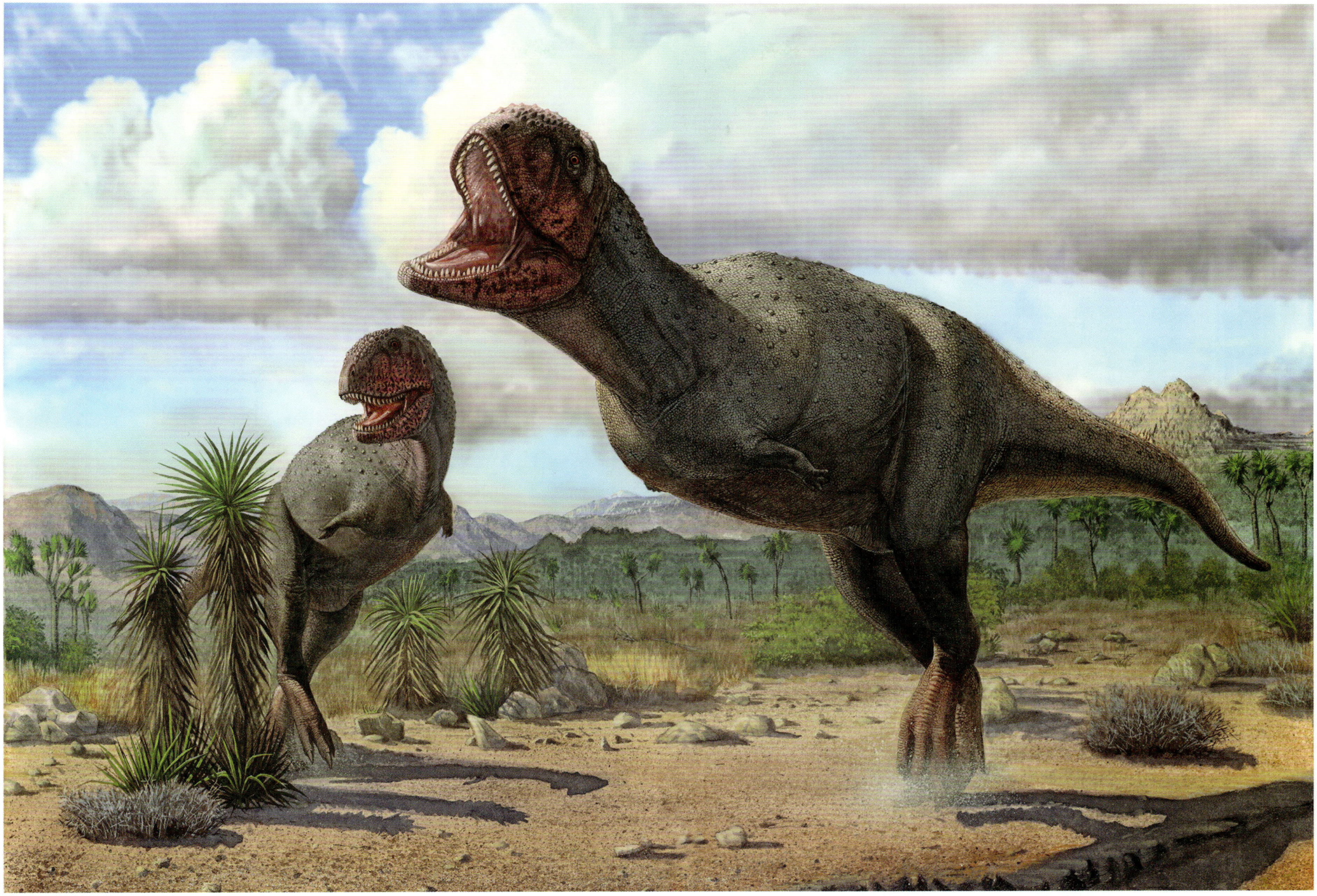

Pycnonemosaurus nevesi
Oils
Maastrichtian Stage, Late Cretaceous, Brazil.

(Overleaf) **Cenomanian Europe: *Neovenator salerii* and hadrosauroids**
Digital

(Pages 23-25) **Dinosaurs of Burgos**
Digital, 2015
Dinosaurs of Burgos, Spain, during the Early Cretaceous. Left to right: Titanosauriform sauropods (based on footprints); small dromaeosauridae theropod (based on footprints); *Arcanosaurus ibericus* (varanid lizard); *Baryonyx* sp. (background); *Demandasaurus darwini* (sauropod, background); ornithopod *Camptosaurus valdenses*; coelurosaurid theropod (based on footprints).

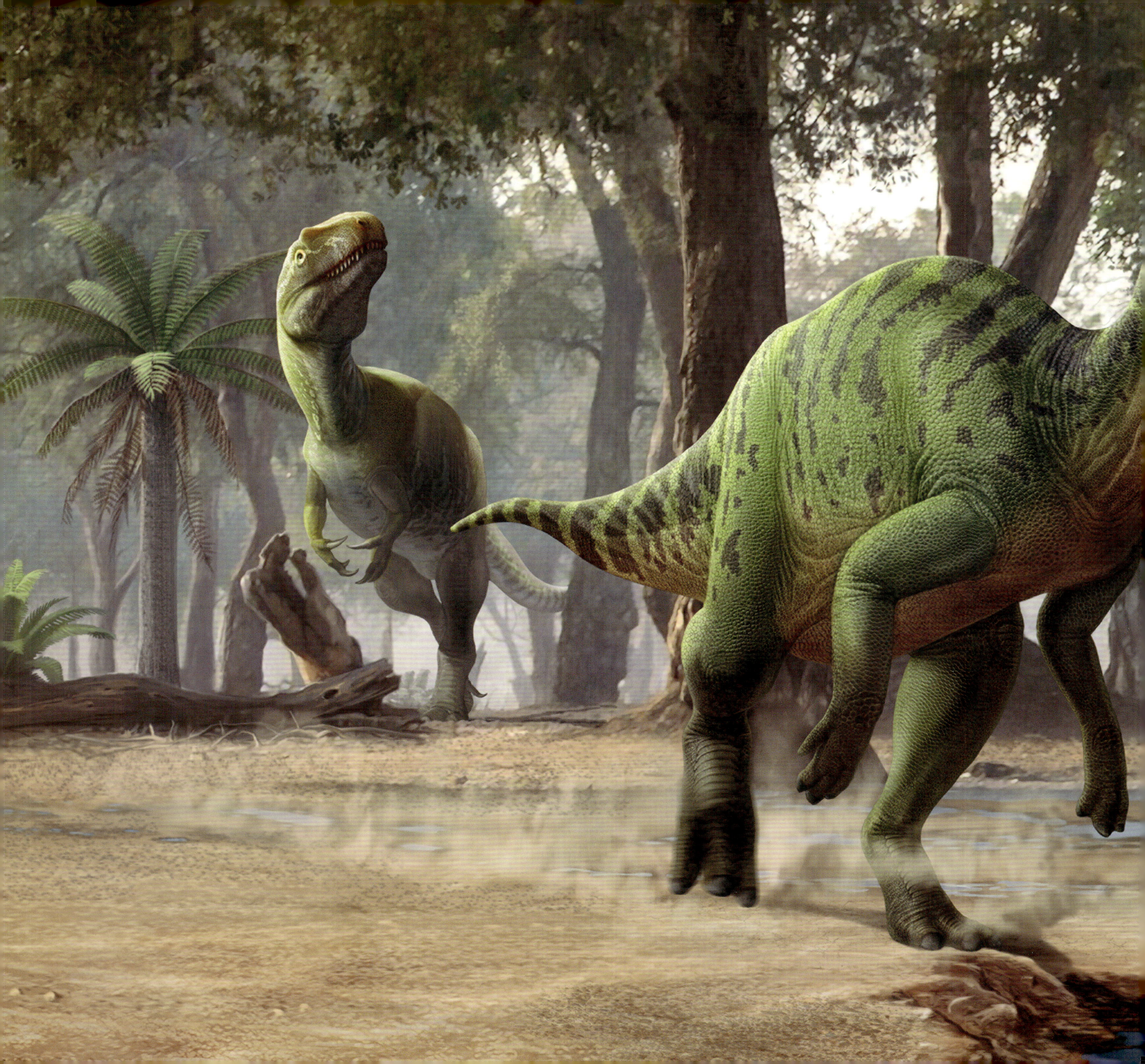

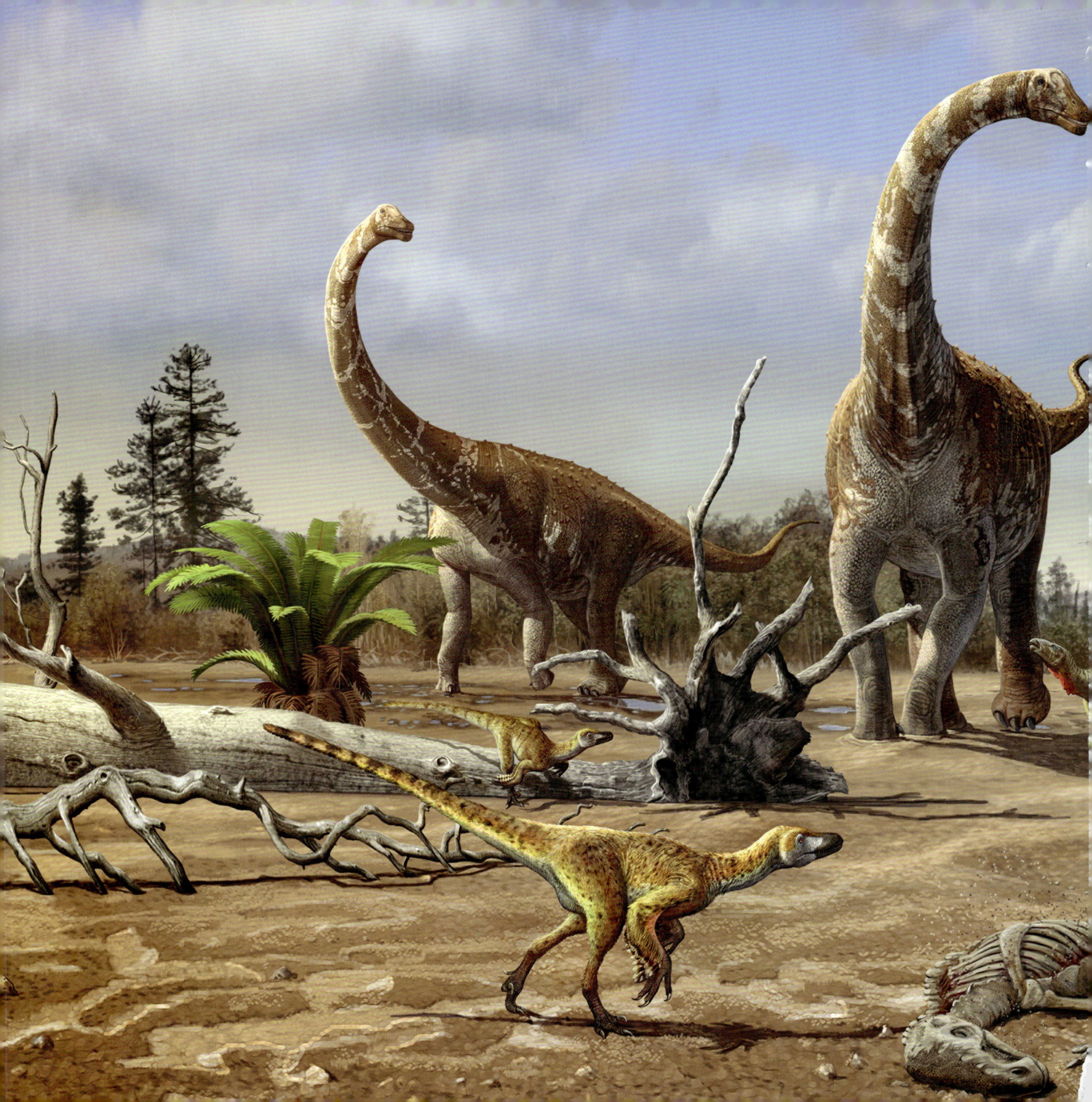

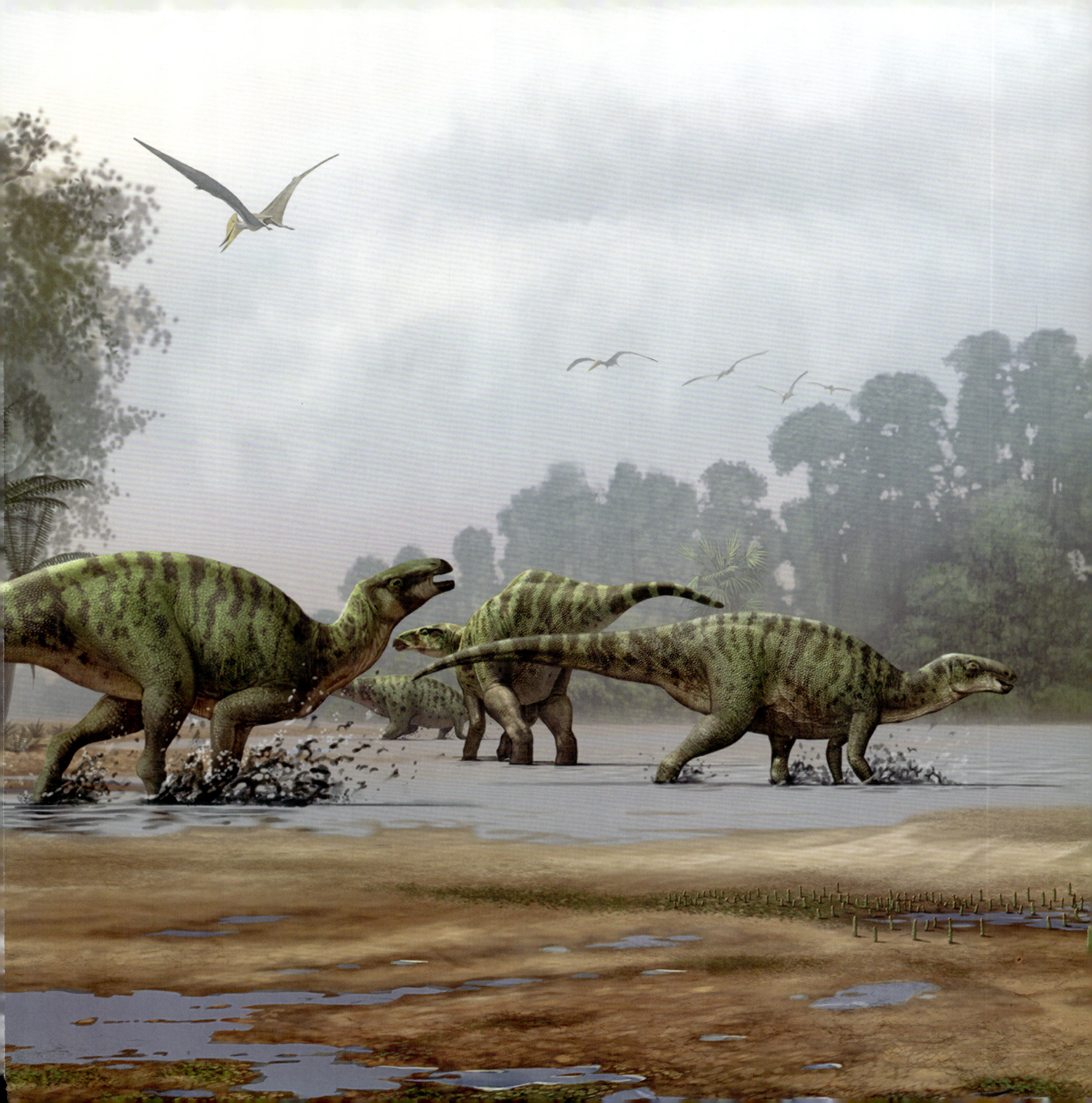

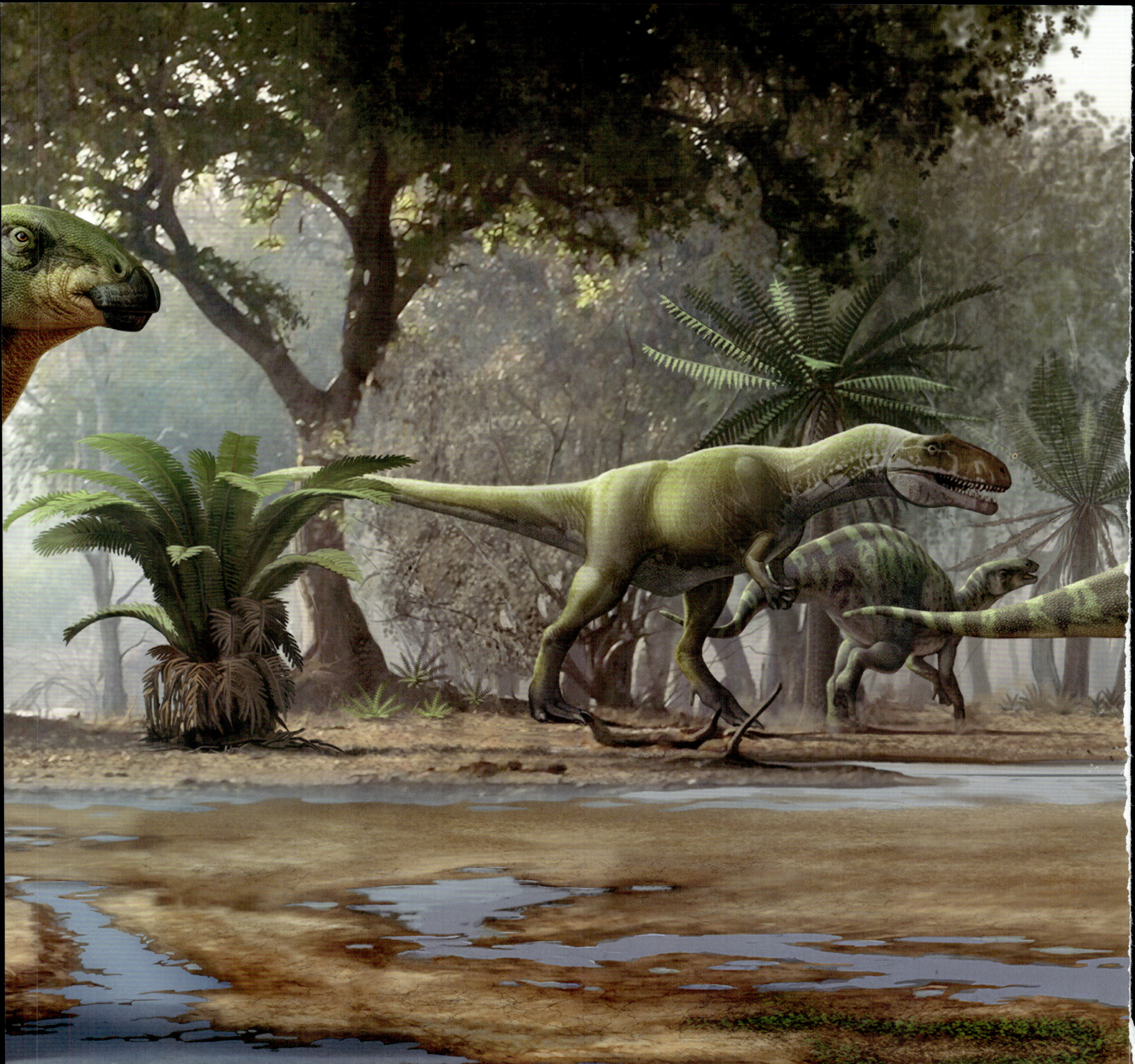

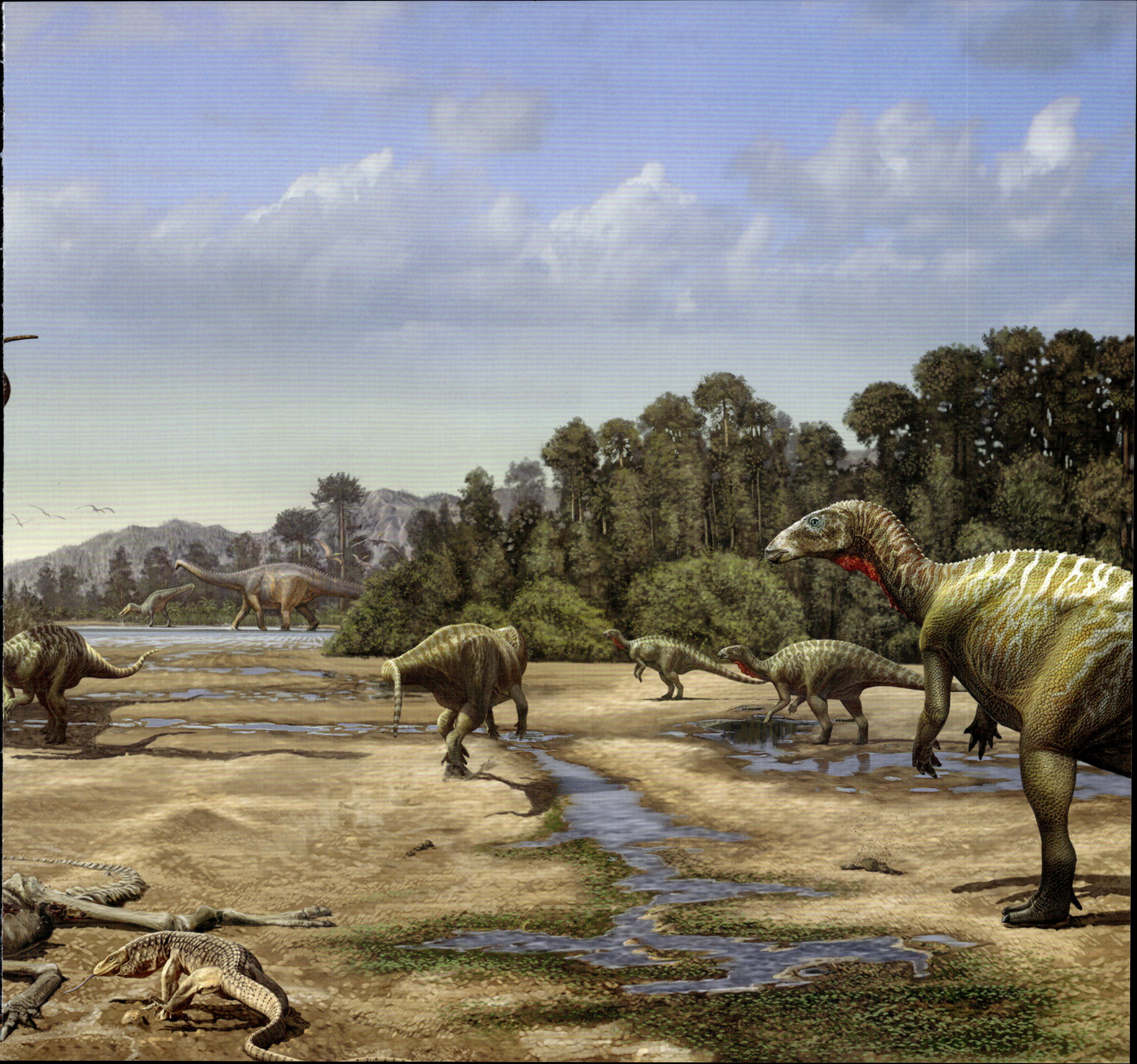

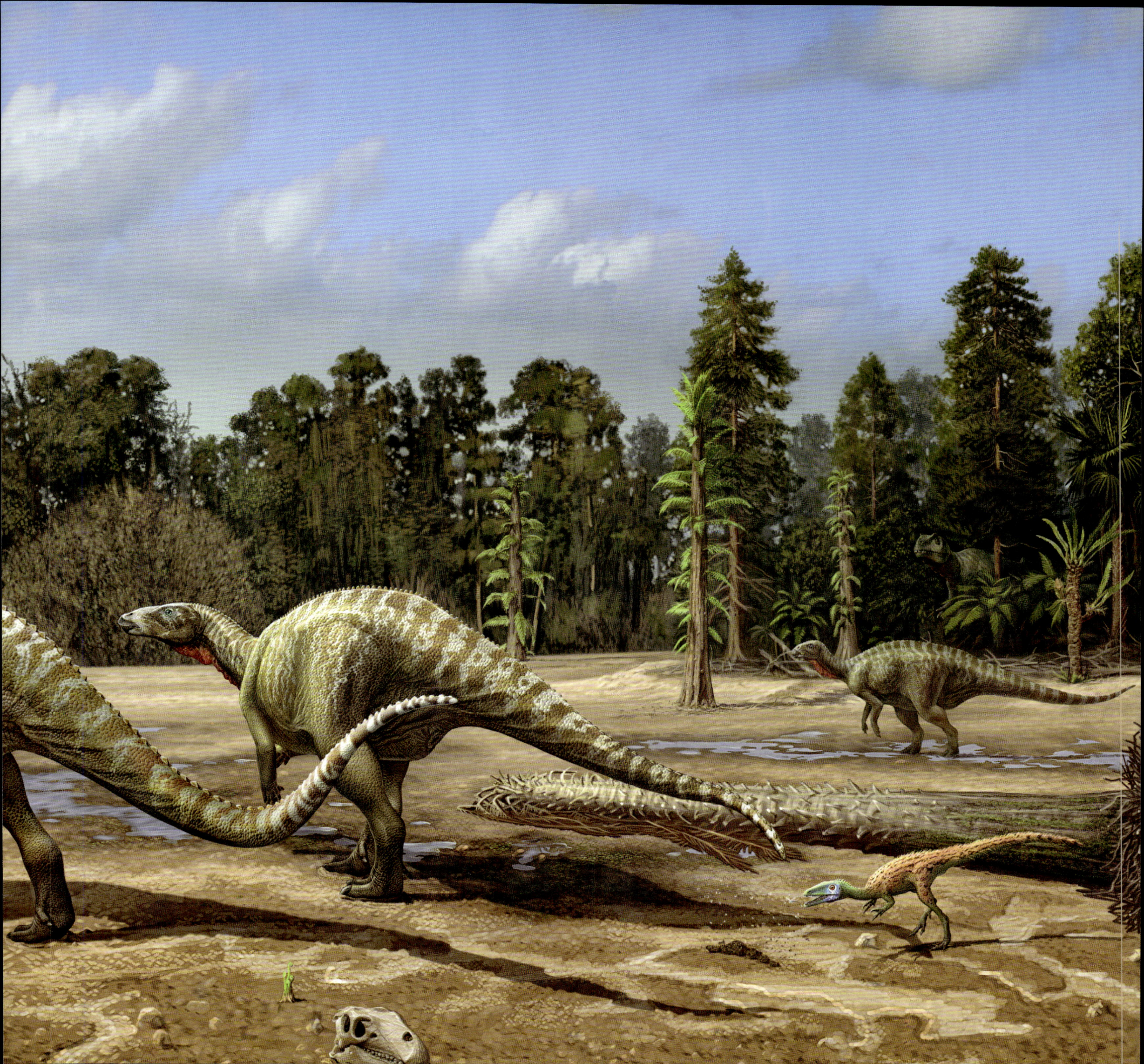

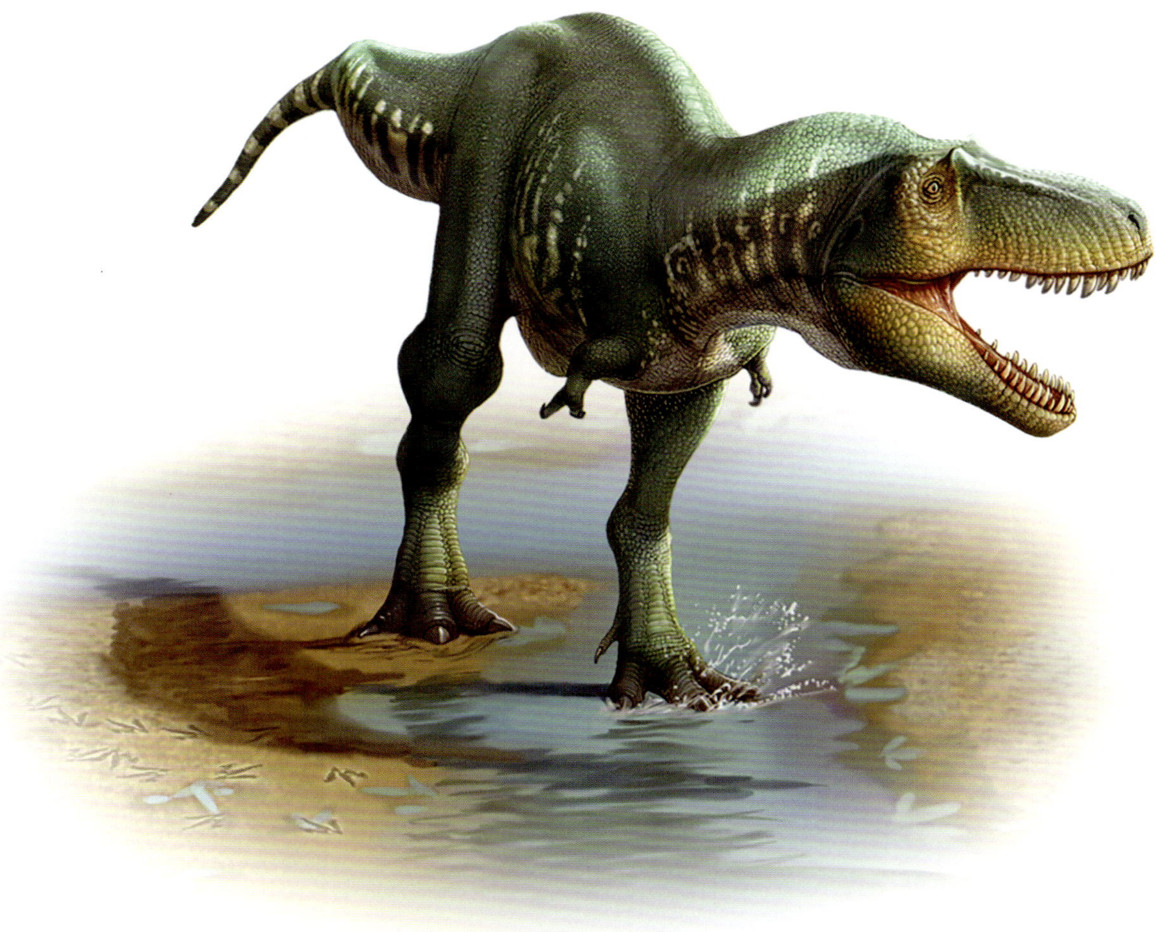

work of John Sibbick and Douglas Henderson. Ooooh, it was magnificent! More recently, the internet has made it much easier to keep up to date with new discoveries in paleontology and trends in paleoart.

Who were your earliest artistic influences?

Varshamov, who was a Russian animal artist and illustrator of children's books, made a very big impression on me. His illustrations appeared in books in the late 80s, and he had a great soft watercolor technique. Flerov also made an impact with his illustrations that were featured heavily in the children's encyclopedias of the time and in the Moscow Paleontological Museum (PIN), where you can still see them today. I also want to mention Burian: his artbook came into my possession in 1986, and I practiced my drawing by copying many of his illustrations – probably more than a hundred of them.

Daspletosaurus torosus
Digital, 2013

(Right) ***Sarcosuchus imperator*** **vs** ***Rugops primus***
Digital, 2016
On a riverbank in Early Cretaceous North Africa, the 35ft (11m) long crocodilian *Sarcosuchus* ambushes the abelisaur *Rugops*.

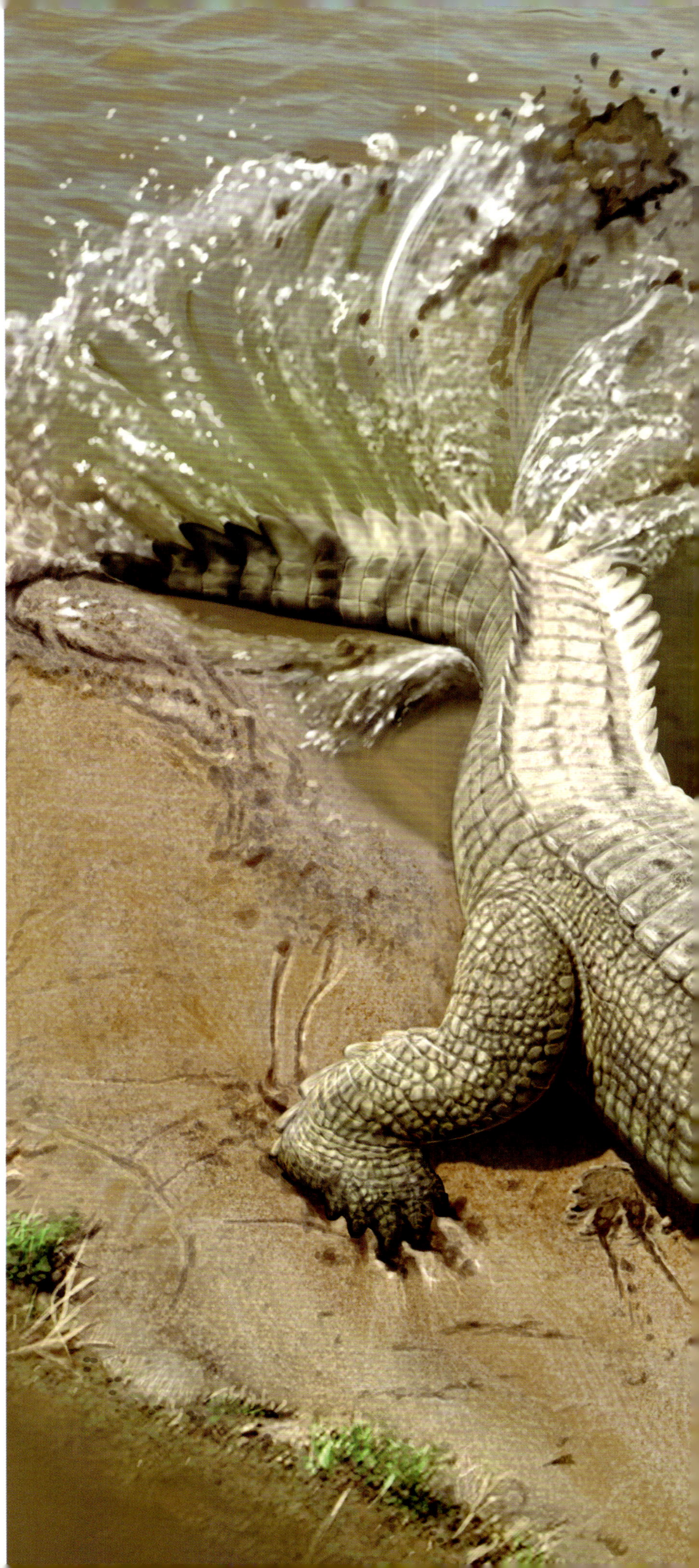

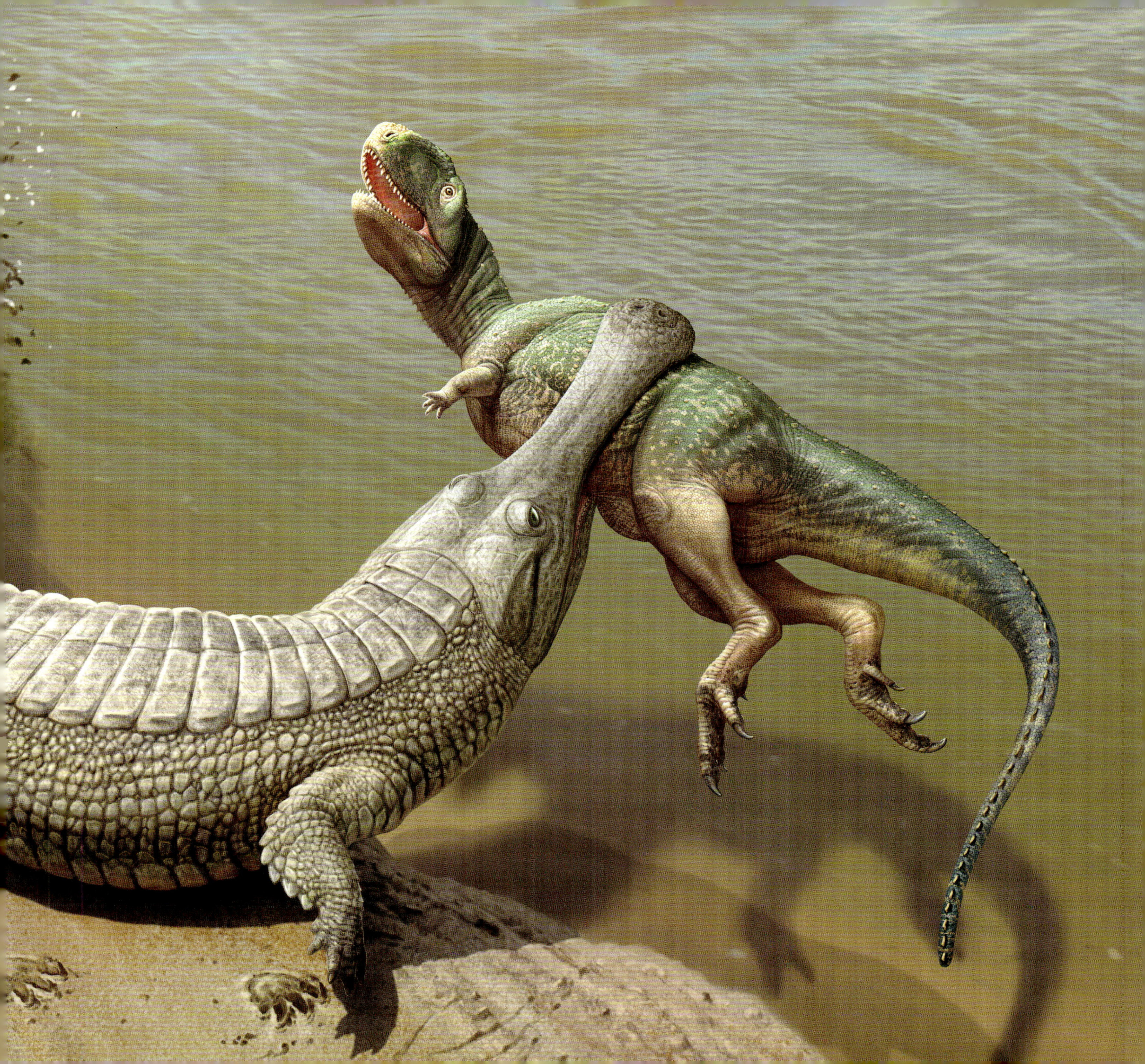

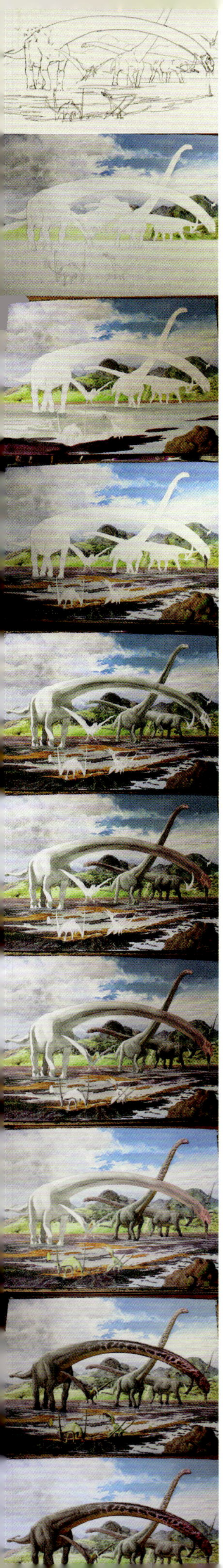

(Below) ***Sercipterus* and *Mamenchisaurus***
Gouache, 2013

(Left) Stages of work on artwork below.

(Opposite below) ***Ornithomimus* and *Panoplosaurus***
Gouache, 2013

(Opposite) ***Torvosaurus gurneyi***
Digital, 2014
Previously known only from the USA, remains of *Torvosaurus* were discovered in Portugal in 2000; further material was found in 2013, in the forms of eggs and embryonic remains and referred to *Torvosaurus*. The Portuguese species was named after artist James Gurney, creator of the *Dinotopia* book series.

Your artwork often has the feel of landscape paintings that just happen to include dinosaurs in them. What sort of references do you use to bring these landscapes to life?

It's possibly more of a stylistic approach than use of references: in college I studied classical painting – my textbooks were full of the art of Ivan Shishkin and Alexei Savrasov. Burian had a similar style, too. As a student many of my works were in classic oil techniques, but I now prefer mixed media using watercolors and gouache.

You're also an artist who made the transition from traditional artwork to digital pretty recently. What prompted the change and how did it impact on your art?

We must all evolve to survive and I'm no exception; after all, once upon a time we used fingers and charcoal! But the main impetus was to save time and keep up with the requirements of my customers, especially timeframes. I switched to a graphics tablet three years ago. I do sometimes still use traditional methods, either

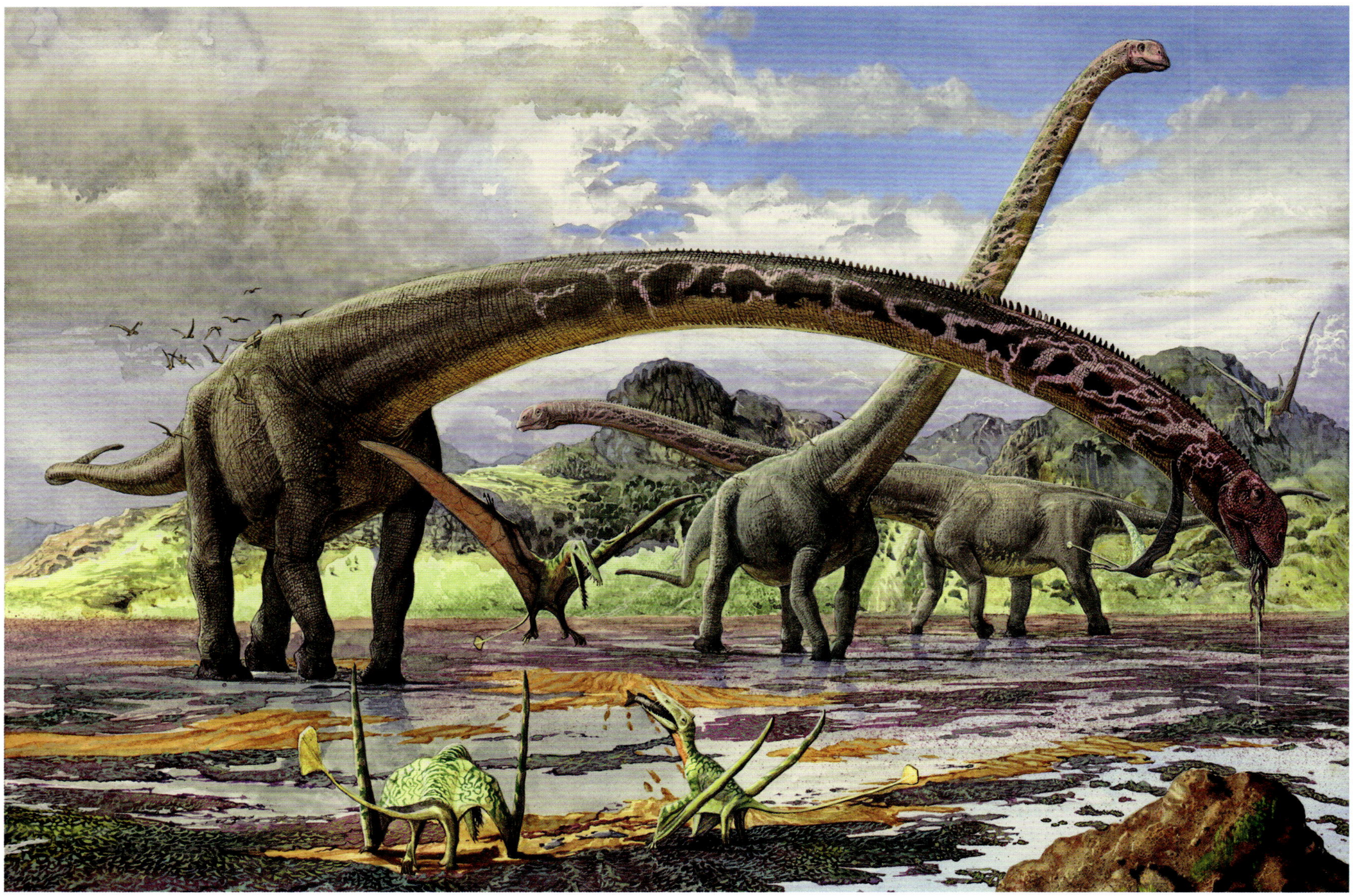

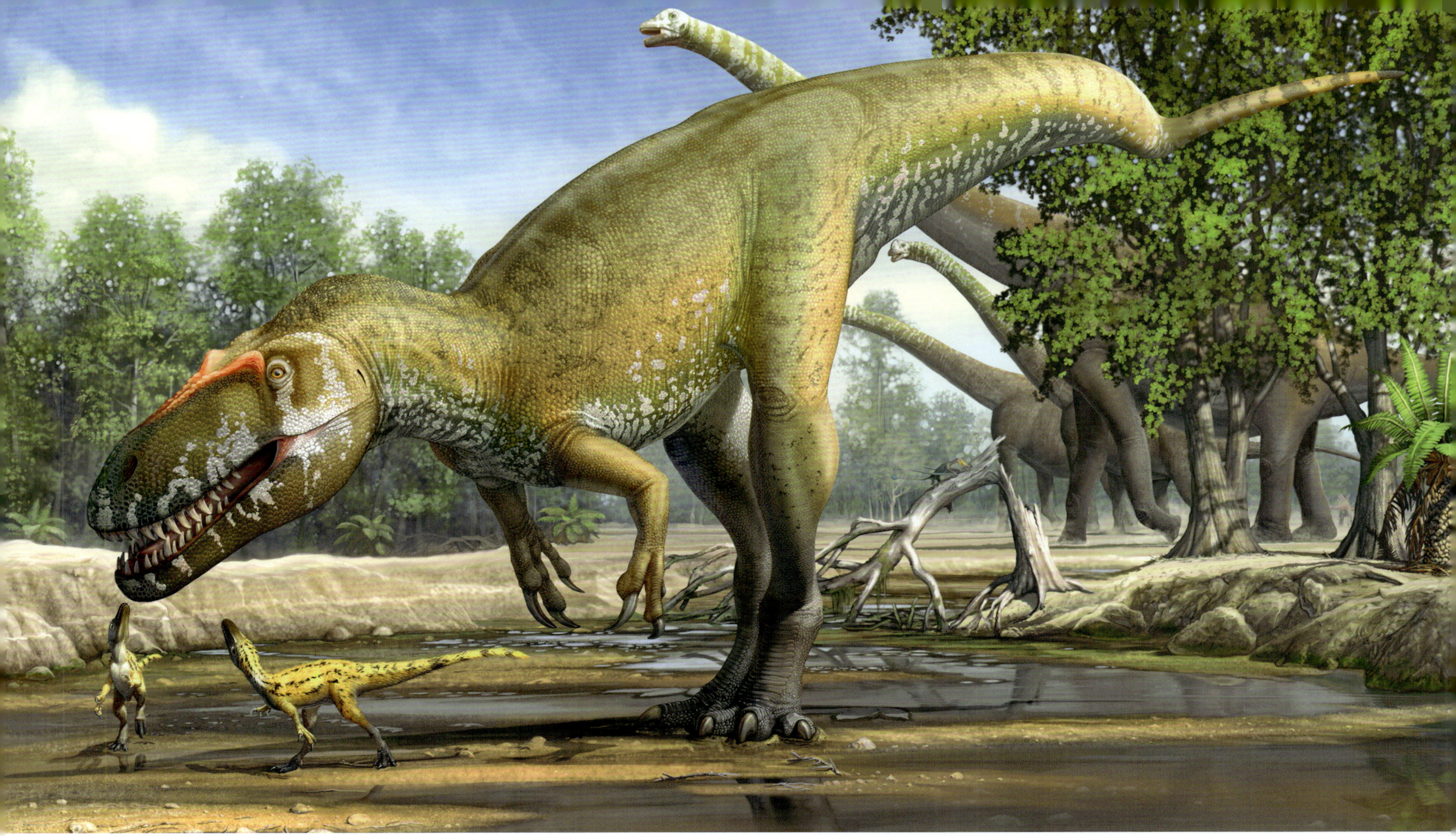

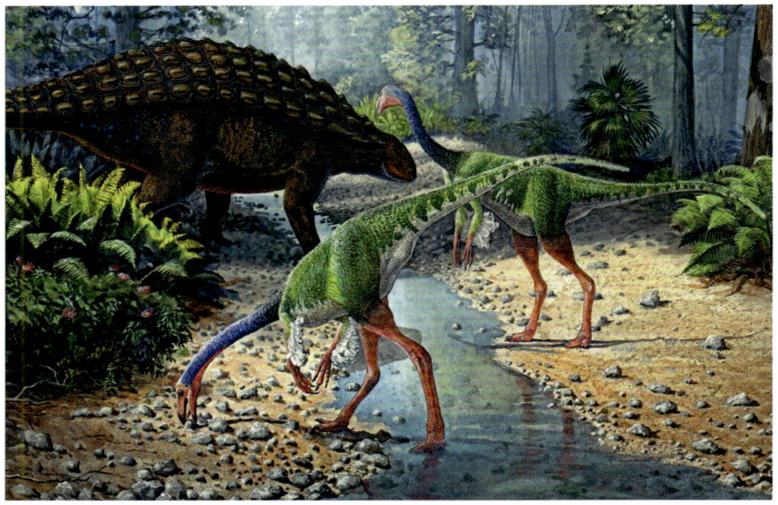

because I feel a piece requires it or if requested by the customer. I'm still not entirely happy with the look of my digital art; I feel there is always room for improvement.

Your image of Torvosaurus gurneyi *was seen worldwide when it was released with the announcement of the new species. How did you get involved in that project?*

That was largely thanks to Christophe Hendrick, who was working on the project alongside paleontologist Octávio Mateus. Together they described the giant from Portugal, naming it *Torvosaurus gurneyi* in honor of the famous illustrator and *Dinotopia* author James Gurney. I'm a great admirer of Gurney's work, so this was a big deal for me, as well as being my first experience working with professional paleontologists. However, I approached it as a standard illustration gig, so I wasn't totally unprepared when I saw it appear in the news, being published in popular scientific journals, and being presented at international competitions (including the sixth International Contest of Scientific Illustrations of Dinosaurs 2014 and the International Dinosaur Illustration Contest [CIID] 2014, where it was awarded the jury prize).

Is there any reason why you rarely illustrate big mammals?

It tends to be dictated by what my clients commission, and of course the highest demand is for dinosaurs, which I'm already known for. However, I've been diversifying recently, and my latest project – which I'm currently still working on – includes 20 illustrations of Cenozoic mammals and birds.

On a related note, your portfolio now includes various other underwater organisms, such as early whales, marine reptiles and frogs, as well as fish. All these are digital images; was it this change in medium that prompted you to begin illustrating prehistoric life below the water as well as above it?

Again, this was just a straightforward commission. These were done as part of a large project of more than 30 illustrations for the Primorsky

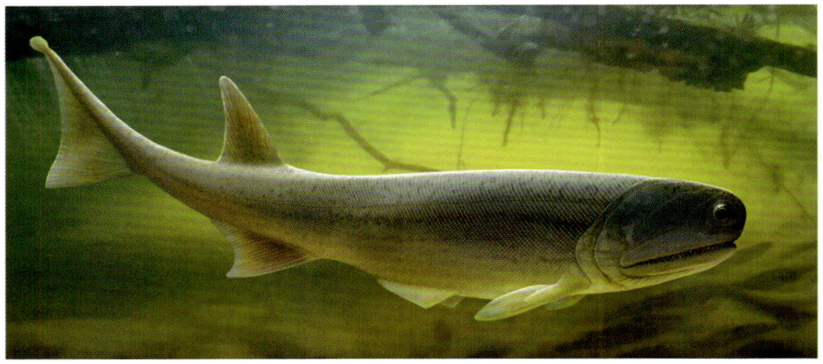

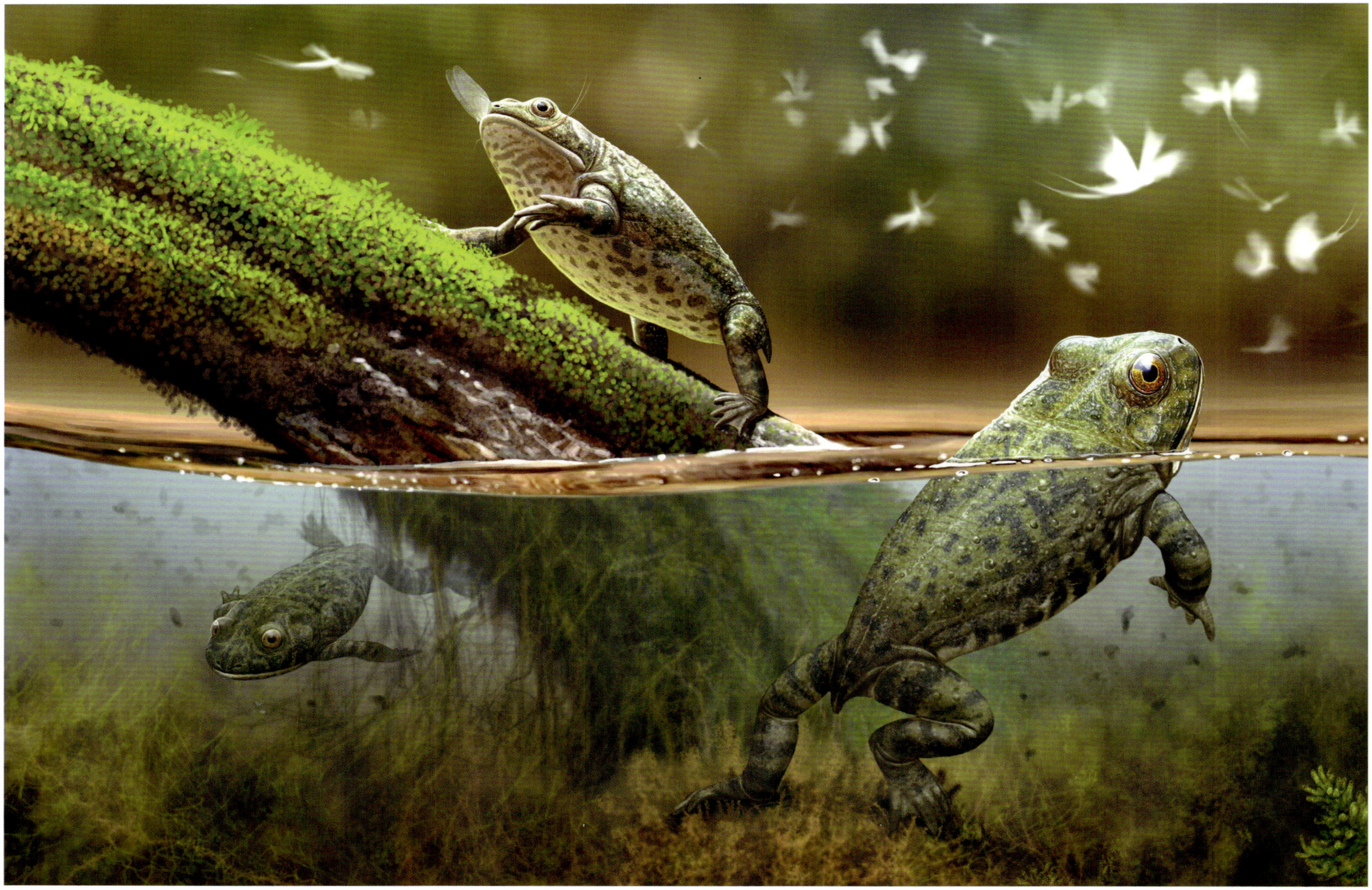

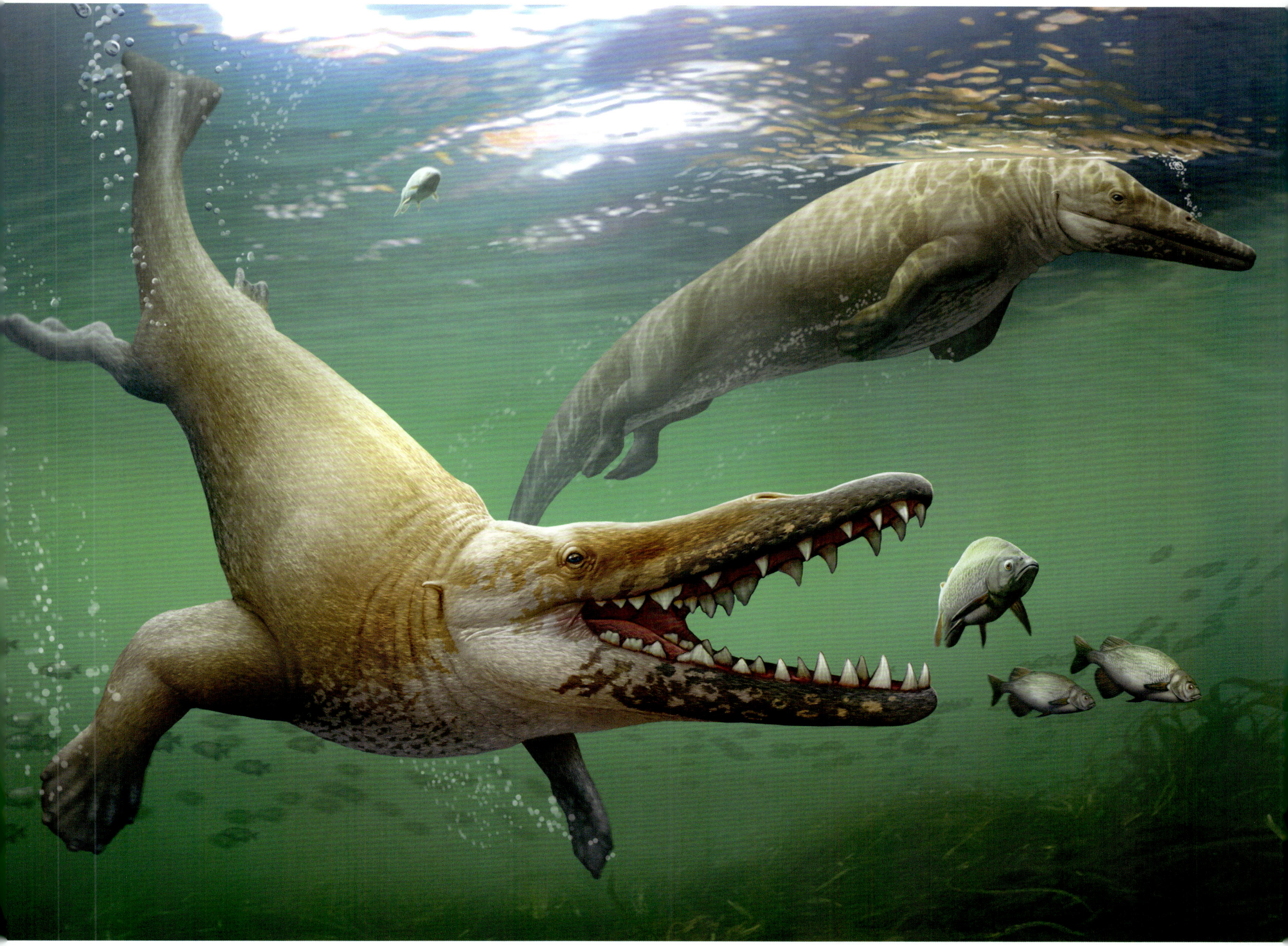

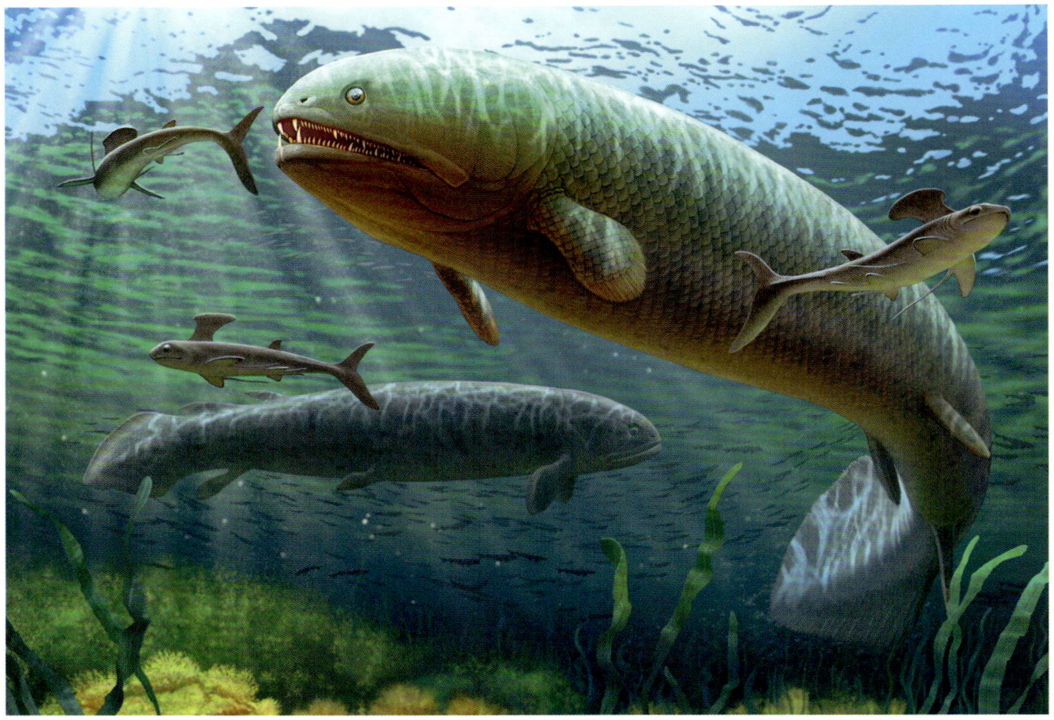

Oceanarium. It covered both marine and semi-aquatic organisms from the Cambrian to the Paleogene, but a large proportion of the series was devoted to the Devonian period, so the fish featured prominently. My approach was to look through hundreds of reference photos of modern fish to draw inspiration for my reconstructions; as a result, they're perhaps more photo-realistic in style than some of my other paintings. And, since it wasn't my area of expertise, I worked under the guidance of Andrey Atuchin, who also contributed many illustrations to the same project.

(Previous spread; Top)
Cheirolepis trailli
Digital, 2016

(Previous spread; Below)
Triadobatrachus massinoti
Digital, 2016

(Previous spread; Right)
Georgiacetus vogtlensis
Digital, 2016
An early whale about 40mya, from the southern USA. Its first remains were uncovered during the building of a nuclear power plant in Burke County, Georgia.

(Above) ***Rhizodus hibberti***
Digital

(Right) ***Ventastega curonica***
Digital

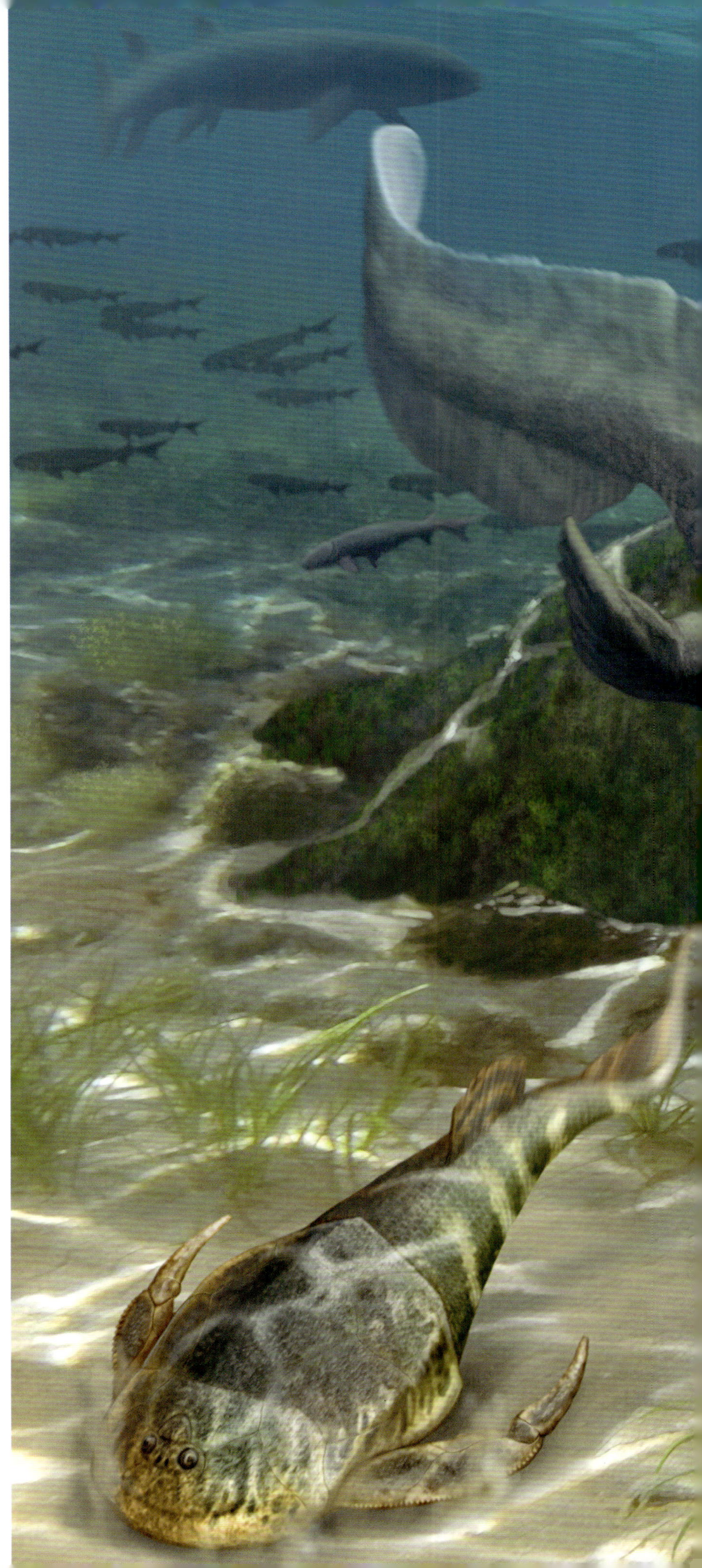

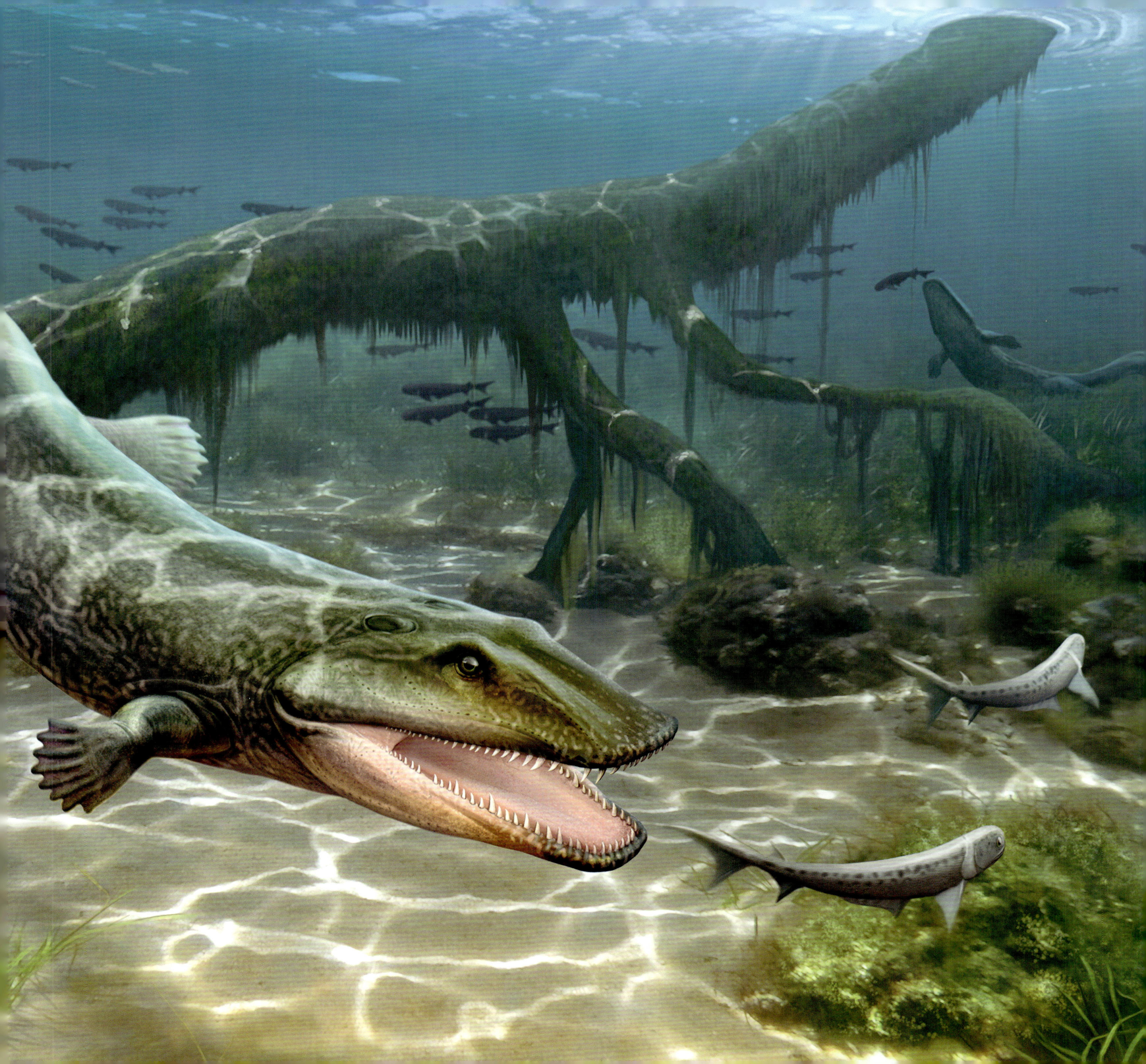

Fallen *Thalassodromeus sethi*
Digital, 2013

(Opposite) ***Epidexipteryx hui* vs *Nephila jurassica***
Digital, 2013
This strange little dinosaur was discovered in the Daohugou Beds of Inner Mongolia and named in 2008; the rocks were dated between the Mid- and Late Jurassic. The specimen preserved the animal's four long, ribbon-like tail feathers, leading to its name, which means 'Hui's display feathers'.

(Opposite below) ***Alioramus altai***
Digital

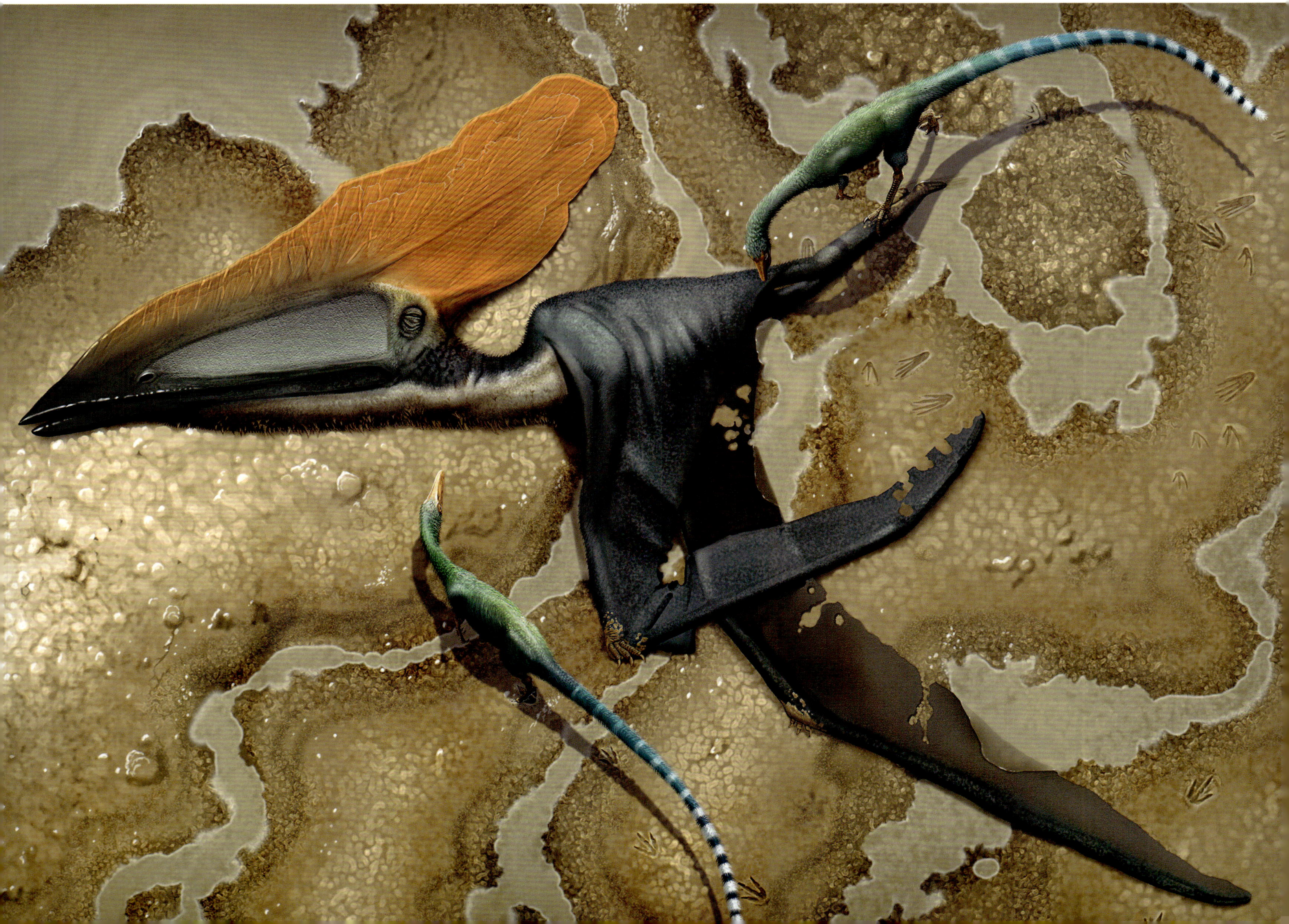

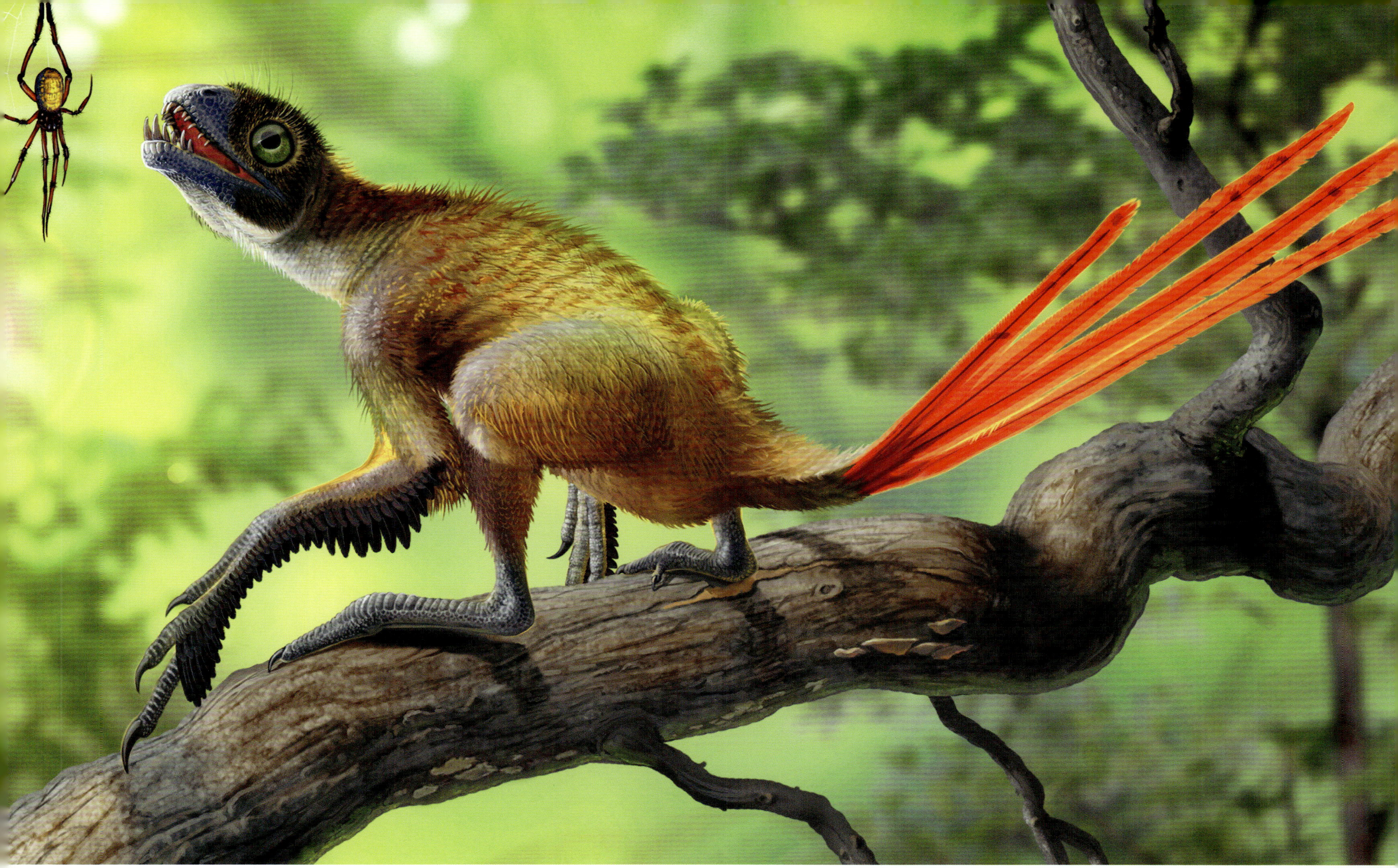

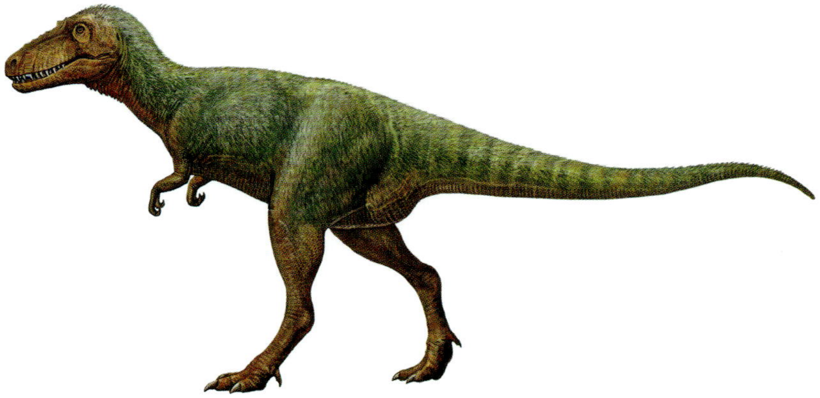

You also seem to enjoy painting 'big' dinosaurs – you rarely seem to work on smaller raptors and the like, which are so fashionable at the moment. Do you feel that's where you're most comfortable – with the classic giants?

One of the most appealing aspects of dinosaurs is their gigantism – it's what attracts children (and therefore the many publishers seeking to satisfy this interest). So commercially, large dinosaurs tend to be perennially popular. There are some exceptions – *Epidexipteryx hui*, for example.

Well, you do seem to really like Oviraptorids. You've illustrated quite a few of them. Is it their weirdness that interests you?

There are indeed a great many! I'm one of those artists that still draws the scales on my theropods, but I decided to experiment with feathers, depicting feathered dinosaurs with colors very much along the lines of modern birds. Oviraptosaurs were the ideal candidate for that!

OVIRAPTORIDS

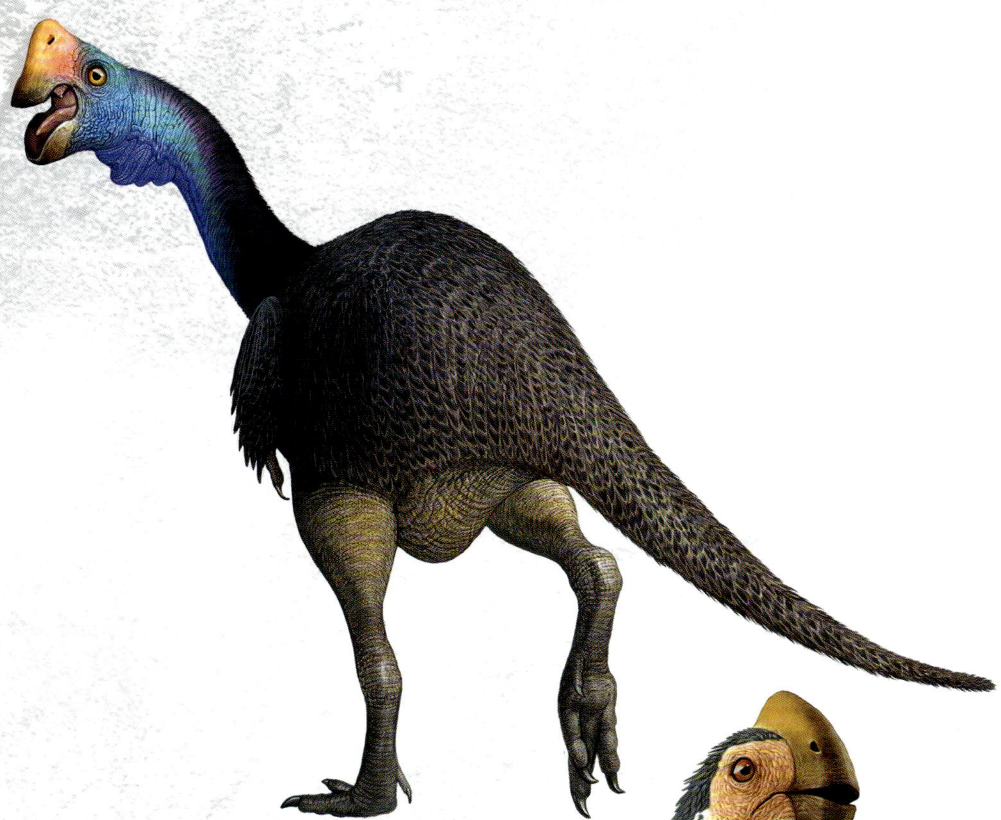

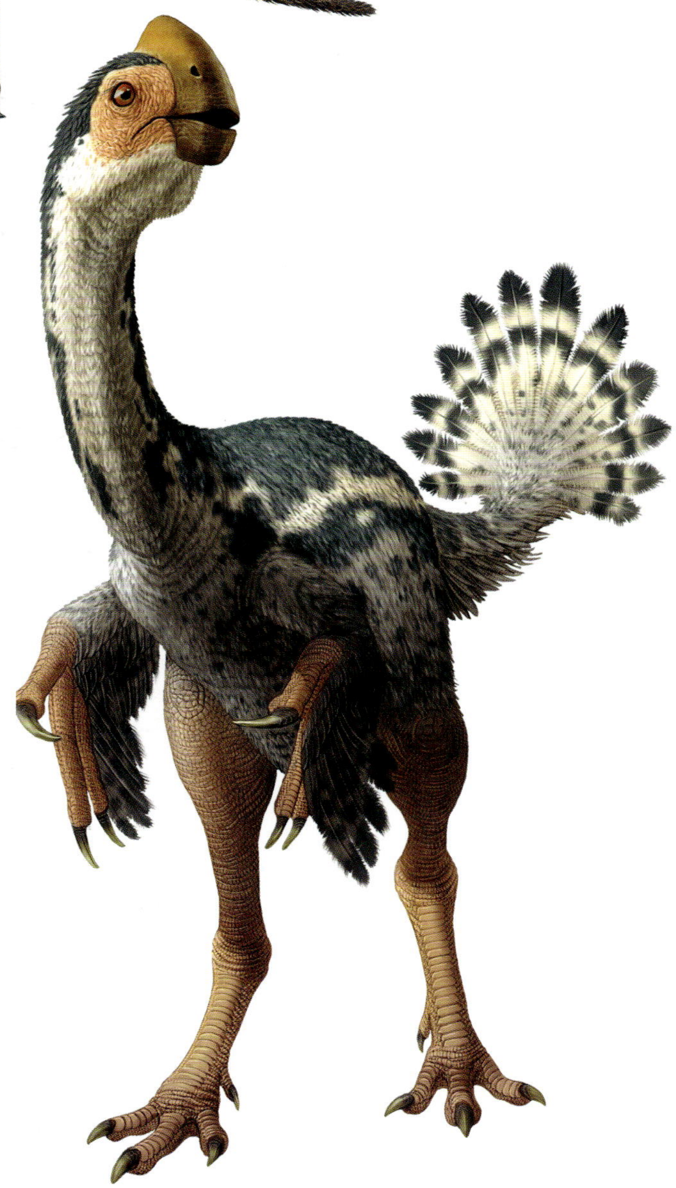

(Left) ***Nemegtomaia barsboldi***

(Right) ***Nomingia gobiensis***

(Opposite top) ***Conchoraptor gracilis***

(Opposite bottom) ***Ajancingenia yanshini***

Oviraptorids are among the weirdest of the maniraptoran dinosaurs, the group that includes the bird-like dromaeosaurs and troodontids as well as birds themselves. So far as we know, oviraptorids are unique to Late Cretaceous China and Mongolia. Other closely related groups (included with oviraptorids within the larger group Oviraptorosauria) also occurred in central and eastern Asia and North America. Fragmentary records might indicate that oviraptorosaurs occurred in Europe and Australia too.

Overall, oviraptorids were long-legged, long-necked maniraptorans with long arms and three-fingered hands. Most were 5-8ft (1.5-2.5m) long, the largest species perhaps weighing 160lb (75kg) or so. *Gigantoraptor* from the Santonian of northern China (it may or may not be an oviraptorid, but is certainly an oviraptorosaur) is exceptional, however, at 24ft (8m) in length and weighing around 2.2 tons (2 tonnes).

The elongate legs of oviraptorids suggest that they were reasonably good runners, though not specialised for high-speed running. Hand length is variable within the group, with both long-fingered and short-fingered species. All three of the fingers are tipped with large, strongly curved claws, and long feathers grew from the upper surfaces of the second and third fingers at least.

It seems that oviraptorids (and probably all oviraptorosaurs and non-bird maniraptorans) were extensively feathered across the entire body. This feathering is well preserved in *Caudipteryx*, a turkey-sized oviraptorosaur from the Early Cretaceous named for the large, long feathers that project from the end part of its tail. A fan-like arrangement of tail feathers seems to have been typical of oviraptorosaurs and might explain why they evolved a proportionally short, muscular tail rather than a long, slender one – maybe the tail was elevated and shimmied during mating displays, the tail feathers acting like those of a peacock. A feather-supporting

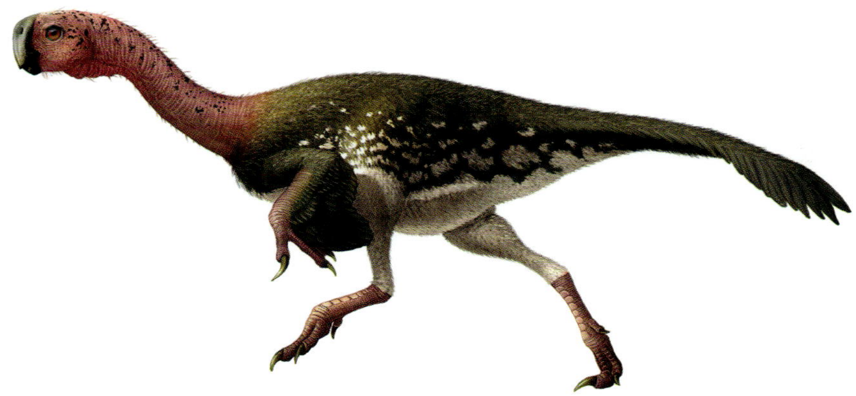

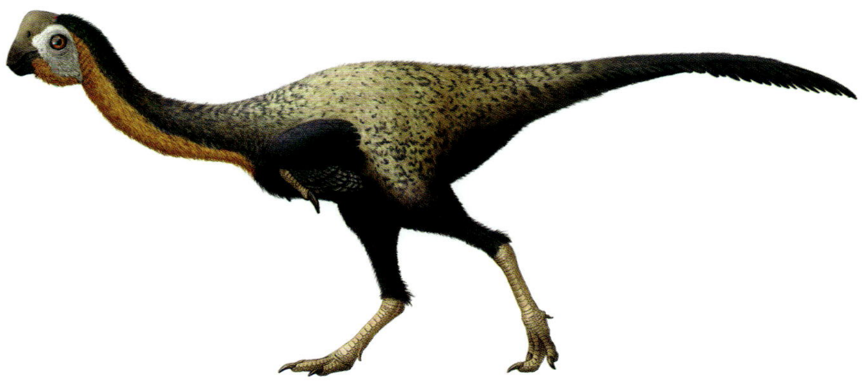

role for the tail is consistent with the presence of a fused group of vertebrae at the tail's tip in at least some oviraptorosaur species.

The oviraptorid skull is short and deep, toothless, superficially parrot-like, very lightly built with numerous pneumatic openings, and sometimes equipped with a hollow crest along the upper midline. The nostrils are located high up at the front of the snout and the palate is equipped with a pair of triangular, tooth-like projections. The crests vary in shape and size from one species to another and not all have one, which might be linked to sex or age. In life, these crests were surely sheathed in keratin and were likely not dissimilar to the casques of modern cassowaries.

Oviraptorid diet is contentious. The strongly built nature of the jaws has led some experts to propose that these animals were crushing objects, perhaps shellfish, eggs, seeds or nuts, but the overall form of the skull and beak suggests a mostly herbivorous diet. However, a well-preserved specimen of *Oviraptor* has a lizard in its gut cavity, while a nest of *Citipati* includes the skulls of two juvenile predatory troodontids. Maybe these animals were omnivores, behaving like large pheasants or chickens.

Oviraptor – the namesake member of the group – has a name that means 'egg thief', a name bestowed on it after its 1923 discovery on a now-famous American Museum of Natural History expedition to the Flaming Cliffs of Mongolia. The fossil was associated with a nest of eggs (the first good dinosaur nest to be discovered) thought to belong to the small horned dinosaur *Protoceratops*. The assumption was therefore made that the *Oviraptor* had been caught and killed during the act of nest robbing, hence its name. However, this preconception was upended in 1993 when an egg identical to those discovered in 1923 was found to contain the embryo of not *Protoceratops*, but an oviraptorid. The *Oviraptor* discovered in 1923 was in association with its own eggs.

Several oviraptorid specimens discovered in associated with egg-filled nests are now known. They mostly belong to *Citipati*, a large Mongolian oviraptorid closely related to *Oviraptor*, and are preserved in a textbook 'brooding' pose, the legs folded beneath the body and the arms and hands folded at the sides. When *Citipati* was alive, the region was mostly desert, so it seems that these dinosaurs were both protecting their eggs from predators and providing them with thermal protection: keeping them cool during the day and warm at night. Such was the strength of their nesting instinct that these adults evidently stayed with their eggs until they were overwhelmed by the sandstorms that apparently killed them.

The nests themselves were scraped out in the sand; up to 22 eggs were then laid in a circle, in pairs, and in as many as three layers. Oviraptorid eggs were elongate ovals; in *Citipati*, they were 18cm long, but apparently smaller in other species. Those 1923 eggs originally associated with *Protoceratops* are somewhat smaller, approximately 12cm long. Study of the embryonic remains led to them being assigned to *Citipati* too.

Gigantoraptor has also been associated with nests and eggs; these nests were 10ft (3m) in diameter and contained eggs 1.6ft (0.5m) in length but similar in structure to those of *Citipati*. They could only have belonged to animals as large as *Gigantoraptor*.

One oviraptorid fossil (representing an as-yet unnamed oviraptorid) consists of a partial pelvis preserved with two *in situ* eggs within its pelvic canals. Modern birds tend to lay one egg at a time and have only a single functional oviduct; the ancestral condition present in other reptiles is for both ovaries to be functional and for eggs to be laid in a single batch. This discovery indicates that oviraptorids possessed two functional ovaries and hence were not fully bird-like. The eggs were laid in pairs, presumably as the female sat in the center of the nest and rotated in a circle. The narrower end of the egg was directed inwards.

Some particularly interesting information on oviraptorid eggs came to light in 2015. A study on the microscopic structure of eggs associated with *Heyuannia* from China revealed how the eggshell was originally blue-green. Bird eggshell derives its color from the addition of two pigments that are added as the eggs move down the pelvic canal; one comes from bile, the other from haemoglobin. In the *Heyuannia* eggs, the eggshell was found to contain biliverdin (derived from bile), and protoporphyrin (derived from haemoglobin). These are the same pigments present in the blue-green eggs of such extant birds as emus and the American robin. The fact that oviraptorid eggs were blue-green is consistent with the idea that adults sat on top of these eggs to brood them: animals that bury their eggs and leave them concealed do not need egg camouflage of this sort and hence produce white eggshell.

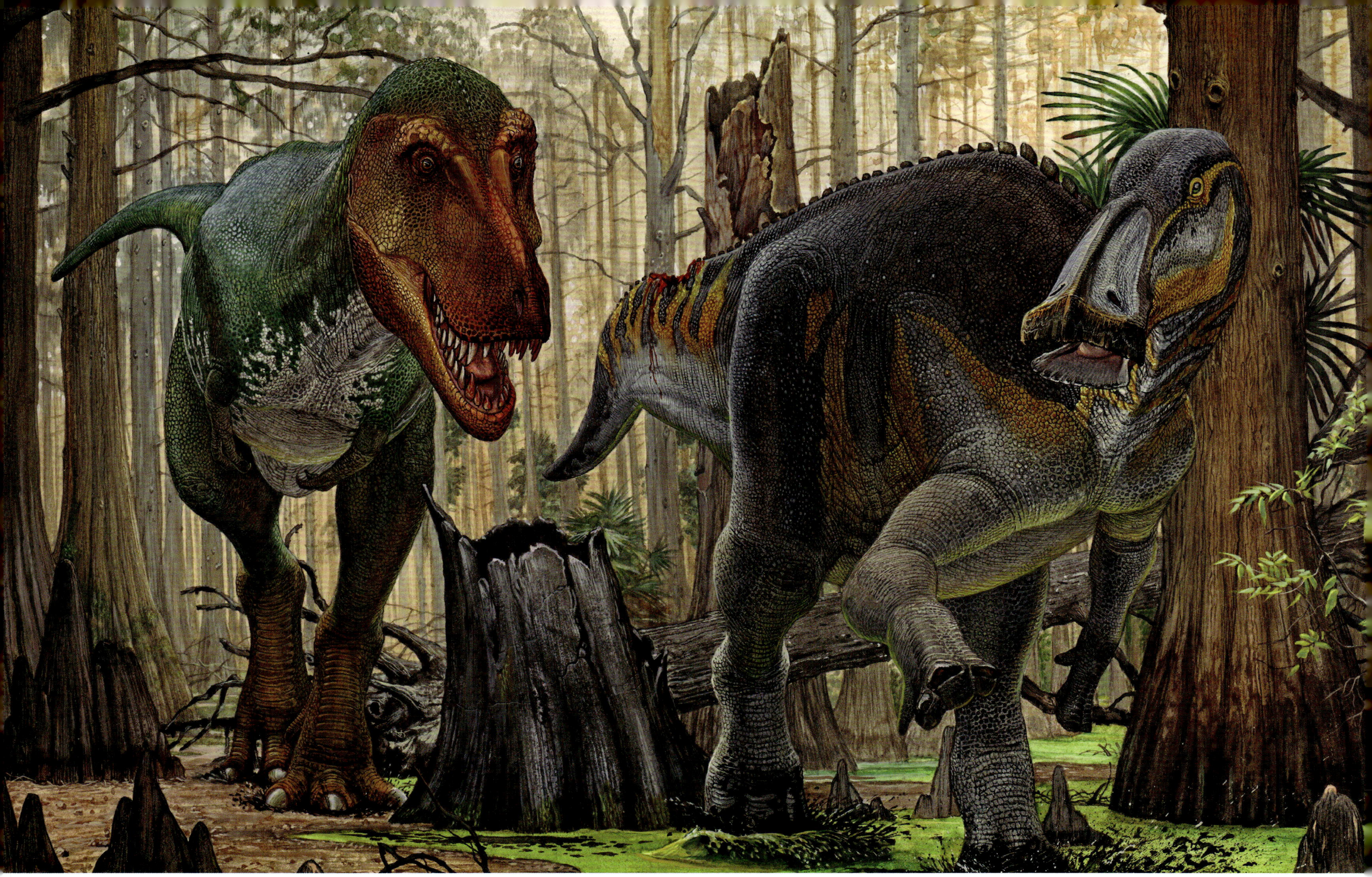

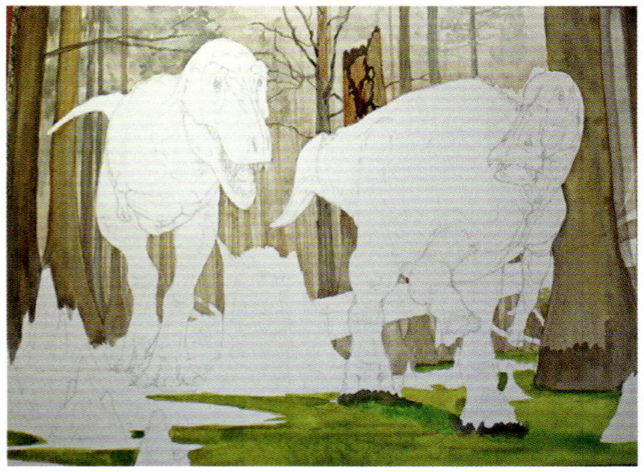

Do you do much sketching? Go to museums or out into woodland with a sketchbook and pencil?

I used to do a lot of sketching – I still have a whole folder of these from my early years, although many of course are showing their age. I mostly sketch digitally now, and this tends to get built up gradually into what becomes the final piece. Sometimes the earlier sketches get sent to the customer as part of the process of finding the direction that the piece will take.

You still, even now, produce traditional painting? Even with the advantages that digital tools provide, do you miss getting your hands dirty with paint?

Oh yes, I'm still very fond of traditional techniques, although I find I use them less often now, mostly due to lack of time. My wife gave me a large easel recently, and I bought a canvas and frame. I plan to use it for a traditional-style oil painting. The technique may be old, but it is still relevant and in demand today.

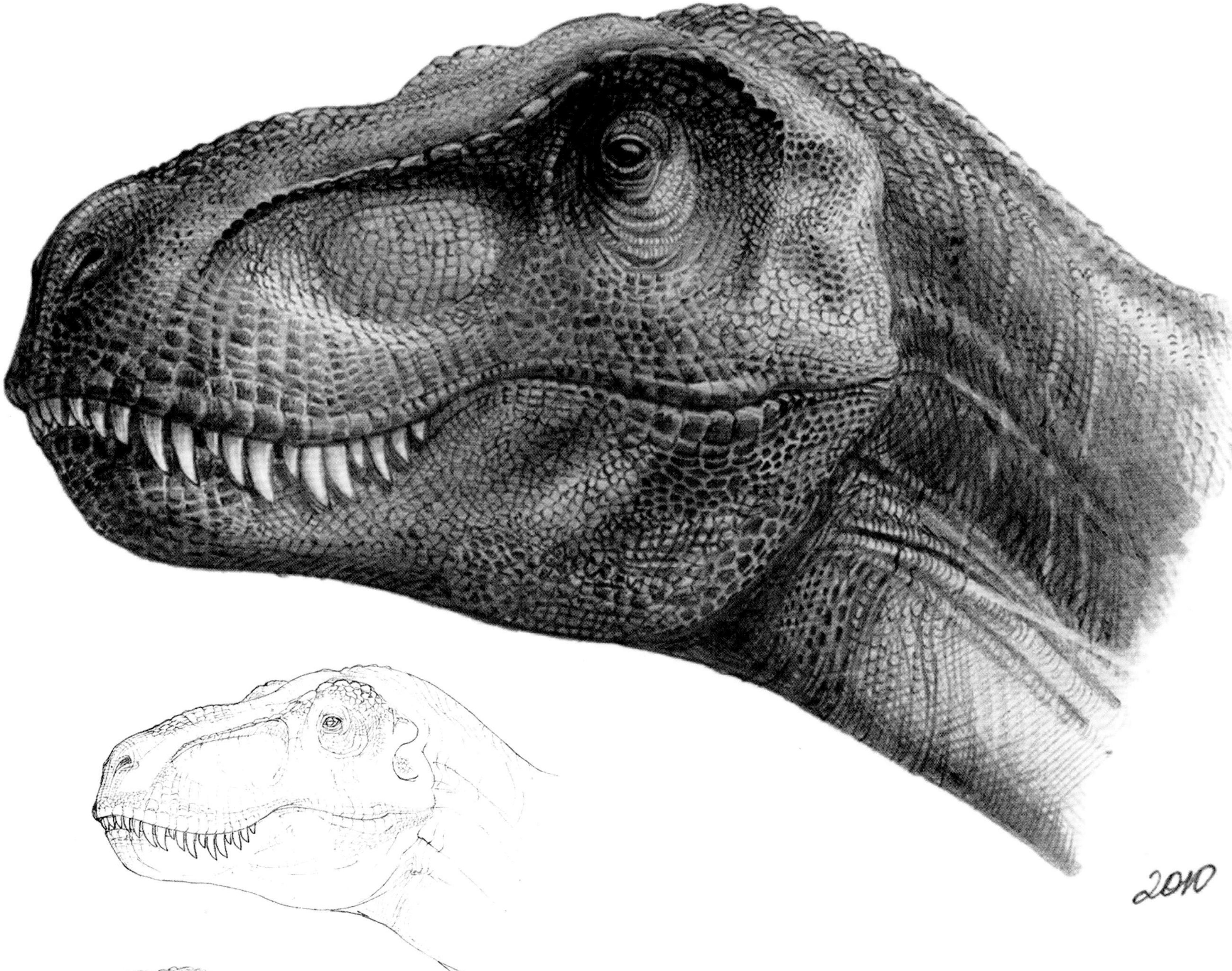

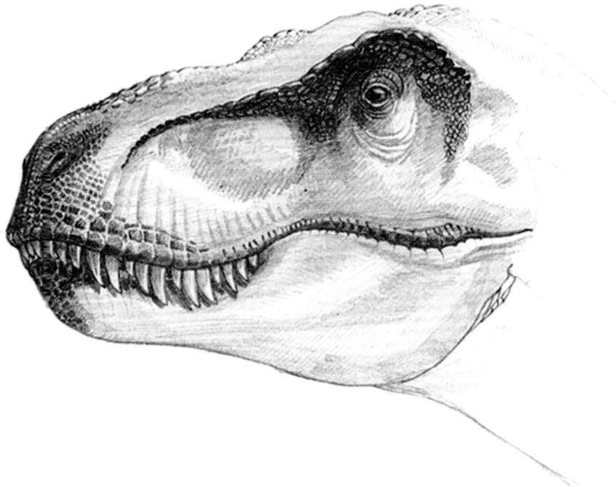

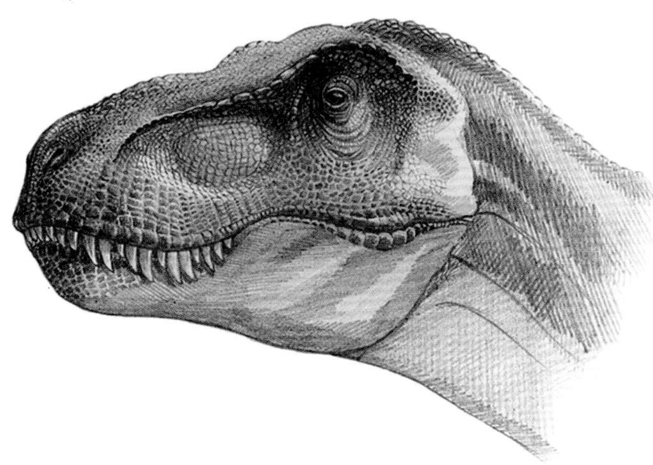

***Tyrannosaurus rex* Portrait**
Pencils

(Opposite) **Stan: *Tyrannosaurus rex* vs *Edmontosaurus annectens***
Gouache, 2014
Based on the *T-rex* specimen known as "Stan", the tyrannosaur pursues the hadrosaur *Edmontosaurus* through the swamps of North America at the very end of the Cretaceous. An *Edmontosaurus* specimen on display in the Denver Museum of Nature and Science sports damage to its tail vertebrae; the spine on one bone has been snapped off, while others have teeth marks, apparently left by an attacking tyrannosaur.

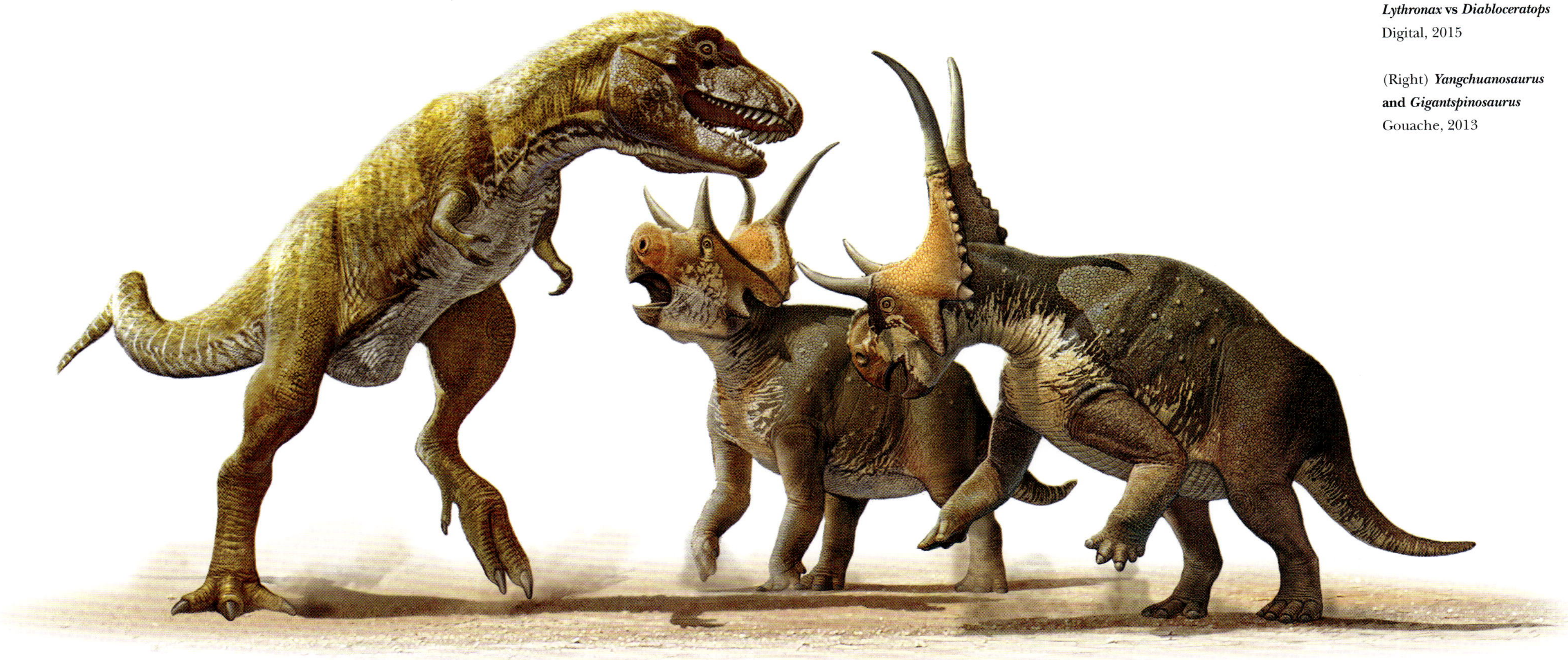

Lythronax* vs *Diabloceratops
Digital, 2015

(Right) ***Yangchuanosaurus* and *Gigantspinosaurus***
Gouache, 2013

(Below) **Symbiosis: *Giganotosaurus carolinii* and *Alnashetri cerropoliciensis***
Gouache, 2012
The little alvarezsauroid theropod *Alnashetri* cautiously picks scraps from the open jaws of the giant carnivore *Giganotosaurus*. This speculative behavior is seen between birds and crocodiles, and fish and sharks.

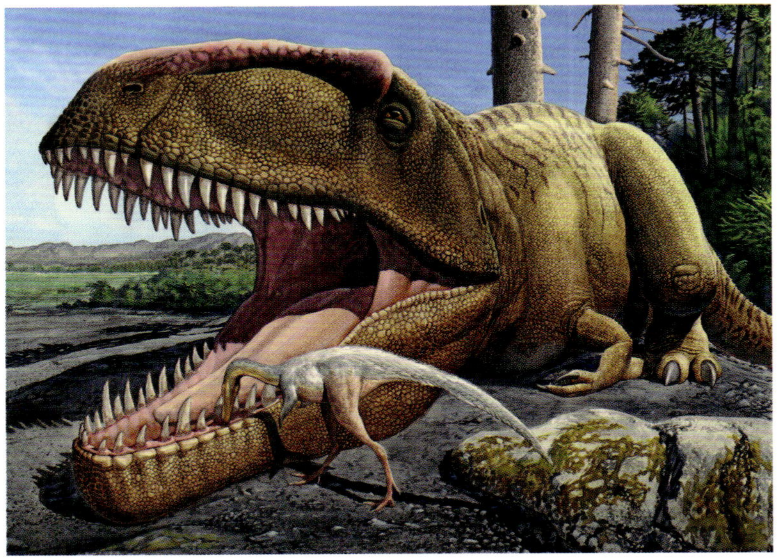

Some of your art has the feel of early and classical natural history illustrations from the 19th century – were those artists an influence on your own development?
Yes, I was really influenced by Charles Knight in particular. His paintings left a strong impression on me. I think most artists sort of accumulate different visual styles and influences, mix them up and what ends up on paper is a sort of cocktail: new imagery with shades of what went before.
You're friends with Russian paleoartist Andrey Atuchin; what advice did he give you when you first started out as a paleoartist?
I met Andrey in 2010, through the Dinoweb forum, which we both subscribed to and where I'd just publicly posted my work for the first time. Andrey asked if I was a professional artist, and I found out he was working on a book for Dougal Dixon. He gave me some guidance on anatomy, and helped steer my work – focusing more on the avian forms. We later met up in Moscow at the Paleontological Museum. The following year, he suggested I enter the international paleoart competitions – he ended up winning all of them (I think there were three in total), but I came in second. So he's really pushed me in my career. We have since collaborated professionally, too – on the Primorsky Oceanarium project I mentioned previously, and for a new paleoart book we've jointly created.

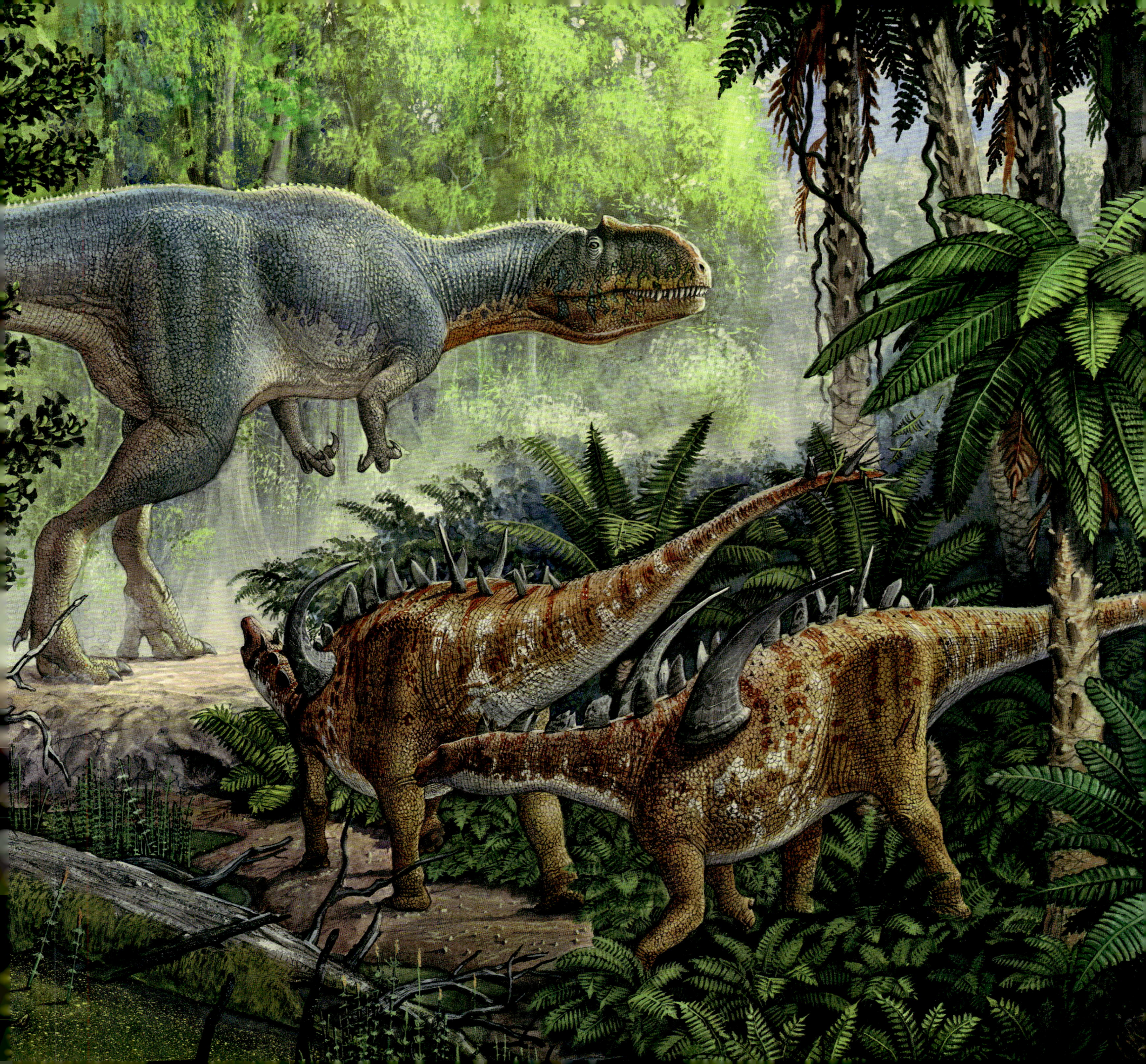

EMILY WILLOUGHBY

USA

Despite a childhood love of artwork, Emily fully intended to be a scientist first; as such she graduated with a Bachelor's degree in Biology in 2012. However, her interest in art and paleoart in particular was rekindled by the sensational discoveries of feathered dinosaurs in the late 1990s. This dovetailed with another of her childhood passions, birds and birdwatching, and she began to garner a reputation as a fine artist of dinosaurs, particularly feathered genera. From 2006, her work began appearing in a variety of magazines worldwide, including *National Geographic*, *Discovery Channel Magazine* and *Popular Science*; and in several books, such as *Dinosaurs: Face to Face* and *The Birdwatcher's Bible*. She has also provided artwork for a number of academic papers, including the announcement of the discovery of *Dakotaraptor* in 2015, and was co-author of *God's Word or Human Reason?: An Inside Perspective on Creationism*, published in January 2016. She is currently doing a PhD in personality, individual differences and behavior genetics, with a focus on human intelligence. She also continues to indulge in another of her great loves – bird photography.

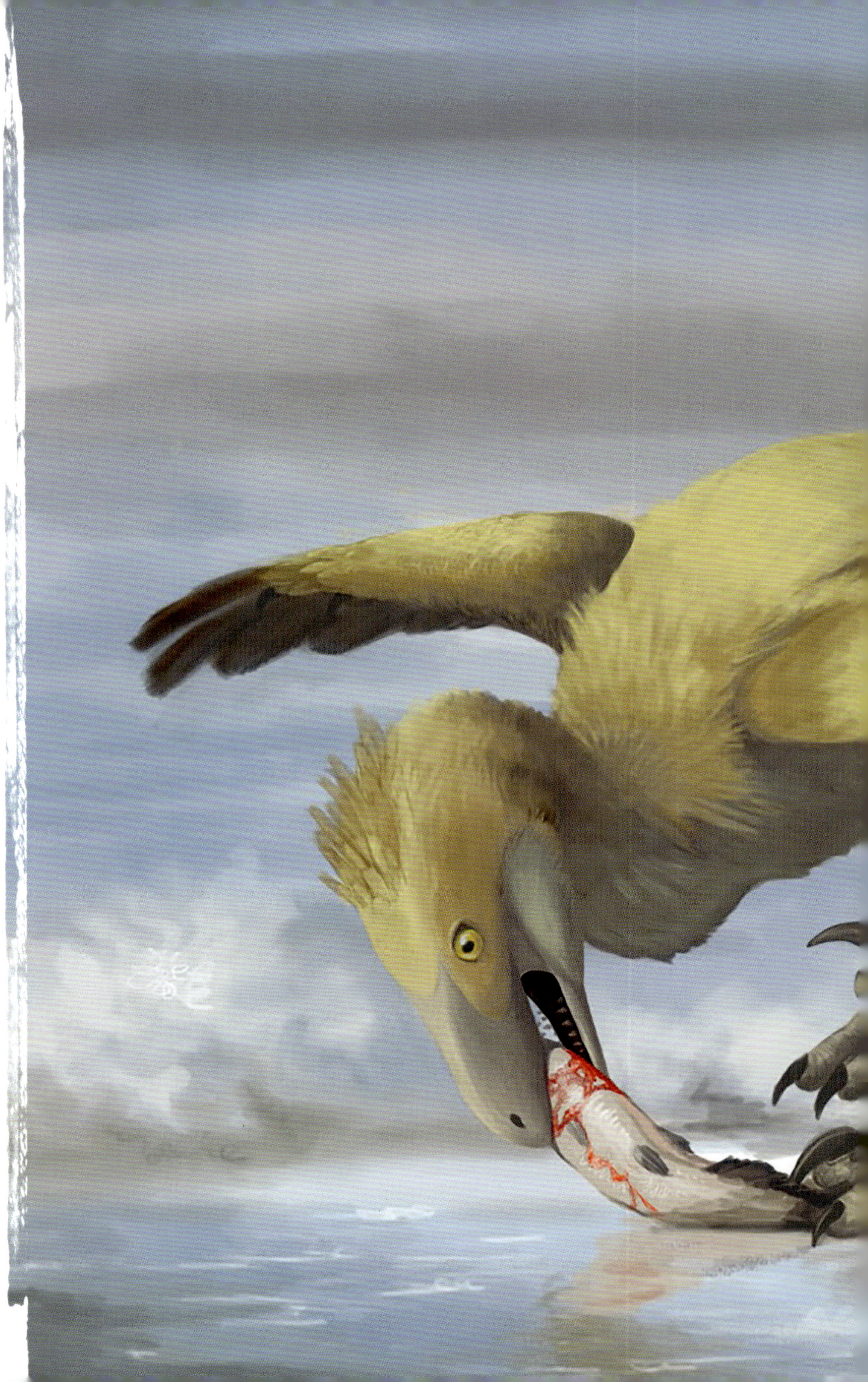

***Deinonychus* Sushi**
Digital, 2013

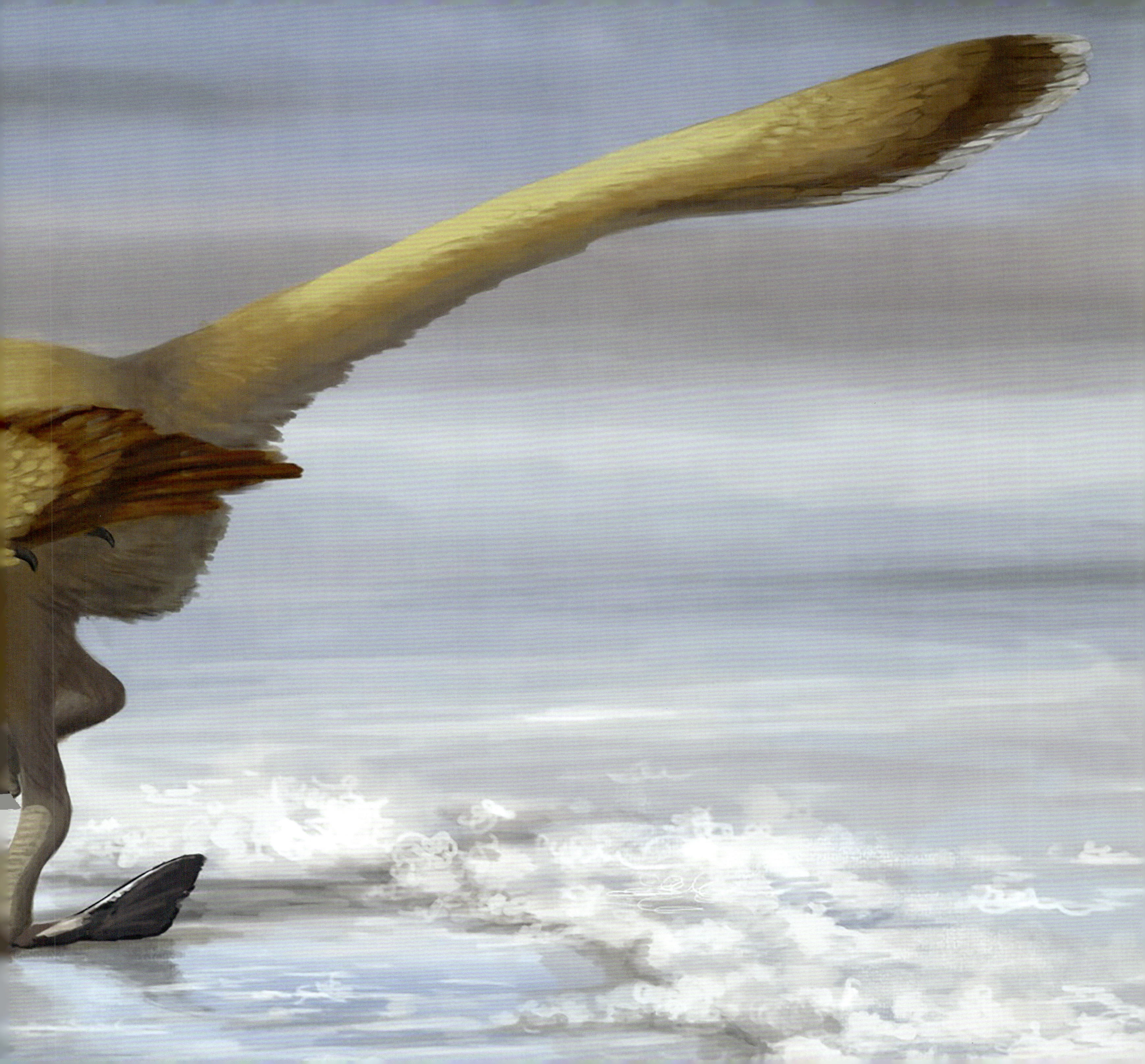

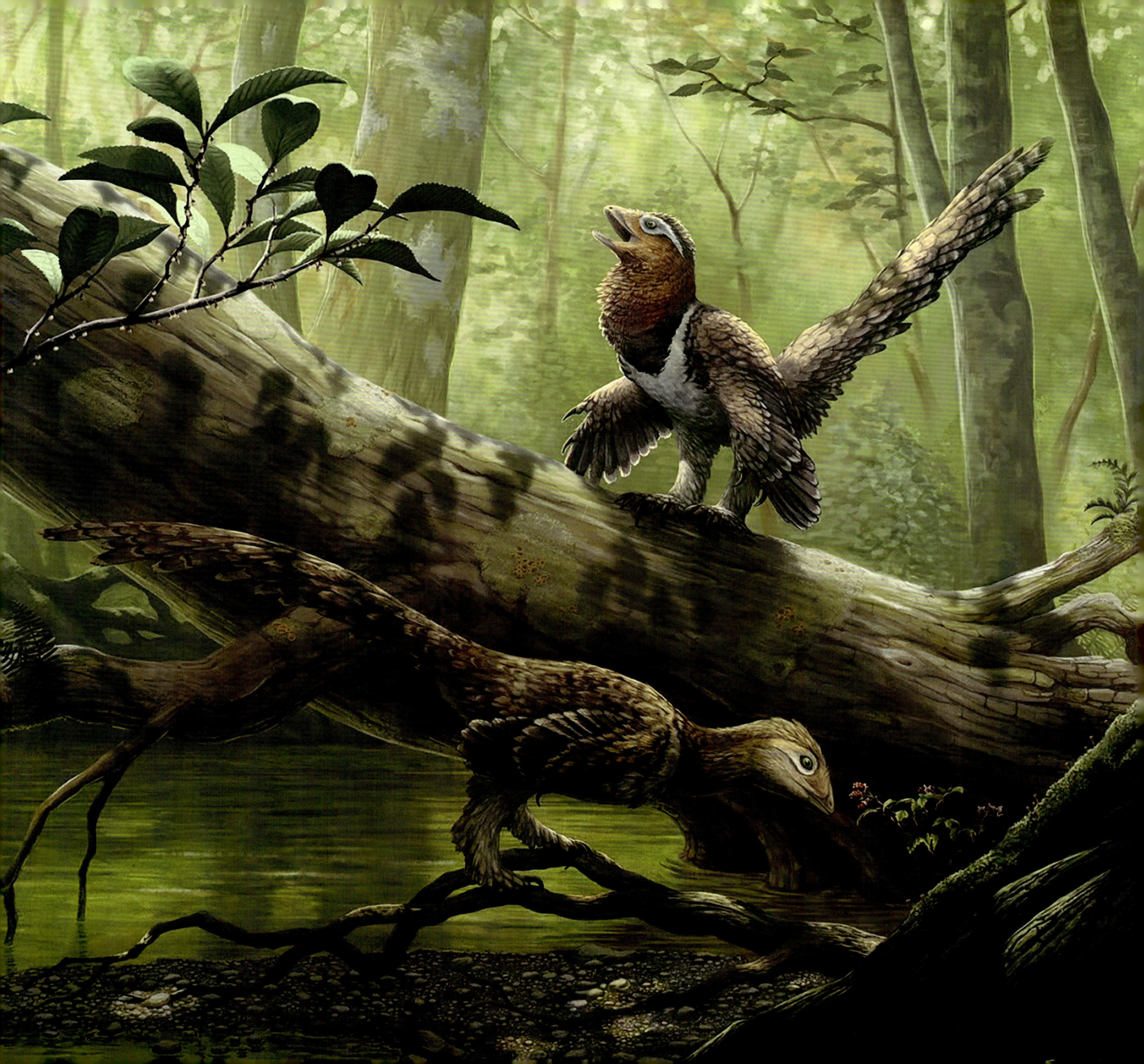

(Left) ***Balaur bondoc***
Digital, 2015
Best known for its twin 'sickle claws', *Balaur's* second claw was actually an enlarged hallux – the backward facing toe seen in birds that enables them to grasp branches. It is also possible *Balaur* was actually a flightless bird about the size of a pheasant. Maastrichtian Stage, Late Cretaceous, 70mya. Hateg Basin, Romania.

(Right) **The Earliest Birds**
Gouache, 2014
A visual representation of the question, "Who was the earliest bird?" Was it *Archaeopteryx* (left) or the more recently described *Aurornis* from China? The complexity and confusion regarding the classification of such paravians – a diverse group of small theropod dinosaurs that almost certainly included the ancestors of true birds – has made the question somewhat moot, as it remains unclear if either animal was a bird or just something very close to it.

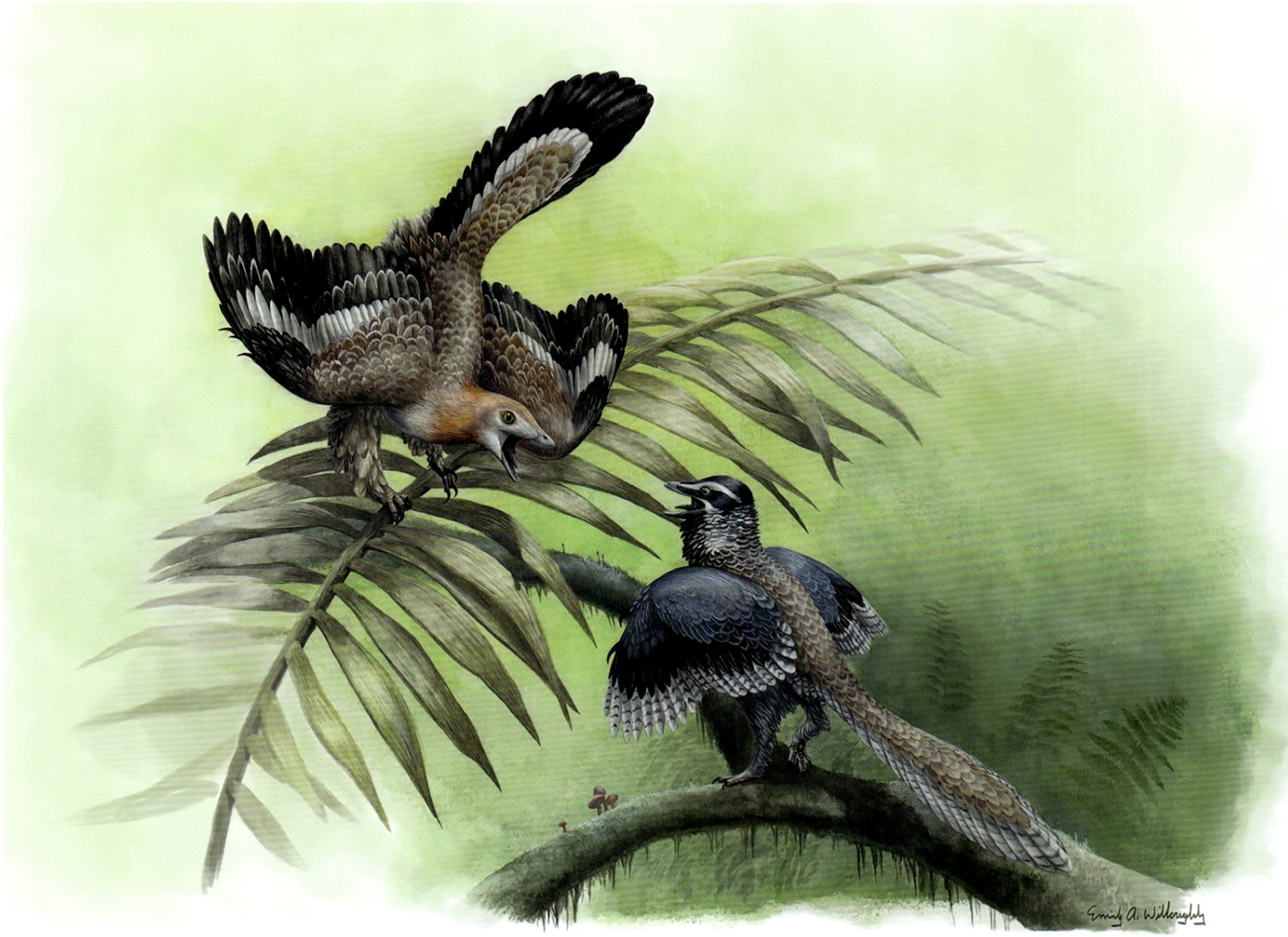

You're perhaps most closely associated with the reconstruction of feathered dinosaurs, but you also have an abiding interest in modern birds. Did one inform the other, and if so, which way round?

Though I have always been interested in both birds and non-avian dinosaurs, my passionate focus on these subjects developed mostly independently. Paleontology emerged as a dominant interest in high school, and my interest in birds developed into a fully fledged hobby following an excellent ornithology course in college. Though they had separate origins, they certainly engage in a great deal of horizontal transfer nowadays.

You're also a pretty decent ornithological photographer; how much does that influence your artwork?

My bird photography has become an invaluable resource for paleoart in more ways than one. Not only does it give me reference images for composition, feather texture, anatomy and more, but it also exposes me to the habitat, behavior and motion of birds in the field, which has myriad applications for reconstructing extinct dinosaurs as real breathing, moving animals.

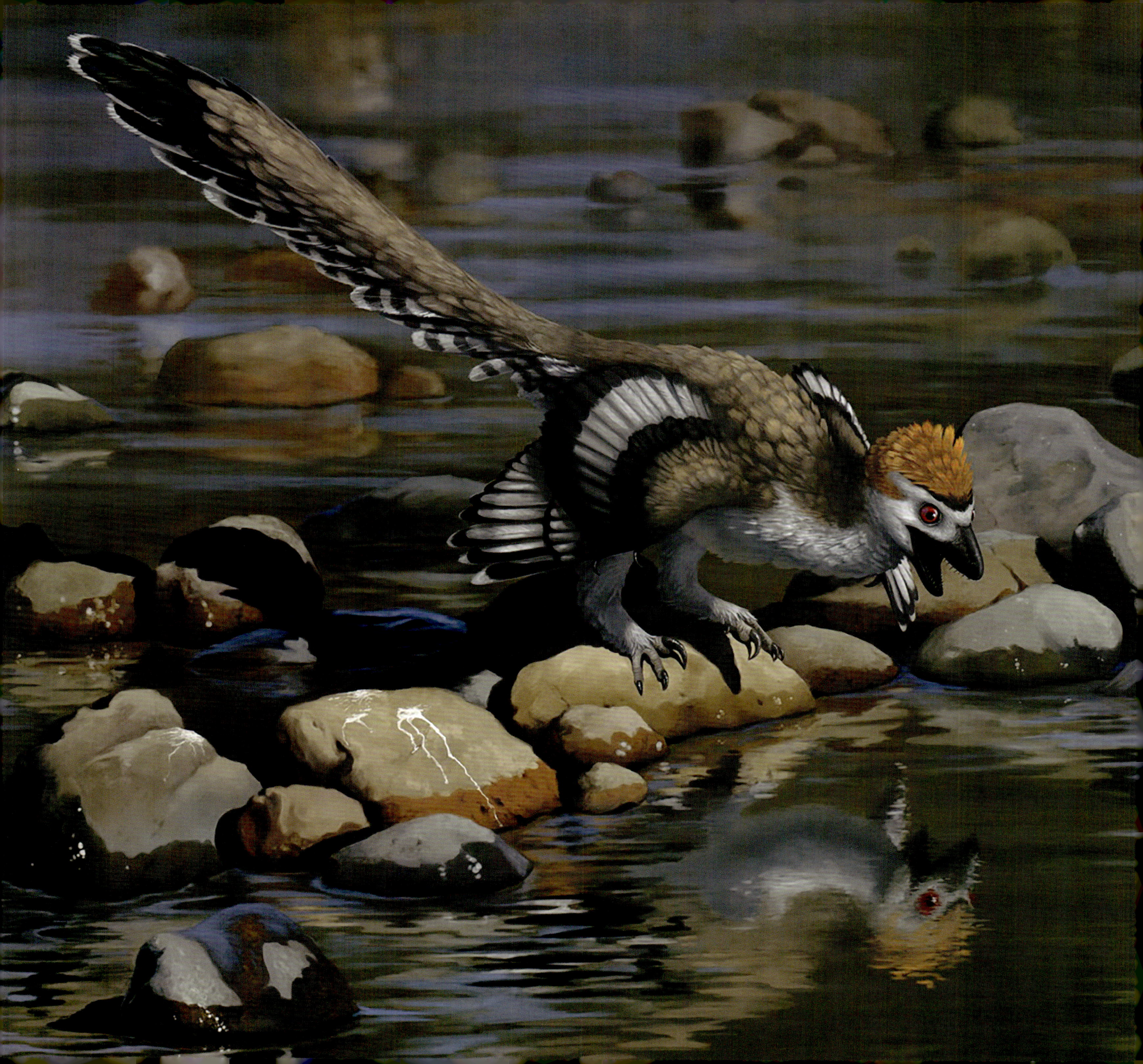

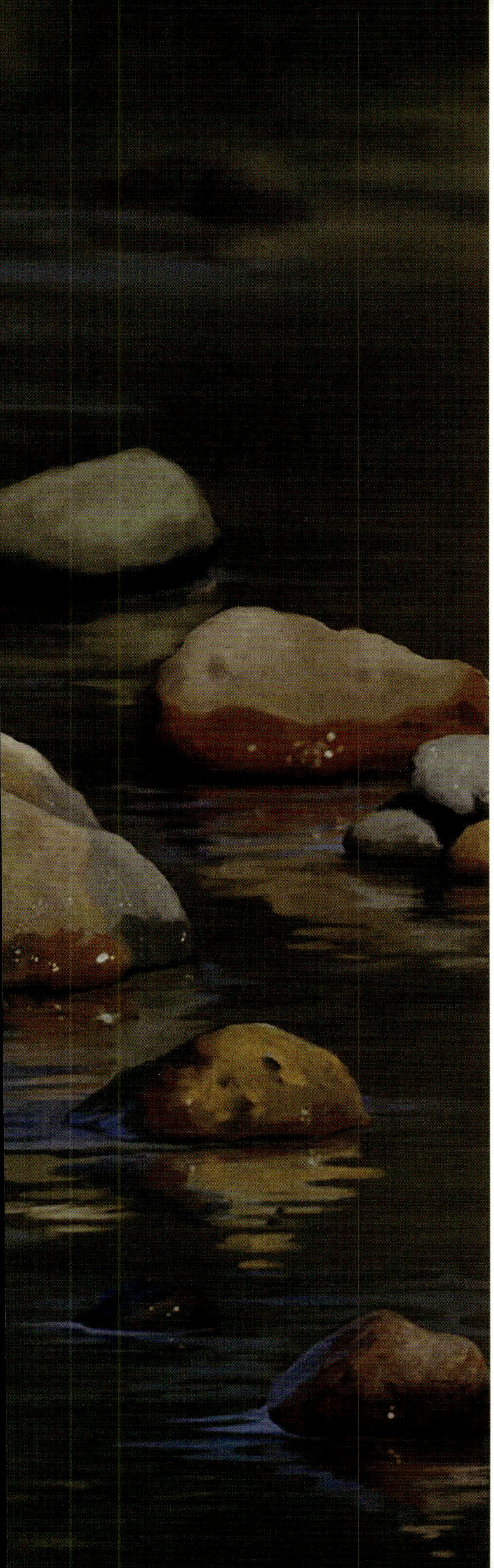

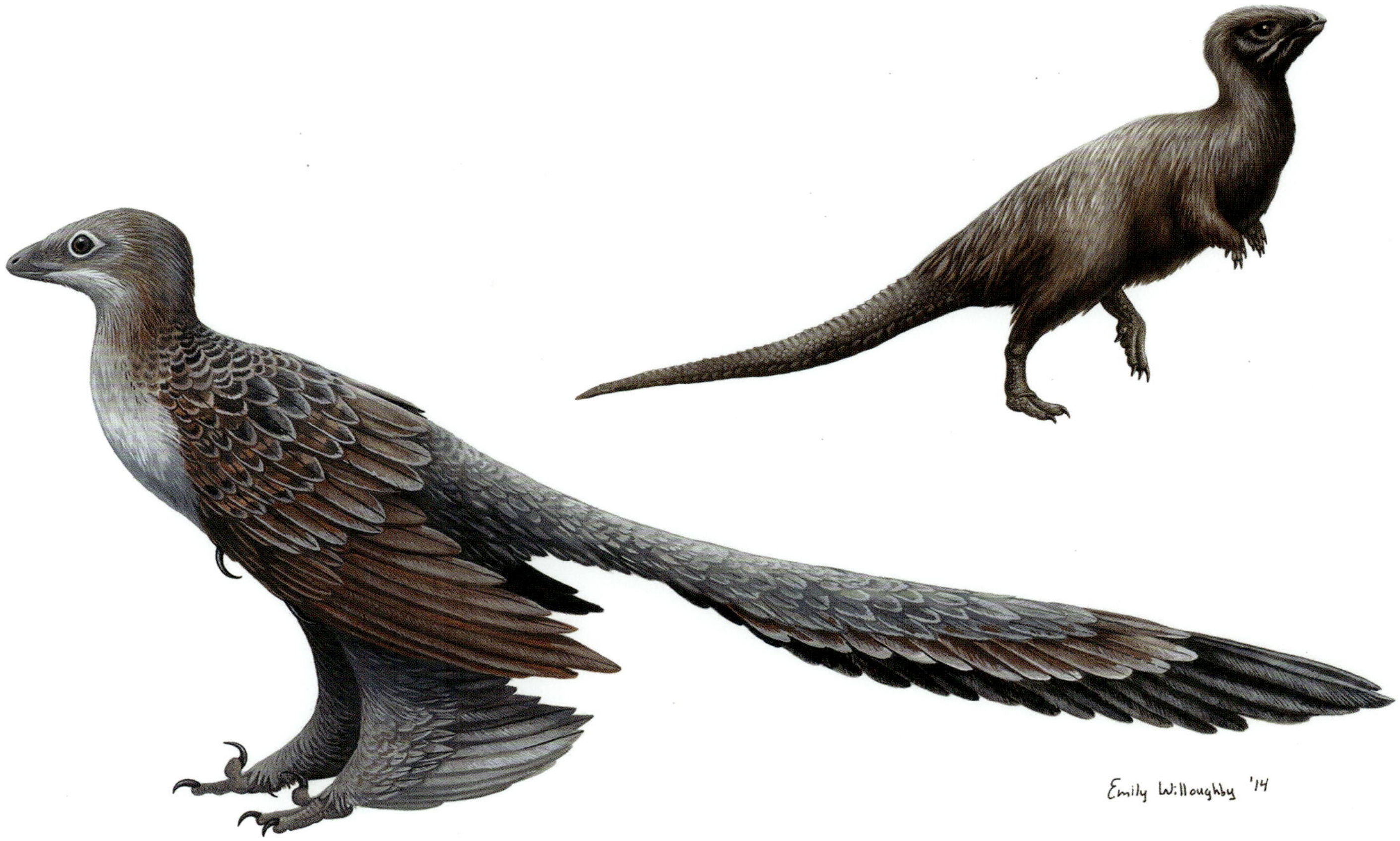

(Left) **Reflections on *Zhenyuanlong***
A male *Zhenyuanlong* encounters his own reflection and, seething with rage, begins a threat display, hoping to drive off the intruder. Similar behavior is seen in modern birds encountering windows or mirrors. Aptian Stage, Early Cretaceous, 125mya. Yixian Formation, China.

(Above right) ***Kulindadromeus***
Gouache, 2014

(Above) ***Changyuraptor***
Gouache, watercolor, 2014

Do you cast a particular bird when you're illustrating a particular feathered dinosaur?
Like many paleoartists, I've given in to the temptation to model a feathered dinosaur from an extant bird numerous times. I try to limit that practice nowadays, though, preferring instead the challenge and authenticity of constructing a unique but believable color scheme from scratch. I do think it's reasonable to draw inference from motifs common to groups of birds that may have had similar niches and lifestyles to extant birds. For example, my recent reconstructions of the tropical archipelago-dwelling *Archaeopteryx* are influenced by color and pattern motifs common to extant shorebirds.

However, I dislike the practice of dressing up an extinct dinosaur in a shape and pattern identical to that of a living animal, and I think this has turned into an over-used meme in contemporary paleoart. Near-birds like dromaeosaurs and troodontids were certainly very avian in appearance and behavior, but they were not modern birds. We have become so concerned with proving that dinosaurs were birdlike, that birds are dinosaurs, that we sometimes forget their features that make them beautiful and unique on their own, and in many important ways totally unlike anything else that's ever walked this earth – or flown above it.

How do you approach a dinosaur where there's no close modern analogy, such as the case of Microraptor*?*
Microraptor is an incredibly unique dinosaur, with nothing quite like it alive today. In some ways, we can think of *Microraptor* as a mish-mash of characteristics analogous to extant birds – for example, the legwings reminiscent of fancy pigeons like the saddleback, and coloration and probable lifestyle similar to that of modern crows or grackles. On the whole, though, a lack of straightforward modern analogue means that it's all the more important to carefully study

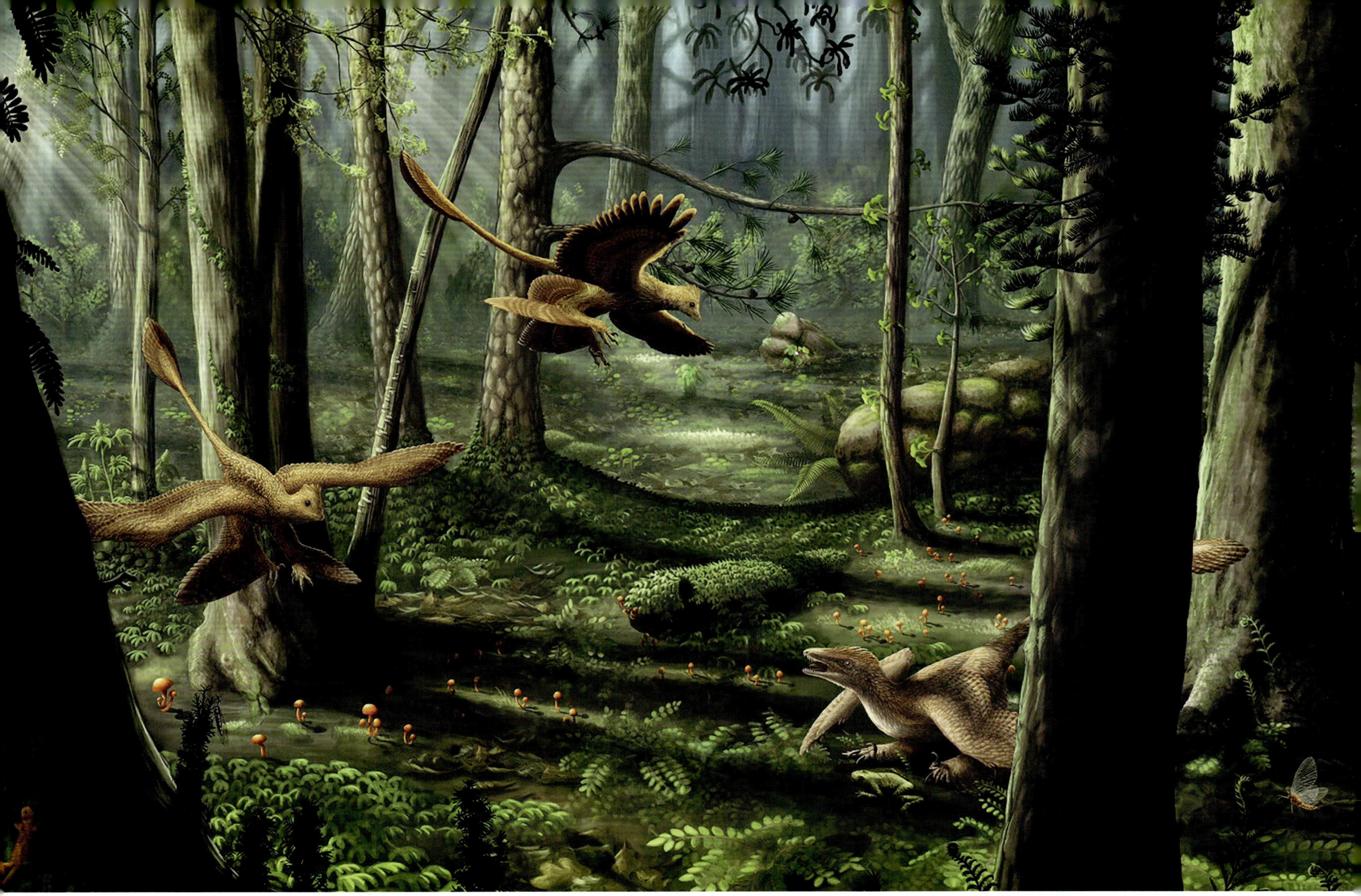

the fossils and the known data we have on the animal's morphology and lifestyle. We know a tremendous amount about *Microraptor* from an abundance of specimens, including plumage variation, diet, and even coloration. A great deal of imagination is needed to incorporate all of this information into creating a likeliness that actually looks like a realistic living animal.

How much anatomical detail do you go into when preparing a reconstruction?

This depends largely on the requirements of the piece, and on the amount of data we have on the taxon, but for a full-scale work intended as a representation of the current state of scientific rigor, the answer is: as much as possible. The variation in available data is vast – for some taxa

Liaoning Scene: *Microraptor* and *Sinornithosaurus*
Digital, 2011
Hypothetical scene set around 122mya in the Jehol Group of Early Cretaceous China. Included are the salamander *Liaoxitriton zhongjiani* (lower left, on tree); the snake fly *Alloraphidia*, the frog *Callobatrachus* – prey of *Sinornithosaurus millenii*; and the mayfly *Epicharmeropsis* (lower right). The two microraptors are generic, but based on *Microraptor gui*, although this species was not contemporaneous with *Sinornithosaurus*.

(Top left) ***Microraptor* Threat Display**
Digital, 2012
The colors on all the illustrations on p49 are modeled on studies of *Microraptor* specimens so well preserved that melansomes were detected, indicating the animal was an iridescent black.

MICRORAPTOR

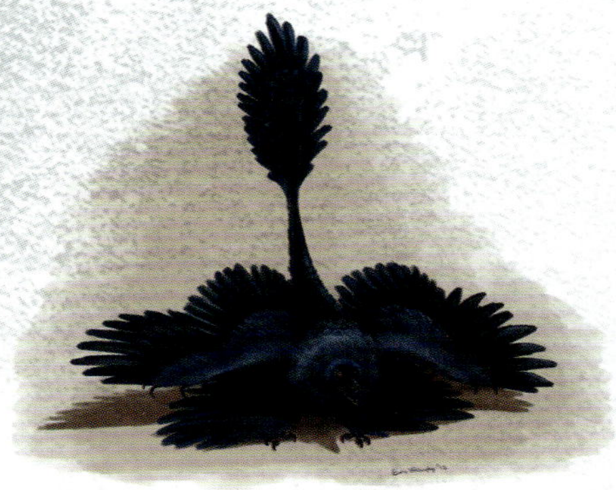

MICRORAPTOR
Genus: *Microraptor*
Species: *zhaoianus*
Location: Liaoning, China
Named: 2000
Age: Early Cretaceous Period (early/mid Aptian Stages), 120 million years ago
Length: 2.5ft (0.7m); wingspan: 2.6ft (0.75m)
Weight: 1.3-2.2lbs (0.6-1.0kg)
Diet: carnivorous

This crow-sized, feathery *Microraptor* caused something of a sensation when the first good skeleton was revealed to the world in 2003. Not only was this small Chinese relative of *Velociraptor* extravagantly feathered, it possessed surprisingly long feathers on the hindlimbs and feet as well as on the forelimbs and tail. Indeed, it soon became famous as a so-called 'four-winged' dinosaur. Several additional beautifully preserved specimens have been discovered since, and a huge amount of research has been published on the behavior and lifestyle of this small predator.

All studies conducted so far have concluded that those four fully feathered limbs are evidence of some kind of gliding or flying lifestyle. The feathers, and the wing surfaces, certainly look adapted for flight: the feathers have asymmetrical vanes (meaning that the part of the vane along the leading edge is wider than that part on the trailing edge), and are long and slender, especially those attached to the fingers (in the forelimbs) and that part of the foot close to the toes (in the hindlimbs). How these feathered surfaces were held during flight, and consequently what sort of flight might have been adopted, has been much debated. The earliest idea is that the arms and legs were held out to the sides during gliding. However, the bones of the leg and hip do not permit a sprawling pose to be adopted without dislocation, so later studies argued that the legs were more likely held perpendicular to the animal's long axis. A 2013 study that tested a model *Microraptor* in a wind tunnel found that this 'legs-down' pose improved glide performance. Another idea is that *Microraptor* instead held its fore- and hindlimbs in some kind of 'biplane-like' configuration, though this idea is not consistent with the way the feathers are arranged.

All of these concepts rest on the assumption that *Microraptor* became airborne after climbing and leaping from height. While there is some support for this possibility, *Microraptor* does not really look like an animal specialized for climbing or perching. It is, in fact, not conspicuously different in overall anatomy from related species that were surely committed ground-dwellers. What seems most likely is that *Microraptor* was predominantly terrestrial, but that it could also climb and jump about among low branches; it was not a 'flying squirrel dinosaur', but a low-level generalist. How much this gliding ability contributed to its hunting strategy remains unknown.

Microraptor's eyes are also proportionally extremely big. So big, in fact, that the authors of one study suggested that *Microraptor* might have been habitually active at night. The idea that at least some small theropods were night-active is both sensible and likely. However, other lines of data seem incongruous with this idea. *Microraptor*'s feathers are so well preserved that the tiny structures that contain pigments (melanosomes) are preserved and visible under the microscope and are of a shape linked with iridescence. Many modern birds use iridescence to communicate or remain visible to members of the same species, but no known nocturnal predators are iridescent, leading to the conclusion that *Microraptor* almost certainly didn't hunt at night.

Three *Microraptor* species have been named, the differences concerning small details of tooth, hand and hip anatomy as well as body size. The possibility that at least some of these represent the same species has been mentioned by some experts. The almost identical *Cryptovolans* is also very likely the same animal as *Microraptor*.

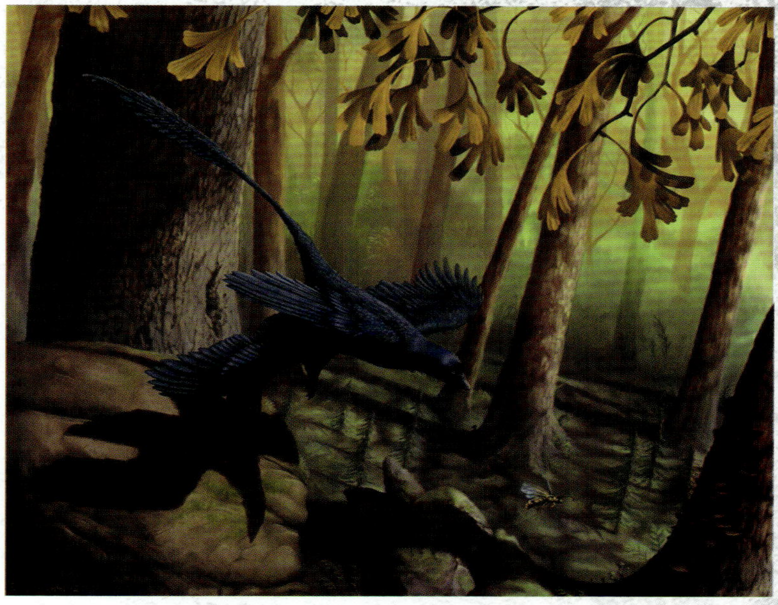

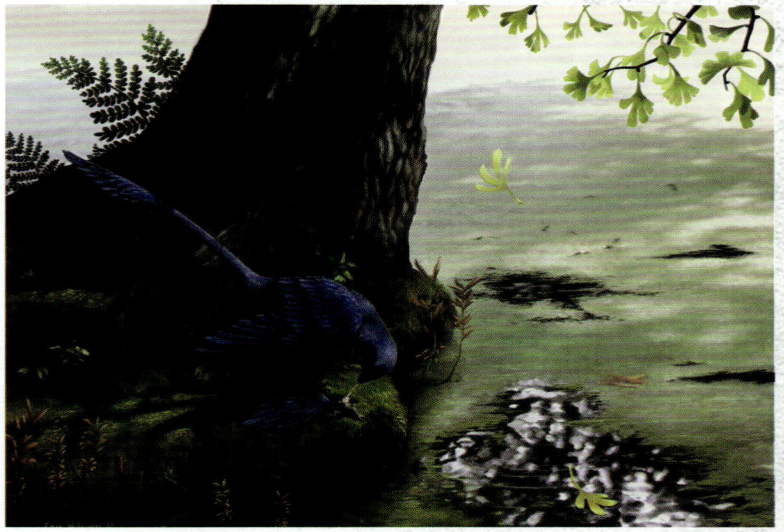

(Top) ***Microraptor* Take-Off**
Digital, 2012

(Above) ***Microraptor* Piscivory**
Digital, 2013
This illustration was based on the discovery of several of the small fish *Jinanichthys* in the gut of a *Microraptor* specimen recovered in 2013.

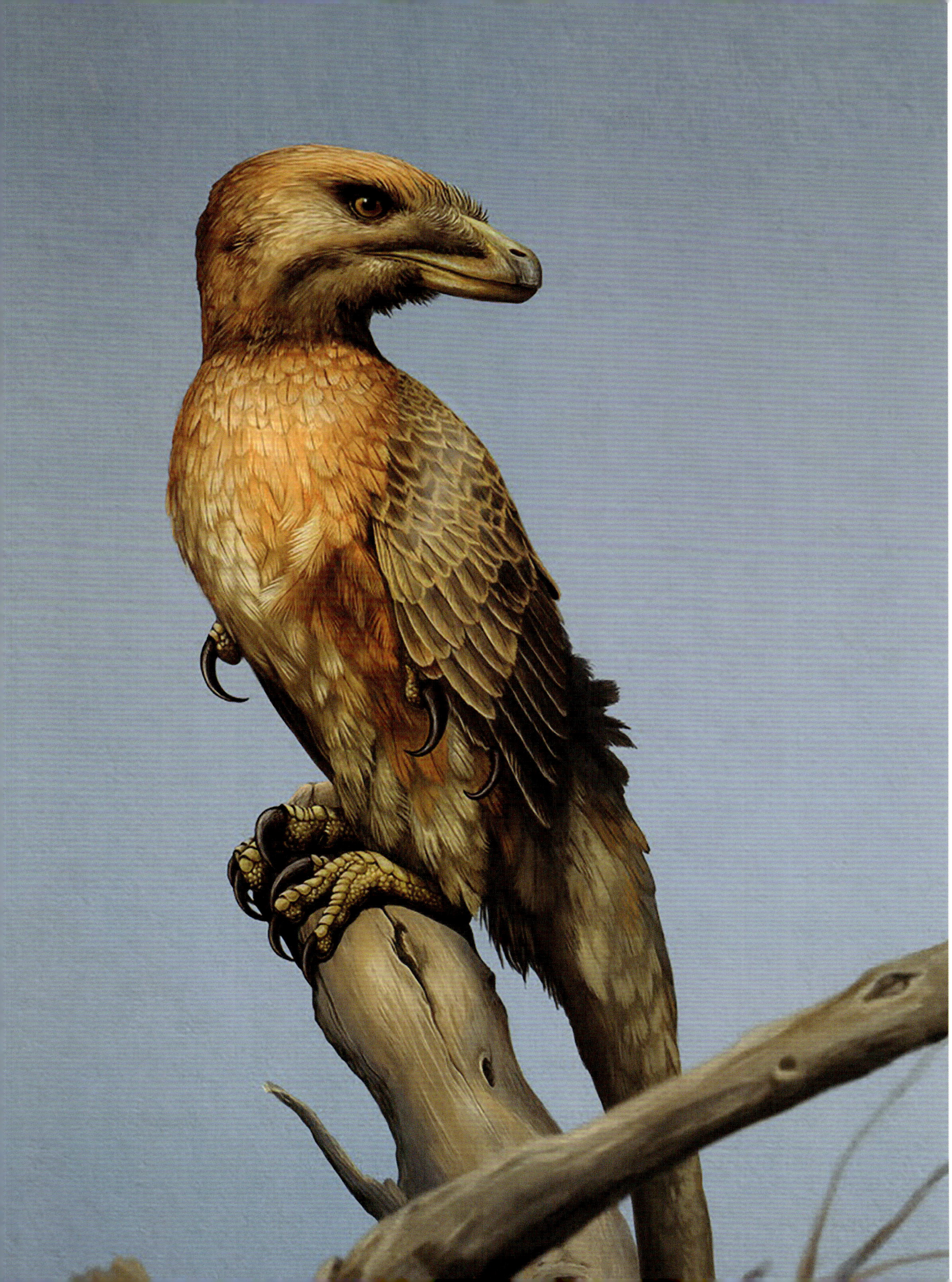

like *Archaeopteryx* and *Microraptor* I have counted the flight feather imprints on the fossil. For others, like *Pyroraptor*, all we have is a handful of bone fragments and must rely primarily on phylogenetic inference, wherein fine details are largely speculative.

You're currently studying behavioral genetics with a focus on personality and intelligence. What empirical inferences do you think can be made about those dinosaurs closely allied to birds from what we know of avian intelligence and behavior beyond just imagination and idle speculation?

When it comes to media and armchair speculation, claims of dinosaur intelligence are greatly exaggerated. This is in no small part due to the influence of a particular franchise that has long overstayed its relevance. Dromaeosaurs probably could not have solved complex puzzles, and even evidence of social behavior and communication is highly speculative. Phylogenetic and brain size evidence indicates, on average, a level of intelligence in the most bird-like of non-avian dinosaurs to be around that of modern ratites – ostriches, emus, and so on.

However, there was certainly large variation in intelligence and behavior among dromaeosaurs and troodontids, which show significant variety in abundance, size, morphology, and diet. It would not surprise me at all if some taxa were social while others were not. We are also only at the inception of really understanding bird intelligence and the structure of bird brains. For example, the idea that birds – which lack a neocortex – have similar neuronal organization to higher mammals is a relatively new idea, and certainly has interesting implications for the brains of birdlike dinosaurs. Intelligence in animals is likely less a consequence of brain shape and structure and more a function of how the neurons are arranged and communicate with one another, which is impossible to detect from fossil braincases. A lot remains unknown…

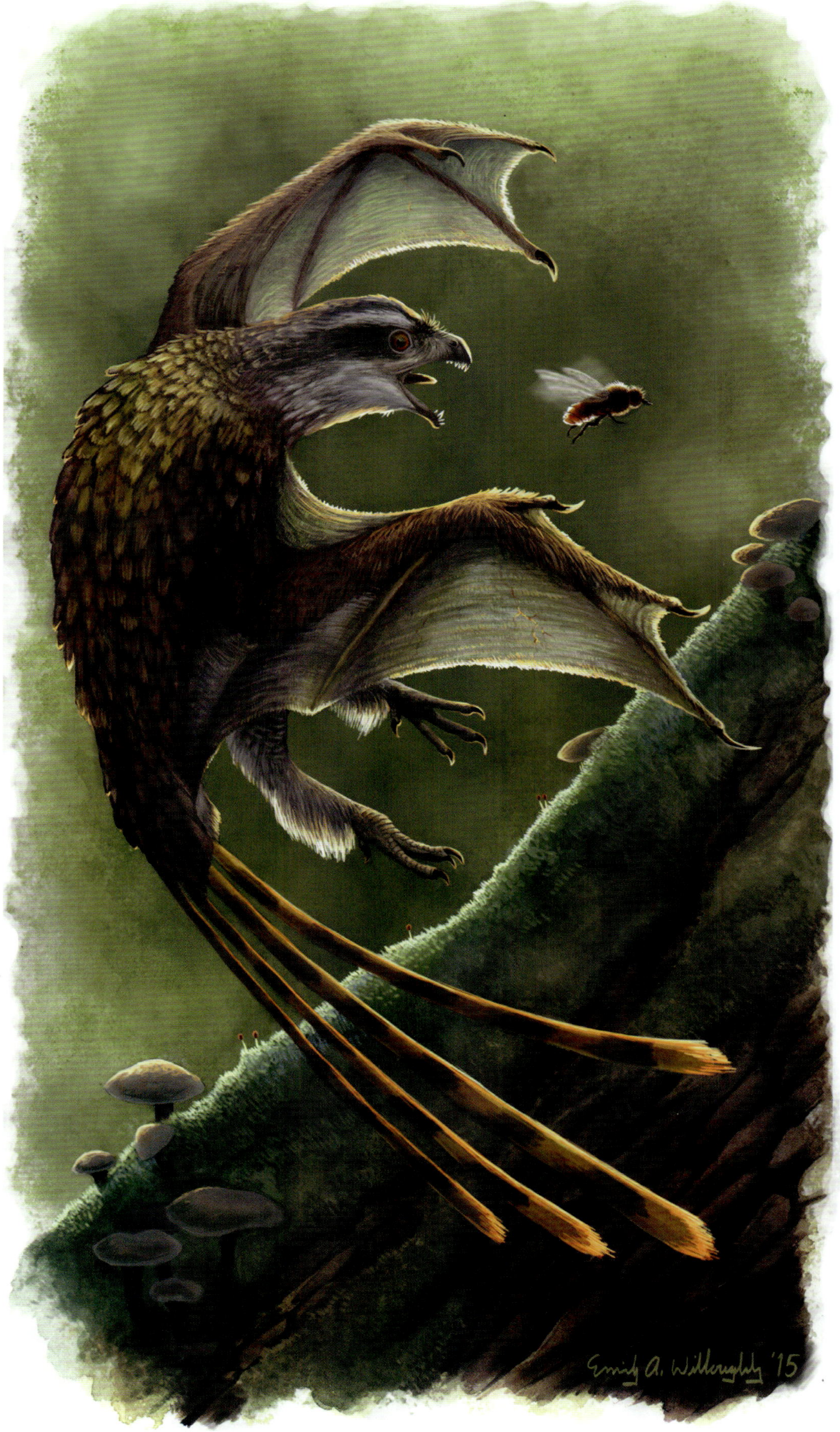

but dromaeosaurs probably weren't in the business of turning doorknobs!

Do you think there are any transferable skills from your art that can be carried over to your studies (beyond doodling)?

Scientific illustration has exposed me to many facets of academia – the best and worst – that will prove to be valuable as I work on my PhD. Most notably it has given me a healthy appreciation for finding and interpreting primary literature. It has also introduced me to concepts like phylogenetic bracketing and parsimony, which apart from being important to critical thinking should also be valuable tools in every paleoillustrator's skillset.

What's your starting point when you begin an illustration? Do you have a different approach when composing traditional and digital art?

(Left) ***Yi qi***
Gouache, 2015
Yi qi is a very strange and recently discovered member of the Scansoriopterygidae, an unusual group of small arboreal theropods. Although "bat-winged", it is still unclear if *Yi* could actually fly and it is shown here in an extended leap, pursuing an archisargid fly, *Calosargus*. Tiaojishan Formation, Mid-Late Jurassic, China.

(Below) ***Balaur* Perched**
Gouache, Digital, 2015
The supposed second 'sickle claw' of *Balaur* lacks the talon-like shape of the sickle claws seen in most deinonychosaurs, suggesting it was indeed an adaptation for climbing rather than a weapon.

(Opposite) **The Noble Savage**
Digital, 2014
Speculative reconstruction of a sub-adult *Deinonychus*. Studies of specimens that may represent an immature individual suggest that the infamous sickle claw (*Deinonychus* means "terrible claw") was more recurved in younger animals and could have been used for climbing.

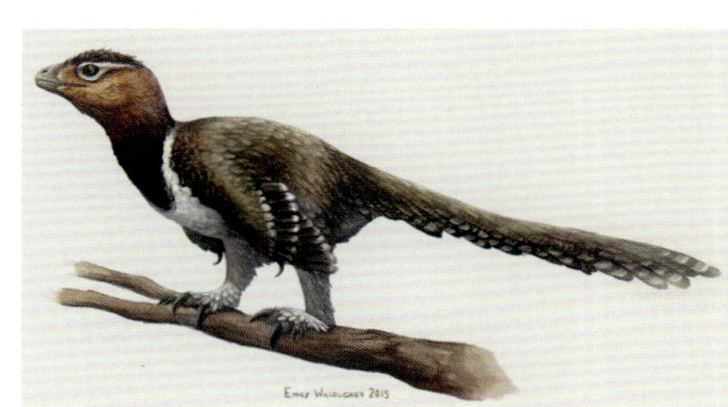

My processes for traditional and digital art have shifted and continue to evolve as I discover more techniques through experimentation, exposure and experience, but my starting point is always the same: research, research, and more research. I will usually start with the bones and then expand outward to details of ecosystem, integument, morphology and lifestyle that may be known about the taxon at hand. Then the collection of reference material begins, from environment to texture, motion, anatomical diagrams, and – of course – a healthy stack of bird photographs.

The feathered revolution has been perhaps the most significant movement in dinosaur paleontology since the warm-blooded controversy of the 1970s and beyond. At what point do you believe feathers (or feather-like structures) first evolved?

A really detailed treatment of that question would involve delving into a great deal of pedantic semantics (it depends on how you define 'feather', for instance), but the short answer is that current data seems to indicate that filamentous integument is likely basal to Ornithodira. We now have evidence from *Kulindadromeus*, pterosaurs,

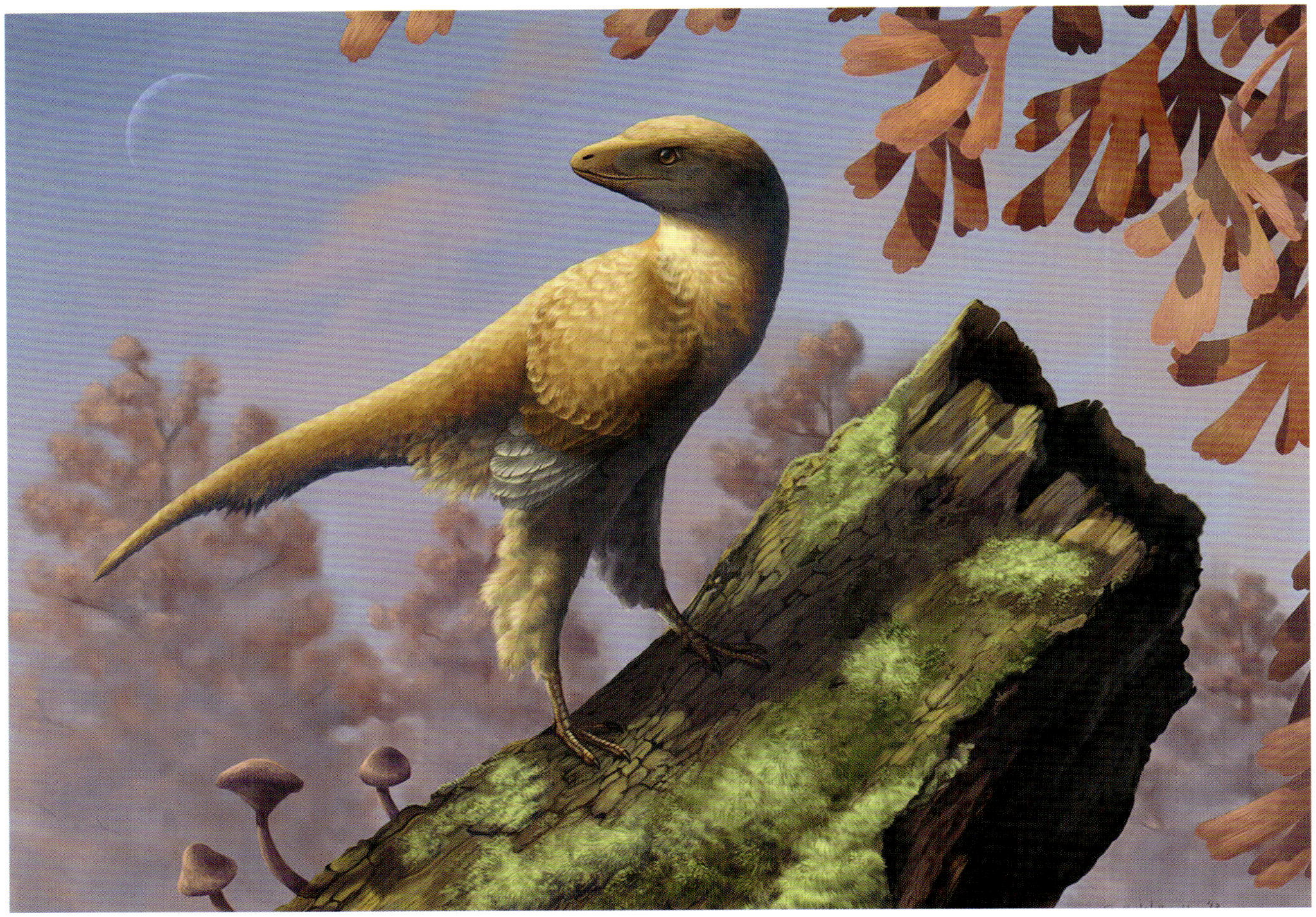

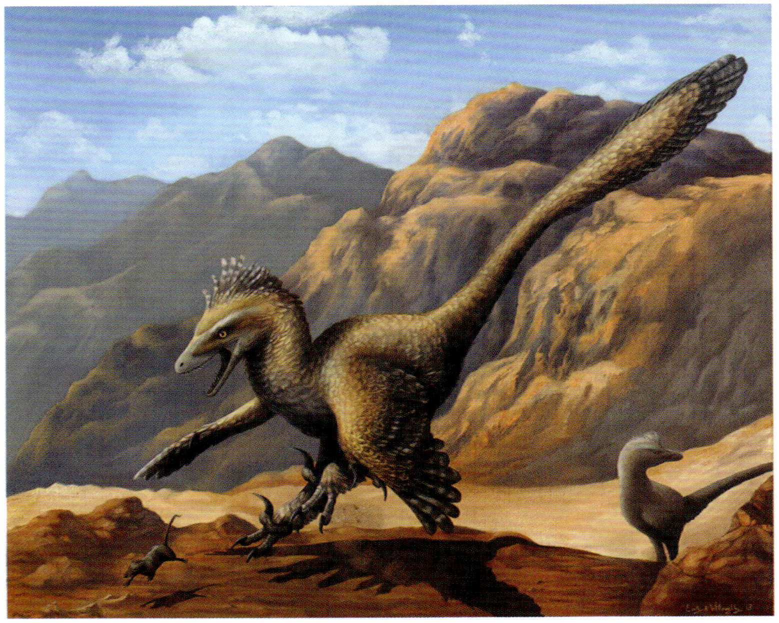

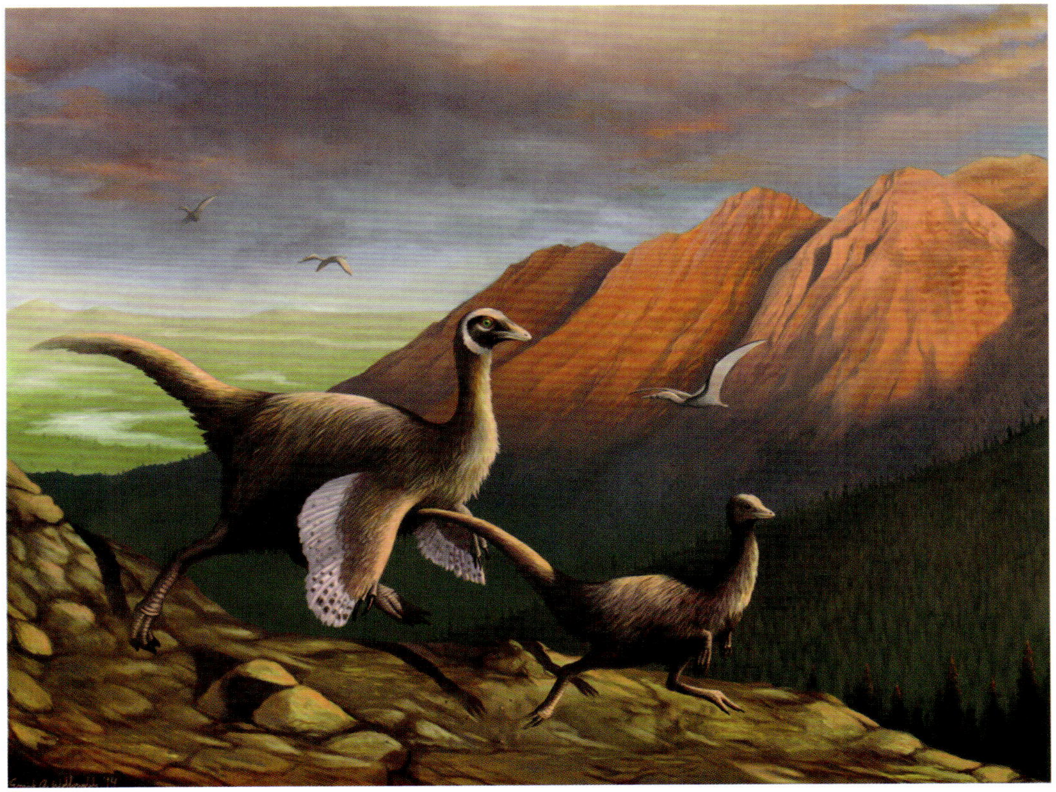

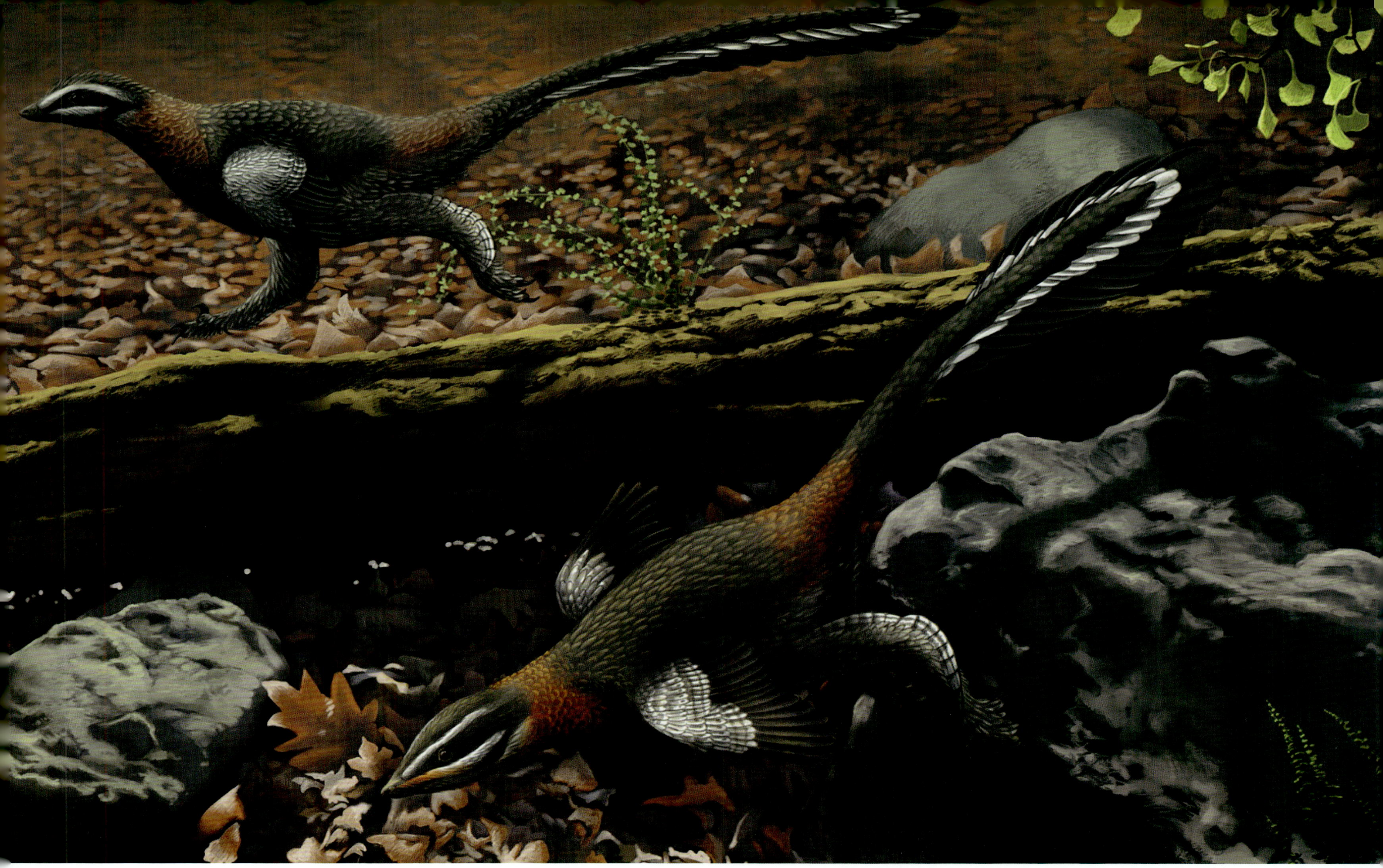

Mei long **Is Not Always Asleep**
Digital, 2012
The first specimen of this troodontid species was a very young animal found in what appeared to be a sleeping posture (its name means "sleeping dragon" in Chinese). These are adult reconstructions being a little more lively.

(Opposite page; Top) ***Eosinopteryx***
Digital, 2013
A tiny troodontid from the Late Jurassic Tiaojishan Formation of Liaoning, China.

(Opposite page; Bottom left) **The *Velociraptor* Hunting Dance**
Oils, Digital, 2005, revised 2009 and 2013
A *Velociraptor* pursues the small mammal *Zalambdalestes*. Late Cretaceous, 71-75mya. Djadochta Formation, Inner Mongolia.

(Opposite page; Bottom right) ***Ornithomimus* and Chick**
Digital, 2014

and various Ornithischians that some kind of feathery structures were present far outside of Coelurosauria in a number of fairly disparate cladistic groups. Whether these structures are homologous to the feathers in Mesozoic theropods and modern birds remains an open question, but my money is on it being so.

Are you in favor of the ground-up evolution of flight or trees-down?

While I think this dichotomy is useful for illustrating various uses for early wings, I don't think it's very likely that evolution definitively favored one over the other in the development of modern powered flight. It's often said that evolution is a bush, not a ladder, and in the case of bird evolution, it was likely an unruly, chaotic batch of kudzu. As we now know from *Xiaotingia, Aurornis, Anchiornis* and others, the base of what we think of as "birds" was not one thing, but rather a shrieking aviary of evolutionary

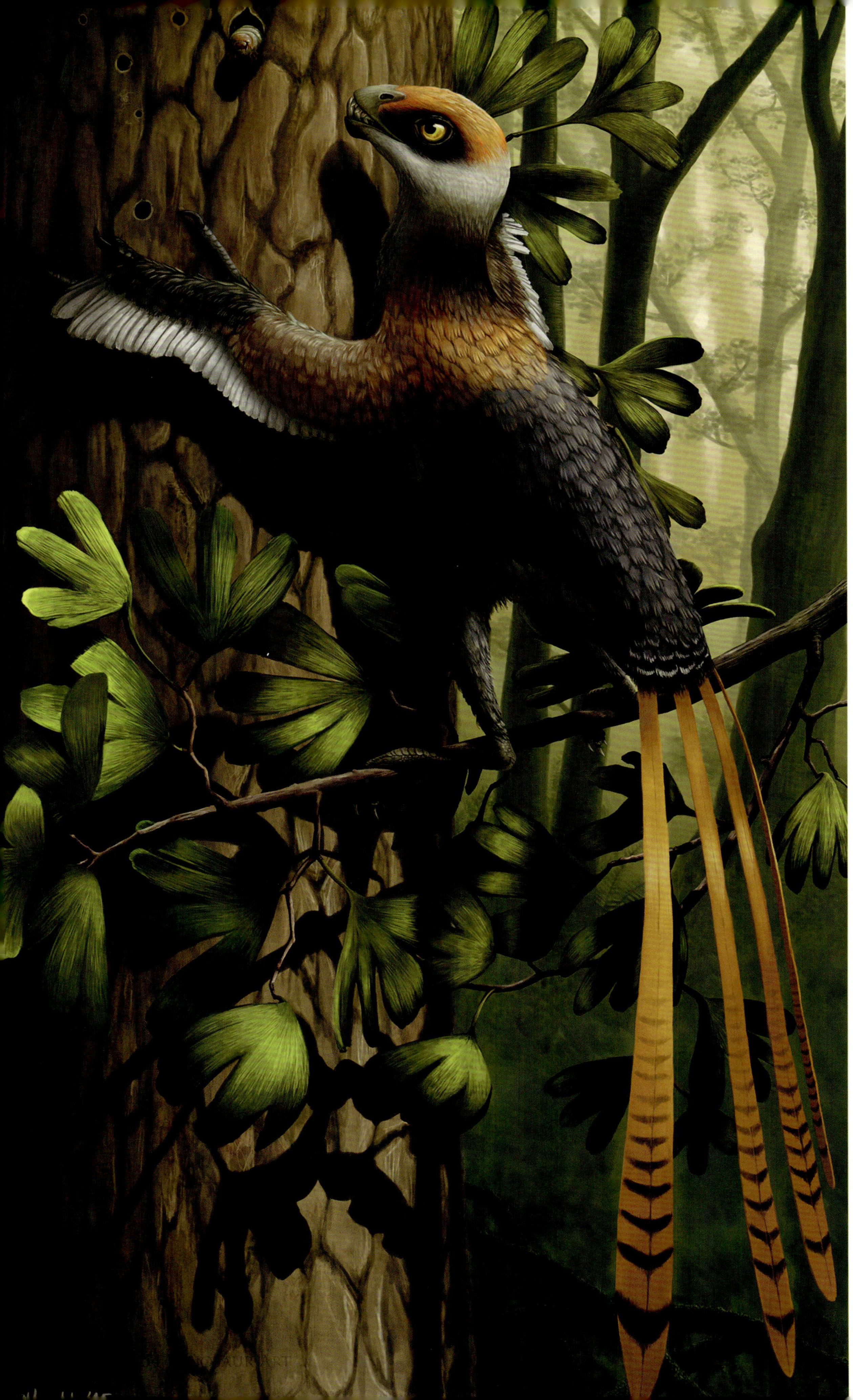

tinkerings. Just as modern birds use a large variety of techniques for getting off the ground – including ground-up launching, trees-down parachuting, and wing-assisted incline running – I think that the late Jurassic mechanisms that led to powered flight probably consisted of several of these techniques operating in tandem.

What hole in the fossil record would you most like to see filled?

Apropos of *Kulindadromeus* and the idea of feathers being basal to Ornithodira: I'd love to see this question answered definitively once and for all.

How did your upbringing in a creationist tradition ultimately translate into your current understanding of evolution?

It's ironic that stifling my curiosity about evolution as a child would play such a large role in developing a passionate interest for it later, but such is human nature. Curiosity and pure adolescent impudence led me from a parochial view of reality to the elegant beauty of concepts like phylogeny, genetic variation, natural selection and parsimony. Taken together, this became my first experience with what it meant to fall in love with the pursuit of knowledge. The sense of wonder and excitement that I felt at the consilience I found in biology was far greater than anything that a literal reading of Genesis had given me. By the end of my first semester in high school I had fully embraced evolutionary theory, and my interest in evolution would go on to define my life in nearly every way up to the present.

(Left) ***Epidexipteryx***
Digital, 2015

(Right) ***Caudipteryx* with chicks**
Digital, 2015
A mother *Caudipteryx* leads her chicks to safety across a shallow river. On the opposite bank, the cause of her concern, a pair of *Yutyrannus*, decide whether to pursue. Over the river glides a pair of the basal bird *Changchengornis*. Early Cretaceous. Yixian Formation, China.

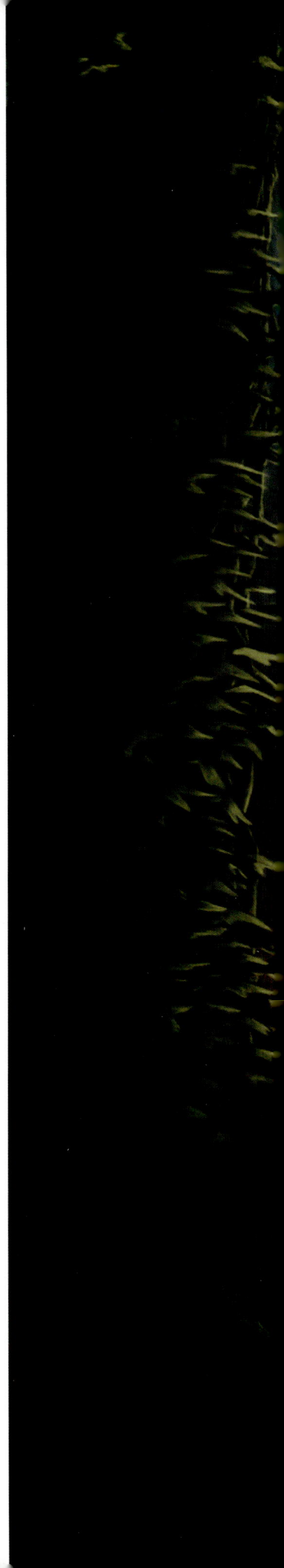

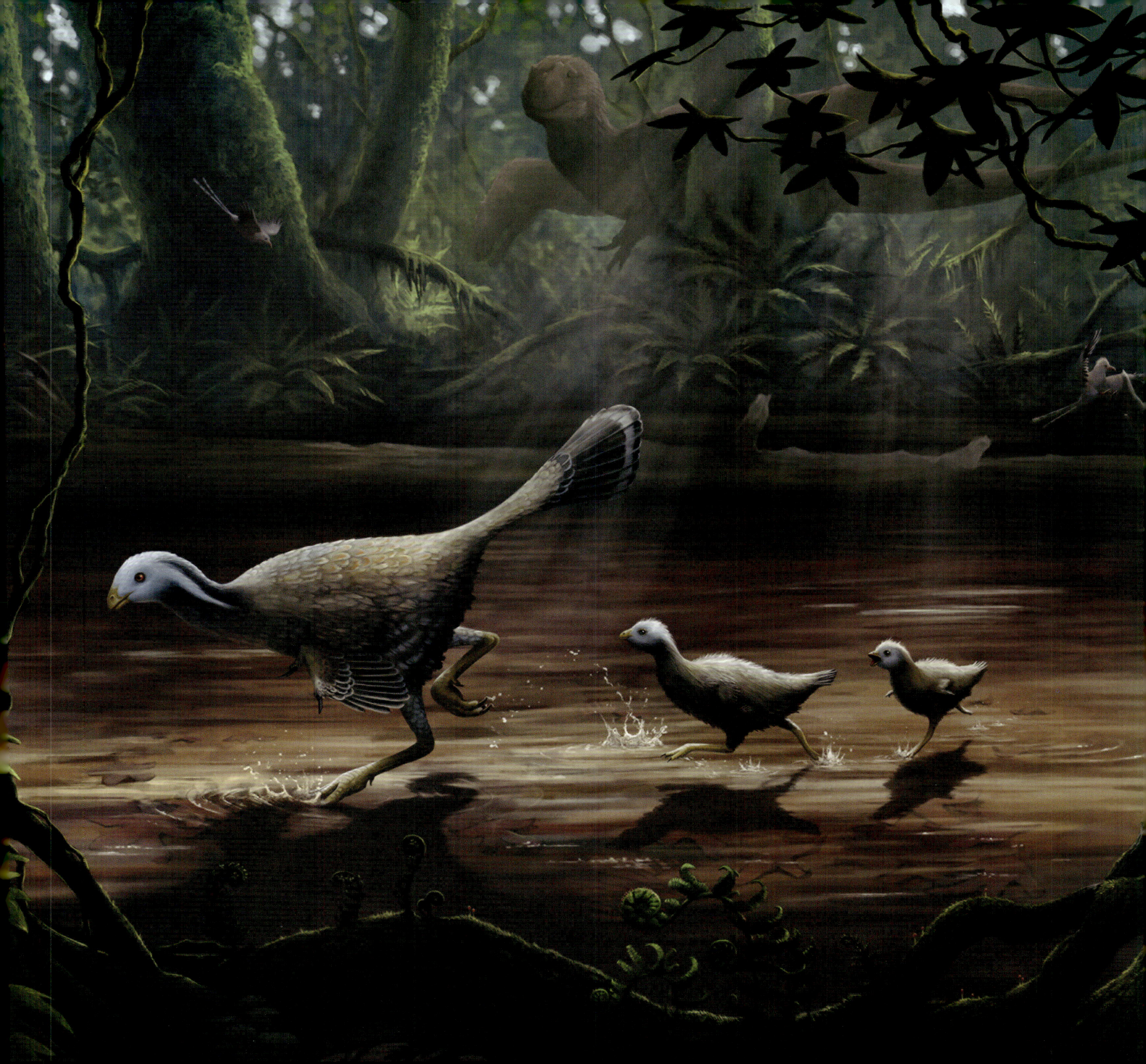

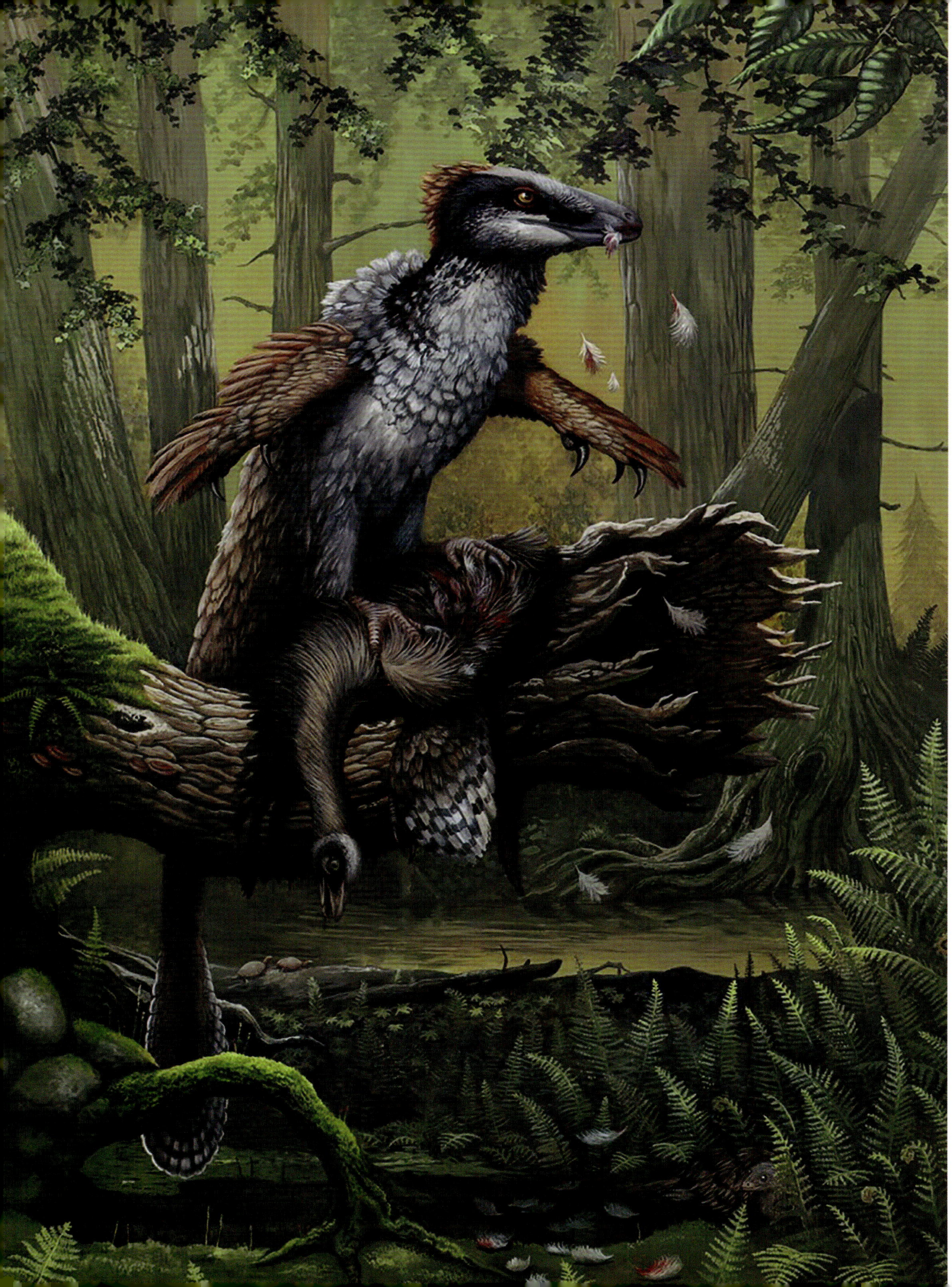

The ardent beliefs of creationists aren't that different from the unswerving beliefs of the BANDit cadre of paleontologists. Is that a fair assumption?

My experience with creationists as well as other brands of science-deniers, from the anti-vaccine movement to the rejection of behavior genetics and human intelligence, has led me to the conclusion that there is very little difference between religious ideology and that motivated by social, political and emotional factors. BANDits are a unique case in that a few decades ago their ideas were still a relatively reasonable (if unlikely) interpretation of the data, but today it seems to require sophisticated mental gymnastics to cling to some of these claims. It is difficult to imagine what further evidence is even possible to better support a theropod origin of birds than what we already have. One of my mentors growing up once told me that scientists rarely change their minds – they just die off. I am confident that in a few decades, the BANDit movement will be more or less relegated to the dustbin of forgotten failed hypotheses.

I am (perhaps unrealistically) somewhat more optimistic about creationists, and in fact have devoted years of my career to publishing a book enshrining that optimism. Whether it will have an effect is yet to be seen, but when creationism threatens education and policy, particularly in the southern US, it needs to be contested by those patient enough to take an approach that might actually work.

You were the first artist to reconstruct Dakotaraptor. *How did that come about and how did you feel as an artist about that project?*

Dakotaraptor was one of my most exciting recent projects. It came about from a happenstance discussion with the lead author of the taxon's description, who shared some tidbits about the discovery that later bloomed into an offer to create some illustrations for the paper. I was very enthusiastic about the project because it was such a novel and impressive find. The animal itself embodies everything I love about Dromaeosauridae – elegance, power and predatory grace – scaled up to massive proportions. Illustrating an exciting new taxon before it's been revealed to the public is one of the most compelling things about paleoillustration to me. However, the project also led to some complications related to omission of credit upon the long-awaited publication, which was corrected too slowly for my liking. Ultimately the experience left me with some ambivalence about professional paleoart, and further revealed the dark underbelly of the trade: to many, particularly the general public and journalists, artists are treated as second-class citizens and our works all too often taken for granted.

You have a rather unique style; who were your influences?

As with many of the paleoartists of my generation whose interests developed at the tail end of the Dinosaur Renaissance, Greg Paul's work, particularly *Predatory Dinosaurs of the World*, was a major early influence on my own. His dinosaurs, particularly his theropods, had such an amazing sense of elegance, fluidity, and life that was like a breath of fresh air after so many tail-dragging depictions. Later on, I found stronger artistic influence in the works of John Conway, Jason Brougham, and Douglas Henderson, who remains my all-time favorite paleoartist.

(Left) ***Dakotaraptor's Ornithomimus* Dinner**
Digital, 2015
A *Dakotaraptor* exhibiting behavior seen in modern raptors – removing the feathers of its prey to make the flesh more accessible. A baby *Ornithomimus* hides in the undergrowth. Maastrichtian Stage, Late Cretaceous. Hell Creek Formation, USA.

(Right) ***Acheroraptor***
Digital, 2013
Portrait of *Acheroraptor temertyorum*, a dromeosaur from the Hell Creek Formation on North America.

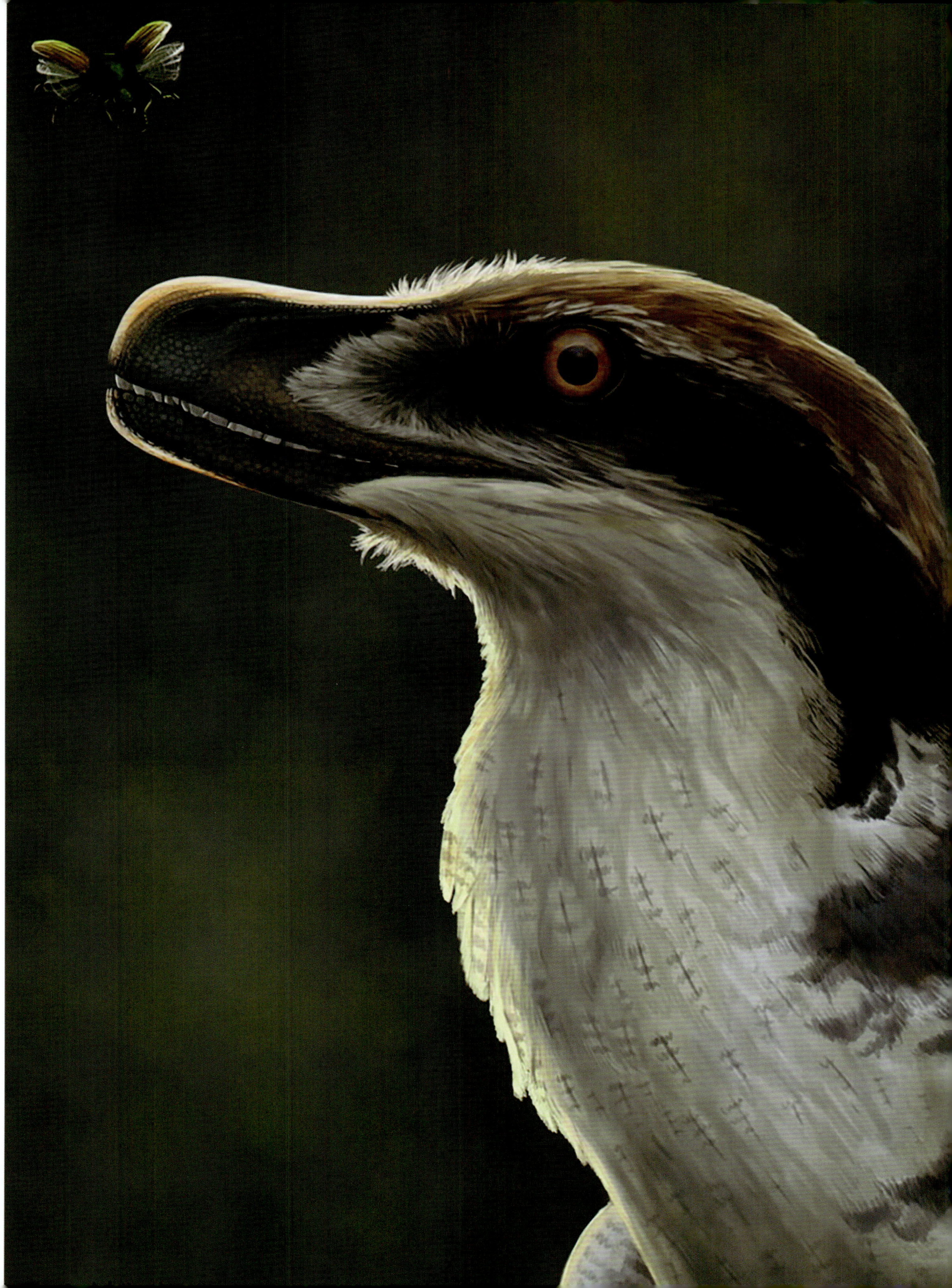

PETER SCHOUTEN

AUSTRALIA

A self-taught artist, Peter is considered not just one of the finest paleoartists but also one of the best natural history artists in the world. He worked as a technical illustrator at the school of zoology at the University of New South Wales before beginning a hugely successful career as a freelance wildlife artist. His work has won numerous awards and been exhibited around the world, while his books remain critically acclaimed and hugely influential. Amongst the most significant are *A Gap In Nature, Astonishing Animals and Feathered Dinosaurs: The Origin of Birds.*

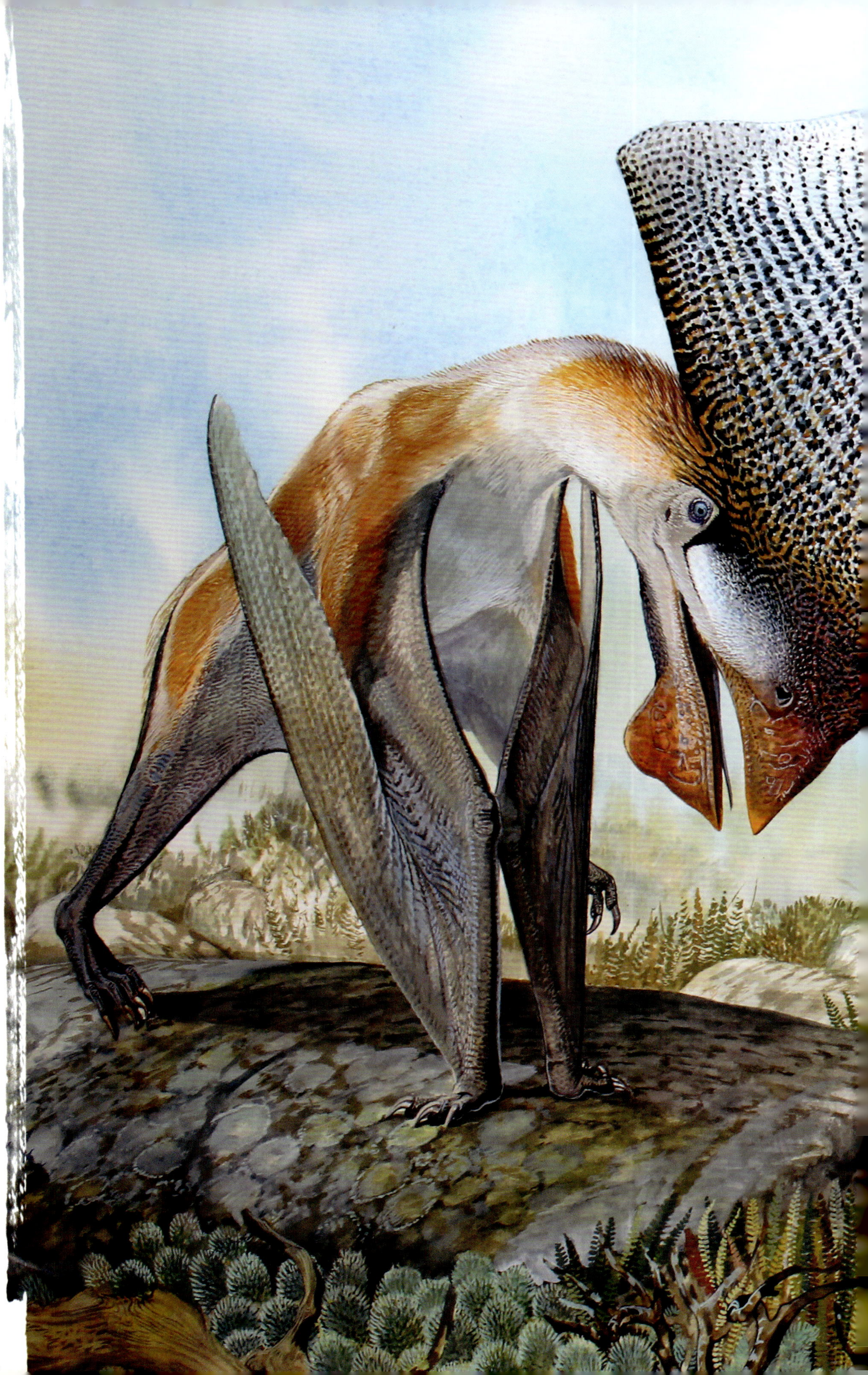

Tupandactylus
Watercolors, Gouache, 2016

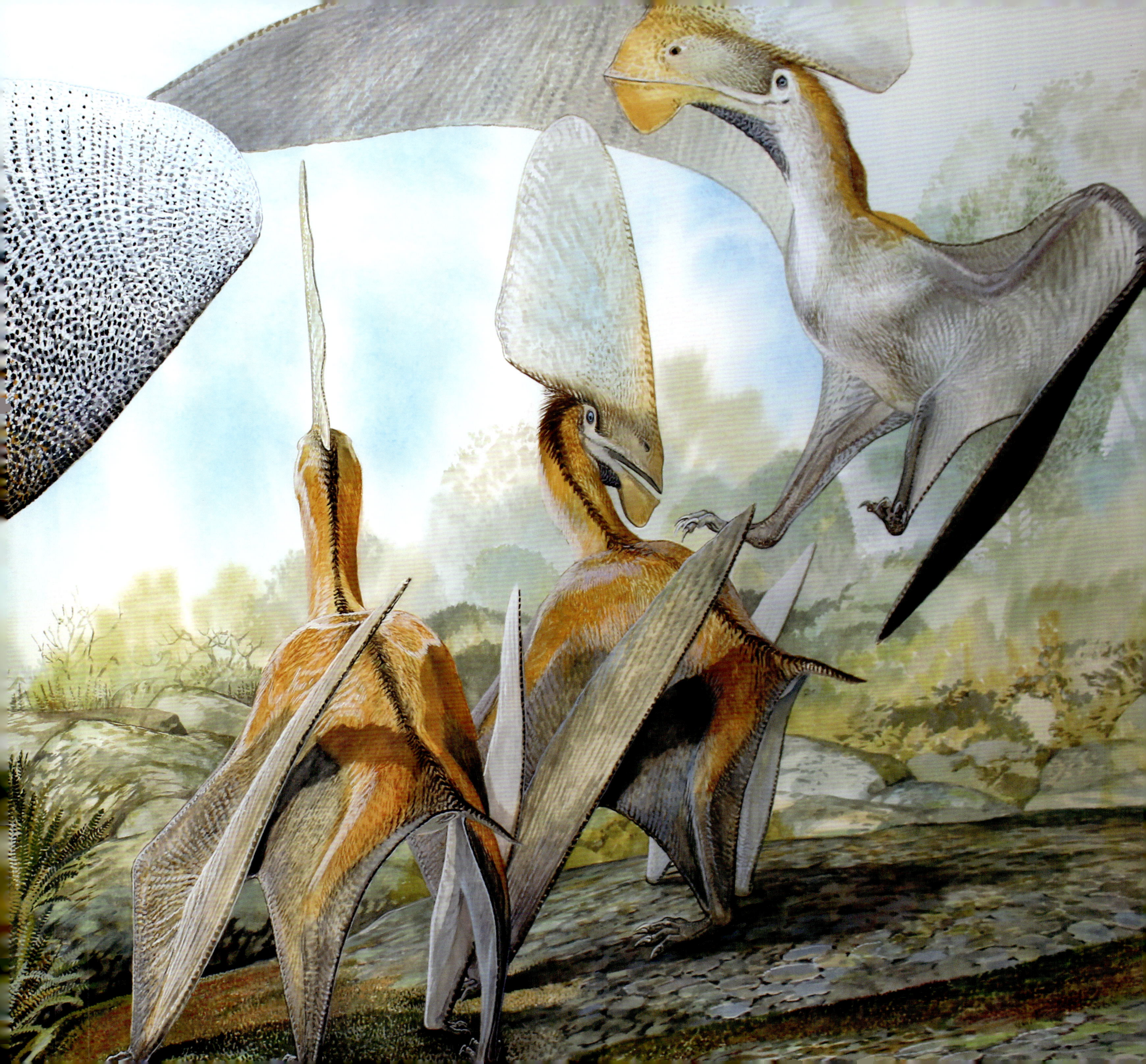

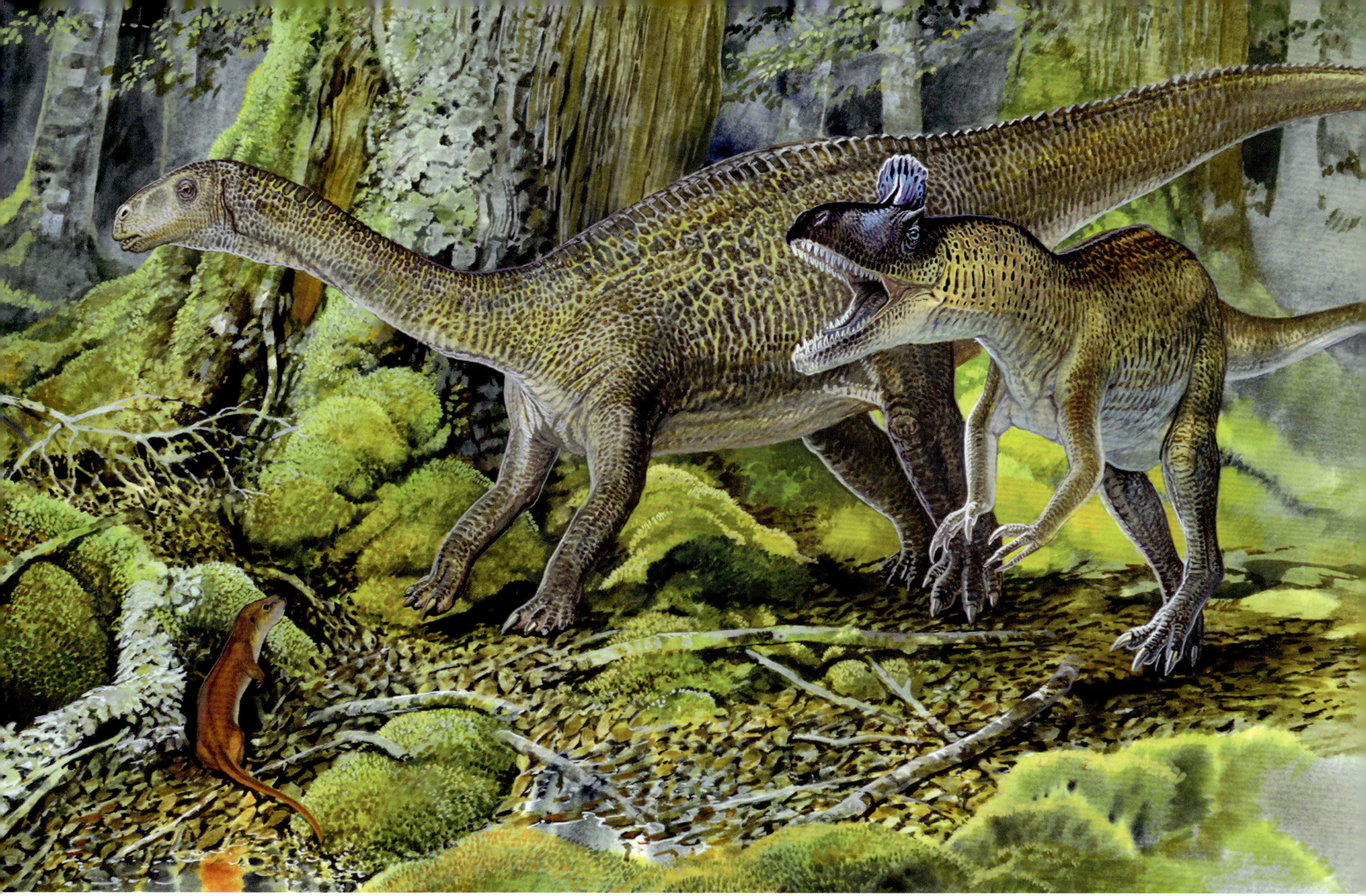

You've been an illustrator for a long time. How did you get started?

I know that this is probably a common answer among paleoartists, but I started drawing dinosaurs when I was a child. My dad was a good oil painter and I guess I inherited some of his ability, although my expertise was in drawing. I was keen to start painting. However, my school years were bereft of art instruction and, on leaving, my abilities were restricted to black and white pencil work.

At this time, I started on a small collection of images depicting Australian megafauna. Seeking evaluation on the scientific accuracy of my drawings, I approached Dr (now Professor) Mike Archer at the University of New South Wales. He was so impressed that he suggested that we collaborate on a book: *Prehistoric Animals of Australia*. I was employed by Archer as a fossil preparator. This involved the extraction of fossils from their matrix, preparation and repair of fossils and, most importantly for me, illustration of fossils for publication.

My time in the palaeontology department was

Hanson Formation
Watercolors, Gouache, 2012
Early Jurassic of Antarctica. Left to right: a small tritylodontid cynodont; *Glacialisaurus hammeri*, an early sauropod; the crested theropod *Cryolophosaurus ellioti*.

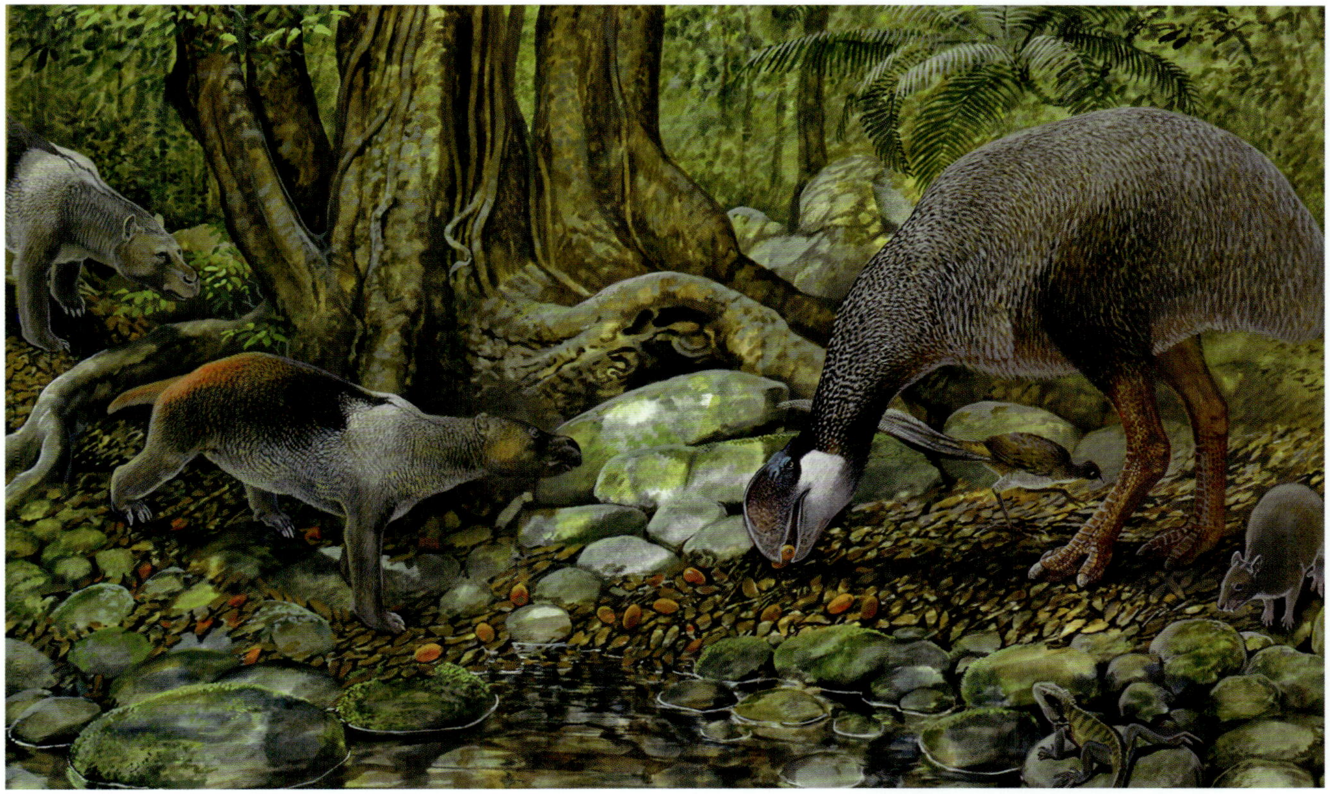

realism and animation of Matternes' subjects were without equal. Although long extinct, these animals had life. I wanted to paint like Matternes.

Other strong influences were Charles R Knight and Robert Bruce Horsfall. Even after 100 years, their depictions of megafauna still stand up. Their black and white drawings were of particular appeal to me as that was also my principal medium. I should also mention the Czech artist Zdeněk Burian. Although his depictions of dinosaurs are a little old fashioned by today's standards, they were rendered in a loose, painterly style that imbued his subjects with a particular animation. His series on fossil elephants is particularly good. Finally, I would like to mention the great bird painter William T Cooper. Bill Cooper was unsurpassed as a bird illustrator. His depictions of birds were not only scientifically accurate, they conveyed information of the animals' habits and habitats, and are beautifully presented works of art. His collaborative monographs with Joe

critical to my understanding of animal anatomy and morphology. Not only did I have access to fossils, I was surrounded by a team of the most knowledgeable scientists in the country who never tired of my ceaseless questions. After completion of a second book on Australian prehistory, *The Antipodean Ark*, I left the palaeontology department and struck out on my own as a freelance artist.

You've got a classic style reminiscent of some of the great natural history artists of the past. Who were your influences?

One of the great pleasures of my childhood was to receive a book as a Christmas or birthday gift. Of course, there were many requests for dinosaur books, but I also collected the Life Nature Library series. On opening the volume *The Land and Wildlife of North America* I remember being totally mesmerized by four double-page dioramas of Cenozoic mammals by Jay Matternes. The

(Above) **Riversleigh Zone B, Early Miocene**
Watercolors, Gouache, 2011
Left to right: large marsupial *Neohelos tirarensis*; the giant flightless bird *Bullockornis planei*; the lyrebird *Menura tyawanoides*; the small kangaroo *Balbaroo kangaroo*; and the living water dragon *Physignathus leseurii*.

(Right) **Riversleigh Zone D, Late Miocene**
Watercolors, Gouache, 2013
Left to right: the kangaroo *Ganaguroo* sp.; the lizard *Tiliqua* sp.; the predatory marsupial *Ganbulanyi djadjinguli*; and *Yarala burchfieldi*.

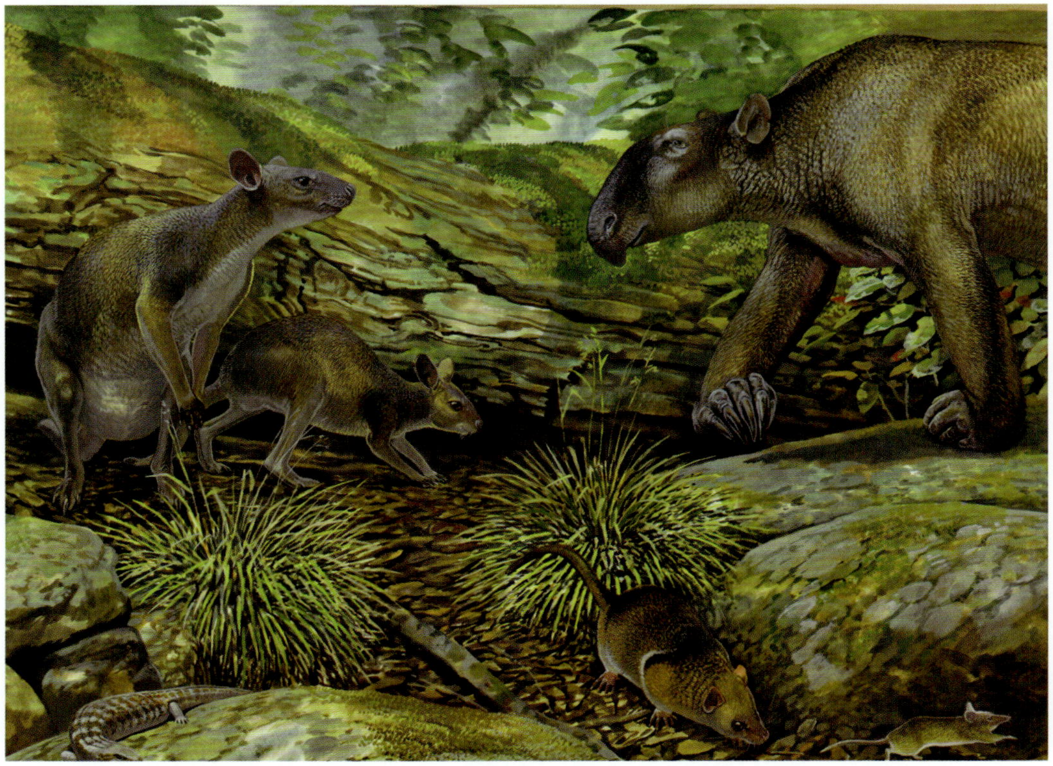

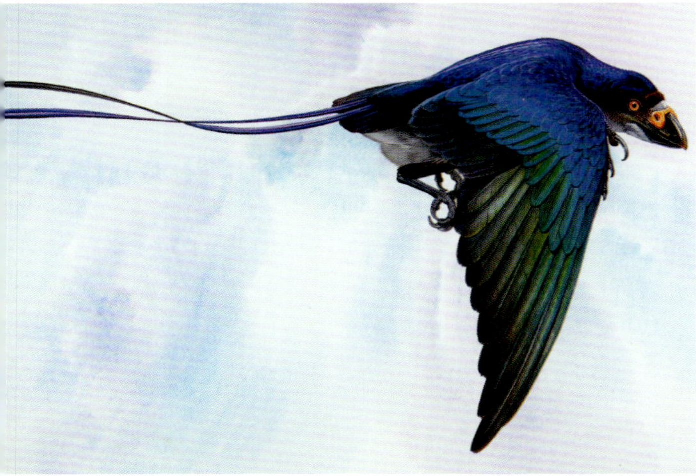

Forshaw will always have pride of place on my bookshelves. Sadly, none of these great artists are with us anymore, but their legacy will continue in their art.

How do you prepare for an illustration? Do you do a lot of sketching or thumbnails?

Before I start any painting, I research my subject thoroughly. With palaeo I source scientific papers covering the original description of the species, the geological formation in which it was found and other animals that may have shared its world. Gaining knowledge of its morphology and palaeoenvironment allows me to draw analogies with other extinct or extant species. This then influences the outward appearance, habits and interaction, if any, with other species. Furnished with all this knowledge I will then think of a composition that might best illustrate the features of that species and how it sits in a landscape. It can take up to three days of research

Confuciusornis sanctus
Watercolors, Gouache, 2006

(Right) **North Island, New Zealand**
Watercolors, Gouache, 2013
Fauna 500 years before the arrival of people (BP). Left to right: North Island flightless goose *Cnemiornis gracilis*; snipe rail *Capellirallus karamu*; North Island giant moa *Dinornis novaezealandiae*; the huia *Heterolocha acutirostris*; stout-legged moa *Euryapteryx curtus*; Scarlett's duck *Malacorhynchus scarletti*; New Zealand musk duck *Biziura delautouri*; and Mantell's moa *Pachyornis geranoides*.

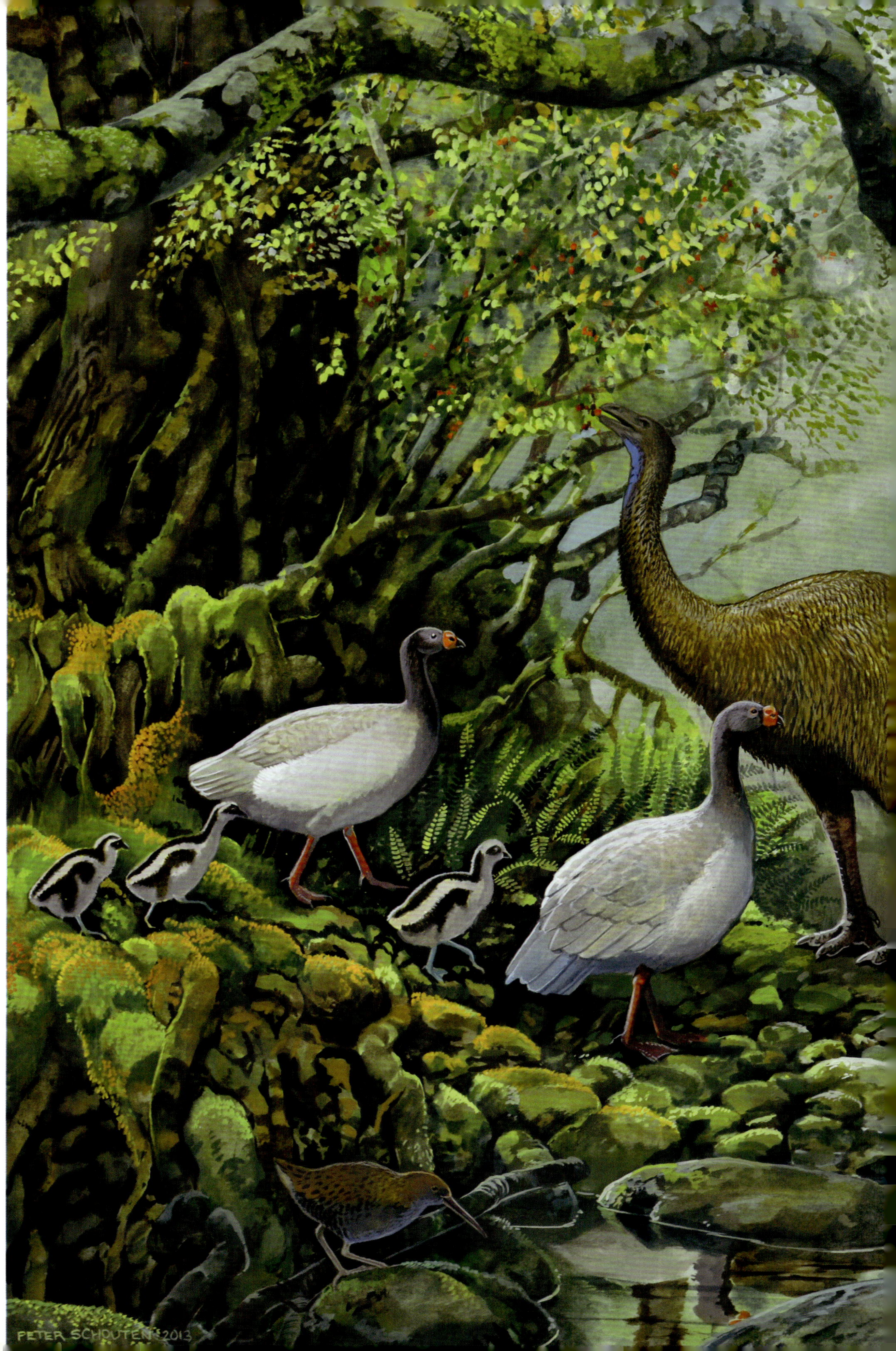

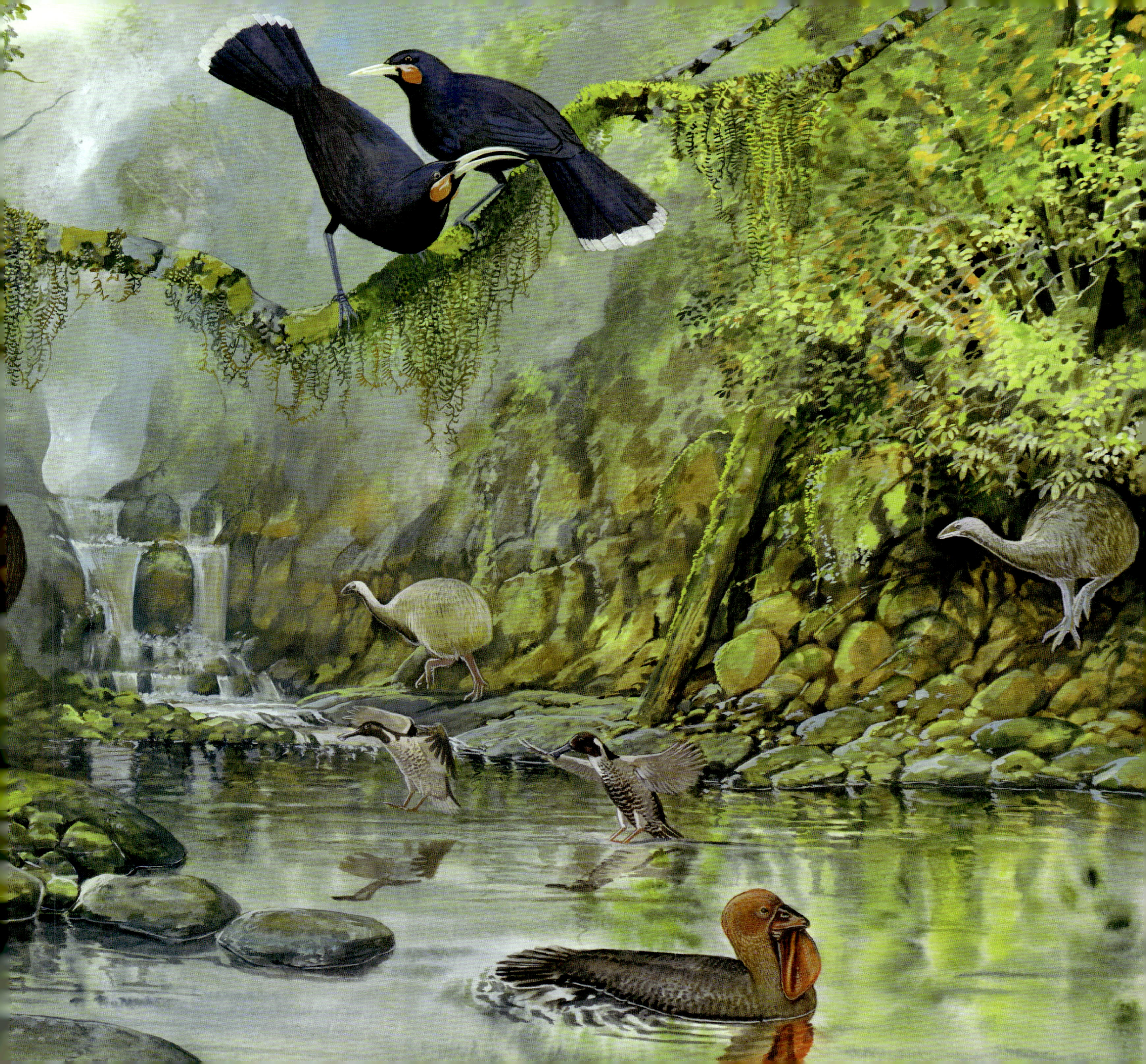

HOMO FLORESIENSIS

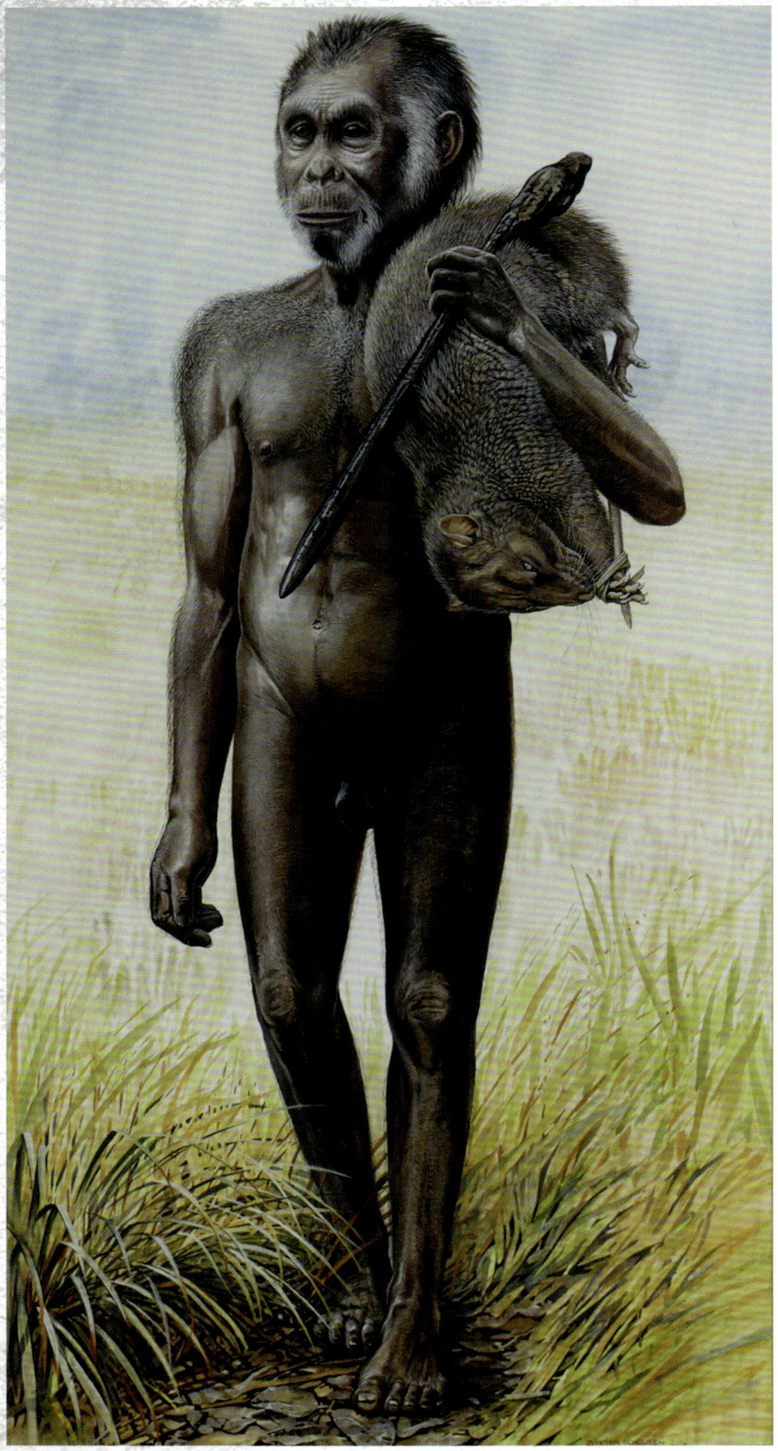

Homo floresiensis
Watercolors, Gouache, 2004
"Hobbit" and prey, Verhoeven's giant tree rat *Papagomys theodorverhoeveni.*

HOMO FLORESIENSIS
Genus: *Homo*
Species: *floresiensis*
Location: Flores, Indonesia
Named: 2004
Age: Middle-Late Pleistocene Period (Ionian/ Tarantian Stages), 100-50,000 years ago?
Length: 3.6ft (1.06m)
Weight: 55lbs (25kg)
Diet: omnivorous

Homo floresiensis made headlines worldwide when its discovery was announced in 2004. Discovered a year earlier at Liang Bua, its remains indicate an extinct member of the human lineage. With *Lord of the Rings* so popular at the time, it was unsurprising that the diminutive hominid was soon nicknamed "the Hobbit."

Since then, the fragmentary remains of nine individuals have been recovered, including a complete skull. They show that *H. floresiensis* had, relative to modern humans, a small brain (similar in size to a chimpanzee's), and proportionally large teeth. These features, amongst others, seem to be a by-product of insular dwarfism, a characteristic of organisms isolated on islands.

The small brain did not prevent Flores Man from exhibiting apparently sophisticated behavior. Associated with the remains of *H. floresiensis* are advanced stone tools and evidence for the use of fire. Animal bones found in the same cave exhibit cut marks consistent with butchering.

Other anatomical features include a high forehead, absent chin, and a posture suggesting 'shrugged forward' shoulders. The legs were short, while the feet were exaggeratedly long and flat with a very short big toe.

The age of Flores Man is somewhat contentious. While the bones were aged between 100- and 50,000 years old, the stone tools found with the remains were dated back as far as 190,000 years. It's also something of a mystery how these hominids arrived on Flores in the first place. The island remained isolated during the Pleistocene, despite the much lower sea levels present during the glacial phases as a result of a deep oceanic strait that created a 12-mile gap between the islands and the mainland. One hypothesis is that a population of *Homo erectus* – present on the Asian mainland at around the time that *H. floresiensis* is believed to have arrived on Flores – somehow arrived on Flores and then underwent the sort of evolution typical of island species. Indeed, some studies of the dentition suggest a direct relationship between the two. However, more recent studies suggest a link to Africa's *H. habilis.*

Flores Man wasn't the only organism to undergo such an evolution. The island was also home to a pygmy species of *Stegodon,* a long-tusked elephant common in southern Asia during the Pleistocene, whose bones were found associated with *H. floresiensis,* evidence for butchery on its bones suggesting that it was one of the hominid's main prey items.

Other animals present on Flores at the time included a giant tree-dwelling rat, the Komodo dragon, and a 6ft (2m) tall marabou stork.

Exactly when *H. floresiensis* became extinct is unclear. Its disappearance has been linked to the arrival of *H. sapiens* on the island, but the suggestion has also been made that a massive volcanic eruption that occurred about 12,000 years ago might also, or alternatively, have been to blame. However, it's looking increasingly likely that Flores Man was actually long extinct by this time and that it did not persist until as recently as was originally proposed. Intriguingly, however, legends do persist on Flores of a race of small cave-dwelling people who are believed to have existed until recently. Might these be something to do with the persistence of *H. floresiensis* to recent times?

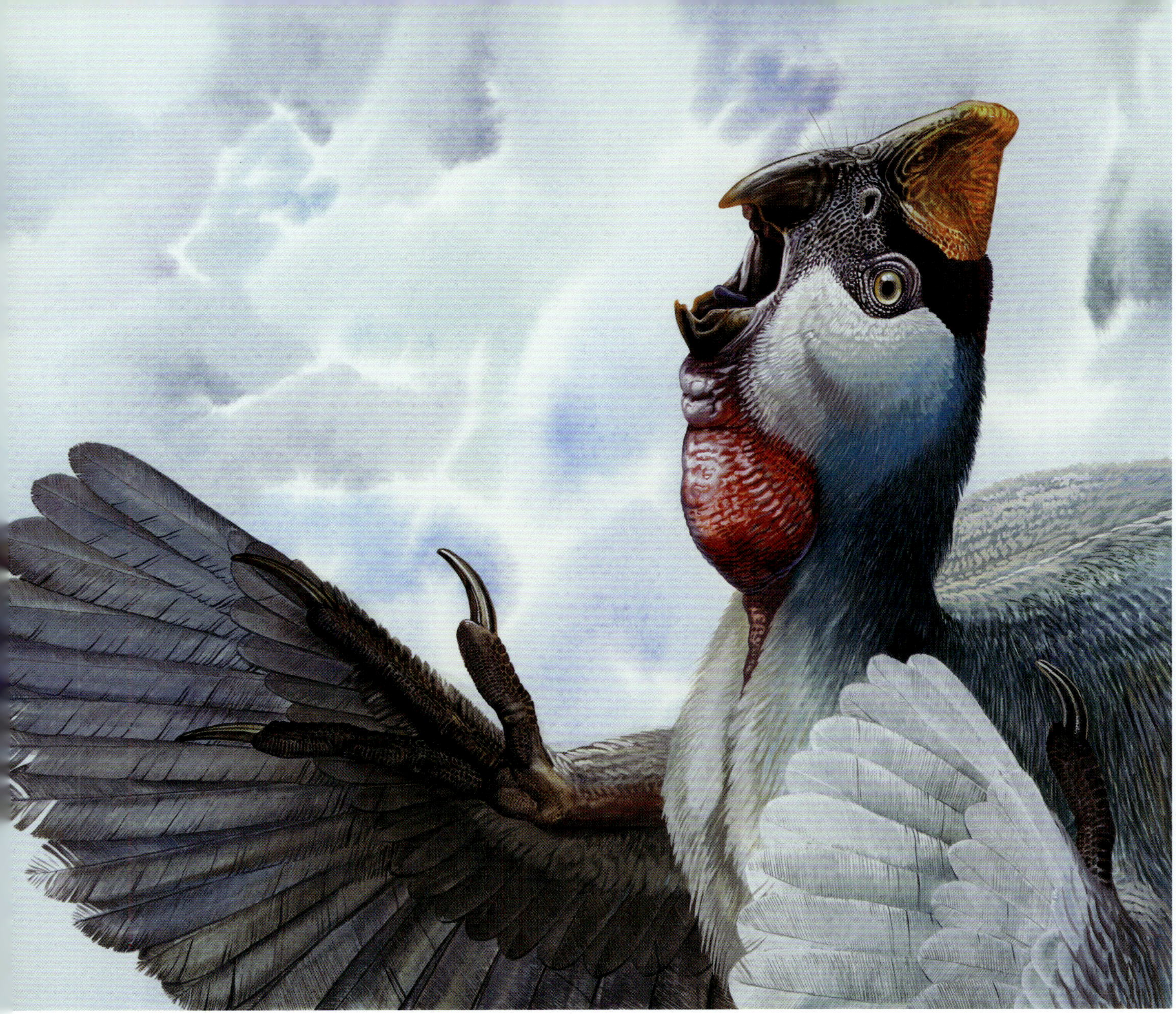

before any preliminary sketches are attempted. I should say, at this point, that I never look at other previous reconstructions of the subject animal, even my own. The science of palaeontology is one that is in a state of constant change, and I prefer to formulate my own impression of an animal based on the most up-to-date knowledge that is available.

The next step is to stretch my watercolor paper and apply a watercolor wash as the paper is drying. This gives me the suffuse, soft colors that you will see in the background of most of my compositions. Preliminary sketches are applied after the paper dries, and I generally use an Aquarelle colored pencil for this purpose. Sketching is done on the finished surface as I find it imbues the subject with greater animation.

Apart from the improvements any illustrator undergoes, has your technique changed significantly over time?

The greatest change for me was the movement from black and white into color. As I touched upon earlier, I was quite proficient in drawing but sadly lacking in any painting ability. Due to the demands of publishers for color images, I forced myself out of my black and white niche by adopting Aquarelle colored pencils. The pencils could be used in a standard way and then transformed into watercolor by the application

(Above) ***Nemegtomaia barsboldi***
Watercolors, Gouache, 2006

(Right) ***Guanlong wucaii***
Watercolors, Gouache, 2006

(Next spread; Left)
Cañadón Asfalto Fauna
Watercolors, Gouache, 2016
Cañadón Asfalto Formation, South America, 164.7-161.2mya. The turtle *Condorchelys antiqua*; an indeterminate crocodyliform; a *Volkheimeria chubutensis* being feasted on by a pair of *Piatnitzkysaurus floresi*; a herd of *Patagosaurus fariasi*; the abelisaur *Eoabelisaurus mefi*; and a flock of the heterodontosaurid *Manidens condorensis*.

(Next spread; Right)
Carnotaurus satrei
Watercolors, Gouache, 2016
Abelisaur from the lower section of the La Colonia Formation, Late Campanian-Early Maastrichtian Stage, Late Cretaceous 72-69.9mya. South America.

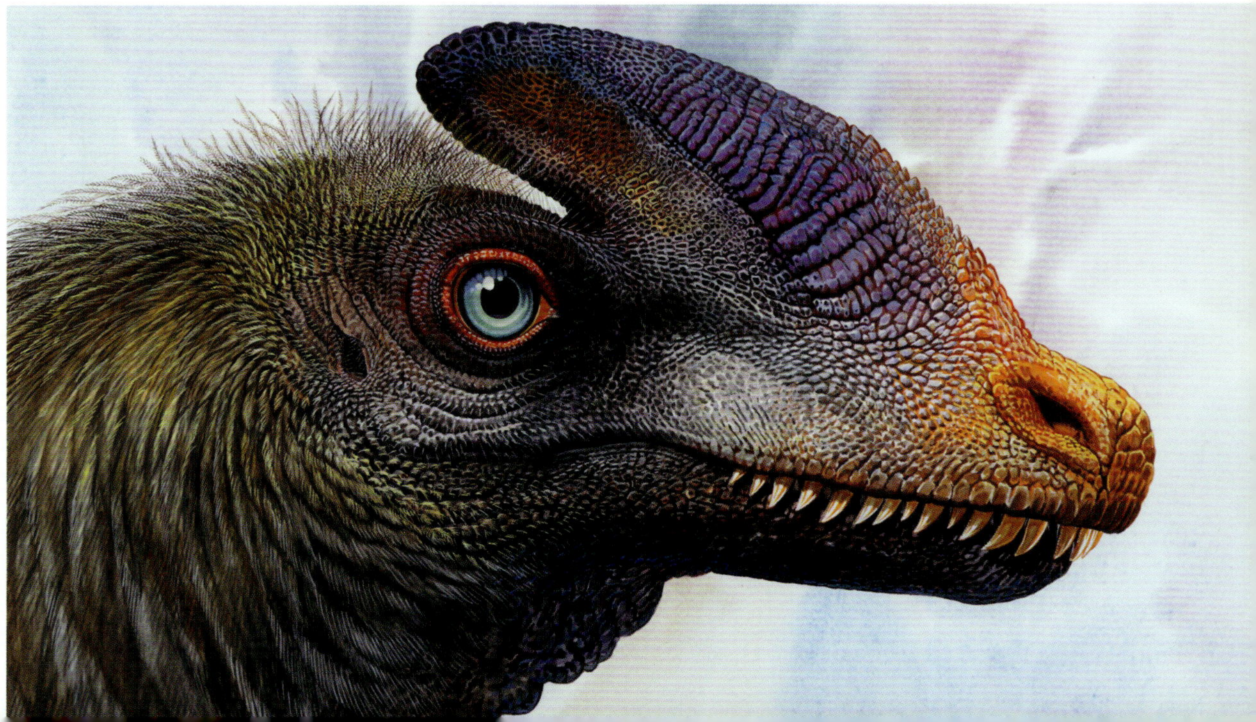

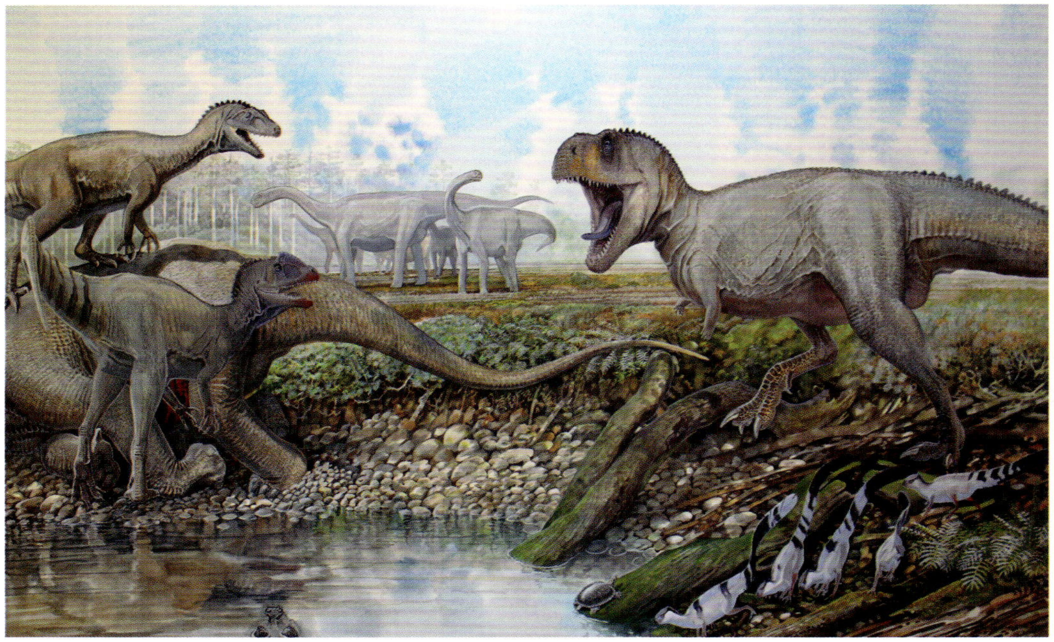

of a moistened brush. This stage was transitional into the full use of watercolors, and then gouache.

What is your preferred medium?

Watercolor and gouache on heavy weight, hot-pressed Arches paper. I use the watercolors for broad, soft washes and the gouache is applied for fine detail work. The fine work is achieved using 0-000 imitation sable brushes. I don't bother with expensive brushes anymore as I find the cheap ones will last just as long. In saying that, however, I do keep a good-quality sable for signing off.

Is there a certain freedom to illustrating extinct animals that you don't have with your work on extant ones?

That's a hard question to answer. Depictions of extant animals require a level of detail that enable the viewer to identify that species. This can usually be checked for accuracy using photographs of live animals or comparison with museum study skins. So for me there is not much freedom in the depiction of the animal; however I can take greater liberties with the composition and surrounding details. I should say that I treat recently extinct species, that are represented by study skins, as if extant. However, fossil species are a different matter.

There is no freedom in the structural morphology of fossil species. You would think that the outward appearance of these species might provide a bit more freedom, however, on reflection I don't think that is the case. The outward appearance of a fossil species is dictated by the same environmental constraints as a living animal. Scraps of evidence can sometimes be gleaned from the fossil itself, such as a skin impression or the presence of feathers or fibers and, in rare cases, color. Some liberty can be taken with features used in intraspecific courtship or agonistic display, but even here it is still necessary to look to a modern analogue as a model. Behavior, interaction with other species and the depiction of environment are also constrained by available evidence, ultimately affecting the composition.

To answer your question, I think there is less freedom in the depiction of fossil species.

Do you have particular groups of animal you particularly enjoy illustrating?

My greatest joy comes from tackling an animal

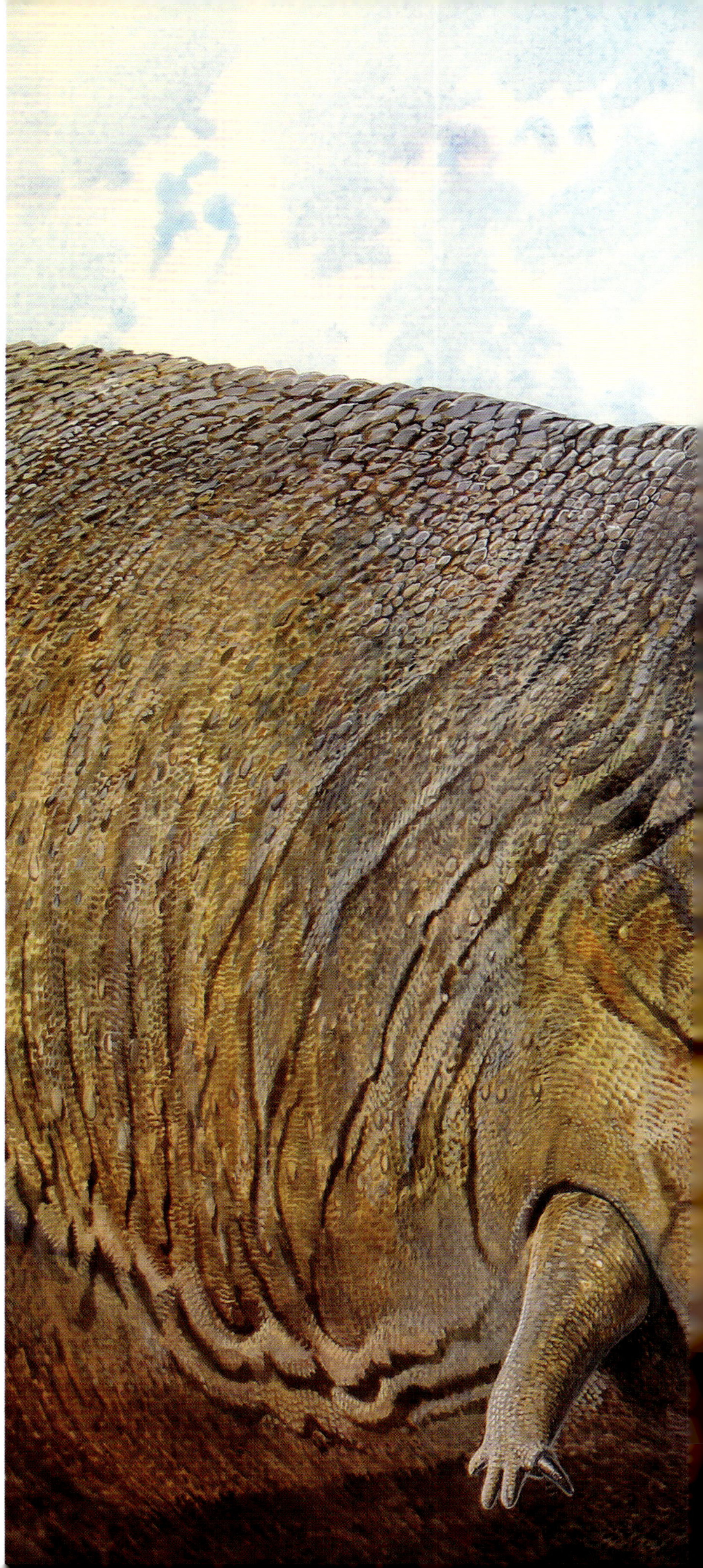

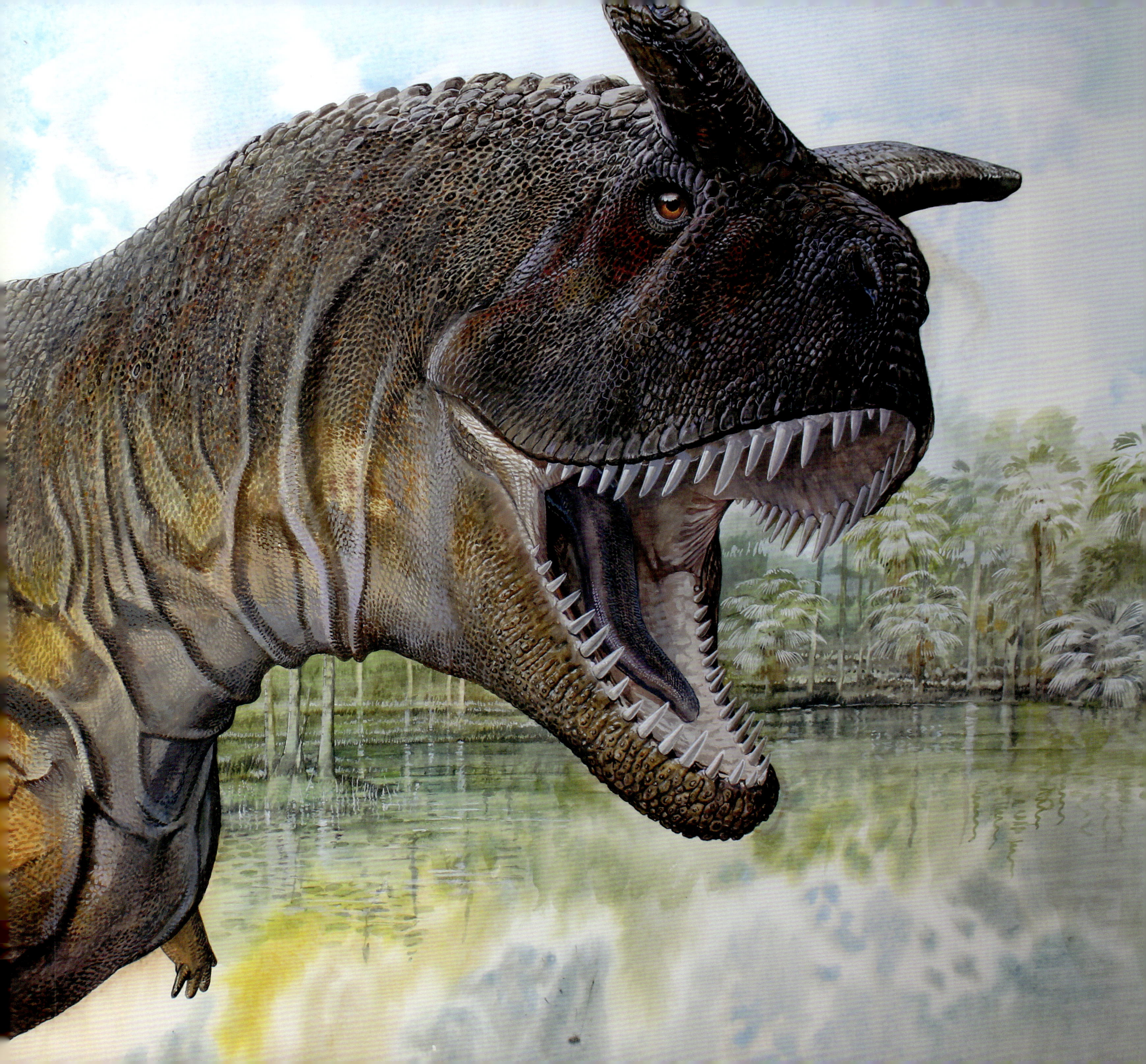

that I have never seen before. This may be an extant species new to science or a fossil species from a group that I have never illustrated before. Novel forms of established groups are particularly attractive. The spine-covered sauropod *Amargasaurus* or the outrageously crested pterosaur *Tupandactylus* are two that spring to mind.

What are your least favorite?

LBB (little brown birds) and LBM (little brown mammals). With diminution of size comes a conservatism of form.

Do you have different approaches to your technical illustration and fine art? Is the former more disciplined?

Technical illustration must, by definition, convey information of the subject being depicted. This can be accomplished through a simple line drawing or a more complex painted composition of multiple subjects set into an environment. These are usually created for a specific purpose, such as publication in a book or as an accompaniment to a scientific paper. Fine art compositions are usually commissioned by a client or created for a gallery exhibition. It is for these reasons that there is less need to convey information of the subject and greater emphasis can be placed on the aesthetics of the overall composition. So, illustration does require greater discipline – however there is no reason why this cannot be done in an aesthetically pleasing way.

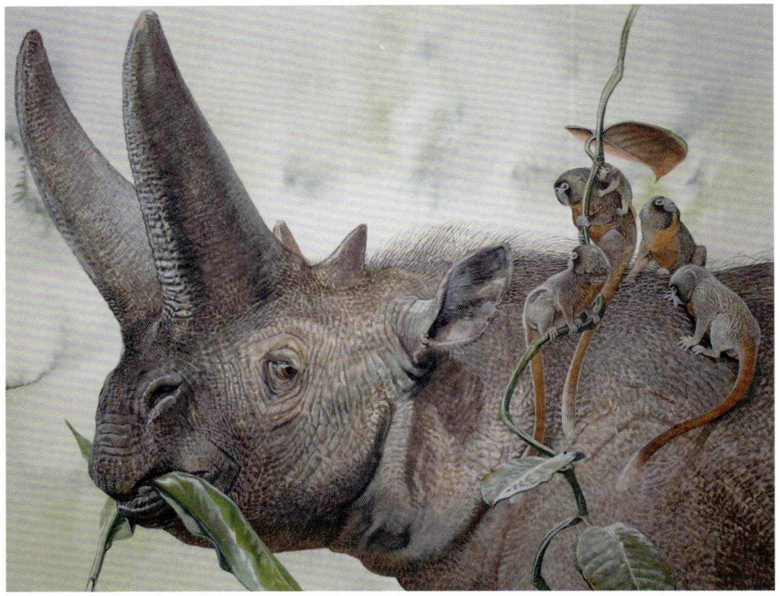

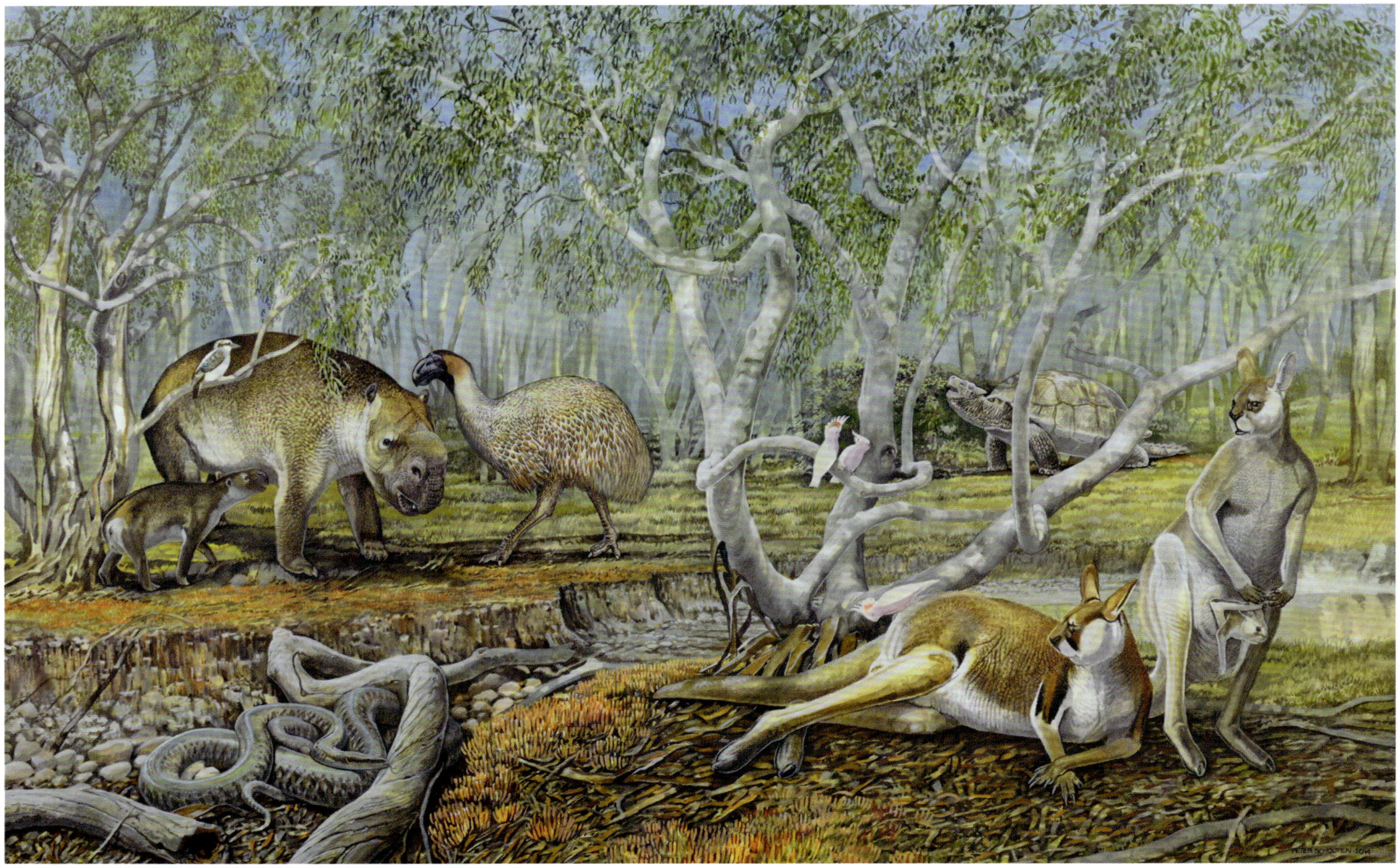

(Above) ***Arsinoitherium***
Watercolors, Gouache, 2013
Arsinoitherium zitteli and the small primate *Proteopithecus sylviae*. Late Eocene 36mya. Jebel Qatrani Formation, Egypt.

(Left) **Arid Woodland, Late Pleistocene Australia**
Watercolors, Gouache, 2014
Left to right: The living kookaburra *Dacelo gigas*; the giant diprotodontid (with young) *Diprotodon optatum*; the flightless bird *Genyornis newtoni*; the giant snake *Wonambi naracoortensis*; the living Leadbeaters cockatoo *Cacatua leadbeateri*; the giant terrestrial turtle *Ninjemys oweni*; and the large kangaroo *Procoptodon goliah*.

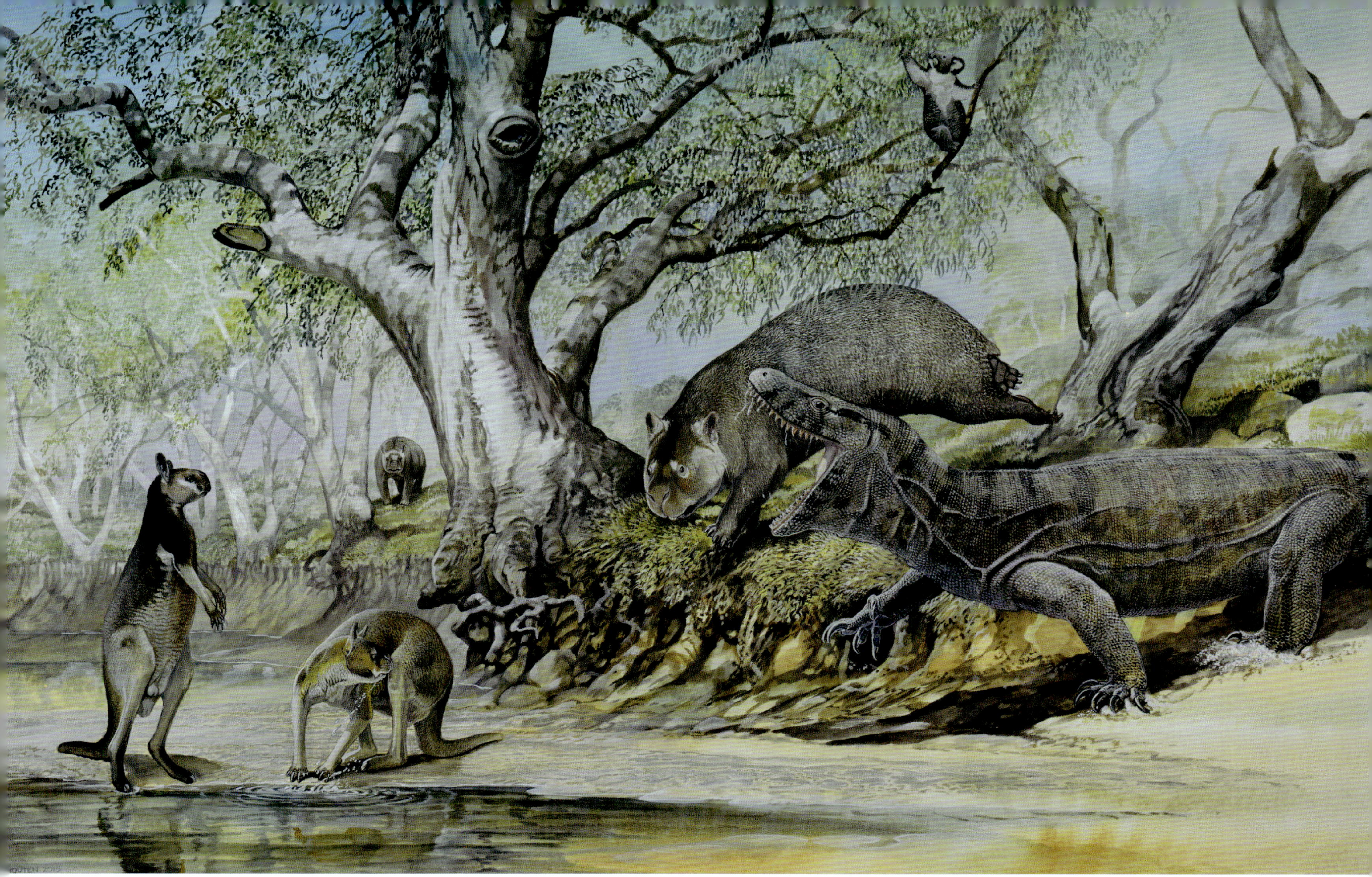

Riparian Woodland, Late Pleistocene Australia
Watercolors, Gouache, 2015
Left to right: the kangaroo *Sthenurus andersoni*; the short-faced kangaroo *Simosthenurus orientalis*; the diprotodontid *Zygomaturus macleayi* (background); the giant diprotodontid *Phascolonus gigas*; the koala *Phascolarctos stirtoni*; and the giant varanid lizard *Varanus* (or *Megalania*) *priscus*.

You're revisiting one of your first books, The Antipodean Ark, *which you originally produced pencil illustrations for. What prompted you to do a new edition?*

I was greatly disappointed with the quality of the images in the original edition. The designer of the original book thought the grainy reproduction of the images gave it a "sketchy" quality – madness! The original was published in 1987 and now, after nearly 30 years, our knowledge of Australasian paleontology has increased exponentially. My confidence at paleo reconstruction has also matured and today I am not afraid to tackle complex illustrations depicting multiple subjects and landscapes. This led me to devise a new approach, in that I am more interested in fossil faunas rather than single species. I believe that the new *Antipodean Ark* is the first time that all

(Below) **Strzelecki Fauna, Australia**
Watercolors, Gouache, 2012
Aptian Stage, Early Cretaceous 120-115mya. Left to right: indeterminate abelisaur; *Koolasuchus cleelandi*, a large amphibian that is the youngest – and possibly one of the last – of a now extinct subclasss of amphibians, the Temnospondyli that were thought to have vanished at the end of the Triassic; the lungfish *Ceratodus avus*.

(Opposite) ***Spinosaurus***
Watercolors, Gouache, 2016
The Kem Kem Beds of Morocco, Early Cenomanian Stage, Early Cretaceous 99mya. Left to right: the 'pancake crocodile' *Laganosuchus maghrebensis*; the knifefish *Palaeonotopterus greenwoodi*; the small polypterid *Sudania* sp. (near submerged log); the small polypterid *Bartschichthys* sp.; *Spinosaurus maroccanus*; the large coelacanthid *Mawsonia lavocati*; shoal of *Calamopleurus africanus*; and the lungfish *Neoceratodus africanus*.

major fossil sites in a given zoogeographic region will be represented in an illustrated form.

The Feathered Dinosaurs *was your first real 'dinosaur' book; do you have a particular approach to dinosaurs, especially those less avian?*

I never stop learning. Every time I illustrate a dinosaur I learn something new. Currently I am illustrating a lot of large Gondwanan dinosaurs and I am learning a lot about how skin moves over muscle, how it might fold along a neck or where it might crease due to bodily movement or the effects of gravity.

Feathered Dinosaurs taught me a lot about the movement of feathers and filaments. It also emphasized the need for a different approach to smaller dinosaurs. There now seems to be an accumulation of evidence that most small theropods and ornithischians had an insulated covering of some sort, and this needs to be taken into account when reconstructing these animals. By looking at modern birds and mammals with integumentary insulation we see that they have greater "volume" than a similar-sized animal without insulation. This must be considered when attempting a reconstruction.

Your work on Homo floresiensis *drew a lot of media attention. How did you become involved in work on those reconstructions?*

I was approached by Bert Roberts at the University of Wollongong to see if I may be interested in creating an image to accompany the media release of an exciting new discovery. Initially he was cagey about the subject matter until he had my assurance of absolute secrecy. When I discovered that it was a new species of hominin I leapt at the opportunity to illustrate it. Much correspondence followed, accompanied by copious notes and photos of the fossil skull. I was asked to wait until the descriptive paper had been accepted for publication and only then was I instructed to start. My jaw dropped when I heard the deadline – two weeks! At this stage the sex of the individual was unknown so I chose to illustrate a male. The day before I was to send

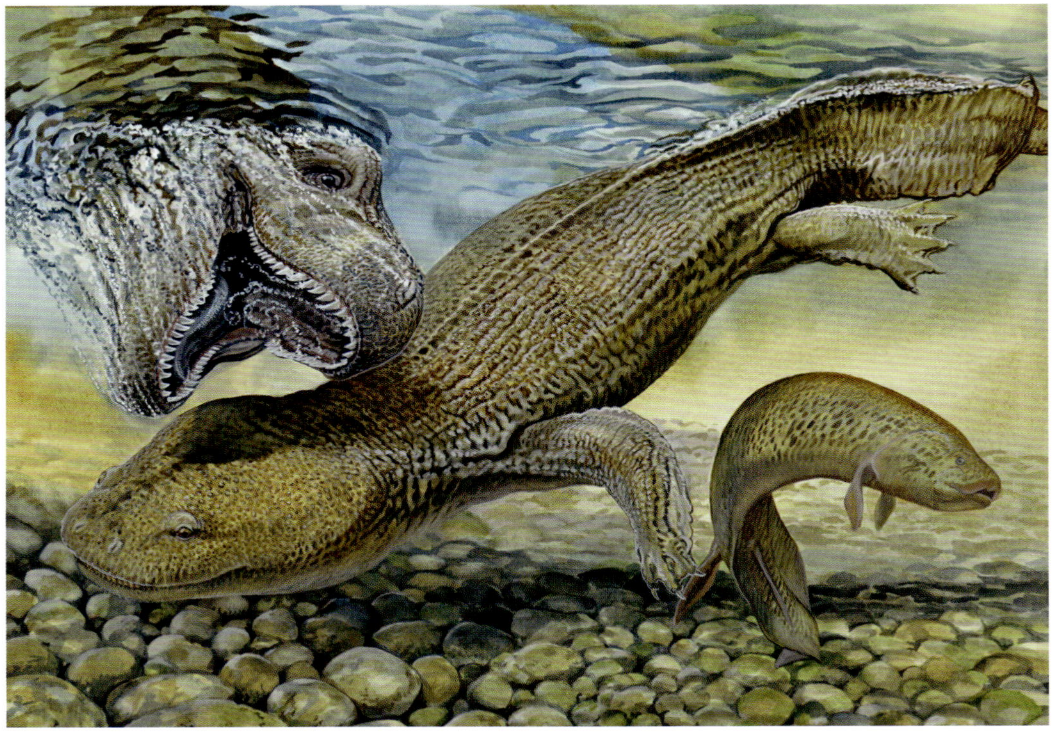

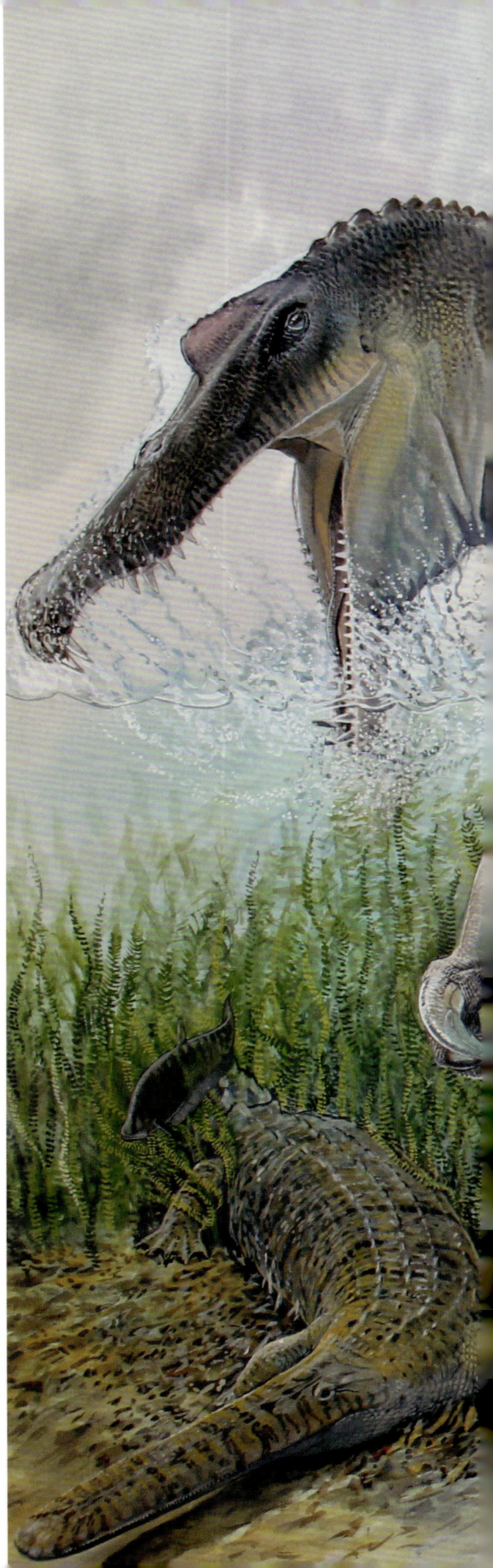

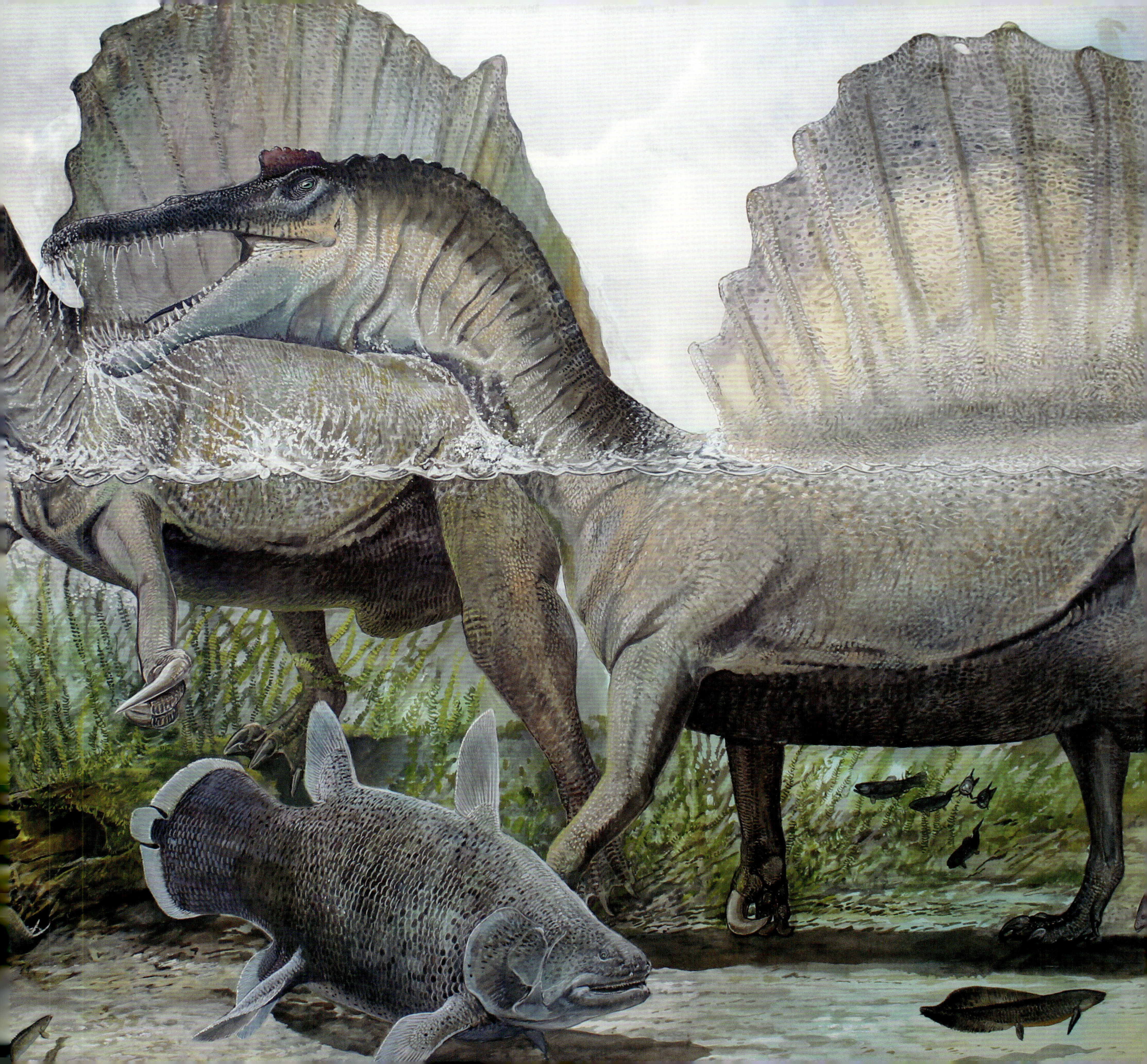

the artwork to my photographer I was informed that the recently excavated material indicated that the individual was female – fuck! Normally adjustments could be made to accommodate this new information, however there was no time left. It had to go to press as it was. In the end it did not matter that much, as numerous individuals were found in the deposit, including males.

The media coverage was incredible. It was front page around the world. I had a constant stream of enquiries regarding the usage of the image and, curiously, an inordinate interest in the genitalia – mostly from US media wishing to airbrush away the offending organ!

What's your particular artistic and academic interest in megafauna?

In 1962, at the age of five, I was hospitalized with polio. On request, my mother would supply me with reading material to relieve the boredom. This usually meant lots of books or comics that featured dinosaurs in some way or other. On one occasion, I received a small paperback book entitled *The How and Why Wonder Book of Prehistoric Mammals.* I was entranced. The cover featured a composite illustration of animals I had never seen before: *Uintatherium*, *Arsinoitherium*, a mammoth and *Megatherium.* At the time I was unaware that this rather naive composite, by John Hull, was both temporally and geographically inaccurate. It didn't matter to me; I was hooked.

Megafauna is the subject of a new book that I am doing with Professor Ross MacPhee of the American Museum of Natural History, currently entitled *Hugest, Fiercest, Strangest.* This book

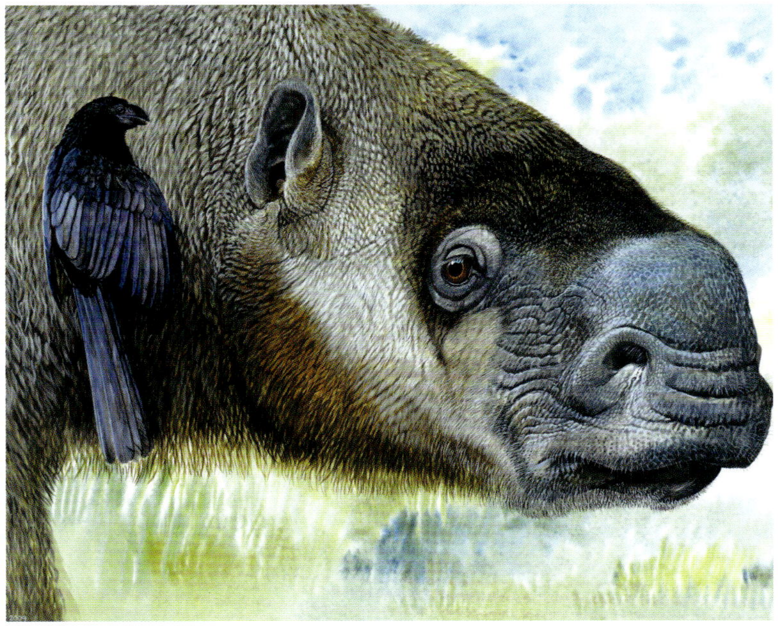

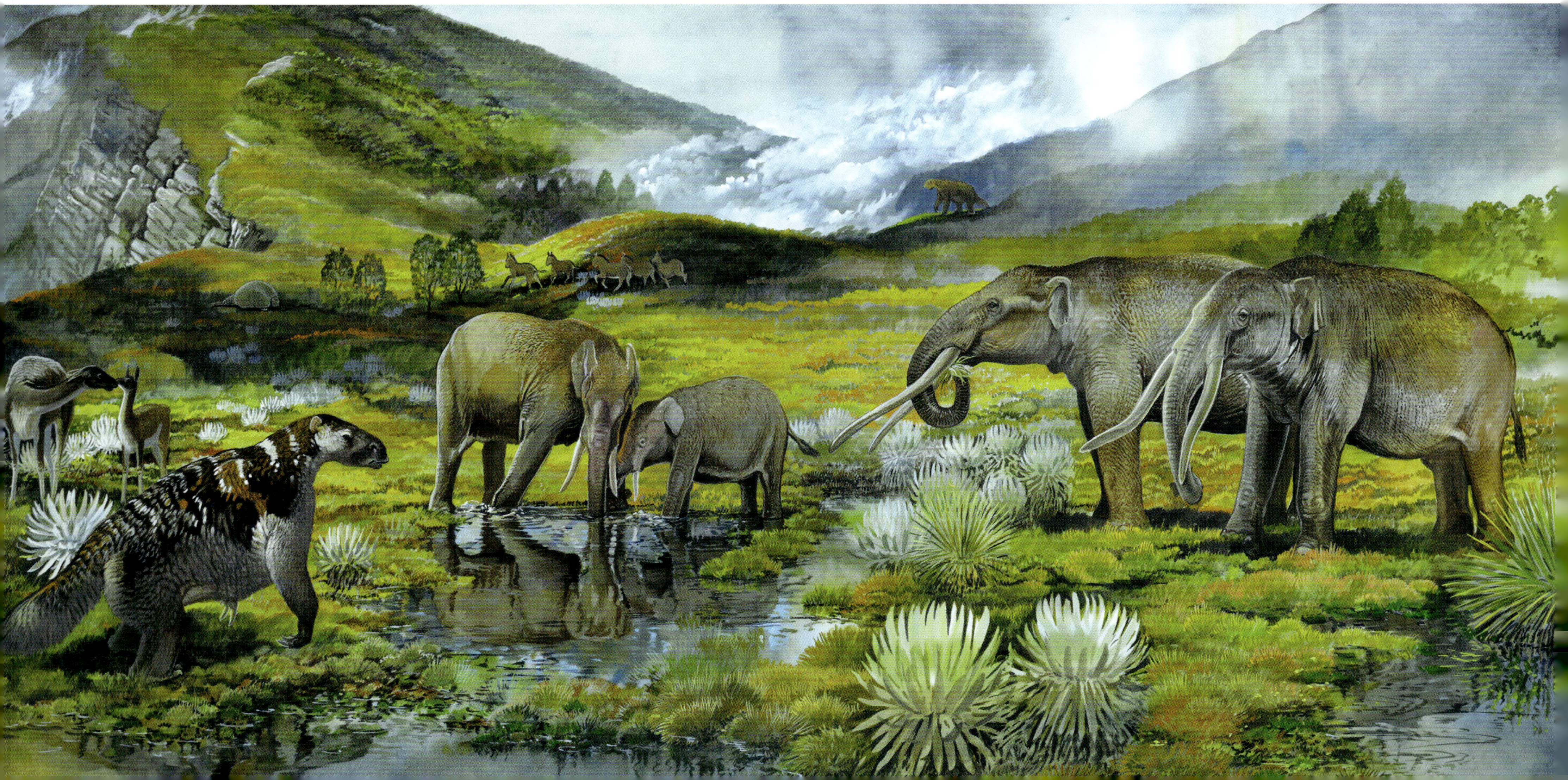

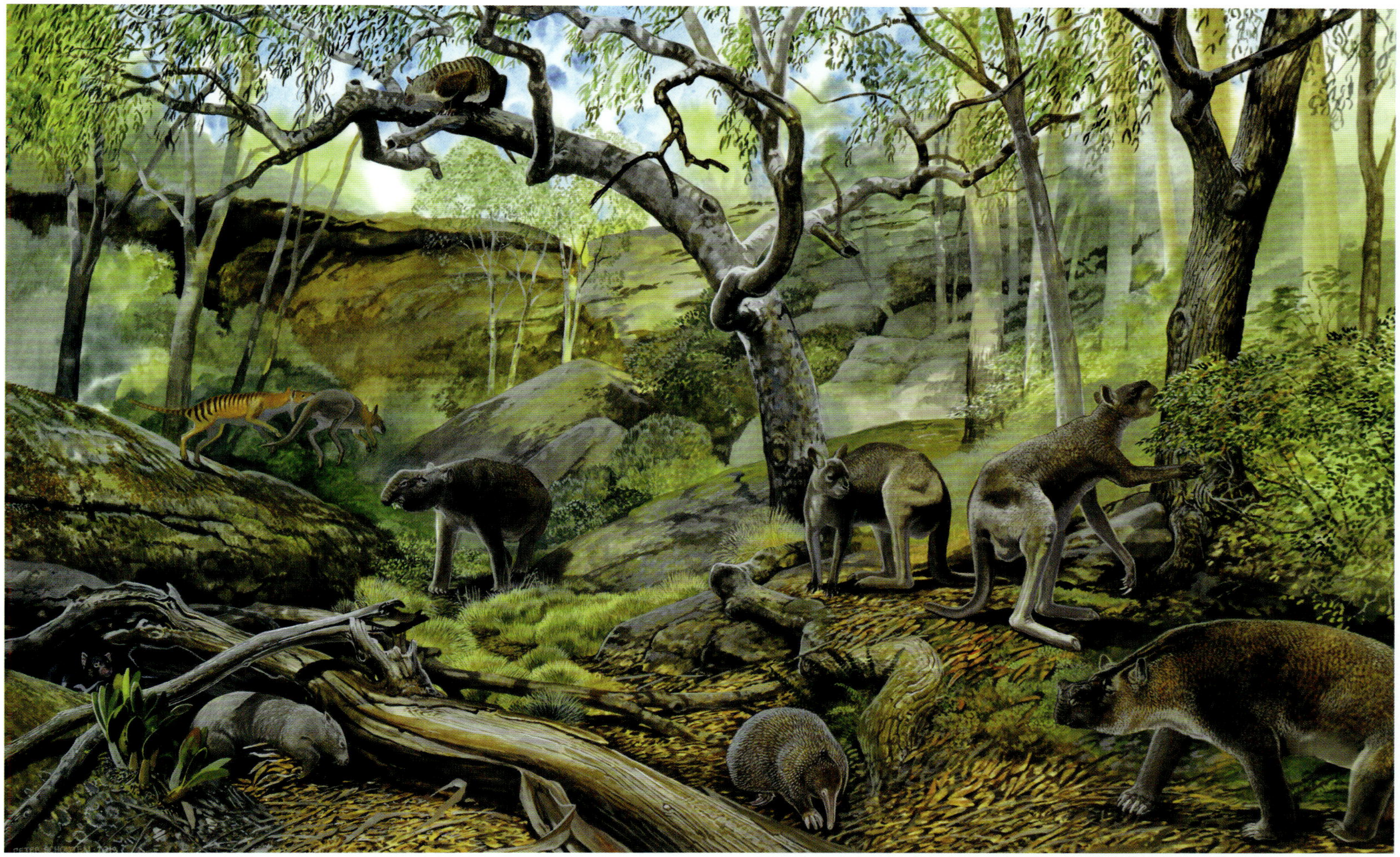

Naracoorte Caves, Late Pleistocene Australia
Watercolors, Gouache, 2013
Left to right: the Mainland devil *Sarcophilus harrisii laniarius*; the wombat *Warendja wakefieldi* (lower left); the 'marsupial wolf' or thylacine *Thylacine cynocephalus* pursuing the red-necked wallaby *Macropus rufogriseus*; the giant wombat *Diprotodon optatum*; the 'marsupial lion' *Thylacoleo carnifex* (in the tree); the echidna *Megalibgwilia ramsayi*; the large kangaroo *Simosthenurus occidentalis*; and the diprotodont *Zygomaturus trilobus*.

(Opposite top) ***Lestodon***
Watercolors, Gouache, 2009
The ground sloth *Lestodon armatus* attended by the extant smooth-billed ani *Crotophaga ani*.

(Opposite bottom)
Central Andes Páramo, Late Pleistocene
Watercolors, Gouache, 2010
Left to right: the llama *Palaeolama weddelli*; the ground sloth *Scelidotherium leptocephalum*; the giant armadillo *Glyptodon* sp. (background); the elephant-like Andean gomphothere *Cuvieronius hyodon*; the horse *Equus andium*; and the giant ground sloth *Megatherium tarijense* (background).

chronicles the movement of modern humans around the planet and the impact that we have had on global megafauna.

Which of your books are you most proud of?

I guess that would have to be *A Gap in Nature*. For me this was an important project. I have had a long-standing interest in conservation and the plight of our endangered species, so when the opportunity arose to chronicle recent anthropogenic extinctions, I jumped at the chance.

The decision was made to create a travelling exhibition to accompany the release of the book, and as a result of that I decided to paint all the animals life-size. This was not a problem for most of the subjects as they would fit comfortably within the confines of the art paper that I use. However, what to do about a 9m Steller's sea cow? Initially I created a 1:10 scale painting, but somehow it wasn't right. I scrapped it and threw myself into the challenge of creating a full-scale painting. At the time, I was living in a small city terrace house with hardly enough room to swing a cat let alone a 9 meter sea cow! The painting was created on five large panels, with no way of joining them together. To complete the work the panels were freighted to a warehouse large enough to display the five panels and, for the first time, I saw the painting in its entirety.

The exhibition was successful in an unexpected way. On opening night I wandered through the gallery and could not help but notice the silence of the room. The viewers would converse in hushed tones and dutifully read all the information panels and, on leaving, many were seen wiping tears from their eyes. Wow! I never expected such a result. I guess the point I am trying to make is that the decision to paint all the animals life-size made them instantly relatable to the viewers, so that the impact of seeing a collection of 103 animals that have disappeared due to actions of man really hit home.

Are there any animals you've not illustrated that you'd love to work on?

I would love to illustrate every animal on the

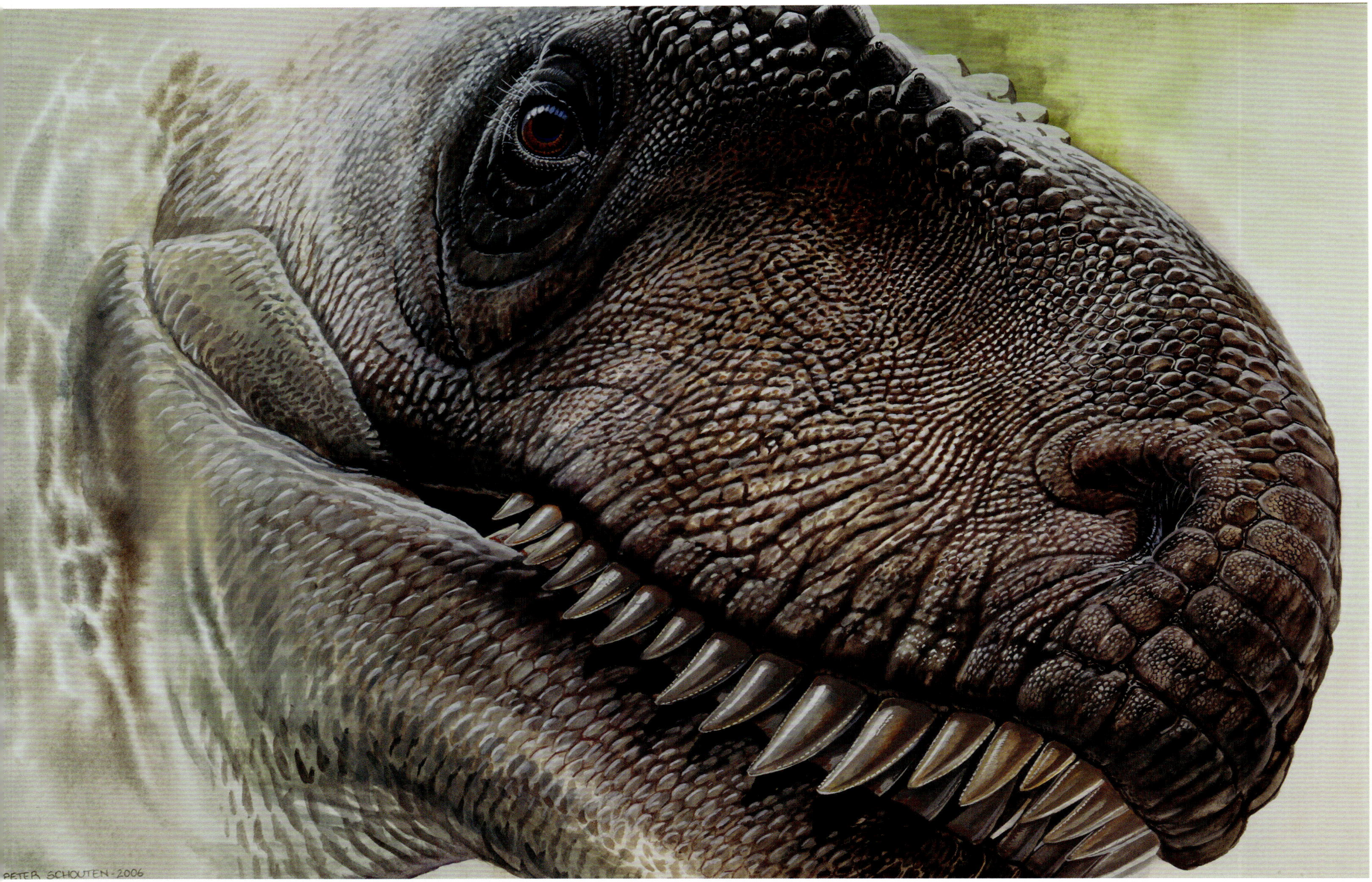

planet, of course; that is not possible. Realistically, I would like to have another go at deep sea fish. I dabbled with them in *Astonishing Animals* and was blown away by their incredible forms and adaptations to such an extreme environment. They surely must be the closest things we have to alien life forms.

The other area of interest for me is life in the Triassic. This period gave rise to many important vertebrate groups, including mammals, pterosaurs, dinosaurs and the marine sauropterygians. I am very keen on the mammal-like reptiles and, as yet, have not had the opportunity to illustrate them.

Appalachiosaurus montgomeriensis
Watercolors, Gouache, 2006

(Right) **Valdarno Basin**
Watercolors, Gouache, 2015
Late Pliocene-Early Pleistocene 3-2mya. Near Florence, Italy. Left to Right: Bush-antlered deer *Eucladocerus dicranios*; the macaque *Macaca sylvanus florentina*; and the long-tusked gomphothere *Anancus arvernensis*.

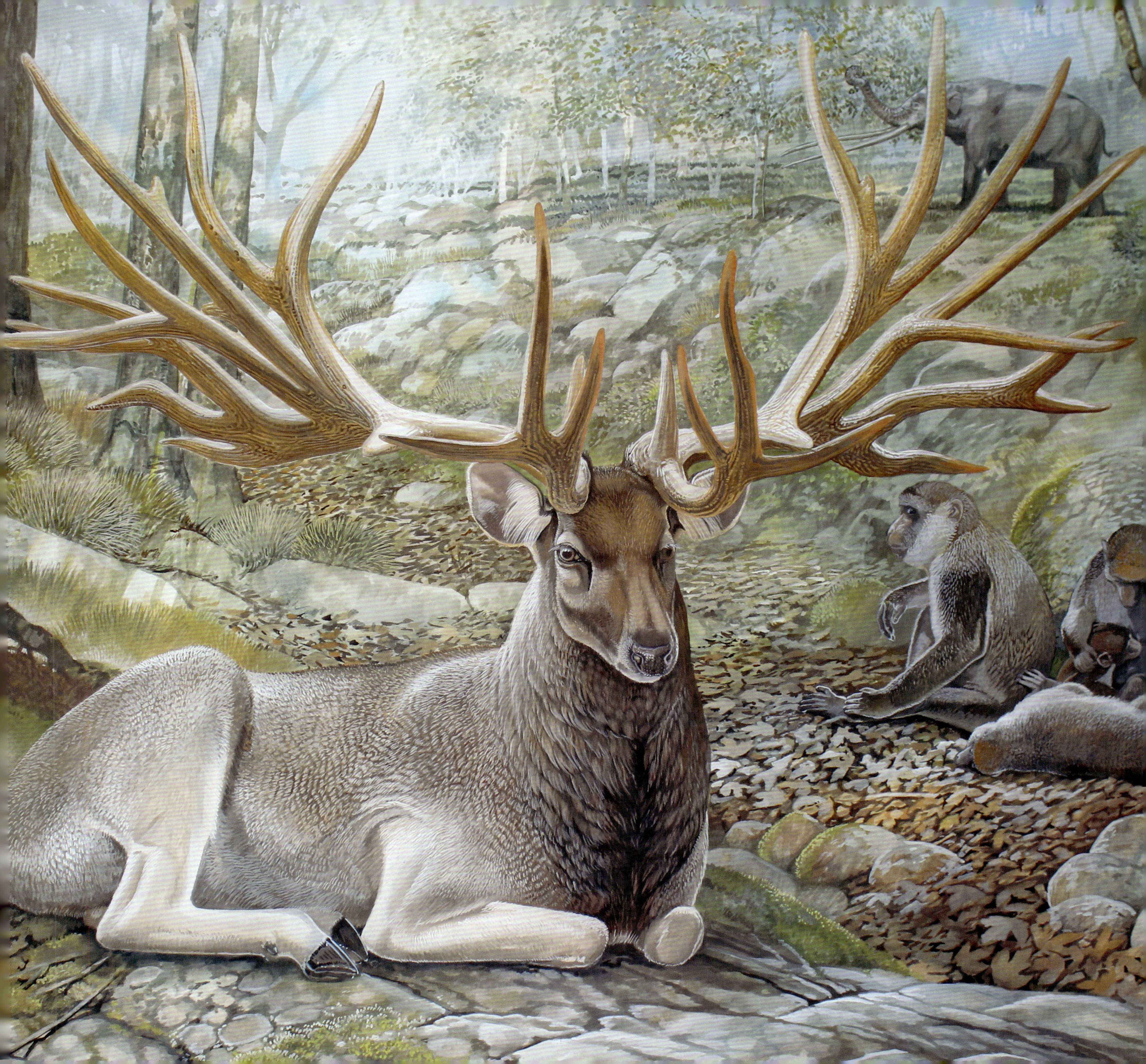

ANDREY ATUCHIN

RUSSIA

Andrey graduated from Kemerovo State University as a biologist in 2006. He then did postgraduate work at the university's department of zoology and ecology as an entomologist until 2010. Since 2004, he has also been working as a scientific illustrator specializing in natural history and paleoart. Since 2008, he has participated in paleontological excavations yearly as a volunteer and research assistant with the Amur Earth History Museum, Kemerovo Regional Local History Museum, and Denver Museum of Nature and Science. Andrey has collaborated with leading paleontologists in Russia and throughout the world; he has produced artwork for numerous publishers, museum exhibits, academic papers and paleontological press releases, with a client list that includes *National Geographic Russia*, the Denver Museum of Nature and Science, Queensland Museum, Cleveland Museum of Natural History, and the Natural History Museum of Utah; and his work has also appeared in several encyclopedias. His work has also won first prize in several international paleoart competitions in Brazil, Spain and Germany.

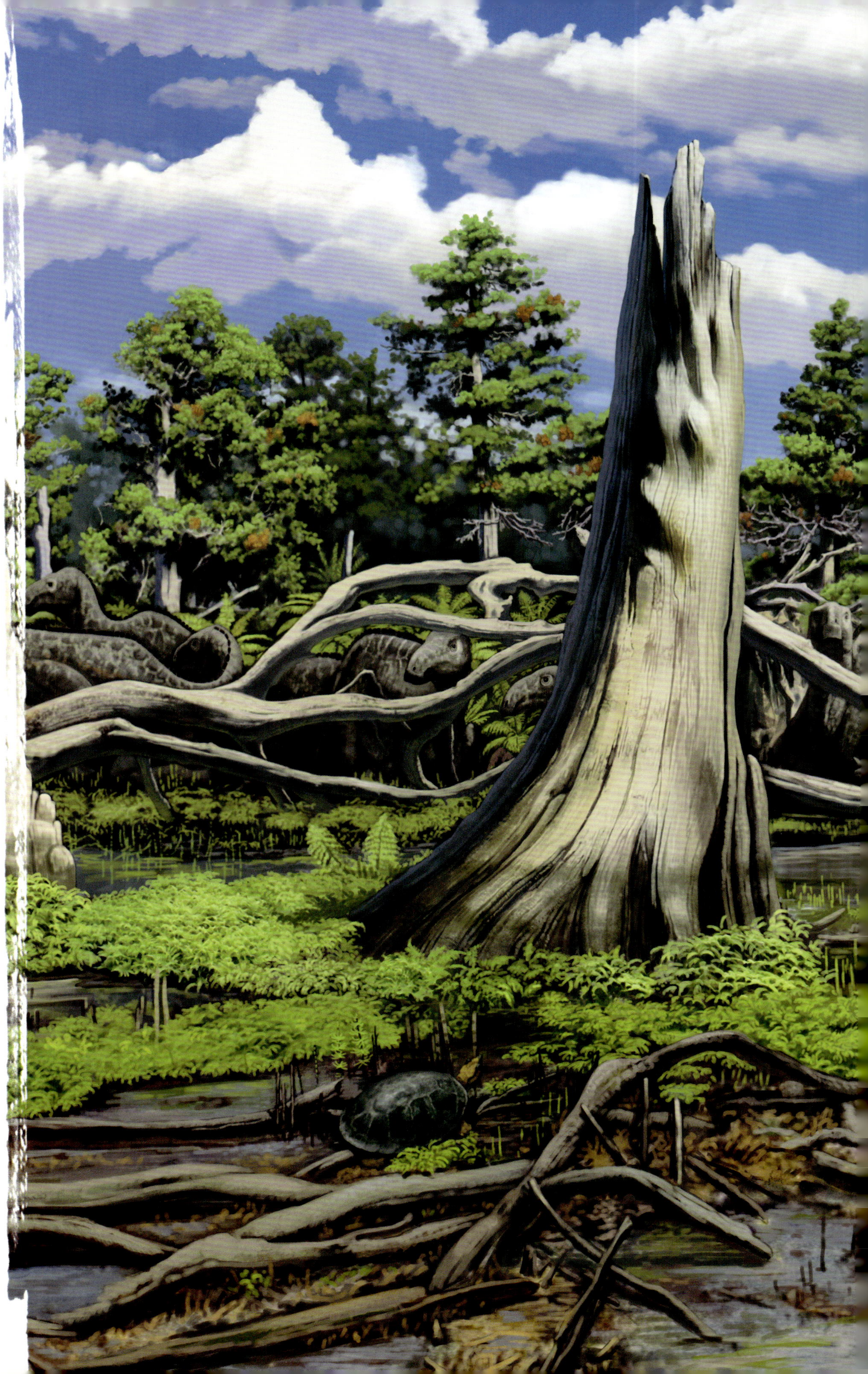

Europelta
Digital, 2014
The nodosaur *Europelta carbonensis* at home in a swampy coastal floodplain. Lower left is the turtle *Trachyaspis*; in the background is a herd of the iguanodont *Proa valdearinnoensis*; and the goniopholidid crocodile *Hulkepoholis plotos*. Lower Albian Stage of Early Cretaceous. Escucha Formation of northeastern Spain.

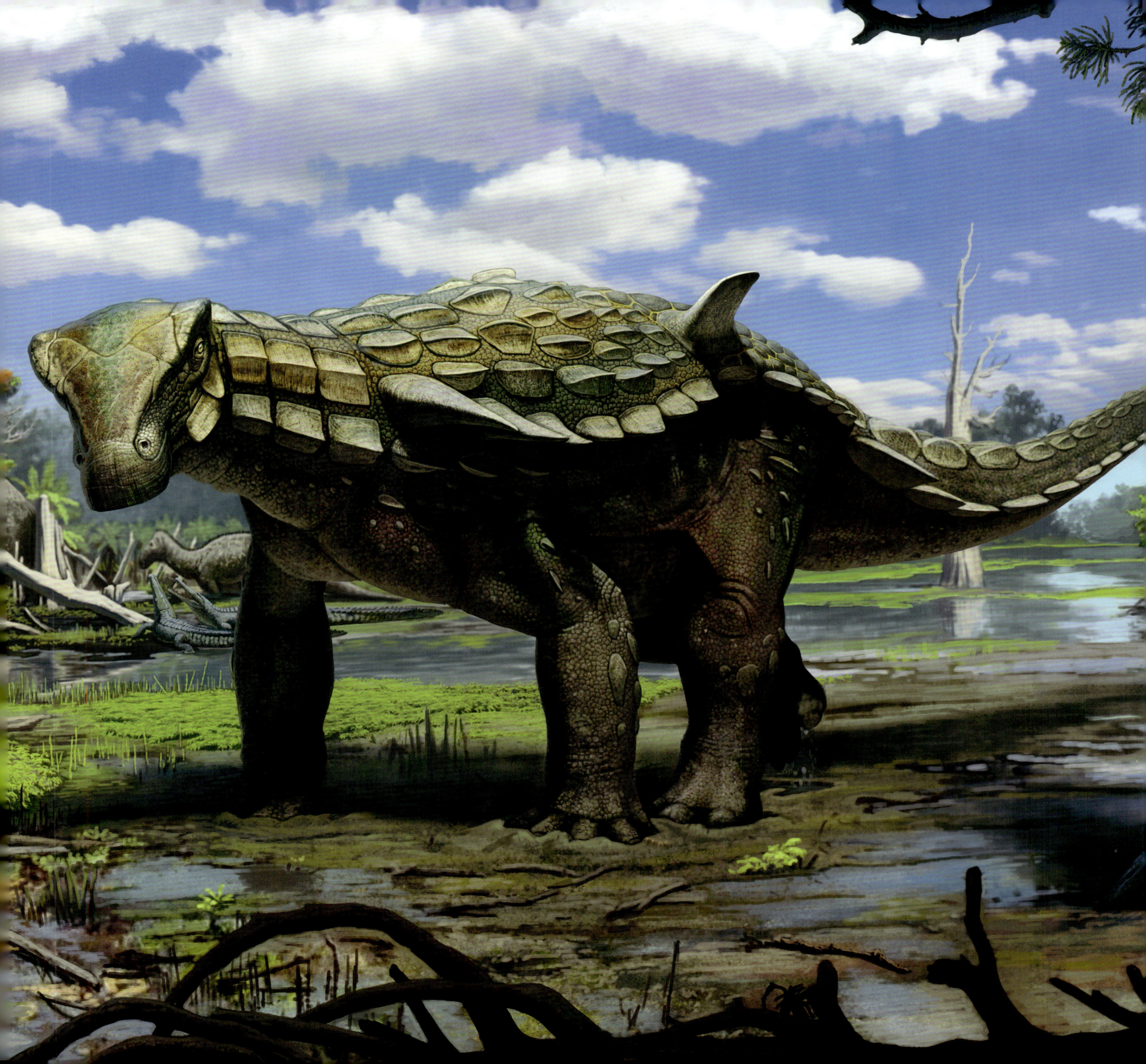

(Right) ***Dollocaris ingens***
Digital, 2016

(Below) ***Hallucigenia sparsa***
Digital, 2016
A truly bizarre type of Xenusia, a group of lobopodian worms, which as their name suggests have lob-like limbs. When first discovered in the famous Burgess Shales of British Columbia (dated from the Mid-Cambrian Period 508mya), the strangeness of its anatomy led researchers to initially reconstruct it upside down, with the dorsal spines as the legs. Subsequent discoveries rectified the situation.

(Opposite) ***Opabinia regalis***
Digital, 2016
Another denizen of the Burgess Shales, *Opabinia* was 1.6-2.8in (4-7cm) long and used its strange trunk to probe the sediment for particles of food.

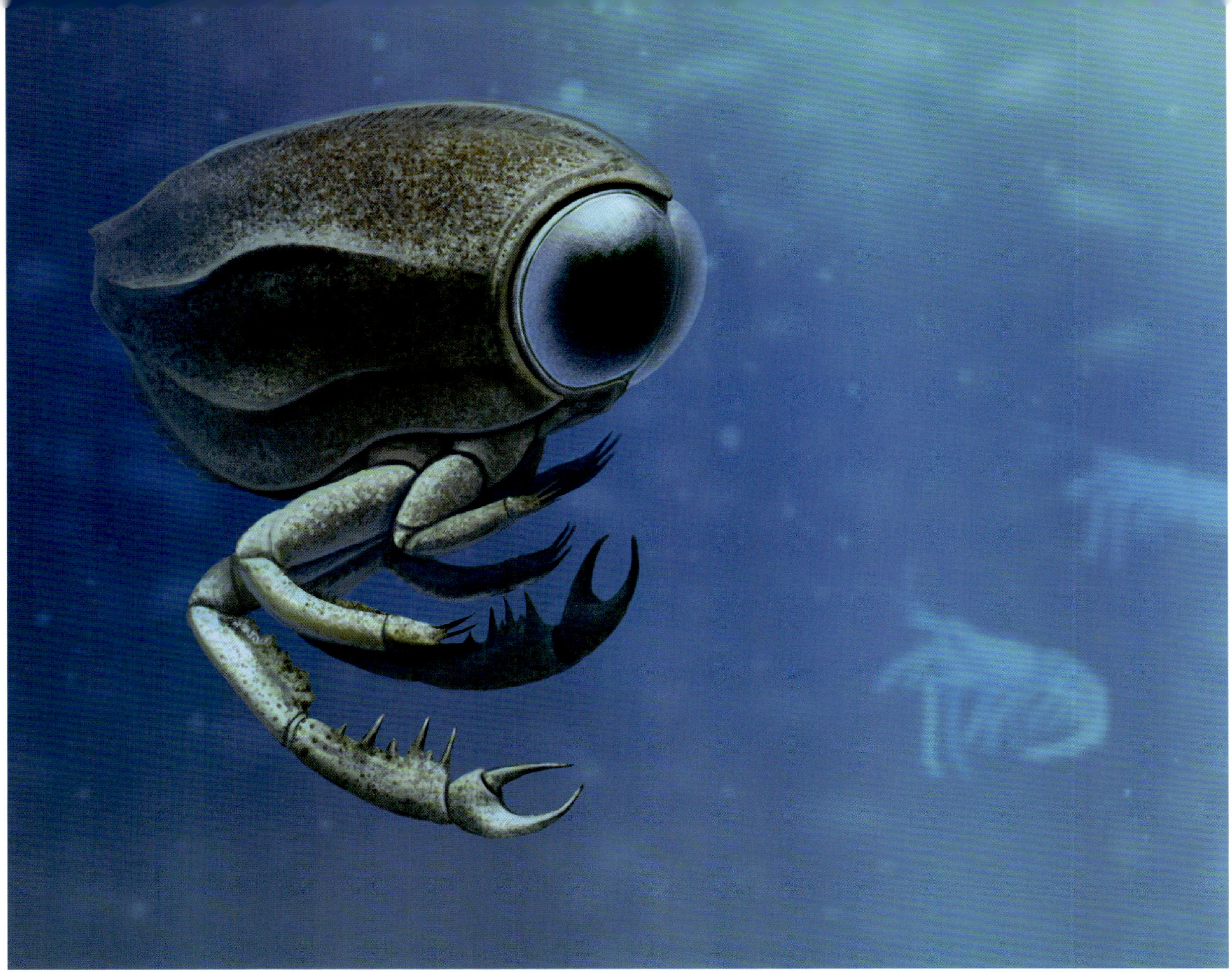

You've illustrated some pretty strange and wonderful organisms that, at first glance, look completely made up, Dollocaris *being a great example. How do you approach something like that artistically? Are they fun to do?*

Actually, these creatures only look weird for people who see tadpoles in a puddle and think they come from another planet. I graduated in biology and undertook a lot of research in the zoology department as an entomology major. So, I'm well acquainted with invertebrate zoology and zoologists, and am certain that anyone who's seen a cool invertebrate through a binocular microscope wouldn't have any trouble accepting *Dollocaris*' eyes or whatever. To be honest, the word "strange" would never cross my mind when I see an animal like that – I tend to think, "Wow, this is really gorgeous!" instead.

You can find plenty of modern invertebrates that are strange enough that they might be mistaken for aliens. Paleontology provides us with extremely striking things too, but it isn't particularly difficult to bring them to life and draw them. I take great pleasure in drawing these beautiful creatures, and I'm always inspired by the variety of shapes and textures they display.

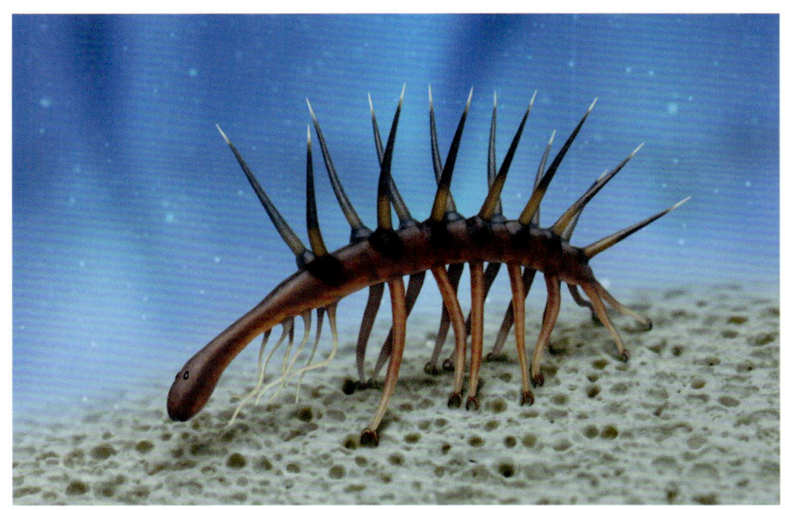

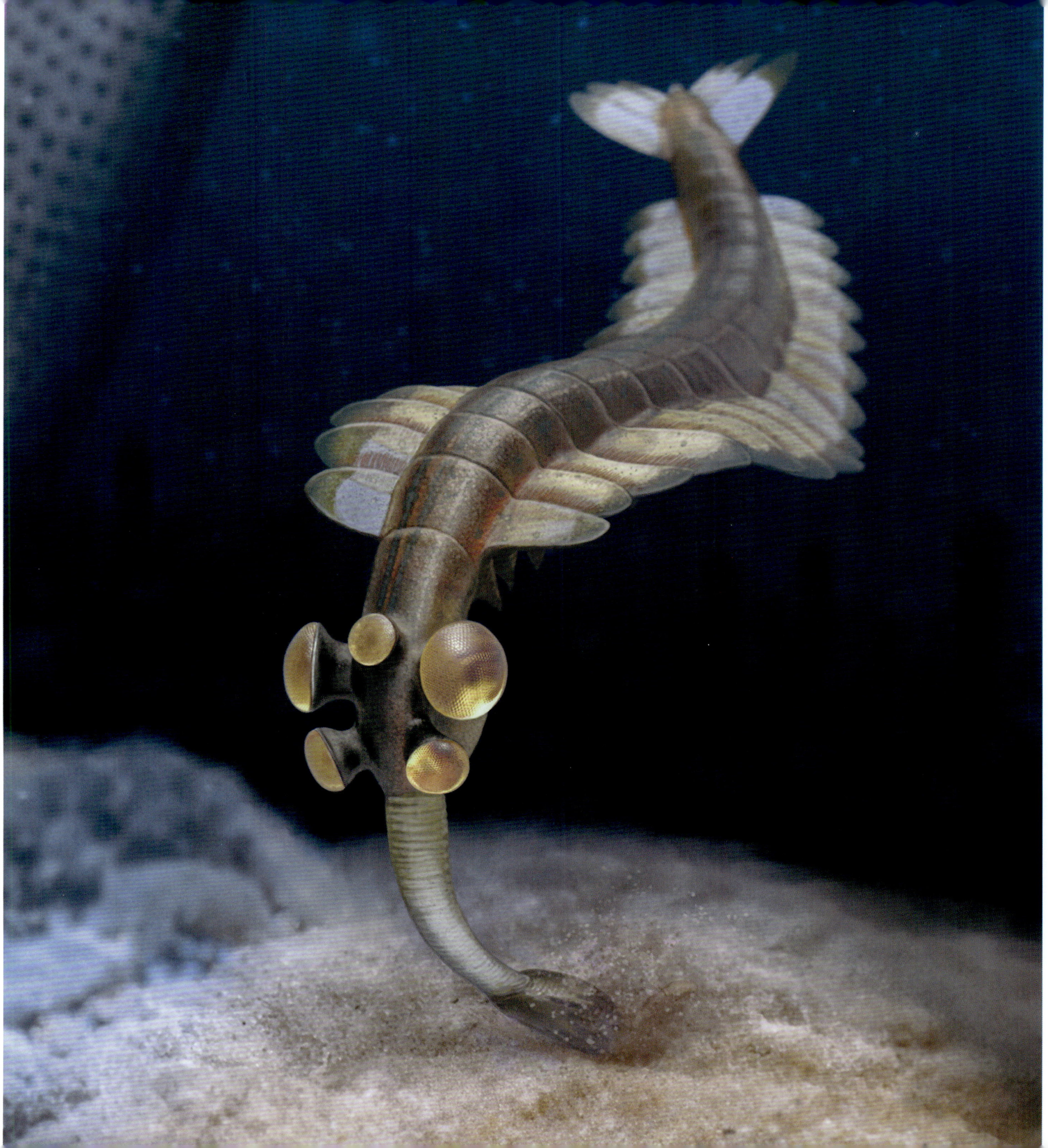

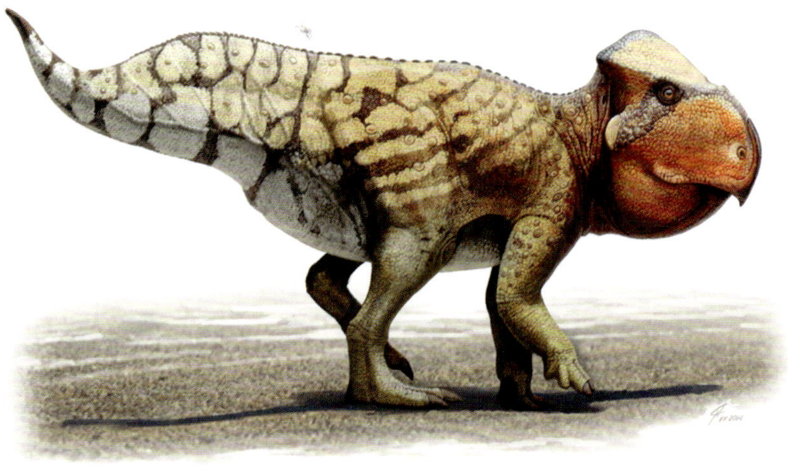

You seem to enjoy illustrating ceratopsians – are they your particular favorites?
Ceratopsians are incredible animals and it always affords me great pleasure to work on them. I enjoy them for their vast diversity of forms, horns and frills; there is always something new and astounding. However, my usual answer to this question is that my favorite dinosaurs are those I'm working on at any given time. Of course, there are dinosaurs and other animals I may favor slightly more than others, or ones that I find particularly inspiring to draw; those I can always count on and be sure to get a great picture. Ceratopsians are part of this group, but not the only members.
Did you set out to be a paleoartist or was that just an accident?
I became a professional paleoartist accidentally, but it's a long and winding road that led me here. Initially, it was just a childhood passion for dinosaurs. Mix with this some rare Soviet books and magazine articles about Mongolian dinosaurs and excavations, a set of plastic Polish dinosaur toys my sister gave me as a present, and you start to see how these might have come together to push me in that direction. I vaguely remember seeing something on TV in the early-mid eighties where they were digging out a dinosaur in North America and lifting it

(Above) ***Udanoceratops tschizhovi***
Digital, 2014
Campian Stage, Late Cretaceous. Djadokhta Formation, Mongolia.

(Right) ***Sinoceratops zhuchengensis***
Digital, 2010
The only known centrosaurine from Asia. Maastrichtian, Late Cretaceous. Wangshi Group, China.

(Opposite) ***Diabloceratops eatoni***
Digital, 2010
Early Campanian Stage, Late Cretaceous. Wahweap Formation, USA.

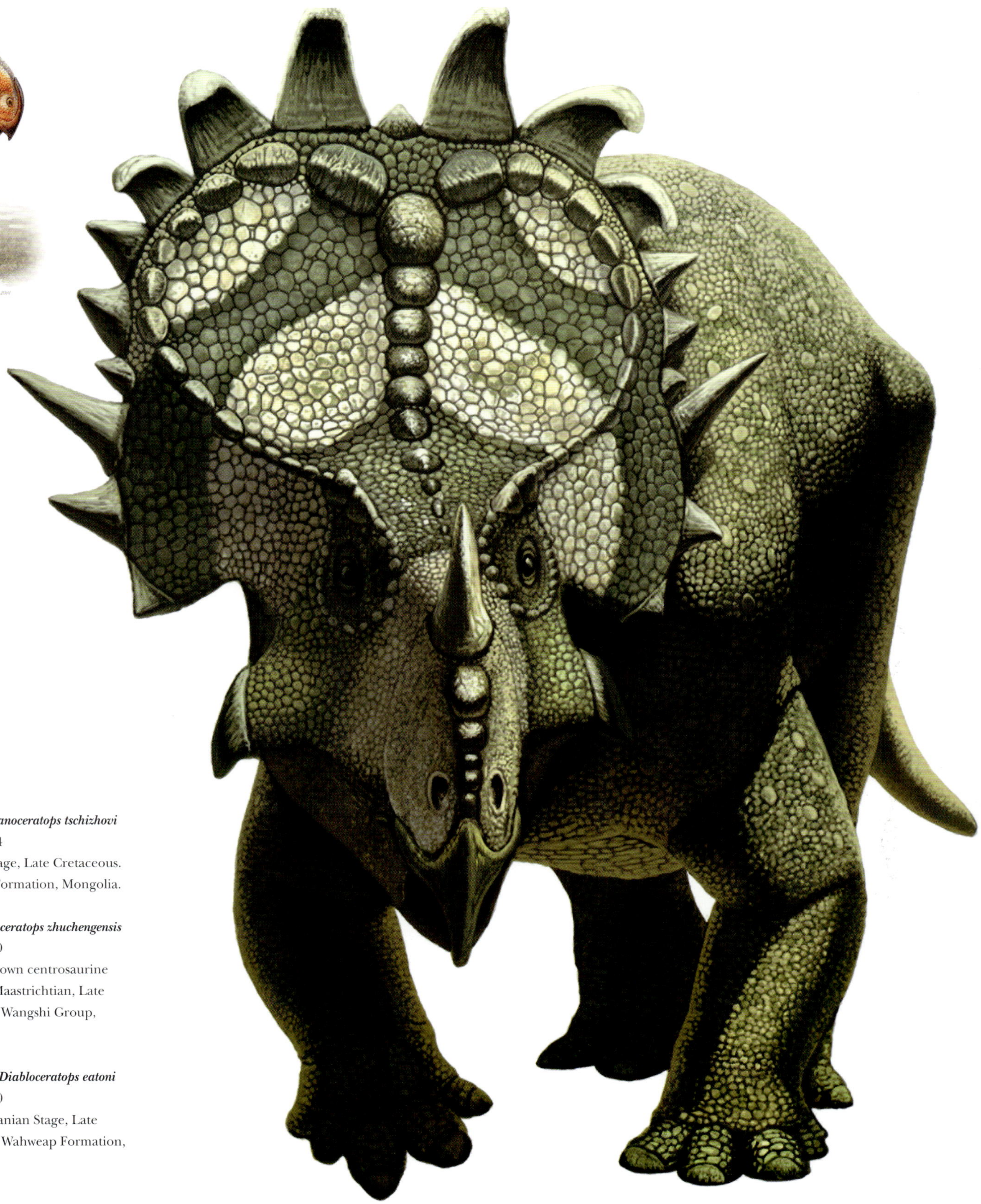

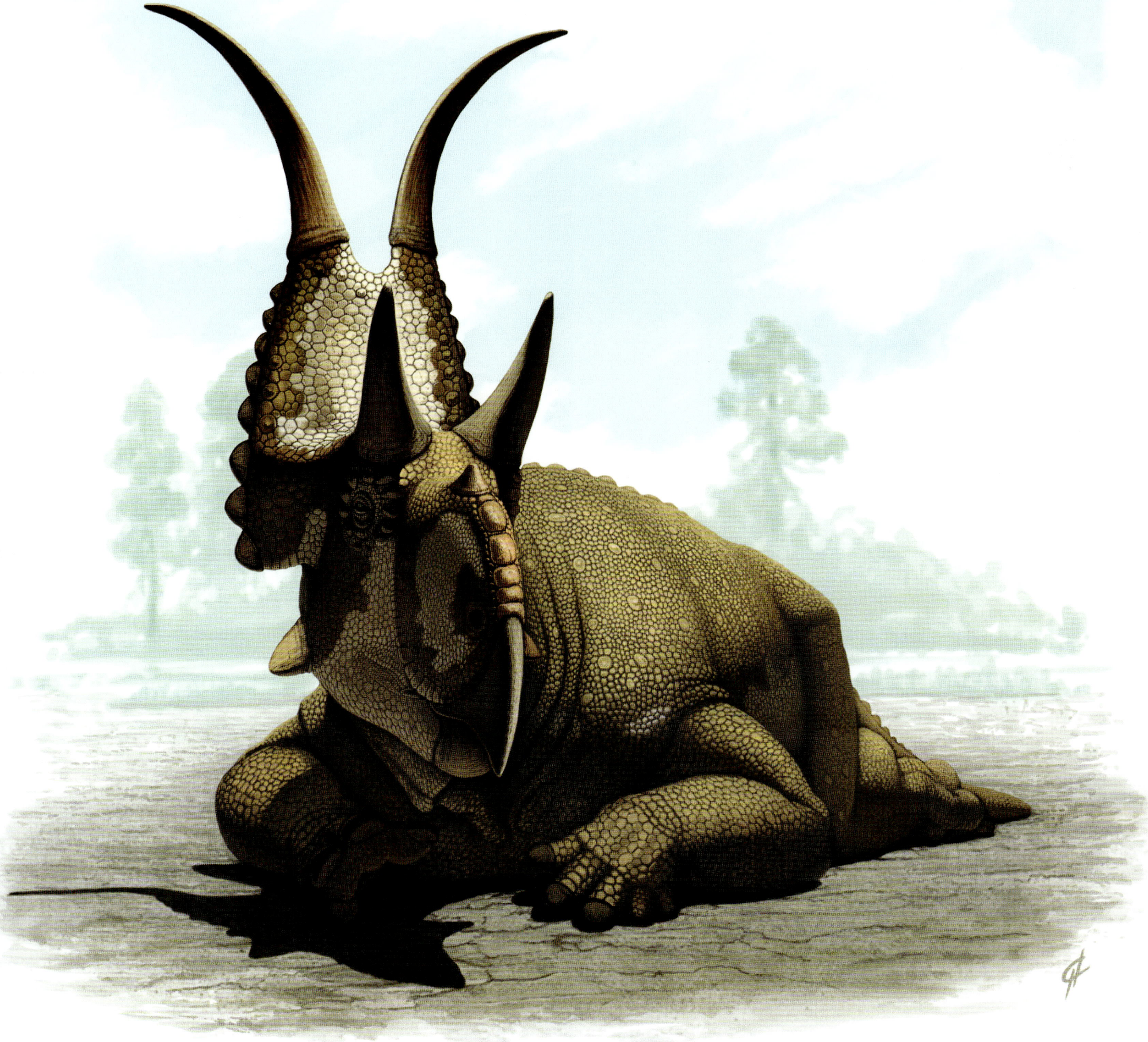

up by helicopter. I was five or six at the time, and was inspired enough by it to draw the scene. Amusingly, this childhood picture became a reality 30 years later when I found myself in North America with a helicopter heaving a dinosaur skeleton up into the sky over my head.

I started to draw dinosaurs regularly at a relatively late age. During my childhood there was almost nothing about dinosaurs and paleontology published where I lived. I was born in a small provincial Siberian town and I did not know about the books of Josef Augusta and Zdeněk Burian that were popular worldwide at that time. I remember after the release of the *Jurassic Park* movie the interest in dinosaurs started to increase rapidly, and at this point a lot of translated foreign books on the subject appeared in bookshops. Even then, it took a while to get to the point where I could actually buy the Dougal Dixon *Encyclopedia of Dinosaurs*: this was the time of the economic crisis after the Soviet Union crashed, and my family simply didn't have the money. There were a lot of skeletons and skulls in that book, which pleased me the most. And having read it, I was aware of how inaccurate the dinosaurs were in the books I'd had before – with the skeletons and skulls of the same animal clearly not matching each other. It was this that gave rise to my dream of a definitive encyclopedia, something that became a bit of a passion project for me.

I did my best to learn to draw in an 'encyclopedic' style in the way I wanted it to look in my own "dream" encyclopedia. I studied at a special arts school for almost two years to gain professional tuition and hone my artistic skills and the quality of my painting. At the same time, I started to collect copies of scientific papers that were sent to me by a relative of mine living in a big city with a huge scientific library. I produced several gouache artworks as a result. In 2000, I entered the biology department of the State University in the capital of the Kemerovo region – my choice of faculty was determined by the location, because I wanted to excavate and research dinosaurs in that region. However, I found the university did not actually offer a paleontology specialization, so I decided to study entomology, which was my second interest.

The internet had arrived at the University just before I did, and this not only gave me access to information that had previously been difficult to

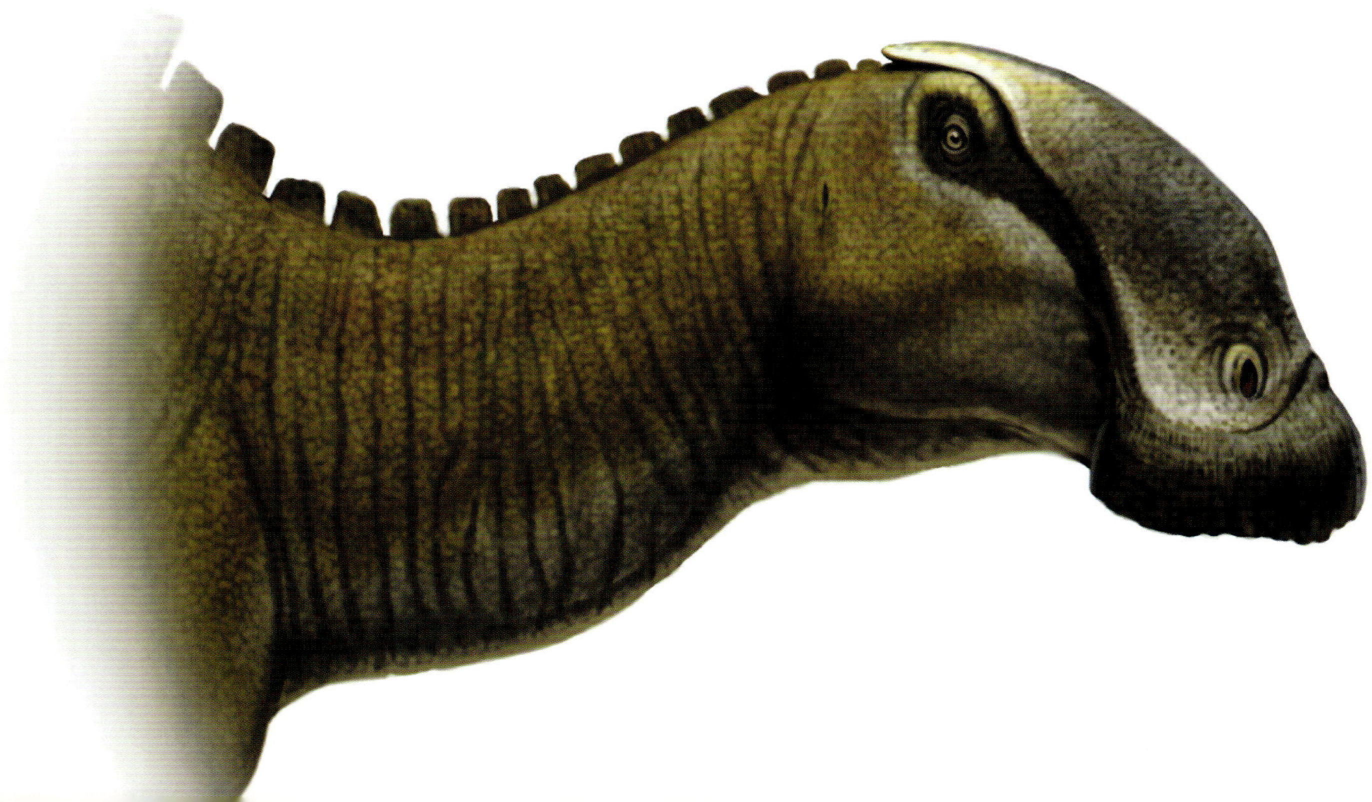

(Below) ***Brachylophosaurus canadensis***
Digital

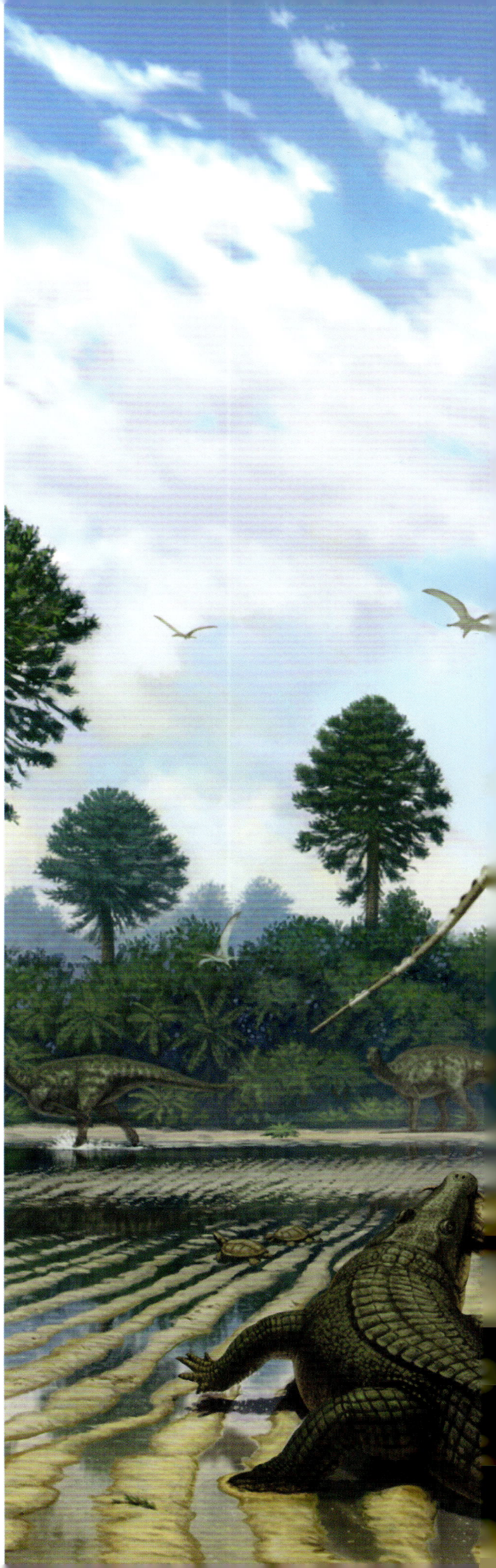

(Right) ***Demandasaurus darwini***
Digital, 2011

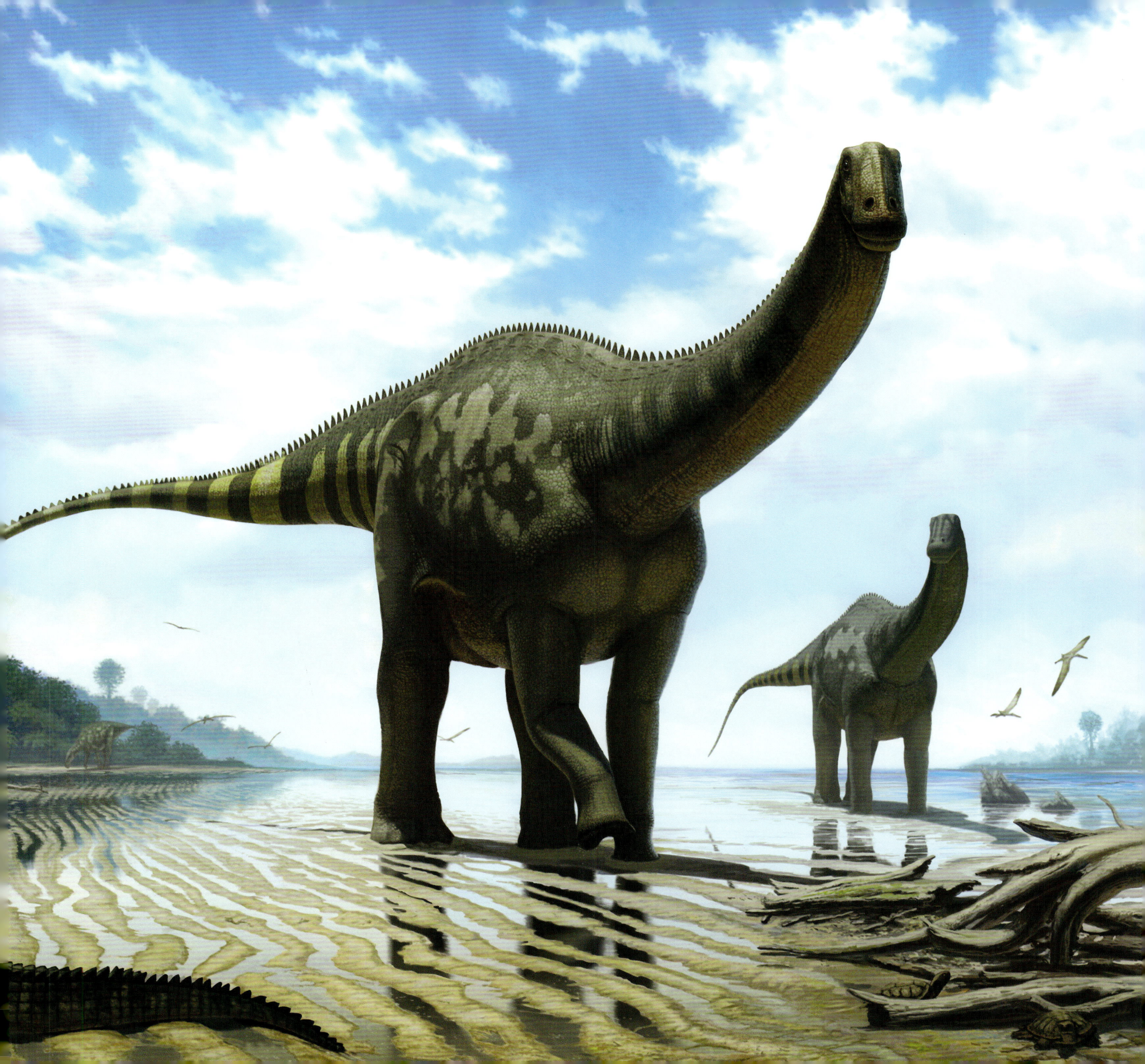

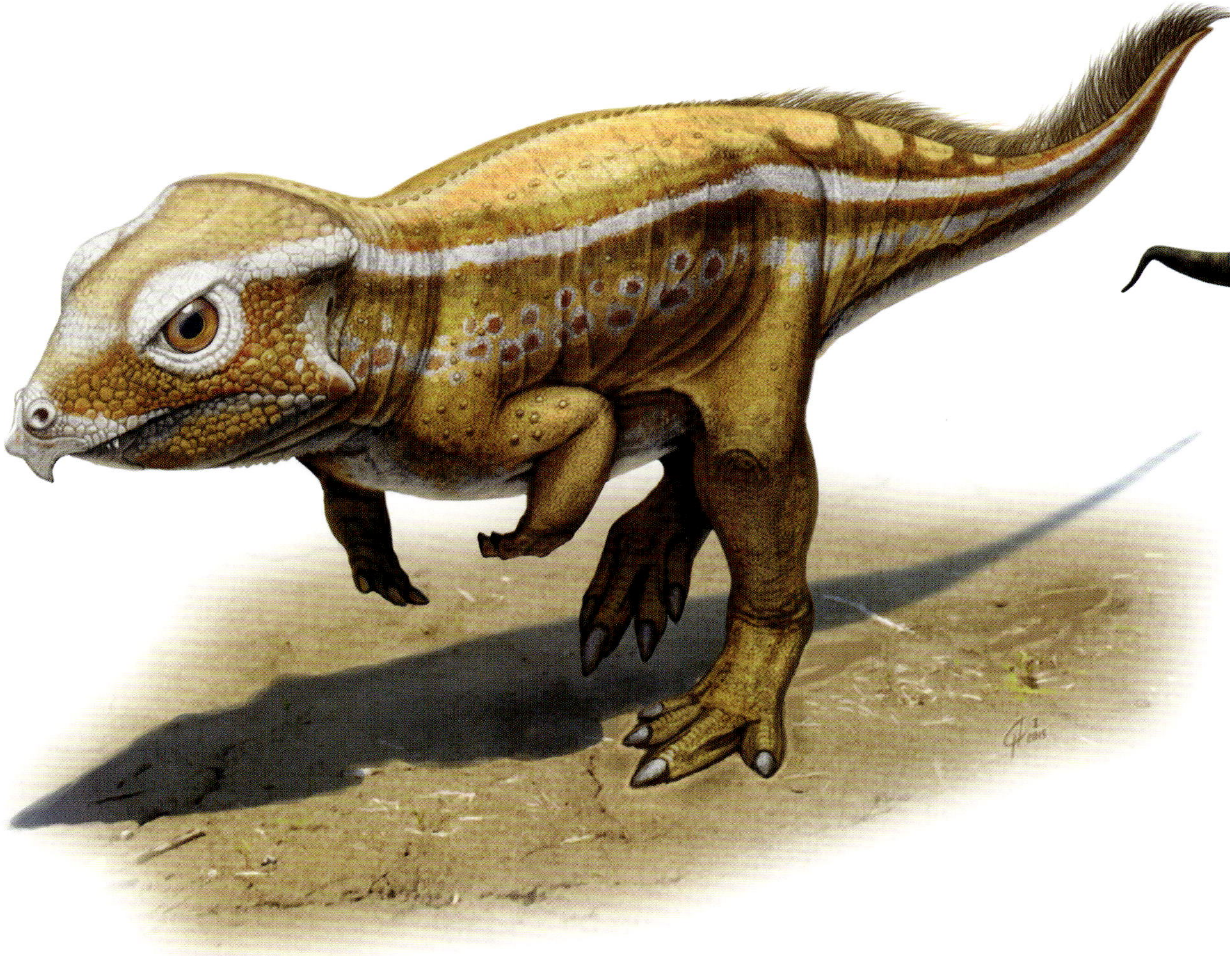

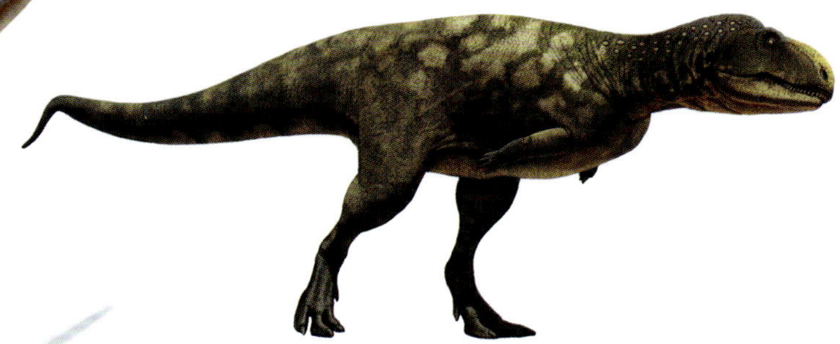

come by, but also allowed my artwork to spread further afield and find itself on foreign webpages about dinosaurs. This paid off in 2004 when the editor of a London publishing company found my pictures and offered me work on Dougal Dixon's book – what a coincidence, the author of that book which had blown my mind so many years ago! Other books, magazines and projects from all over the world followed. This is how I became a paleoartist and it has been my profession and only source of income since that time. The fact I am still afloat is fantastic and has amazed me.

Who were your influences when you first began drawing dinosaurs?

I was born in the absence of Russian paleoillustrators, period. The old classical masters had been and gone. I do remember dinosaurs drawn by [classic Russian paleoartist Konstantin] Flerov and others' interpretations of Flerov's pictures, but I only got to know his works and those of the other Russian classicists at a relatively late age. I am not sure why their books and pictures were unavailable in my region. The exception was Zdeněk Burian, whose work could occasionally be found in certain magazines or books.

Western illustrators' works weren't available in those days. This is why the first artist who inspired me to draw in an accurate, encyclopedic style was [British natural history artist] Denys Ovenden. I saw several dinosaurs,

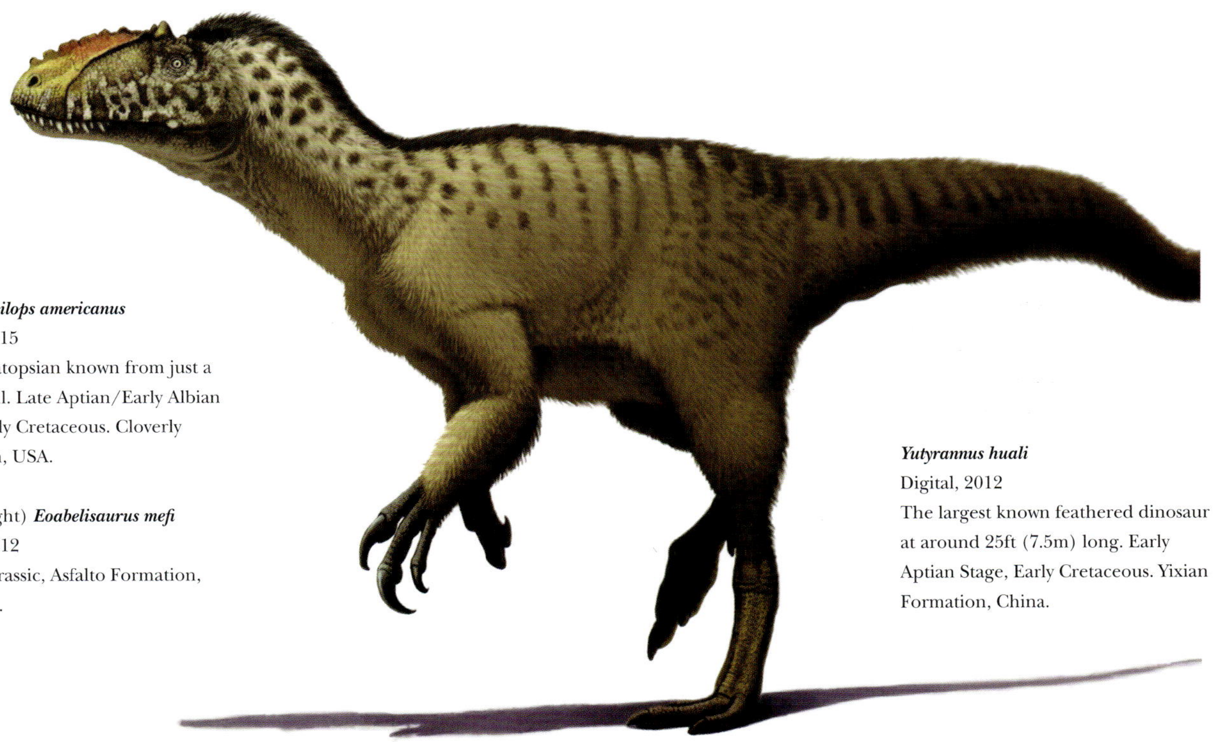

(Top) ***Aquilops americanus***
Digital, 2015
A Neoceratopsian known from just a single skull. Late Aptian/Early Albian Stage, Early Cretaceous. Cloverly Formation, USA.

(Above right) ***Eoabelisaurus mefi***
Digital, 2012
Middle Jurassic, Asfalto Formation, Argentina.

Yutyrannus huali
Digital, 2012
The largest known feathered dinosaur at around 25ft (7.5m) long. Early Aptian Stage, Early Cretaceous. Yixian Formation, China.

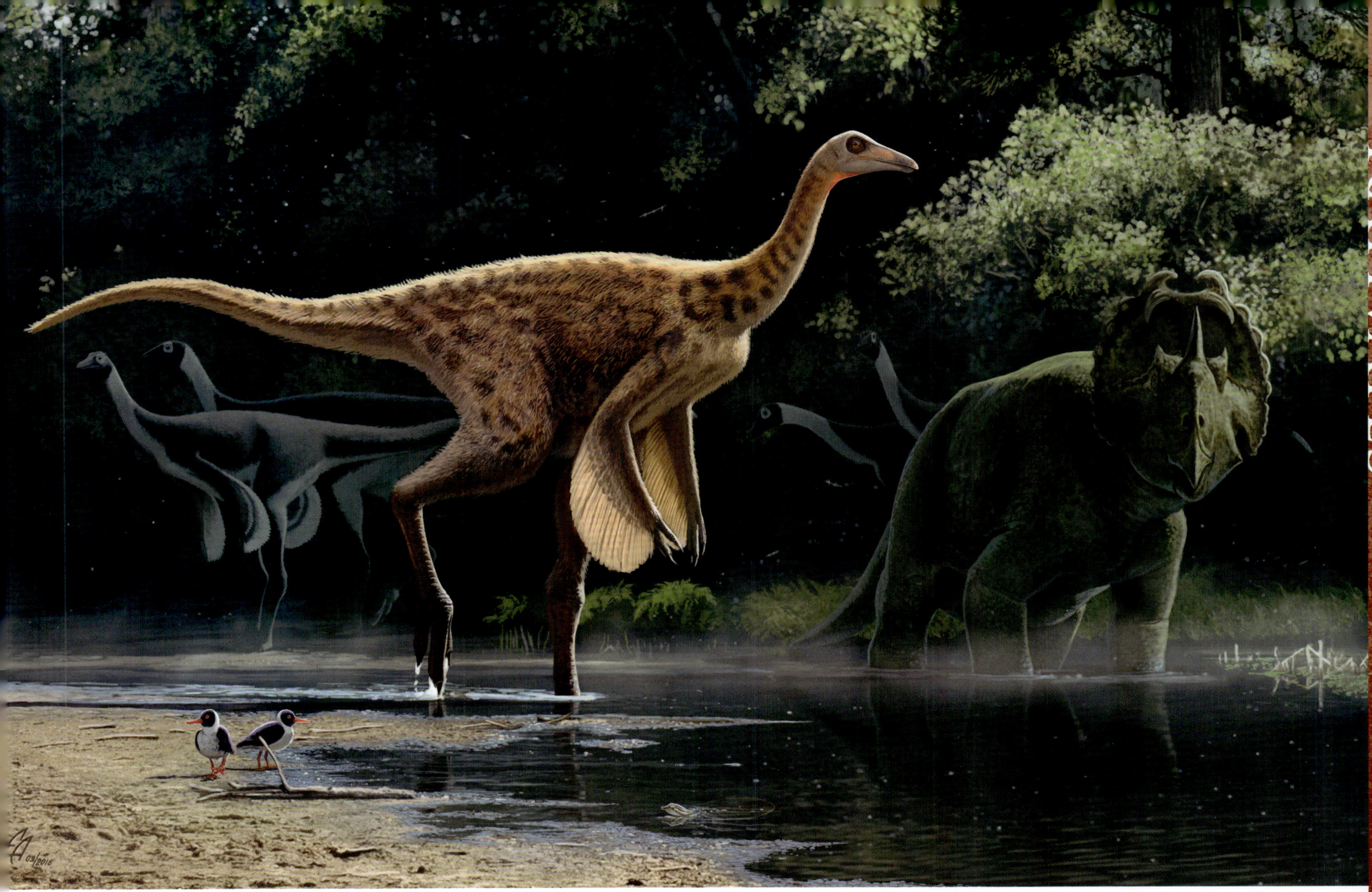

RATIVATES

The new ornithomimid, *Rativates evadens*, from the Late Cretaceous of Alberta, described by my former graduate student Brad McFeeters and our colleagues, is based on a partial skeleton, as so many dinosaur descriptions are. Reconstructing the full skeleton is not as difficult as it may appear because we know that *Rativates* is closely related to *Struthiomimus* (seen running in the background), which is known from a more complete skeleton.

To come up with an image of what it would have looked like when it was alive, we worked closely with our collaborating paleoartist, Andrey Atuchin. Andrey has a deep knowledge of dinosaur anatomy and an understanding of how the soft tissues (muscles and skin) and the ornamentation of living animals reflect their underlying skeleton. We know that some Canadian ornithomimids at least had filamentous feathers. Combining all these factors, Andrey has produced an entertaining and plausible vision of *Rativates* that also gives the viewers some insight into where it lived and what other dinosaurs lived in its environment.

DR. MICHAEL J. RYAN, PHD
HEAD OF VERTEBRATE PALEONTOLOGY,
CLEVELAND MUSEUM OF NATURAL HISTORY

elephants and ancient horses in one translated foreign book about prehistoric life. These pictures were exciting and motivated me to try drawing in the same way. However, I never sought to become an artist; rather, I sought to find, dig for, study and reconstruct dinosaurs. I wanted to be a paleontologist.

You seemed to master computer painting pretty early in your career. How did that impact on your artwork?

Initially, I used only gouache. I had to master watercolors when I started working with the London publisher, as it was part of the contract. Three years later, my wife gave me my first pen tablet as a present. That was a turning point, as I realized that computer graphics could afford me the opportunity to create without the constraints of traditional techniques. It was much easier than working with paints, brushes, water and paper; I could amend a work until I was completely satisfied with it.

It was also more convenient as we had a really small apartment and working in traditional ways became pretty untenable. Nowadays I've got about one square meter of workspace on our heated balcony. So, if I hadn't switched over to digital art, I would probably have left paleoillustration due to the lack of working space alone.

As well as being a paleoartist, you have spent a lot of time doing fieldwork. Did your artwork inspire you to find and work on the actual fossils themselves?

Actually, it's quite the contrary. Personally, there is nothing more inspiring for my productivity as an artist than searching for and excavating real

(Right) ***Parotosuchus***
Pencils, Digital, 2010
A 6ft (2m) long genus belonging to the Temnospondylii, a subclass of giant crocodile-like predators from Africa, Antarctica, Australia and Europe. They are usually considered primitive amphibians. However, they differ from true amphibians as they are often covered in scales and armor, and their actual classification is unclear.

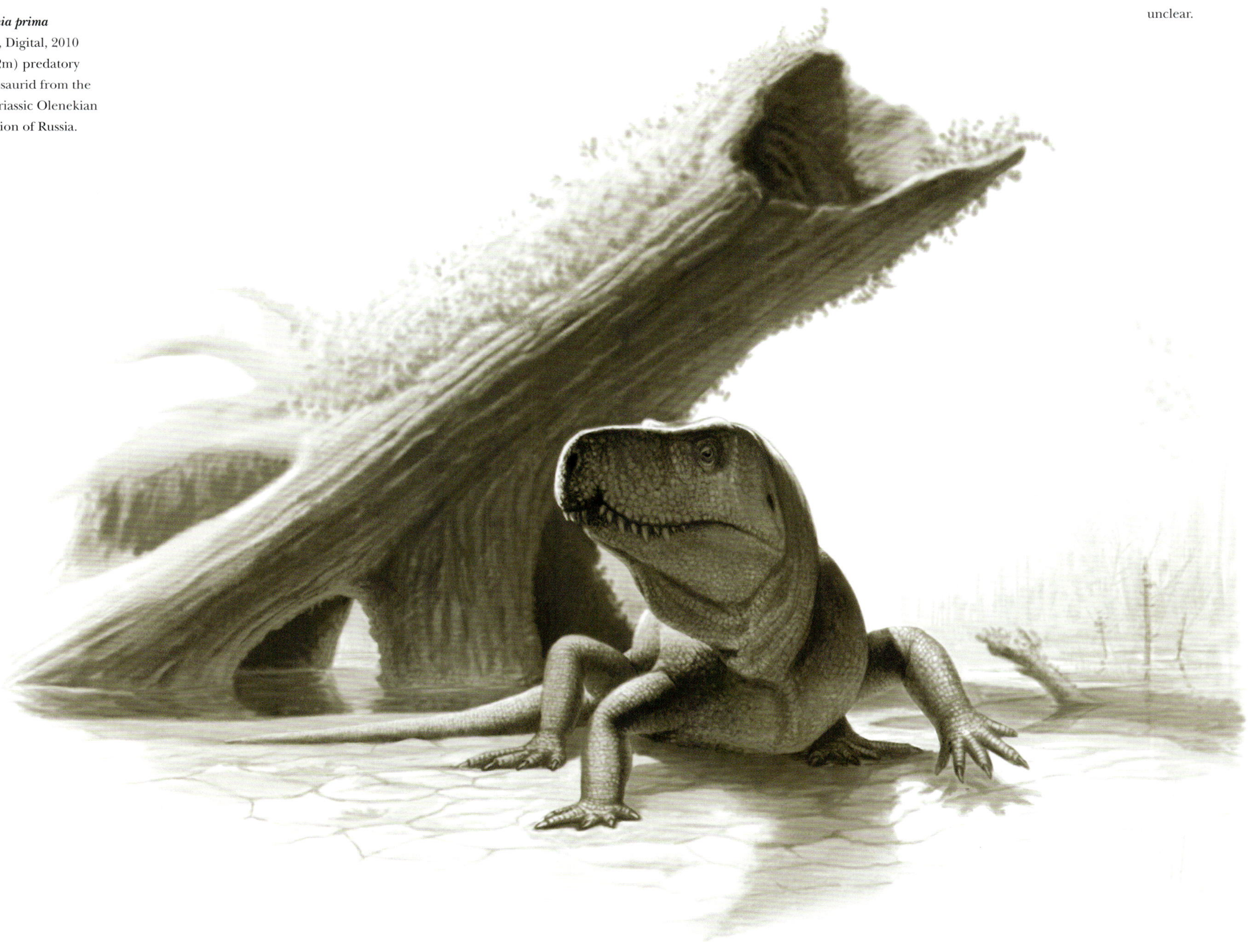

Garjainia prima
Pencils, Digital, 2010
A 6ft (2m) predatory erythrosaurid from the Early Triassic Olenekian Formation of Russia.

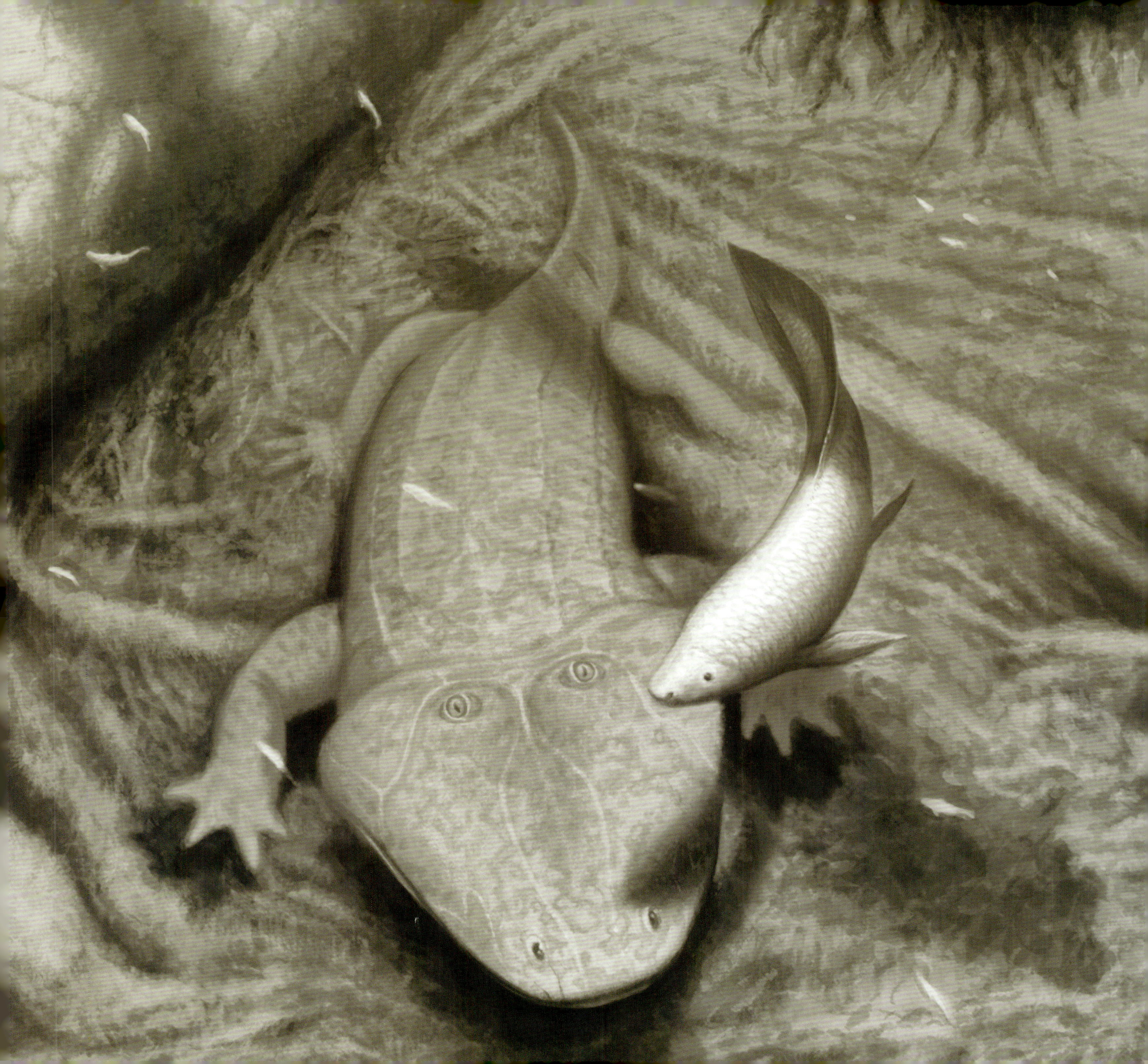

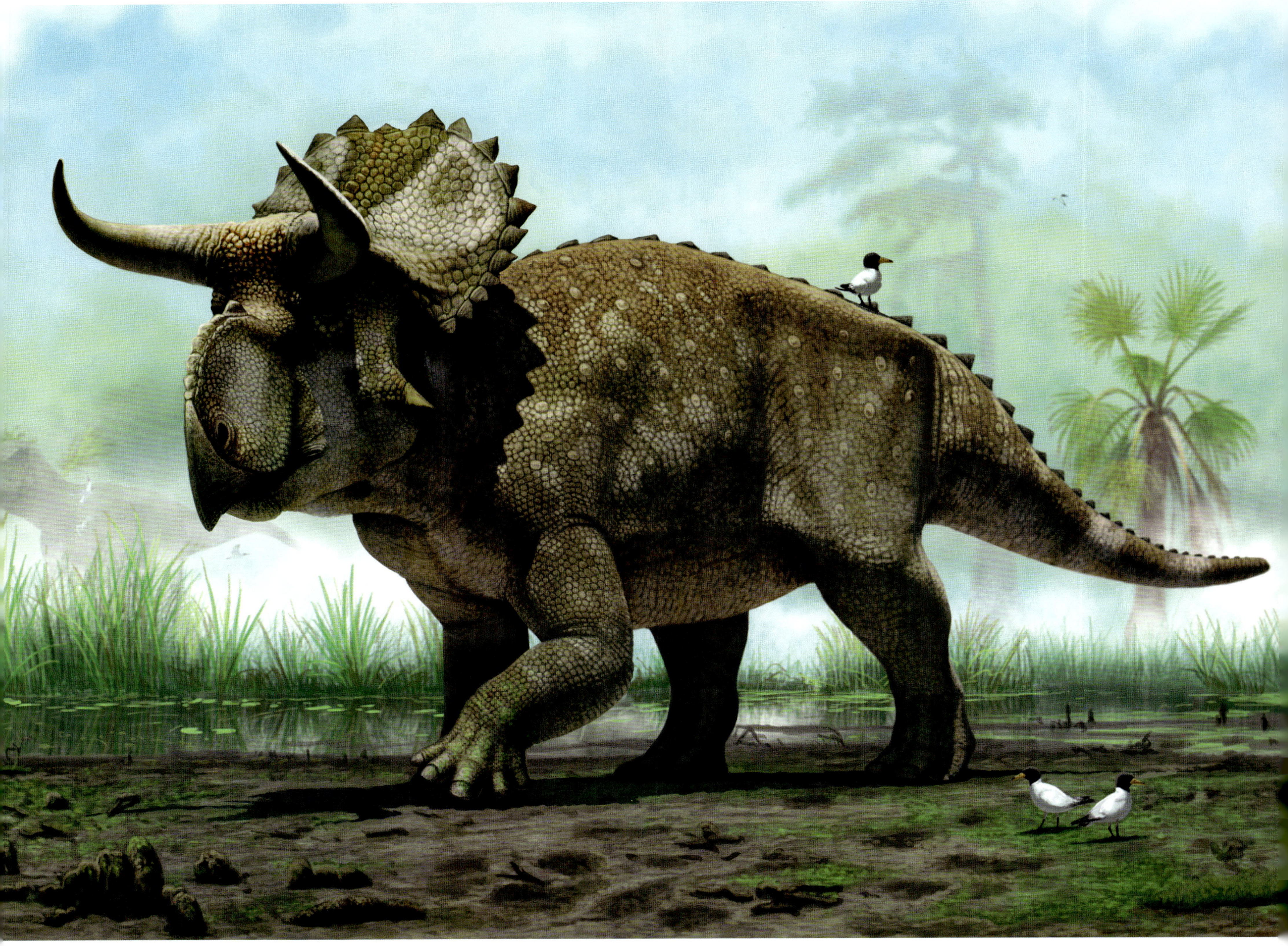

fossils. Fieldwork is a breathtaking experience! You never know what the matrix is hiding, and you're compelled to search further and deeper for bones or other paleontological treasure. As soon as I see a fossil or a new dinosaur or crocodile skeleton – even a trilobite – I immediately think, "I want to depict it as it looked in life." It is fair to say that paleoart itself led me into field paleontology; many paleontologists who had seen my pictures started to invite me on digs.

You've also worked on preparing and reconstructing a number of Psittacosaurus *specimens. Can you talk us through the process of cleaning the bones and then how you set about working up the reconstruction.*

In 2014, a team from the Kemerovo local history museum discovered a new productive bonebed with early Cretaceous fauna near Shestakovo village in the Kemerovo region. They found about a dozen *Psittacosaurus* skeletons of various ages, from juveniles of about 1.5 to 2 meters in length to giant ones about 2.5 to 3 meters long; there were also buried nestlings. By that point, I had gained a fair amount of fieldwork experience, so I was called upon to help. Digging them out was a real pleasure for me, as the bones occurred in a relatively soft clay and were perfectly preserved, intact and articulated. The process is fairly standard: impregnate the exposed bones with a special glue solution, then cover them with several layers of wet soft paper and, finally, several layers of burlap soaked in plaster should cover the surface. This produces a jacket with bones inside.

The museum team transported the jackets from Shestakovo to the museum lab in Kemerovo at the end of the field season, but there was a lack of space there, so they gave some of the stuff we'd discovered to me to look after. For several months, Psittacosaur bones occupied a part of my working balcony. While I worked at my computer, a large half-prepped skull lay behind me. My schedule during that period was as follows: I spent some time drawing illustrations, then took a break, took up my glue and tools (brushes and scalpels), and prepared the skull or other bones. I discovered a tiny baby skeleton, just about 5cm long, with its hindlimbs grasping the adult by the fingers of its forelimb. Such an outstanding find!

During preparation, I recorded what had been found, took measurements, scanned the specimens to create a 3D model, and studied the bones' structure to correlate the possible facial integument. I used all the information from this research as a basis for reconstructions. For instance, it helps to develop integument on the virtual skull in the correct way or to define the shape and location of the keratinous sheaths [on the horns and beak] by using the location of nerve-vascular grooves. These findings not only allow the anatomy of a given individual to be reconstructed, but might also shed light on the cause of their death, their social behavior and even the environment they lived in.

You did the first official work on the new Deinocheirus *reconstruction. The result is an incredibly weird-looking animal. Was that fun to work on? How much of its anatomy was hypothesis and guesswork?*

I've now drawn *Deinocheirus* reconstructions several times. I drew the first one in 2000, when I was inspired reading Barsbold's paper about Mongolian carnivorous dinosaurs. The paper clearly described it as a kind of ornithomimid, but its appearance was less clear – except for what was known about the shape of its hands. Depicting it definitely required a certain amount of imagination!

In 2012, I drew it again, as a large feathered ornithomimid for a book that has not been published yet. Shortly after that, information appeared on the Internet about the existence of the skull in some private collection, then actual photos of the skull and leg bones surfaced. That hump on the sacral bone, the extraordinary pelvis, the duck-shaped beak – they certainly blew my mind! I immediately imagined this exceptional giant wading through a flooded forest with

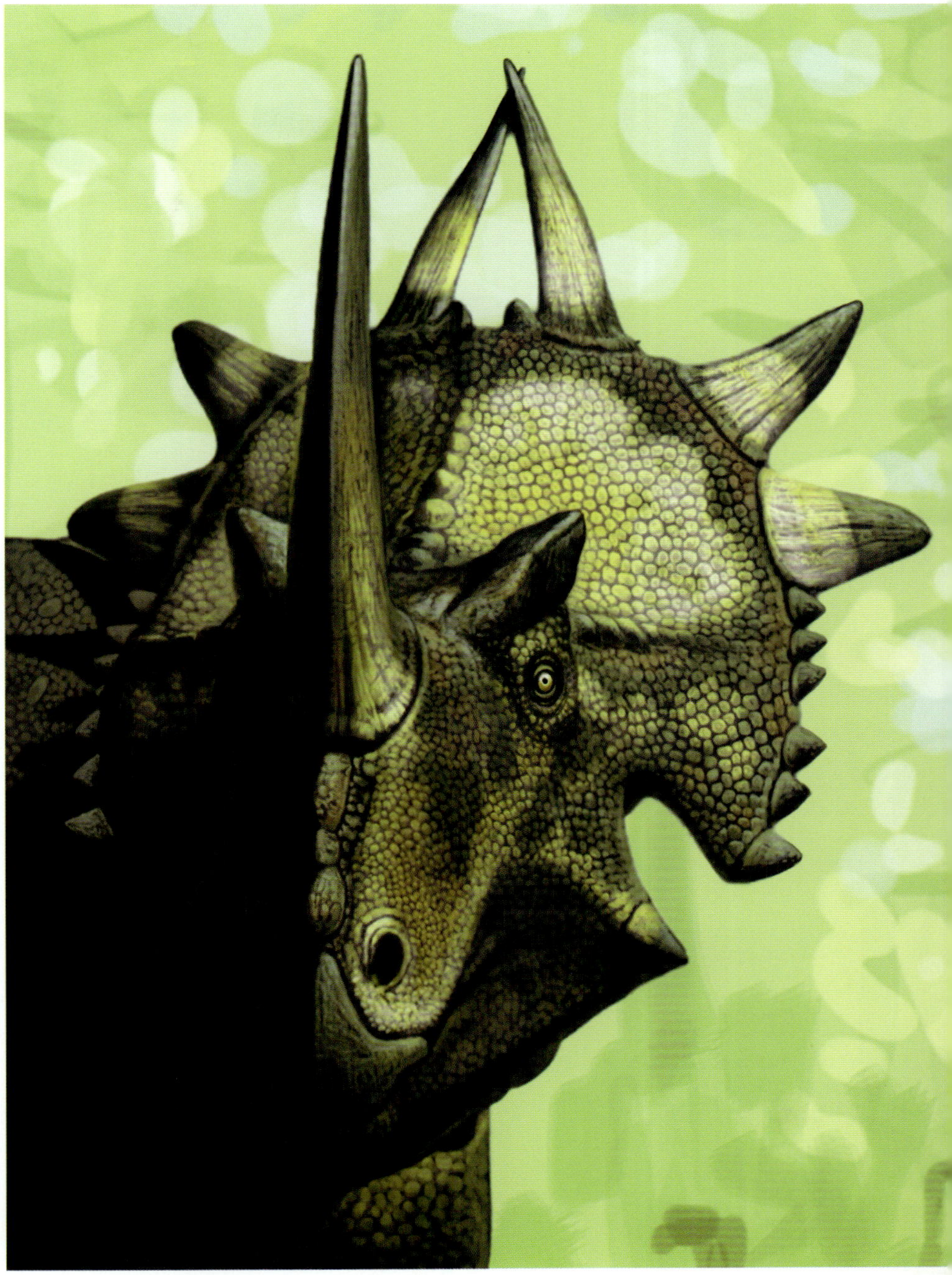

Rubeosaurus ovatus
Digital, 2014
Previously assigned as a species of Styracosaurus, this ceratopsian dinosaur was reclassified in 2010 and renamed. Middle-Late Campanian Stage, Late Cretaceous. Upper Two Medicine Formation, Montana.

(Opposite) ***Nasutoceratops titusi***
Digital, 2015
Late Campanian, Late Cretaceous. Middle Kaiparowitz Formation, Utah.

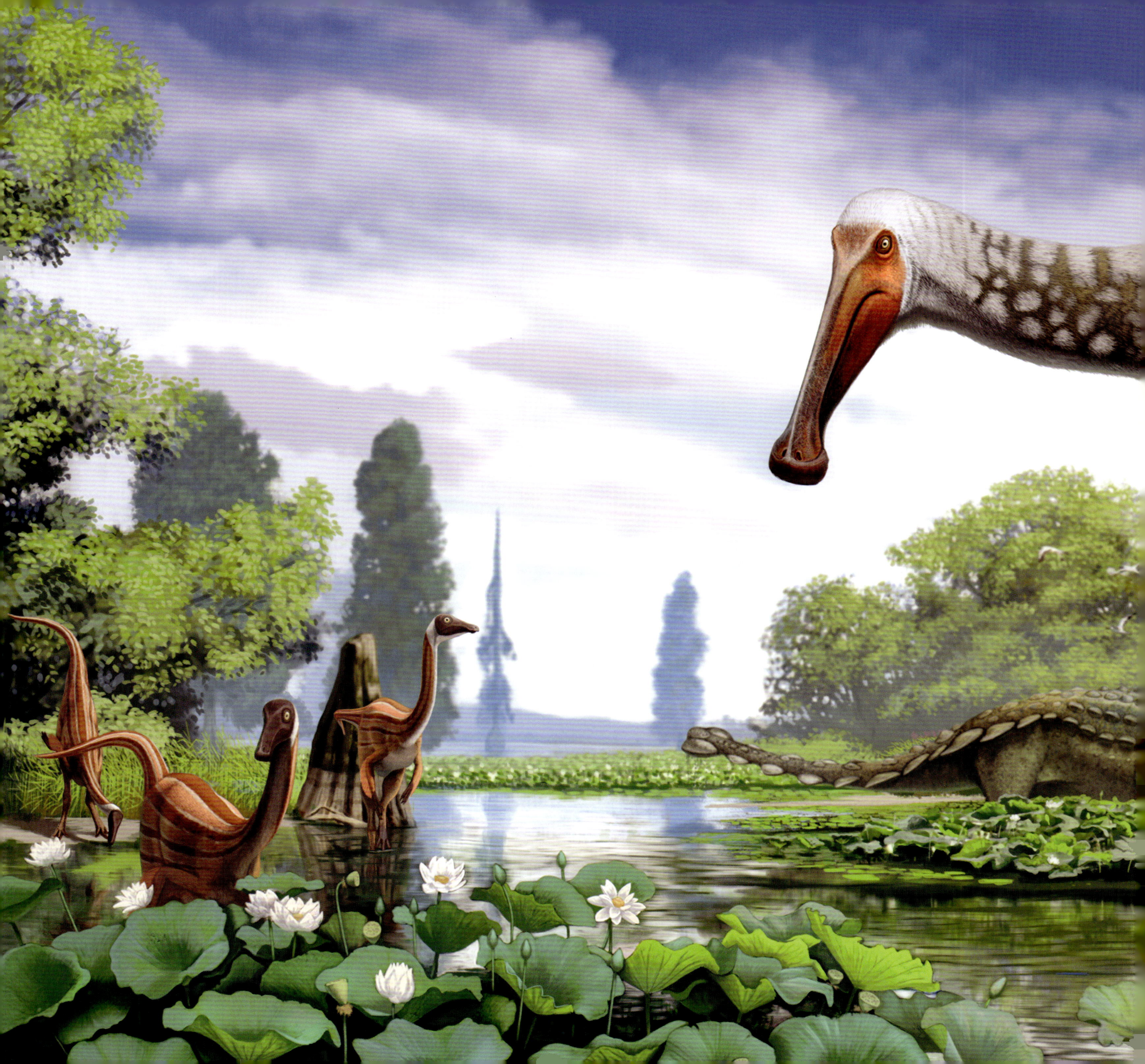

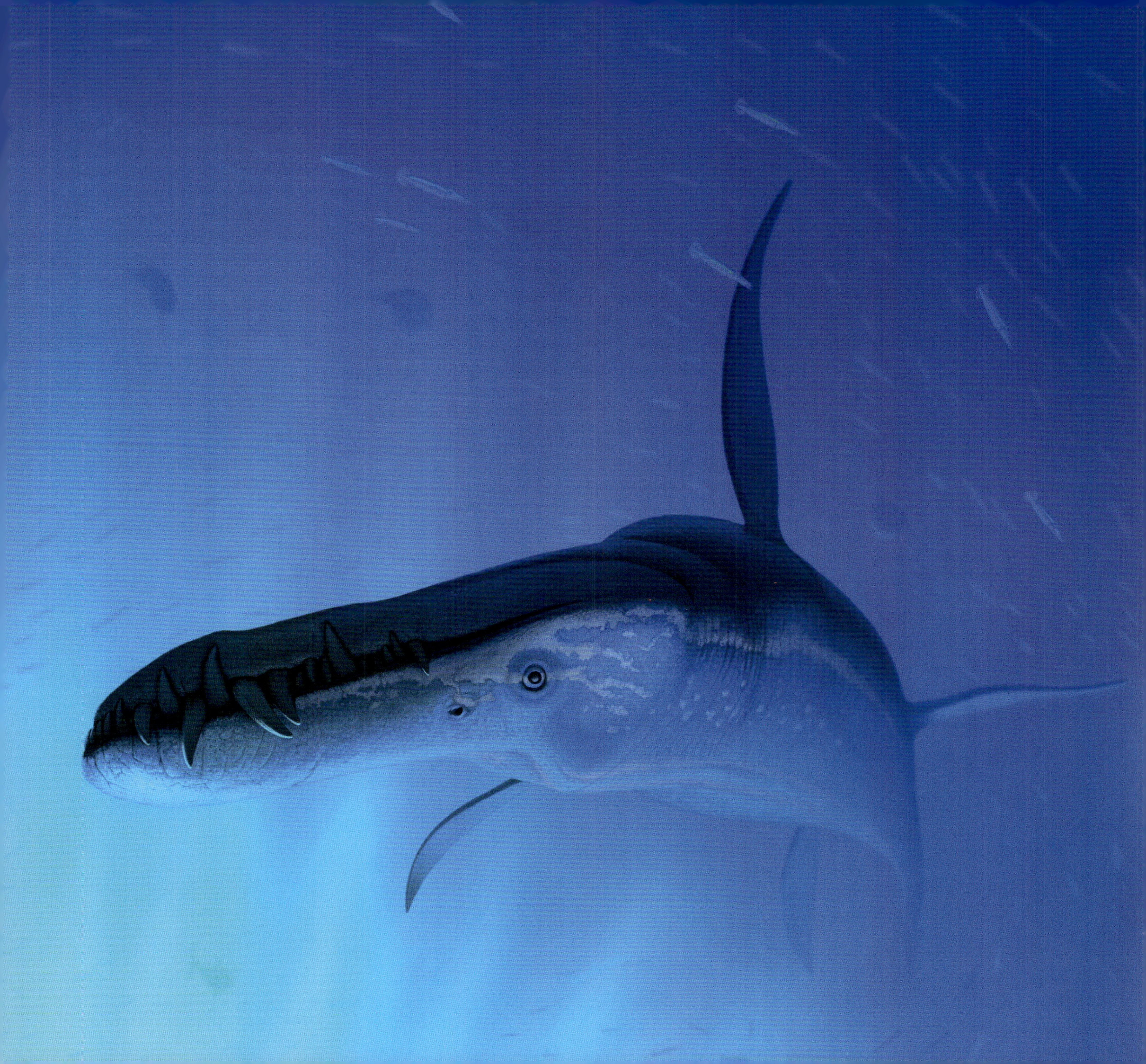

PSITTACOSAURUS

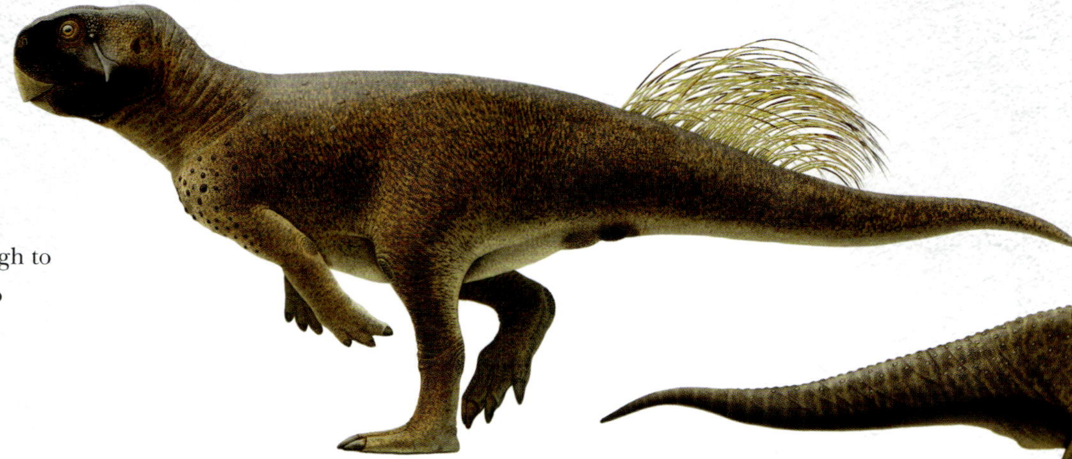

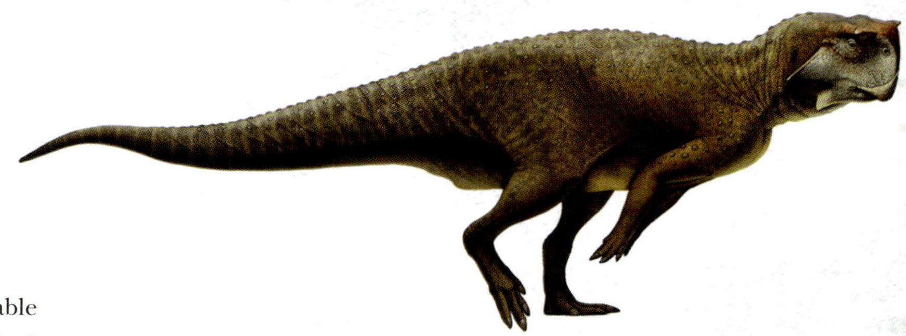

PSITTACOSAURUS
Species: Various
Location: China, Mongolia, Russia and perhaps Thailand
Named: 1923
Age: Early Cretaceous (Barremian through to Albian Stages), 123-100 million years ago
Length: 3-6.5ft (1-2m)
Weight: 13-25lbs (6-15kg)
Diet: herbivorous

Psittacosaurus is amongst the earliest known representatives of Ceratopsia, the dinosaur group best known for such giant, horned, quadrupedal kinds as the famous *Triceratops*. Though *Psittacosaurus* was small, lacked true horns, and was bipedal. Its name – meaning 'parrot lizard' – refers obviously to its deep, superficially parrot-like, beaked face.

In scientific terms, *Psittacosaurus* is one of the best known dinosaurs: hundreds of specimens have been discovered that come from rocks deposited over more than 20 million years and in a variety of environments, including deserts, cool woodlands and tropical forests, representing more than ten species. With some species' specimens ranging from tiny hatchlings to adults two or three decades old.

In overall postcranial anatomy, *Psittacosaurus* was not unusual compared to many other ornithischians. The forelimbs were short with four fingers (unlike most ceratopsians, which had five), while the hindlimbs were longer and more powerful. Its proportions indicate that it was fully bipedal, its forelimbs being too short to be any use in walking or running. The shortest was *P. ordosensis* and the longest *P. mongoliensis*.

It was recently discovered that at least some individuals of some species possessed long quills or spines on the upper part of the tail. So far, only a single quill-bearing specimen is known. The quills are long and curved and formed a tall fringe along the tail's upper surface.

This tail-quilled specimen is also remarkable in that it preserves part of the animal's original pigmentation. Its face and cloacal region were especially dark, and the animal was clearly darker overall on its upper surface than its underside, a pattern suggesting adaptation to life in a dense forest with lots of shade. The specimen also seems to possess a large web of skin between the ankle and base of the tail, another previously unknown feature.

The main area of variation within *Psittacosaurus* is the skull. While vaguely parrot-like in profile, the bones of the snout are fixed in place (in parrots there is a joint between the upper jaw and braincase). The lower jaw of *Psittacosaurus* was, however, somewhat more mobile than might be predicted: an elongated jaw joint meant that it could be slid backwards or forwards during chewing. The head is broad and deep, with flanges of bone that extend outward from the cheeks and sometimes form long, horn-covered spikes. Some species, such as *P. sibiricus*, possess additional bumps and ridges over the skull and around the eyes. The teeth are chisel-shaped, self-sharpening and formed grinding batteries, though they are confined to the rear of the jaws, replaced at the front by the beak. Some *Psittacosaurus* remains have also revealed the presence of a gizzard complete with gastroliths, stones that were swallowed and used to mill plant material. All these features indicate a diet of tough plant material, including seed pods and nuts.

Psittacosaurus had a relatively large brain compared to many other dinosaurs. The brain's structure indicates acute senses of smell and vision, and suggests a degree of intelligence in keeping with complex social behavior. Indeed, direct evidence for this comes from mixed-age associations, the most spectacular being the preservation of 34 juveniles together with a near-adult that was apparently serving as a guardian or babysitter (it does appear to have been mature enough to be a parent). Several other clusters of juveniles are also known. One of the primary reasons for such associations may have been protection from predators.

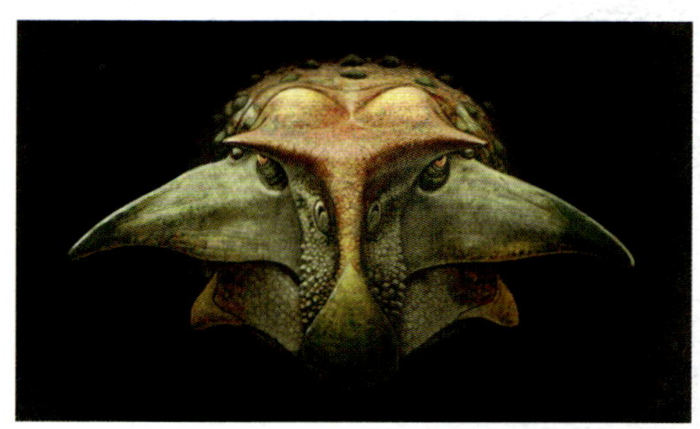

(Above left) ***Psittacosaurus* Update**
Digital, 2016
Psittacosaurus reconstruction modified after recent studies provided incredible detail of this genus' anatomy and appearance (see Introduction).

(Above right)
Psittacosaurus sibiricus
Digital, 2015

(Below) ***Psittacosaurus sibiricus* Portrait**
Digital, 2015

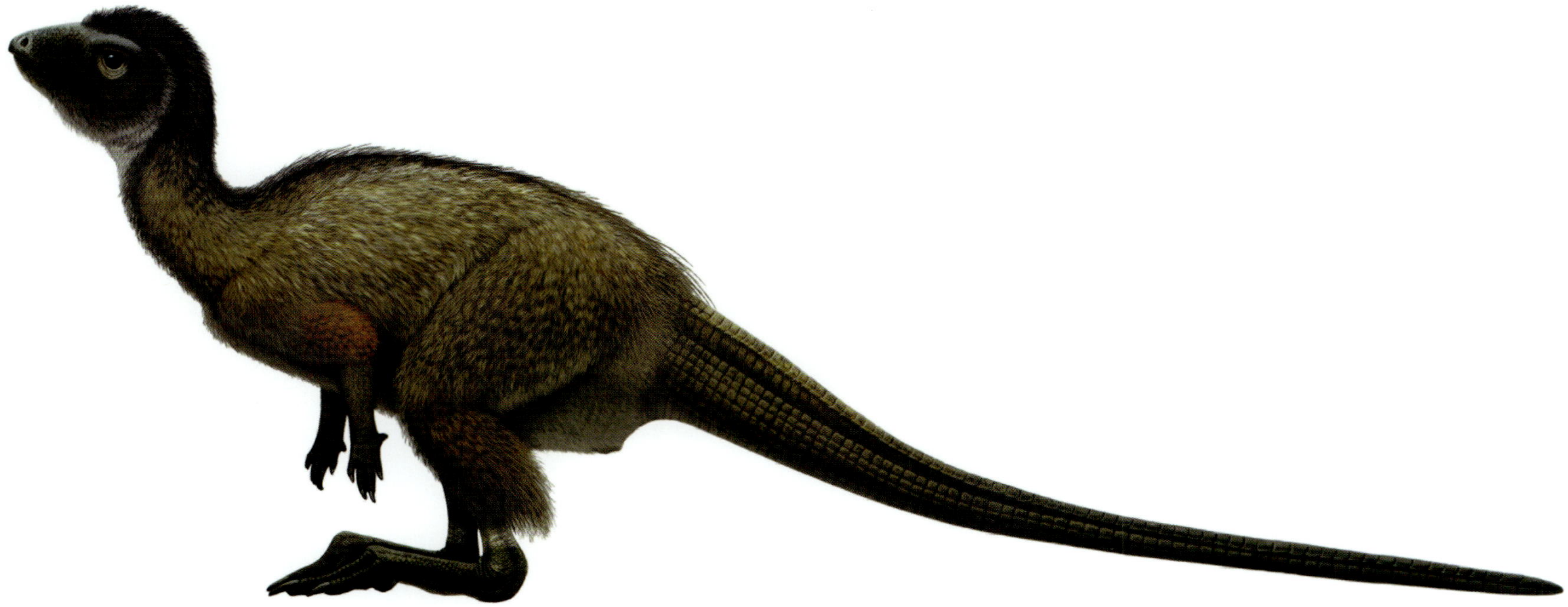

lotuses such as those found in Mongolia. The picture for the book was reworked accordingly.

Since then the official paper has been released, containing precise descriptions and a clearer picture of the skull. I've had to correct my illustrations again because of slight differences in the skull formation that became apparent in the new photos. I believe we now have a fairly clear idea about most parts of *Deinocheirus*' skeleton. Perhaps the biggest challenge that remains for me in reconstructing its color and integument.

You also worked with paleontologists on Kulindadromeus. *Like the* Deinocheirus *illustration, you provided an environment for the animals, rather than just having them simply standing in isolation. Do you think it's important to give the animal a context, that it gives the viewer the sense that this was a living animal? And how much information came from the taphonomy of the fossils themselves?*

It depends what you want to demonstrate. I mean, if the purpose is to focus on the anatomy, the background should be minimized. On the other hand, it is important to give more detail to a background when an animal should be shown in an environmental context. In the most cases, depicting a creature in the context of its likely surroundings helps the audience to get a better sense of the animal. As a biologist, one tends to think of any animal as part of its environment, so taking a holistic approach to studying it is fairly standard.

I first drew *Kulindadromeus* without a background, because my priority was to reconstruct its appearance including its integument, feather-like structures and the scutes on the tail. Besides which, not much was known about its environment at that point. Further study showed it most likely inhabited a lake surrounded by volcanoes and probably some temporary ponds and puddles. This allowed me to develop in-context pieces for *Kulindadromeus*, and because of the environmental studies it was also possible to include additional details. For instance, in this ecological setting, paleontologists also found beautifully preserved tadpole shrimps' (*Triops*) imprints, caddis fly cases and imprints of several plants. These all went into the piece along with *Kulindadromeus*.

The bottom line is artwork that includes the environmental backdrop looks more spectacular.

How much research do you do on the environments in which you set your reconstructions?

This is a huge part of my work and usually it is extremely exhausting. I have to search and read tons of publications and ask for help from paleontologists. I find it difficult to draw the background and landscape; it's a headache for me. I couldn't attempt to create an accurate environment without the advise of different specialists, as their data and recommendations are very useful. This is why I enjoy working with a team of professionals.

Do you do a lot of preparation for your larger pieces of artwork? Do you spend time sketching and composing the image or are you one of those artists who works a great deal in your head?

Generally, I laboriously work through all scientific papers, information, photos, drawings or real fossils if they are accessible and it takes a lot of time. Sometimes I also do a preliminary reconstruction of an animal in profile to make it clear how it looked. When I need a really detailed and thorough understanding of an animal's form, I sculpt a model from polymer clay or use 3D modeling.

(Previous spread)
Deinocheirus mirificus
Digital, 2014
This strange and enigmatic dinosaur had been known since 1965, solely from a pair of massive arms equipped with large claws and assigned to the ornithomimosaurs – the famous 'ostrich mimics'. Its appearance was the source of much speculation until 2010, when more complete remains were uncovered. Few researchers could have guessed at its giant sail-backed, duck-billed and deep-jawed bodyplan.

(Above) ***Kulindadromeus zabaikalicus***
Digital, 2014

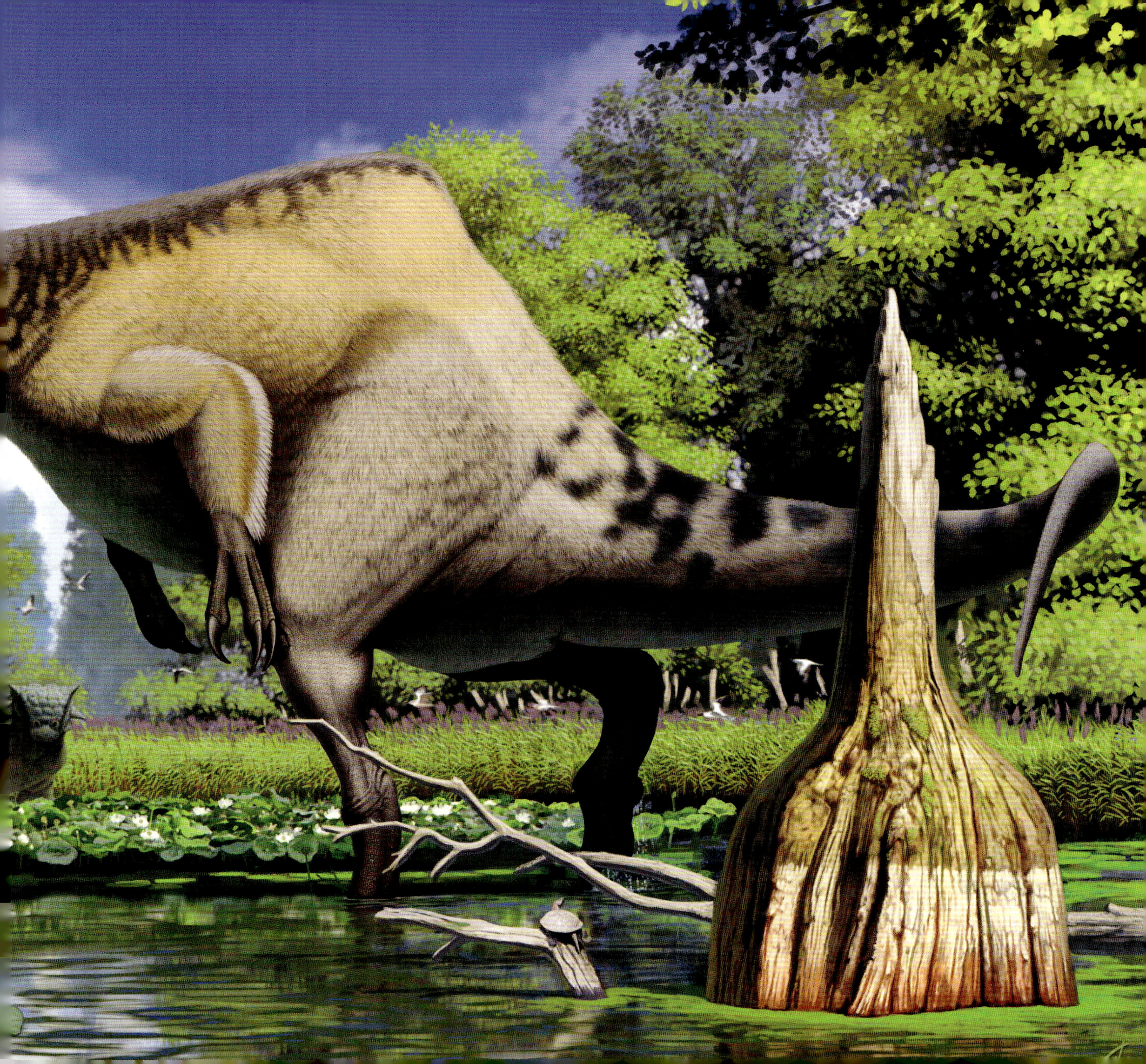

I occasionally draft using pencil and paper, but it is unusual for me to draw many sketches. I've tried to do more sketches by hand as it's helpful in improving technique, but the sketchbook I bought for this purpose has remained relatively unused. I think the problem is I just don't like doodling. More frequently, the whole process of creating a new piece of art takes place in my mind; I think up various sketches and reject some of them. As a result, I've got a picture I want to transfer to paper or digital form. It is such a pity I can't connect a printer to my head, as it is sometimes impossible to fully realize the exact image I imagined.

Your more recent illustrations, such as the portrait of Spiclypeus*, are super-detailed. What's the process for producing such finely crafted artwork? What software do you use?*

I am fond of super-detailed artwork. I'm also keen on reconstructing animals precisely in traditional sculpture or 3D modeling by using their fossils. An initial three-dimensional study gives me much more to go on than do photos, which often only show part of the fossil, often at an unhelpful angle. This isn't something that's easily done in your head, in abstract; for want of a good reference, a large number of my early reconstructions and those of other artists are incorrect. So, sculpting a model allows one to understand how the head looked at various angles, perspectives and in different sorts of light. I model the skull and then put over muscles, other soft tissues and keratinous structures; it is a very absorbing and laborious task. Afterwards, I use all this information as a reference for the artwork. Nowadays, technology allows us to be more exact, with greater ease; I found using 3D scans of bones and skulls very helpful. For the *Spiclypeus* artwork, I made two sculptures (one of them made of clay in 2012 and another one in 3D made recently).

What I described above is just the preliminary process: subsequent work is done in Photoshop. Mostly, I select the regular soft round brush and use brush strokes, in a technique similar to painting in oils or acrylic. I draw the details of the whole texture and scales, taking into consideration the coloration. If the time schedule is not too tough, I work through almost every scale, analyzing how it should look in a certain light, where shadows and reflections of other scales and background should be. It is arduous and risky when you are drawing a highly detailed picture; it may become flat and horrible as a result. This is why using a physical sculpture as a reference assists me to control drawing the details while keeping the general treatment of light and shade on the figure. As a result, the artwork looks super-detailed but keeps the whole figure coherent at the same time. I use filters, blurs and other tools were necessary, but try to draw the most part of a picture with strokes, so the artwork looks more like a traditional painting. My motto is always "the less digital in your digital painting, the better". Digital graphics offer a great amount of opportunities, but it tempts artists to become lazy. Thus, I endeavor to control my technique to retain the traditional painting core in it.

As a field worker, is there anywhere in the world you would really love to go prospecting for fossils?

Anywhere that it's possible to find a lot of well-preserved fossils – of dinosaurs, in particular. I loved having the opportunity to go prospecting in Utah in 2015. Unfortunately, what we have in Russia barely can be called "prospecting", because there are no badlands; deserts in Russia and all their interesting fossils underlay the Quaternary clay and loam, covered by swamps or forests. This is why dinosaur excavations here usually take place at certain types of location: quarries, highway excavations or steep riverbanks. I am looking for opportunities to go prospecting in various sites in the USA, Canada, Australia – probably in Africa and South America as well. I have always been fond of fieldwork and life in a camp since my university fieldwork training back when I was a biology student. It brings me a lot

(Opposite) ***Pliosaurus* (*Liopleurodon*) *rossicus***
Digital, 2011
Middle Tithonian Stage, Late Jurassic. Chuvash Republic, Russia.

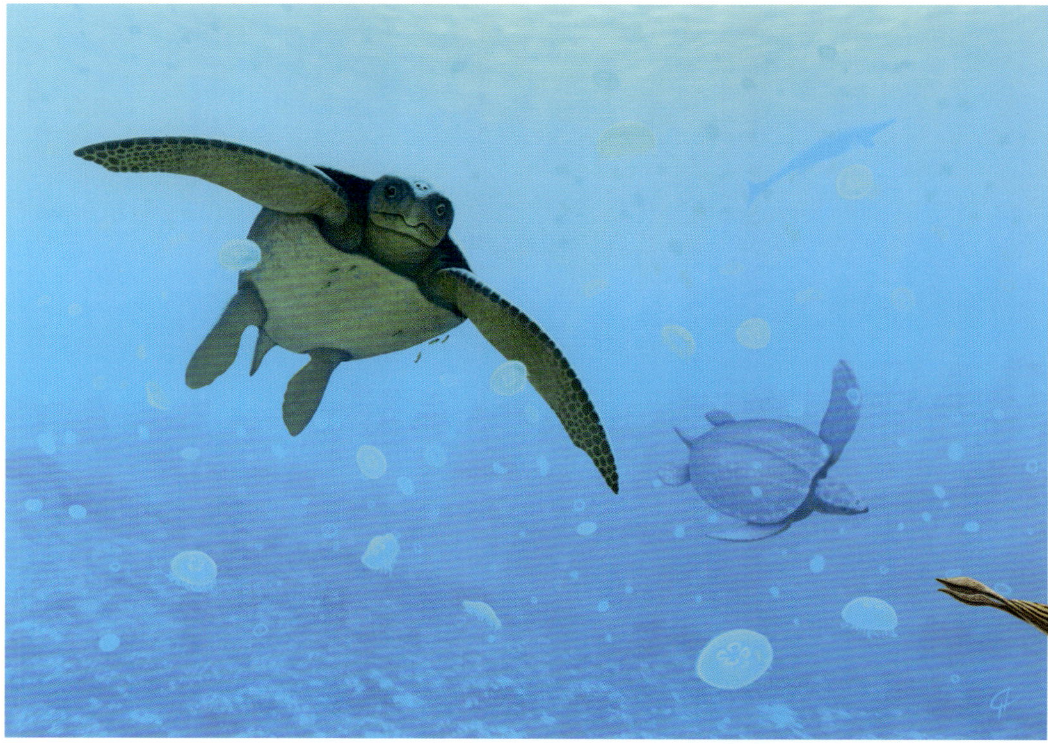

(Below left) ***Protostega gigas***
Digital, 2011
At 10ft (3m) long, *Protostega* is the second largest known sea turtle. Santonian Stage, Late Cretaceous, 83mya. Smoky Hill Chalk Formation, Kansas.

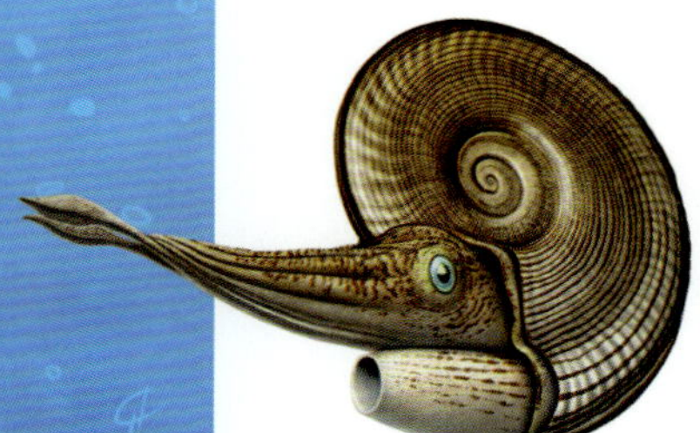

(Below) ***Sublunuloceras***
Digital, 2016
Ammonite from the Lower Oxfordian Stage, Upper Jurassic.

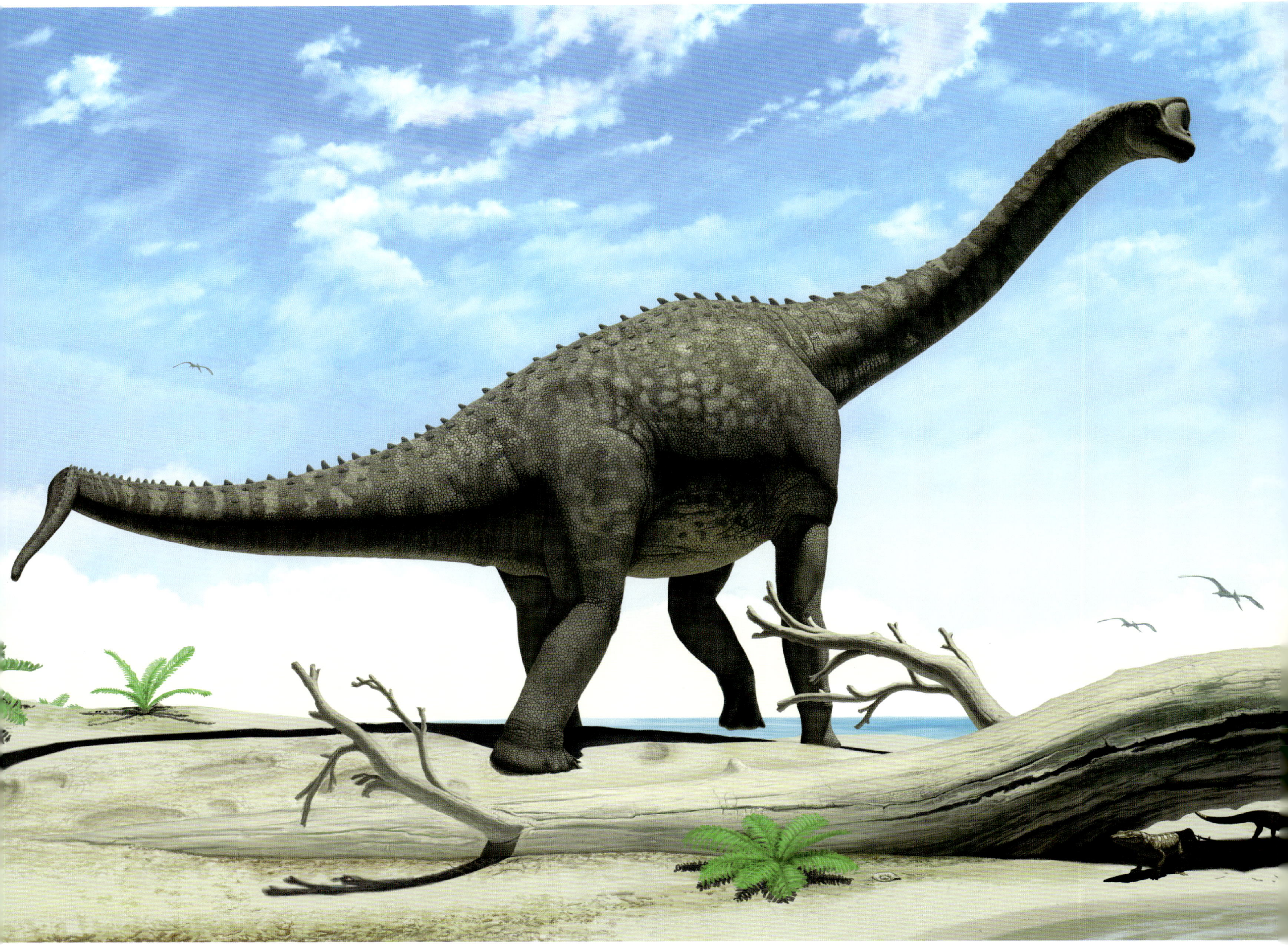

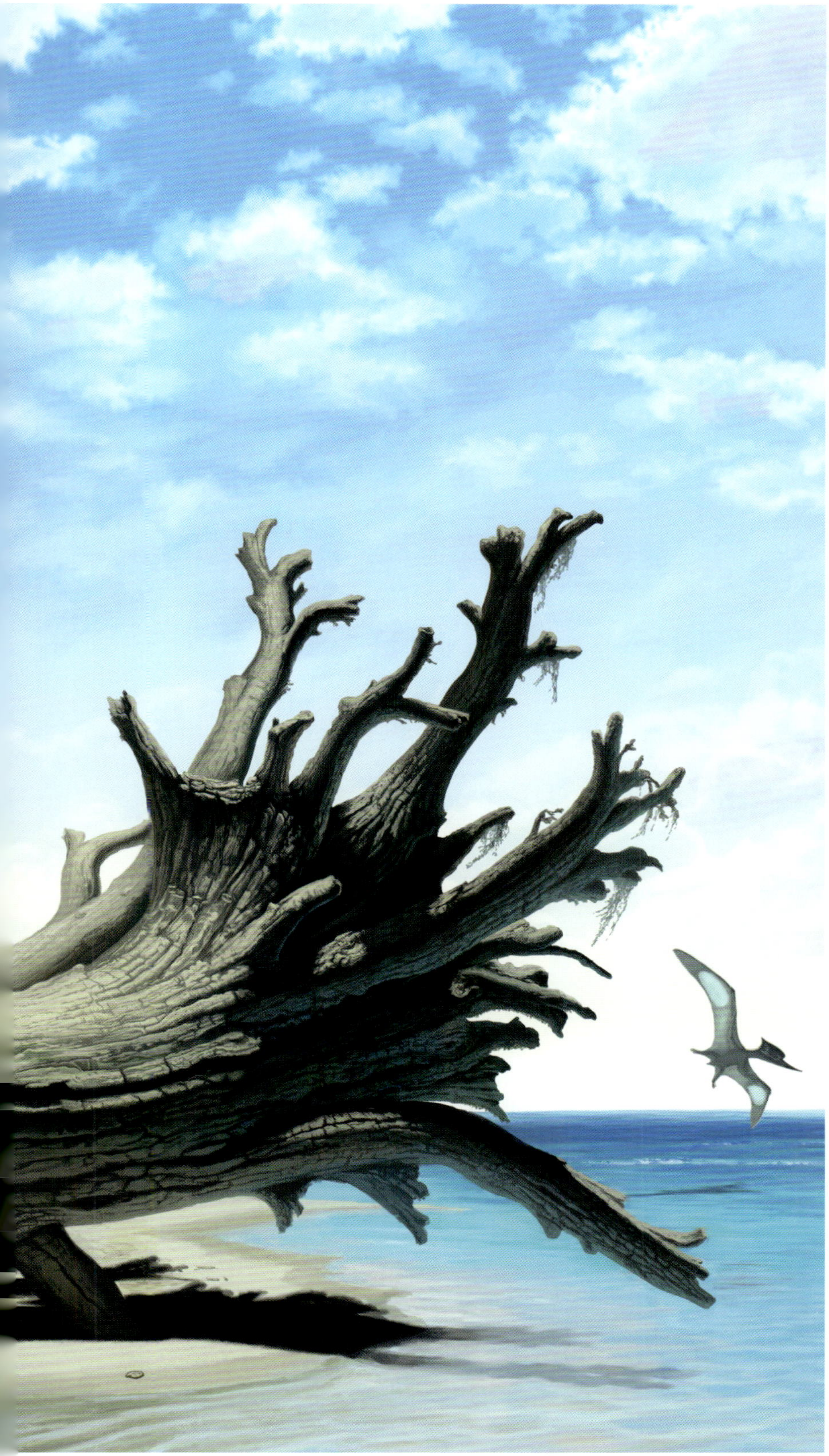

of energy and inspiration; I definitely benefit greatly from it.

You have obviously done a lot of work with Russian fossil animals, many of which are overlooked elsewhere. Is that something you set out deliberately to do?

It seems so. From where I'm standing, all the fossils we dig out and the new locations we've found seem little known outside Russia – and even here, many Russians are unaware of the animals that once inhabited different parts of this country's vast territory across different geological eras. There used to be a belief that there were no dinosaur skeletons found in Russia, only fragments of bone. I haven't been able to verify if this story is true as I don't know where it originated, but apparently [American paleontologist] Othniel Charles Marsh once visited Russia and said, "Russian dinosaurs, like the snakes of Ireland, are remarkable for their absence". This is one of the motivations for me to illustrate poorly known Russian dinosaurs and other extinct animals: they are real, and they do indeed exist!

I've illustrated many articles in magazines, and have published several illustrated books about Russian dinosaurs, Permian animals and Mesozoic marine reptiles in collaboration with one Russian journalist who specializes in paleontology. I hope that plenty of exciting things might be found here and that I'll be one of the people to reveal them to the world. Actually, I still have something I've yet to show, as I'm still working on the reconstruction of a huge Psittacosaur. Those pictures of it you saw are just preliminary artwork; I'm still working on an accurate reconstruction of its skull.

You have a big following on social media. Do you think the likes of Facebook and Instagram are now vital tools for aspiring paleoartists?

Social media "likes" don't matter so much in terms of my self-esteem, but they are a crucial way of promoting one's work and boosting its profile. More and more people can discover you and your art; browser search engines bring up your images in search results more frequently as it improves their page rank. Social networks can be a great boost for novice paleoartists who want to share their work with the world. They can also be a means for professional paleoillustrators to find clients. Social media has superseded the need for me to maintain a personal web page; I've abandoned the one I had. Most of my clients find me through social networks or via Google. It also makes it easy and convenient to stay in touch and communicate with a lot of the friends and paleontologists with whom I collaborate. Many I met first through social media, and subsequently in real life. I can hardly function without social networking in particular, and without the Internet I would not be a paleoartist.

On a personal level, it has helped me keep going through hard times and depression. The ability to share news or events instantly allows me to work and keep myself afloat. It's an odd profession and not always well paid, so staying in the public eye is crucial in order to get commissions. I'm actually amazed that I have been working in this field for 12 years and am still at it. It's particularly hard being a paleoillustrator in Russia: most paleontology happens in the West, which presents a language barrier and makes it harder to access the relevant papers and literature. The Iron Curtain has come down, but Russians are still shut off, even if it may not be obvious from the outside. It is terrible, but seems to be the case that the Iron Curtain is returning. I would not be able to work as a paleoillustrator if problems with the Internet and social media should occur.

Europasaurus holgeri
Digital, 2011
This sauropod from the Late Jurassic of Germany is relatively small – just 19ft (5.7m) long – compared to some of the family's other members, which are among the largest terrestrial animals ever known. It has been suggested that *Europasaurus* is actually a dwarf island species, an evolutionary trait seen in many large animals isolated on islands.

JASON BROUGHAM

USA

As well as being a talented artist and sculptor, Jason is a Senior Principal Preparator at the American Museum of Natural History in New York. He has worked on a number of the museum's exhibitions, including the recent Dinosaurs Among Us exhibition on feathered dinosaurs and their evolution, while his art has appeared in *Natural History* and *Discover* magazines, *The New York Times*, and on TV shows for National Geographic and NOVA. He also illustrated *Inside Dinosaurs* from the Inside Series published by the American Museum of Natural History (AMNH) and Sterling Publishing. He studied Comparative Morphology at the University of Michigan.

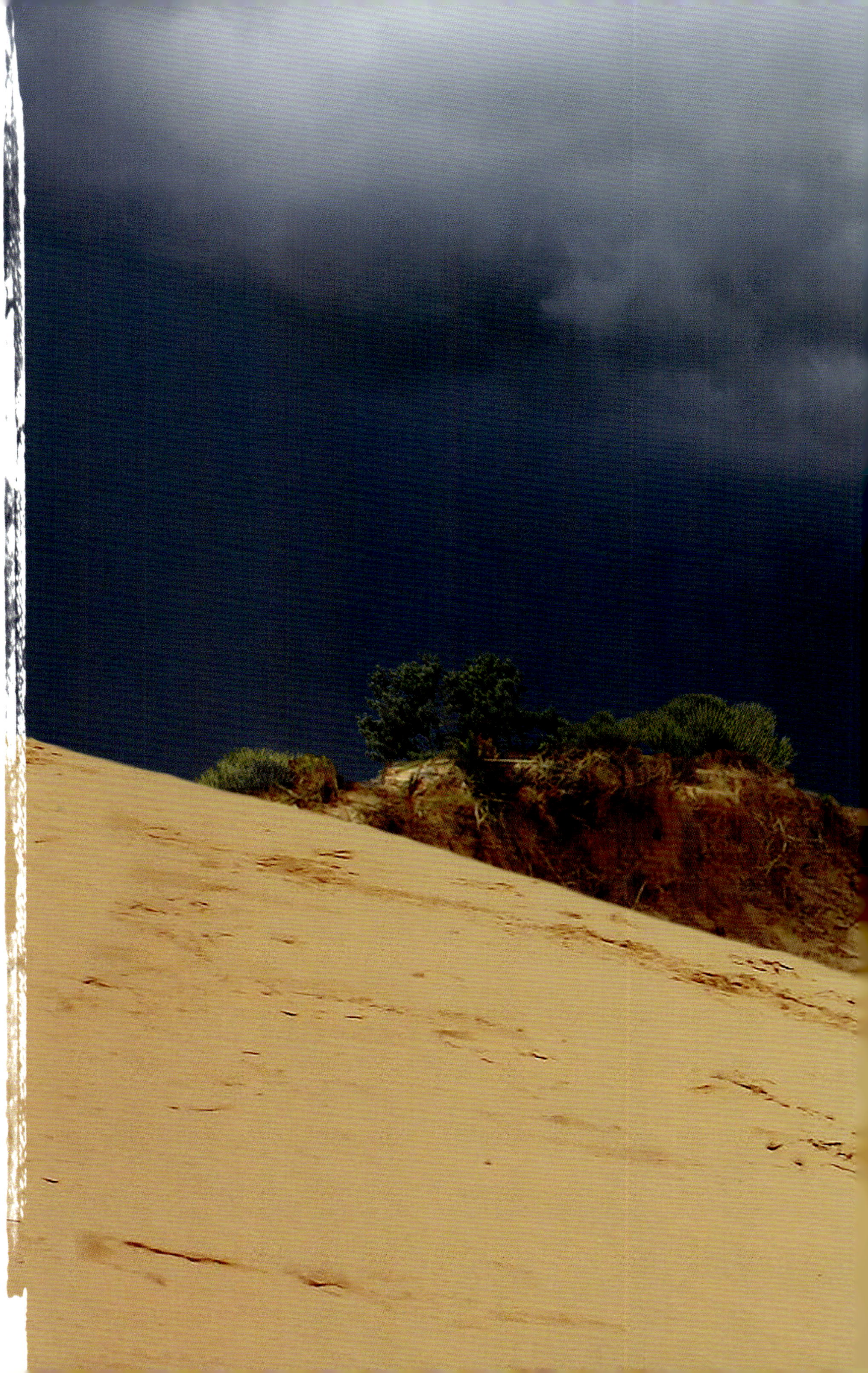

Velociraptor mongoliensis* and *Protoceratops andrewsi
Digital
A scenario based on the "Fighting Dinosaurs" specimen, where the two stars may have tangled just as a storm was brewing. The subsequent strong rainstorm and sand dune collapse interred them in a deep sand flow. Djadokhta Formation, Gobi Desert, Mongolia. Late Cretaceous.

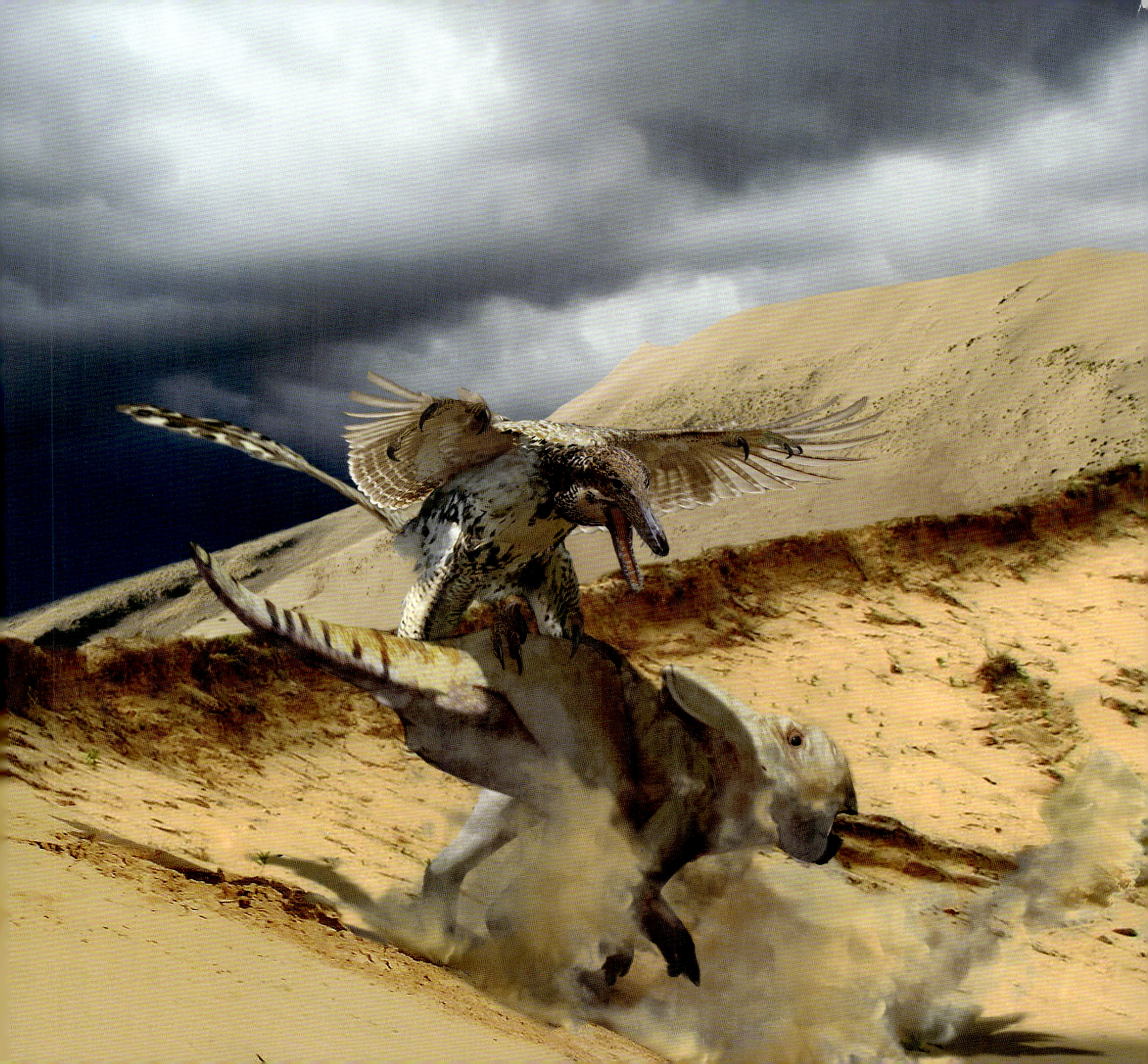

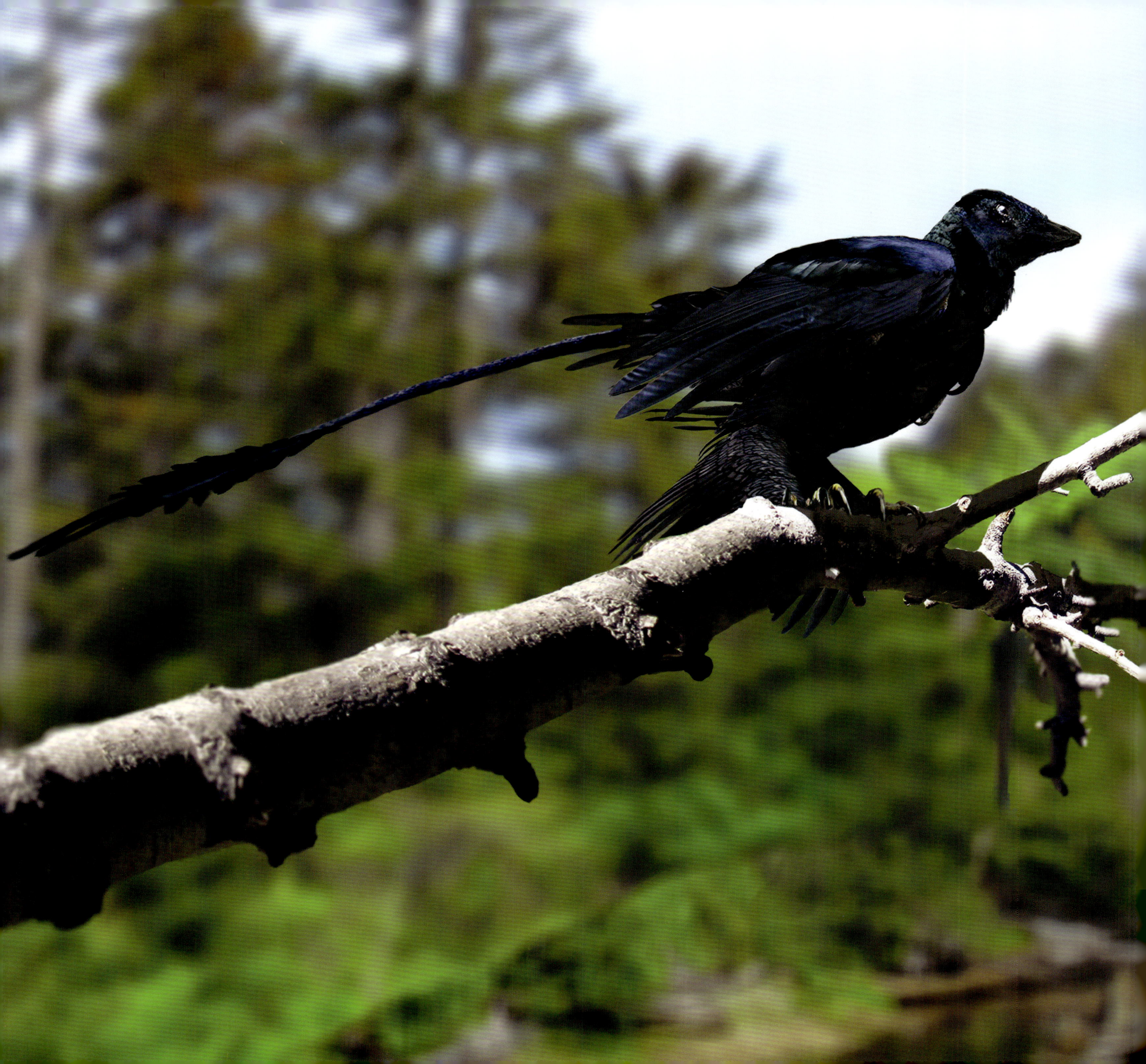

How has your interest in prehistoric animals and ecosystems influenced your work on modern zoology and ecology, and vice versa?
The feedback between the two has been really rewarding. In reconstructing extinct organisms and ecosystems I always wanted to make them seem real, like living things, and that is not easy. I felt there was no point in depicting an animal or habitat again if I couldn't at least convey some novel (or new to me, at least) insight that I'd observed. I study living animals and habitats. I go to the zoo to do life drawings, I watch videos and freeze frames and, above all, I watch the behavior of the birds I pass every day on the way to work. After I started working on dinosaurs I became an avid birder and, now, it is one of the biggest thrills in my life.

It might be sort of like the *World War Z* or *Game of Thrones* books (neither of which I have actually read). The authors set out to make an ultra-realistic work of art. Along the way they ended up researching and finding new appreciation for the ways the real world functions (or functioned): from how the plumbing in a fortress works to the physical and spatial factors that drove the development of military tactics in different centuries.

For example, I wondered how small deinonychosaurs (troodontids and dromeosaurids) might have raised their young. Did the parents feed their brood when they hatched, like hawks? I did a few sketches depicting that. But then I researched the scientific literature and found out my sketches were probably incorrect. We have evidence that suggests it was much more like the pattern in ratites like rheas and emus, where the father raises the young alone and never feeds them. Instead, the brood is precocial; they begin to walk very soon after hatching and will hunt alongside their father, foraging for themselves in his territory. At night the young huddle with their father for safety and warmth. Now ratite breeding fascinates me, I am a huge fan, but I would not have ever looked into these details about the real, living animals, had I not had a question about the extinct ones.

Another example: many forests in the Mesozoic had podocarps and tree ferns, both of which are exotic-looking to those of us in North America. To get some idea of how they look I researched forests in New Zealand; I even asked a friend to take photos for me there and, now, if I see a mamaku (*Cyathea medullaris*, a tree fern) in a greenhouse it's like I just saw a movie star! I am so excited to be in its presence. The enigma of an extinct organism makes me look for answers in living relatives, which makes both more interesting: a feedback loop.

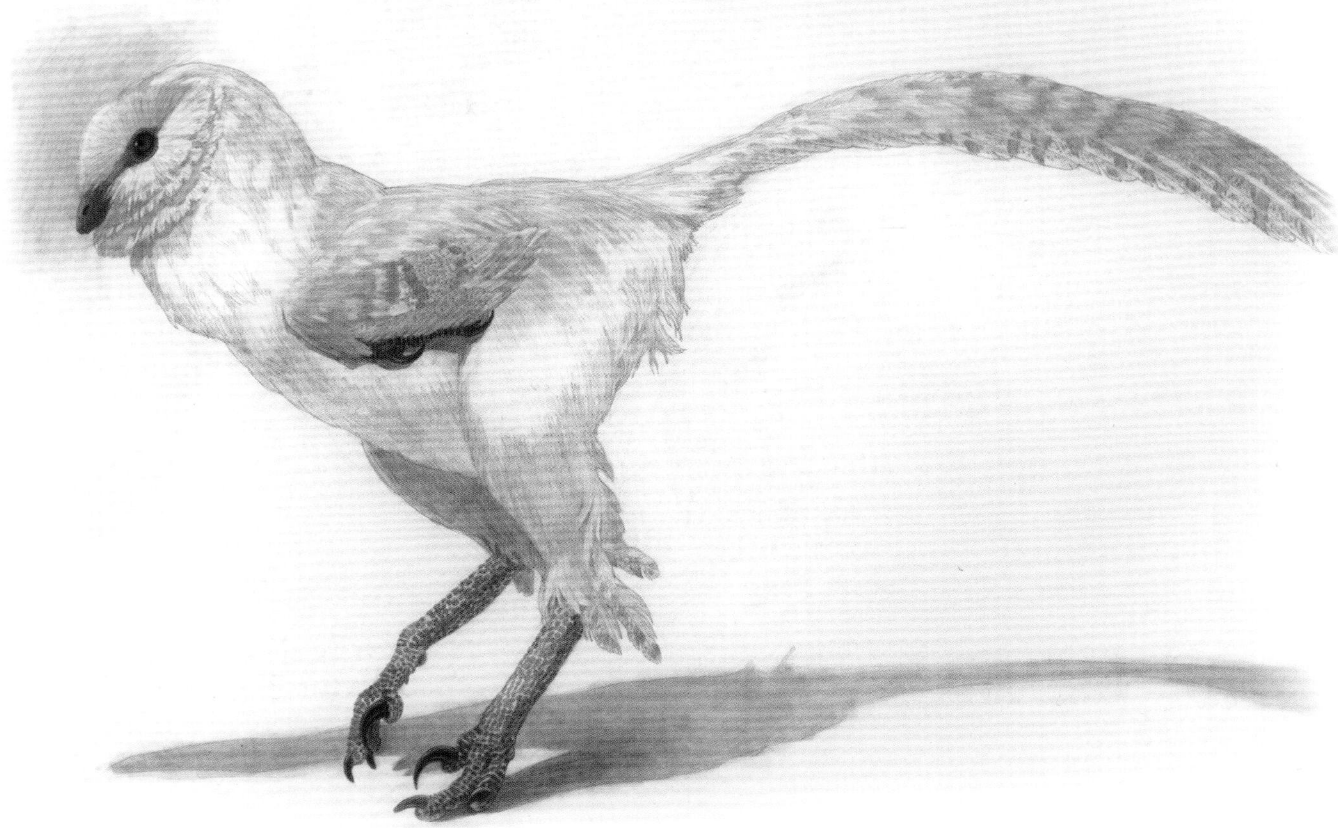

(Above) ***Sinornithoides youngi***
Pencil
Illustrating a hypothesis first suggested by Octávio Mateus; that some troodontids may have had hearing adaptations convergent with those of owls. Ordos Basin, Ejinhoro Formation, Nei Mogol, China. Early Cretaceous.

(Opposite) ***Microraptor zhaoianus***
Digital
The first dinosaur known to have had iridescent black feathers in life, something like a modern grackle or drongo. Yixian Formation, Liaoning, China. Early Cretaceous.

What lead to your choice to specialize in Maniraptorans?
It was topical! The real fossil of NGMC 91 – the one called "Dave" – came to AMNH in 2001 and I got to examine it closely. It is a juvenile dromaeosaur, probably *Sinornithosaurus*. That fossil is just absolutely incredible to behold. I fell in love with maniraptorans then. I often stop to think that generations of paleontologists passed who, if they had one wish, probably would have asked for a fossil of a non-avian maniraptoran with feathers. I will always be grateful that I was alive and in the right place when hundreds of these exquisitely preserved feathered fossils were discovered. The enthusiasm from the new discoveries made me go back to *Archaeopteryx*, which was discovered in

1861, and really appreciate it, as well.

These species are small and, therefore, easier for me to picture behaving like birds do today, in contrast to gigantic sauropods or tyrannosaurs. In drawings, you can make good compositions with these small maniraptorans using cones and leaves and the like.

You're a Senior Principal Preparator at the American Museum of Natural History. Is there such a thing as a regular day in a job like that?

In 1998, I walked into the Exhibition Department for my job interview. There were bowling ball-sized models of viruses hanging from the ceiling, their surfaces studded with scale-model peptides and antigens and so on. The shop was preparing a show called Epidemic. Everyone was just like, "Hey, I need to airbrush my trypanosome, when will you be done in the painting booth?" One person was plugging thousands of cilia into the coat of a translucent *Paramecium*. I said, "I need to work here." It is now far more familiar to me; we've done it a million times. But there still are many moments where we are rolling a gigantic, two meter-long leafhopper model down the hall and it dawns on me that this is a most unusual sight.

We do two shows a year, and preparing for each one is like a college-level course in a subject I may have known almost nothing about – Polar exploration, say, or the voyages of Captain Cook, or the different traditions of body ornamentation from around the world. The curators come in and teach us about the content of the shows, we go to our collections and research library to get reference materials. It is very enriching.

You did a great deal of work on the Dinosaurs Among Us exhibition at the AMNH, especially on the three-dimensional reconstructions. What sort of process was involved in generating the models?

It is always a collaboration. The curators introduce us to each species and tell us their early thoughts on its depiction. There are 12 preparators, and they all build different models, fossil mounts and other exhibits. Our editors develop the stories and the designers then work out each species' placement and relationship to text or audio that will explain it. We research the science literature, we may consult our own permanent exhibits and fossils or other materials in our collections. We are usually working on sketches, scale models, mock-ups, and measured drawings a year to six months before the show, and every iteration is corrected by the curator and supervised by the designers.

With dinosaurs, including extinct birds, I always begin with skeletal measurements. I must be certain that the limb bones are precisely to scale, as well as the skull, and that the vertebral column is as accurate as we can get it. The measurements of the segments of the limbs will be transferred to the armature, which is typically welded from tubular steel. I will say, however, that feathered animals are much trickier to get to look convincing. This is because the skeletons of many birds will give a very misleading idea of what the living animal would look like. An articulated chicken skeleton gives the impression of an emaciated, wiry predator with fearsome spikes for hands. Think about it: in reality the beast is fluffy, with a full, rounded form that softens the appearance of the scaly feet. Those forms, by the way, cannot be even nearly approximated by covering a chicken skeleton in an even coat of fibers, nor by painstakingly gluing on feathers. The feather tracts of living birds are complex and precise, each at different angles and in subtly converging directions, describing different planes and volumes, and all of this changes with the movements and postures of the animal. If you really examine the wings of a chicken, every feather is at least slightly different in size, shape, geometry, and proportions, and has only one match, its mirror image, on the other side.

We dealt with that issue a lot on our 2005 exhibit Dinosaurs: Ancient Fossils, New Discoveries. We experimented with prototypes, testing many techniques. We settled on casting the feathers in hard plastic resins. For outstretched wings, we made molds from bird specimens, cast them in resin, and cut and modified them to make the final models. With folded wings we sculpted feathers in clay, molded and cast them. There were a few times that I displayed the models to viewers and I would tap on the wings to demonstrate that they are hard. A few times viewers said they had thought the feathers were real, which was the highest compliment we could have gotten.

For the latest show, we made scale models, or maquettes, to establish the three-dimensional feather tracts and shapes before any work began on the full-size models. That way we did not need to have a welded steel version of every rib in the armature buried deep inside the final model, you would never see any trace of it beneath the feathers. We had already worked out the surfaces and then blew them up. That was new.

Did you have a particular favorite model to work on?

I got to do *Archaeopteryx*, which I have always wanted to do. I combed over every single detail. Of course one always hopes to see something no one has seen before. Instead I concluded that [the paleoartist] Peter Schouten got his restoration 100% correct. I am a huge fan of his, and hats off to him.

Is it safe to assume you worked closely with the museum paleontologists pulling together the exhibit? Did you have Dr. Mark Norell looking over your shoulder?

Absolutely. I am very lucky to. First of all, Mark taught me everything I know about dinosaurs. And a few other subjects as well. The first dinosaur reconstruction I ever attempted was in 2000, a *Protoceratops* model I prepared under Dr. Norell's supervision. He is fun to learn from and, when a model was starting to come together, he might exclaim, "Cool!" I had a million questions. He would tell me two or three papers to read, and one or two fossils that showed an anatomical feature. I would go to the AMNH research library or collections and

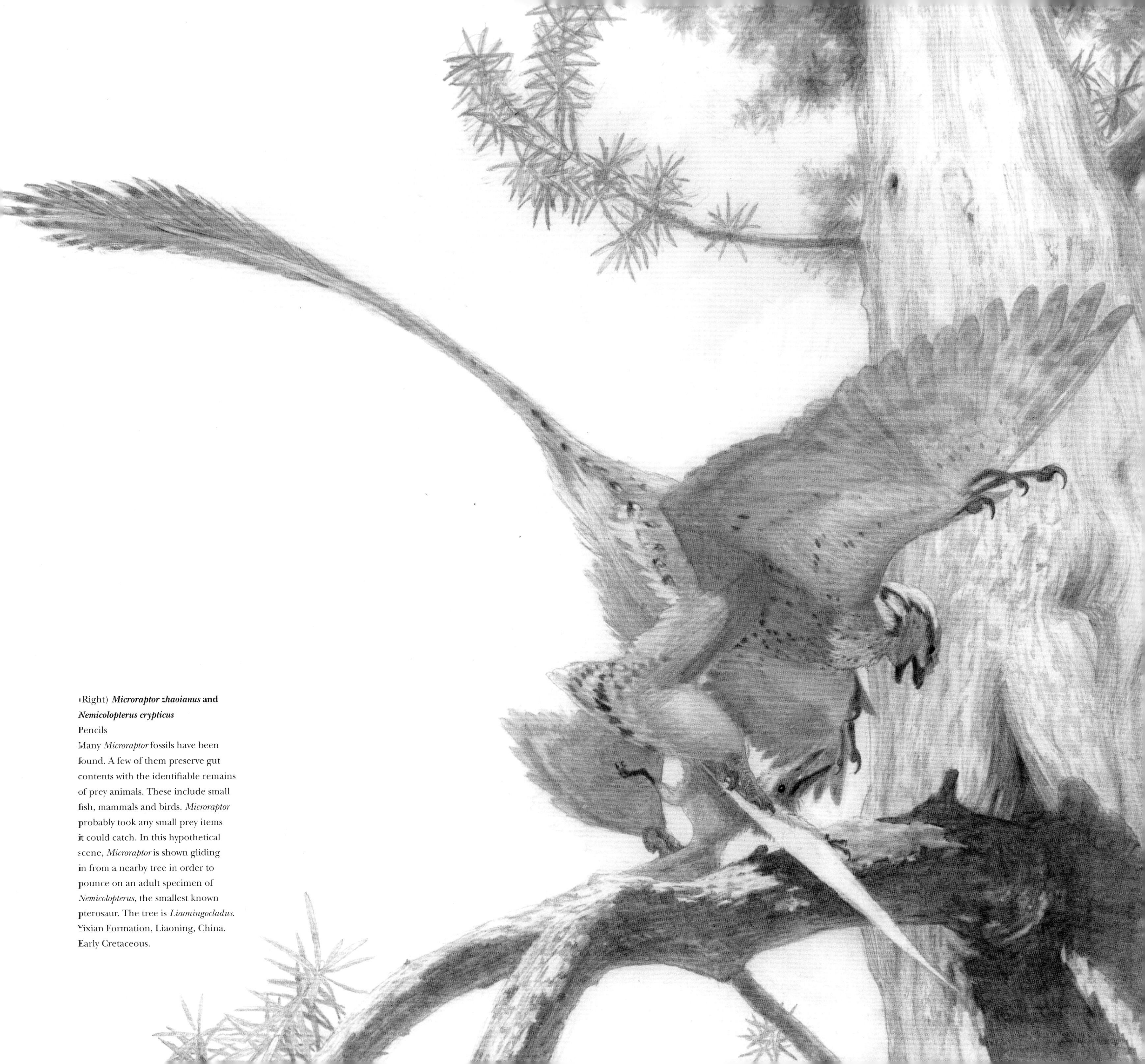

(Right) ***Microraptor zhaoianus*** **and** ***Nemicolopterus crypticus***
Pencils
Many *Microraptor* fossils have been found. A few of them preserve gut contents with the identifiable remains of prey animals. These include small fish, mammals and birds. *Microraptor* probably took any small prey items it could catch. In this hypothetical scene, *Microraptor* is shown gliding in from a nearby tree in order to pounce on an adult specimen of *Nemicolopterus*, the smallest known pterosaur. The tree is *Liaoningocladus*. Yixian Formation, Liaoning, China. Early Cretaceous.

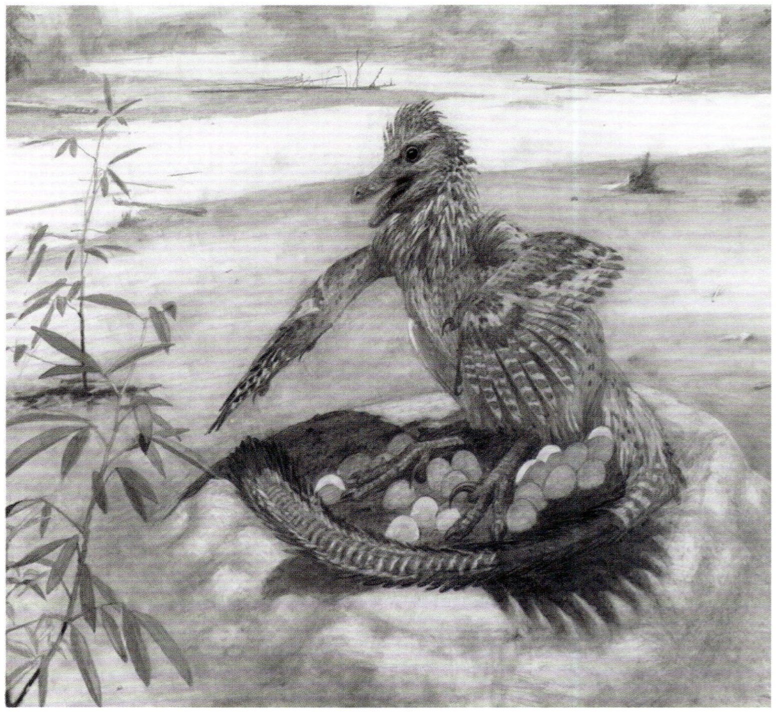

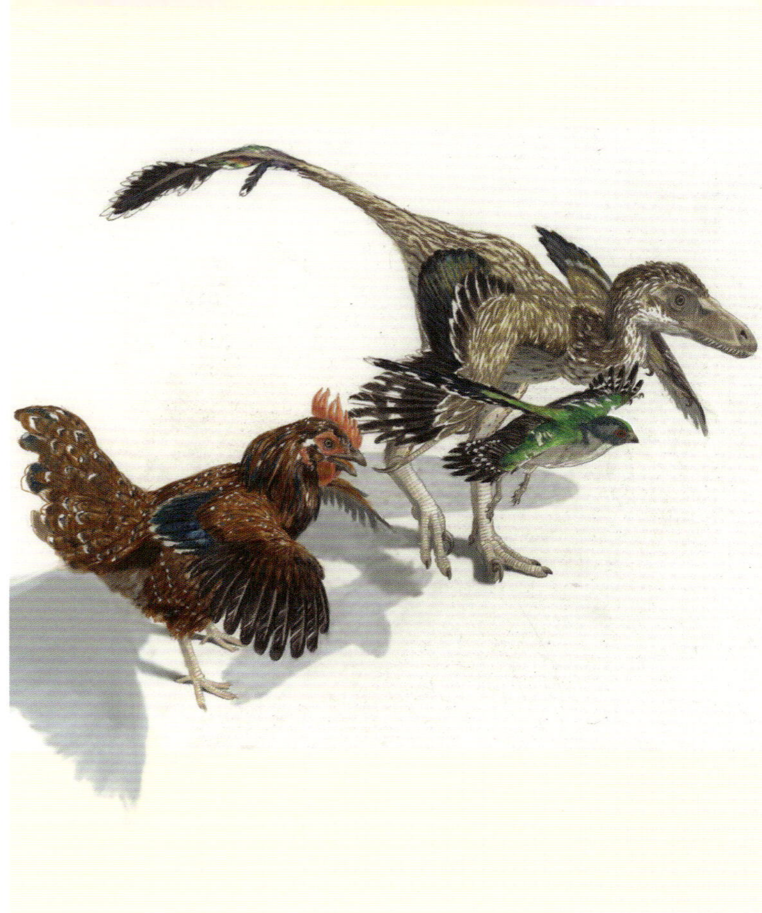

get them, and I would understand.

I have always read the monographs on the species we reconstruct, and tried to get thoroughly grounded in the science literature. I was lucky to have Mark to ask, though, because he knew how all the debates had unfolded and he often pointed me to totally pivotal papers that were less well-known. Working with Mark is sort of like having access to a professor's office hours; he has steered me out of my confusion many times.

A large number of the world's top paleontologists have worked on our shows, and not just the ones currently at AMNH.

As a museum preparator, do you think that reconstructions of extinct animals are more important in bringing an animal to life than the skeletons that seem more prevalent in museums?

That's a good question. I love real material, the bones themselves. They are indispensible. And, frankly, museums filled with real bones are probably the most authoritative and aesthetically

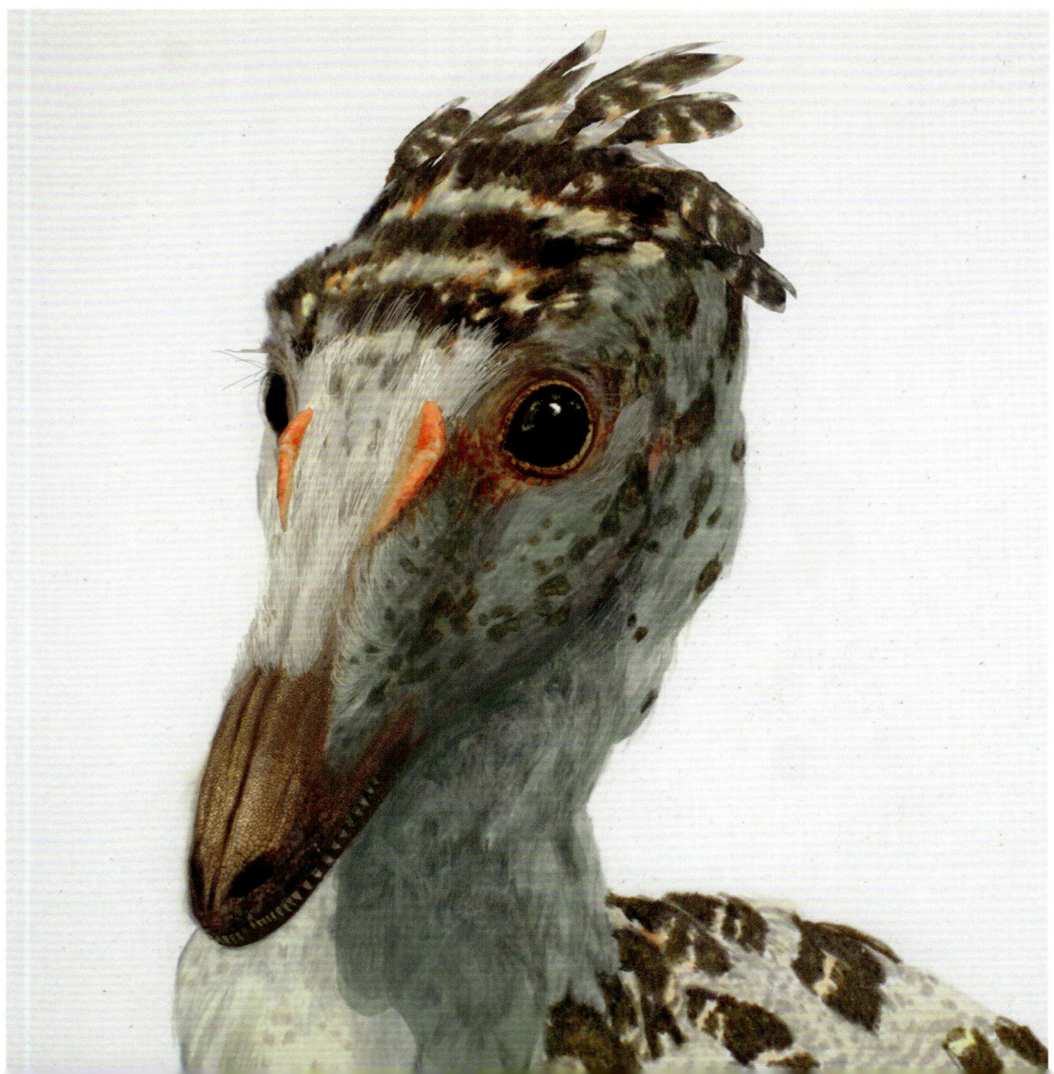

(Far left) ***Troodon formosus* Nesting**
Pencils
Several fossils of male dinosaurs still on their clutches of eggs are known from around the world. Remarkably, *Troodon* males brooded large clutches of eggs alone, and the young hatched in an advanced state of development, probably able to walk on their first day. Here a *Troodon* rooster shields the eggs from the strongest sunlight on an especially hot day, and adopts a posture that birds use today to cool his own body. Two Medicine Formation, Montana, USA. Late Cretaceous.

(Top right) ***Gallus*, *Zhongornis* and *Bambiraptor***
Watercolor
Maniraptoran theropods from three different ages of earth history. *Bambiraptor* is a dromaeosaur from the Late Cretaceous Period, *Zhongornis* is a very primitive (probably enantiornithine) bird from the Early Cretaceous, and *Gallus* is a primitive bird – a chicken – from the modern day.

(Left) ***Troodon formosus***
Watercolor
Theropod dinosaurs had feathers. Did they, like ostriches today, even have eyelashes? Judith River Formation, Montana, USA. Late Cretaceous.

pleasing, in my opinion, to my tastes. But, often, bones do not convey what the animal looked like in life, like I said about chickens. Living humans look very little like their skeletons, to my eye. Birds are even worse. If all birds were extinct I am pretty certain that a reconstruction of, say, a pigeon, would look reptilian, emaciated and scary.

How much did your art influence your academic career?

Well it *was* my academic career. I started out a Biology major, then moved into scientific illustration, then finished with a Master's in Fine Art, as a figure and portrait painter. To be honest, I was not a real painter. I loved subject matter too much and the process of painting not enough. It got complicated, too, because, to address this problem I developed a style of painting that was highly improvisational, lots of daring brushstrokes, to try to force it to be more about painting. I was not scientist material, either, I don't think, because I did not have much talent for devising experiments or thinking about data mathematically. I was between disciplines somewhere.

I was surpassingly lucky that I brought my portfolio into the museum, and they were hiring, because, if there was a good fit for me in the world, this was it.

You produce art in both two and three dimensions, traditional and digital. With artwork, many artists have more or less abandoned traditional methods; in your case, was it a holistic development to include digital images or a more determined choice?

I resisted trying digital. So much so that it became kind of conspicuous. I was still cranking away with colored pencils, of all things, when a friend got so frustrated that they bought me a digital drawing tablet. It was like an intervention. All the little details that drove me nuts but that I could not practically fix in paintings or drawings, now I definitely could. However, one can spend literally one's whole life tweaking things in digital, flipping back and forth, and touching up, and hoping to make the picture spring to life. And all that time can make you stop seeing it with fresh eyes, the way the viewers will. I still have a real challenge getting a sense of depth in digital; it is much easier in drawing, I think.

Did one discipline lead to another or had you always been interested in both illustrating and modelmaking?

In art history, in Beaux-arts education, they always wanted students to draw, sculpt and paint, concomitantly, and I always did. I will say that sculpture came much more easily for me than 2D work. My father was a sculptor – there was a clay oven in my house. I grew up on modeling clay. Perhaps that was why I pursued painting: more of an adventure.

Though, as soon as I walked through the museum door, 'sculptures' became 'models'. In a sense, that semantic change is an important conceptual change. In the museum I am not just representing things I see in three dimensions, I am also illustrating scientific ideas in three dimensions, and they can be revised.

Who were your formative influences?

In natural history art I put Douglas Henderson above all others, for the insights he finds. He goes out into Yellowstone every week and sketches in the field! He truly understands trees. When he drew primitive tetrapods in the water, he had their limbs splay out in that weird way from their

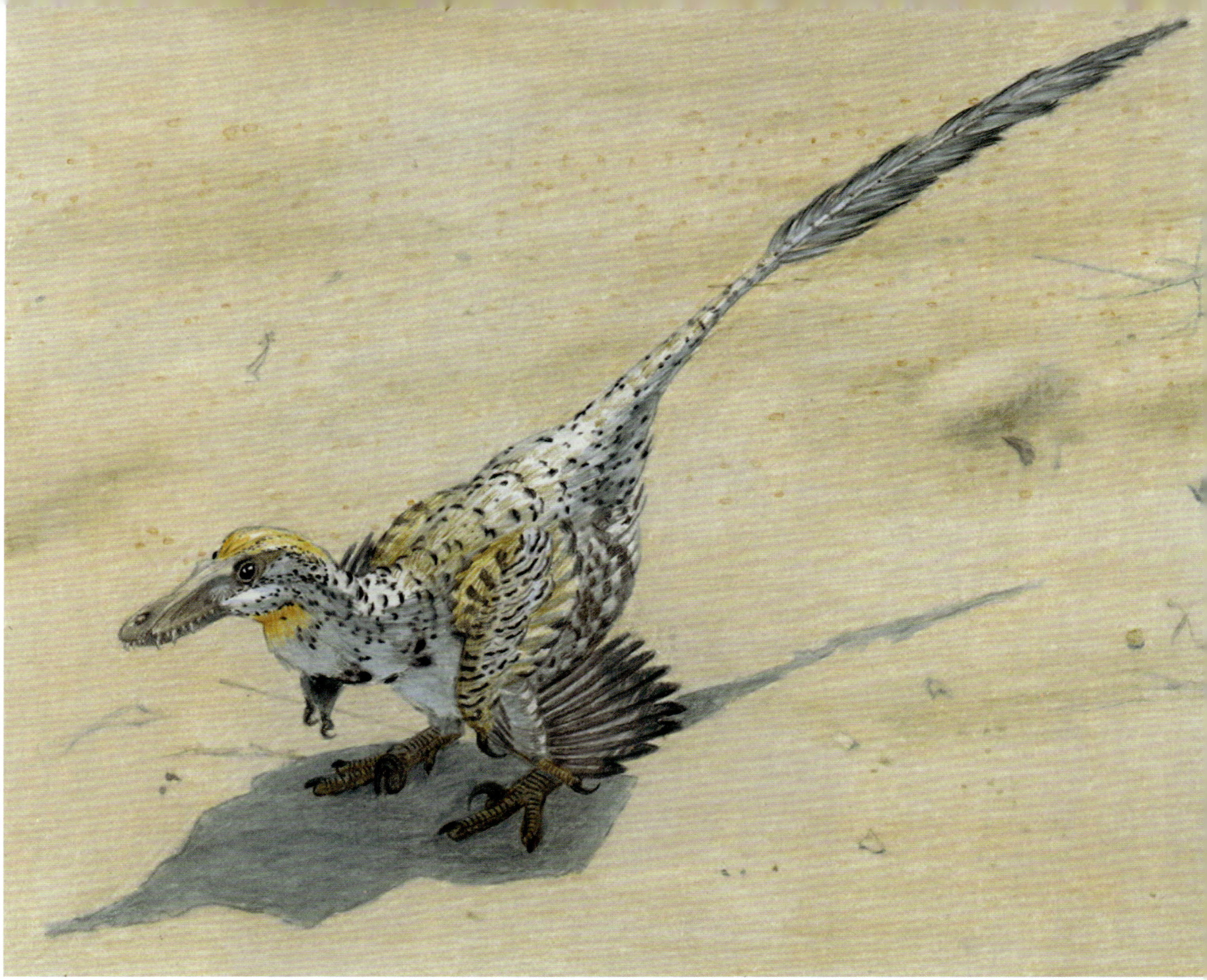

Velociraptor mongoliensis
Colored pencil
Fossil evidence demonstrates that *Velociraptor* had large feather follicles along its forearm (like those of winged birds today) and several fossils of other species in the same family as *Velociraptor* preserve full feathery body coverings. Therefore, this predator was almost certainly fully feathered. Djadokhta Formation, Gobi Desert, Mongolia. Late Cretaceous.

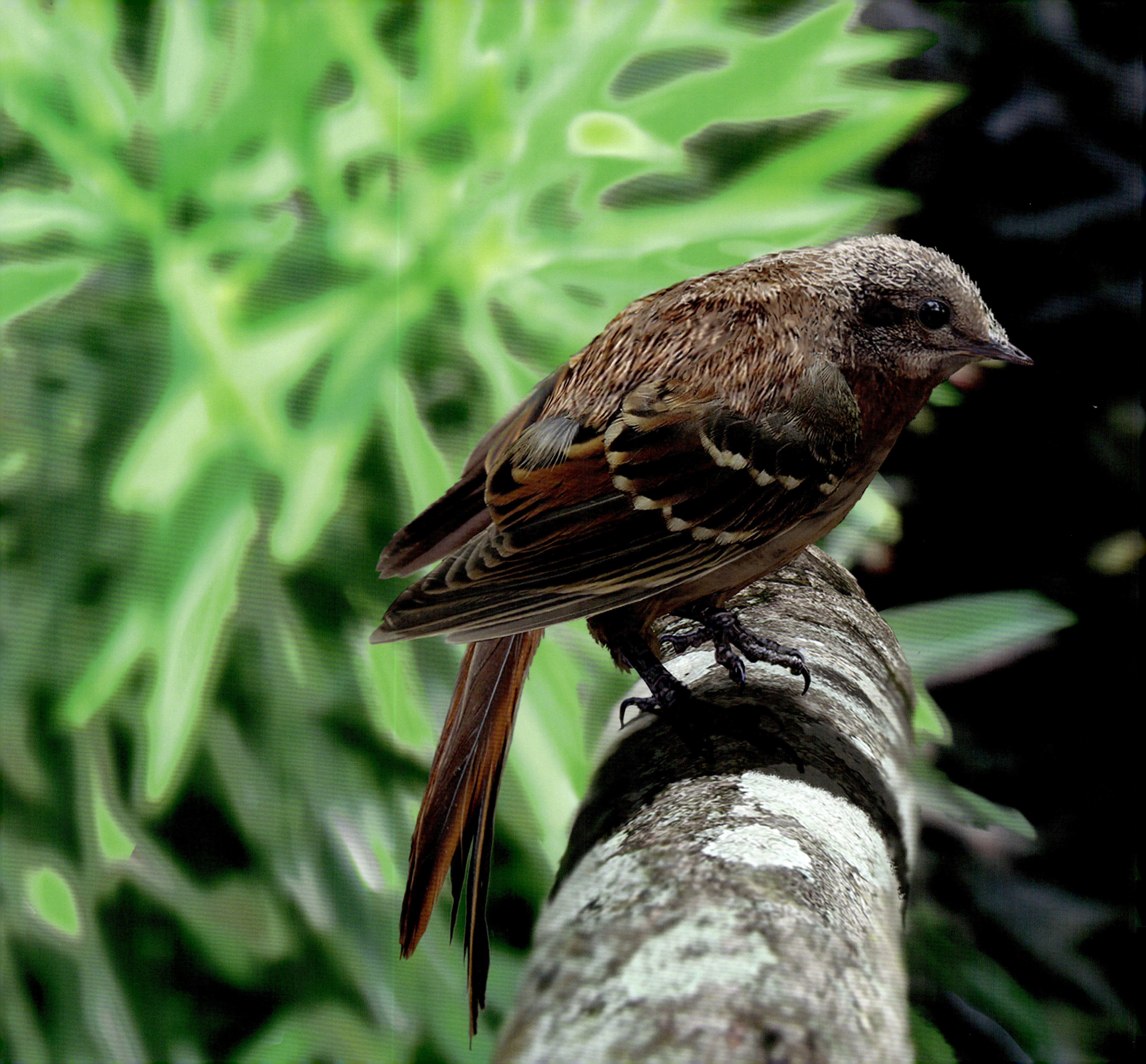

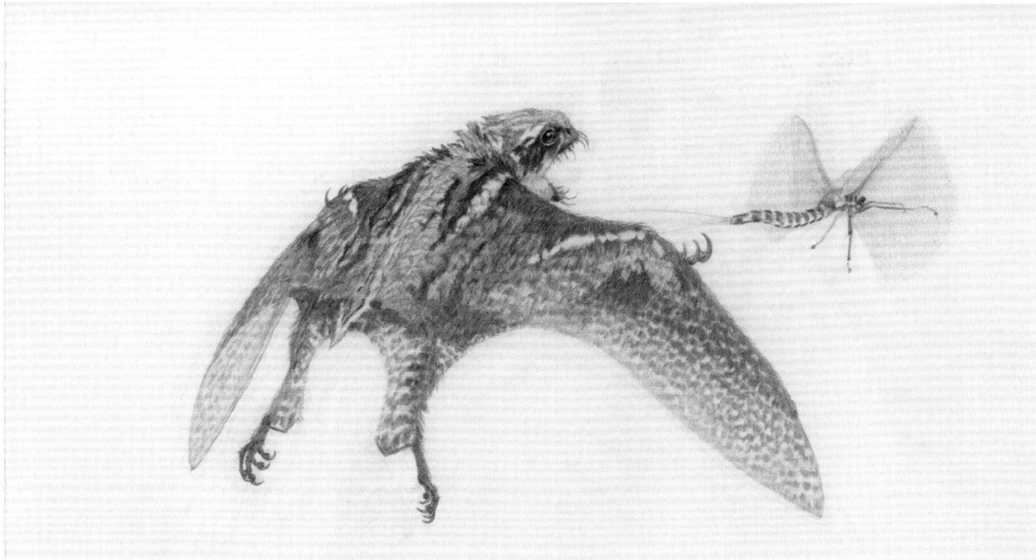

(Left) "***Liaoxiornis***"
Digital
An enantiornithine fledgling of uncertain species, based on several fossils (including GMV-2156/ NIGP-130723), from the lower Yixian Formation. Genus formerly known as *Liaoxiornis* (and also *Lingyuanornis*). Depicted here perched in a tree from the Jehol Biota with *Liaoningocladus* foliage. Yixian Formation, Liaoning, China. Early Cretaceous.

(Above right) ***Jeholopterus ninchengensis***
Pencils
A furry, bat-like pterosaur. Tiaojishan Formation, Nei Mongol, China. Early Cretaceous.

buoyancy in the water, just as one sees in frogs or salamanders in an aquarium. I don't think anyone thought of that before him.

To me the AMNH's most inspiring artist was probably [James] Perry Wilson, whose dioramas are just towering accomplishments. I could stare at his painting of [rock formation] El Capitan (the backdrop for the coyote diorama in the museum's Hall of North American Mammals) for a hundred years and never stop finding new passages I hadn't noticed before that are just brilliant. And it would be a treat to do so, too – that painting is absolutely beautiful.

You have a very loose art style. What materials do you use, traditionally and digitally?

I came from fine art, and [Eugène] Delacroix said that if you aren't skillful enough to sketch the gesture of a man in the time it takes him to fall five stories, you will never be a great painter. A colleague once said to me my work is very loose. I feared he was displeased but, then, he said that was only fair, since reconstructions are hypothetical.

Recently I started working with charcoal again, for the first time in many years. It is no fun to clean up. It drives me nuts with sharpening the points, but nothing else I've found gets the total range from blackest black to stark white.

I think I was always better at capturing the gesture and presence of subjects than the surfaces. I still have that; to me the poses of dinosaur reconstructions are very important. I like all of mine to be observed from analogous animals. Other artists want to see every scale on the skin. Both are very valuable, but my eyes and brain just demand the former.

How much does your background in comparative morphology dictate your work? Does it have a greater influence on one discipline than the other?

That was the only way I could do it. One needs to see the range, the context of animal form.

It was also the first time I think I might have earned Mark Norell's approval. In college I took a very challenging comparative anatomy class with the late Dr. Carl Gans. He taught anatomy in the context of cladistics, which is a theoretical method that seeks to reconstruct evolutionary history in the most empirical, testable way possible. In class we went through the entire vertebrate radiation, and we spent many many hours in the lab dissecting a series of animals representing the evolutionary branches. Our lives became all about lancelets through the microscope and shark dissections on our lab benches. We had to know every nerve, every blood vessel, every process on every bone or cartilaginous branchial arch, and the separate disarticulated bones of the skulls of things like bowfin fish, alligators and pigs. It was a real boot camp. Dr. Gans was tough, but that class was absolutely fascinating. I mentioned Gans to Mark and Dr. John Flynn (a mammal evolution curator) in my early days at the museum, and they exclaimed, in unison, "You were a student of Carl's?! Oh, you'll be fine!"

When I felt inspired by my shark dissections in art classes, it generally went down terribly. It overlapped with human anatomy studies for figurative art, surely, but it was like my own private secret. Artists did not like science and vice versa; my two worlds were separate, until the AMNH.

A paper was recently released that suggested that birds survived the K-Pg extinction because they didn't have teeth and were able to forage more effectively. Do you have any thoughts on why maniraptorans didn't make it beyond the Cretaceous?

I know exactly what you mean, but Carl Mehling is my good friend and colleague in the Vertebrate Paleontology Department, and is a stickler for taxonomic wording so, in tribute to him, I will note that birds *are* maniraptorans, so they did make it. But, as you say, the non-avian ones did not make it. Also I would not attribute it to the teeth, as many squamates, choristoderes, crocodilians, mammals, and fish with teeth made it.

But first, I would be not at all surprised if future excavations of the earliest Paleocene deposits in Patagonia, New Zealand or Antarctica, showed that a small number of non-avian dinosaurs did survive for a time after the K-Pg Event. Kirk Johnson's superb *Plants and the K-T Boundary* demonstrates that plant communities in the distant Southern Hemisphere recovered quickly and with few or no extinctions. If there were a few refugia that still supported ornithopods or something I would not be surprised but, being small, widely isolated populations, their eventual extinction is also no surprise.

Second, extinction is not super-well understood. Predicting which animals will and which will not die out in a mass extinction is not currently possible. But there are some rules of thumb. Large animals that require very large ranges of habitat to meet their needs are vulnerable. Small animals that reproduce very quickly and have generalized feeding habits tend to do the best. Primitive birds were good matches for the latter. Yes, there were non-avian dinosaurs that were very small, but it is not clear how many of those were still around by the K-Pg. Most of the really small ones we know of are from the Lower Cretaceous and Jurassic.

Third, the devastation was extreme. In North America, the sedimentary basins in some places hold no spores or pollen except for one species of fern for thousands of years after the bolide impact. Picture that: all of interior North America with no plants besides bracken ferns. In habitat that is so degraded it is remarkable any animals survived. I think the work showing an extremely bad, worldwide thermal flash from space (re-entering ejecta creating a broiler sky for up to 20 minutes) after the bolide impact is interesting, but too deadly. If it had been that severe I don't think birds could have made it, either. Certainly not the three or four lineages that apparently did survive. I hope no one ever tries the experiment to see if whistling ducks, feeling broiler heat over their heads, will keep diving, over and over, to put out the smoldering fires on their backs. I think they will not know what to do, and die.

I think there must be a role for contingency, just sheer chance. Some surface organisms were sheltered by forest canopies, in tree hollows, the mouths of caves, or overhanging tree trunks. I always think about the hemispheres and their seasons, too. If the bolide struck Earth in the austral winter, they may have had very high

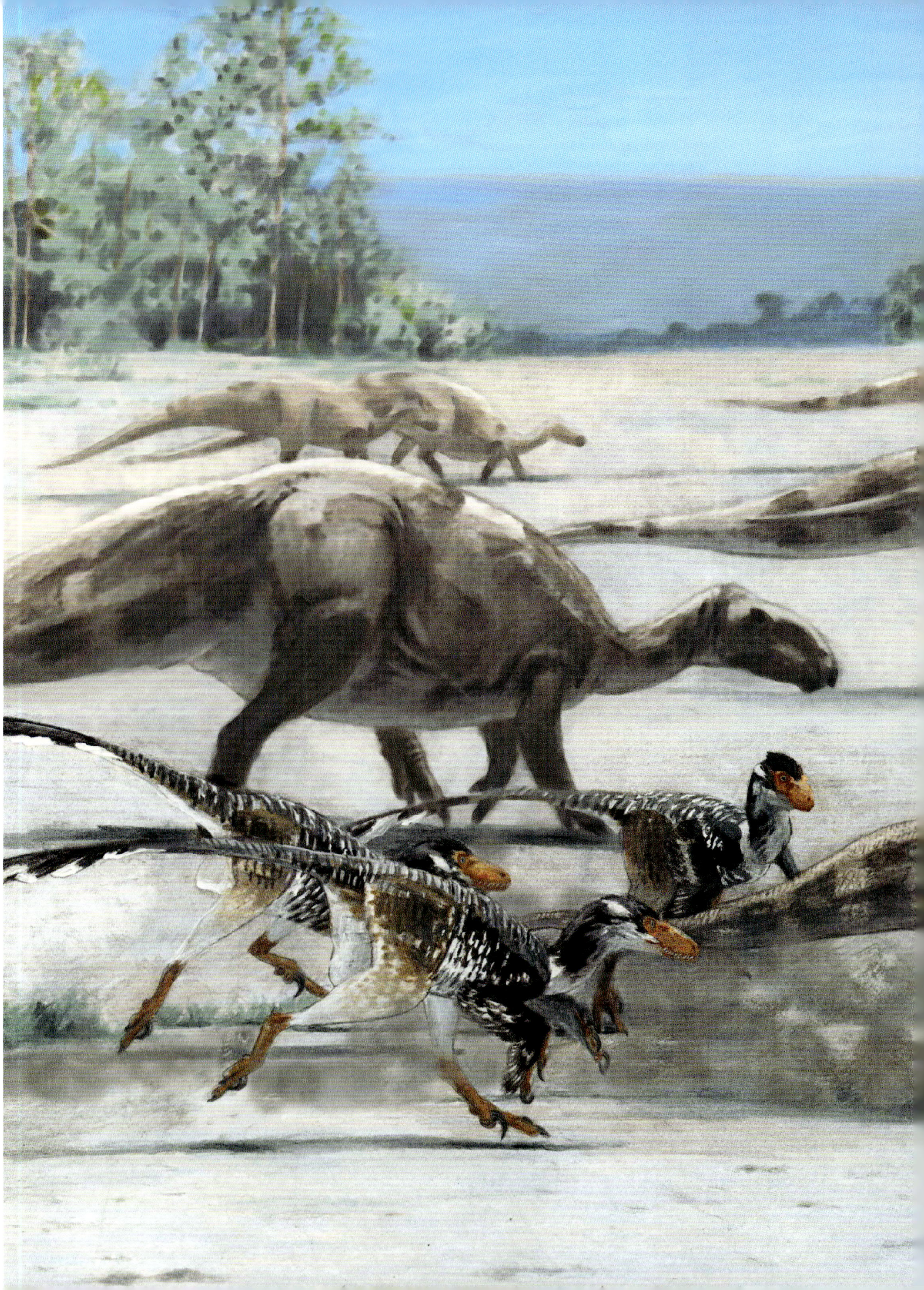

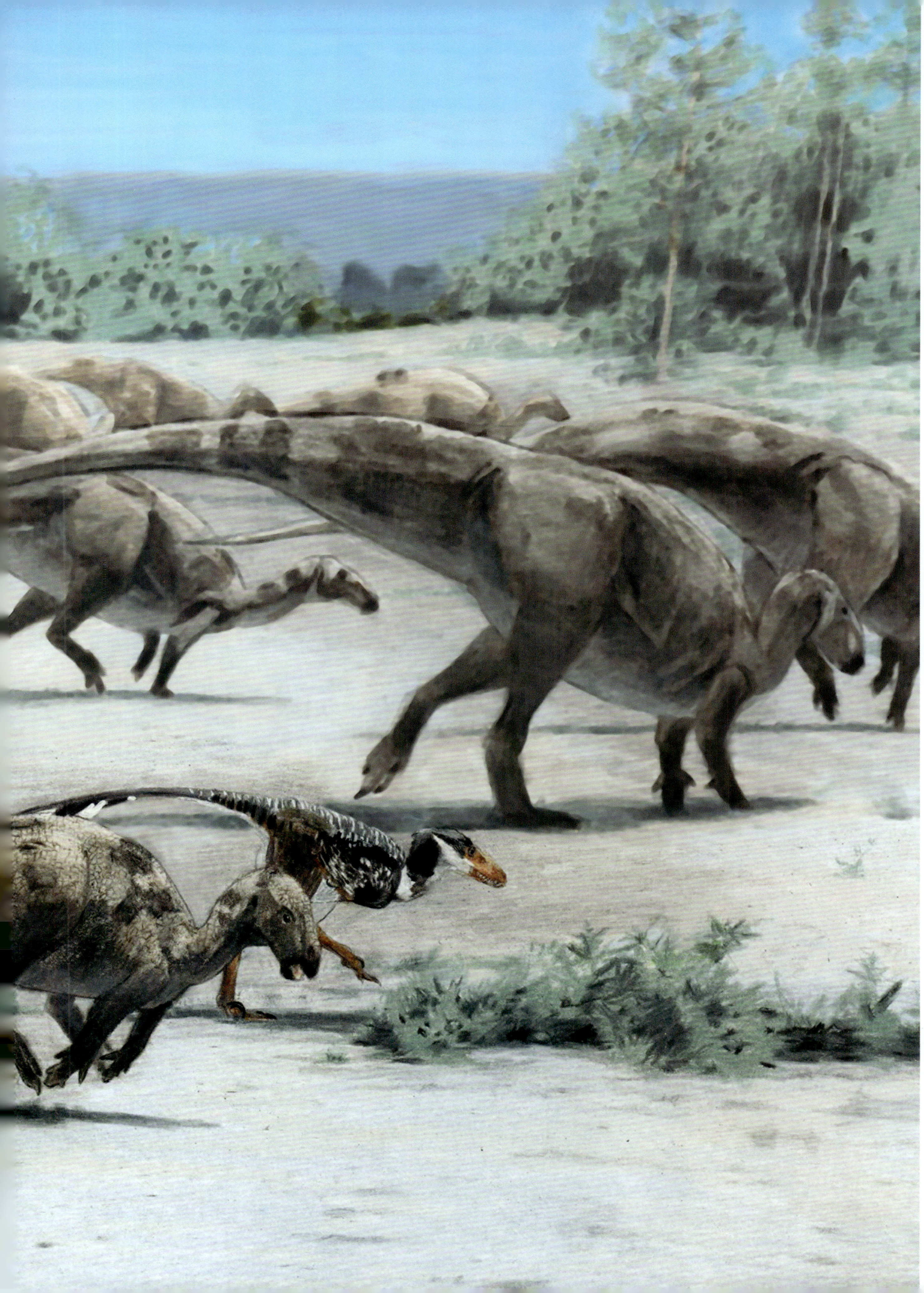

survival at higher latitudes, as the forests, insects, turtles, etc. would already have been dormant.

The ones that survived were most likely not predatory and definitely not large-bodied. Last time I looked, for one (warm-blooded) predator to survive, 100 herbivores of similar body mass must survive. In a crunch, the big, hungry predators run out of food first. A lot of Cretaceous maniraptorans, like Dromaeosaurs, were probably just that.

The lineages of birds that made it were probably generalists, like anatids and galliforms today, eating invertebrates, seeds, plant shoots and even submerged aquatic vegetation. That may have set the more derived birds apart from the other maniraptora. Ducks and geese are very primitive, and they can practically live on grass shoots and algae. They made it through.

It is weird, though, and not fully explained, why oviraptorids and ornithomimids died out. I've always thought the former probably cracked gymnosperm cones for seeds, and there is good evidence that the latter fed on aquatic organisms, much as ducks do. That's where the incandescently hot sky scenario probably does explain the extinction of all large-bodied taxa.

You've done a lot of work on Microraptor. *What are your thoughts on its lifestyle, particularly its flying abilities or lack thereof?*

Well, that has been a story in itself, and an informative one about the scientific process.

Antlers Formation, *Deinonychus antirrhopus* and *Tenontosaurus tilletti*
Watercolor
Fossils of *Tenontosaurus* have been found together with *Deinonychus* in deposits from an ancient river floodplain. The bones show signs of predation. Scientists have studied whether several *Deinonychus* scavenged the large ornithopods, or hunted in packs, or if, like monitor lizards and birds of prey today, each predator individually tried to catch the prey, with no cooperation. Predators often attempt to isolate and attack the youngest, smallest members of social or herding prey animals. Antlers Formation, Oklahoma, USA. Early Cretaceous.

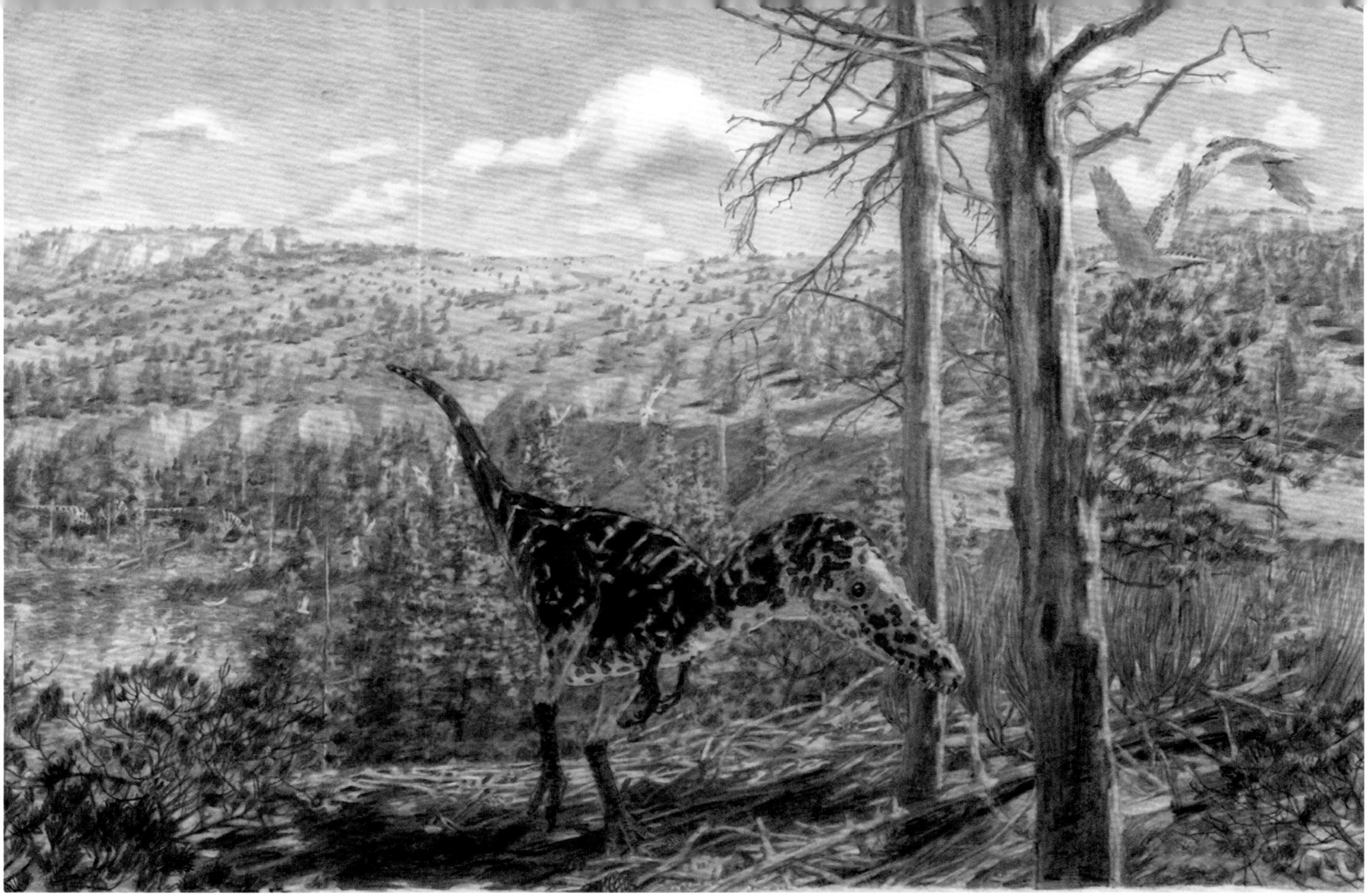

Alioramus altai
Nemegt Formation, Gobi Desert, Mongolia. Late Cretaceous.

Above all, we must never forget, *Microraptor* is an enigma. It has four wings! It has wings on its legs! How could that possibly work? No one knows for certain. We've put it through many wind tunnel tests and aerodynamic computer models and we can't say with certainty it even glided. But I am very interested in what animals can do beyond what is definite from their anatomy. Flying foxes, for example, are big, heavy fliers with no keel on the sternum. And I have a big file of photographs of penguins that have climbed up and perched in trees on Auckland Island and whatnot. But here is where Norell's tutelage is so helpful. Literally on the back of a napkin, he once proved to me that there is no real chance of ever getting an actual ancestor of birds preserved in the fossil record. The preservation areas (at least seasonally dry, stagnant water basins) are partitioned from the area where evolution would have occurred (tropical rainforests). Everyone seized *Microraptor* like it was the answer on bird evolution, but it is way too young, It is pretty clearly a side branch of a side branch. Like a gliding squirrel or colugo is to the glorious bat radiation.

When *Microraptor gui* was first reported it was described as an arboreal animal, based on features of the foot skeleton and claws. I was fortunate that Dr. Xu Xing was at the AMNH then and advising me on his discovery himself. I reconstructed it as an arboreal animal the first time, climbing trunks and gliding from tree branches. We had no information on the coloration then, so I looked at birds in analogous habitats from today: taxonomically diverse, warm temperate forests with pronounced dry seasons. I found many of the birds there, like hornbills, etc. were banded or spotted with patterns of dark and light, and drab colors were most common overall. Years later, new methods produced evidence that *Microraptor*'s feathers were very dark and slightly iridescent, something like a grackle! That is how we show the animal in the new exhibit. The new model is actually made from new casts of the same model from 2005, but painted differently, and with an altered tail, based on the new scientific evidence.

Later studies, once there were many more *Microraptor* specimens from which to take data, re-analyzed the evidence on the feet and talons and, now, it seems the feet are more like those of ground birds. That makes perfect sense to me. But we still don't know if it could fly, or glide, or what. Many ground birds retain large wings, including the kagu of New Caledonia, which has about the same wingspan and mass as *Microraptor*. Studies have shown that, in living birds, almost all of the launch energy comes from the legs: they don't need to fall out of a tree to accelerate enough to get airborne. Most paleogeeks know that *Microraptor* has proportionately very long arms, but it also has very long legs, which may have made for strong jumping abilities. Anyone who's flushed a pheasant knows that birds can take off explosively from the ground. And a pheasant is about the same size as *Microraptor*, and quite a primitive bird as well! I liked imagining *Microraptor* as an arboreal creature, but ground-based is pretty cool, also. It lived amongst trees, anyway. Its habitat was the forests that surrounded a giant lake system, whether it ever climbed those trees or not.

You have a particular interest in the gymnosperm plant group bennettites and have blogged about them in an effort to encourage more reconstructions amongst paleoartists. Do you think paleoflora is an area overlooked amongst paleoartists in general?

Thank you for bringing that up, I feel like a lone voice! In 2005 the AMNH reconstructed the Lower Cretaceous Jehol forest of the Yixian Formation in a large diorama. There is a longstanding method for preparing dioramas, going back to the halls of African and North American mammals. The scenic artists do their best work if they pick one specific actual place and document it in detail. Just taking a wall and painting in the trees and rocks tended to make the scene look generalized. Painting it like a formal landscape was usually more convincing and gave the sorts of specific insights that make great natural history art. In short, it was more inspired. So we were all trying to figure out a rough analog, a forest type that might look roughly the same. The redwood forests in the Sierra Mountains in California? The exotic podocarp and tree fern forests of New Zealand? Ultimately, the backdrop painters chose the Pine Barrens in New Jersey, and a team went there to collect references and do field sketches. They said there were ponds there where the pine pollen floated on the water, 10cm thick in some places.

I kept reading about the Yixian forests for years afterward, as more and more data was published on the climate, topography, lake environment, and plant communities as worked out by fossil abundances. I concluded that there actually is *no* extant analog. There were pines and podocarps, sort of, and likely members of the cedars and cypresses, like we can see in the Northern Hemisphere, but also may plant types that have left no living relatives. The ginkgos in the Jehol did not look like modern ones. And, like, 25% of the leaves in the fossil beds there are bennettites, and we aren't even certain what growth form those took! The forest was also super-diverse, with many families and even several phyla of trees contributing to the canopy.

When I started researching paleobotany I learned right away that what the artist wants – the look and size of the mature extinct plant – is almost unattainable. Fossil plants are known from seeds, cones, leaves, twigs, and fossilized wood. Each one gets a different scientific name, and debates over which ones belong together, as organs of the same plant, go on for decades. Moreover, the same whorl of leaves could have grown on a tree the size of a redwood or a low scrubby bush, or both – as with oaks or junipers today. So, it is a super-hard area to figure out. But I will say this: several habitats that dinosaur fans may think they know well – the Morrison Formation of *Allosaurus* and *Apatosaurus*, the Yixian Formation, and the Chinle of *Coelophysis* – have probably never had their vegetation fully reconstructed. That means that they have never been depicted quite as they really looked. To me that is fascinating.

Bennettites are a good example, just because they have never been completely figured out. Some authors think they grew to be tall trees in some habitats, while others think they were probably just a meter high or so, like shrubs. Some seem to have grown in saltwater deltas, like mangroves, and some (cycadeoids) had gigantic female cones (*Williamsonia margotiana*) that looked basically like magnolias. Small oval seeds that may have been bennettite ovules were found in the gut of the first specimen of *Jeholornis*. And sauropods and stegosaurs probably grazed on bennettites. But that has almost never been depicted.

***Aurornis xui* in Thicket**

A remarkable bird-like, paravian dinosaur that lived before *Archaeopteryx*. Here a male is depicted displaying to a female in a thicket of bennettites. Tiaojishan Formation, Liaoning, China. Late Jurassic.

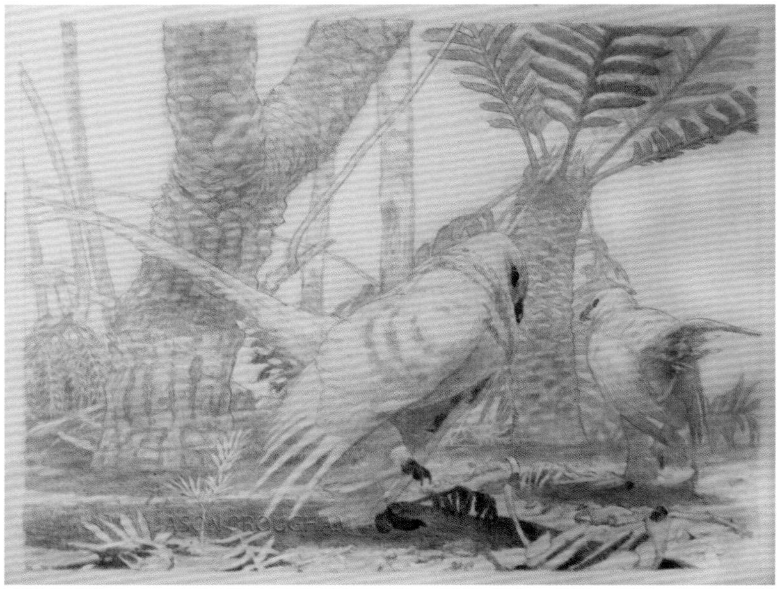

VITALI KLATT

GERMANY

Born in 1972 in the Republic of Uzbekistan, Vitali first became interested in dinosaurs at the age of 10, constructing his first models. In 1992, following the collapse of the Soviet Union, he emigrated to Germany where, in 2001, he entered the Academy of Fine Art in Karlsruhe and began to develop as an artist, winning a three-month scholarship to study in Limerick, in the Republic of Ireland, in 2006. After graduating from the Academy in 2010 with a Master's degree in Fine Art, he fulfilled a childhood dream, setting up Paleoworldstudio and becoming a full time model builder.

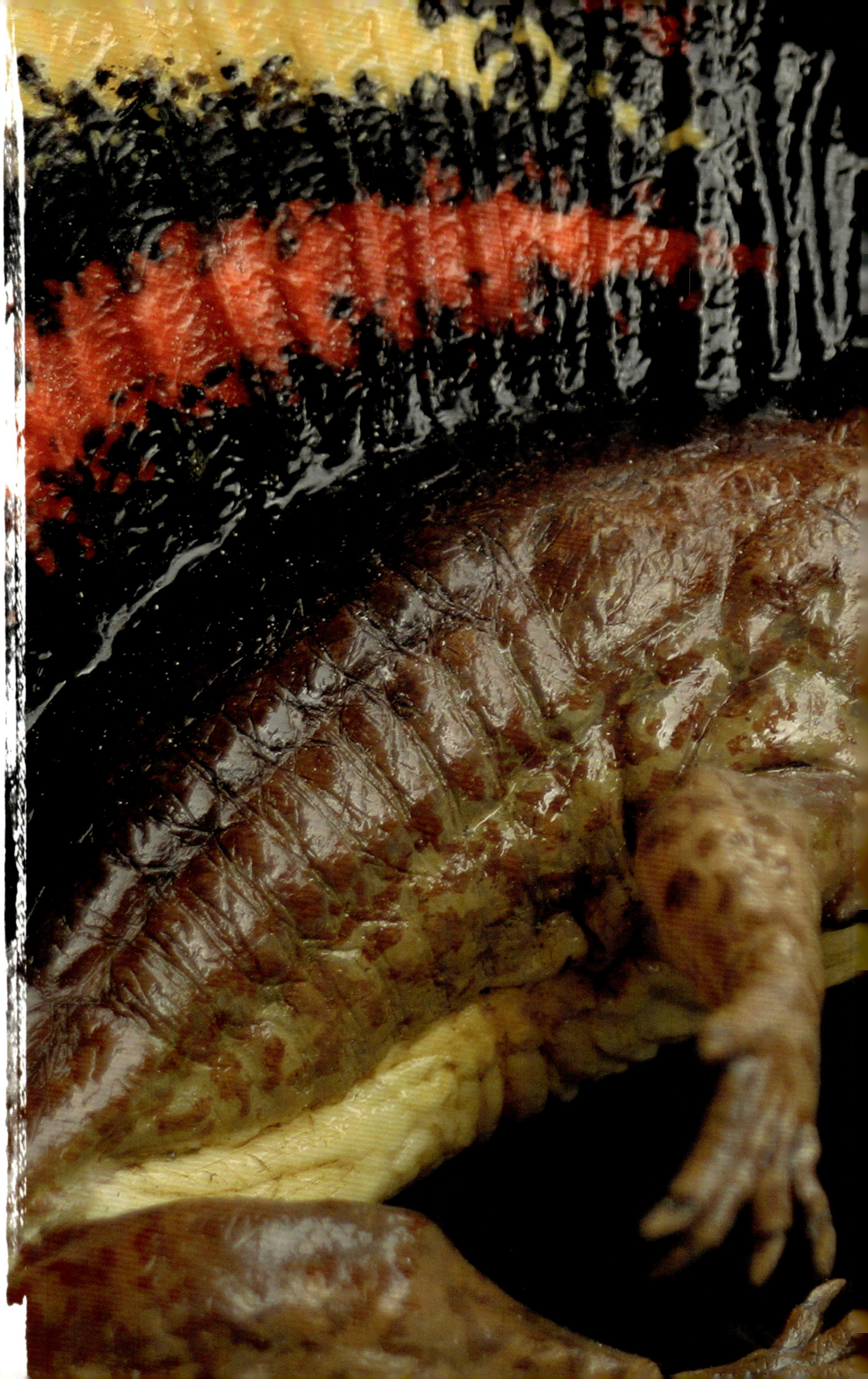

Dimetrodon limbatus* vs *Ophiacodon retroversus
Birezin, 1:10 scale, 2015

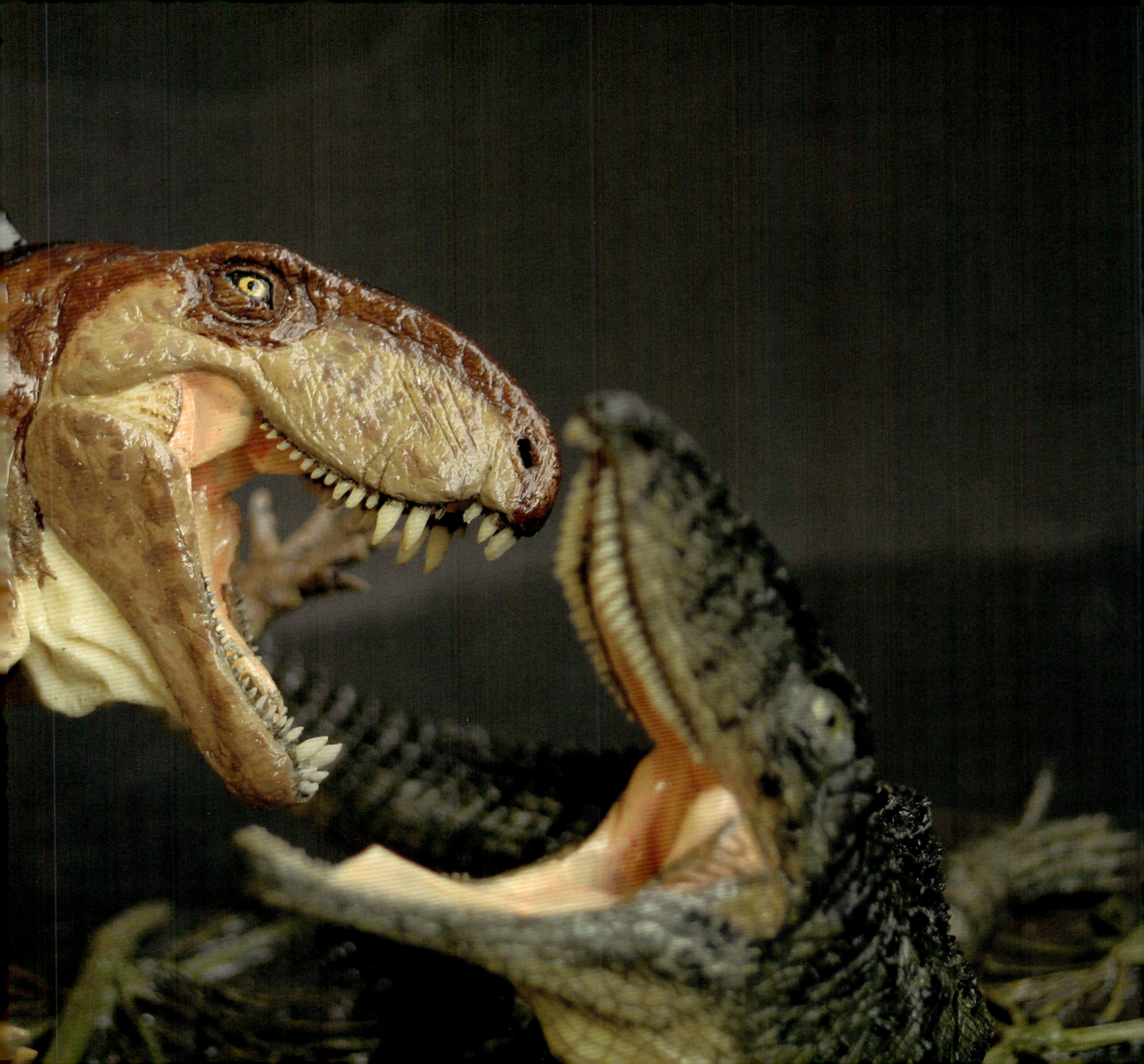

When did you first start sculpting? Did you always intend to build sculptures?

I started modeling from my childhood. I modeled from plasticine, mostly building prehistoric animals. However I didn't plan to be a sculptor or a painter. I wanted to be a paleontologist. Life was different. As a result, I have graduated from the Academy of Fine Arts in Karlsruhe, and about five years ago I started modeling animals seriously.

Can you explain your methods when building an animal? How do you start?

At the beginning, of course, I collect all the known material, animal skeleton pictures, reconstruction of skeletons etc. If possible, I take pictures myself in available museums. My friends from paleoforums also help me a lot.

Then, I make a wire skeleton; I often try to model anatomically accurate limb bones then model rough muscles and, if necessary, I 'saw' the model up, breaking it up into its component pieces. Most sculptors do this at the end, when the model is completed, but I like to do it before finishing. I insert tubes into those areas where I've cut and where the parts of the figure will be linked. It is easier to model on separate parts than working by hand on the whole thing. Once that's finish, I sheathe the model with leather, then I make silicone molds and the model is cast in plastic.

Do you do a lot of anatomical research to ensure the musculature is as accurate as you can make it?

I always thought that I don't just do figures but reconstructions. For a precise reconstruction you need to know not only the shape of the skeleton, but what muscles are attached and where. If I can get a three-dimensional model of the skull, I'll use a 3D printer to cast the skull in minature. I know muscle locations from the lessons on anatomy, but to be more accurate I always look through the academic literature.

What are the most difficult organisms to reconstruct?

Permian reptiles! In the words of V. Yu. Reshetov, "The detailed reconstruction of the earliest representatives of vertebrates, including the reconstruction of more superficial muscles, as a rule, borders on fiction." It's tough because the integument and limbs positions of Synapsida still remains rather a mystery.

What sort of materials do you use?

For initial modeling, I use Super Sculpey in both colors: soft pink and solid grey. I mix them to get a soft grey of the right consistency. For muscles I use FIMO colored clay and, for the casting of the finished figures, German plastic Birezin G26.

What types of tools do you use?

I generally use a single tool – a small, sharp knife. But also a brush for smoothing and I have a whole arsenal of presses to help pattern the skin structure on the figure.

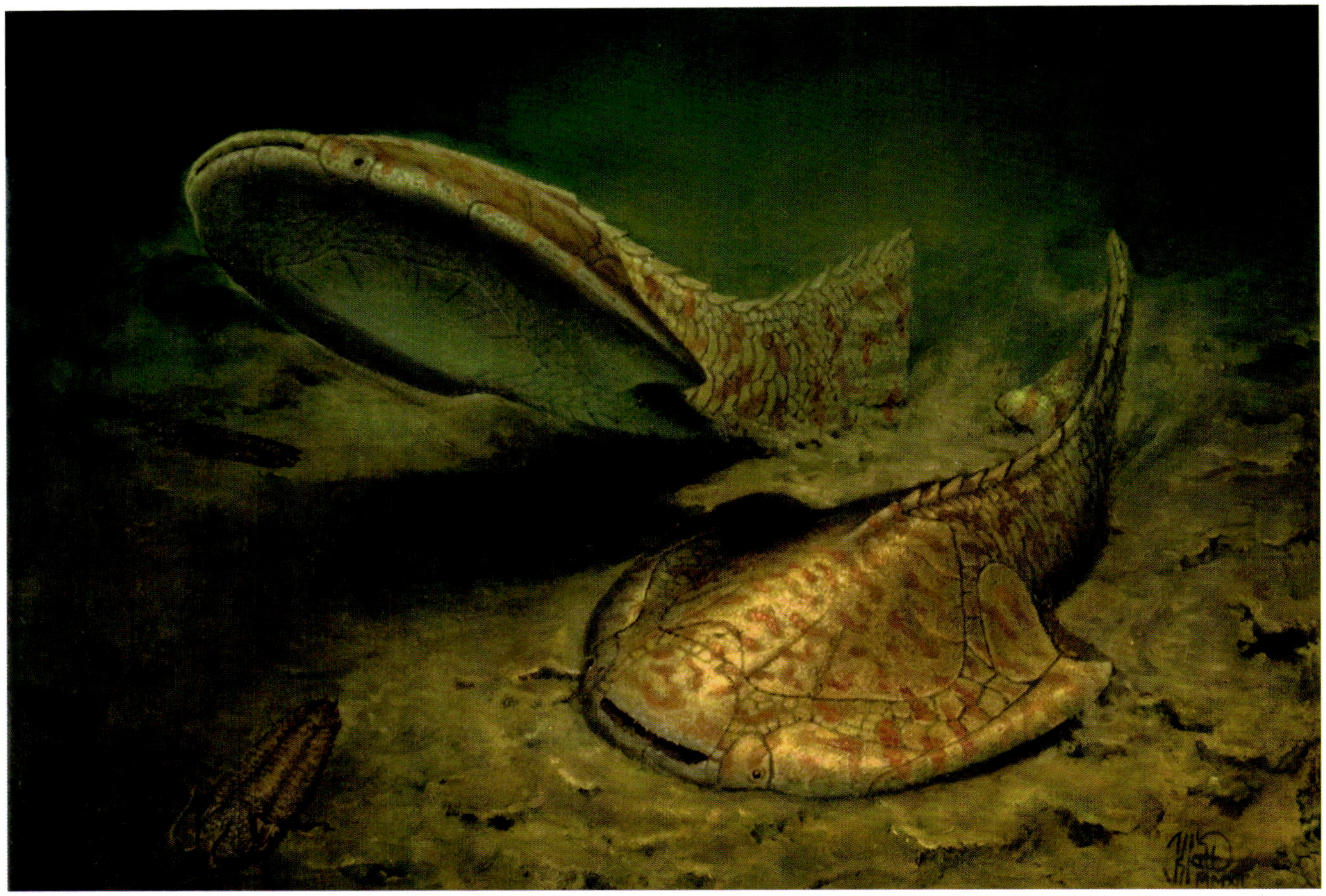

(Above) ***Drepanaspis***
Watercolors, 2012

(Below) ***Diplocaulus***
Birezin, 1:10 scale, 2015

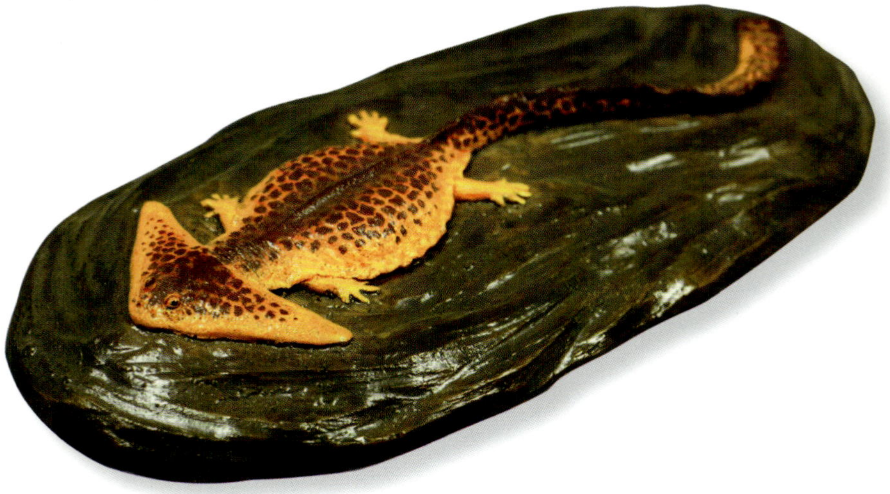

How long does your average sculpture take?

Hard to say. It depends on the complexity of the model, but on the whole I'd say about two weeks. However, many of my fans would say that it takes me an eternity! I've got many figures and whole compositions that I started but just don't have the time to continue.

Do you always work to the same scale, more or less?

I try to adhere to a strict scale for its reconstruction. For example, the Permian animals are scaled at 1:10; Mesozoic reptiles 1:40; and Cenozoic mammals 1:20. The choice is not accidental; the fact is that the many ancient animals were not

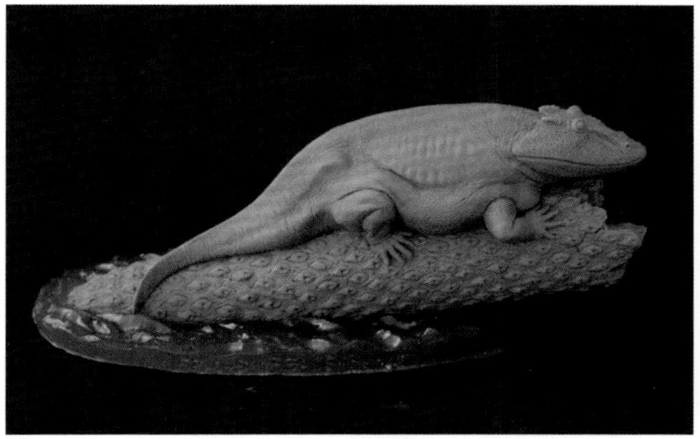

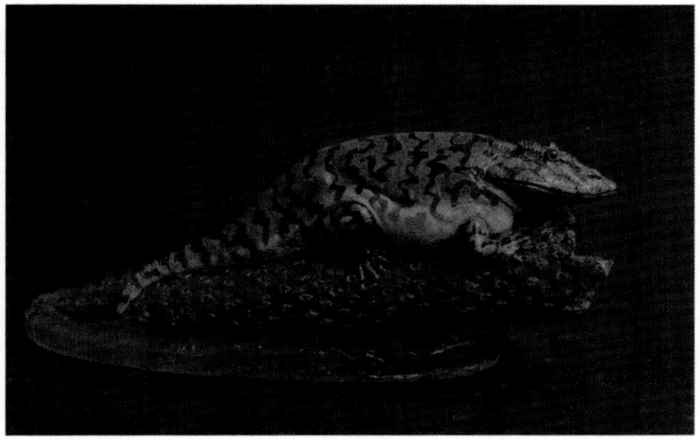

Eryops megacephalus

Resin, 1:10 scale, Painted and Unpainted

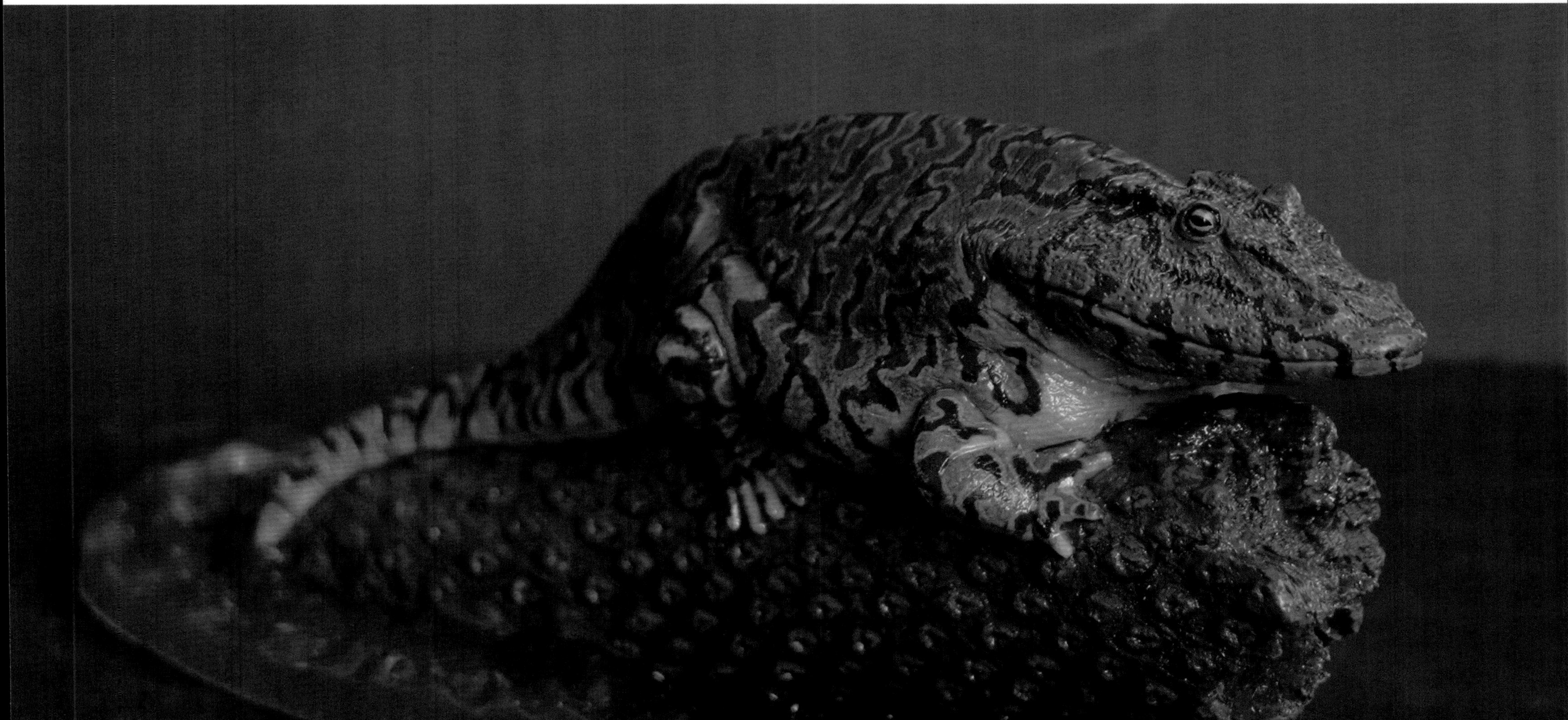

big and a smaller scale would cause them to be molded too indistinctly. On the other hand, many dinosaurs are well known by their gigantism and a larger scale would complicate their production. The Cenozoic scale, however, is comfortable – somewhere in the middle – although the Australopithecines are actually quite small works.

What are the advantages and disadvantages of working in three dimensions?

What are the advantages of the sculpture over the painting and vice versa? Even Michelangelo seems to have thought over that dilemma! I think that the matter is not in the superiority of one over the other, but your personal preference; I prefer to model prehistoric animals. Of course, the main difficulty of modeling is that it is necessary to turn the model to get to one side or the other – it is almost impossible to model the entire figure at any one moment. You also have to be careful not to spoil the parts that you've made ready, which can be difficult when you've fixed the model in position, but then

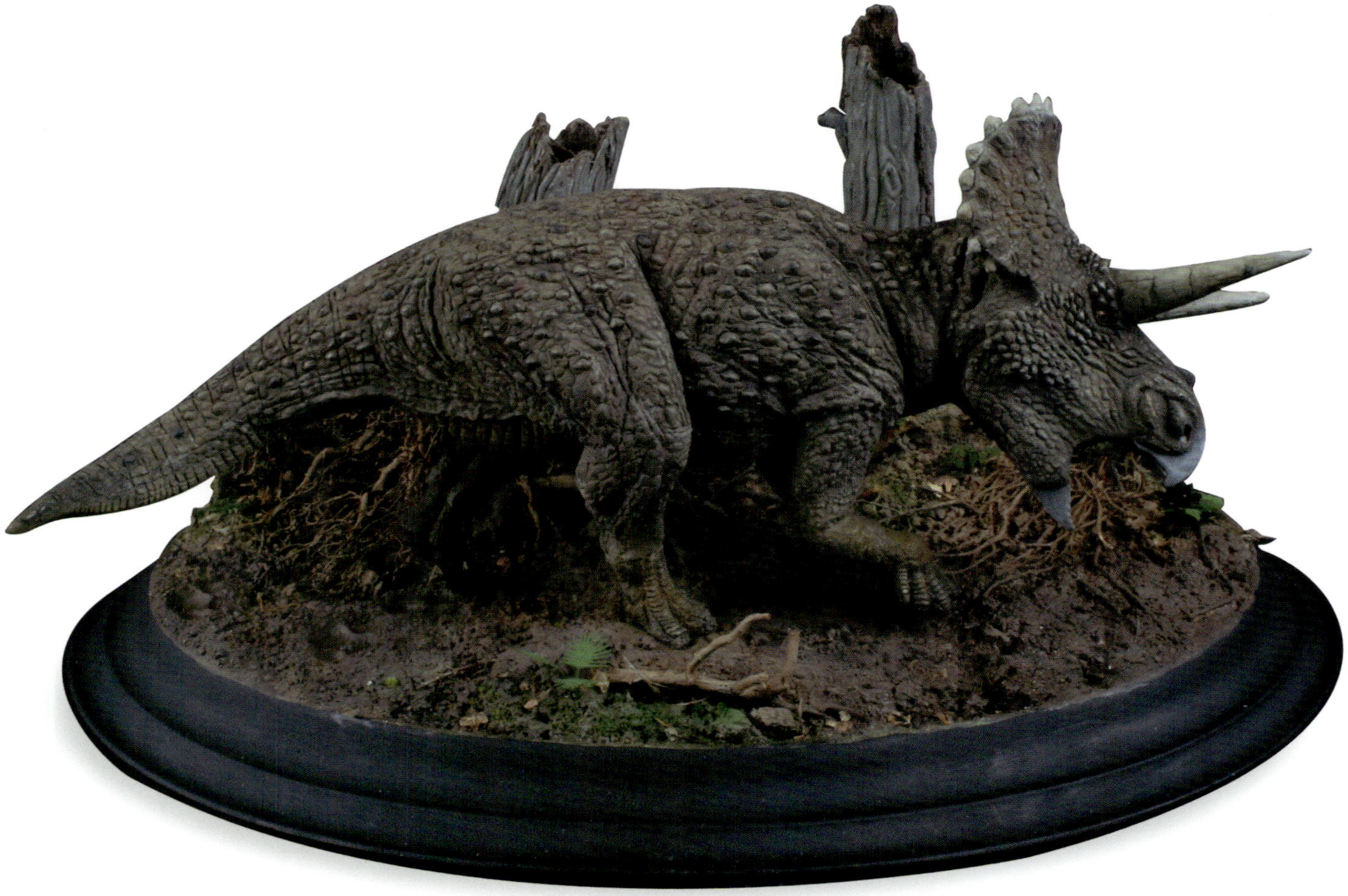

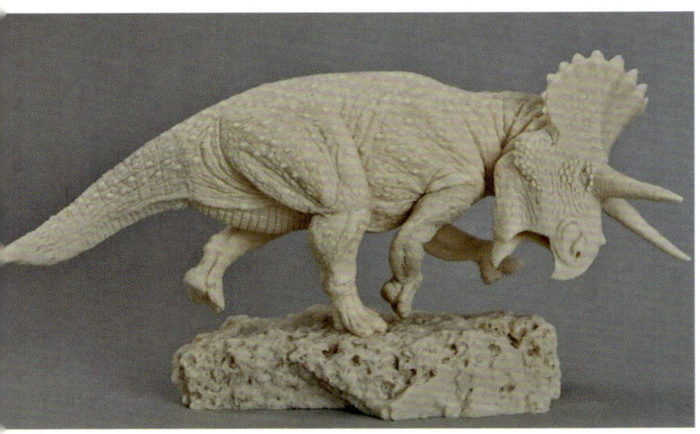

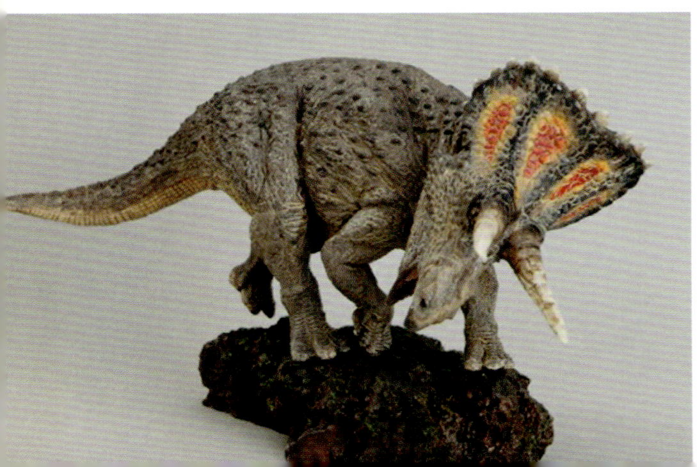

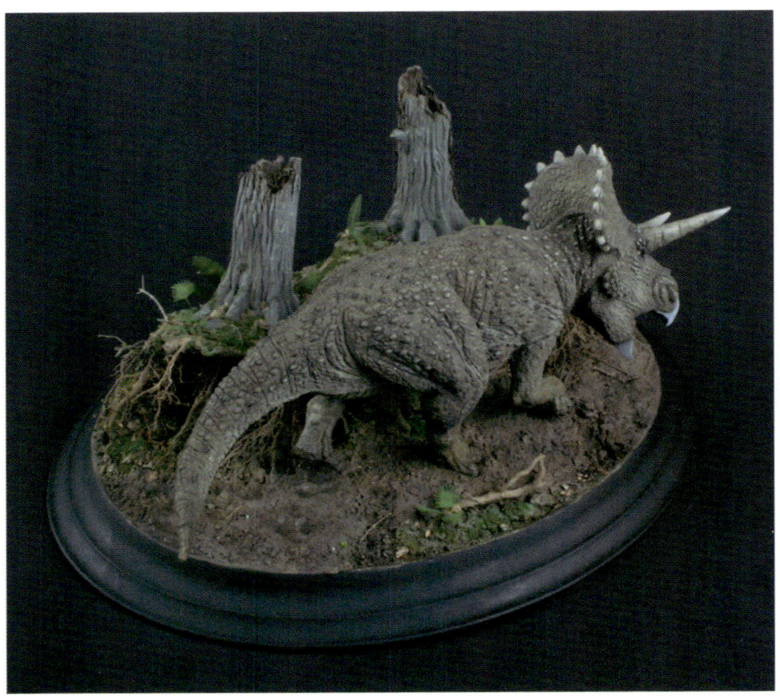

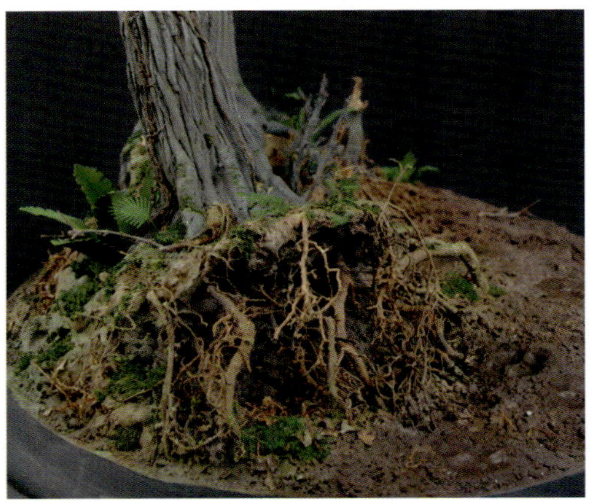

Turanoceratops
Resin, 1:10 scale, 2013
Diorama made by Hans Henrik

(Above) **Base Detail**

EMBOLOTHERIUM

EMBOLOTHERIUM
Genus: *Embolotherium*
Species: Various
Location: Mongolia
Named: 1929
Age: Late Eocene (Priabonian Stages), 37-33mya
Length: 8ft (2.5m) at the shoulder?
Weight: 2.5 tons (2.26 tonnes)
Diet: herbivorous

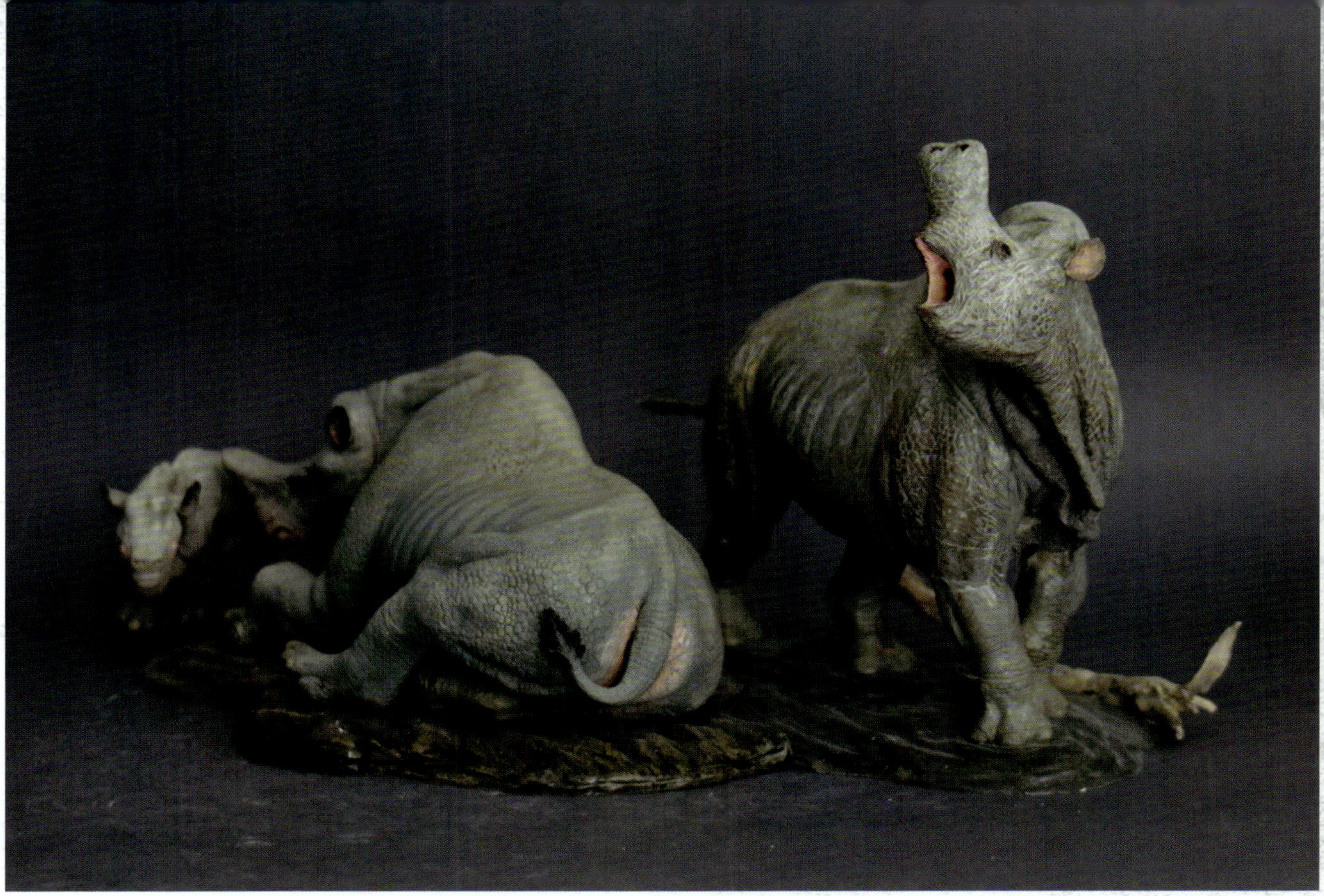

***Embolotherium* Family**
Biresin, Resin, 1:20 scale, 2015

Brontotheres are part of the placental mammal group Perissodactyla, the so-called odd-toed hoofed mammal group that also includes living horses, rhinos and tapirs. By Late Eocene times brontotheres had diversified into several groups, some of which included gigantic big-horned kinds such as *Embolotherium* in eastern Asia and *Megacerops* (long known as *Brontotherium*) in North America.

Embolotherium is known largely from a dozen skulls, a number of lower jaws and some fragmentary post-cranial elements found in the deserts of Outer and Inner Mongolia. Several species have been named, but it's likely that they represent just one or two actual species, the observed differences representing normal inter-species variation. Indeed, our understanding of brontothere species-level diversity has long been afflicted by what's known as 'splitting', individuals belonging to one species being identified as five or more as a result of differences that are actually due to sex, age, health or genetics.

Embolotherium is instantly recognizable thanks to its giant skin-covered hollow nose horn. This widens at its top end and is positioned some distance back from the tip of the snout, a configuration which once meant that *Embolotherium* was reconstructed with a horn shaped like a shovel projecting from mid-way along its face. It now seems that a large amount of cartilage, muscle and skin surrounding the horn base and nose streamlined the horn into the rest of the head and that its giant nasal cavities were confluent with the horn's base. The result is a massive structure that would have looked more like a thickened column than a horn. Exactly where the nostrils were positioned remains unknown; they might have been at the base of the column or even at its top.

Embolotherium does not seem to exhibit sexual dimorphism in horn size or shape. While in North American brontotheres like *Megacerops*, males seemingly had larger horns, and pathologies like damaged ribs indicate that their horns were used in intra-species combat, the fragile nature of *Embolotherium*'s horn would seem to preclude this. Rather, the large nasal cavities and their connection to the hollow horn suggests that the structure acted as a sound generator, the noise resonating in the horn. Rather than physical fighting, *Embolotherium* may have preferred to settle its differences with acoustic battles.

The eyes of *Embolotherium* are located well back on its face and below the base of the horn. This is a rhino-like configuration, and studies of rhinos actually show their eyesight to be pretty good in this configuration. It is also inferred based on various features of the skull that brontotheres had good senses of smell and hearing. Their teeth were simple and adapted for the chewing of soft, leafy plant material.

Little is known of *Embolotherium*'s skeleton, but if we combine what we know with our knowledge of better-understood brontotheres like *Megacerops*, we can assume that the vertebrae in the shoulder region had especially tall bony spines that would have raised the withers and provided huge muscles capable of supporting the large head.

Brontotheres thrived across Europe, Asia and North America throughout the Eocene, even occurring inside the Arctic Circle. However, they were extinct by the start of the following Oligocene epoch, their disappearance seemingly associated with the drying and cooling of the planet that occurred at the end of the Eocene. This triggered a decline in the tropical forested habitats brontotheres were adapted for.

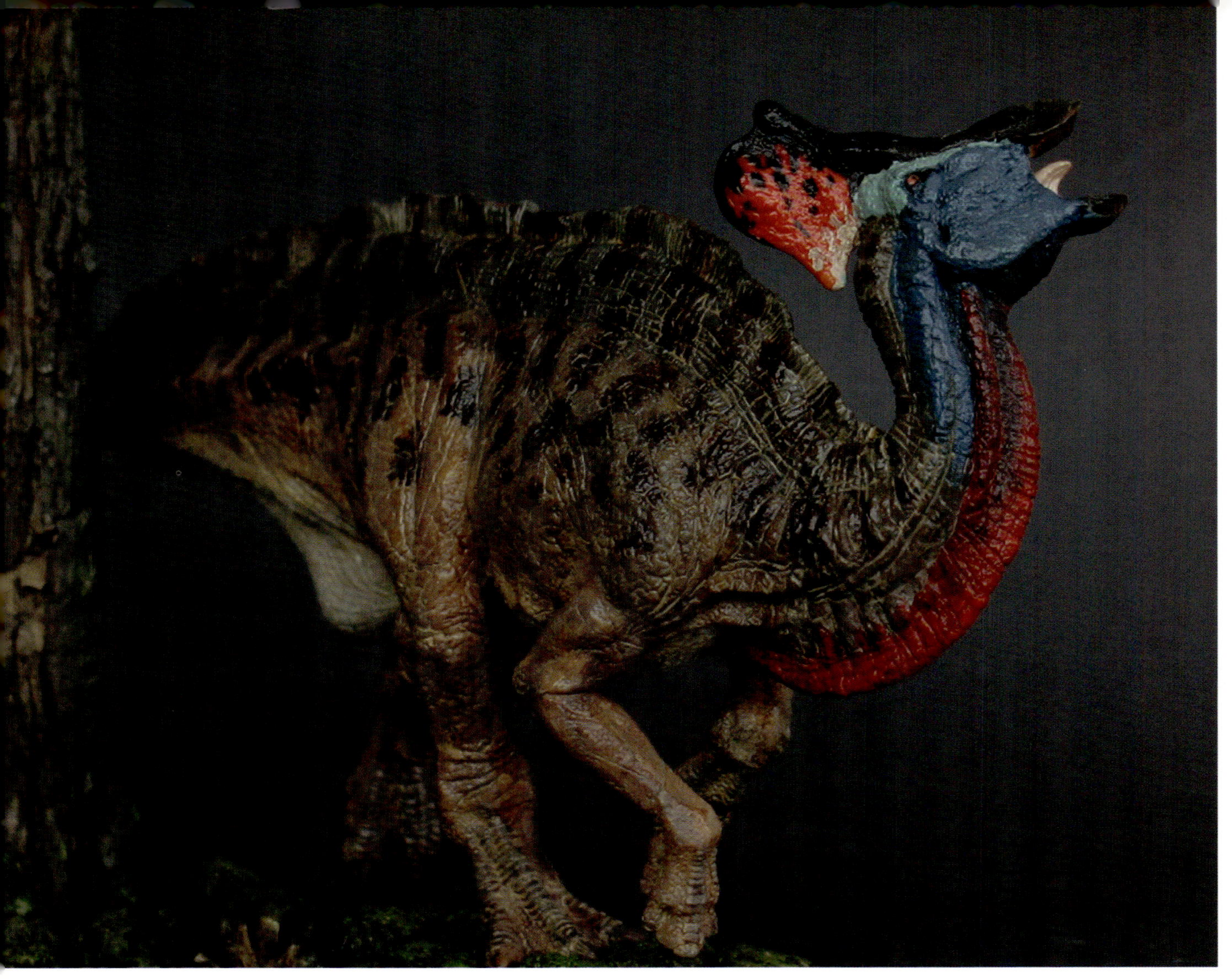

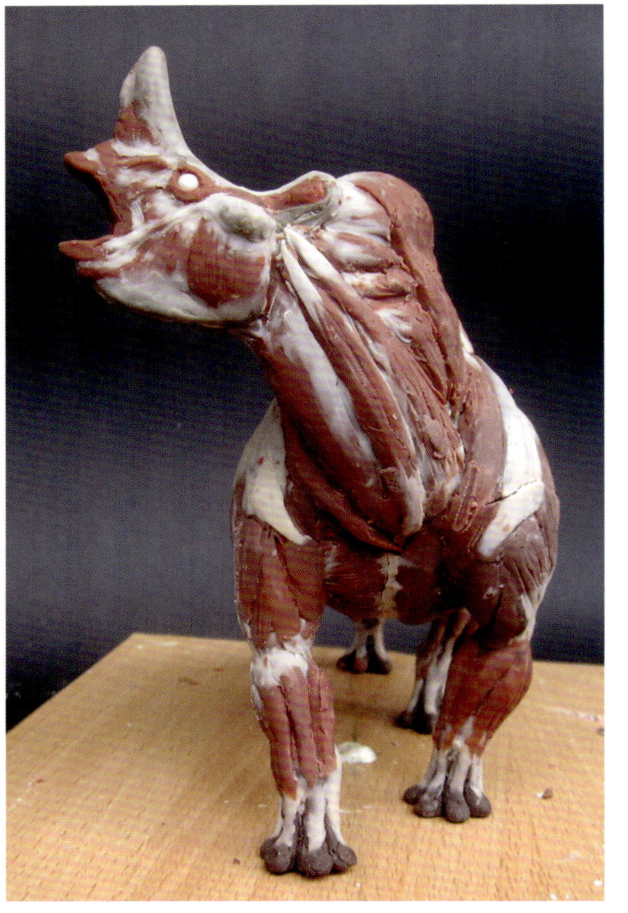

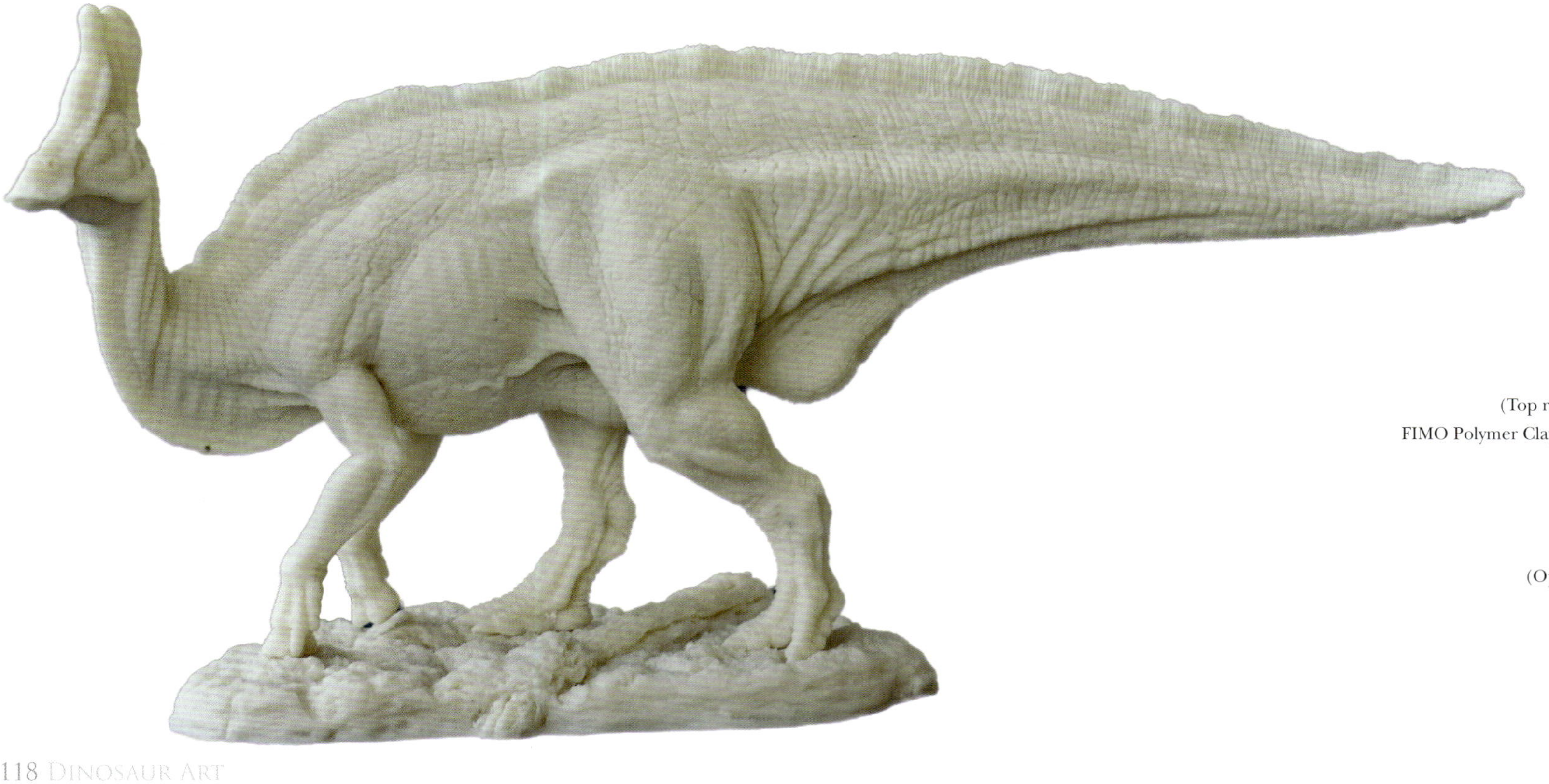

(Top left) ***Olorotitan***
Resin, 1:40 scale, 2013

(Top right) ***Embolotherium* Musculature**
FIMO Polymer Clay, Super Sculpey, 1:20 scale, 2013

(Left) **Unpainted *Olorotitan***
Resin, 1:40 scale, 2013

(Opposite) ***Australopithecus afarensis***
Resin, 1:20 scale, 2014

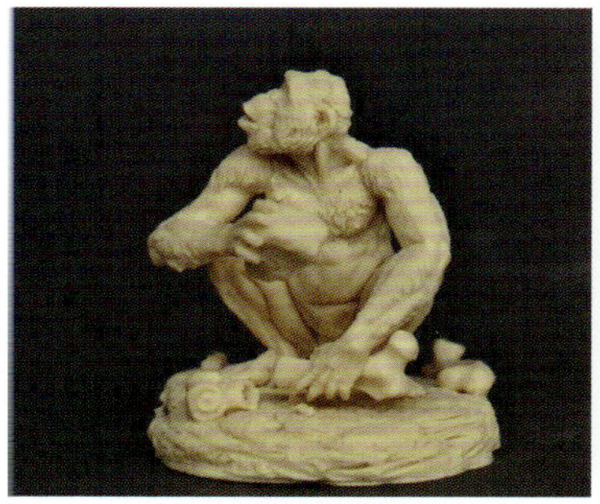

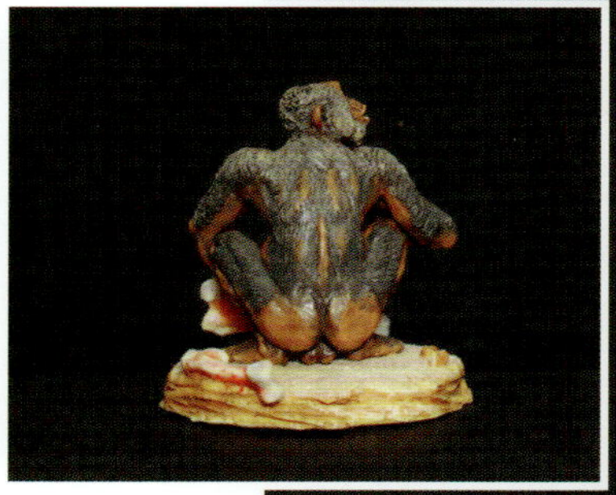

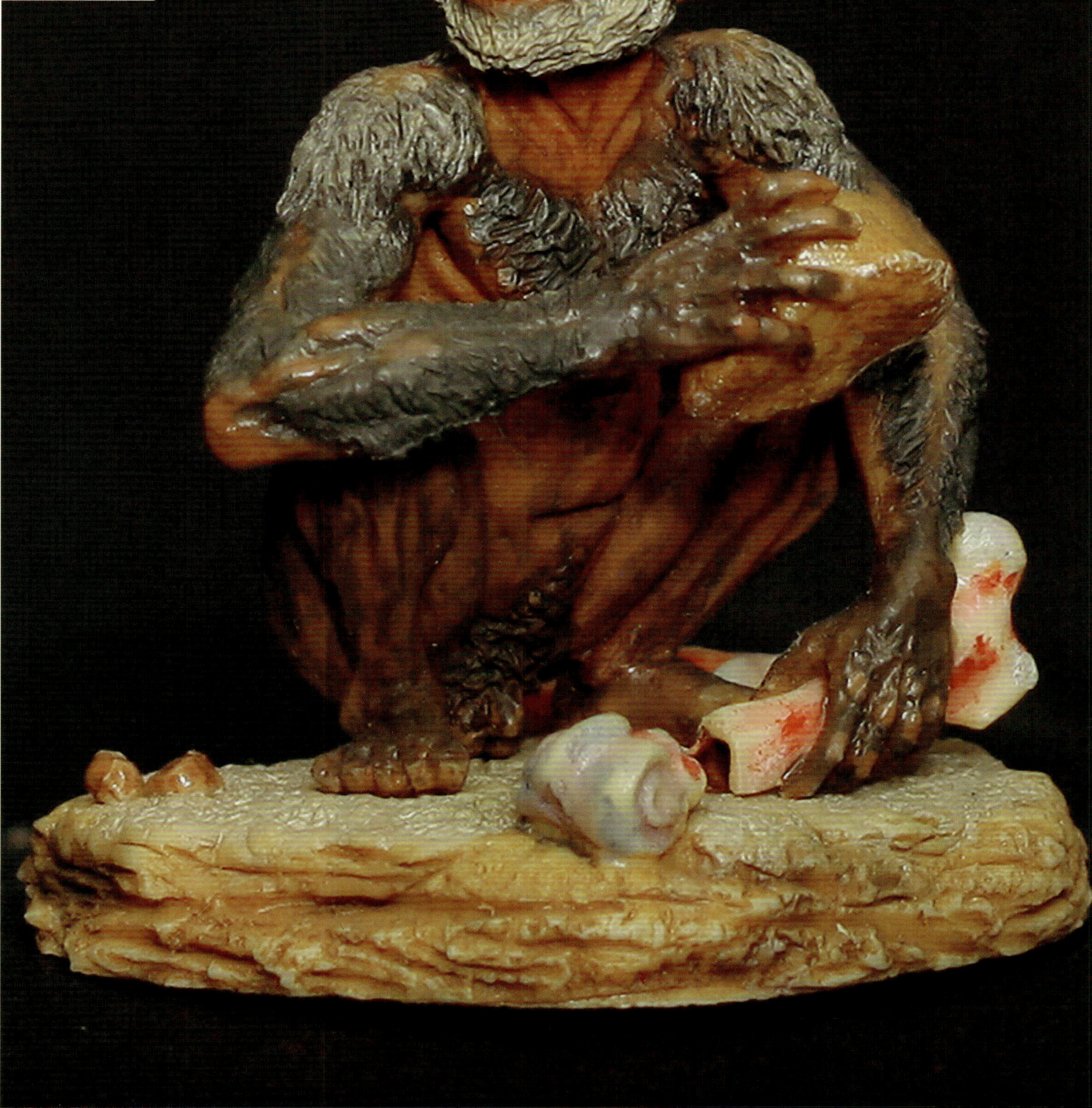

you either have to turn it or to try to get at those more difficult places. There's also the observance of symmetry. While modeling one side you can be as imaginative as you want, but working with the opposite side you have to enforce the strict laws of mirror reflection. However, compared to illustration, modeling doesn't require you to consider the play of light and shade on the figure but, on the other hand, it's easier to position the subject in its native biosphere. Each direction has its own charm.

How do you make your color choices when painting one of your sculptures?

Mostly, I proceed from the existing natural examples. Animals have adopted their colors not by chance but through a long period of selection that adapted them to the conditions in which they live. If we consider that prehistoric animals occupy the same biological levels as modern ones, their coloring must have been similarly appropriate. I believe that large animals do not require bold coloring since, due to their size, they are visible from afar and in general most of the animals try to be invisible. For example, in my opinion, an *Allosaurus* brightly painted like a parrot looks interesting but is not realistic.

Have you ever wanted to attempt a full-size reconstruction?

To model an animal in its natural size has always been my dream. I already have plans for this and I'm currently working on small flying lizards. They are not large, but they are in their full, natural size.

You seem to enjoy placing your animals in dynamic poses – whilst it might make them more interesting, doesn't it make them far more difficult to do?
As a child, I remember I was very inspired by Charles Knight's *Leaping Laelaps* picture. The scene was very vivid, like a fight between two giant cats. I enjoy dynamic poses, the energy and life in them. However, in pursuit of that energy, there is a strong temptation to give the model a very unnatural anatomical form, as Knight did with his dinosaurs. The realism of a reconstruction has to prevail over its dynamism, which may not be the greatest difficulty, but should always be the first one.

The real difficulty is the correct approach to the muscles in motion. You need to try to imagine what muscles are bulging out of where on the animal's structure and this can be especially difficult to model on an animal with no modern analogues. Luckily, the anatomy of terrestrial vertebrates is generally broadly similar, so if you think about any new position, it can be enough to look through images of other animals in a similar motion.

Have you always been interested in prehistoric animals? Was it dinosaurs in particular that triggered that interest?
I have been interested in prehistoric animals since the age of five. Naturally these were dinosaurs. Even at that age I could recognize them by name. And like Alan Grant in *Jurassic Park*, Triceratops was my favorite! But I became really passionate at about the age of 10.

(Top right) ***Inostrancevia* vs *Scutosaurus***
Resin, 1:10 scale, 2012

(Right) ***Tarbosaurus* vs *Tarchia***
Resin, 1:40 scale, 2012

(Opposite) ***Dimetrodon limbatus* vs *Ophiacodon retroversus*, Unfinished**
Birezin, 1:10 scale, 2015

Do you still produce artwork in two dimensions?
At first, as a professional artist, I expressed my view of the prehistoric world only in painting. Now, however, I've completely switched to the models. But sometimes I still want to paint.
Do you use any digital software to help with your work?
Before I start to model, I always generate it on my computer. Sometimes I have to collect a complete skeleton from separate pieces in the right size for me. And if there is a skull in three views, I can, as I mentioned before, make a primitive 3D model on the computer, which can then be printed. However, on the whole, everything is done with my hands and the future composition is based not on the screen, but in my head.

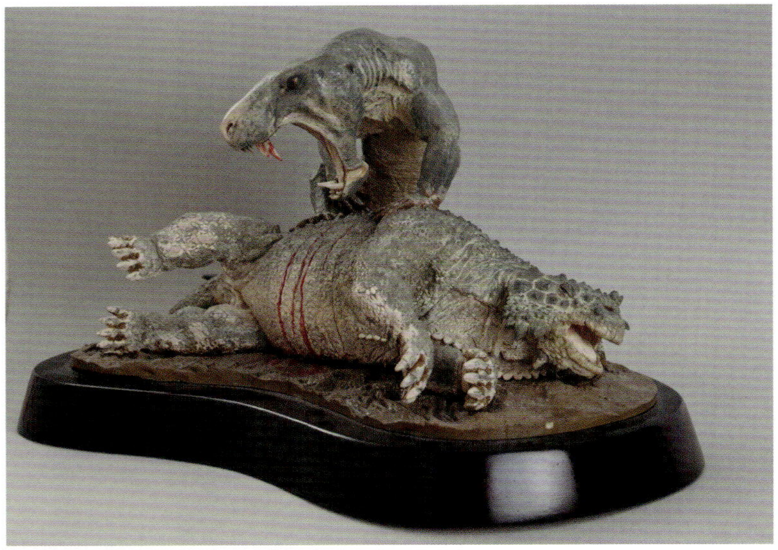

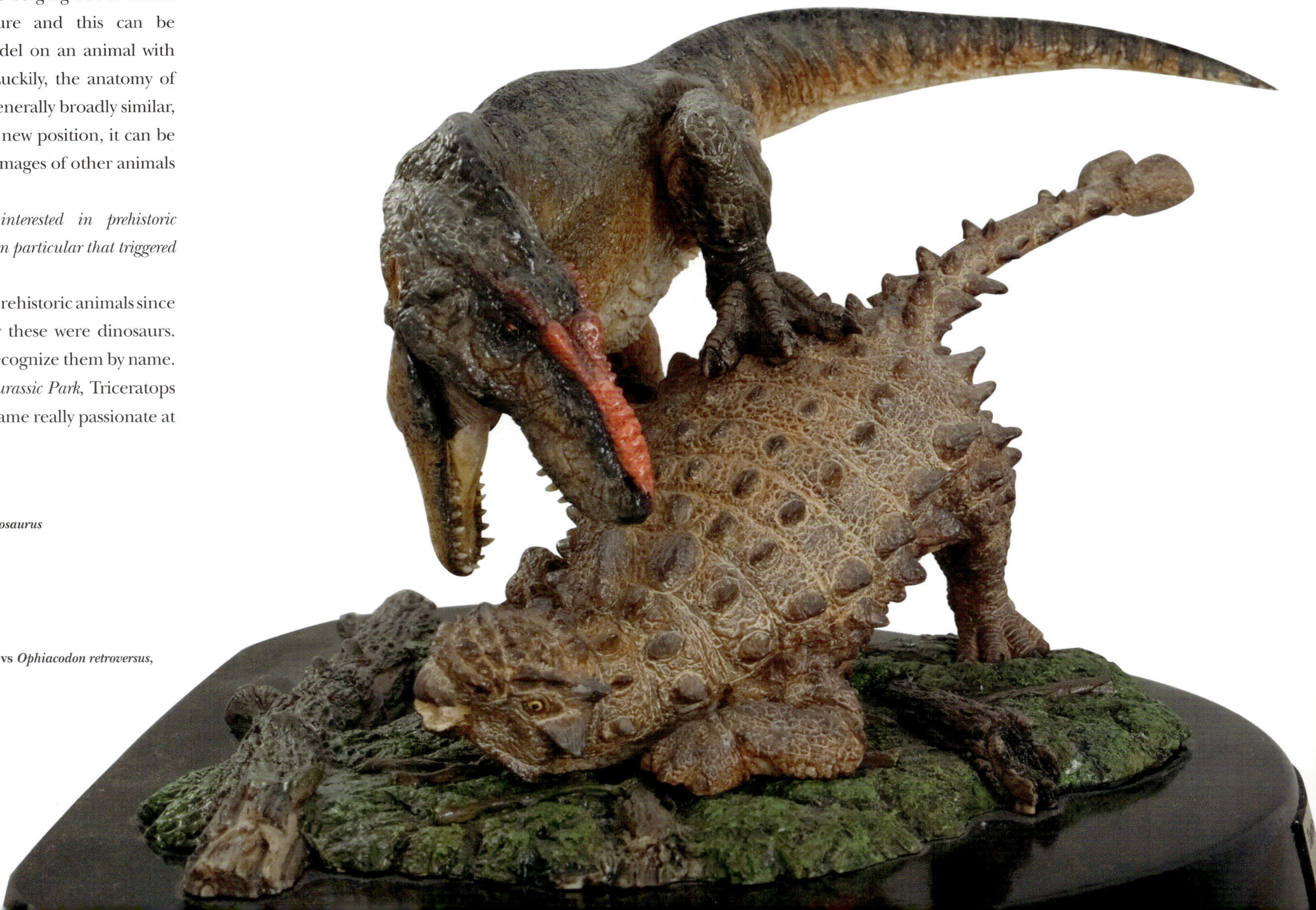

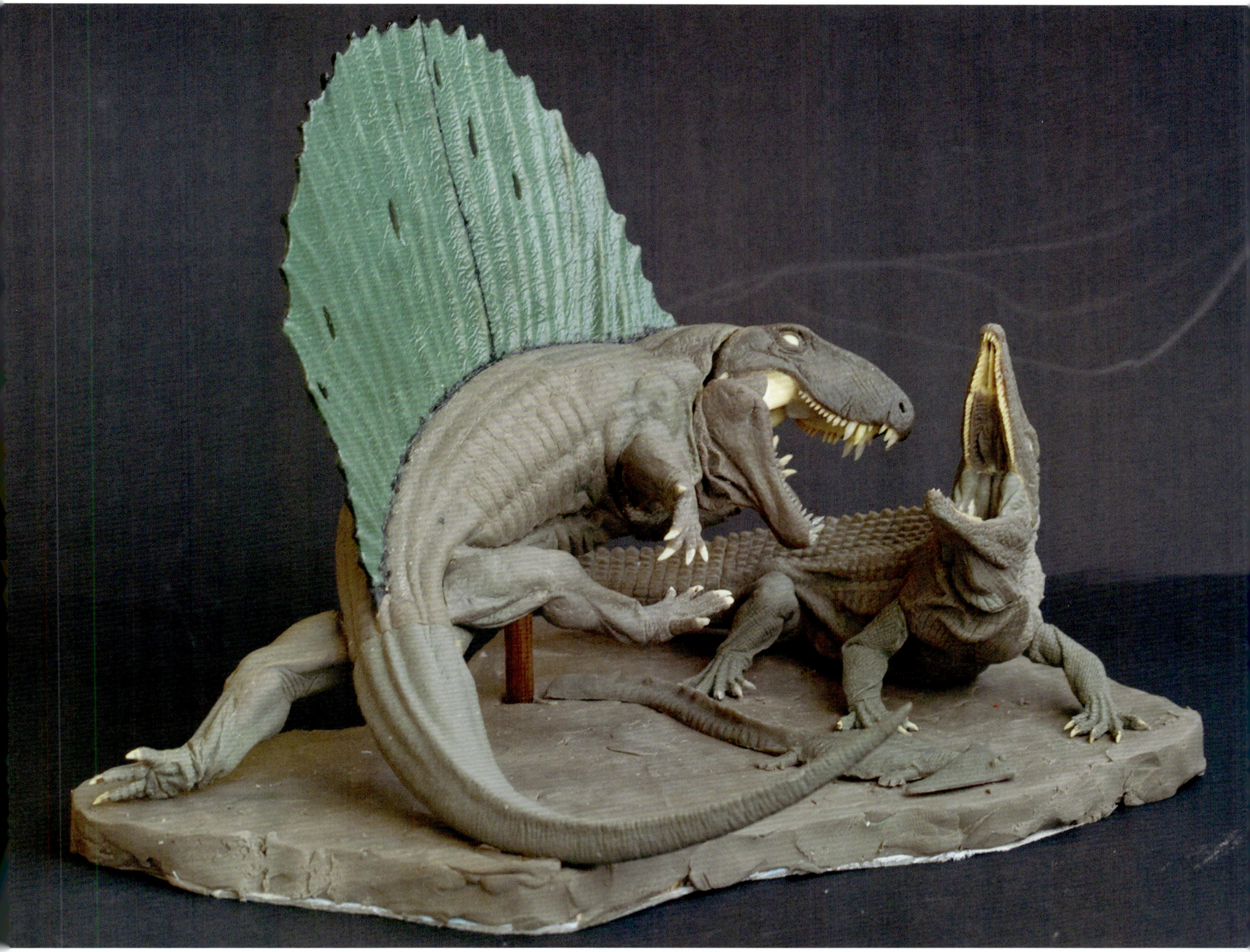

TOM BJÖRKLUND

FINLAND

Born in 1963, Tom grew up in a small industrial town in eastern Finland (the "lake district", not to be confused with the region of the same name in the UK!), where he spent much of his time pursuing the local wildlife. He began his formal artistic career studying Art History and Applied Arts, planning to combine both theoretical and practical skills (especially carpentry, in the case of the latter) and become a conservator. However, he chose to invest his energies into becoming a full-time artist, continuing his studies at Svenska konstskolan i Nykarleby, a Swedish-speaking art school on the west coast of Finland. After graduating, his career initially relied on private commissions; he also began to exhibit his work and accept illustration assignments. Since then, his art has appeared in a number of natural history and children's books, and magazines such as *Suomen Luonto* ("Nature of Finland"). He has contributed to exhibitions at the Finnish Museum of Natural History and the Moesgaard Museum in Aarhus, Denmark, and illustrated guideposts for Finland's National Board of Antiquities. Together with author Seppo Vuokko, he also received the State Award for Public Information (2010) for the book *Mammutin Aika* ("The Age of the Mammoth").

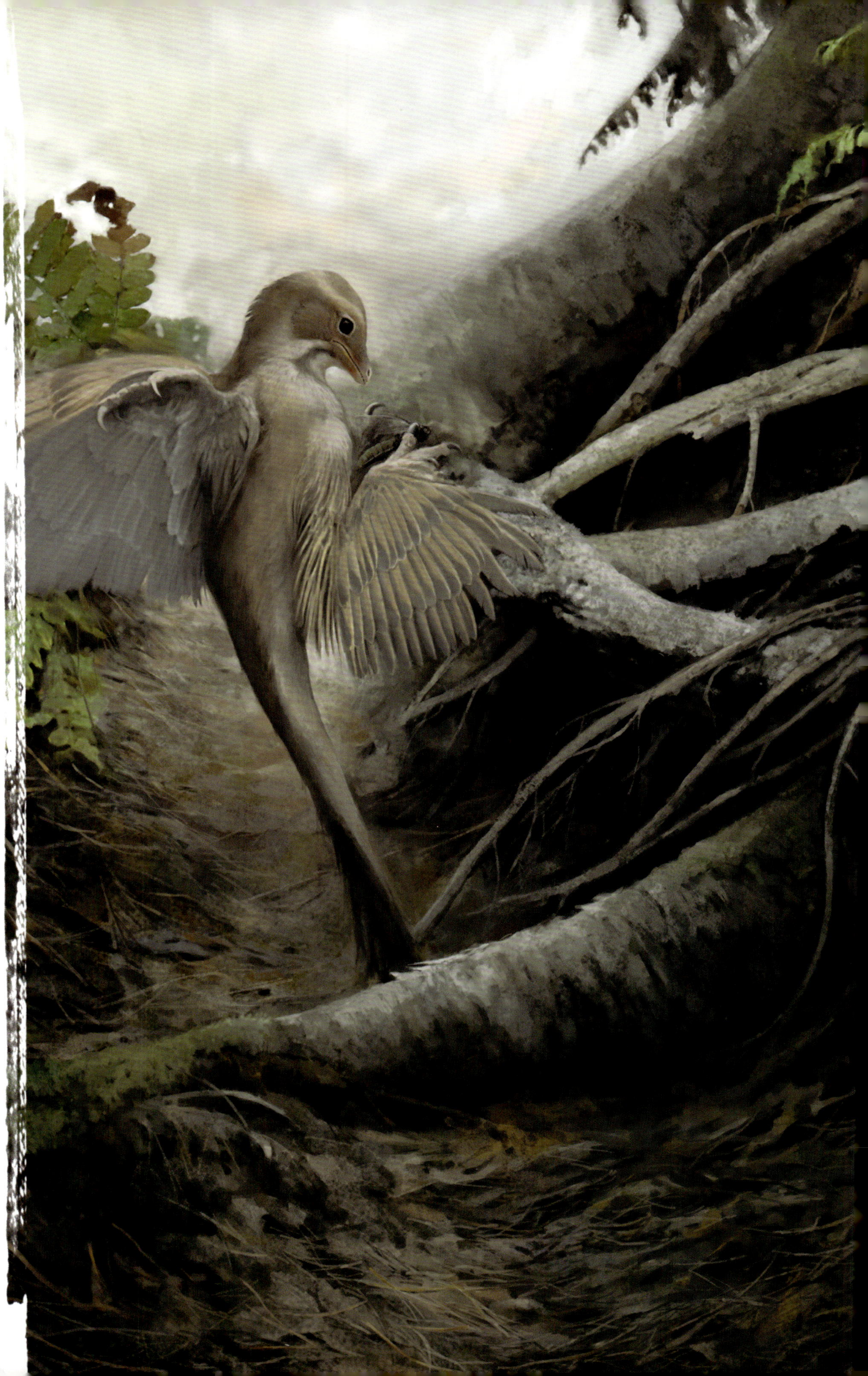

Four-Winged Paravian Dinosaurs
Digital, 2015

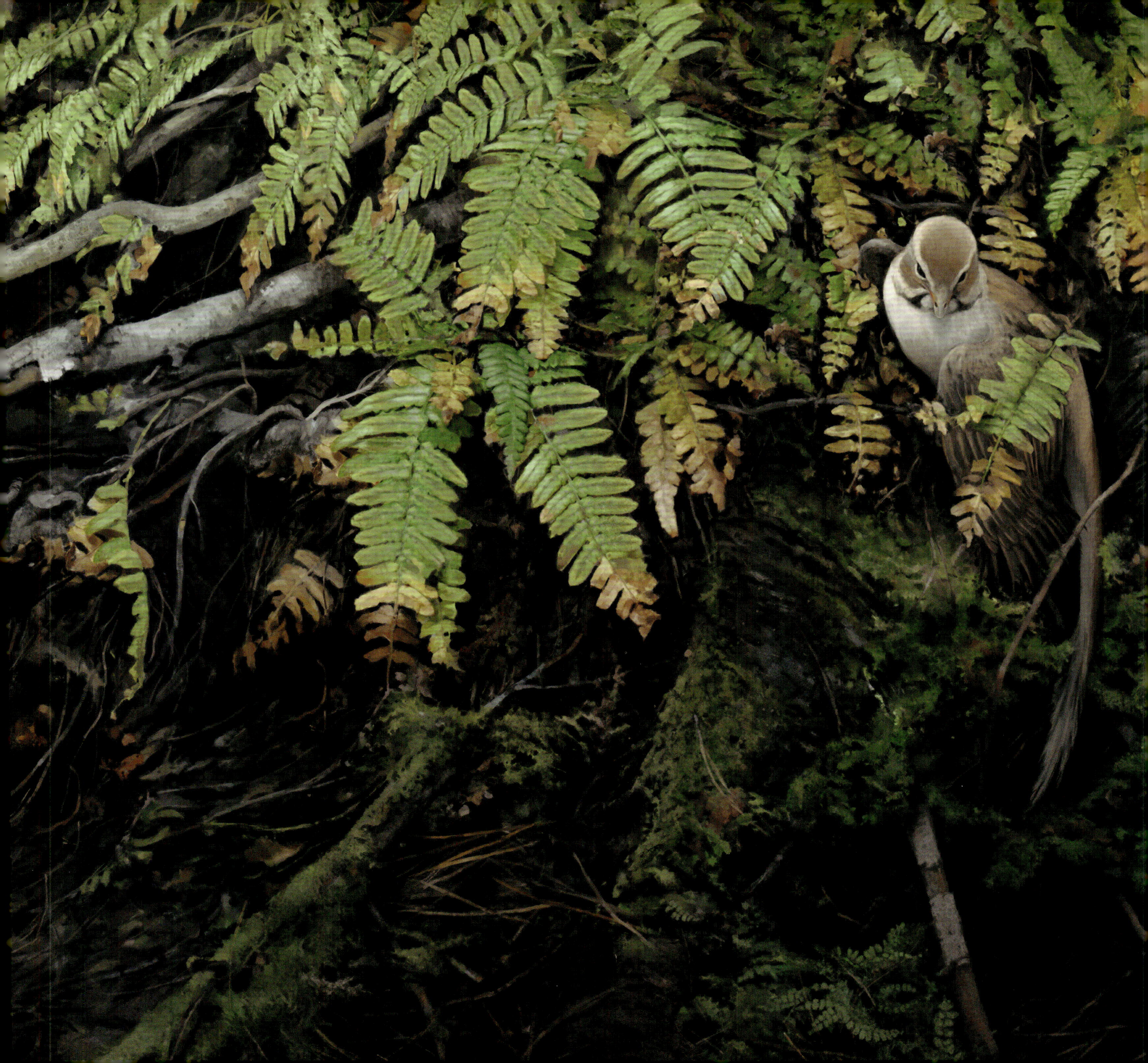

When did you realize that you had a talent for art?
I'm not sure that's something I have realized yet – or whether or not I actually have a particular talent for it... But there must have been a moment when I realized that this was what I wanted to do; that I simply wasn't capable of doing anything else. This, I believe, happened quite early in life. I have had my doubts, though, along the way, and have tried to find more secure ways to make a living, but somehow it hasn't worked out so well. So, I feel that rather than thinking of my possible talent, I have just followed a path I haven't been able to turn away from.

What are your artistic influences?
Of course I look a lot at other artists' work and I'm very interested in trying out various kinds of techniques and ways of expression in order to develop my own style. Learning never ends and art, like everything else, is not a result of an individual's work: it's cumulative knowledge and culture gathered and evolved over hundreds of generations.

Naturally, I get inspired by art I feel I can learn from. But it isn't only about how to use my brushes or how to handle colors; it's about the whole artistic process. Technical mastery is, of course, admirable, but it's only superficial. The real meaning and importance of art comes from the subject matter, the message, the story that gives the images life, that makes us think. I could say that many artists from the latter half of the nineteenth century have affected my views on painting in many ways; Bruno Liljefors is one of the greatest wildlife artists ever, in my opinion. But I am even more inspired by works of contemporary artists like Tony Gragg, Gerhard Richter and Anish Kapoor (and many more, including far less renowned artists). Not because their style would be something I'm striving towards, but because of the whole creative process, power of expression and the impact of their work on the field of art, and on society.

Microraptor gui
Digital, 2016

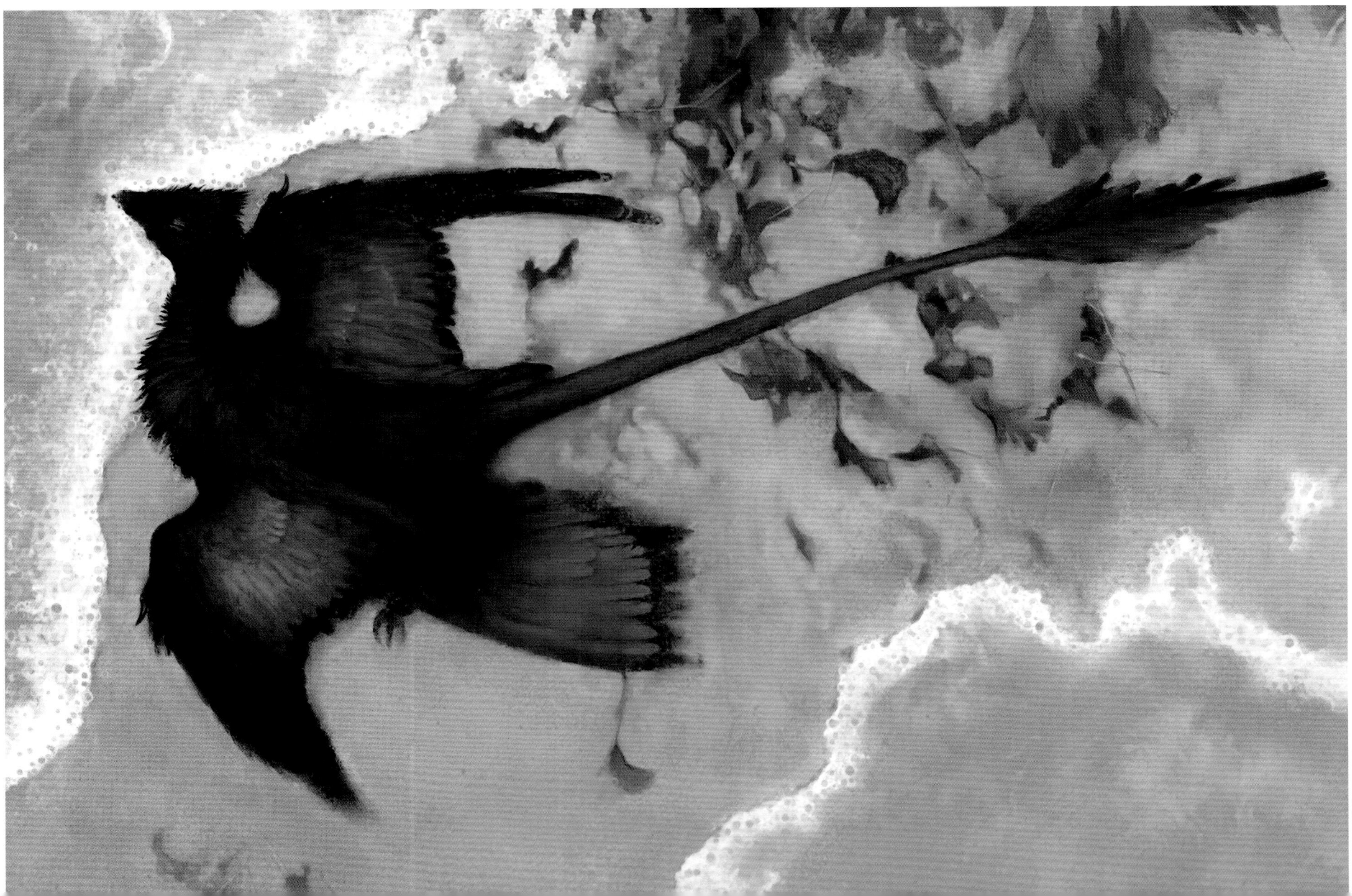

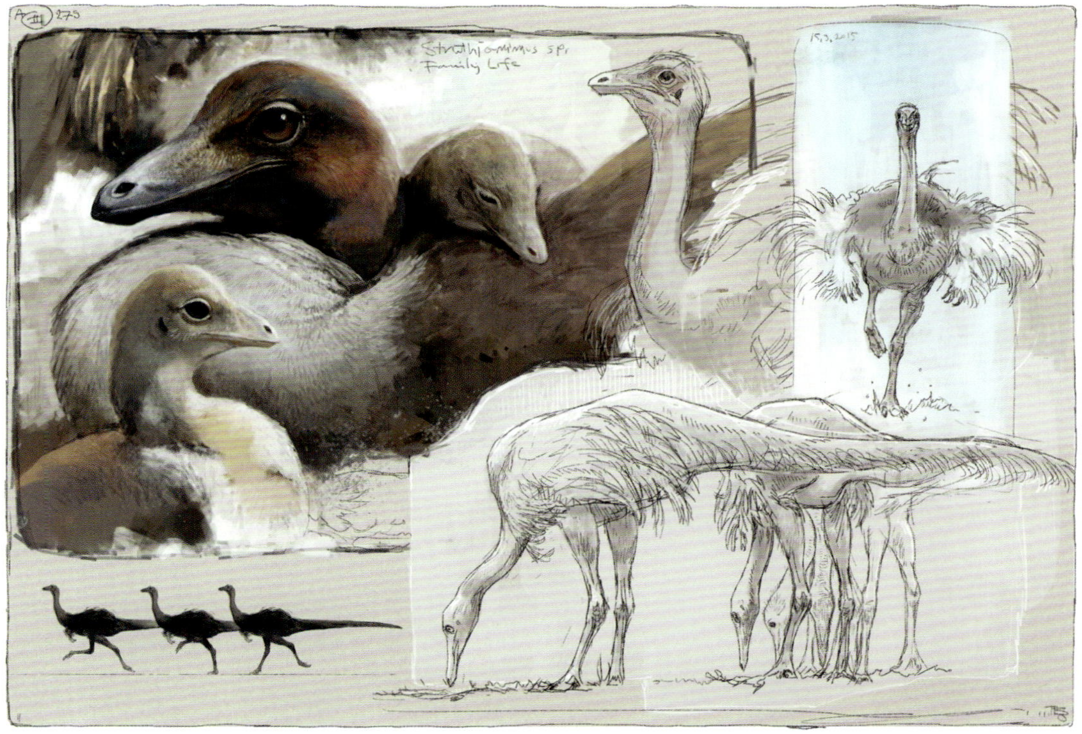

(Left) ***Struthiomimus* Family**
Digital, 2015

(Below) ***Troodontids***
Digital, 2016

Your color palette is muted, with lots of neutrals; it's particularly noticeable in the avian species and goes against trend towards brightly colored plumage. What is behind your color choices?

The muted palette has become my trademark to such a degree that my audience expects it from me. My color choices could be explained by the environment I live in. Although a Finnish summer is as green as can be, and the sharp blue of the sky is reflected in the sea and the tens of thousands of lakes which characterize much of the country, it lasts only for a few months, and for most of the year the landscape is dominated by delicate shades of greys and browns. In winter the palette is often cut down to black and white. When illustrating dinosaurs, I tend to lean towards the same palette. Although the iridescent black plumage of the *Microraptor*, for example, is based on the latest scientific studies, I do tend to use a rather

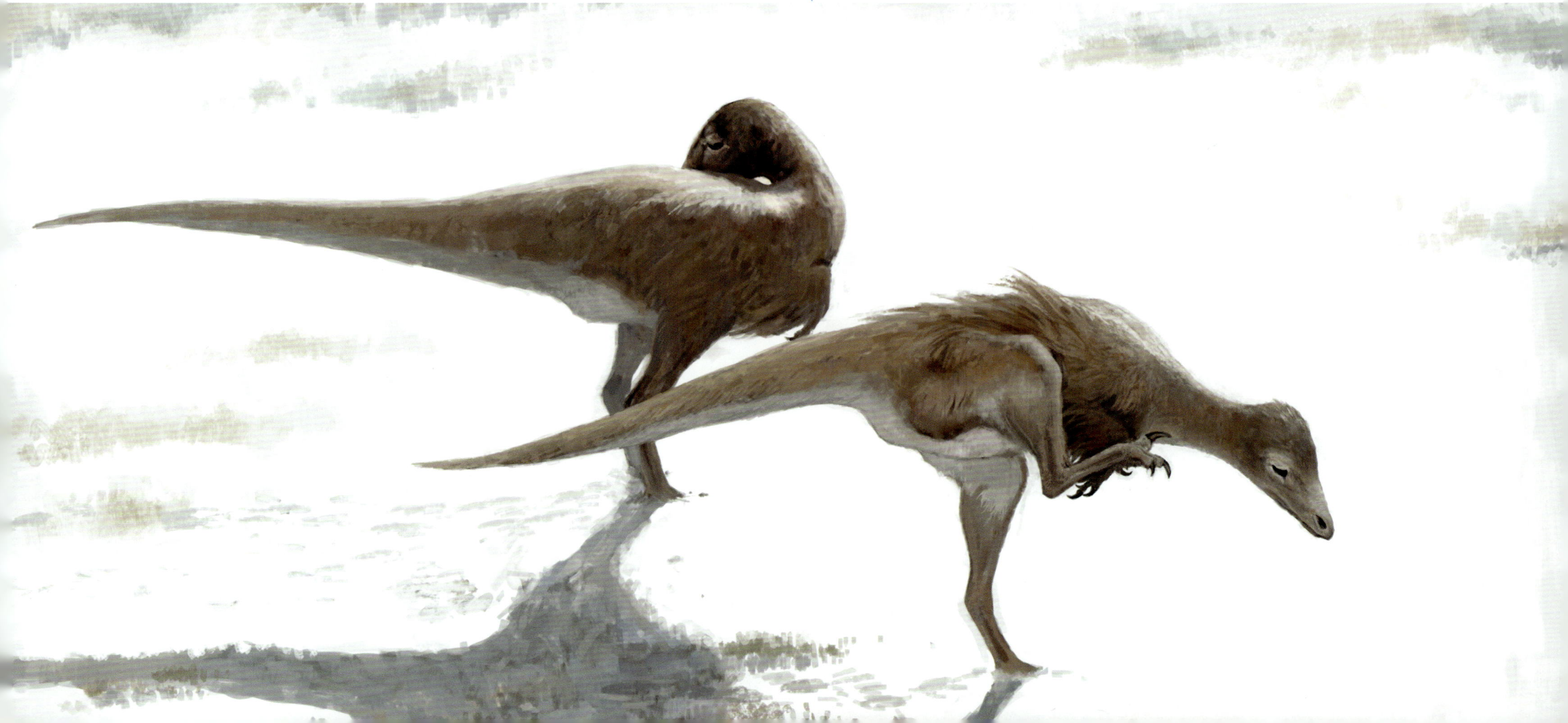

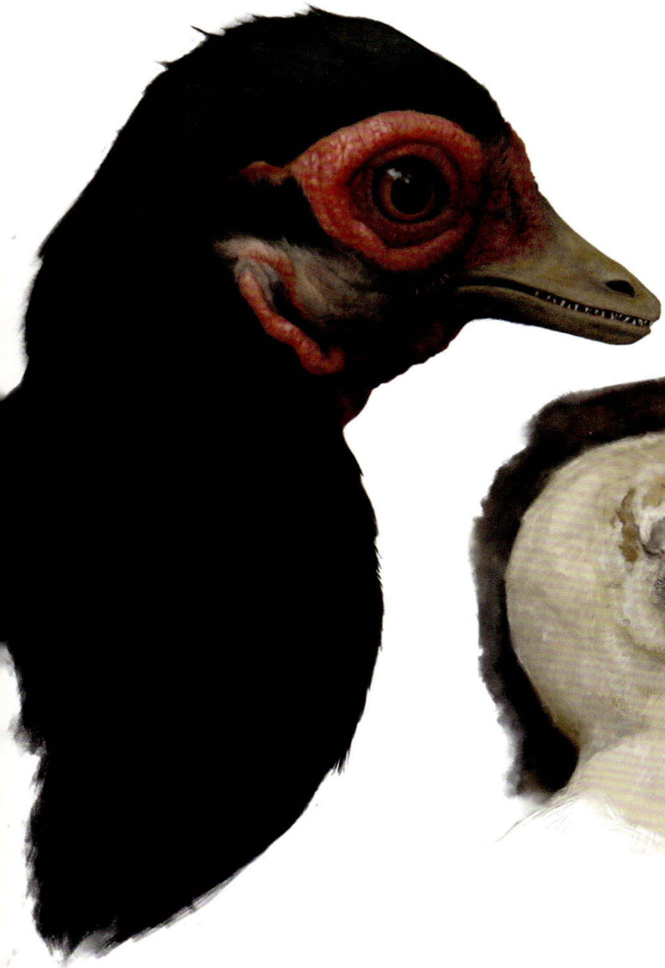

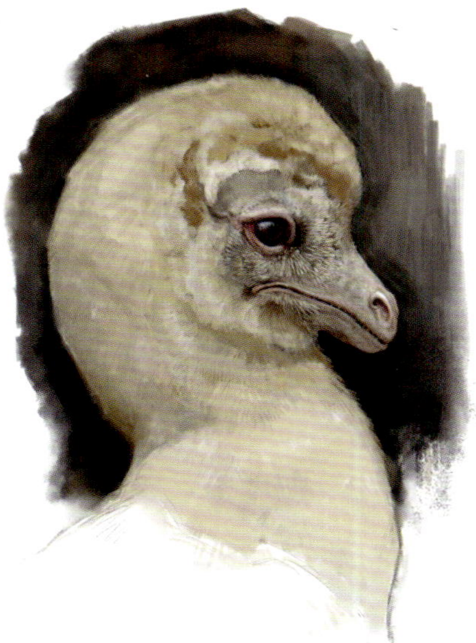

small supply of colors even for other dinosaurs. It's partly because of my personal references when it comes to color choices, but I also like to concentrate more on the anatomy of the animals, which we know more about than we do of their possible coloration. But that's just me; I don't mind at all that other paleoartists often use bright colors in their interpretations.

Is there something special about birds? You seem to have a particular affinity with them.

I haven't actually been a bird artist for very long, or wildlife artist in general for that matter. I kept art and my interest in nature apart for a long time, and didn't even realize that there was a distinct genre of bird art and I certainly didn't know how big a thing it was. I was watching birds on my own outside the birdwatching community and it could have stayed that way for ever if it hadn't been for a keen birdwatcher who got curious about this guy sitting at a wetland area sketching waterfowl (at that time I sketched birds only occasionally, in the same way as any other motif I found interesting).

(Above left) ***Archaeopteryx* Study**
Digital, 2014

(Above right) **Juvenile Theropod Study**
Digital, 2016

(Right) **Territorial Call**
Digital, 2015

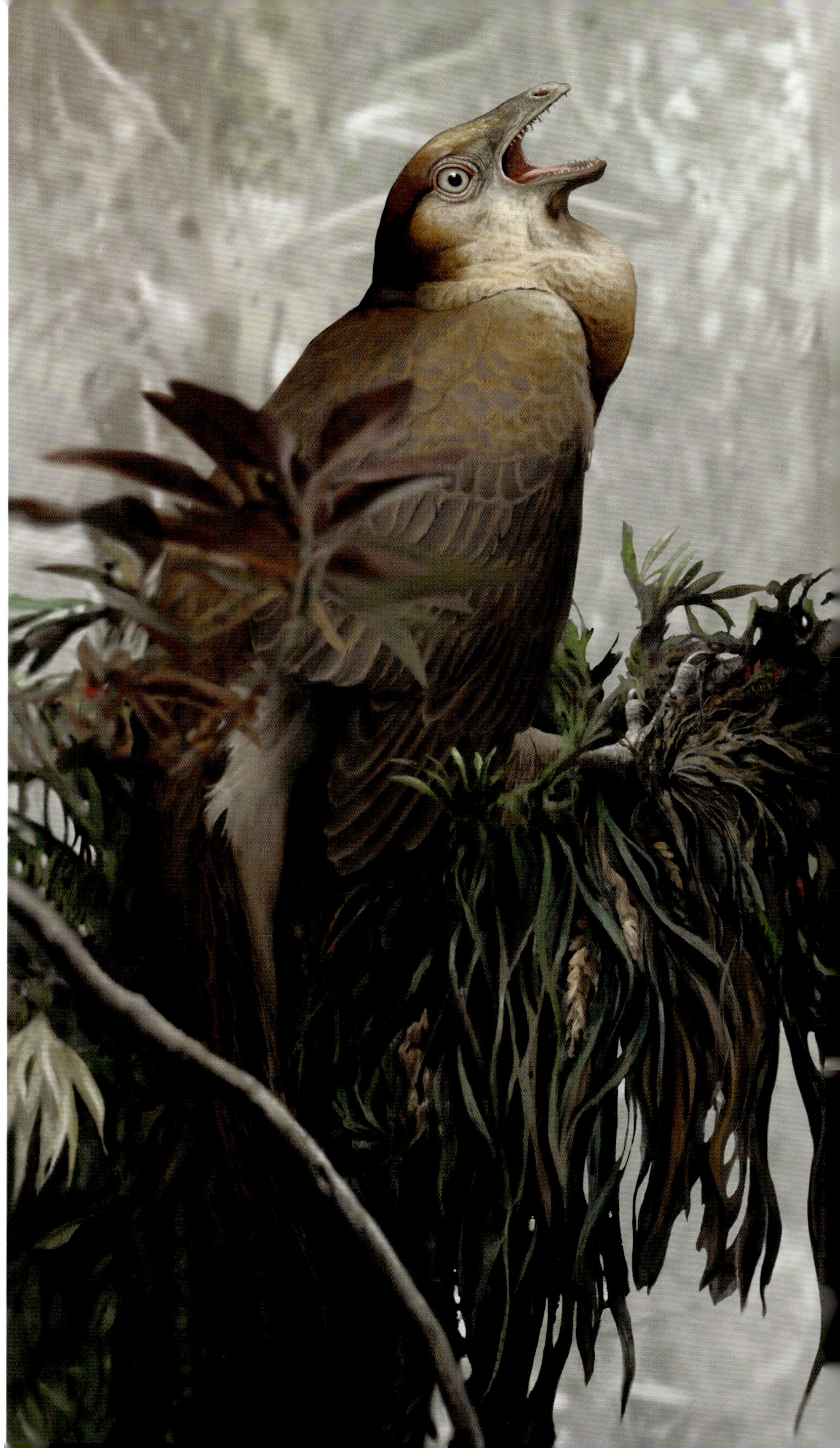

HOMOTHERIUM
Genus: *Homotherium*
Species: Various
Age: Early Pliocene to Late Pleistocene; 4mya to 17,000 years ago
Height: 1.1m (3.6ft) at the shoulder
Weight: 190kg (420lbs)

Homotherium is one of the best understood, most successful and most geographically widespread of sabertooths, the extinct cat group technically known as Machairodontinae. Sabertooths vary substantially in skull shape, tooth anatomy, body size and proportions, and experts have recognised several subgroups within this assemblage. *Homotherium* is a Homotherini, one of the so-called 'scimitar-toothed' sabertooths.

Homotherium fossils are known from Europe, Africa, Asia and both North and South America. A large number of species have been named, mostly defined by variations in the upper canines and skull. *Homotherium* specimens discovered in Europe and Asia are grouped within the species *H. latidens*; *H. ethiopicum* and *H. hadarensis* are known from Africa; *H. serum* is the North American species; while *H. venezuelensis* is, as the name suggests, known from South America. A number of other species have been named, but they are mostly represented by fragmentary remains and there is some uncertainty as to whether they can be distinguished from those known from better material.

Homotherium was similar in size to an adult male lion, but had a somewhat different build. It was more lightweight, its forelimbs were longer but more powerful, while its back sloped downward to the shorter back legs and short tail. The sloping back was most pronounced in *H. serum* and would have given it a hyena-like appearance. The forelimbs also sported a very large dew claw, but the other claws were shorter and blunter, and less retractable, than is usually the case in cats.

The neck was long and flexible, offering a wider range of movement than in modern cats. The skull was long and large with protruding incisors, shearing, blade-like carnassials and elongate, blade-like upper canines. *Homotherium* is often said to have especially compressed 'scimitar-like' upper canines that are not as long as those of other sabertooths, like the famous *Smilodon*. This is certainly true of the American species *H. serum*. However, at least some species have longer upper canines that are of a form more typical for sabertooths as a whole. Later species also possess enlarged orbits and an enlarged visual cortex in the brain, suggesting excellent vision.

Combined, the long forelimbs, sloping back, shorter hindlimbs, and blunt claws suggest an ability to run over long distances (quite different from *Smilodon*, seemingly better suited to be a sprinting ambush predator). After running down its prey, *Homotherium* would presumably use its powerful forelimbs and large dew claws to pin the struggling victim, while the especially mobile neck would allow the precise positioning of the head as the killing bite was delivered. The nature of these adaptations suggest a bite to the throat, the canines puncturing the veins and arteries around the windpipe of its prey. The projecting incisors may have been used to pluck or scrape flesh from the kill, thereby avoiding damage to the canines. The scissor-like carnassials could similarly have sheared meat from bone. It seems that *Homotherium* was relatively poor at processing bone and would have left the skeletal parts of a carcass behind.

Our ideas on prey choice in *Homotherium* are speculative. However, some especially intriguing possibilities are raised by the fossils of Friesenhahn Cave in Texas. Here, the remains of 30 *H. serum* individuals – representing both adults and cubs – were found alongside the remains (mostly teeth) of several young (c.2 years old) mammoths. Several dire wolves (*Canis dirus*) were also present. The implication, circumstantial as it is, is that Friesenhahn Cave was a homothere den where adults brought body parts of young mammoths to their cubs. Lions will kill elephants of around 2-4 years old, but elephant killing is such an ordeal for lions that it involves both large pride size and a hunt time of some hours.

Homotherium, it seems, was far better equipped as an elephant-killer. Its long teeth, unusual proportions and dextrous forelimbs probably made it better able to grab, subdue and dismember young mammoths, the remarkable teeth presumably making it easier for it to puncture the mammoth's tough hide and reach the vital organs. The large eyes also suggest that *Homotherium* used darkness to its advantage: perhaps it was a nocturnal hunter that was able to remain ecologically separated from *Smilodon*, its Ice Age relative and neighbor.

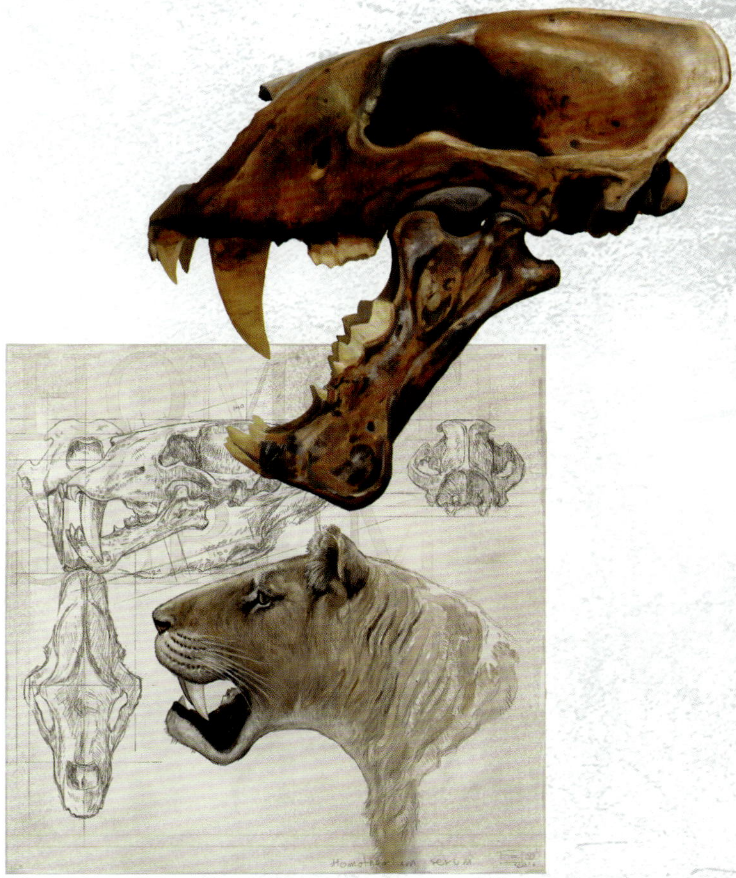

***Homotherium serum* Study**
Pencils, Gouache, Digital, 2000-2016

The birdwatcher was Arto Juvonen, now an internationally recognized and award-winning bird photographer. His strong opinion was that, since I was an artist and a birdwatcher, I naturally should be painting birds. This happened in the early nineties in the midst of the economic depression – not a very good period of time for an aspiring artist. However, when, after a slow start and various illustration jobs, I finally gave my first exhibition, I sold almost everything within the first hour of the exhibition and I understood that it could be possible to make a living painting birds. Birds are definitely works of art themselves, literally, making captivating subjects for sketches and studies. On the other hand their interactions with their environment and other species make excellent motifs for more complicated compositions.

You've done paintings of modern birds which you've "translated" into Mesozoic versions. Can you talk about your process of transforming one into the other?

Since I have loads of bird paintings lying around, I felt it practical to start using them as references for avian theropods, or any theropods, or even to repaint them, placing the scenes in Mesozoic settings. I don't use this method regularly, and not very seriously. I prefer not to repeat myself. But it's kind of fun to think how it would look if evolution had taken a slightly different direction or if another group of avian theropods would have survived the disaster at the end of the Cretaceous period. It's a bit dangerous, though, to draw parallels between modern birds and the feathered avian and non-avian creatures of the Mesozoic. They were different kinds of animals, after all.

Where do you get inspiration for your depiction of Ice Age peoples? Do they have modern counterparts?

When I depict people from the Pleistocene and the early Holocene I try to balance between two goals. On the one hand, humans during those ancient times probably would appear quite peculiar to us, both in terms of their look and

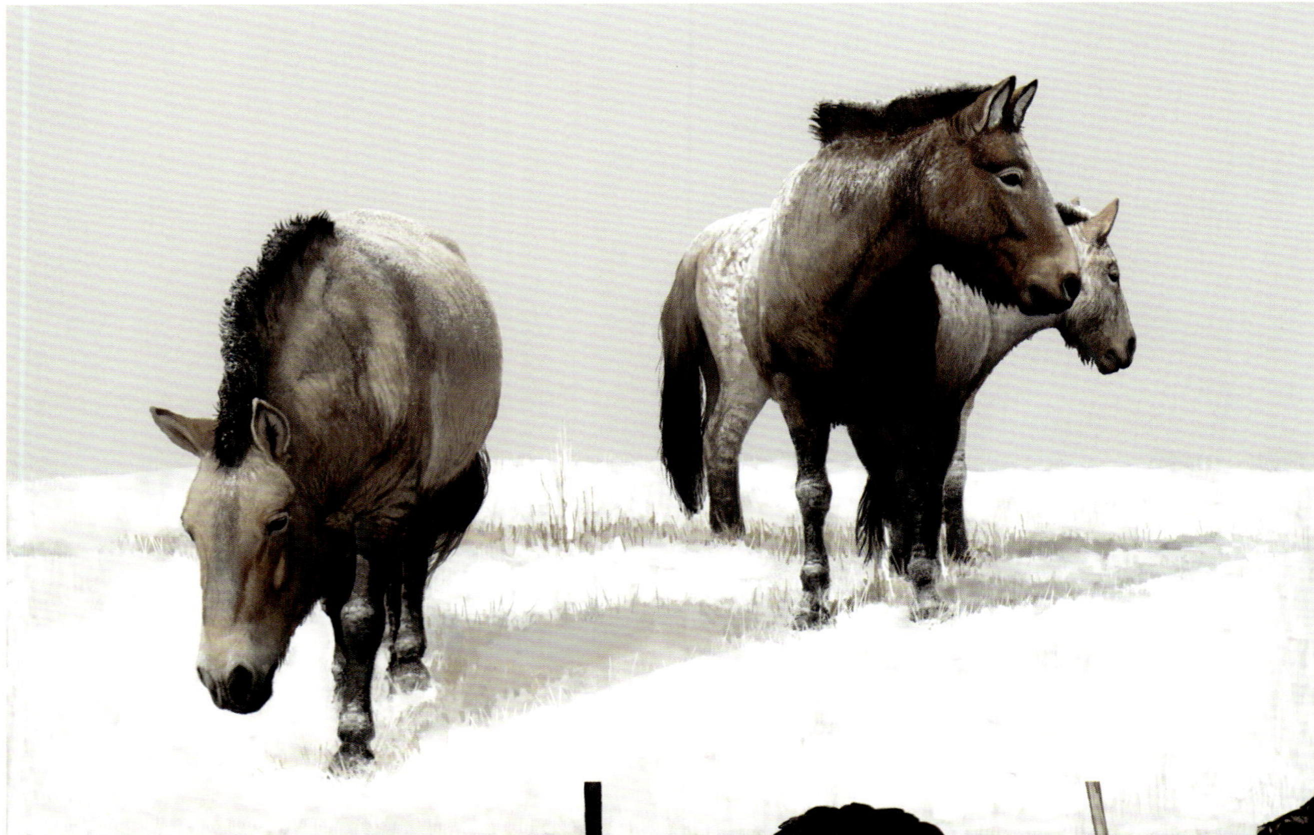

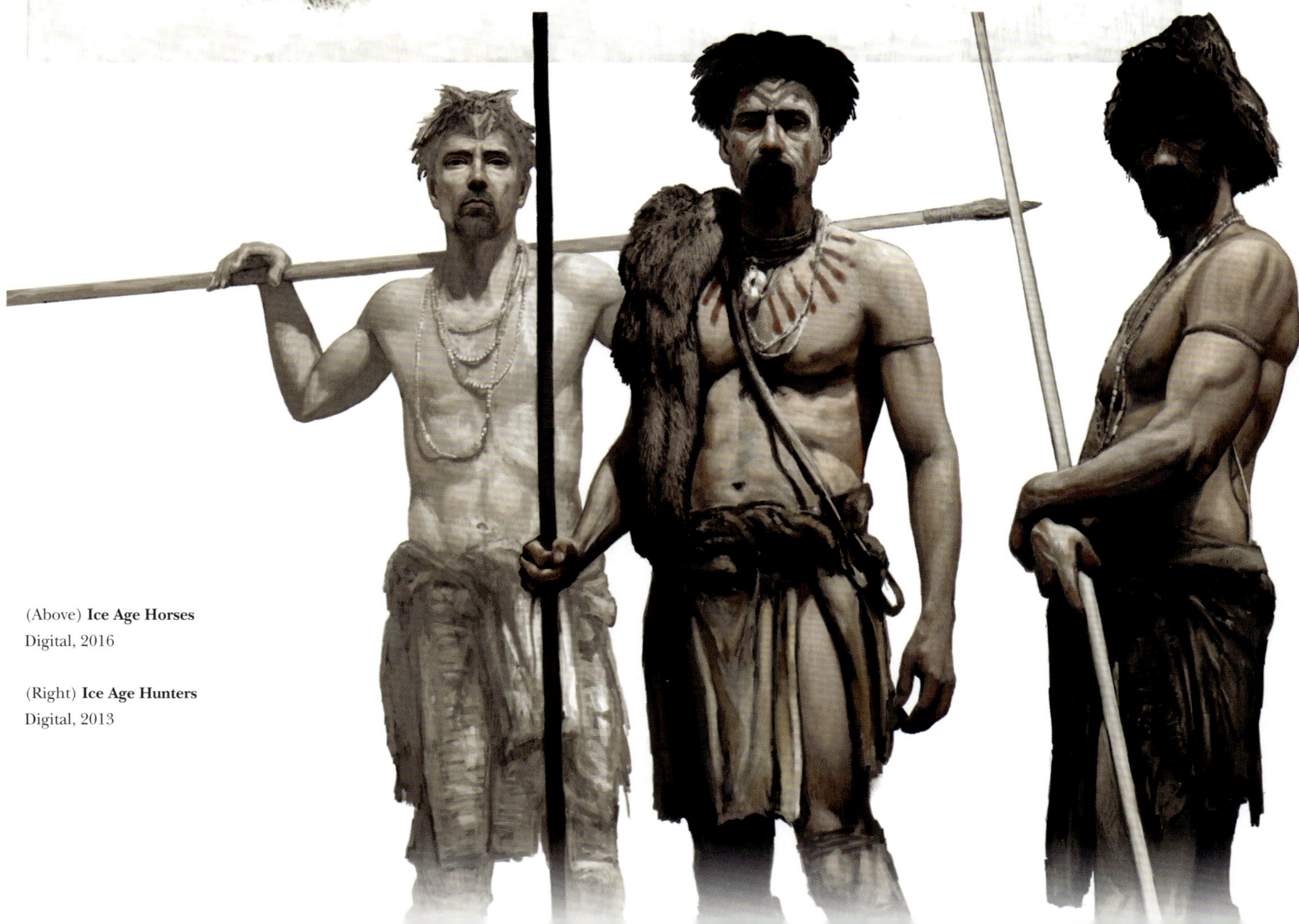

(Above) **Ice Age Horses**
Digital, 2016

(Right) **Ice Age Hunters**
Digital, 2013

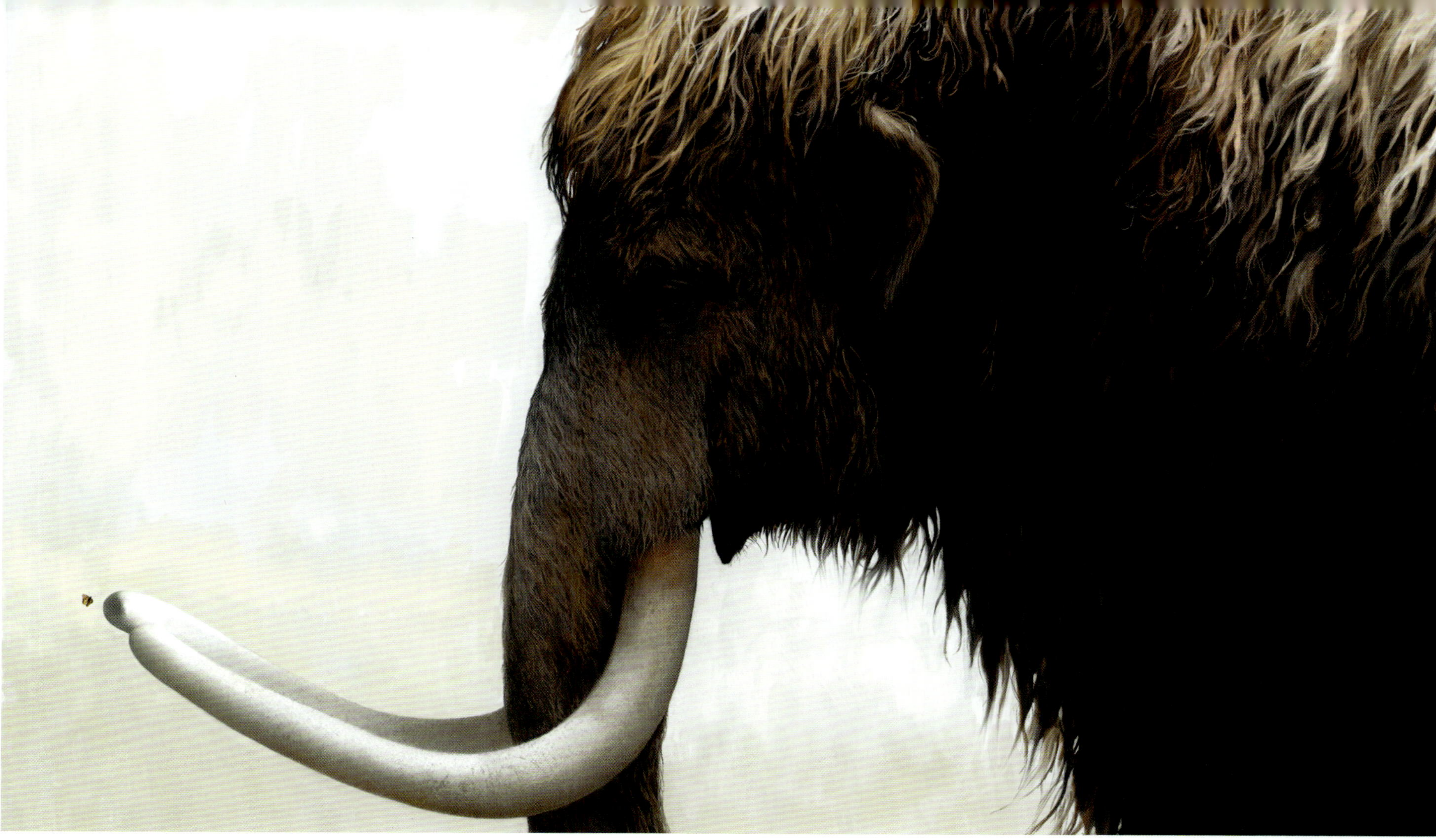

their behavior. According to what we know now, based on DNA analyses, our ancestors may have sported rather interesting combinations of skin, eye and hair coloration. Their patterns of life, economics, rituals and beliefs were surely something totally unthinkable for us living in modern, relatively well-organized secular states. On the other hand, I want my depictions of ancient humans to feel familiar too. I don't want them to look simple-minded and brutal, still on their way to becoming – in modern terms – sophisticated and humane, which is what people commonly think. Despite the differences I mentioned, people living tens of thousands of years ago were pretty much like we are. And we shouldn't fool ourselves, the layer of refinement we think we possess can so easily be whipped away. It has been, repeatedly, and it will, over and over again. As individuals, falling back to a primitive state of mind and behavior happens to all of us on a daily basis, even if only briefly, but as long as society, with its network of rules, spoken and unspoken, keeps together it doesn't matter so much.

So, in answer to your question, I want my "cavemen" to have a personality and to look like anyone we could know, with a tint of "wildness" and primitiveness. And in order to do that, they do have real life, modern counterparts. As models, for practical reasons, I often use members of my family, myself included. Friends and neighbors may also appear in my illustrations, or anyone I think could do fine in a certain role. Unfortunately, because of the attitudes I mentioned before, not everyone will appreciate the idea that they have an appearance that would sit great as a stone age clan member.

Did your Finnish upbringing have any bearing on your interest in the Ice Age?

I wouldn't like to say that the Nordic, and especially Finnish wildlife isn't interesting enough to be depicted in paintings. But the truth is that we don't have anything like, let's say the African savannah, with the fantastic opportunities it presents for framing the great drama of life. Not at the same magnitude, anyway. But while African wildlife is something I like to admire from a distance, I don't want to draw or paint it. It's not my world and for me it's important to depict things I have a connection to; that are a part of my heritage. So, since we don't have much of our original wildlife left, I can travel back in time and see all

Woolly Mammoth and Painted Lady
Digital, 2015

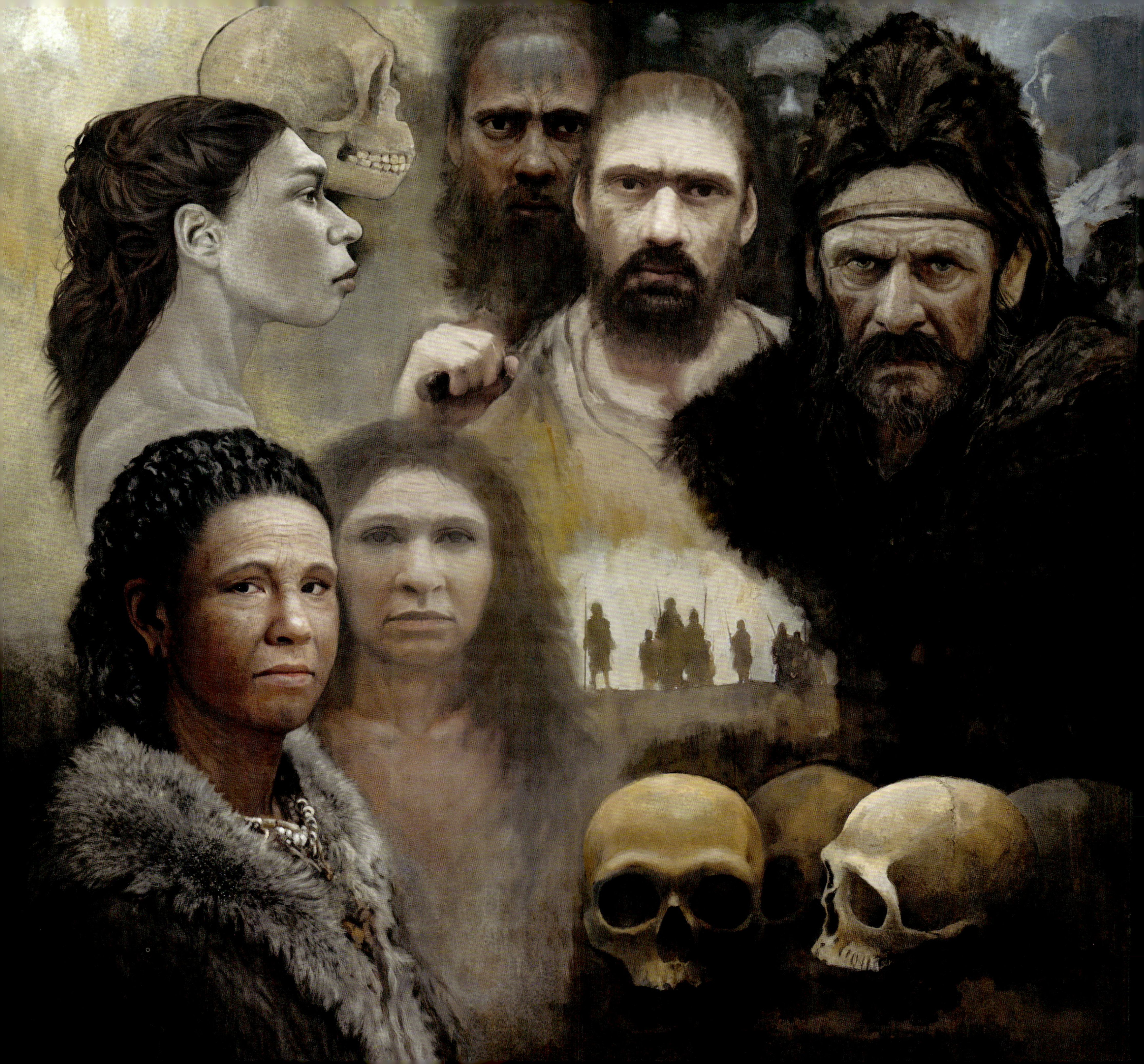

those large herds of bison and horses, reindeer and antelopes, and of course mammoths and all the big carnivores, through the eyes of my ancestors. Finland is definitely marked by the Pleistocene glaciation periods; you can see the evidence everywhere. Unfortunately, the ice also scraped away most of the softer material, including fossils, leaving only the hardest bedrock. It means we have very little evidence about life in Finland during prehistoric times. On the other hand, it kind of gives me the freedom to illustrate things the way I like.

Is Homotherium a particular favorite of yours?

Yes, *Homotherium* – the scimitar cat – is one of my favorites, although I haven't painted it that often. I find the species intriguing; it had a wide distribution covering various habitats, but much of its behavior is unknown. The scientific name, *Homotherium* – man's beast – gives a hint of the relationship between the scimitar cat and humans, although we don't know if they regularly predated on hominids. They may have not been great sprinters, but they certainly could have been a threat for slow moving creatures like our ancestors. A reconstruction of *Homotherium serum* (based on the Friesenhahn cave finds) was made at the Finnish Natural History Museum in the early 80s. It was colored black, which in my mind makes it look a bit like a big Labrador retriever. I saw it a lot when I was working on an illustration project at the museum. The museum also has a copy of a *Homotherium* skull which I have sketched. Many of the large carnivores of the Ice Age are more or less familiar in their appearance, but the scimitar cat was something else, especially in Europe (*H. latidens*), in the absence of *Smilodon*.

At what point did paleoart become a part of your repertoire?

I have a special interest in both nature and history, so any topics relating to wildlife or to human culture can pique my curiosity. Also, the harsh reality is that as a freelancer I must be prepared to accept all sorts of assignments, and it just so happened – this was in the late 90s – that I was asked to illustrate a museum exhibition with the theme "After the Ice Age", which led to a few more commissions along the same lines. I think it was about that time I got the idea to illustrate life during the Ice Age as my personal project. Later on, I was involved in the production of a larger permanent exhibition, The History of Life, which naturally included illustrations covering life forms starting from the early beginning of life on Earth. Dinosaurs and other ancient animals don't get my attention in the same personal sense as the Pleistocene and especially the last glaciation period, but they are as important from an educational perspective, the production of educational material being my bread and butter at the moment.

Can you talk a bit about your process? How much preparation work do you do?

I have no set routine when I work. To tell the truth, I'm not a very organized person and much of what I do is based on intuition. However, experience has taught me that often the fastest way of doing things is through proper preparation, especially when a realistic approach to the subject in question is required. It depends a lot on what I'm doing. Ideas for personal work often come suddenly, without planning. The inspiration can be a special situation I have witnessed, interaction between animals, a landscape or a face of a person I have seen through the bus window. Also, with regards to my own projects, I don't start painting if I haven't already got an idea of the composition and adequate references.

In the case of commissions, the situation is different. The client normally has a specific plan for the images that may not be my personal choice of how to do the job. I have to force myself to use elements in the composition that I wouldn't usually, and there can even be – since we are talking about scientific illustration – different opinions on how the finds on which

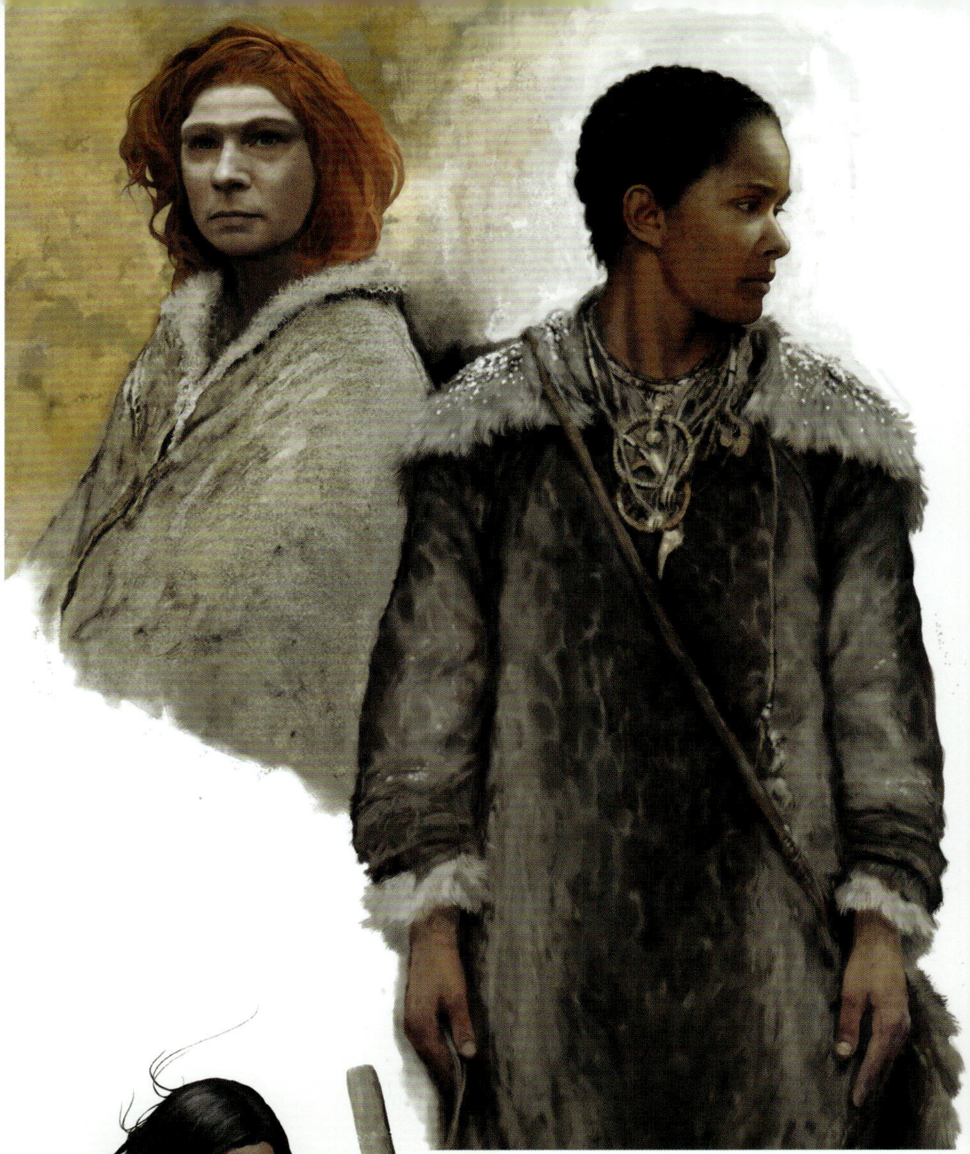

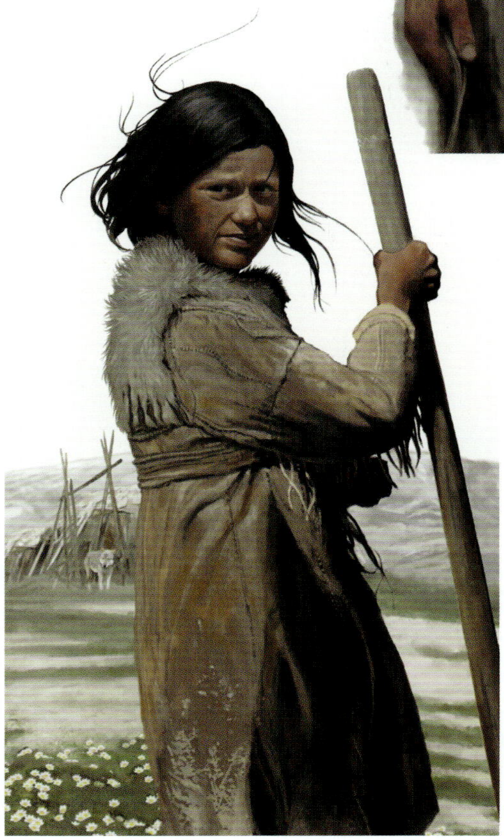

(Above) **Ice Age Women**
Digital, 2017

(Left) **Ice Age Girl**
Digital, 2017

(Opposite) **Neanderthals**
Digital, 2017

the painting is based should be interpreted.

But as a professional I have to be prepared to deal with all kinds of problems, both artistically and those related to the subject matter. It's not always fun, but it's certainly a challenge. I normally start the practical preparations by collecting and studying facts about the subject matter, including consulting experts. I also gather as much reference material as I can, preferably via first-hand experience. It can be a complicated process, from searching for suitable settings and models, to building miniatures. The preparation can be time consuming, but the work pays off when you start drawing and painting.

You have a photorealistic style and a strong sense of light and shade. Can you talk a bit about that? What references do you use?

As per definition – in terms of the specific genre of art – photorealistic paintings should be based on photographic material, although the same kind of impression can be reached by painting from life, too. My understanding is that to be accepted as true photorealistic art, it must be possible to compare the painting (or other work) with a photographic reference image in order to measure the skill of the artist, principally anyway. When striving to create as realistic and accurate images as possible, there

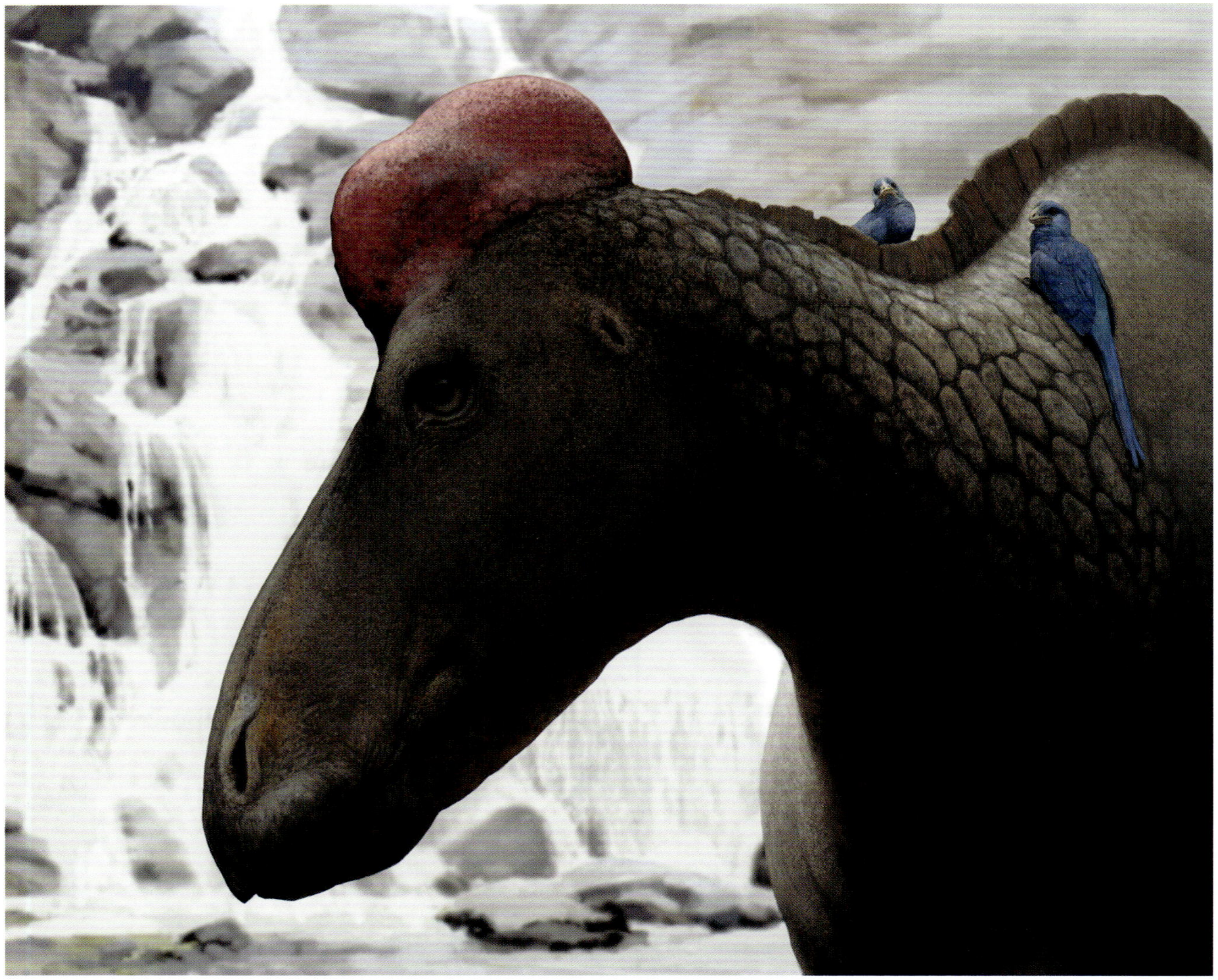

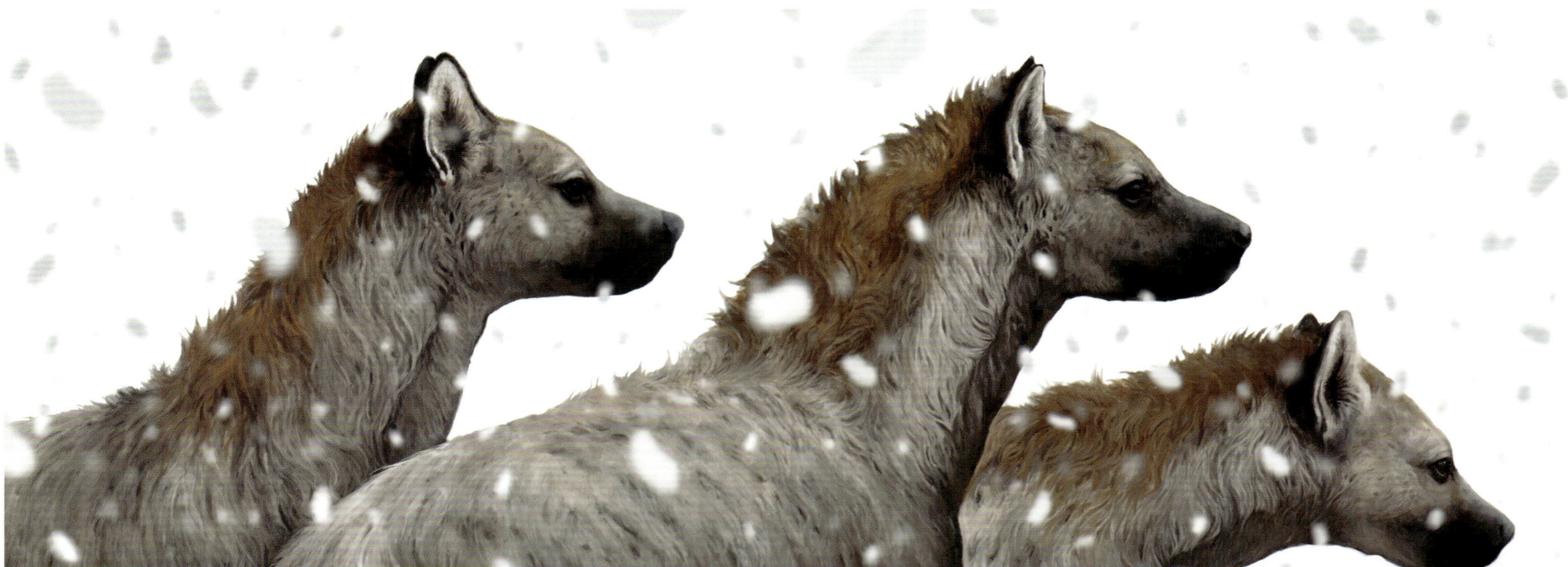

has to be something solid upon which to base everything. It's not a question of imagination, or the lack of it - it's about knowledge. While an experienced and skilled artist can render believably realistic images purely from their imagination, I think this is only possible up to a point; nobody can store so much visual data in their brain that they can reproduce absolutely anything without reference to real life.

I'm not necessarily a fan of photorealism as an art form in and of itself, but at its best the technique can be quite powerful, and give images a sense of presence – so you feel that you are looking at something that really did exist. It doesn't necessarily require a meticulous recreation of every tiny detail; often, suggestive brushstrokes can be more effective. Here, the use of light and shade certainly plays a big part.

At what point did you move to primarily digital art? What prompted you to do this?

I have been working digitally for about five or six years now. It all started quite suddenly, when I felt I had to find a more effective way of working. I was tired of the piles of paper, sketches and studies gathering all over my working space, and I saw the benefits of working digitally in terms of keeping my stuff in order (of course, I have by now realized that it's possible to make a complete mess on the computer, too). Also, I now never run out of

(Left) ***Edmontosaurus***
Digital, 2016

(Below left) **Ice Age Spotted Hyenas**
Digital, 2015

(Below) **Ice Age Hyenas Pursuing Reindeer**
Digital, 2017

(Right) **Woolly Rhino and Magpies**
Digital, 2016

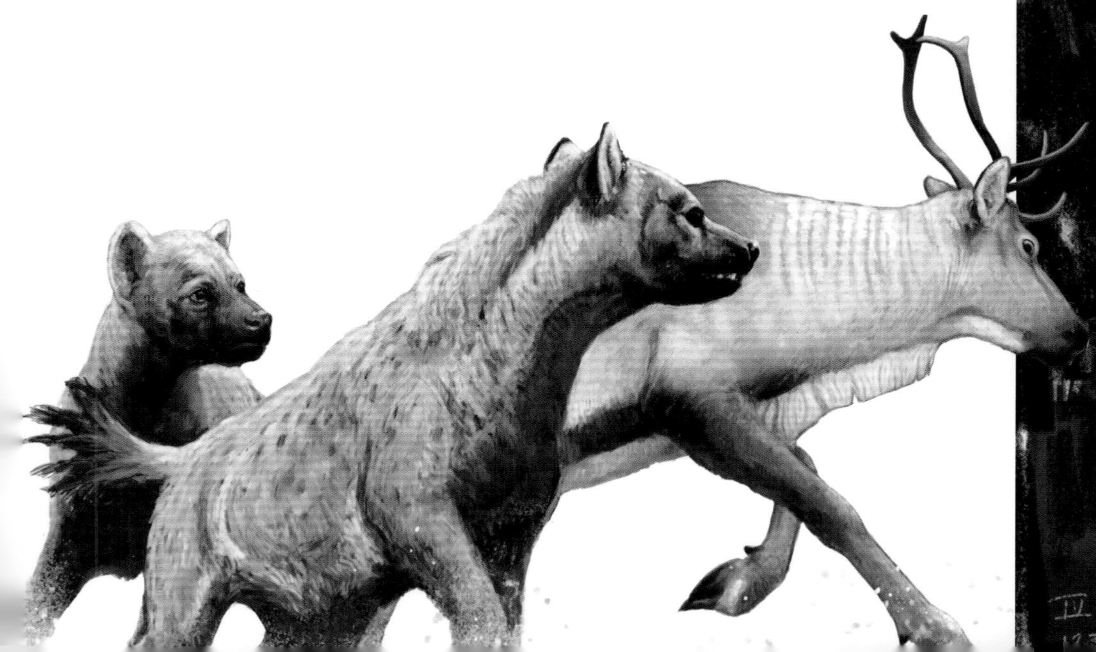

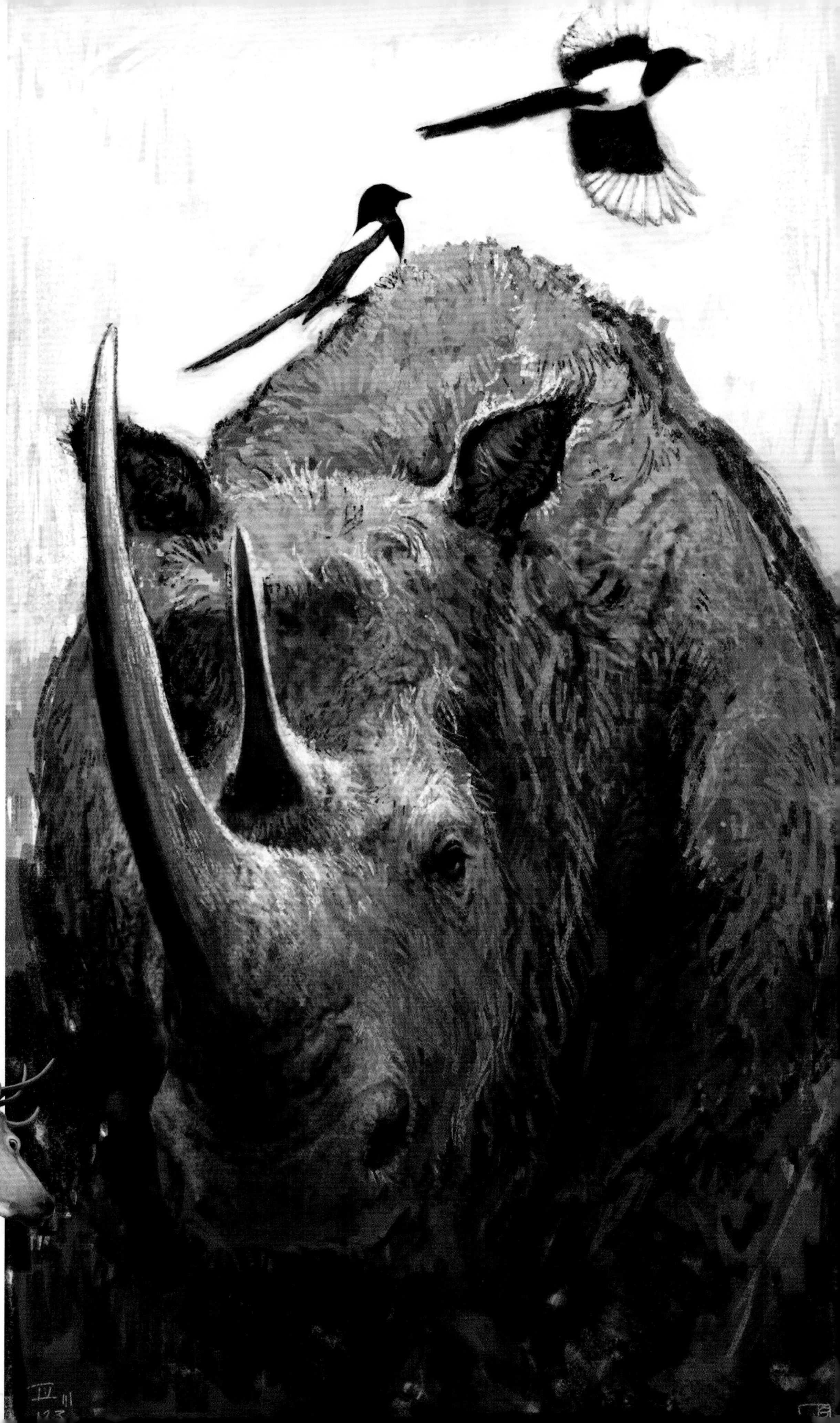

paints, brushes, paper and canvases. I work from home, and with young kids in the house, I value the fact that I can start working within seconds, which allows me to take advantage of every minute I can spare for work. Traditional painting often means that I have just got the paints on the palette only to return and find them dried up after an inevitable interruption.

In the beginning my plan was to start making prints, not by reproducing my traditional paintings but by creating original graphic art (although often based on the same motifs as my acrylics and watercolors). However, as I was regularly asked to do illustration work, I thought I could try digital painting for that purpose too. So, when I was asked to do a set of book illustrations I accepted the task on condition that I could make the paintings digitally – only a few years ago, it wasn't that common yet, and the clients could be quite skeptical. Until then, I had used my computer mainly for writing and reading e-mails, and needed a chance to train. The problem was that, being a family man, I didn't have too much time for practicing without pay. So, the commission made it possible for me to learn a new craft and even get paid for it (there was a risk, of course, but I couldn't afford to worry about it too much). Then I just had to find the right software. Photoshop seemed to be the most common one used by professionals, but for me it looked too complicated. As it happened I found a review of ArtRage (on the Lines and Colors art blog) and as I thought it sounded promising I purchased the software along with a 27" iMac and a Wacom intuos4 large pen tablet. Learning the painting process didn't require much, if any, of a learning curve. It immediately felt natural, very close to traditional painting.

Do you think that working digitally has had an impact on your art – either stylistically, or in terms of the constraints of possibilities inherent in the medium?

I have a lot of experience in traditional media, so my idea of how I want my paintings to look is quite fixed, and ArtRage is designed to simulate real life materials, therefore my digital paintings don't differ substantially from my traditional paintings and drawings. As I see it, one's style isn't only determined by the medium; it's more about how the artist looks at things, plans the compositions and chooses the subject matter. Although traditional and digital media seem worlds apart they still are just tools, and the difference between, let's say, oils and digital painting is in my mind smaller than between oils and charcoal. Painting with a computer isn't about pushing buttons, which is unfortunately a widespread misunderstanding; the artist's hand still holds a pen or a brush and the craftsmanship required is pretty much the same. In addition to that comes, of course, all the stuff with pixels, resolution and file formats, but as an illustrator, nowadays they are things you would have to deal with anyway.

Digital painting isn't easier than traditional techniques; often the painting process itself isn't even faster. The benefits come mostly from more practical issues, such as the digitization of the infrastructure. I'm not restricted to working within the limitations of my studio, or inhibited by geographical distances. I can make paintings which can be printed in really large sizes and deliver them within seconds to the other side of the world, unthinkable not so long ago. Naturally this could be done with traditional work too, but the reproduction process would make it much more complicated than working directly in a digital format. So, basically, even if learning a new technique forces one to rethink the creative process to some extent, I can't say that digital painting has affected my style – time and experience have done more. But digital painting definitely has changed a lot of things – not least lowering the costs related to work – and it has opened up new possibilities.

Are there particular subjects that you prefer to paint using traditional media?

All in all, I paint the same kind of motifs traditionally as I do digitally, mostly because my customers expect that. But my background as a painter is a little different. During my art studies I developed an interest for non-figurative painting. To make a rude simplification, from an artistic point of view, depicting a motif realistically doesn't require much more than copying reality as it is: craftsmanship, certainly, but that's about it. Working in either an abstract or a concretistic manner demands different insight in the handling of composition and color. It's interesting how the "laws of nature" seem to guide my brushstrokes and my color choices even when I'm not limited to following the reality in front my eyes. Of course, it's impossible to completely reject all the learned experience and muscle memory from figurative painting, but it's still fascinating to concentrate only on forms and colors and to have, as my sole objective, to show not an illusion of something else, but how paint looks worked in different ways, just as what it is, as paint. The patterns created by brushstrokes and the color choices may not form clearly recognizable figures, but nevertheless shapes and colors always affects us emotionally (at least if we keep our minds open), due to the visual iconography we all carry within, based on the cultural references we have inherited. So, this is something I might think of when I have the opportunity to create something freely, namely in traditional media.

Are there any recent fossil discoveries that you're keen to draw?

I couldn't pick any specific fossil, but the new finds dropping in quite regularly, revealing details of bird evolution and the relationship between theropod dinosaurs and extant species, are indeed inspiring. In general, all discoveries regarding details such as skin impressions of any dinosaur (or other ancient creature) give rise to an urge to try new interpretations.

***T-rex*, a Cutie or a Beast?**
Digital, 2016

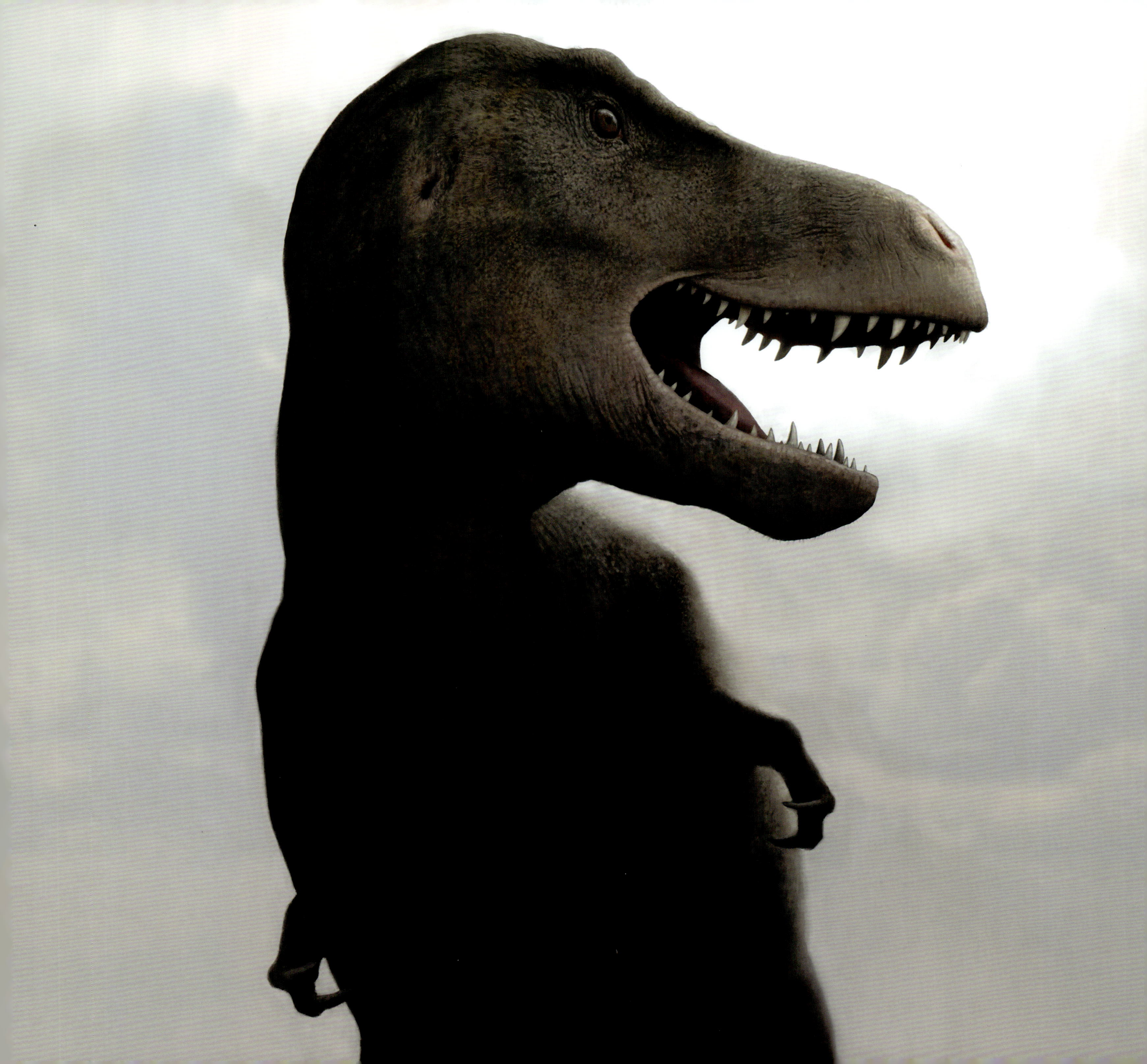

MARK WITTON

UK

Based at the University of Portsmouth, Mark is a researcher as well as an artist and was awarded a PhD in 2008 for his studies of flying reptiles. He continues to publish scientific papers on pterosaurs, but has found an unexpected career as a palaeoartist and consultant, with clients including the BBC, Twentieth Century Fox, the Natural History Museum (UK), and *National Geographic*. He designed several of the species for the 2013 feature film *Walking With Dinosaurs 3D*. He has published two critically acclaimed books: *Pterosaurs: Natural History, Evolution, Anatomy* (2013) and *Recreating an Age of Reptiles* (2016).

Teleocrater
Digital, 2017
Originally named in 1956 from fragmentary remains found in 1933, this member of the archosaurs – the group that includes crocodylians, pterosaurs, dinosaurs and birds – is known from the Middle Triassic Manda Formation of Tanzania (147-135mya). Fresh remains described in 2017 revealed a number of interesting anatomical features that provided valuable insights into the evolution of the dinosaur-bird lineage of the archosaurs.

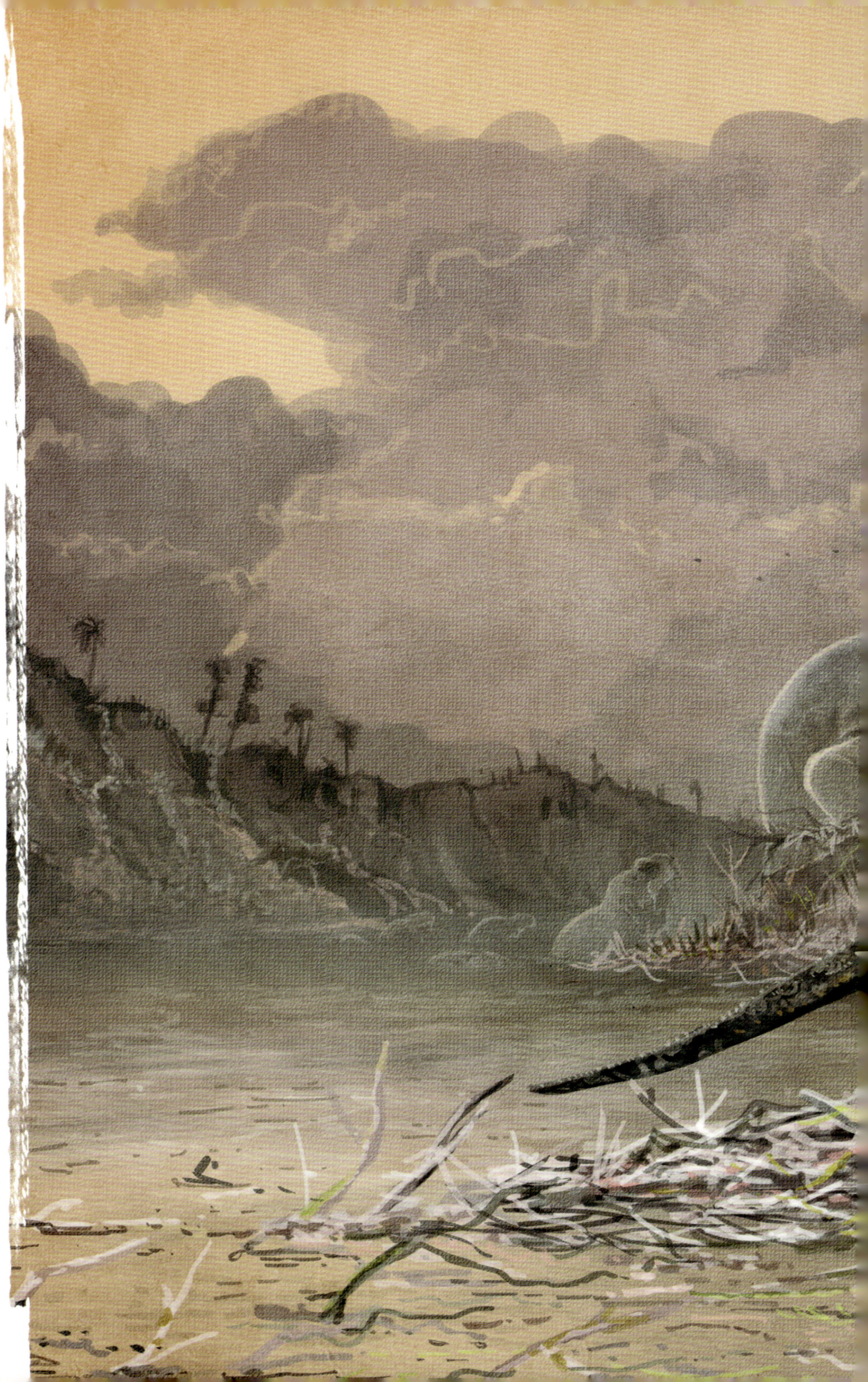

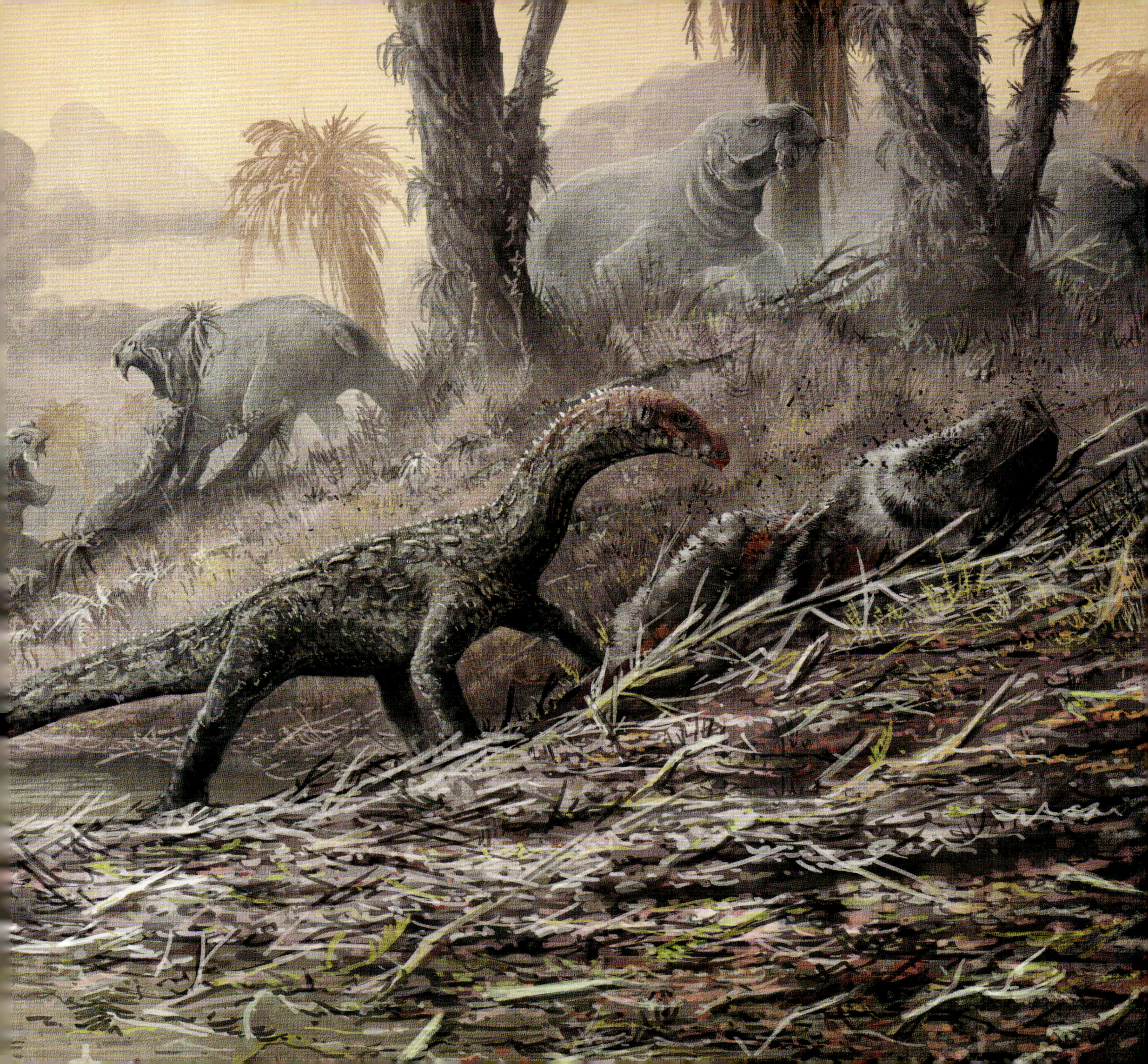

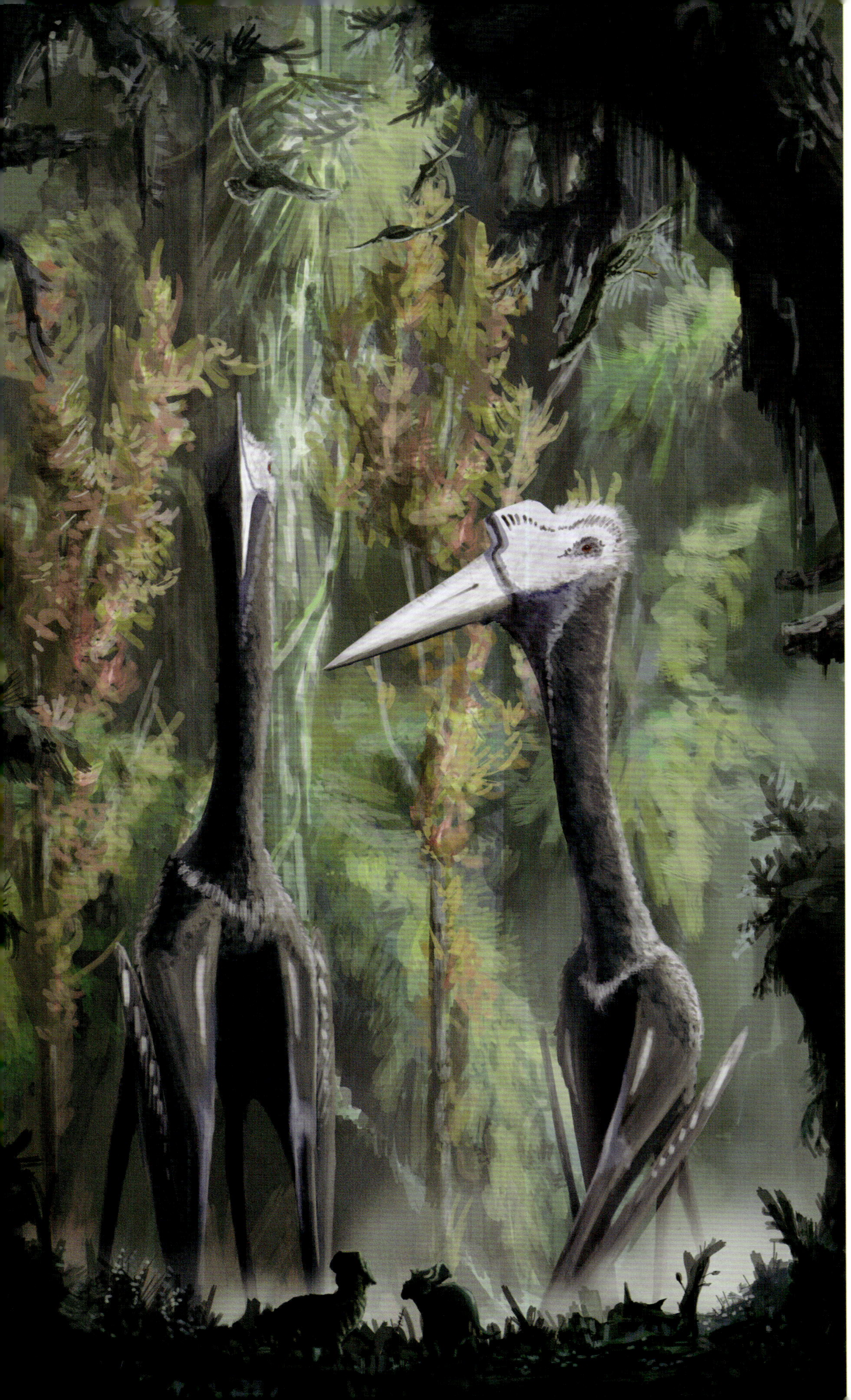

You're most closely associated with pterosaurs; when did your love affair with them begin?

Pterosaurs were just another fossil animal until I entered the third year of my undergraduate studies at the University of Portsmouth. My dissertation project focused on the sedimentology and paleontology of the Cretaceous Wealden Group beds on the Isle of Wight, which are known for, among other things, yielding the razor-toothed pterosaur *Istiodactylus latidens*. The skull of this animal is really odd: it's short, broad, much of it is occupied by a giant bony 'window' (the nasoantorbital fenestra), and the toothrow is restricted to a short, broad muzzle. The teeth also tightly interdigitate, forming a zigzagging cutting row. I found it such an intriguing animal that I asked Dr. David Martill, an expert on pterosaurs working at the same university, if he would take me on as a PhD student to study pterosaurs in more detail. I got my doctorate based on my pterosaur studies in 2008 and I've stayed with them as a research subject since.

Do you have a favorite pterosaur?

I don't know that I do, to be honest. I know it's a cop-out response, but it's hard not to get attached to most species through the research, art and outreach projects I've worked on. So, much as I might think *Dimorphodon* is a neat

(Left) ***Quetzalcoatlus***
Digital, 2016
Background: Javelina Formation forest. Mid-ground: the 4.6m-wingspan, super-famous azhdarchid pterosaur *Quetzalcoatlus* sp. Foreground: lunch. Late Cretaceous, Maastrichtian Stage, USA.

(Below) **Maasai giraffe, human, *Arambourgiania* & *Hagzegopteryx***
Digital, 2015
The 2015 version of the giraffe vs. azhdarchid vs. person image, now in it's fifth iteration. The giraffe is a big bull Maasai individual, standing a healthy 5.6m tall, close to the maximum known Maasai giraffe height. The pterosaur is a 10m-wingspan *Arambourgiania philadelphiae*. On the right is the Transylvanian azhdarchid *Habzegopteryx*.

(Right) **Carboniferous Scotland**
Digital, 2016
A scene of (currently unnamed) stem-tetrapods and arthropods from 'Romer's Gap', only now being filled by fossil data.

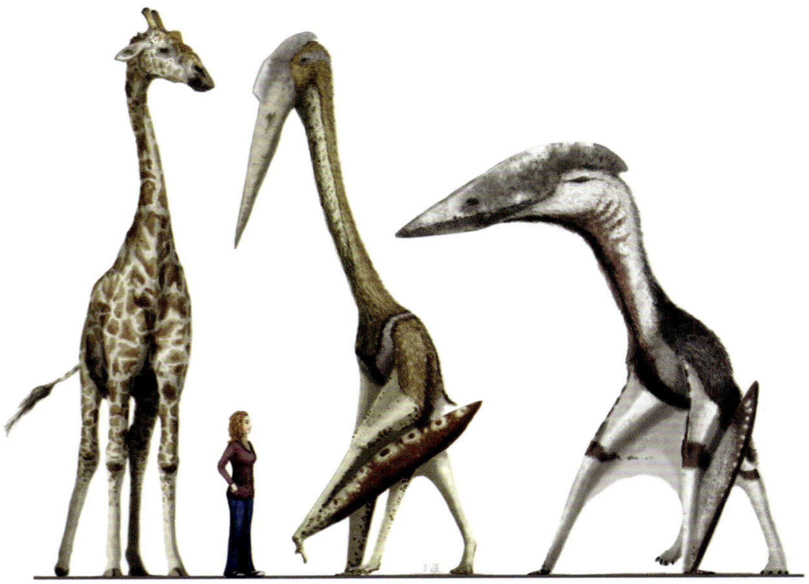

little species that might make for a good pet, I'm easily swayed by the awesome size and charisma of the big azhdarchids, or the spectacular headgear of thalassodromids. The combination of big heads and long tails in wukongopterids is really fun to draw for some reason, and monkey-armed campylognathoidids are pretty cool, too. And hey, have you seen the skull of *Caviramus* or the jaws of *Boreopterus*? They're pretty amazing.

So, no, I guess I don't have a favorite.

Azhdarchids have been the center of much, sometimes heated debate. They've gone from naked condor-like scavengers to giant storks. What's your current stance on their ecology and behavior?

Azhdarchids are, in some respects, poster children for our modern pterosaur renaissance, because reinterpretations of their anatomy, flight capability and ecology have helped shift perceptions of pterosaur paleobiology in a number of areas. But they're also an excellent example of how pterosaur anatomy has long proven confusing and controversial to scientists: since their recognition in the 1970s the same anatomical features have been linked to aerial and aquatic predation, skim-feeding, dip-feeding, sediment probing, dedicated scavenging and wading. These disagreements stem from authors 'cherry picking' anatomies that support a specific lifestyle – a long beak for probing sediment, narrow jaws for skim-feeding – while ignoring the bigger picture.

Back in 2008 my colleague and friend Darren Naish and I published a holistic study of azhdarchid paleobiology, looking at the functional properties of the entire azhdarchid skeleton, as well as flight models, trackway data and the depositional context of their fossils. We proposed a then-radical idea that azhdarchids were a largely continental group which roamed prairies and forests in pursuit of food – probably small animals and nutritious vegetative matter like fruits and seeds. We rejected the older lifestyle hypotheses because, among other reasons, they required highly specialised jaws for things like cutting through water, ripping flesh or extracting buried invertebrates. But azhdarchid jaws are actually quite weak and unspecialised: picking things up seems about all they were adapted to do. Elsewhere on the body, we noted that long limbs with highly

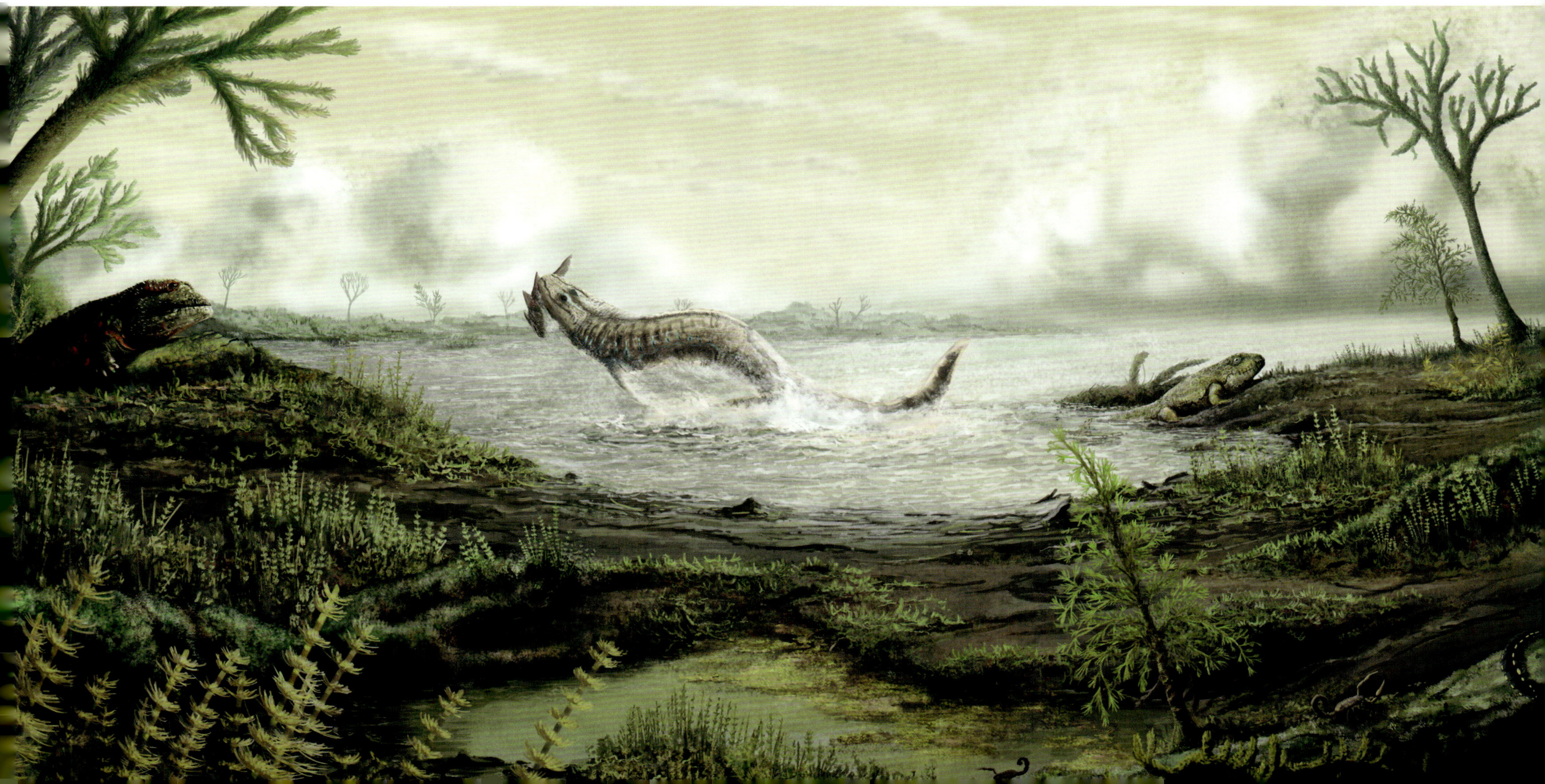

compact feet and short wings would be ideal for locomotion in cluttered terrestrial settings, and that the long, stiff necks of many species rule out a number of lifestyles requiring flexible or strenuous neck action. Azhdarchid fossils and tracks are also biased to terrestrial settings, and we have good evidence that they were eaten by other non-marine species – notably dinosaurs and crocodyliformes. We've built on this model over the years, testing neck strength against skim-feeding forces and so on, and it seems to be holding up. Ongoing work by ourselves and other pterosaur workers is now demonstrating that azhdarchids were less anatomically uniform than we previously anticipated, but this general model seems to apply to most known forms. As I understand it, the 'terrestrial stalker' model (as we termed it) seems to have been generally accepted by our colleagues.

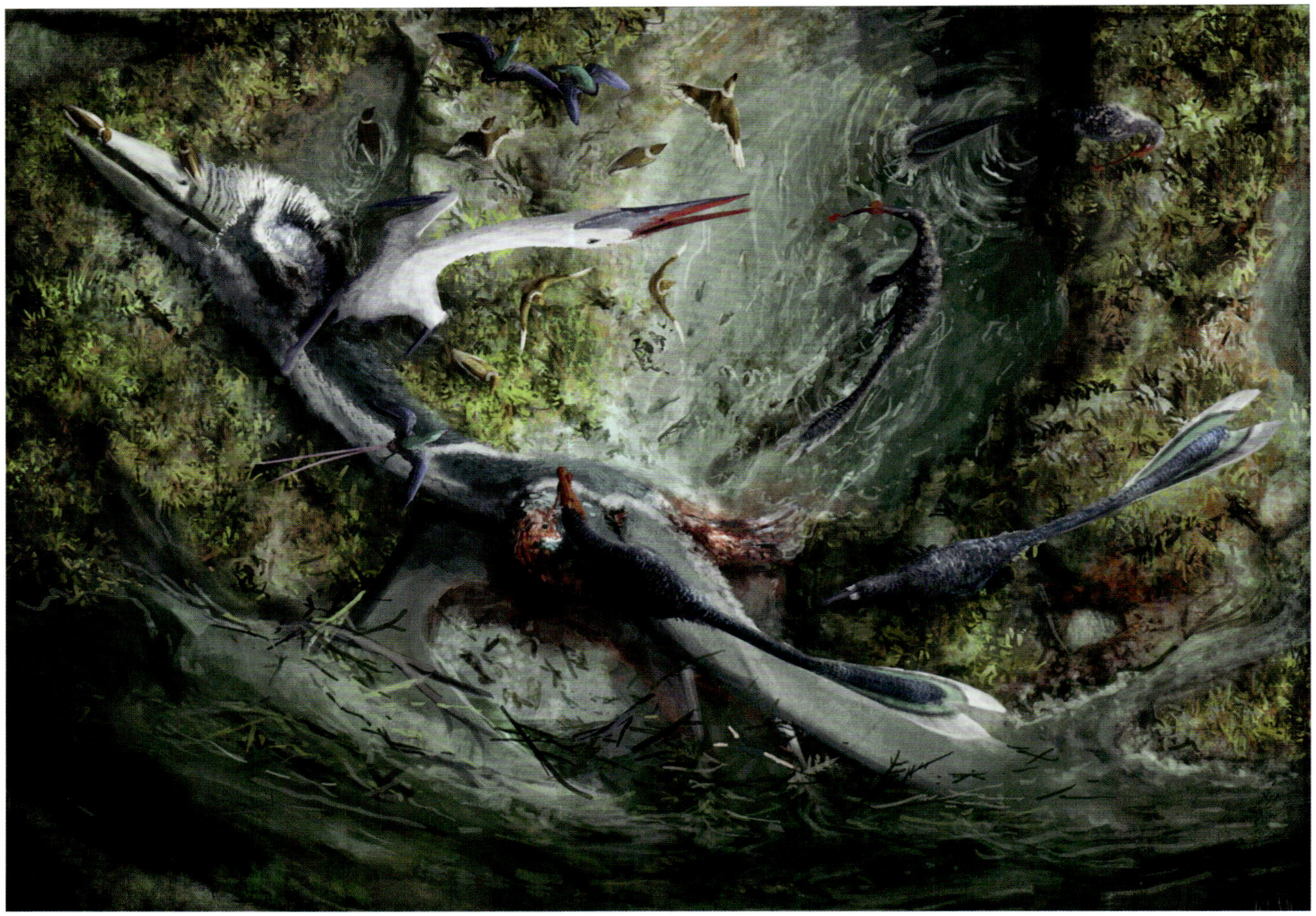

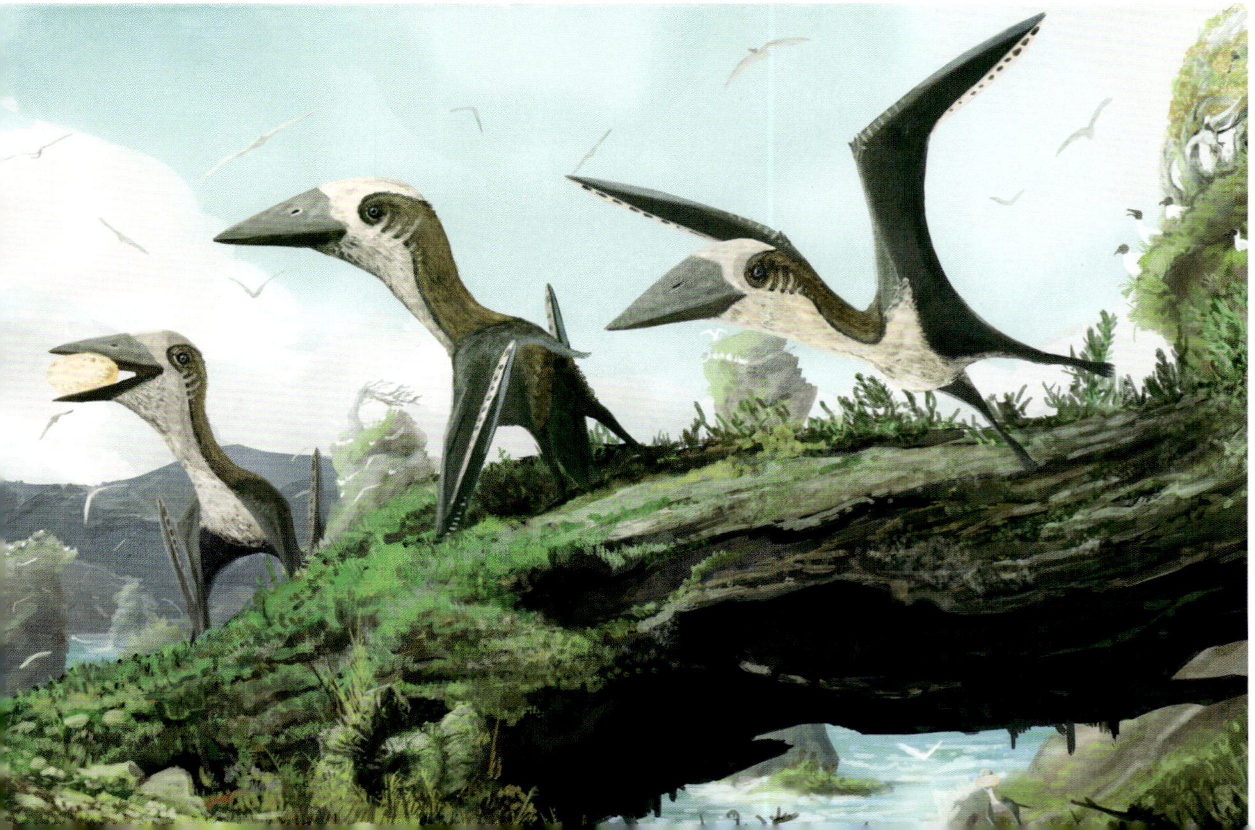

(Above) **Peaky Looking Azhdarchid**
Digital, 2009 revised 2016
The undignified end to the life of a large (18ft [6m] wingspan) azhdarchid: being squabbled over by *Saurornitholestes langstoni* and other local ruffians. Signs of butchery on azhdarchid remains indicate scenes like this did occur, although whether it is the result of predation or scavenging is unclear. Late Cretaceous, Campanian Stage, Canada.

You've discussed elsewhere that azhdarchids, in particular Quetzalcoatlus, *are the pterosaur darlings of the mass media, but their portrayals are often at odds with the actual science. The same applies to the likes of* Pteranodon *in recent blockbuster movies. How different are the two versions – the media and the science – and what, in your opinion, are the worst crimes perpetrated by movies and the like?*

Thankfully, the portrayal of pterosaurs in documentaries is improving over time, due in part to there being greater agreement among experts on aspects of their life appearance and behavior. The portrayal of pterosaurs has really benefited from the contributions of anatomists like Chris Bennett and Michael Habib, as well as anatomically savvy artists like John Conway, who've shown that the skeletons of pterosaurs are not beyond the comprehension of mere mortals. Indeed, there are a number of pterosaur experts who get ticked off at their colleagues for continuing to use the word 'enigmatic' to describe flying reptiles, as if they're a strange alien race of animals that we can never hope to understand. Yes, they're peculiar, but they

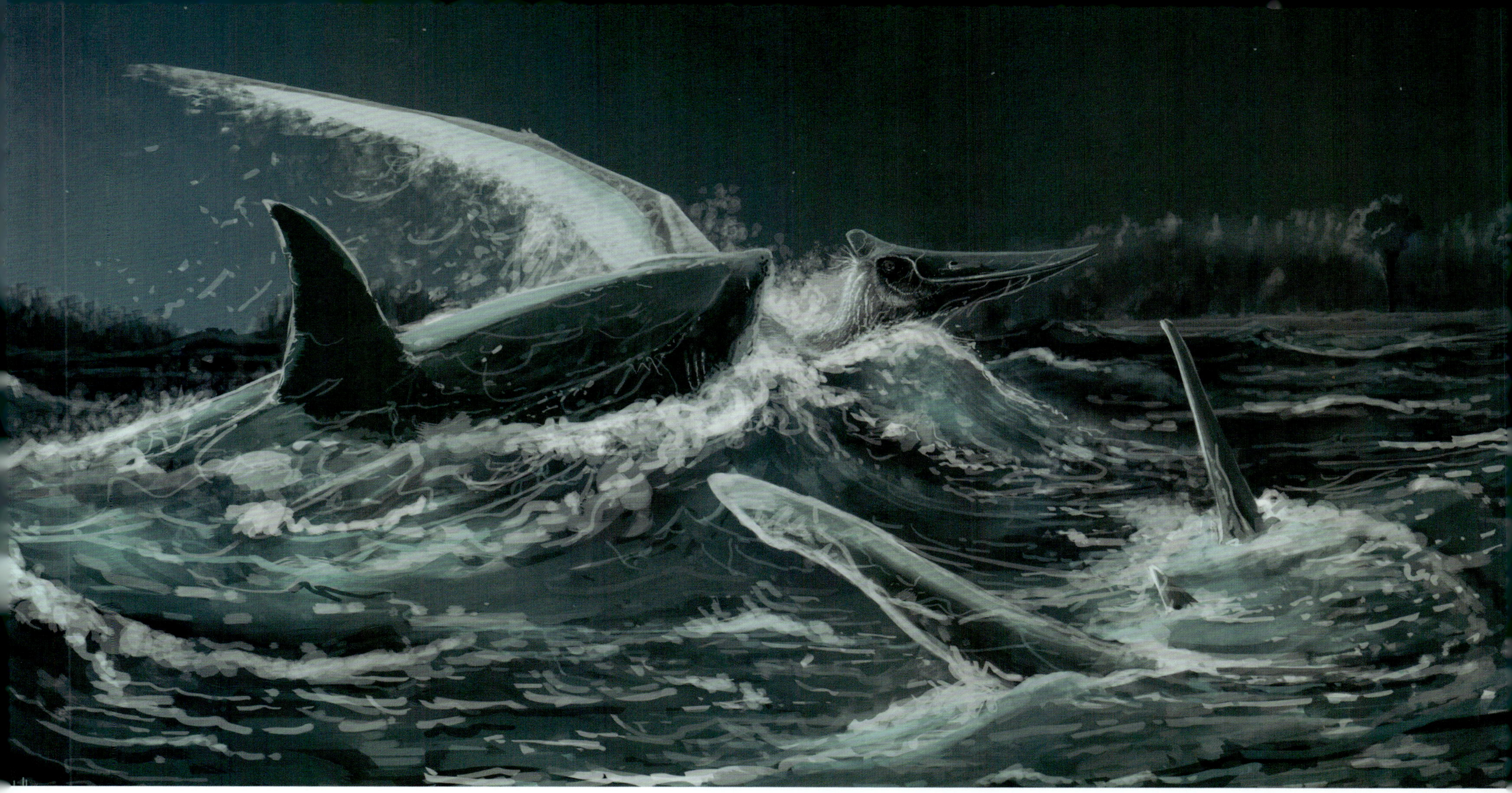

Pteranodoomed
Digital, 2017
A female *Pteranodon* falls prey to the 'crow shark' *Squalicorax* in the rough waters of the Western Interior Seaway that covered much of midwest America during the Late Cretaceous. Santonian Stage.

(Left) **Hornby Azhdarchoid**
Digital, 2016
A group of azhdarchoids perform guerrilla raids on shore-living Campanian bird nests. Late Cretaceous, 77mya. Hornby Island, British Columbia.

aren't *that* peculiar. This message is getting through to documentary makers, and it shows. Their budgets are often the biggest problem: pterosaurs are complicated creatures to restore and animate, and it's frequently difficult to stretch TV documentary budgets to cover the time needed to get them right.

It's a different story in film or drama productions. With few exceptions, they rank scientific concerns low down on their list of priorities, meaning their pterosaurs are ill-proportioned, have bizarre anatomical quirks and move without regard for skeletal anatomy or even the physics of flight. One thing that stands out in so many movies is how powerful people think these animals were. Don't get me wrong – animals like *Hatzegopteryx*, *Quetzalcoatlus* and *Pteranodon* were strong, well-muscled creatures – but they were not capable of crashing through windows, effortlessly carrying large adult people in their jaws or feet (giving pterosaurs raptorial feet is another movie trope, and one without basis in reality), or spearing people with their beaks. This isn't just a pterosaur problem, of course: virtually all movie versions of prehistoric creatures are unstoppable killing machines.

I'm sure that some pterosaurs were fast, dangerous creatures, but they were still only flesh and blood animals. We know that some of the largest pterosaurs had dietary preferences for very small prey (at least some of the time), that their bones were strong but vulnerable to buckling, and studies of their skull mechanics suggest most had weak jaws and bites that likely limited their ability to kill even moderately sized animals. So yes, the movies are right that being cornered by a giraffe-sized animal with a 2m-long beak would be a terrifying experience. It would be a steely person indeed who didn't need to change their undergarments after that encounter! But would that same animal hound us incessantly, smashing through terrain without any regard for its personal safety before hurling itself at us, wholesale, to rip, shed and bite us to pieces? Probably not.

As well as azhdarchids and pteranodontids, there are also quite a few apocryphal 'giant' pterosaurs rumored to be in collections around the world. In terms of

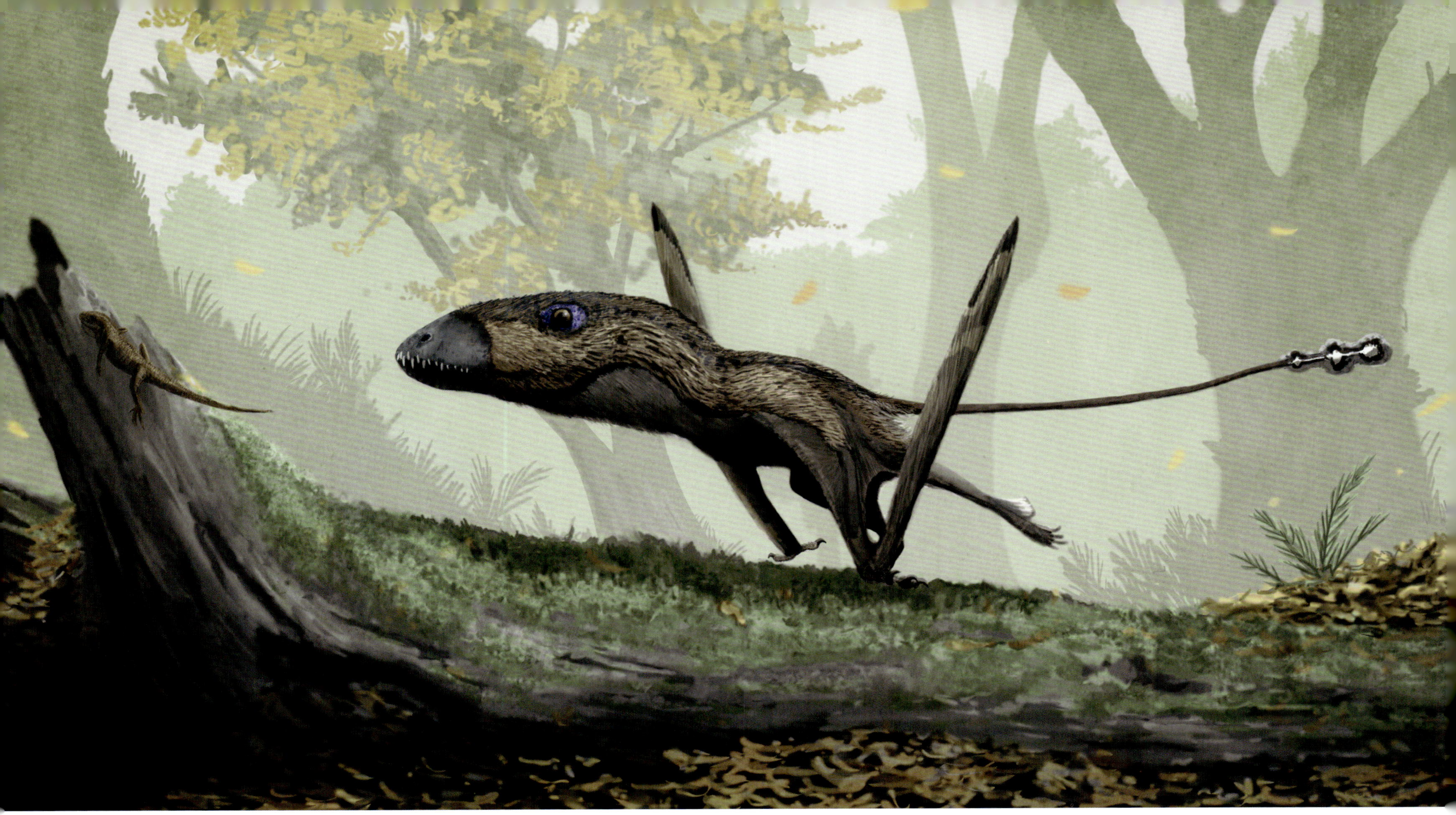

speculative evolution, at what point do you think 'ratite' pterosaurs – those too big to actually take to the air – may have appeared?

Different bodyplans have different prospects for maximum flightworthy size, and we could theoretically take any pterosaur type and make it too big to fly. Not everything would get to the size of a plane before it was too large and cumbersome to achieve flight: as we see in living insects, birds and bats, sometimes wingspans of just a few centimeters are too much for a given bodyplan. So, from that sense, a 'ratite like' pterosaur could have developed at any point in pterosaur history, so long as selection pressures were pushing in that direction.

The animals that many people would automatically assume might have the most 'ratite potential' are the giant azhdarchids that existed at the end of the Cretaceous. But the fact that pterosaurs probably took to the air using quadrupedal launches, rather than bipedal ones like birds, means that strong fliers like azhdarchids would have to get incredibly large before abandoning flight. Whereas birds don't seem to have ever flown much above 70kg, pterosaurs seem to have retained flight to masses well above 200kg. So, we'd need to see some seriously big azhdarchids – well beyond the largest pterosaurs known to us today – before they were simply too large to fly.

Perhaps more interestingly, there are indications that a much smaller pterosaur, the 1.4m wingspan Jurassic species *Dimorphodon macronyx*, is the closest thing we have to a 'flight limited' pterosaur. It doesn't seem to have been flightless, but estimates of its wing loading, gliding potential and flapping power requirements do not suggest it was as efficient at flying as other pterosaur species. As with modern birds that find flight strenuous, *Dimorphodon* seems to have compensated for its lack of aerial prowess with strongly built limbs and a robust

***Dimorphodon* On the Chase**
Digital, 2015
Dimorphodon macronyx pursues a sphenodontian mammal on the ground. Sinemurian Stage, Early Jurassic, England.

(Opposite top)
***Rhamphorynchus* Takes a Dip**
2010, updated 2016
Juvenile, subadult and a big old adult *Rhamphorhynchus muensteri* forage in a Jurassic lagoon. Tithonian Stage, Late Jurassic, Germany.

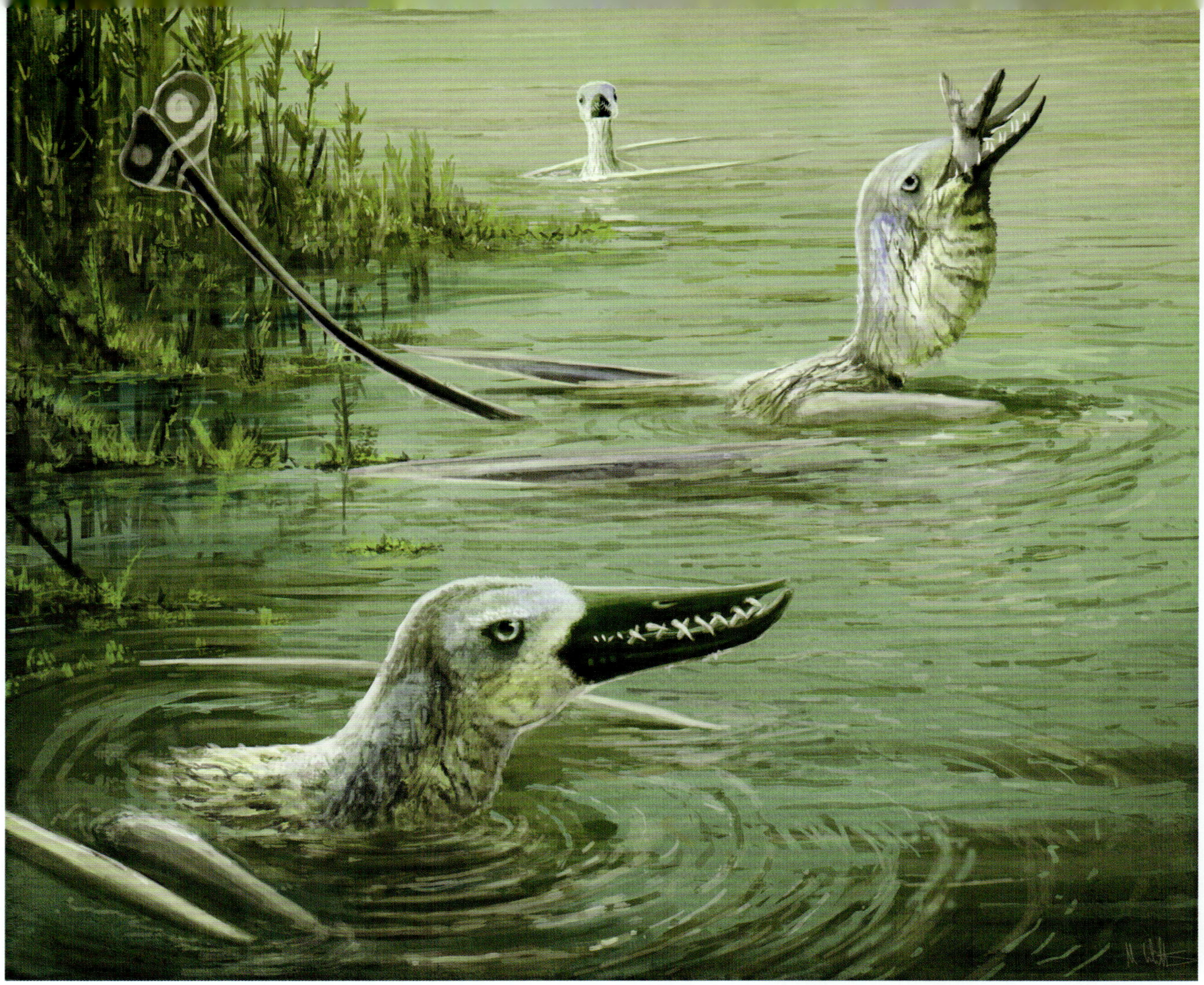

skeleton. It was probably quite happy running around on the ground, only taking wing to evade predators or travel long distances.

Do you think there were any other ground-based pterosaur predators?

Almost certainly. We know that a lot of pterosaurs were competent terrestrial animals from their trackways, and numerous foraging traces associated with their footprints suggest they were taking food from ground level at least as early as the Jurassic. The 'classic' idea of pterosaurs being a group which largely caught insects or fish on the wing is looking less and less likely because we're realising how difficult and specialized these lifestyles are. Being able to fly does not mean that you can suddenly make a living hawking insects or grabbing fish from water. Both lifestyles require a large number of changes to the skull and wings, and we only see these adaptations in some pterosaur groups. It's looking more likely that pterosaurs were a diverse bunch, with many finding food on the ground, others perhaps entering water to seize fish and other aquatic prey while swimming and floating. We've only really scratched the surface of research into pterosaur ecology, and there's a lot more to learn here.

You've written a lot about Rhamphorhynchus. *Was that the first pterosaur you saw as a swimmer? You have illustrated other types swimming, such as* Pteranodon, *but as a marine genus, that's a more obvious choice. What led you to envisage* Rhamphorhynchus *as 'aquatic'?*

There have been ideas off and on about pterosaurs swimming for centuries, but little in the way of serious investigation until recently. Now we have swimming pterosaur tracks, digital models of their floating abilities (they float like regular animals, not birds, which sit on the water in a uniquely avian way) and some ideas of what a pterosaur adapted for aquatic launch looks like. Both *Rhamphorhynchus* and *Pteranodon* fit the model for strong aquatic launchers: they have short legs, relatively large feet, reconfigured upper limb bones, and reduced torso sizes. Moreover, their wings are very long and narrow, a likely adaptation to marine flight, and both are known to have eaten swimming prey – fish and squid. The fact that these animals were good at taking off from the water implies that they must have been entering the water regularly too, perhaps intentionally, and it is this logic that lead to my swimming pterosaur pictures. *Rhamphorhynchus* has a narrow elbow joint too, and streamlining

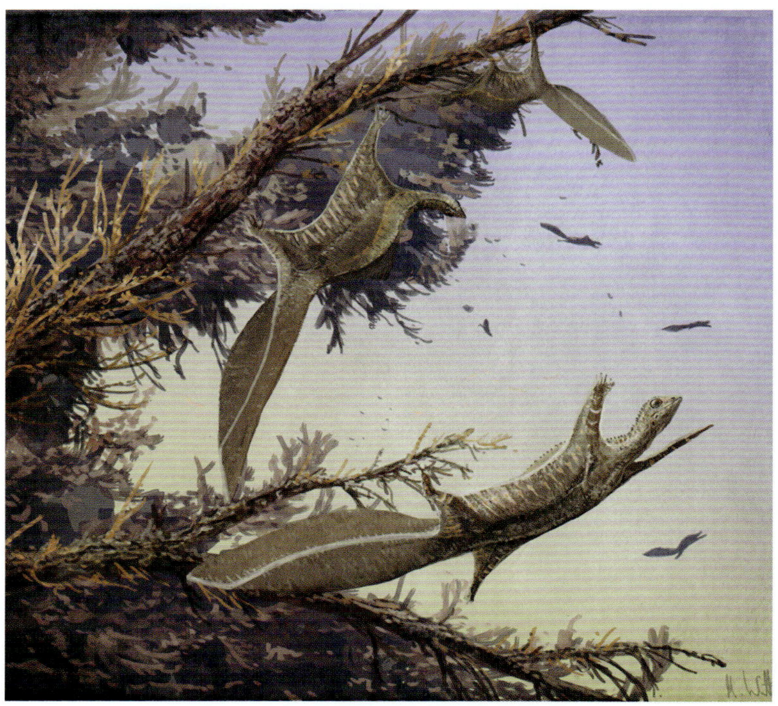

(Left) ***Hypuronector limnaios***
Digital, 2016
A distinctive, strange and controversial species belonging to the equally distinctive, strange and controversial group of reptiles known as the Drepanosaurs. Reasonably good fossils of this small (12cm long) animal have been known for decades from upper Triassic deposits of New Jersey. Here it is restored as a glider. Norian Stage.

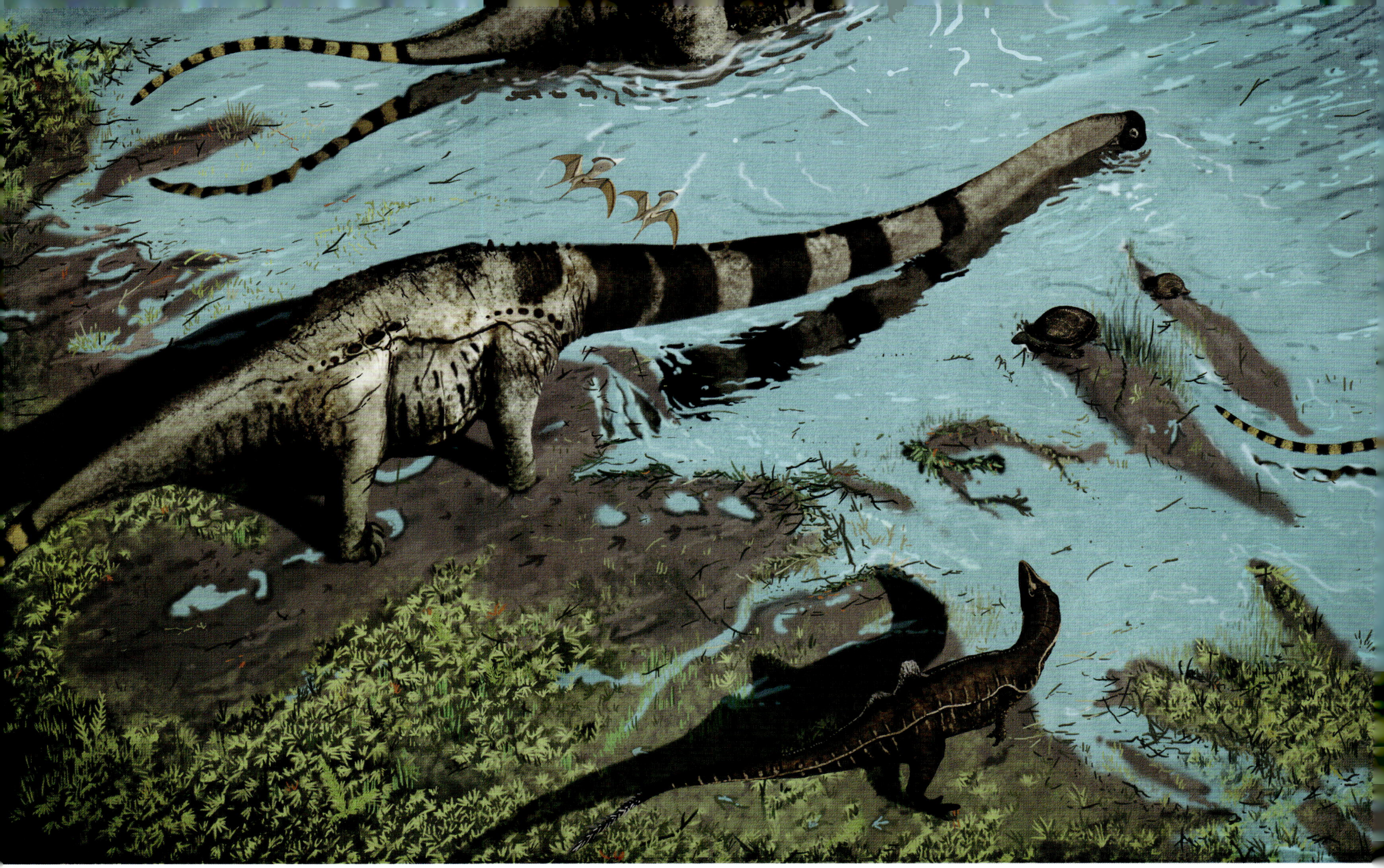

Hastings Beds
Digital, 2015
A speculative reconstruction of a swollen river representing part of the Hastings Beds, the oldest deposits of the Wealden Formation. The animals shown are poorly known: titanosaur '*Pelorosaurus*' *becklesii* (fragments of forelimb), possible
[caption continues opposite]

of the wing bones is a common feature of birds that routinely swim. This is not to say we *know* *Rhamphorhynchus* spent a lot of time in water – we're still getting to grips with pterosaur swimming in the research community – but it doesn't seem like an unreasonable idea.

Another favorite organism of yours is Tanystropheus. *It's so bizarre that it* has *to be fun to reconstruct, but it's interesting there are no modern analogies to it or the likes of the marine Plesiosauria. What made the Mesozoic so ideal for long-necked piscivores?*

I imagine it's something to do with the stock of animals around at that time. For whatever reason, reptiles seem to be very good at elongating their necks – sauropods, certain pterosaurs and birds, tanystropheids, plesiosaurs have all done this. My colleagues Mike Taylor and Matt Wedel have looked into the factors behind neck elongation from the sauropod angle – not exactly comparable to the long-necked piscivores, but close – and noted that there are several aspects of reptile anatomy which lend themselves to having a long neck. They tend to have lightweight heads thanks to the fact they do not orally process their food, which negates the need for heavy jaws, tongues and teeth. Reptiles also seem pretty happy to add bones into their neck skeletons, whereas some clades – like mammals – are extremely rigid in our vertebral counts. Being

TANYSTROPHEUS

TANYSTROPHEUS
Genus: *Tanystropheus*
Species: *longobardicus*
Location: Europe, Middle East, China
Named: 1886
Age: Mid Triassic Period (mid Anisian-mid-Carnian Stages) 245-228mya
Length: 20ft (6m)
Weight: 66lbs (30kg)
Diet: carnivorous

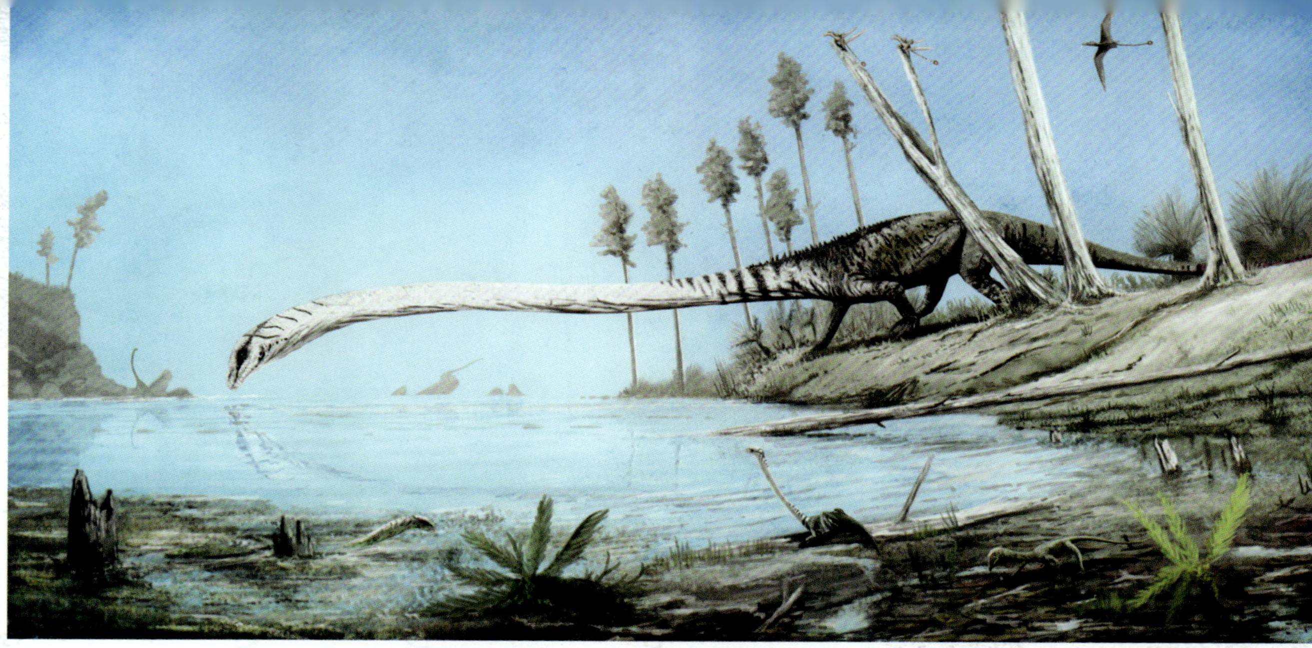

Tanystropheus had an incredible elongate neck. However, rather than being an unusual, geographically restricted one-off, it was both geologically long-lived *and* geographically widespread. The Besano Formation in Italy in particular is famous for the number of complete juveniles discovered there.

Tanystropheus is a member of Protorosauria, a group of reptiles that are in turn part of Archosauromorpha, the huge group that includes archosaurs (crocodylians, dinosaurs, pterosaurs and kin) and all those groups closer to archosaurs than to lizards and snakes. Most protorosaurs were built something like lizards. Several were large (1m long or more), long-necked and therefore closely related to the exceptional, relatively enormous *Tanystropheus*.

The most obvious feature of *Tanystropheus* is its 5-6m-long neck. This was formed of 12-13 hyper-elongated neck vertebrae, the ninth of which was the most exaggerated, it being ten times longer than it was tall. Long, rod-like neck ribs extended along the bottom of each vertebra and would have been attached to muscles used to move the neck. The nature of the joints between the vertebrae indicate that the neck was fairly rigid, though certainly capable of extensive vertical movement at its base. Extra muscle attachment points for the neck were present on the long, broad shoulder blades.

The number of vertebrae in *Tanystropheus*' neck is low compared to the sauropod or plesiosaur neck, a feature which reduced the need for heavy joints and the enlarged bony flanges and ridges that often serve as muscle attachment points. Each vertebra was hollow, a classic weight-saving device, and the neck bones of *Tanystropheus* were not occupied by air-filled sacs and tubes as they were in sauropods and pterosaurs.

The body of *Tanystropheus* is similar to that of less extreme protorosaurs. The limbs were held in a semi-sprawling pose (like those of crocodylians), the forelimbs were shorter and more slender than the hindlimbs, and the limb girdles and digits were robust and well developed. The long bones in both sets of limbs were hollow. The skull was vaguely lizard-like, unusual features including long interlocking teeth and nostrils retracted some short distance from the snout tip. This combination of features has resulted in some significant difference of opinion about the lifestyle and biology of this animal. The interlocking teeth, posteriorly shifted nostrils and super-long neck have been regarded by some experts as evidence of an aquatic lifestyle, an idea also supported by the sediments in which these fossils are preserved and by the presence of fish and squid as stomach contents.

In fact, while the neck is certainly long – making up about 70% of the animal's total length – it does not appear to have been heavy, making up perhaps 20% of the animal's weight (so the remaining 80% present in the body and tail was easily sufficient to counterbalance the neck). Furthermore, the hollow limb bones are a feature typical of terrestrial animals. Animals that live largely in water have dense bones that function as ballast. Long shoulder blades are also rarely seen in aquatic organisms, while the tail of *Tanystropheus* was shortish, slender and compressed dorso-ventrally so as to be wider than tall – again, a contrast to the long, laterally compressed tails of aquatic reptiles.

What seems most likely is that *Tanystropheus* used its long, slender, lightweight neck as a rigid 'fishing pole', and that it frequented coastlines, estuaries and riverbanks, reaching out over the water to grab prey swimming offshore. It does not appear to have been a specialized swimmer, instead being well adapted to walk and run on land. Based on the behavior of their living relatives, we can also say that the fish and squid that *Tanystropheus* preyed on were not only found far from shore, but must have closely approached coastlines, frequently being within reach of a terrestrial bank- or beach-dwelling *Tanystropheus*. It therefore seems that *Tanystropheus* functioned as a sort of Triassic reptilian mega-heron, filling a niche neither occupied by short-necked terrestrial reptiles, nor by those strongly aquatic flippered groups that swam offshore.

carcharodontosaurian *Becklespinax altispinax* (three dorsal vertebrae), eucryptodiran turtle *Hylaeochelys belli* (a shell), and the possible azhdarchoid previously known as *'Paleornis cliftii'* (humerus). *Becklespinax* is modeled closely on *Concavenator*, as they seem closely related and have a similar taste in dorsal ornamentation, though *Becklespinax* has a more vertical anterior sail margin, as indicated by the fossil. Wealden Formation, southern England. Valanginian Stage

Tanystropheus
Digital, 2015
My preferred lifestyle interpretation for *Tanystropheus*: a Triassic croco-heron which snatched prey from shorelines and promontories around coastal waterways. Note the animals perched on rocks out to sea – I have no problem with this animal swimming *per se*, I just don't think it lived in water. Landinian Stage, Middle Triassic, Italy.

big and having support for the front part of the body (either being quadrupedal or aquatic) seems to help too, because neck tissues are heavy and need a stable platform to support them. Mesozoic reptiles were of course often quadrupedal and pretty good at becoming large. And while it doesn't apply to *Tanystropheus* or marine reptiles, many reptiles are also very good at exploiting vertebral pneumaticity to get huge necks with very little skeletal material. As a group, then, reptiles are preadapted for having long necks and we've seen it develop in response to a number of foraging strategies. We think this era of long-necked creatures is odd because we live in a world of short-necked mammals, but it's clear from the fact that so many reptiles independently developed long necks that, for them, it's a pretty easy thing to implement through natural selection.

You make liberal use of integuments and skin coverings, and you've been keen to ensure that the correct skin coverings are used where possible. At the same time, the fossil record for dinosaur skin is pretty patchy. How do you plug the gaps?

Phylogenetic bracketing remains, of course, the tool of choice here, even though we know from modern species that it can't always predict integument types reliably even with good data sets. This is the problem with trying to understand anything biological – there's always exceptions to our predictions. The woolly *Pachyrhinosaurus* is a response to this, playing devil's advocate with the fact that we have scaly skin impressions from a number of ceratopsids, but asking, 'What if there were oddball species, like the hairy rhinos and naked apes we have today?' I'm not trying to 'deconstruct' phylogenetic bracketing, however – it really is the best tool we have for predicting so many aspects of prehistoric animal biology – but it's fun, and important, to explore its limitations.

All this said, we live in an interesting and uncertain time for predicting dinosaur integuments. Some recent fossil discoveries show dinosaurs with extensive coverings of scales *and* filaments, and other studies are now suggesting ornithischian filaments are homologous to those of birds and other theropods. Both undermine assessments of dinosaur appearance where a scrap of scaly skin was considered to represent the integument of the whole animal. There are whole swathes of the dinosaur tree where skin fossils are unknown or extremely rare – sauropods, thyreophorans, early theropods and ornithischians are good examples – and big question marks now hang over the integument of these groups. Were they just scaly, or did they bear filaments, 'protofeathers' or other strange integuments like those we're now seeing in some of our better preserved fossils? It's no longer a question of just wholly scaly or wholly filamentous – there are shades between. And we haven't even mentioned the impact that fuzzy pterosaur fossils have on restoring the ancestral condition of dinosaur skin. We have a lot of gaps in our knowledge to fill here, and I feel we have to be open to the idea that some of these animals may have looked very different to our traditional ideas.

You've depicted some very interesting examples of unconventional behavior in dinosaurs – scavenging ceratopsians and the 'Brontosmash' hypothesis for example. At the other end of the activity spectrum, you've recently discussed how dinosaurs rested. Do you think this kind of behavioral interpretation is important, no matter how hypothetical?

I think a lot of us make paleoart because we want to envisage how these animals lived. If we want to do that, we need to consider the full spectrum of behavior, from routine things like lying down and sleeping to more unusual, rare things like herbivores scavenging or ritualised intraspecific combat. We see a lot of emphasis in paleoart on predator-prey dynamics and, to be

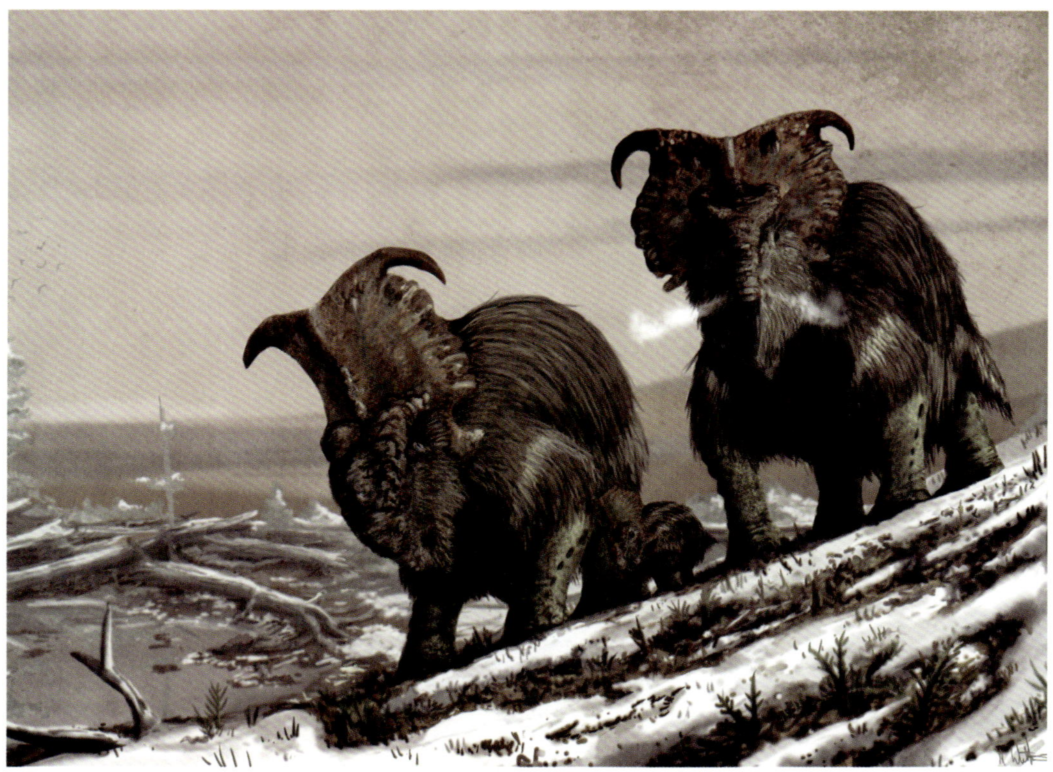

(Below) **Woollysaurs**
Digital, 2013 revised 2015
A family of the Alaskan centrosaurine *Pachyrhinosaurus perotorum*, a species notable for its existence in rather chilly Late Cretaceous climates at paleoaltitudes of 80-90°. Maastrichtian Stage.

(Right) **Brontosmash**
Digital, 2015
Multiple tonnes of *Brontosaurus excelsus* in disagreement. Kimmeridgian/Tithonian Stage, Late Jurassic, USA.

(Next spread; Left) ***Sinornithoides***
Digital, 2013, revised 2016
Three *Sinornithoides youngi*, one standing, one sitting, one sunbathing. The poses are speculative. Early Cretaceous, Aptian-Albian Stage, China.

(Next spread; Right) ***Polacanthus***
Digital, 2013 revised 2015
A Wealden tree vies for attention with *Polacanthus foxii* and some tiny birds. There are two species of birds shown here: a flock of small grey forms leaving the tree, and a suite of smaller brown birds hanging out on the *Polacanthus* itself. These animals are speculative additions to this Wealden scene based as they are on possible and as yet undescribed avialan teeth. Early Cretaceous, England. Barremian Stage.

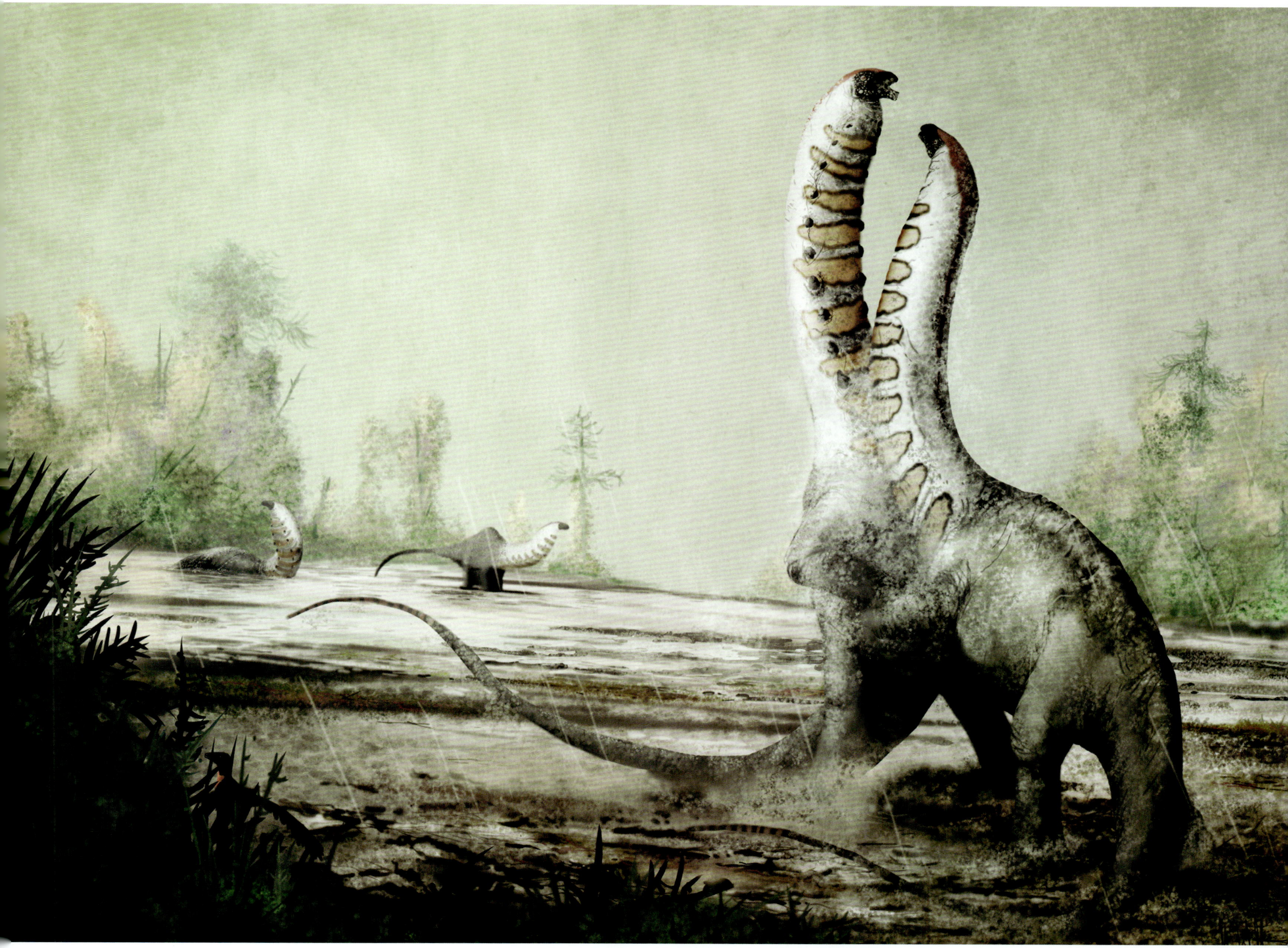

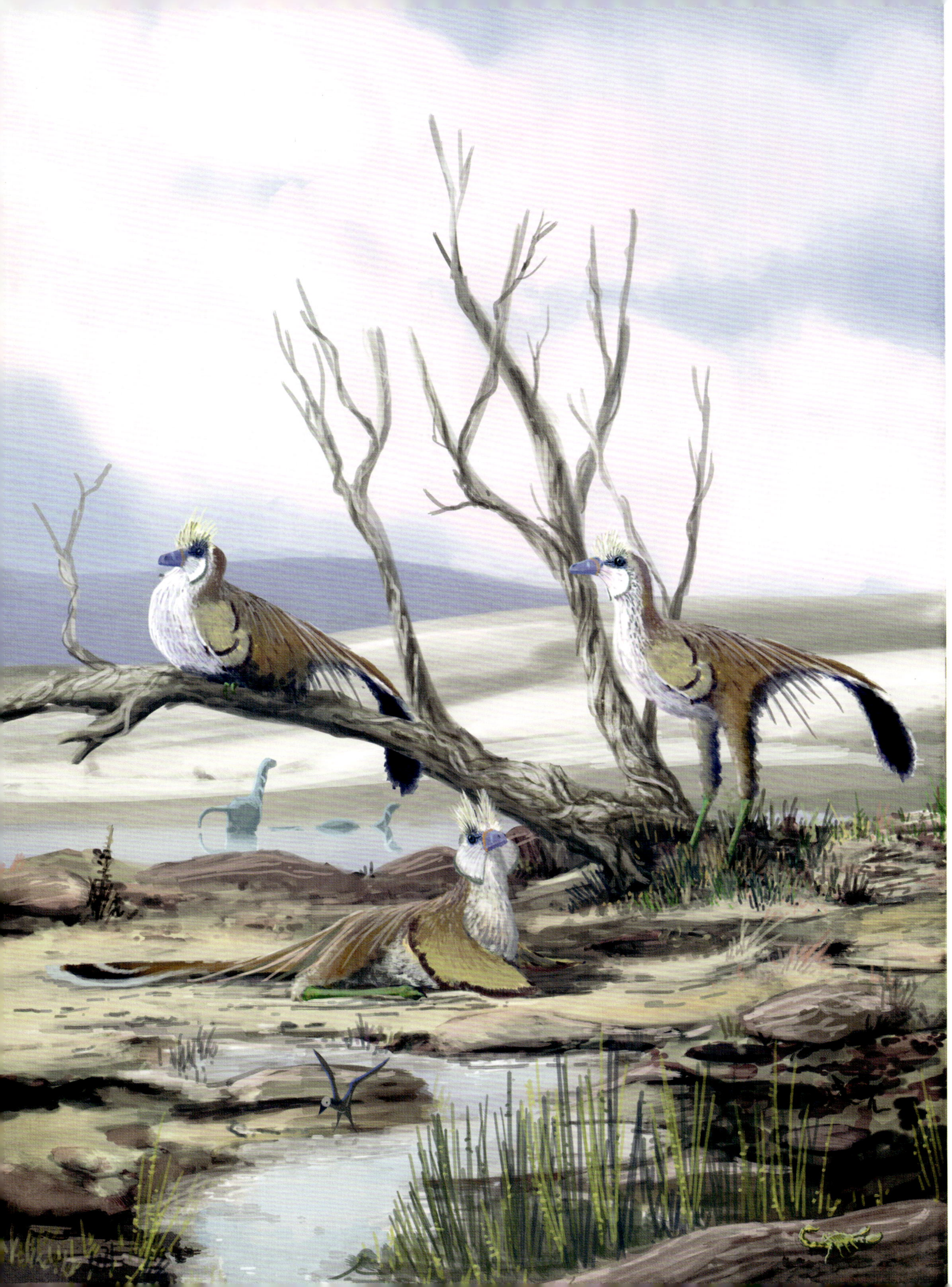

honest, I feel that's been done to death: there are many alternative behaviors we can show, many of them supported by or even directly demonstrated in the fossil record. Moreover, I think we can show a lot more about animal paleobiology away from the predator-prey arena. The Brontosmash hypothesis shows us that long sauropod necks may not just be about reaching tall trees, and emphasises the truly weird neck anatomy of apatosaurines. A sleeping or resting theropod allows us to appreciate its form and anatomy for what it was and consider how they might have behaved when they weren't chasing prey species. Paleontological science is a lot more than just figuring out who ate who, and I think we have a responsibility as artists to portray as many facets of it as we can.

Do you have a particular process when composing your artwork? Do you sketch or thumbnail?

It depends on what I'm reconstructing, and who it's for. Working primarily digitally allows for a very organic creative process where revision and changes are easily implemented, and if I'm painting something I have familiarity with and have only myself to please, I might just work through from the initial concept to the final piece. I generally start work only once I have a fairly solid idea in mind anyway and, although my pictures tend to evolve from that initial idea during the painting process, it's easy enough to keep tweaking or modify the composition as I go. It can be a bit heartbreaking undoing, obscuring or removing work from a painting if it represents a significant time investment, but thankfully this doesn't happen too often. Moreover, all the thumbnails and sketches in the world don't remove the fact that we make mistakes, pursue ideas that just don't work as well in one format as they do in another, or simply change our mind on certain things. One of the key aspects of improving artwork is realising when we have to make changes, no matter how painful they seem at the time.

Working with unfamiliar animals requires some preparation before diving in, however. Though this is initially more to understand the anatomy, range of possible poses and character of the species than to work up compositional ideas. The former is ultimately constrained by science, and thus has to be worked out before we can take the species to the drawing board and place it in an interesting composition. It can be a bit daunting being presented with a wholly unfamiliar fossil animal and a tight deadline, because if I don't understand the creature in question, I may not be able to form an interesting image around it.

Naturally, working with clients necessitates the production of sketches for approval and comment. Mine tend to be very, very rough and quick – enough to tell what's going on (just) and discuss ideas, but nothing like the wonderful concept sketches produced by other artists. This is partly because art is only one aspect of my professional life. I'm also engaged in other projects as an author, editor, referee and consultant, and that doesn't always leave huge amounts of time for producing concept art to polished stages. The time I have for art has to be directed to the finished piece, or it risks taking too long to produce.

Is there anything missing from your canon of work – some thing or place you'd love to explore artistically but haven't had the chance?

I find myself increasingly wanting to explore the parts of "deep time" that we rarely see: those poorly represented ages and species that other artists, for whatever reason, just aren't depicting. I've enjoyed working on paintings of unusual Triassic reptiles and stem-mammals, and had a good response from scientists working on these groups – I think they're happy to see paintings equivalent to those being made for dinosaurs and pterosaurs being applied to more obscure groups. So I'd like to do more on these clades, but would also like to move

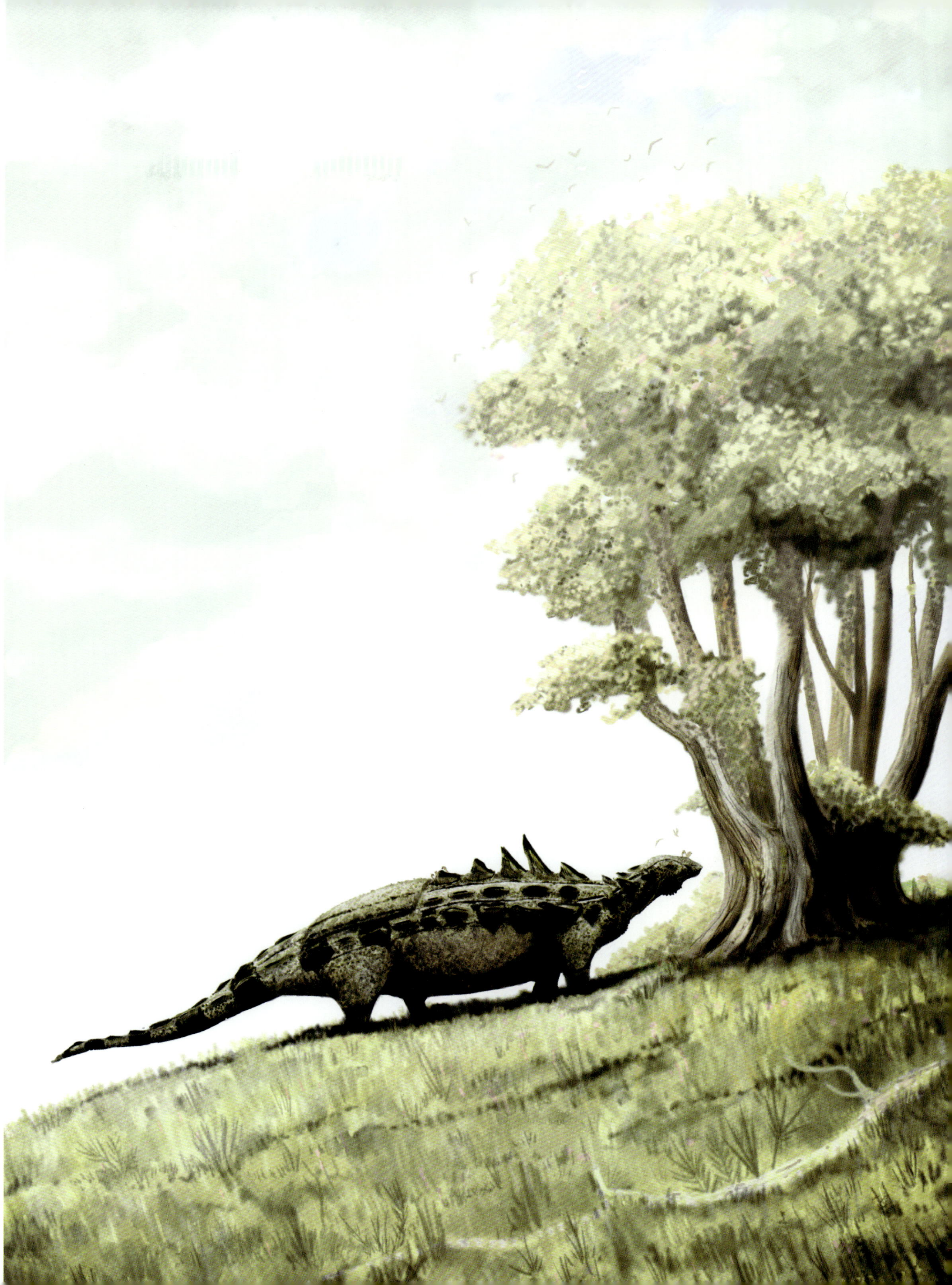

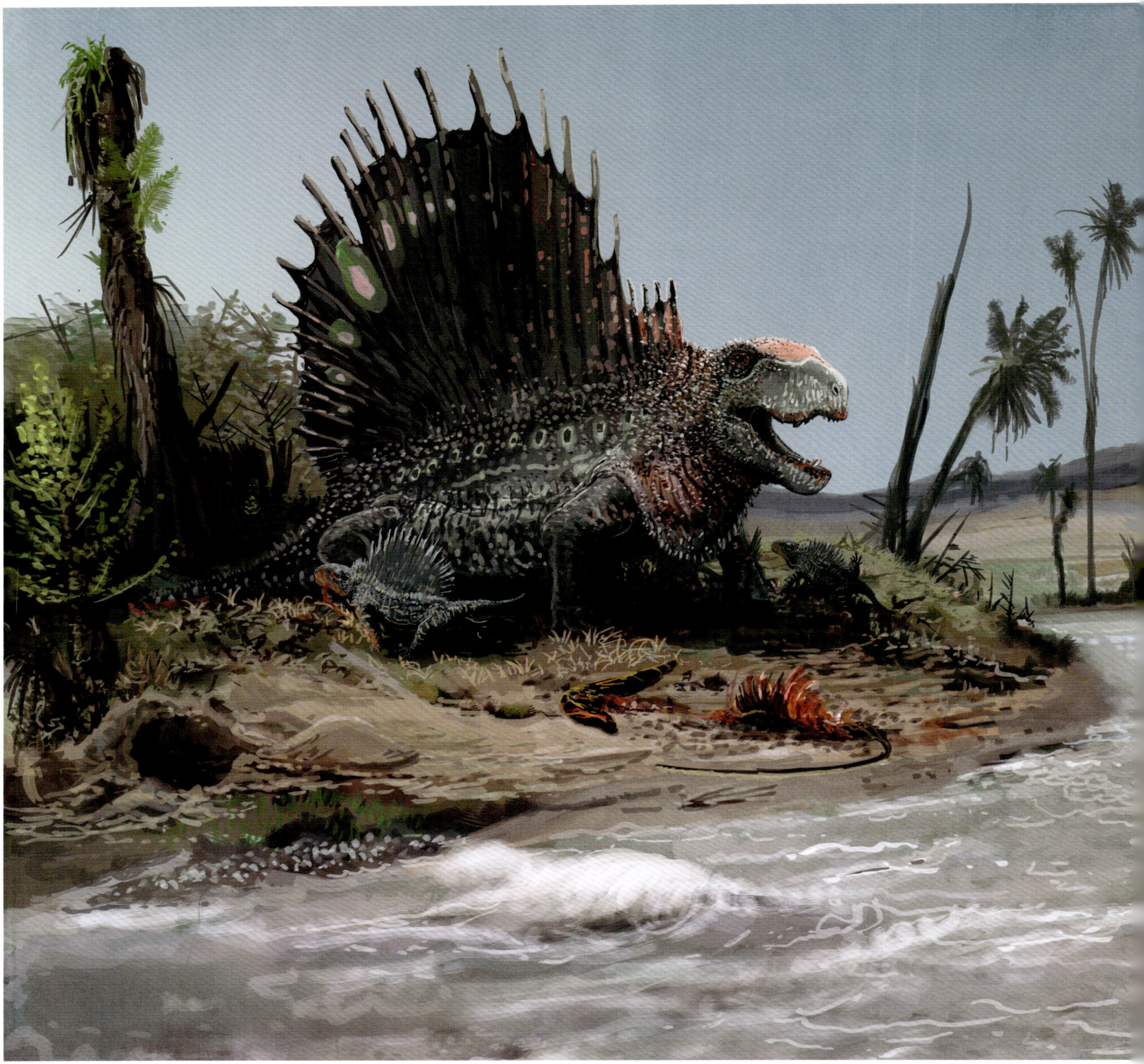

Dimetrodon grandis
Digital, 2017
A modern restoration of one of the classic 'non-dinosaurs', using information from new studies, especially regarding the classic 'sail'. *Dimetrodon* is a predatory sphenacodontid synapsid known from the Cisuralian Stage of the Early Permian Period, 295-272mya. Red Beds of Oklahoma and Texas.

(Opposite top)
Stereognathus ooliticus
Digital, 2015
Two wary *S. ooliticus* keep a moonlit eye on possibly troublesome dinosaurs. Bathonian Stage, Middle Jurassic, England.

(Opposite bottom)
***Triceratops* on the Plains**
Digital, 2015
Turns out that *Triceratops horridus* had some of the coolest scales of any dinosaur: huge interlocking tubercles with low bosses and spikes. No other dinosaur has skin like this – at least, not without supporting osteoderms. Maastrichtian Stage, Late Cretaceous, USA.

backwards in time from the Mesozoic. After all, dinosaurs, pterosaurs and Cenozoic mammals have fairly good representation in art, but early synapsids, archosauromorphs, early tetrapods and Paleozoic seas aren't featured that often. I'd like to help redress that balance.

Who were your influences when you started out? And whose work are you currently a fan of?

Given that I initially focused most of my artistic attention on pterosaurs (I started getting professional attention during my PhD studies, when my brain was full(er) of flying reptiles), it's hard to say whose footsteps I was trying to follow in when starting out. For dinosaurs, you've got the guidance of modern masters like [Gregory] Paul, [Douglas] Henderson and [Mark] Hallett. For mammals, you've got [Mauricio] Antón and [Carl] Buell. But we've never really had a professional paleoartist who specializes in pterosaurs. There are of course some people who have rendered them very well in the past (John Conway stands out as being one of the first people to really 'get' pterosaurs), but there was no obvious 'authority' or text to follow on restoring pterosaurs ten years ago. It's only in the last decade that paleoart-minded folks have made restoring pterosaurs a relatively accessible pastime. The closest person we had to a pterosaur paleoartist before then was Peter Wellnhofer, the scientist who began the modern age of pterosaur research in the 1970s and dabbled in pterosaur art himself. Wellnhofer created skeletal reconstructions and very well illustrated papers, as well as the odd life restoration, and these were undoubtedly important references for anyone making pterosaur art in the early 2000s. His work remains very useful today.

In terms of more general artistic influence, my real drive for paleoart developed in that interval where pre- and post-renaissance dinosaur art was duking it out in books and magazines and we had no internet to check facts with. As with many children of the 1980s, John Sibbick's work was the pinnacle of art for most books and magazines, but I remember noticing, and being enthralled with the few Paul paintings that I saw as a young person. *Jurassic Park* came out when I was nine, and I thought Mark ["Crash"] McCreery's concept art for its dinosaurs was great. I also remember the first time I saw Ricardo Delgado's art in his *Age of Reptiles* comics and you can see an obvious watershed in my drawings from that time. Although his prehistoric animals were in a comic book, they carried a sense of character and anatomical detail that the work of many contemporary artists lacked. I think I'm still in my post-Delgado phase, to be honest: you can still see his influence on my landscapes in particular – dramatic cliffs and waterfalls, distant mountains and so on. As a teenager and early twenty-something, I read a lot of Paul and [Robert] Bakker, and found their art an important, inspirational component of their arguments. I

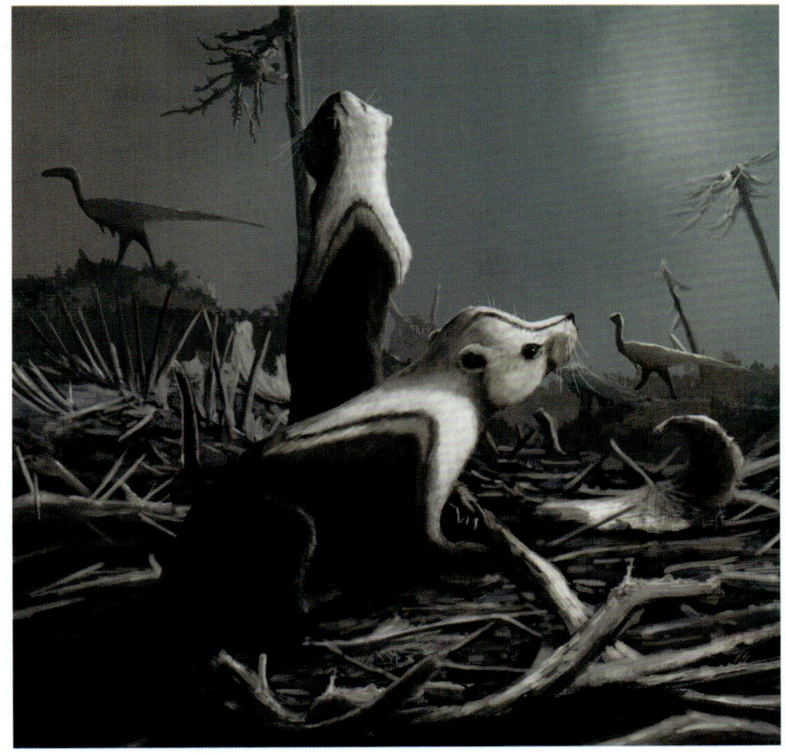

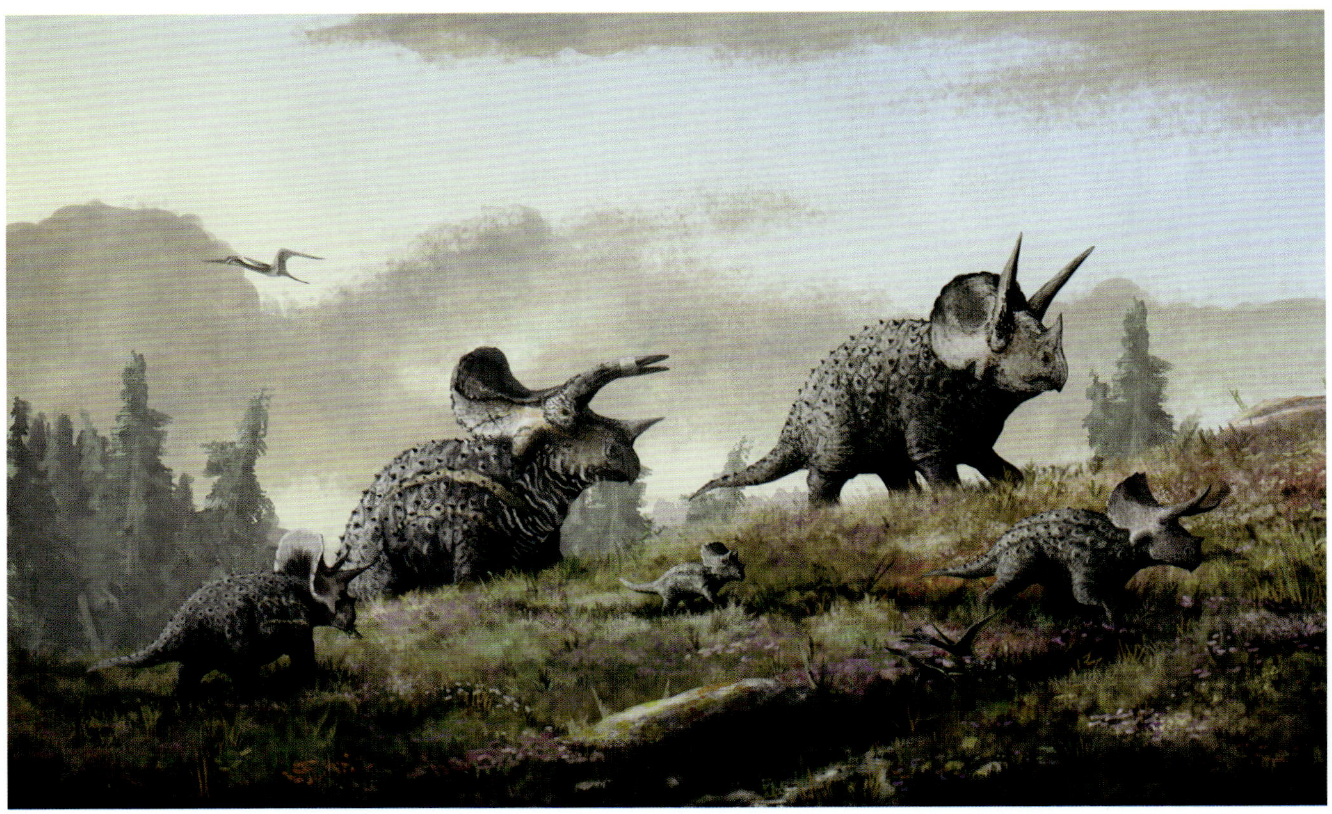

don't think anyone interested in the art of fossil reptiles can deny the importance, and inspiration, of Paul's work. More than anyone else, he's set (or at least standardized) the framework that we all still largely work in.

There are a lot of terrific modern paleoartists, and the pool of talent is so huge that it's hard to pick a few choice favorites. But it's difficult not to stare at works by Conway, Julius Csotonyi, Emily Willoughby or Henderson. And Bob Nicholls is unrivalled, I think, for scenes of extinct marine species. These artists have very different styles, but they really understand how to compose natural scenes and they shy away from over-posed, aggressive animals. But I also find myself increasingly drawn to the classic era of paleoart, and the work of Charles Knight and Zdeněk Burian. We might look at their work as outdated now, but their paintings also show animals which *look* real, and actually inhabited the landscape they lived in. And their skills with real artistic media are enviable – I have enormous respect for anyone who can paint without undo buttons and separated digital layers.

You're another paleoartist who's transited to academic writing. At what point did you decide to put finger to keyboard? Was it always part of your plan or an accident of the research you conducted for your artwork?

I'm a scientist who became an artist, rather than the other way around. My training is in the scientific side of paleontology, and nothing to do with art. I gave up art classes when I was sixteen. Drawing and sketching has been a lifelong hobby, and there's always been a strong link between my interests and artistic output, but it was only with coercion from friends and family that I started distributing my pictures online and became involved in press work for scientific discoveries. So yes, it was always a plan to get involved in research: the unplanned bit was getting so involved in the artwork. I never expected to be reliant on my work to make a living, or for it to be featured in compilation volumes of paleoartwork, that's for sure!

What advice would you offer to an aspiring paleoartist, beyond buying your book?

Paleoart is such a specialized field, with so many skills to learn and practice, that it's hard to give a short, succinct answer here. There's a lot of obvious things to say – keep up with the latest science, learn as much as you can about how fossils are formed and interpreted, get your name out there and, yes, learn as much as you can about modern animals as well as the fossil ones with research papers, dissections, zoo visits and so on. The best paleoartists know how living animals go together, and you can see it in their work. What's more, they know how animals move and how to situate them in their landscapes: getting outside and watching real animals do their stuff is an invaluable aid here. But if I can give some advice based on my own experience, it would be to not be afraid to get stuck into those groups people haven't really explored in detail yet. Indeed, if you're looking to make a name for yourself it can help to be that person who brings poorly represented parts of evolutionary history to life. Why not be that person who's known for early sauropterygians, or for early synapsids which aren't *Dimetrodon*? Researchers often lament the lack of artwork for anything which isn't a dinosaur or pterosaur, so good artwork of alternative species will be noticed – that's not something to be taken for granted when making a living as an artist. Adding another picture of *Tyrannosaurus* to the mountain of artwork of that animal is not the way to stand out. When looking for subjects, remember that there's no such thing as a boring fossil subject, just boring ways to recreate them. Immerse yourself in the literature on these animals, learn what makes them interesting (and remember that what scientists emphasise is not always what artists and the public find exciting) and start recreating things no-one has witnessed for millions of years.

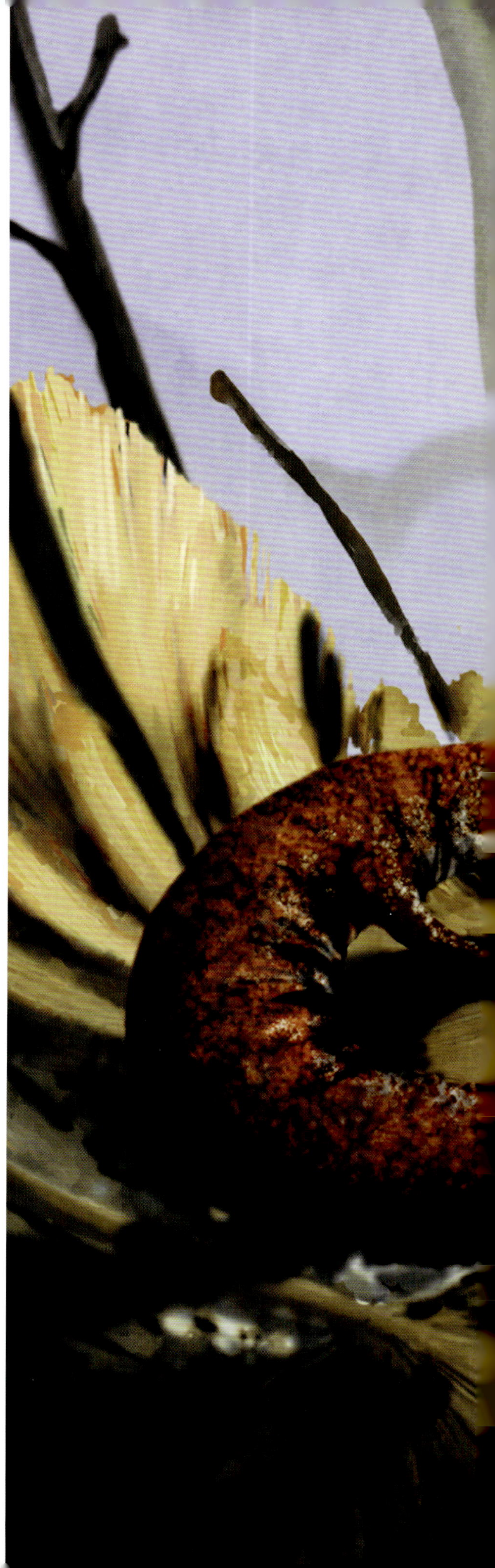

Wesserpeton
Digital, 2013 revised 2015
Two tiny (35mm from snout to vent) *Wesserpeton evansae* get in each other's faces, because some animals are just jerks. Early Cretaceous, Barremian Stage, UK.

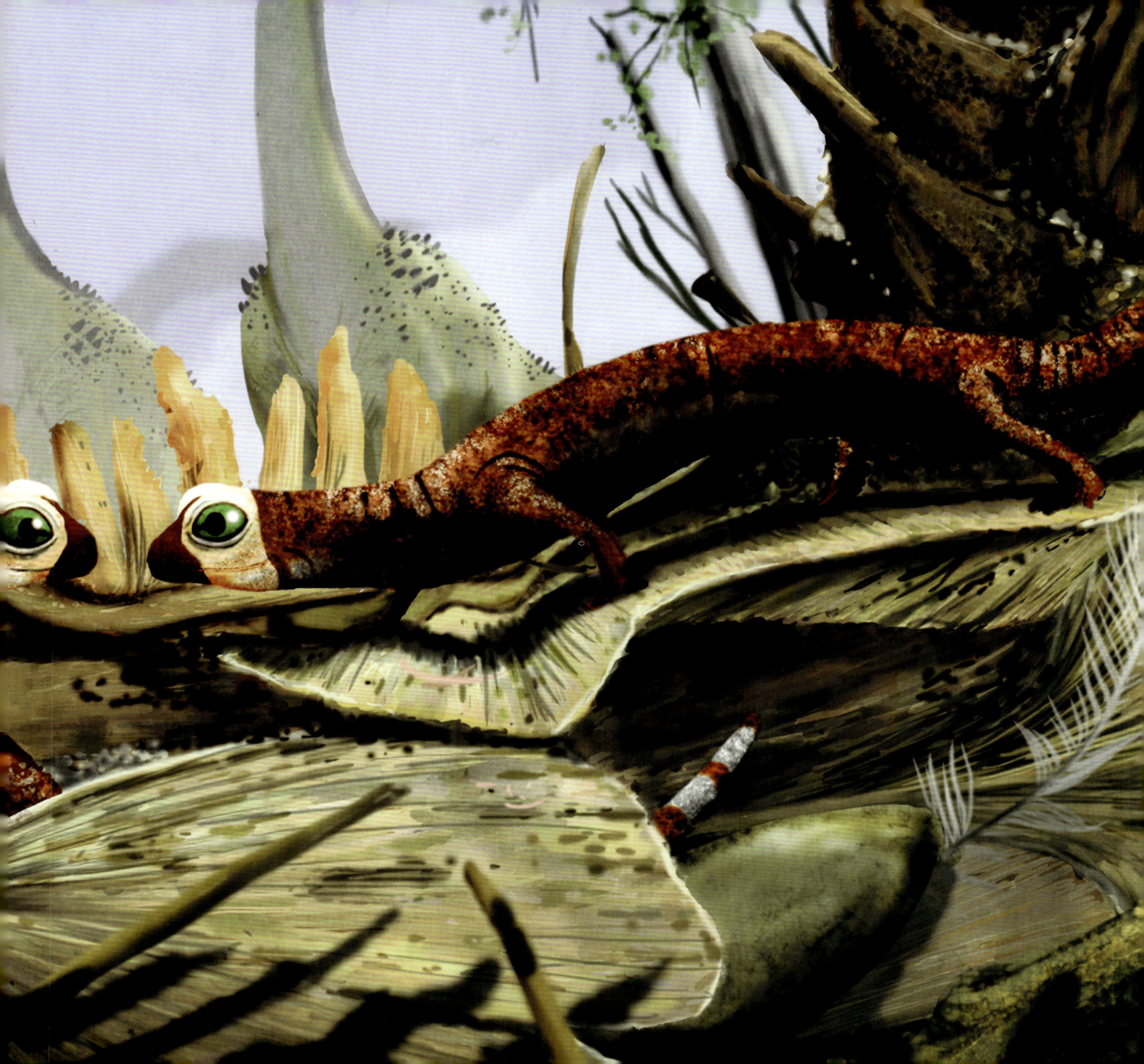

JULIO LACERDA

BRAZIL

Both illustrator and graphic designer, Julio Lacerda became fascinated by paleoart at the age of seventeen. His work has since been published and shown in several countries, including Japan (a pterosaur exhibition at the Fukui Prefectural Dinosaur Museum) and the USA (the academic paper announcing the discovery of *Siats meekerorum*, North Carolina Museum of Natural Sciences). He is also staff artist and writer on the natural history website Earth Archives.

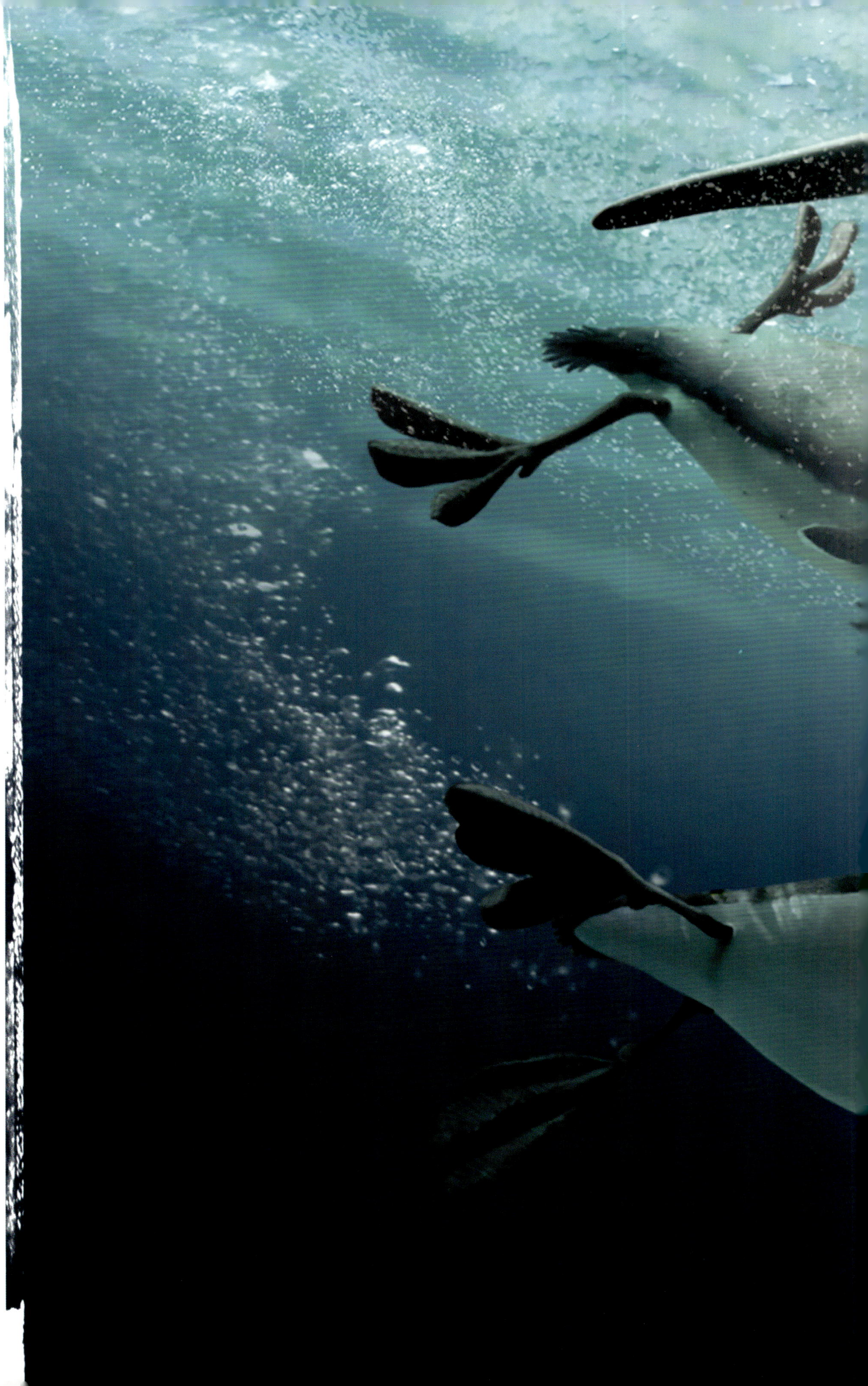

Fish Theft

Digital, 2015

Below the surface of the Cretaceous Inland Seaway, a shallow ocean that covered the center of North America during the Late Cretaceous, a thieving pair of the flightless seabird *Hesperornis* harass a fishing *Pteranodon*. The image was based on research that suggested that the pterosaur may have been quite competent under the water as well as over it.

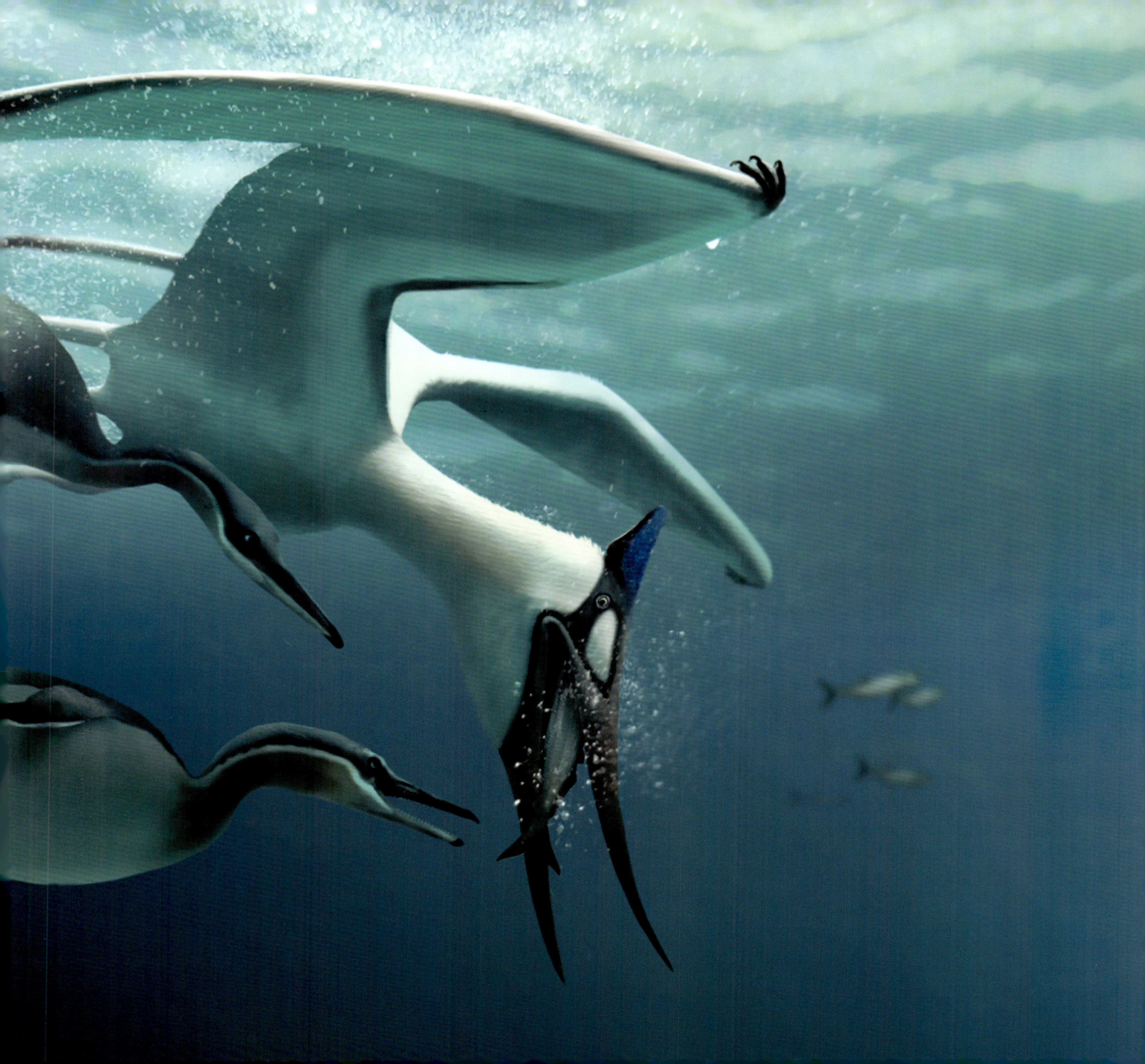

When did you first realize you had artistic talent?
I'd always been an artistically oriented child, something I inherited from my mother, who is a painter at heart. I started drawing at around three years of age and never really stopped.
At what point did you switch to the digital medium?
I had been experimenting with digital illustration on and off for a while, but started really dedicating my time to learn it properly in the last five years.
What programs and software do you use?
I use Adobe Photoshop for the illustrations themselves, but I also often use Blender to create 3D models that help me in creating a scene that I can then export and paint over.
Can you detail your artistic process from start to finished art? How long does an average illustration take?
My painting process is really varied. I love wildlife photography, so occasionally I stumble upon some beautiful pictures that give me inspiration to do something similar; on other occasions, I have a specific idea for a behavior or scenario in mind and try to bring that concept to fruition.

In terms of methodology, I something draw on paper, especially when I do not have a clear direction in mind, and after sketching I scan the drawing and work digitally on it; other times I start from scratch in the digital medium. Regardless of how the painting came into

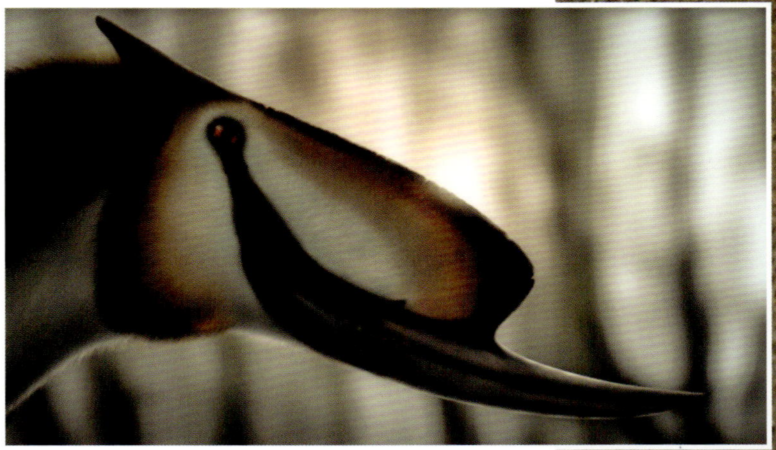

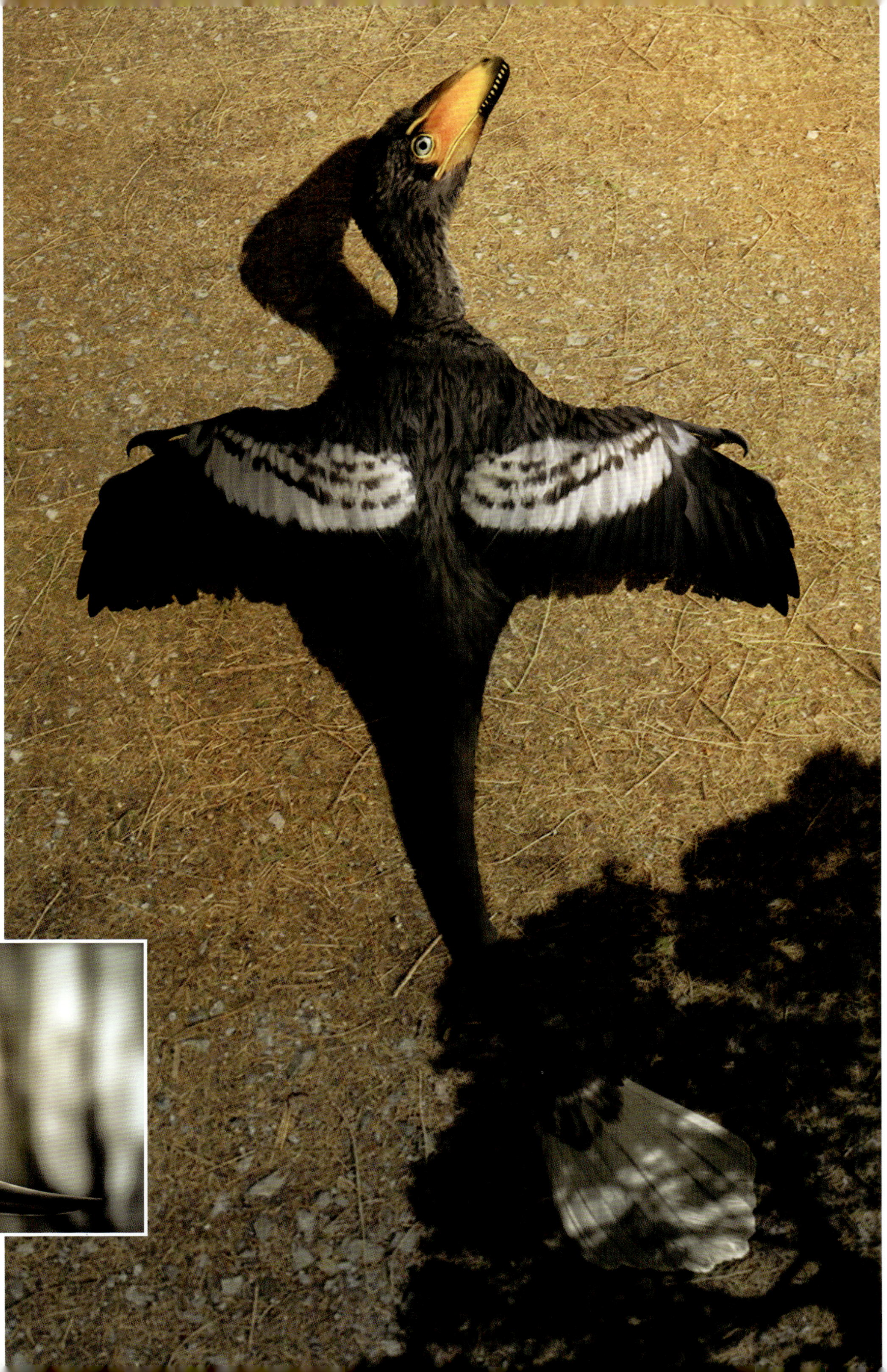

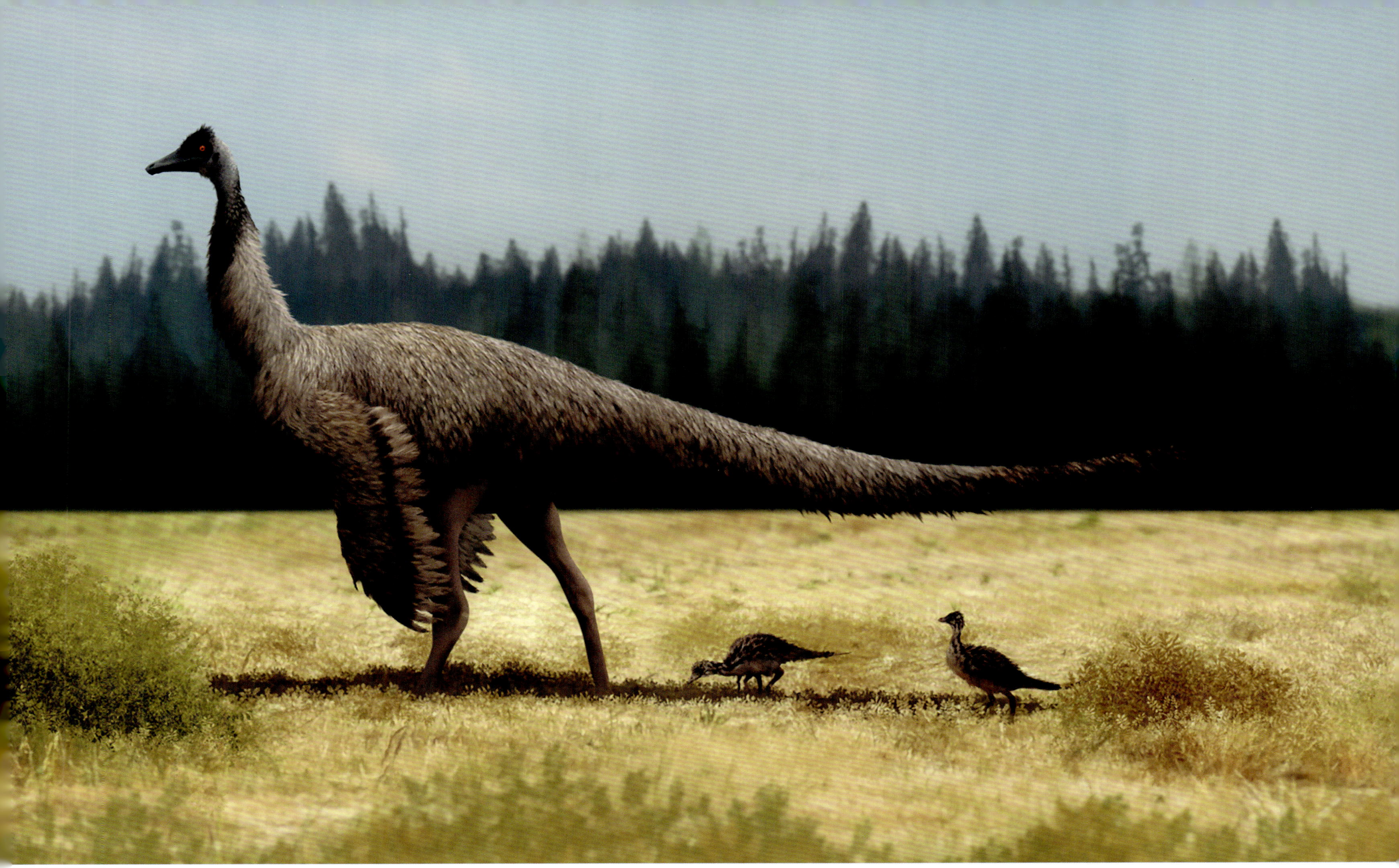

(Far left) **Who Are You Callin' Ugly?**
Digital, 2012
A chance to beautify the "ugly" Chinese pterosaur *Dsungaripterus*.

(Left) **Sun Worshiper**
Digital, 2014
A sunbathing *Deinonychus*.

(Above) **Big Bird**
Digital, 2012
A mother *Ornithomimus* taking her chicks for a walk.

(Right) **Photobombing Level: Cretaceous**
Digital, 2013
Paddling *Austroraptor cabazai*.

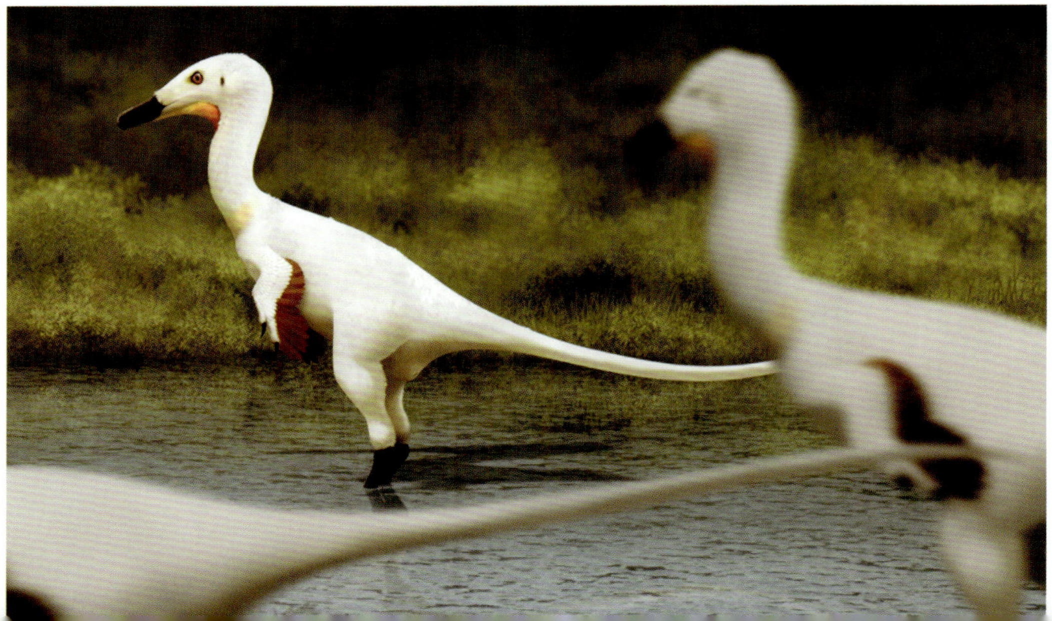

being, that can take anywhere between one day to a week or more, but I guess three days would be the average time for completing a project.

How much research and preparation do you do?

As I said, I usually gather lots of references before starting to work on something; this includes photographs of live animals, fossils, landscapes and scenarios, color palettes, skeletal reconstructions and, sometimes, other pieces of paleoart. I enjoy focusing on the "art" side of it, so searching for inspiration to create the perfect atmosphere and feel of an image is an important part of my creative process.

You have a very 'clean', almost photographic look to your art; was that just how your style developed or did you set out to achieve it?

That wasn't something that I set out to do at the start, but as time passed I felt more and more dedicated to creating the most realistic images I could. On one hand that is a bit limiting, since I now find myself having difficulty exploring different styles; but on the other hand I like to imagine the illustrations as being actual photographs that could have been taken by a time traveller, and bringing this same feeling to the audience is gratifying to me.

Do you have particular sources of inspiration for your compositions?

I always look at the works of professional wildlife photographers for inspiration, both the safari and expedition style of photography, which is very objective and has a clear educational message, and the kind of artistic photography that tries to capture the mood and focuses on the details. Over the years I've learned a lot of photography techniques and I try to incorporate those into my art.

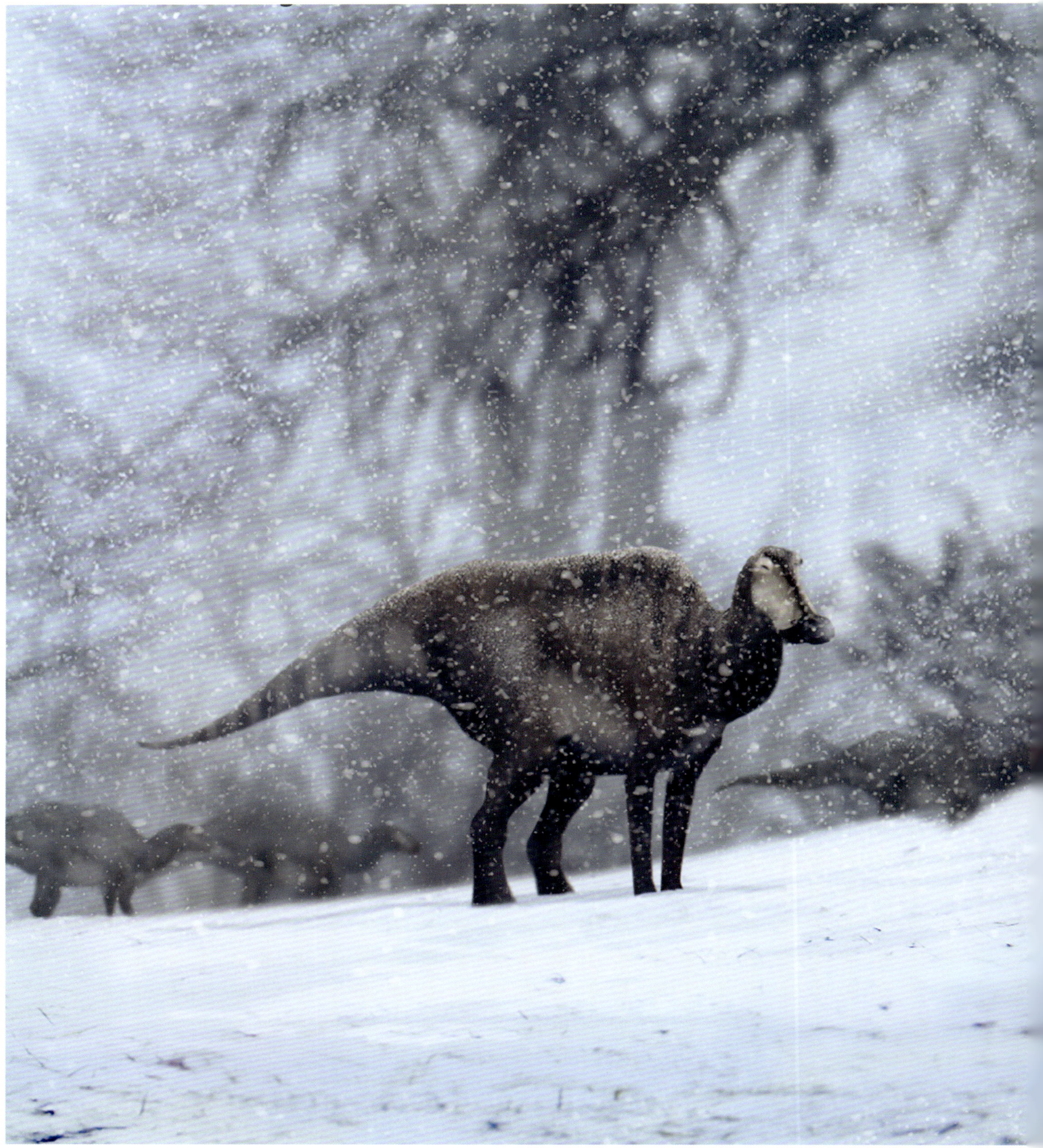

Fear Is For the Long Winters
Digital, 2013
An *Edmontosaurus regalis* encounters a small mammal about to inherit the Earth at the very end of the Cretaceous.

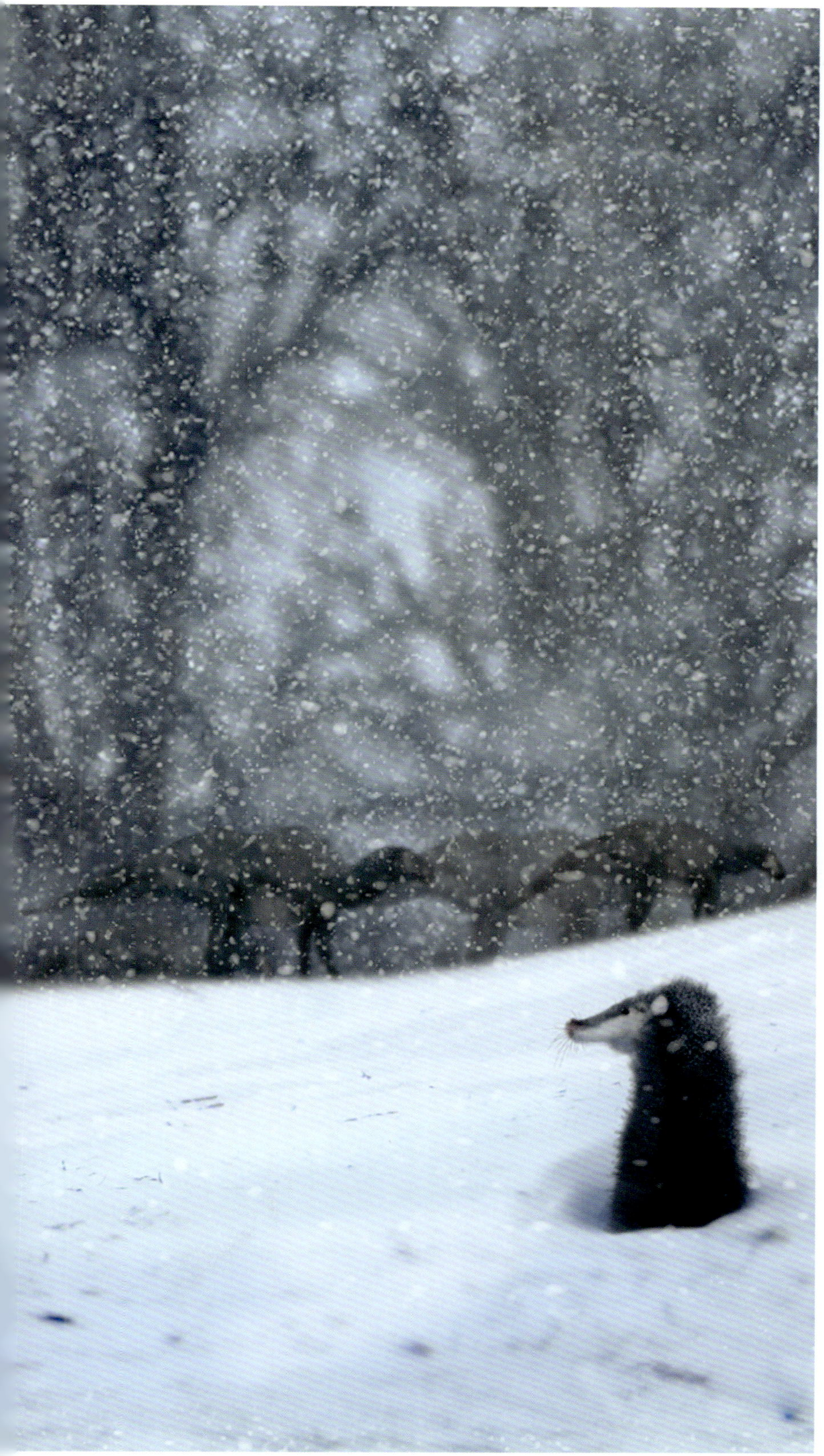

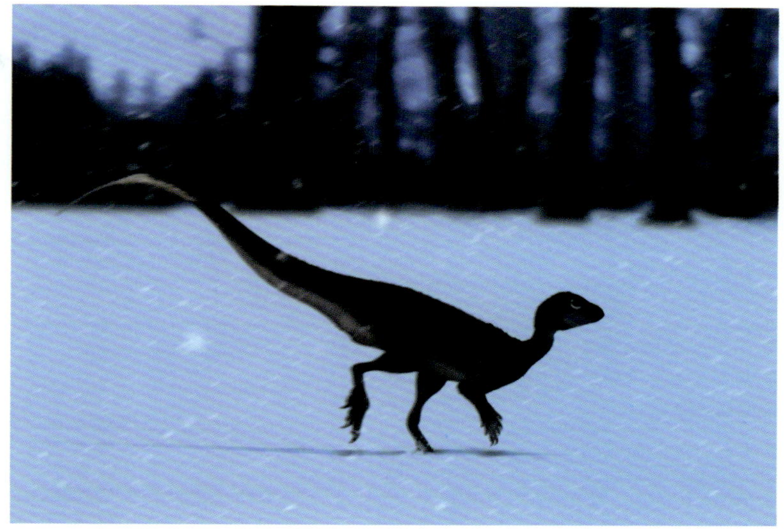

(Left) **There Goes the Sun**
Digital, 2013
A *Trinisaura* flees during the Antarctic winter. *Trinisaura* is one of several ornithopods known from Antarctic and Patagonian sites who may have had to endure polar winters. Snow Hill Formation, Lower Campanian Stage, Late Cretaceous.

(Below) **Royal Wedding**
Digital, 2016
A pair of *Gorgosaurus libratus* courting. Late Cretaceous, Canada.

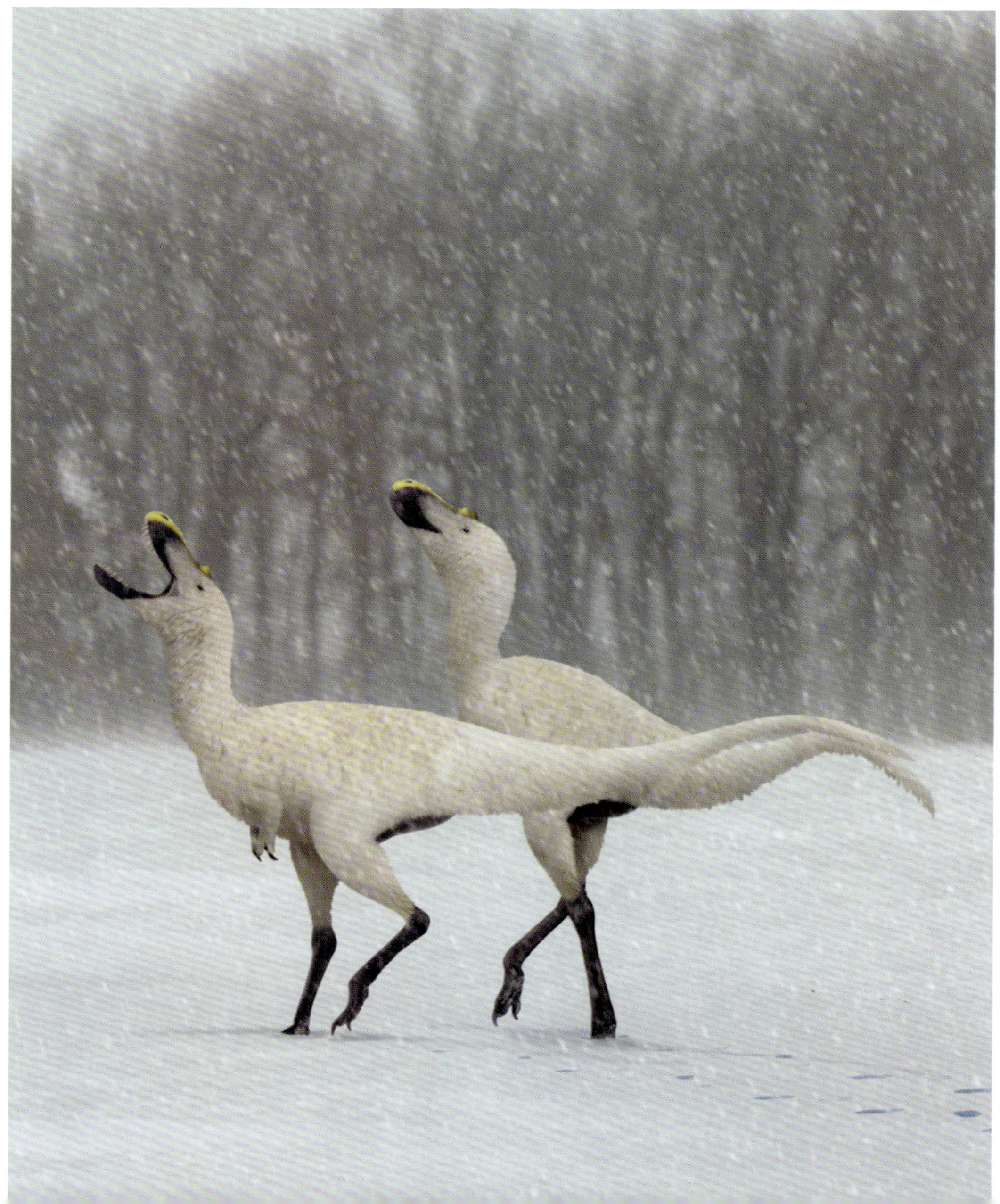

Your illustrations cover subjects on air, land, and sea. Is there one particular setting you favor the most?

I guess my favorites are flying and underwater scenes, probably because of the simple aero- or hydrodynamic shapes, which are delightful to draw; and the fact that I can easily place vibrantly colored animals against the soft background of the sky or water, creating a contrasting and eye-catching composition. I also like to make soothing and peaceful pictures, something that was once very rare in paleoart, and underwater scenes or cloudscapes are a good way to achieve that.

Who are your biggest influences?

I consider some of the great paleoartists of our time as my biggest influences, like John Conway and Andrey Atuchin. Those are people whose work fascinated me and made me try my own hand at drawing dinosaurs. However, I like to keep my eye on this new generation of artists that are popping up, particularly with the help of social media, and every now and then I discover someone remarkable, like Antonin Jury, Paul Heaston and RJ Palmer (to name just a few), who inspires me to keep going and learn

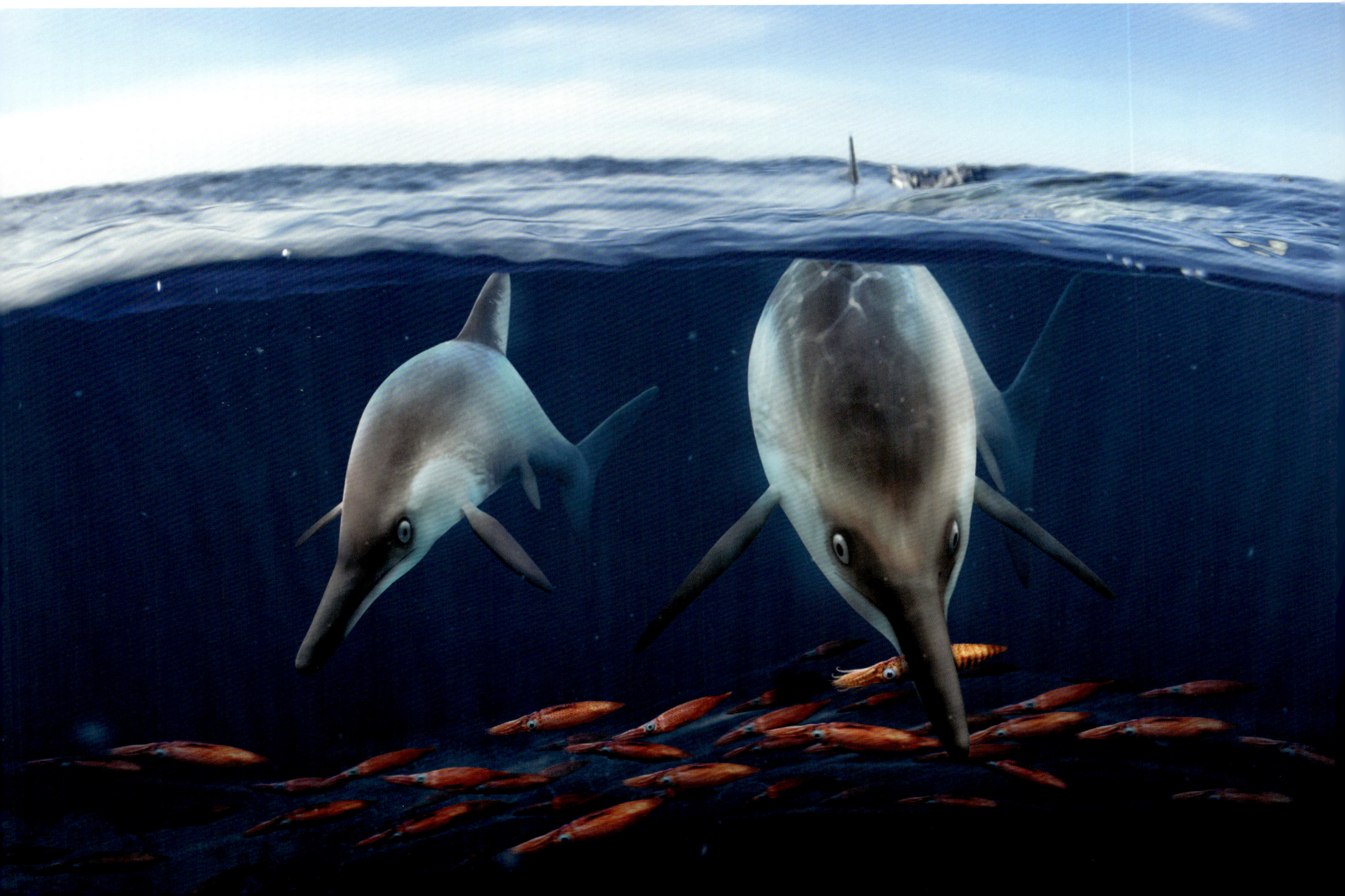

(Left) ***Ichthyosaurus somersetensis***
Digital, 2017
I. somersetensis hunting belemnites in the shallow seas that covered Europe during the Early Jurassic. This species was named in 2016 from fragmentary remains discovered in the 1840s!

(Right) ***Ichthyosaurus larkini***
Digital, 2017
A pod of *I. larkini* herding a baitball of small fish. This species of ichthyosaur was named in 2016 following research that led to a major reclassification of the genus. Early Jurassic, Britain.

(Far right) **Washed Ashore**
Digital, 2012
The pterosaur *Nyctosaurus gracilis* alights beside the carcass of a young *Tylosaurus proriger*.

(Overleaf) ***Yutyrannus***
Digital, 2012
Yutyrannus huali amidst the snow of a chilly winter. The description of *Yutyrannus* in 2012 caused a sensation. Up until that point, most known feathered dinosaurs were small – just a few feet long – but at 30ft (9m) long, this huge theropod is still the largest known dinosaur with a covering of proto-feathers. Studies suggest that winters in the Yixian were cold, so such an integument is hardly surprising. Early Cretaceous, Yixian Formation, China.

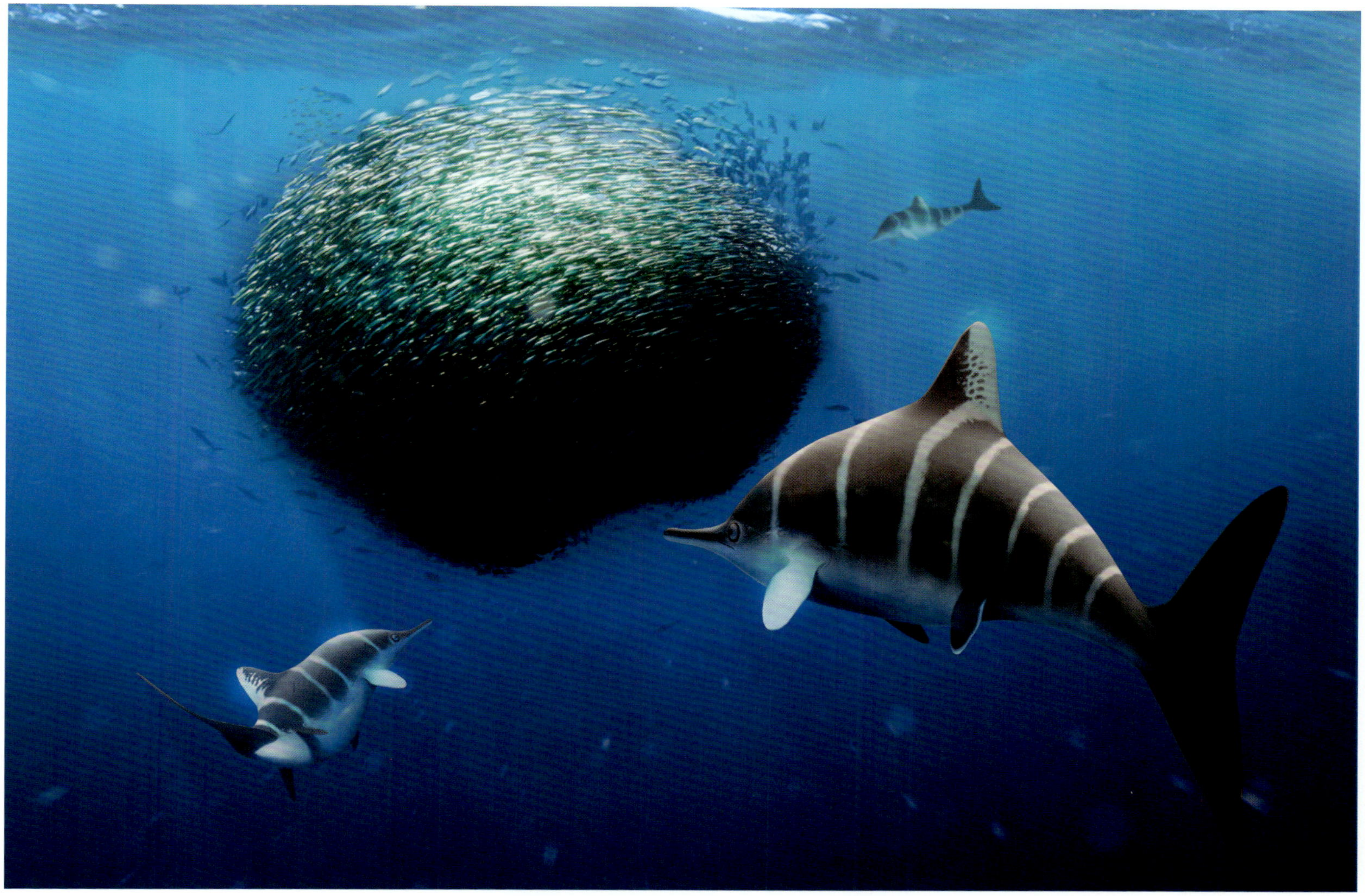

new things in order to keep up.

What recent paleontological finds or ideas have excited you? Do you read something and think, "I have to paint that!"?

I'm always very intrigued by discoveries that hint at previously unknown integuments on dinosaurs, and the implications that always come with such finds. I'm also very interested in unusual hypotheses regarding behaviors that may or may not have been preserved in some way in the fossil record. But I'm usually pretty late to the party when something new has been discovered and by then everyone is drawing it!

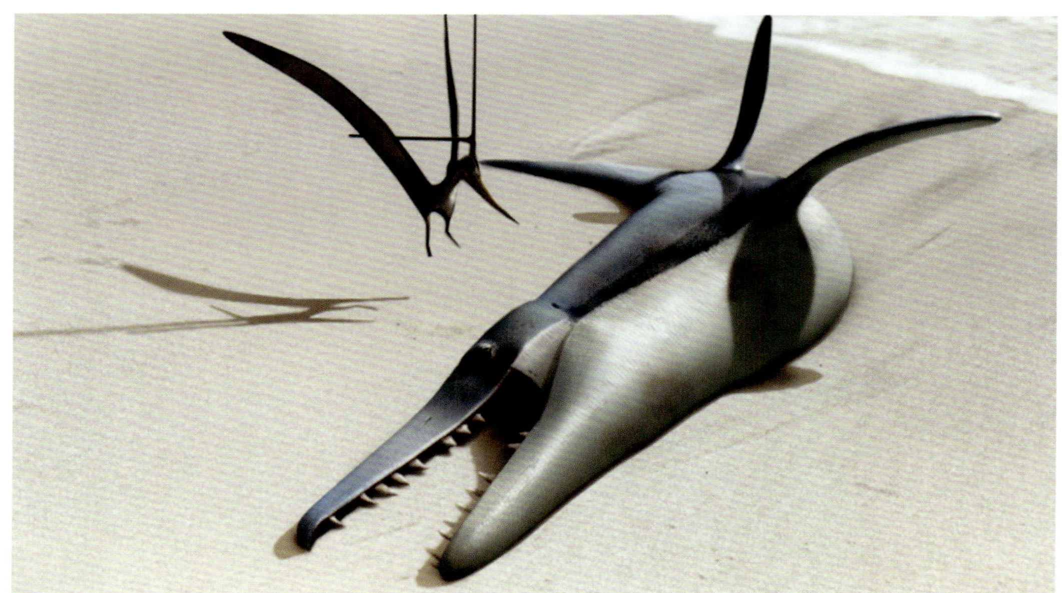

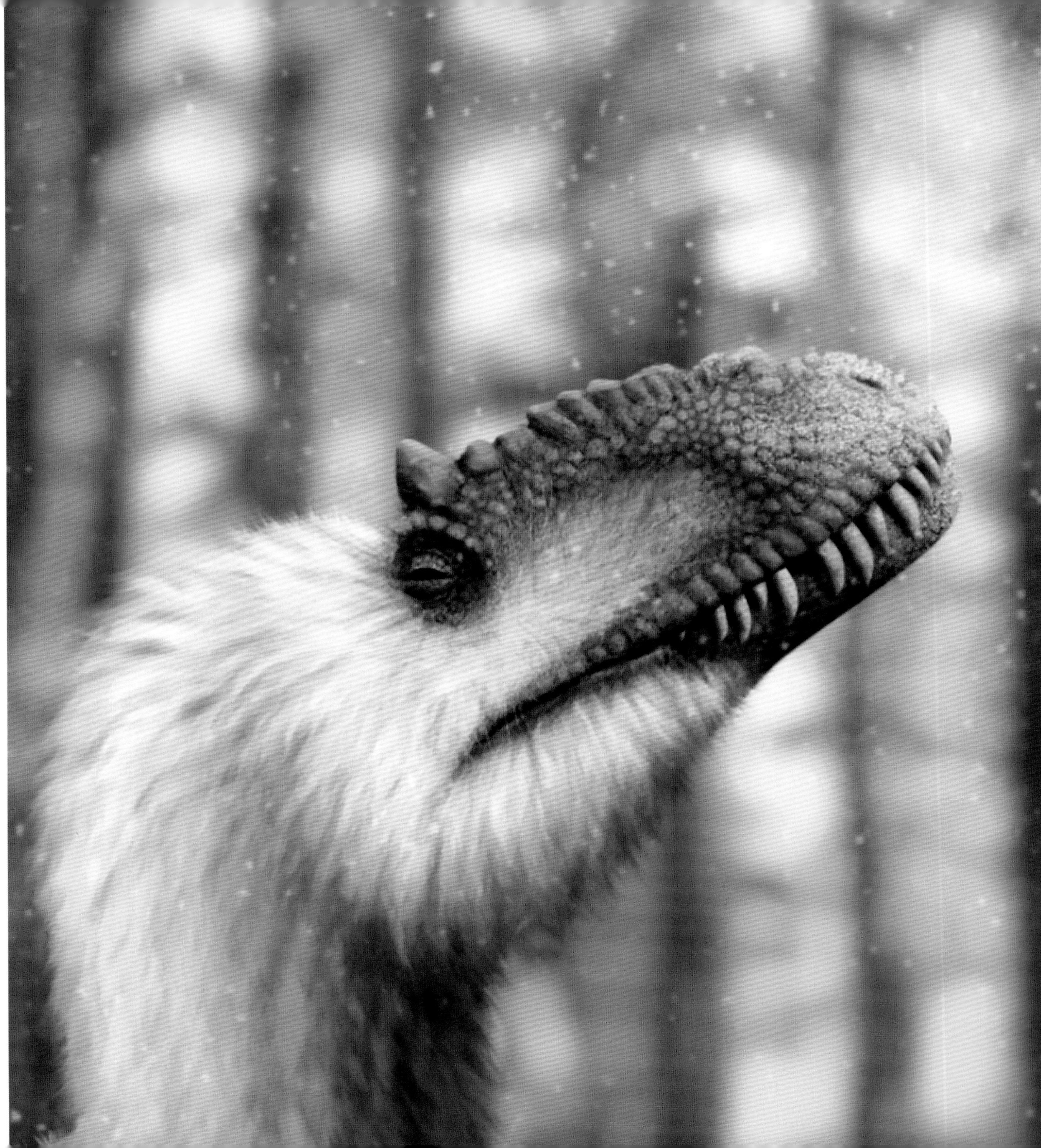

(Right) **The Antlered Flyer**
Digital, 2012
The strangely crested pterosaur *Nyctosaurus gracilis*.

(Far right) **Exquisite**
Digital, 2012
Linheraptor exquisitus, a little-known dromaeosaurid dinosaur named in 2008. The feathering is modeled on quails and willets.

(Below) **Courtship**
Digital, 2012
Courtship behavior in the pterosaur *Pteranodon* (or *Geosternbergia*) *sternbergi*.

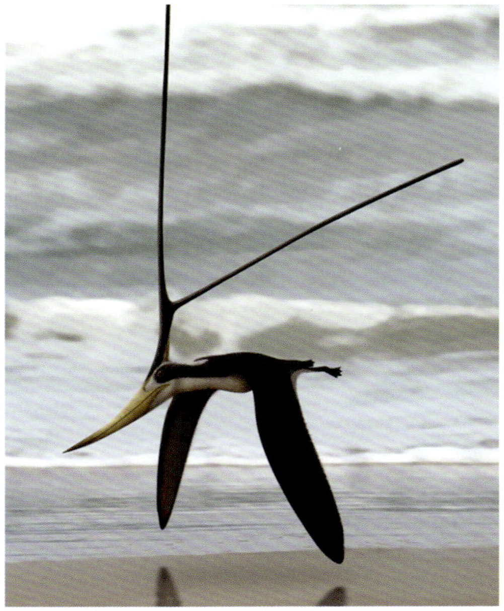

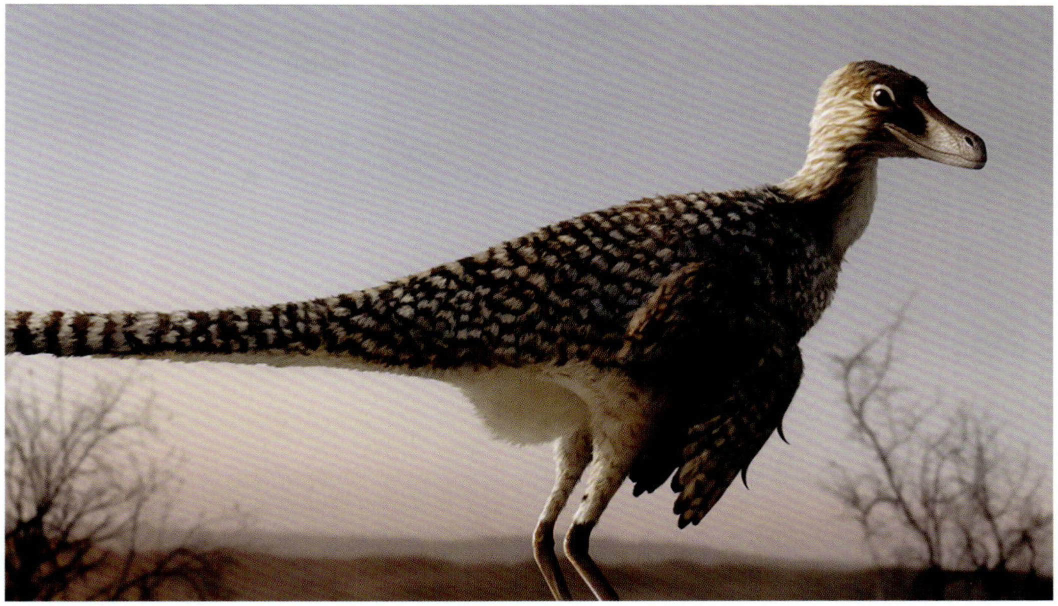

What are your favorite animals to paint?
I have a very soft spot for pterosaurs, which can easily be noticed by how many of them I have in my portfolio! To me they are the right combination of alien and familiar, strange and elegant. They totally feel like something that we could see today and be in awe of, yet we can't. My second favorites are the almost-birds, since they show the fascinating transition between avian and non-avian dinosaurs; they feel so marvellously different and yet not so dissimilar to the birds we have today.
If there was one time you could go back and visit, when and/or where would it be?
As cliché as it sounds, probably the Cretaceous, in any location. The mix of extinct and still-living fauna and flora, as well as the enormous diversity of species and the spectacular range of sizes is so interesting!
Is there a big difference between illustrating dinosaurs and mammals? Do you feel you need to use a great deal more imagination when illustrating dinosaurs?
I'm only now trying my hand at extinct mammals and I have to say, most of the time, it's not as exciting. At their core it seems that

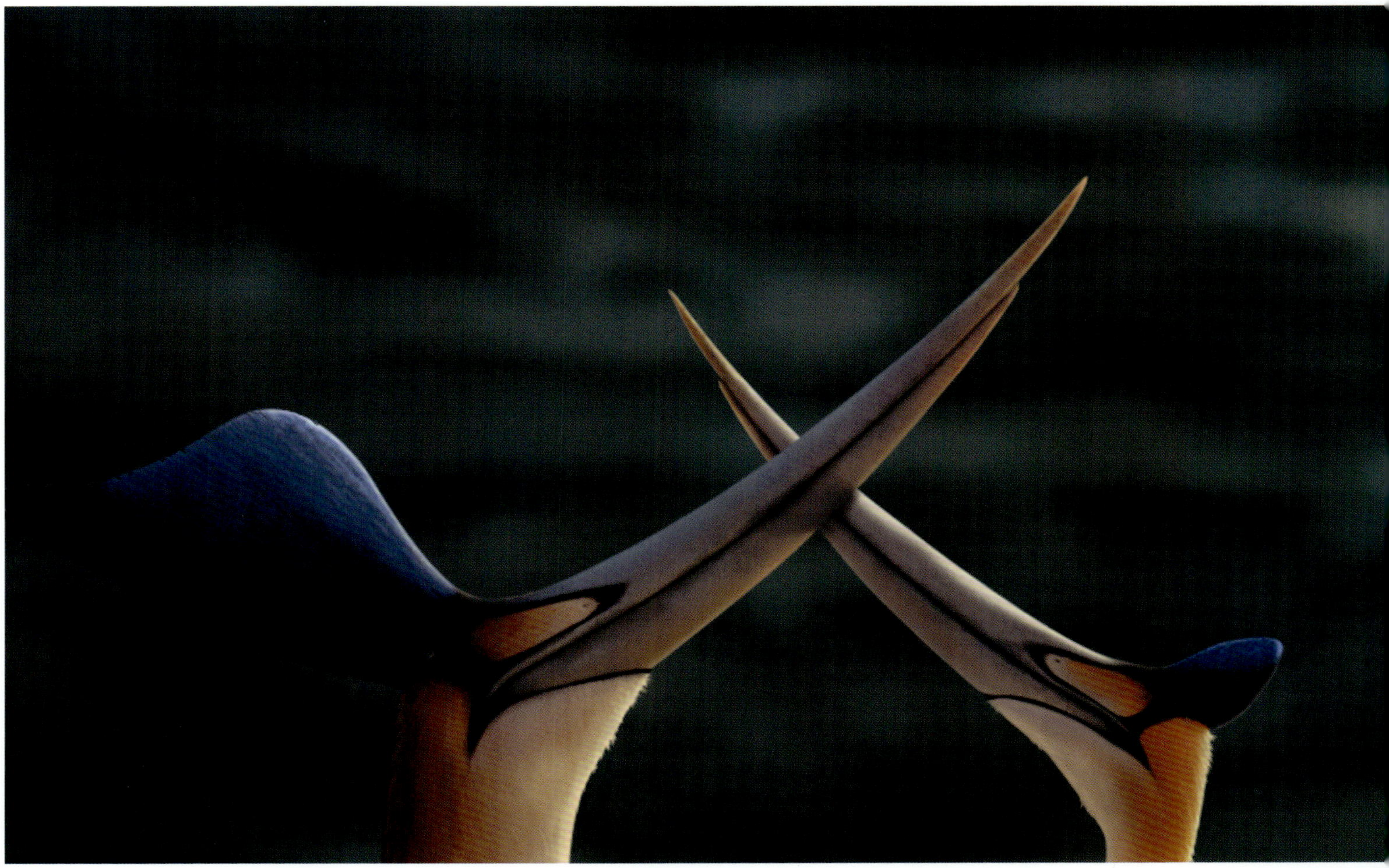

(Right) **The Great Dying**
Digital, 2012
The therapsid *Inostrancevia*, with a melanistic dark coat of fur, looks up at a sudden burst of dust and sulphur thrown up by the distant Siberian Traps. These eruptions are one of the 'smoking guns' that may have triggered the mass extinction event at the end of the Permian Period around 250mya.

(Below) **Terminator Pigs**
Digital, 2016
A pair of the pig-like entelodont *Archaeotherium* fight over territory.

(Opposite) **Magnolia**
Digital, 2014
A *Pachycephalosaurus* scans the horizon beside his favorite magnolia tree. Late Cretaceous, USA.

every one of them is a mix of things that we can see at the zoo today, and as much as they can be beautiful and fascinating in their own right, that doesn't compare to the utter strangeness of dinosaurs in general. I feel like we definitely have more room for speculation when it comes to the 'terrible lizards'.

You're a relatively new artist to the field of paleoart – any advice for newcomers?

Always keep drawing, because as with so many other things in life, we get better by practicing – and not only better when it comes to skill, but also in finding what exactly we most enjoy drawing and how, and that reflects in the quality of our work. Always try to learn new things, both artistically and scientifically, since there's plenty of science involved. And make full use of the internet, the great tool of our generation. All these new discoveries are now at our fingertips, but so are amazing people from the community that can teach us new things every day.

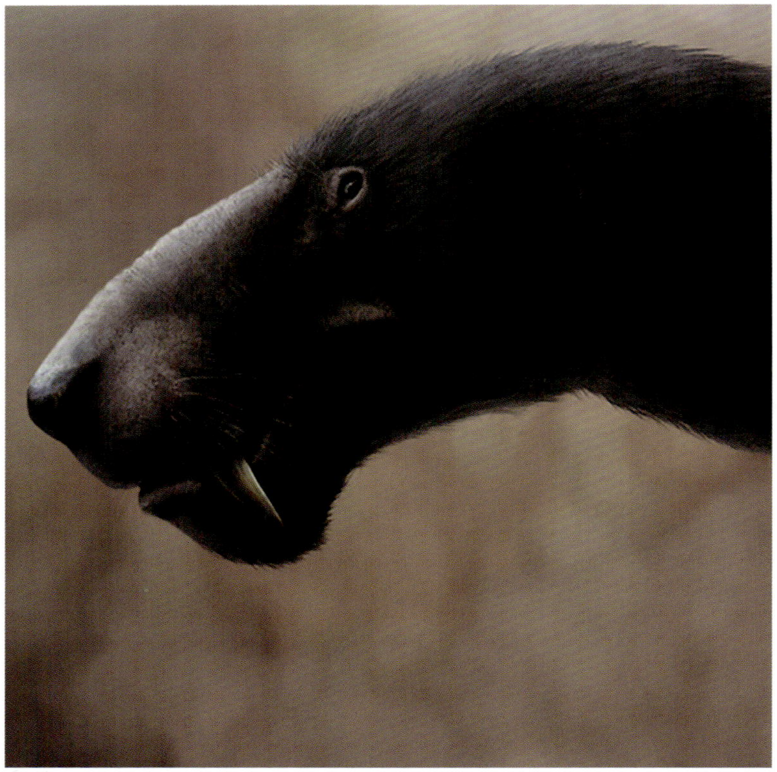

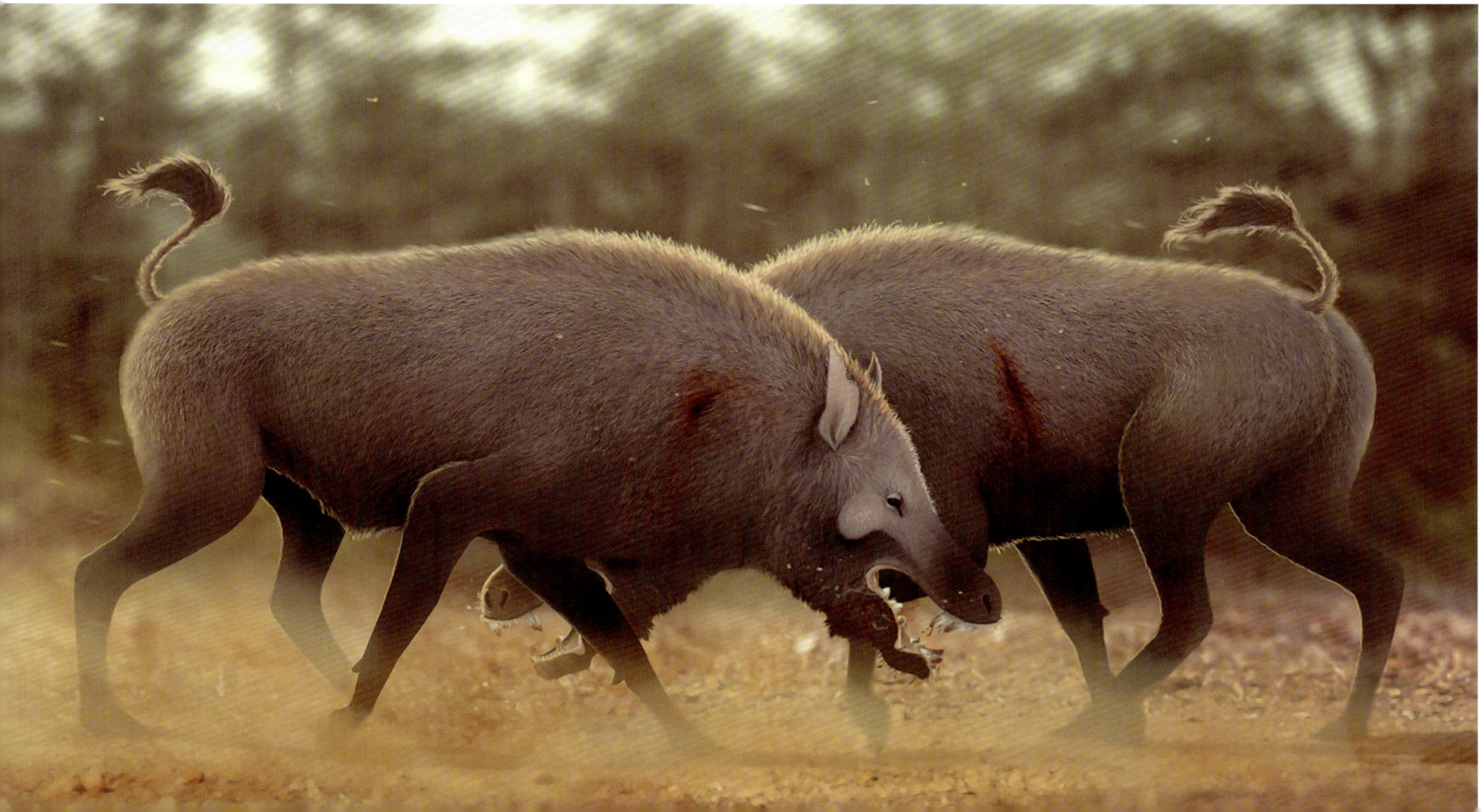

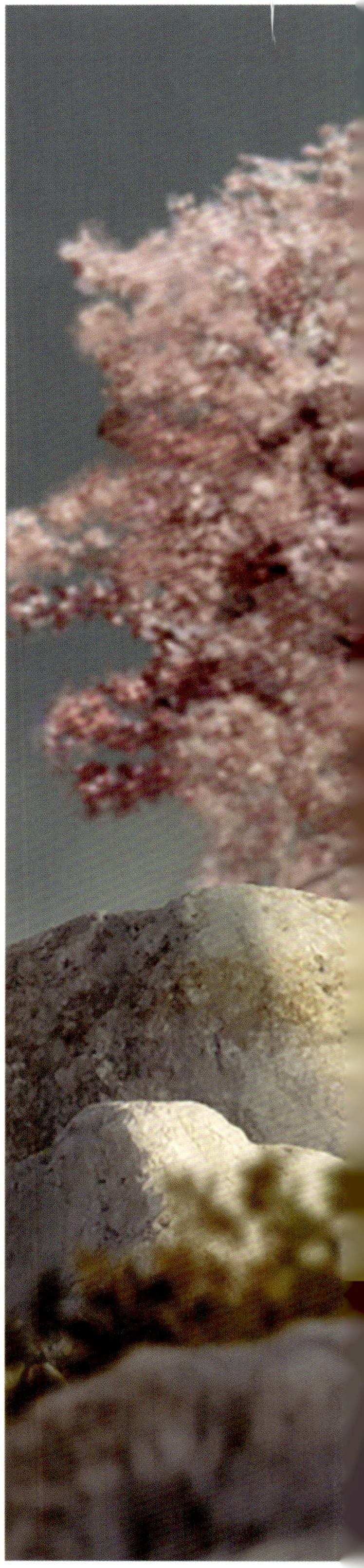

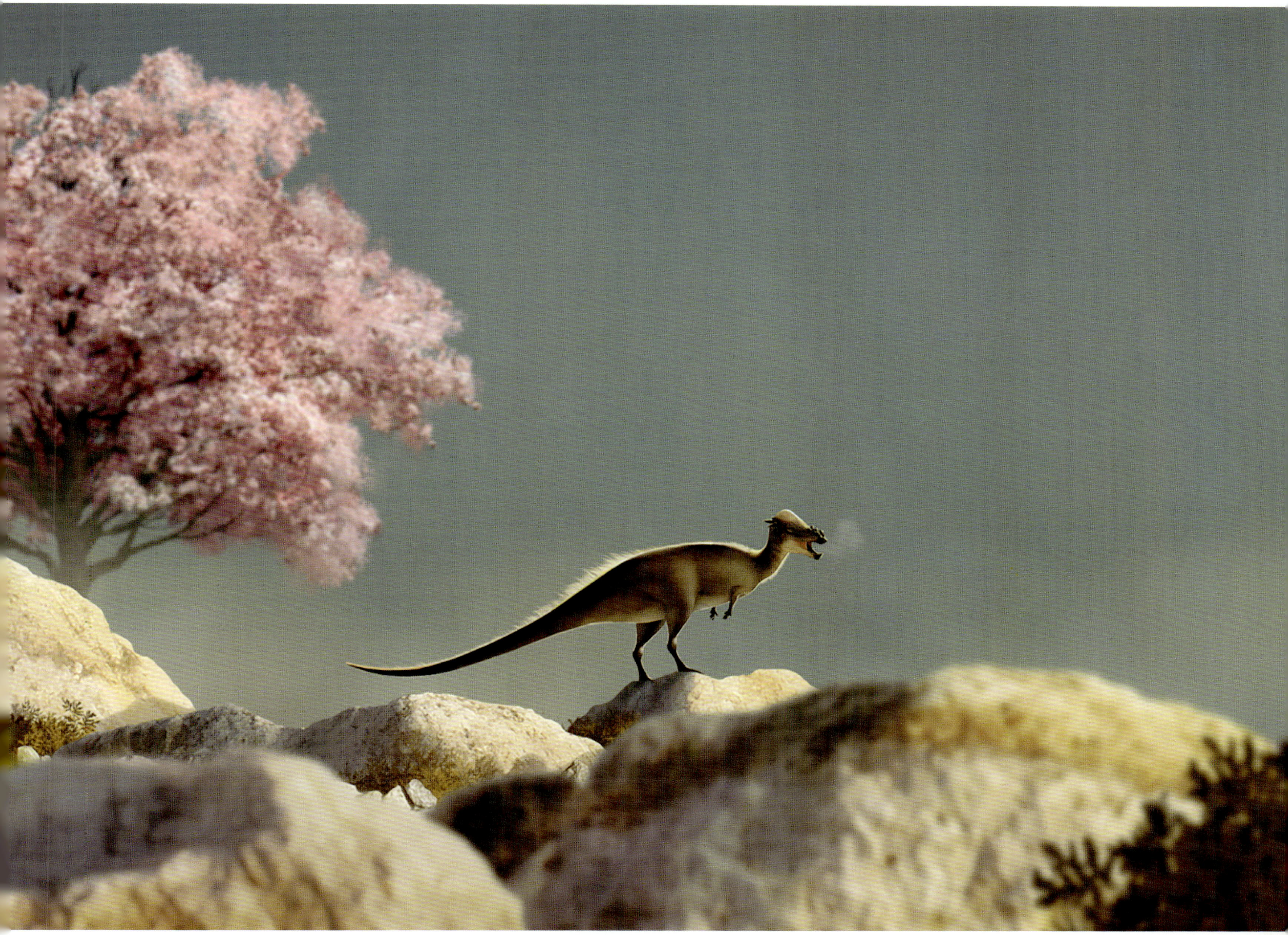

VELIZAR SIMEONOVSKI

BULGARIA/USA

As well as being an exceptional artist of mammals both living and extinct, Velizar is also a trained biologist. Since graduating from Sofia University, he has contributed both as scientist and artist to a number of academic papers, largely on his particular passion: big cats and their various relatives. He has also taught Biology in Bulgaria. Most recently, his artwork has graced *Horned Armadillos and Rafting Monkeys*, a history of the fossil mammals of South America published by Indiana University Press' prestigious Life of the Past series; and *Extinct Madagascar*, from University of Chicago Press.

Merciless
Digital, 2015
Dinictis – a member of the Nimravidae or 'false sabertooths' – is helpless under the brutal attack of a *Hyaenodon*, determined to steal its prey, a *Merycoidodon*. Oligocene, North Dakota.

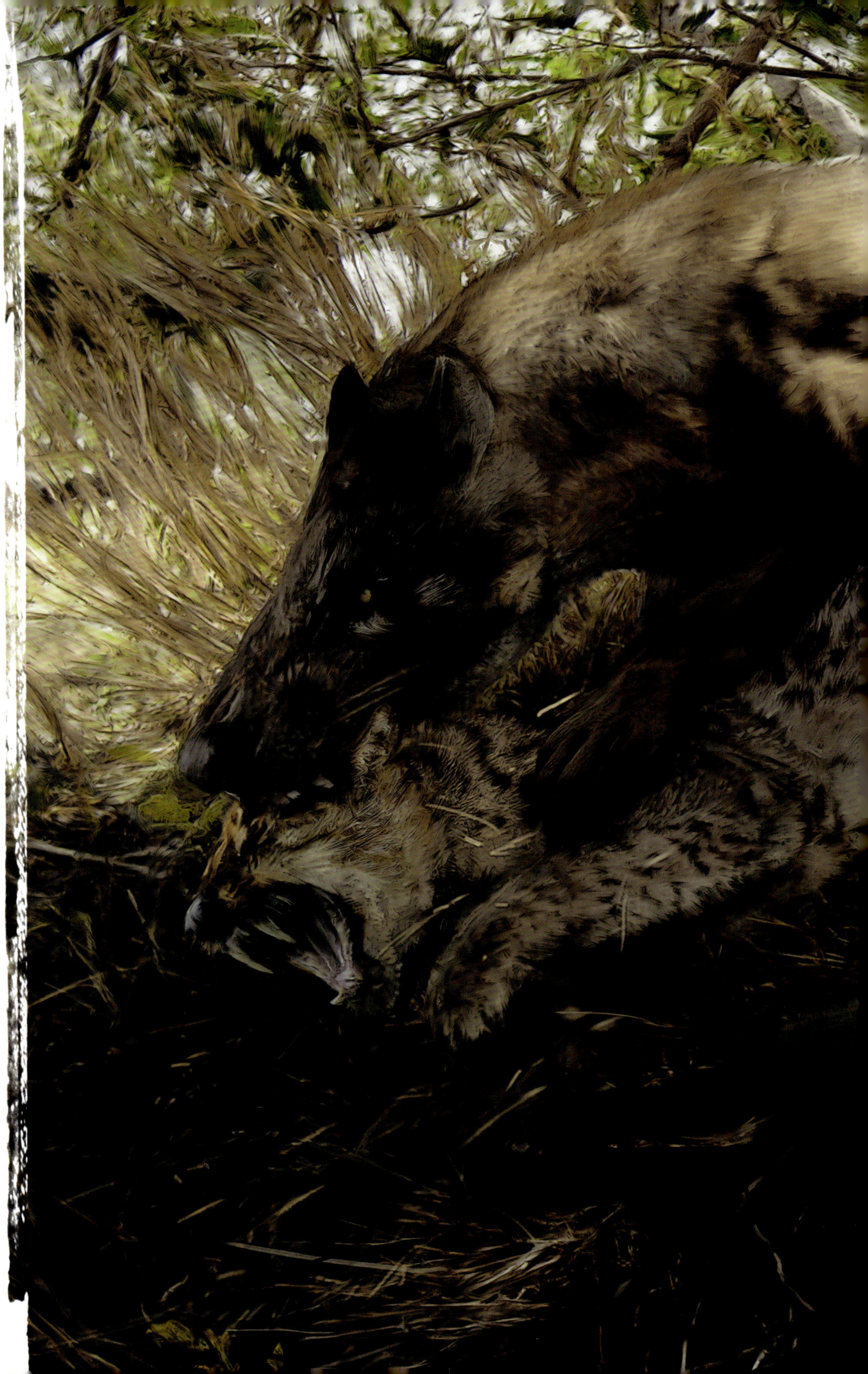

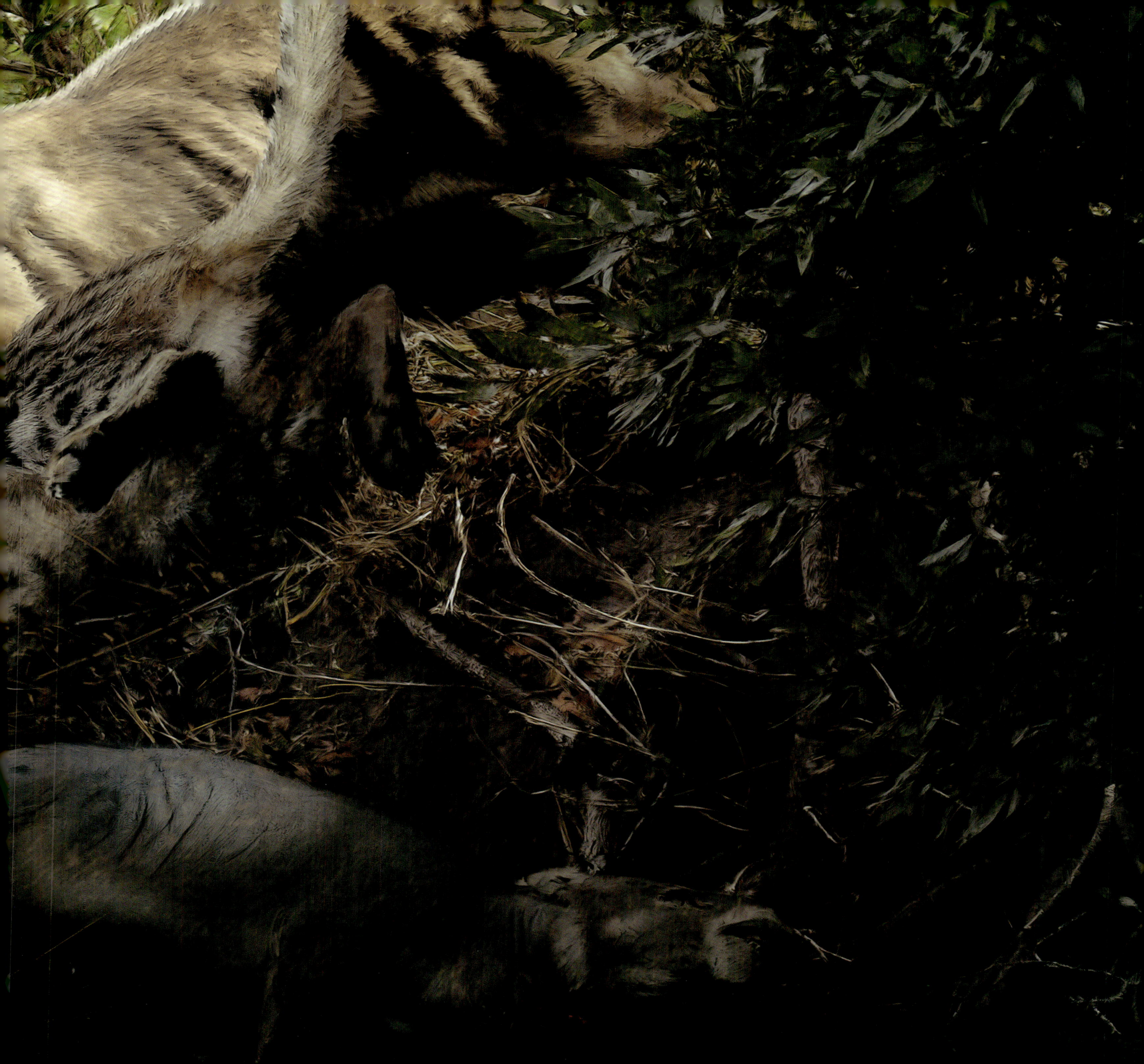

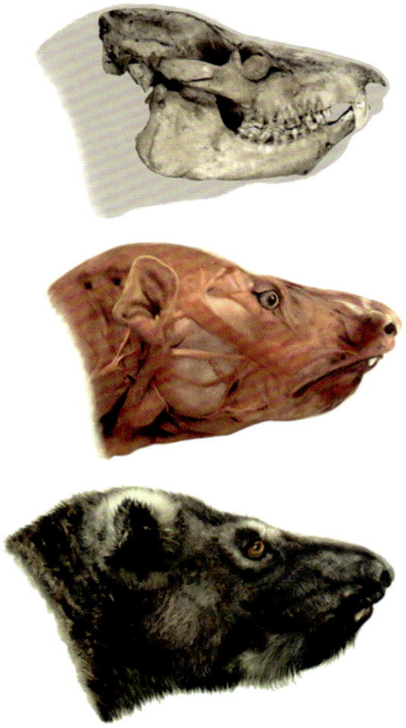

You are unusual in limiting your artwork to the post-Mesozoic. Why is that?

I don't think I am particularly unique in that respect – other artists such as Mauricio Antón and Jay Matternes also focus predominantly on the post-Mesozoic. However, it is true that the majority of paleoartists concentrate on the pre-Paleocene. In fact, there are very few artists who can be considered universal in their coverage – Zdeněk Burian, Konstantin Flerov, and Jorge Blanco are notable exceptions. For me personally, the reason to work mostly on post-Mesozoic subjects is because my scientific interests are centered on mammals.

(Above) ***Megaladapis***
Digital, 2012
Head anatomy of the 'koala lemur' that became extinct on the lemur family's home island of Madagascar about 1,000 years ago.

(Right) **Divided Attention**
Digital, 2015
The earliest known superficially cat-like predator, *Oxyaena*, is stalking a pair of *Diacodexis*, a genus belonging to the Dichobunidae, a family of muntjac-like artiodactyls or even-toed mammals (modern representatives include pigs, hippos, deer, and cattle). However, when a sheep-sized primitive brontothere, *Eotitanops*, appears in the distance, the predator finds its attentions torn between the easy but smaller prey and the larger but potentially more dangerous quarry.

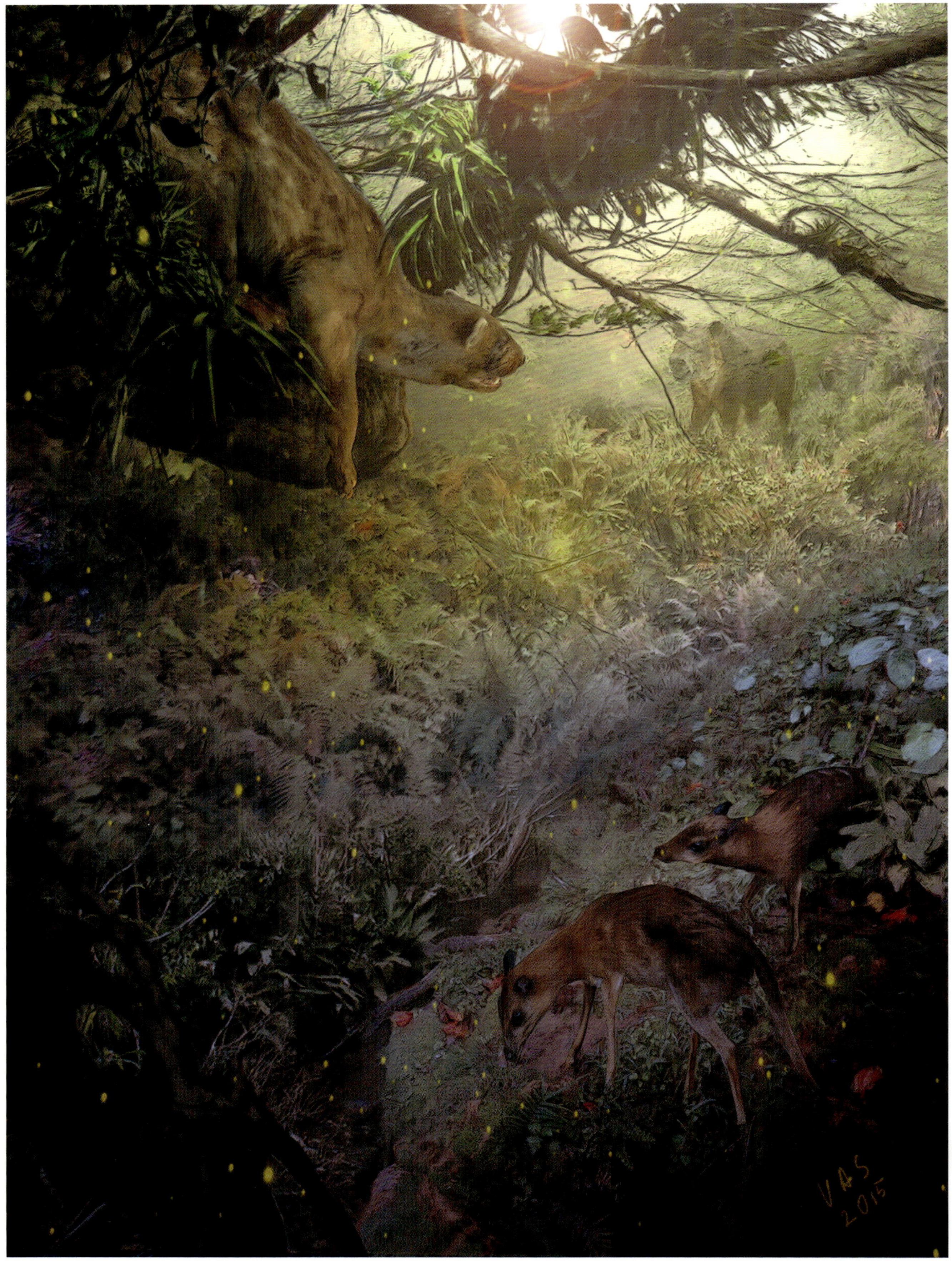

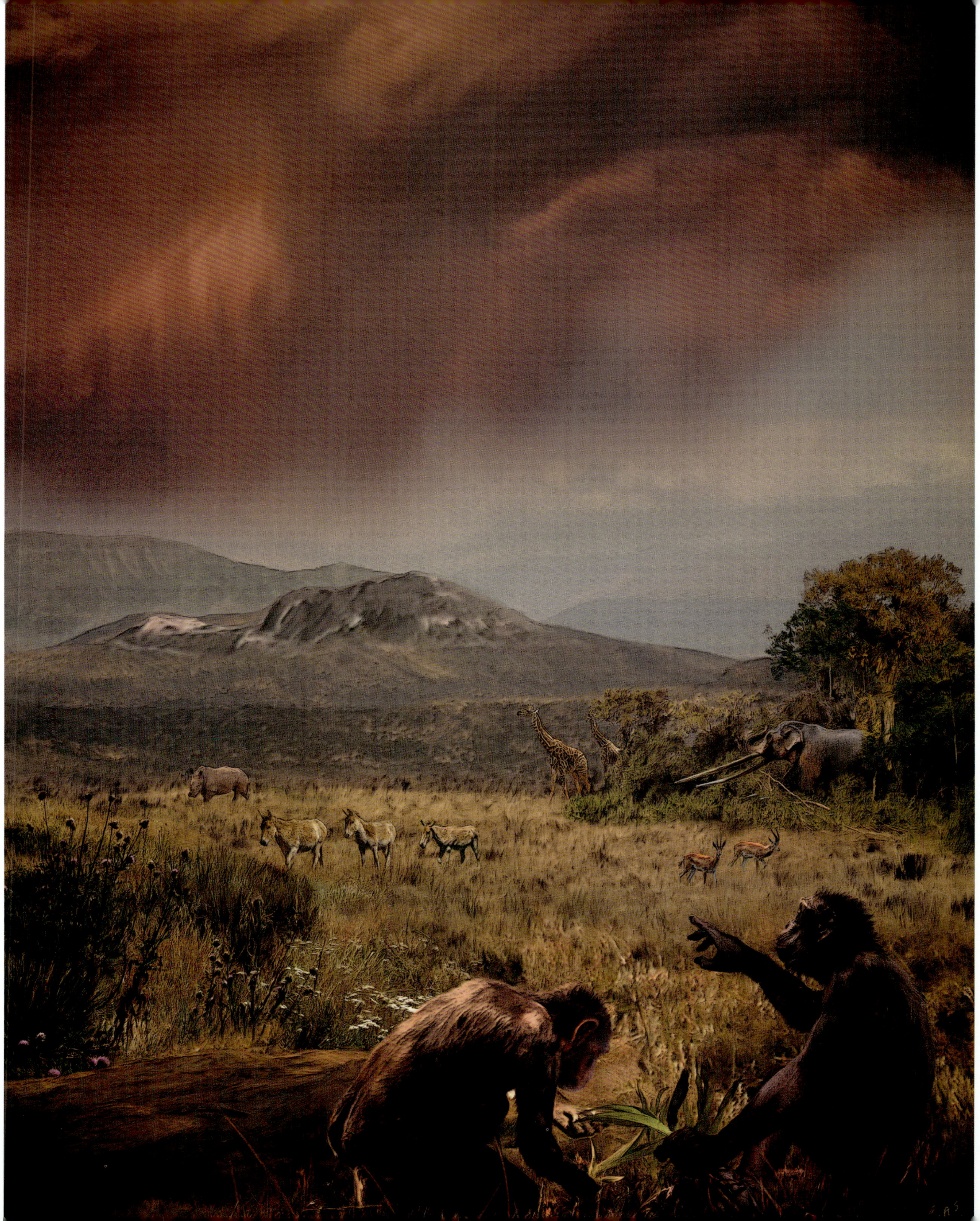

(Left) **'El Graeco'**
Digital, 2016
The habitat of 'El Graeco', *Graecopithecus freybergi*, in what is now the Athens Basin, during the earliest Messinian Stage of the Late Miocene Period.

(Overleaf) **Dorkovo**
Digital, 2012
The Pliocene megafauna of Dorkovo, Bulgaria, five million years ago. The artwork forms the basis of a 30ft (10m) mural at the Pliocene Park Museum in Dorkovo, Bulgaria. Amongst the animals illustrated (left to right) are the tapir *Tapirus arvernensis*, the deer *Procapreolus* sp. and rhino *Stepharnochinus megarhinus* (background); in the foreground, the grouse *Tetrao rhodopensis* amongst rhododendrons, the primate *Dolichopitecus ruscinensis*, the bear *Ursus boecki*, the mastodon *Mammut borsoni*, the primate *Mesopithecus*, and the long-tusked gompothere *Anancus arvernensis*.

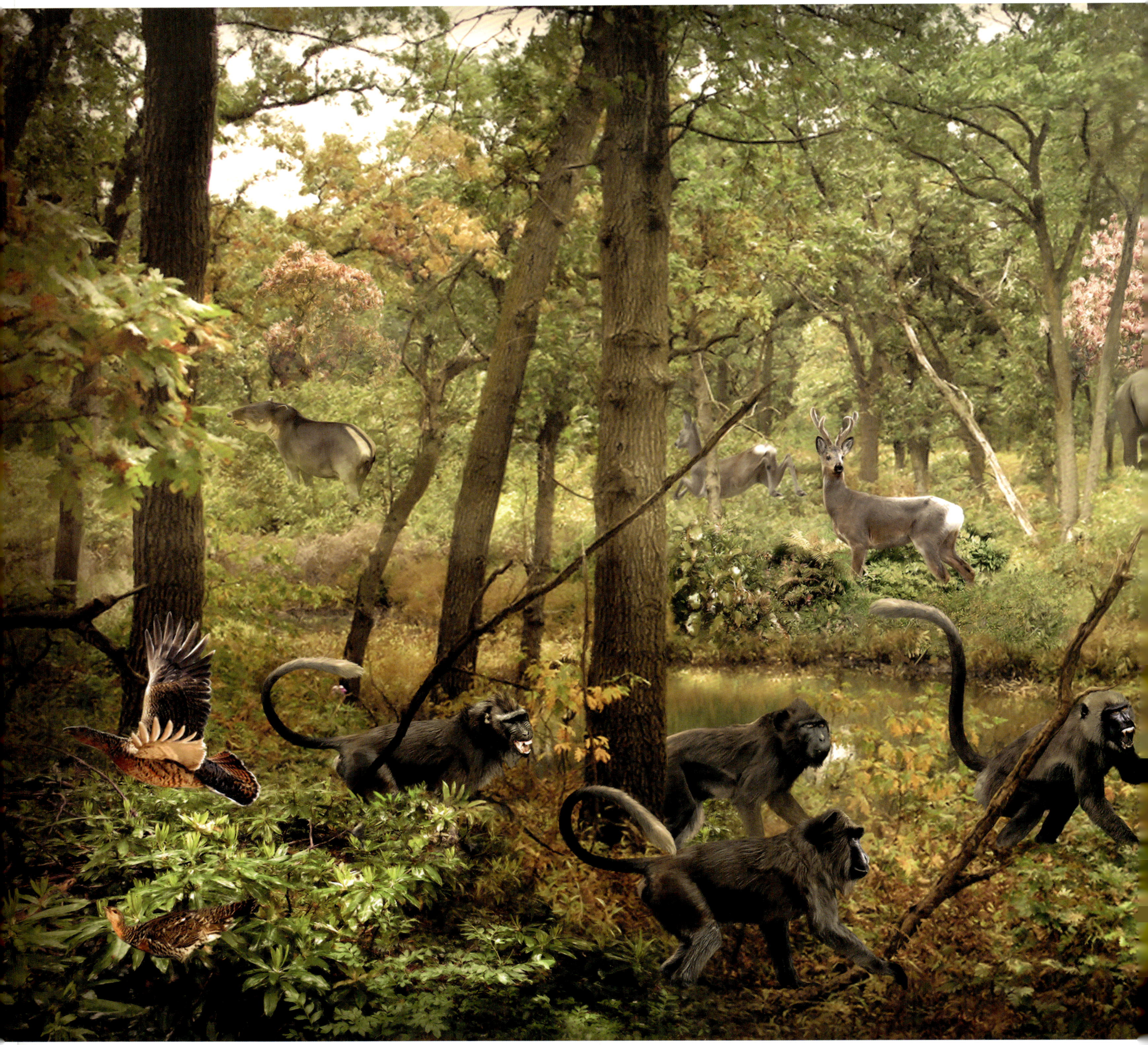

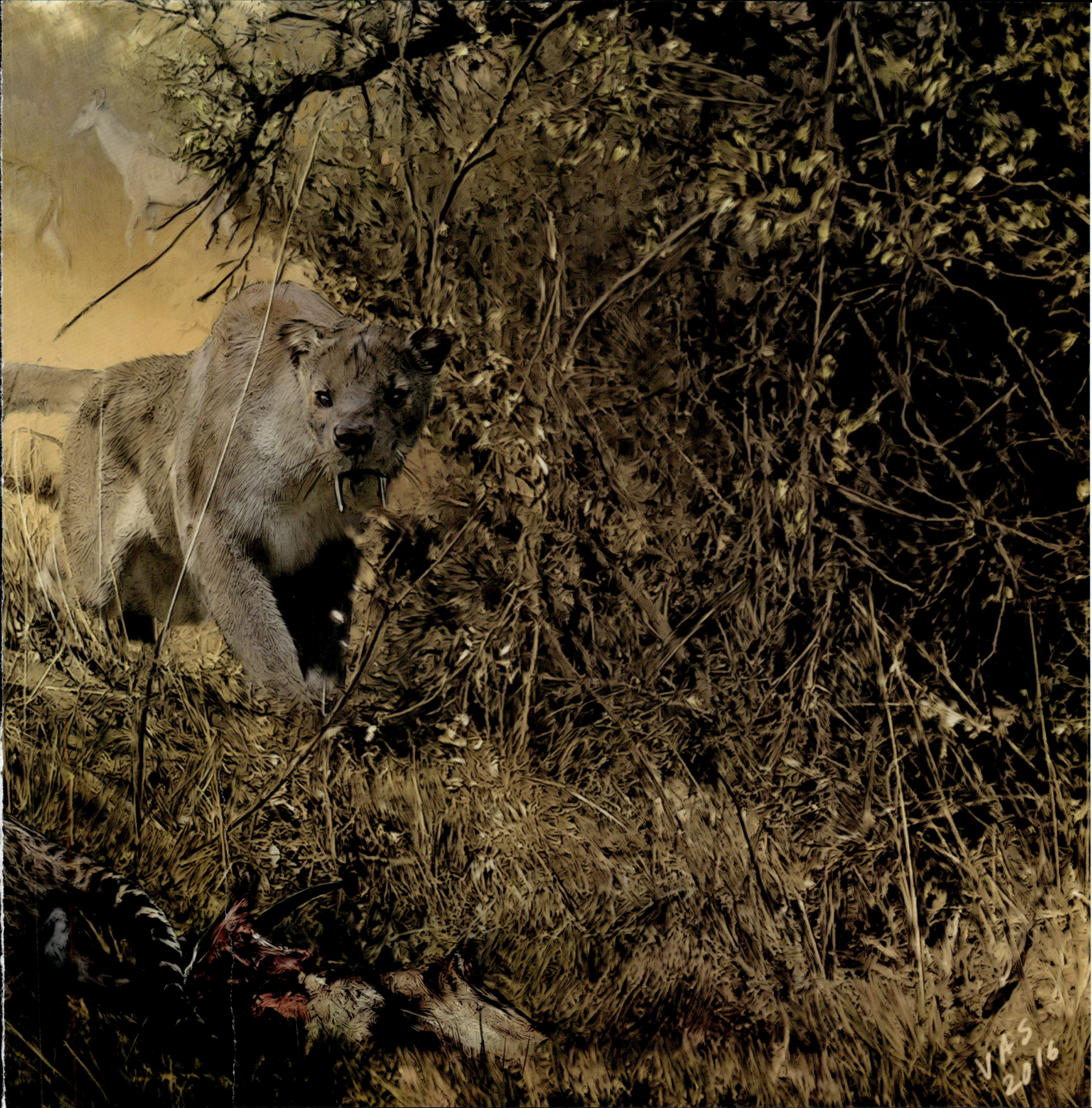
VAS
2016

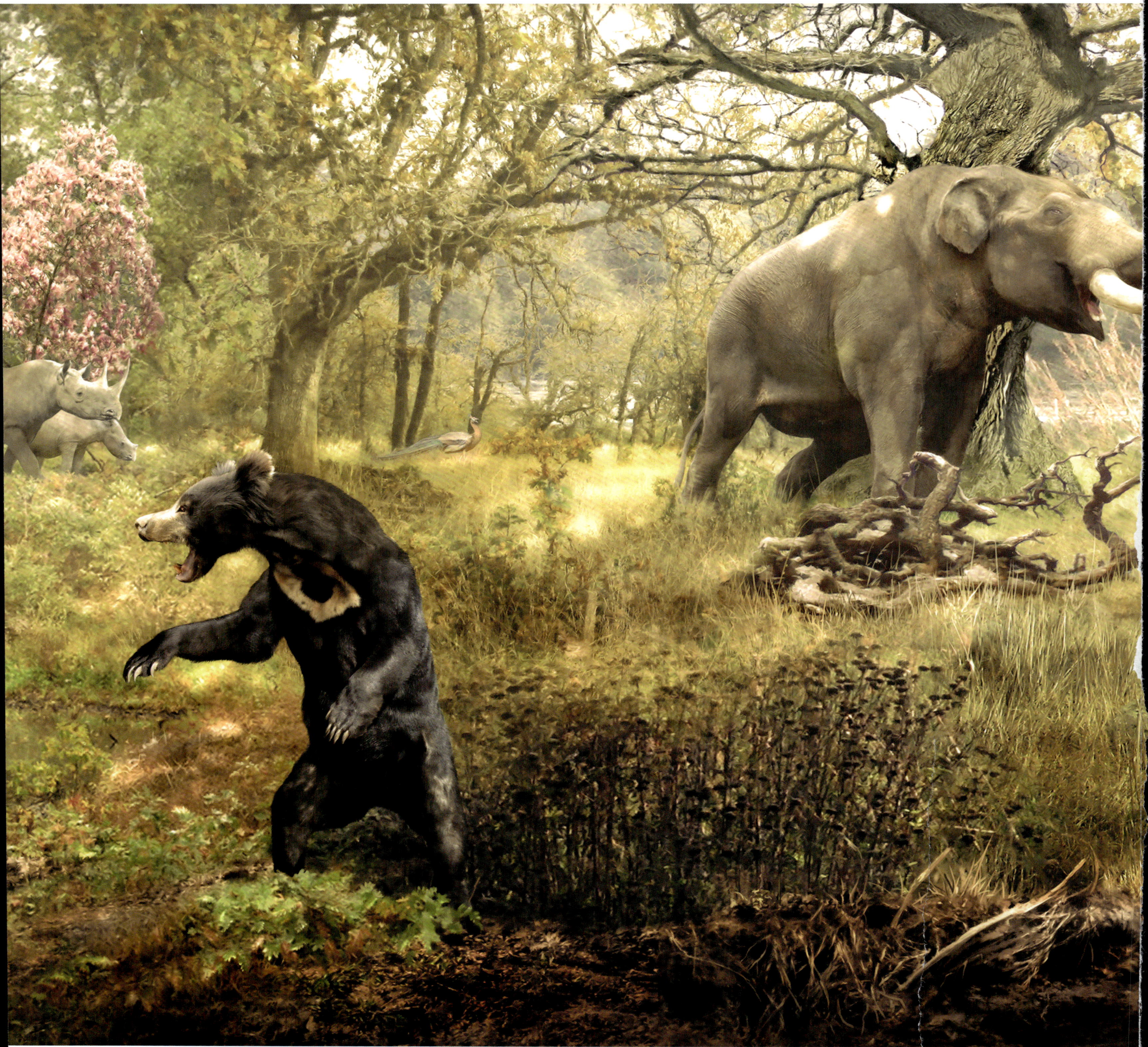

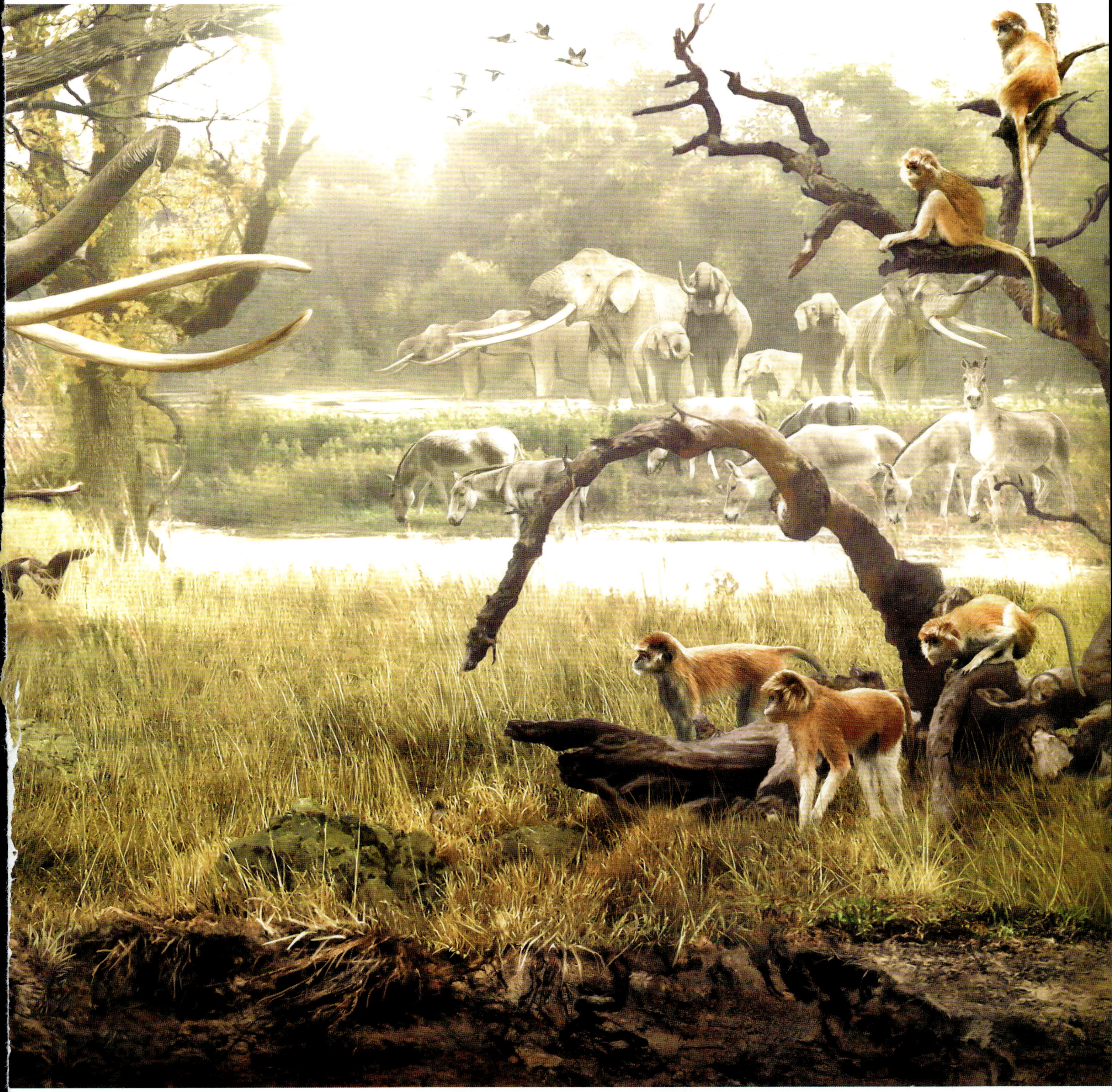

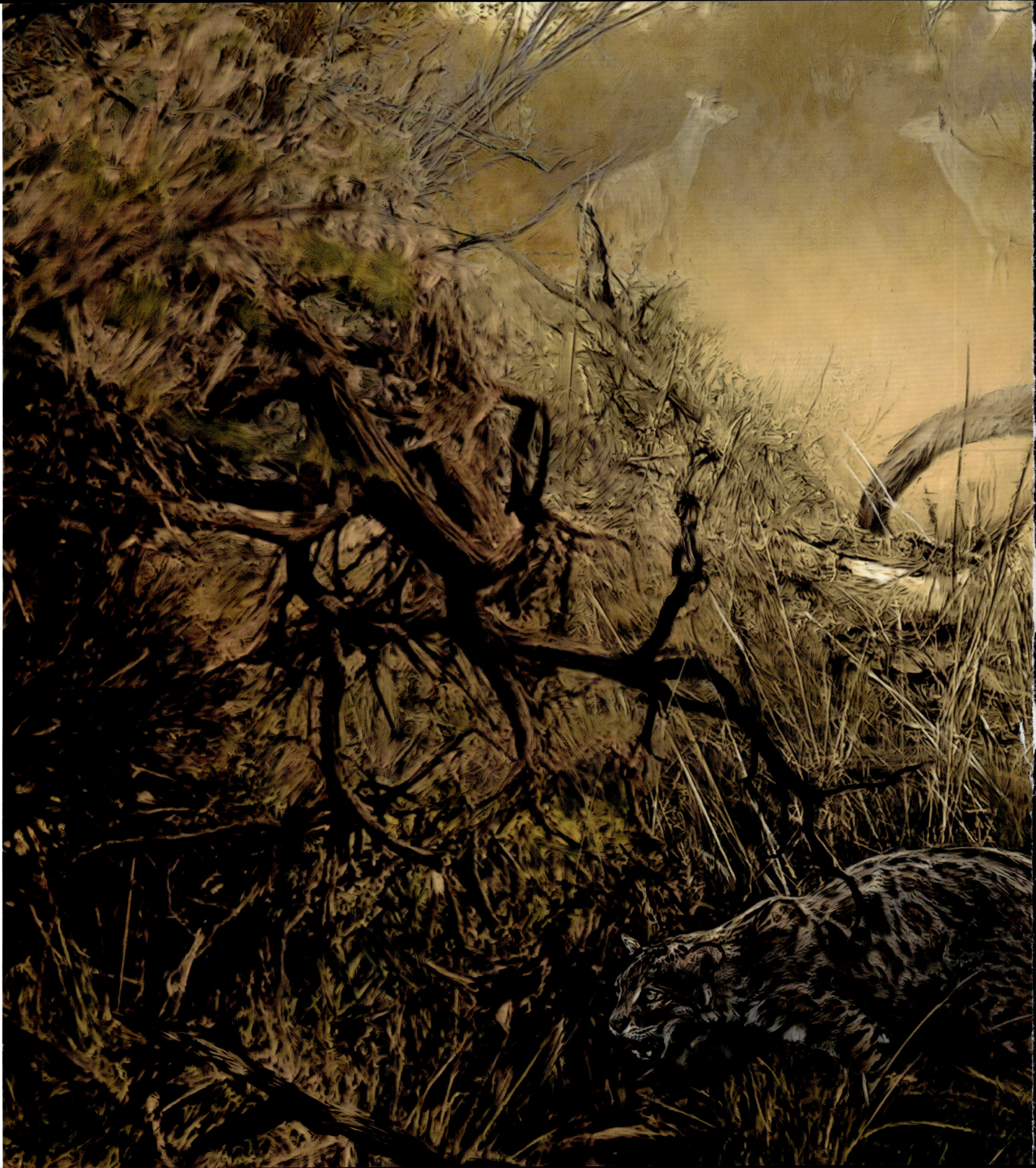

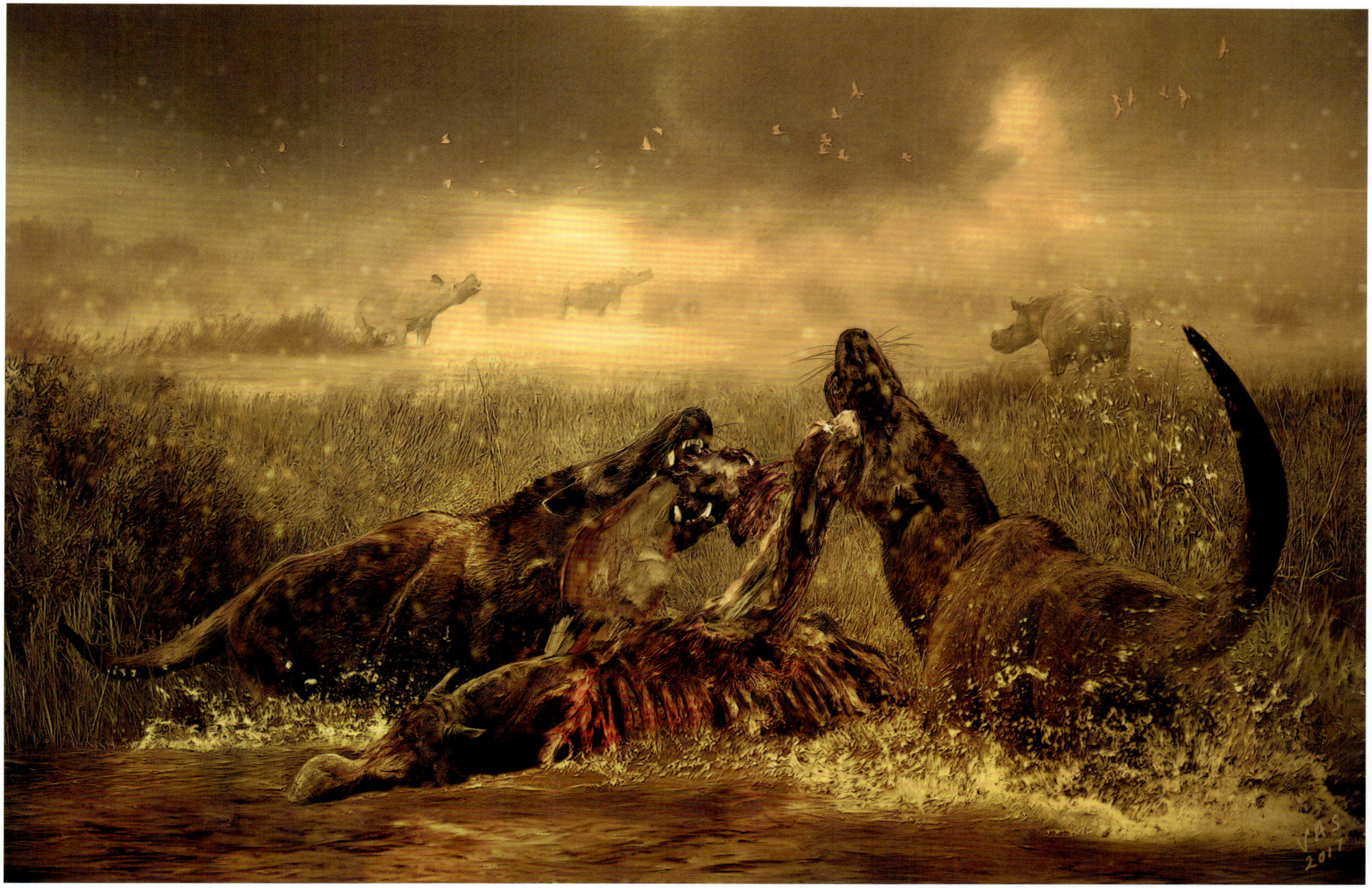

(Left) **Tactical Retreat**
Digital, 2016
A *Miopanthera pamiri*, the earliest known pantherine cat, prefers to retreat swiftly before the curiosity of a *Barbourofelis piveteaui*. Although still relatively small in size, *Miopanthera* established a line of descendants some of which would be among the largest mammalian predators in Earth's history. Late Miocene. Sinap Formation, Anatolia, Turkey.

(Above) **Primeval Feast**
Digital, 2017
A pair of *Andrewsarchus mongoliensis* ripping apart the carcass of a *Gobiatherium*, one of the last of a strange family of herbivorous mammals known as the Uintatheriidae. Eocene. Inner Mongolia.

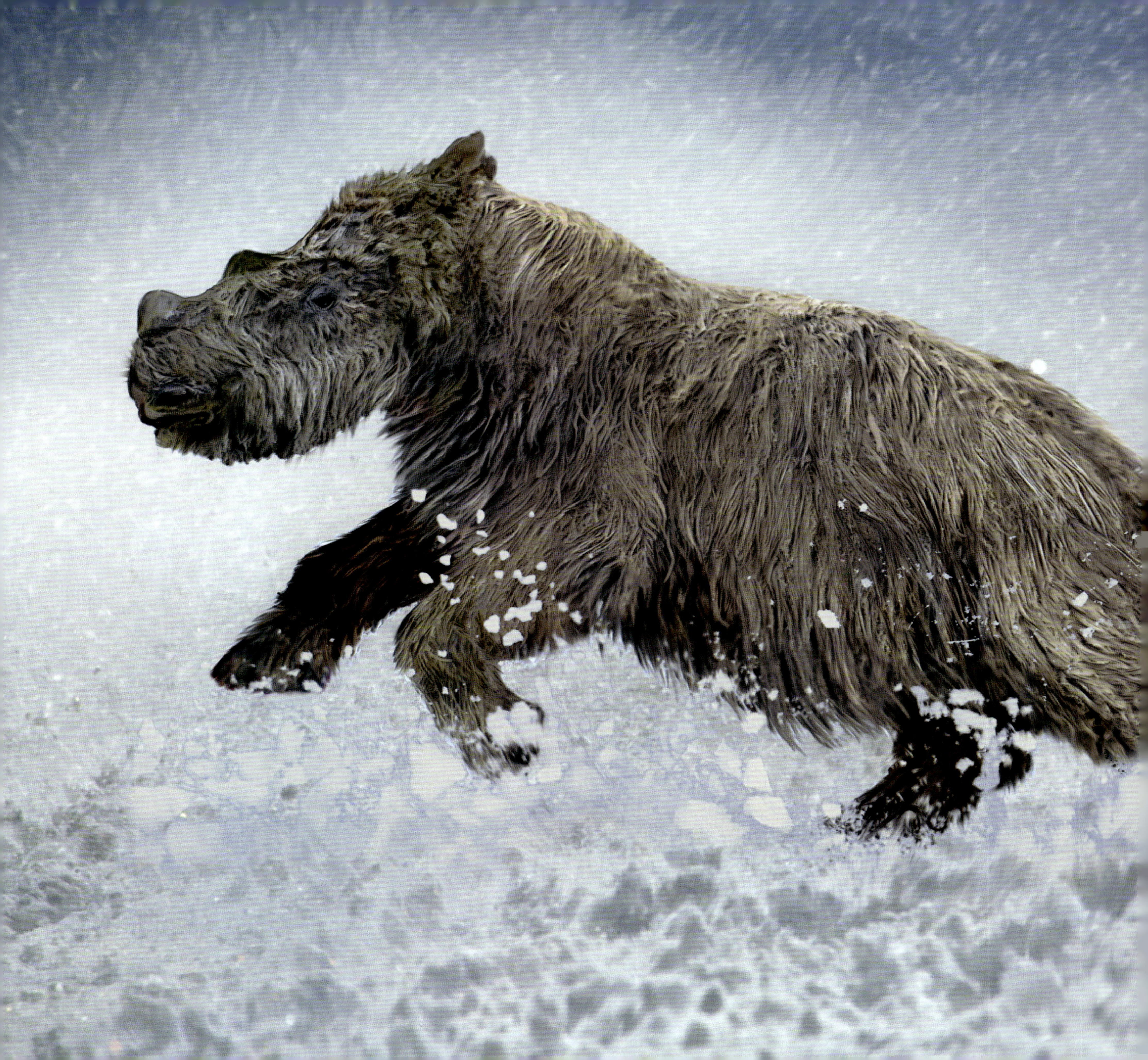

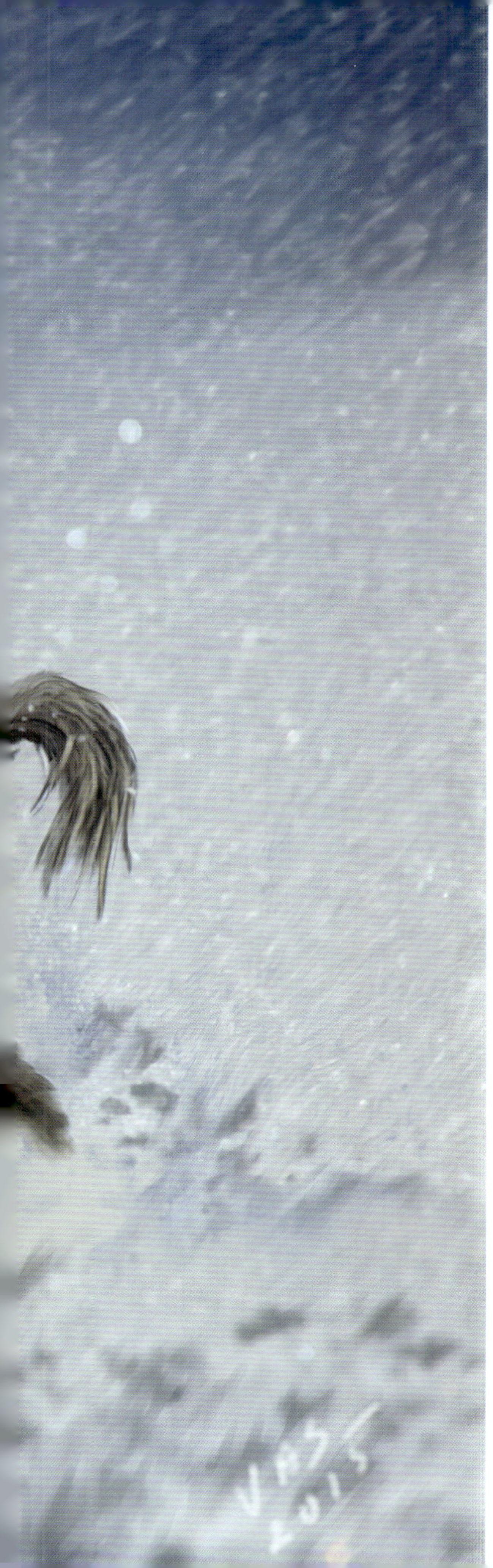

(Left) **Sasha**
Digital, 2015
Reconstruction of the world's only known frozen baby woolly rhino. Estimated to be 34,000 years old, she was found in the Sakha (previously Yakutia) Republic in Siberia.

(Right) **The Spring Fervor of the Lonely Giants**
Digital, 2016
A male Columbian mammoth, *Mammuthus columbi*, mates with a female woolly mammoth, *M. primigenius*. This image derived from a 2016 genetic study that indicated that the two species were interbreeding about 10,000 years ago. Late Pleistocene. Somewhere in the US Midwest.

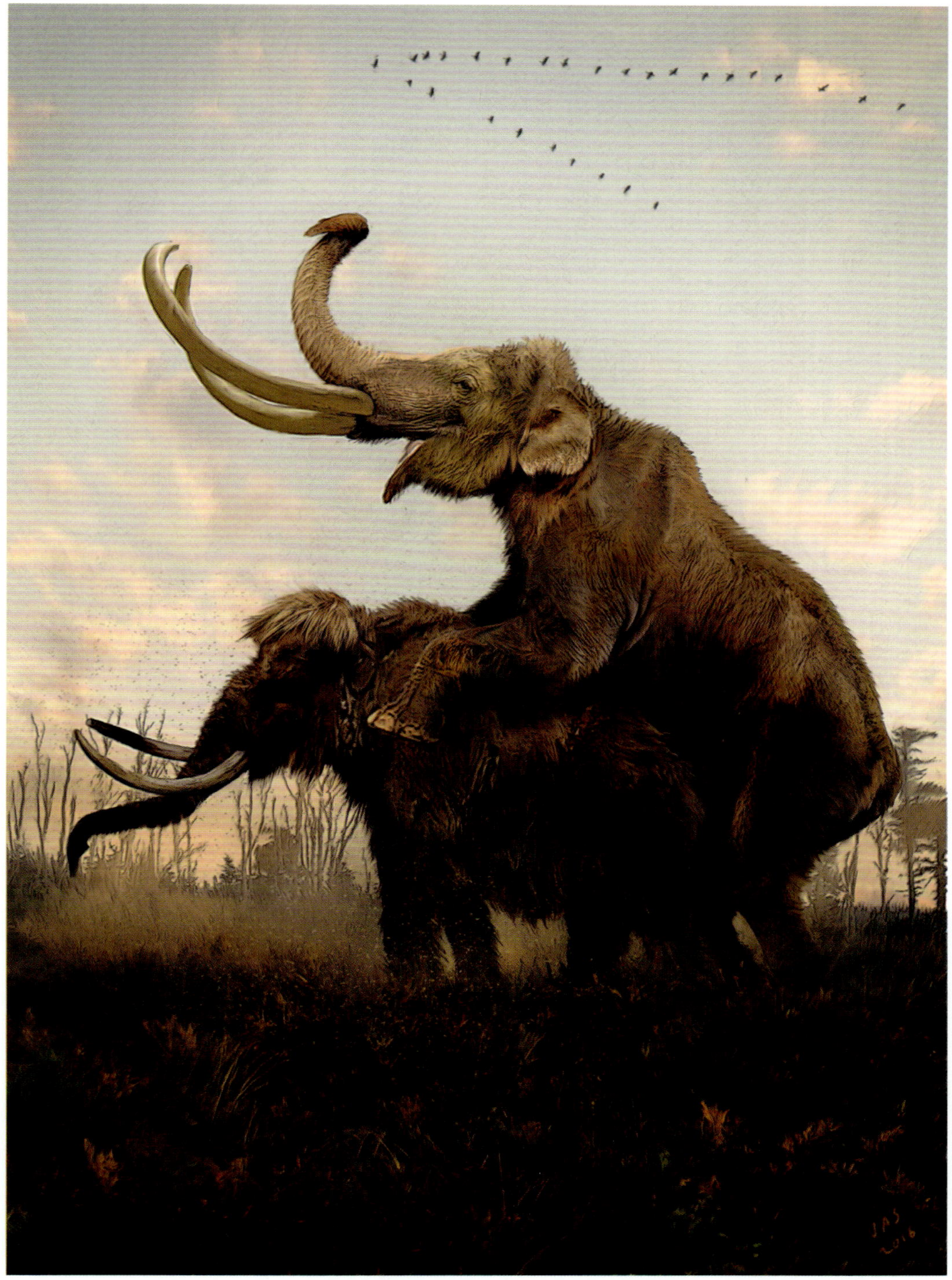

You started out very much as a traditional artist. How much did that influence your subsequent digital style?
At the time when I was developing my technique as an artist, there was no such thing as digital art, so I approach the computer as another tool that I use – just as I would a pencil or pastels – to accomplish what needs to be done for any given piece of artwork.
What prompted the switch to digital?
In 2009 an order came from a client who required the artwork to be digital. I found that I liked the process, appreciated the possibilities it gives, and ever since I've continued to work with and learn digital art.

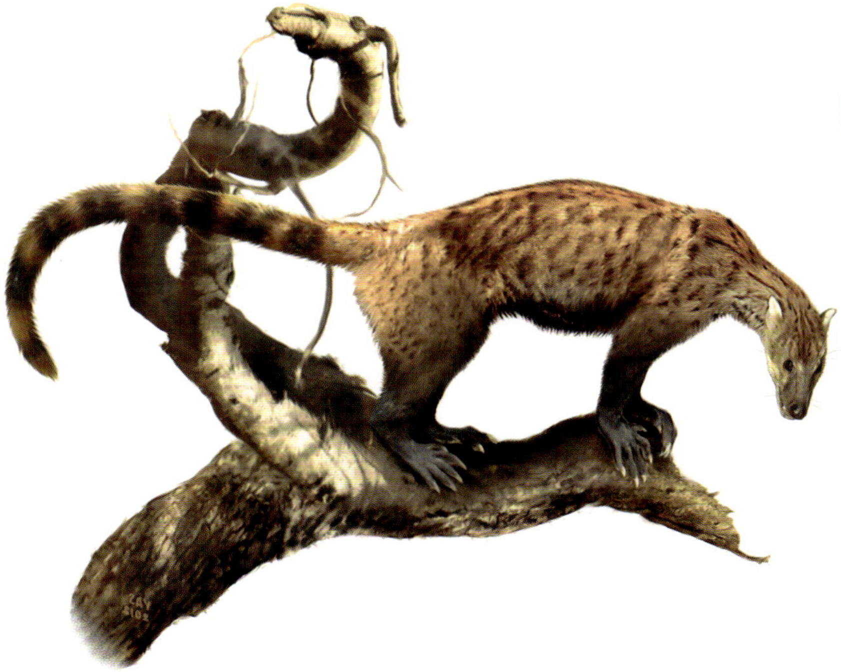

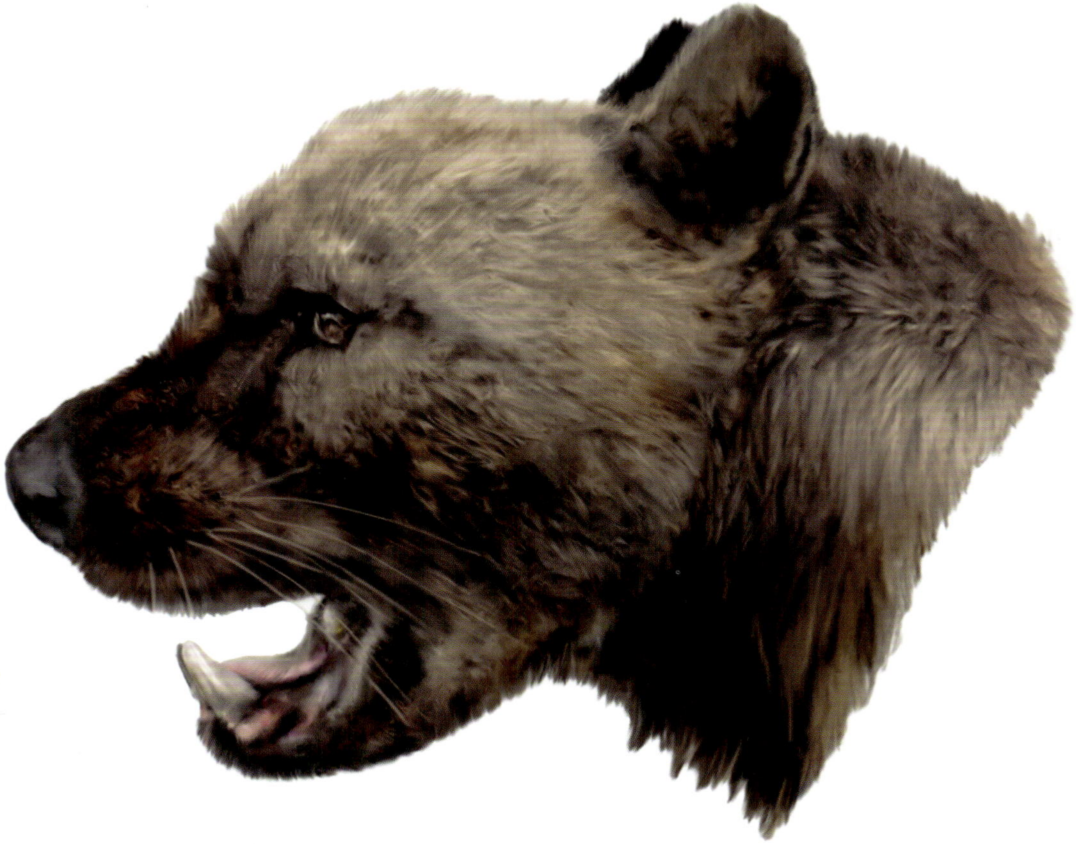

From looking at your childhood art, you seem to have always been fascinated with big cats. How did that lead to paleoart?

I did draw dinosaurs too, as a kid, but didn't save any of the art! But yes, my childhood subject of preference was the big cats, and modern lions in particular.

You have a fairly unique style. What were your influences that led to it?

I am influenced by many artists – the Russian school of animal art, including [Georgii] Nikolskii and Flerov; also the giants of wildlife art: [Wilhelm] Kuhnert, [Maria] Barry and Burian. And there are many others. Although, of the artists specializing in paleoart, Douglas Henderson is the one I have learned from the most. I should also mention some non-wildlife influences, too: [Ilya] Repin, [Ivan] Shishkin and [Frank] Frazetta are just a few examples.

Can you explain your working method?

When I'm working on reconstructing a likeness of an animal – which I do in stages, from skeleton up – my main goal is for it to have a natural posture, which often involves rearranging the positioning of the bones. For the final step, the finished reconstruction, I'm fairly conservative in that I heavily base aspects of the appearance on living animals that are in some way (whether phylogenetically or ecologically) related to the subject. As for the paintings depicting animals in their natural habitat, for me the composition is most important, and then the detailed work, which still has to support the overall composition.

For the actual artwork, I use Corel Painter Essentials 4 and Photoshop; these are older

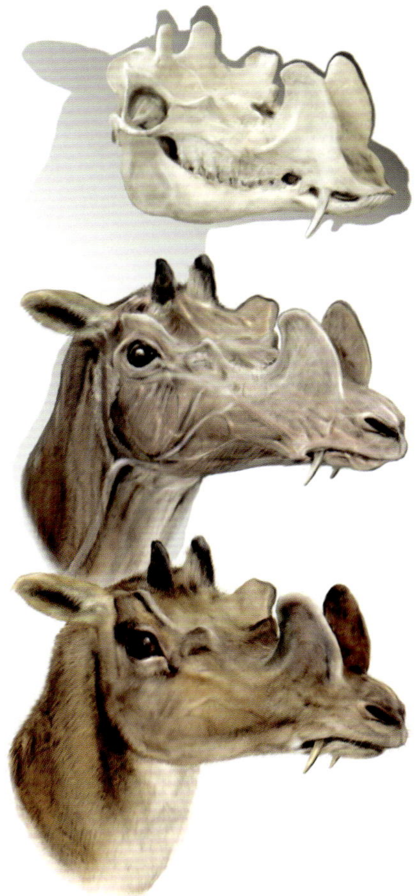

(Above left) ***Vulpavus***
Digital, 2012

(Above) ***Simocyon primigenius***
Digital, 2010

(Left) ***Protoceras celer***
Digital, 2011

(Right) **Silent**
Digital
Maofelis is the first nimravid from Asia to include its skull.

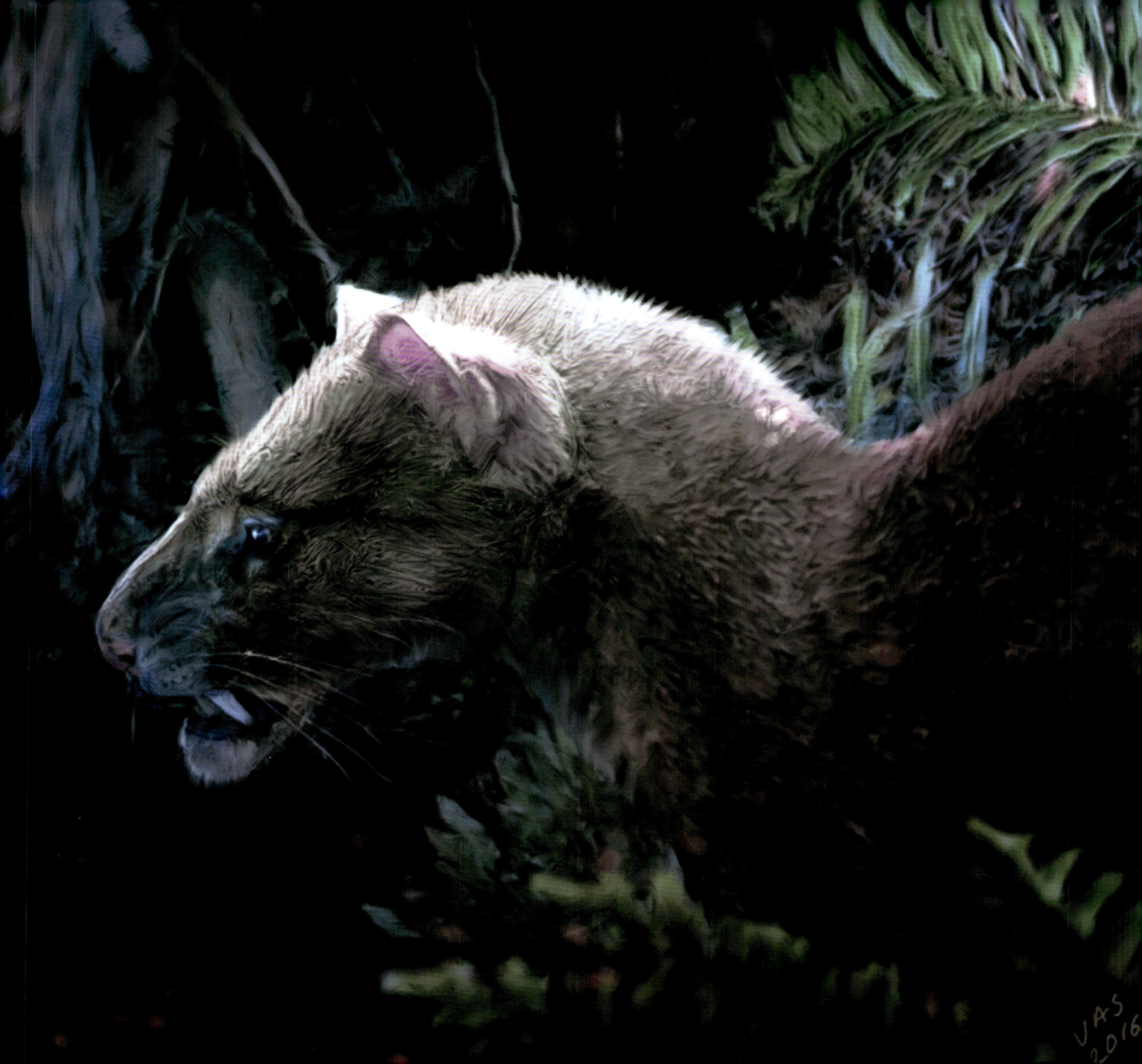
VAS
2016

versions, but I'm hoping to update. There is no particular protocol about starting a piece; sometimes I begin with a pencil sketch and scanning it, sometimes directly via digital sketch on Corel, and I'm now also trying ArtRage 4. Once the general idea is set, I work on the separate elements, one by one, on Corel. Then, I finesse the composition on Photoshop using layers, and further develop the elements. I use reference photos for the details, for example, a leg, an ear, a branch, but also for the textures. Then, I further adjust the details on every element to fit in with the general composition. After that, I paint the whole illustration on Corel, using the various brushes they provide – for the final details I use mainly the airbrush tool. When all that is done I play around with the light, colors etc. on Photoshop. Depending on the composition, size and complexity, it

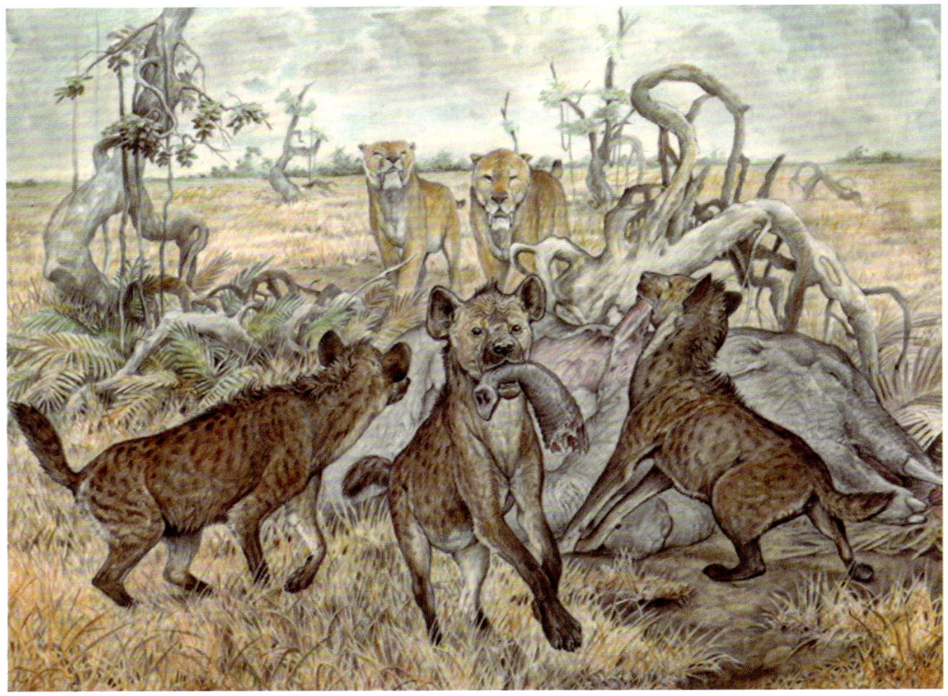

(Above) **Eternal Enemies**
Pastels, 1998
A pack of the hyena *Adcrocuta eximia* flees a gompothere carcass at the arrival of a pair of the huge sabertooth *Machairodus giganteus.*

takes two or three weeks to get a painting done, but sometime more. Now I am working on a picture started in June and I am not nearly close to finishing it [written in November]! It's also a very important thing to point out that although there is quite a lot of hard science included in the major paintings, these are not diagrams but artwork, so I don't mind if I loose a few details if it benefits the composition.

How much did your upbringing and surroundings influence your development as an illustrator?

There have been artists in my family for generations, so I've had encouragement in this direction since my early childhood, particularly by my father. He was a self-taught artist and a librarian, so books, too, have always been a tremendous part of my life: Jules Verne, Karl May, the Strugatsky brothers, [Bernhard] Grzimek, [Gerald] Durrell, and [Joy] Adamson. I knew these writers well before I even went to school,

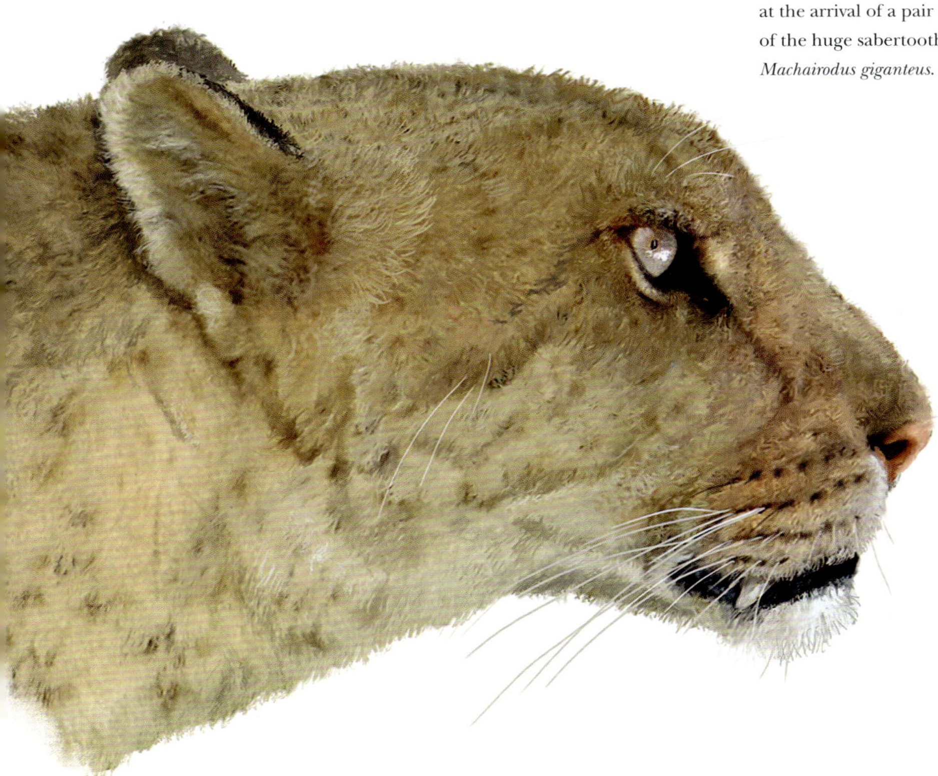

(Left) ***Yoshi garevskii***
Digital, 2013

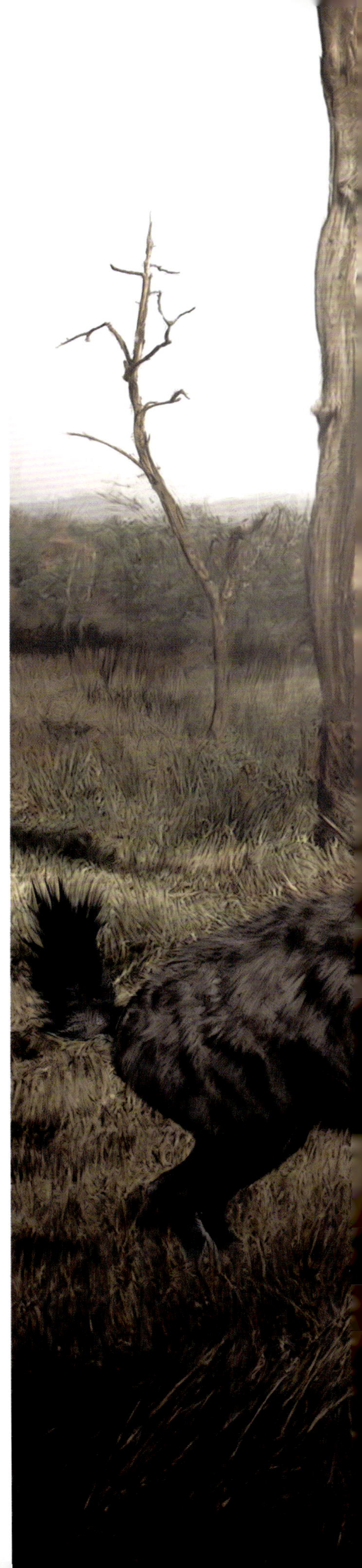

(Right) ***Adcrocuta eximia* and *Machairodus giganteus***
Digital, 2015
Updated version of the image above.

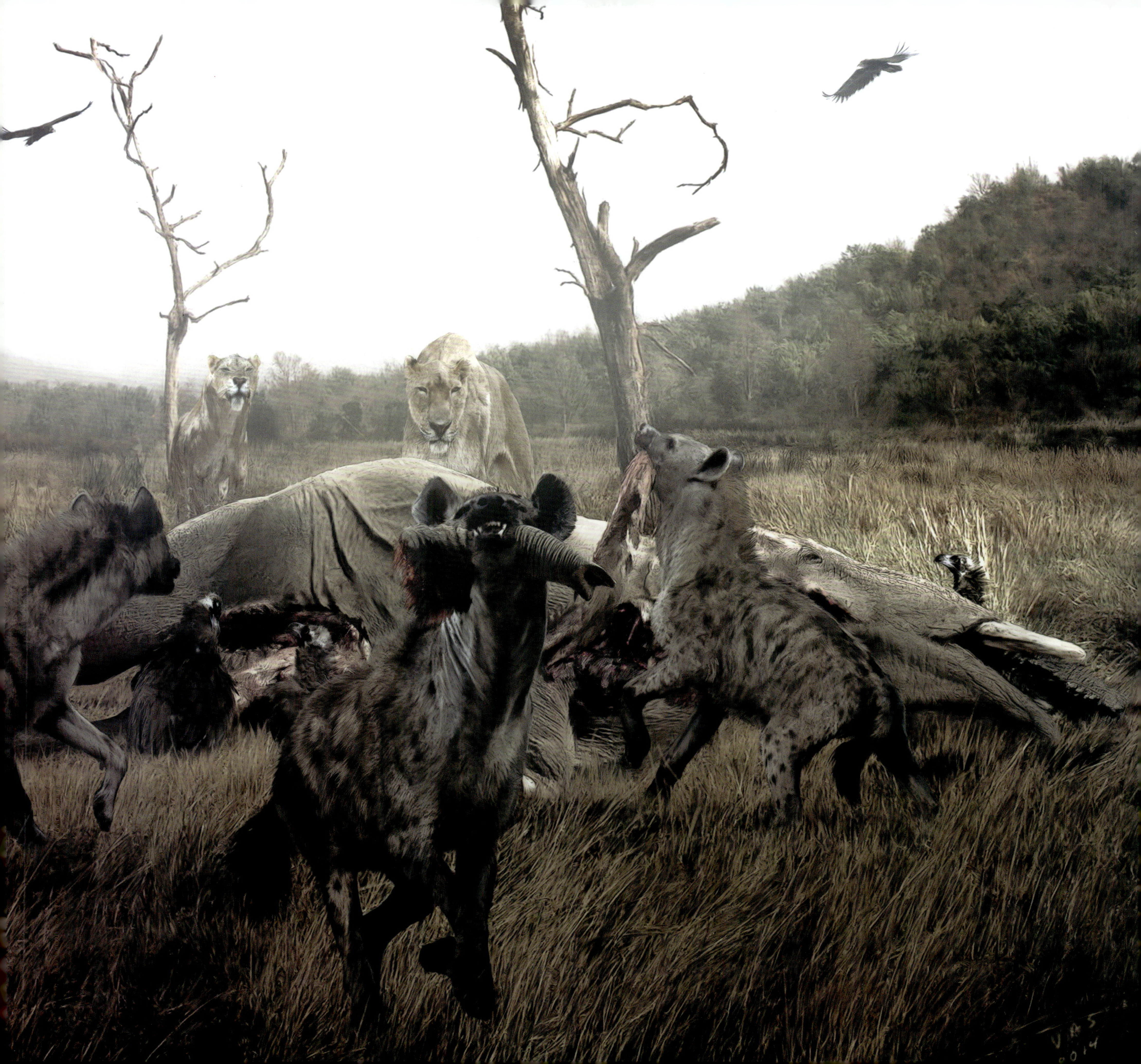
VAS
2014

BLUE BABE

In the summer of 1979, near Fairbanks, Alaska, a gold-mining operation was using hydraulic hoses to clear a cliff face of frozen silt. However, instead of precious metals, the miners uncovered the frozen carcass of a Steppe bison (*Bison priscus*).

Efforts to extract the body, subsequently dated at 36,000 years old, were hampered by the ice and frozen ground, despite warm summer temperatures. Once the bison's body was freed, it was decided to sever it from the head and neck, which remained trapped. The carcass was taken to the University of Alaska and refrozen while efforts continued to extract the head. Once freed, it rejoined the rest of the body and was then subjected to study by paleontologists.

Phosphorous from the bison's tissues reacted with iron from the surrounding soil to produce the mineral white vivianite. On contact with the air, the white mineral turned blue. This partly explains the specimen's popular name – Blue Babe – though this is of course also a reference to the fictional ox ridden by American folklore's giant lumberjack, Paul Bunyan.

Subsequent research revealed that the bison, a male with large horns, had been killed by an American lion (*Panthera atrox*). There were claw and tooth marks on Blue Babe's hindquarters, and the ribs and spine were exposed, the skin having been rolled back by feeding predators. There was even blood still frozen in various parts of the carcass. The remaining skin revealed the presence of a layer of fat and a winter undercoat, both of which suggest the bison had been killed in fall or winter, the two layers helping insulate Blue Babe from the bitter cold of the Ice Age winter. Other animals had scavenged the lion's kill. There were signs left by wolves, foxes, wolverines, and ravens. However, the carcass froze quickly enough to keep it in reasonably good condition.

Blue Babe remained at the bottom of a small valley, and during subsequent summers was covered in silt. However, the soil remained cool enough to prevent serious deterioration and the carcass was eventually preserved in the permafrost.

A few years after its discovery, Blue Babe was restored, its skin treated to prevent deterioration, and today it remains mounted in an exhibition.

The Steppe bison was an extremely widespread species, with fossils known from Europe, Asia (including Japan), Alaska, and Canada. It was, on average, 6ft (2m) at the shoulder and weighed about 2,000lb (900kg). It first appeared about 1.8mya, probably evolving in South-East Asia before spreading into North America via the Bering land bridge. Its primary habitat was the Mammoth Steppe, a vast area of cold, dry tundra rich in grasses, herbs and small trees. The dominant animal here was, unsurprisingly, the woolly mammoth. The steppes spanned virtually the entire Northern Hemisphere during the final stages of the Ice Age, until gradual climatic warming and the retreat of the ice sheets triggered the disappearance of the habitat and the many animals it supported, including *B. priscus.* The species – at least in its pure form – eventually vanished about 9,000 years ago. In North America, the Steppe bison was replaced by the modern species *B. bison*, and in Europe by *B. bonasus*, the wisent or European bison. In fact, the wisent seems to be a hybrid descendant of the Steppe bison and cattle, meaning that Steppe bison genes live on in a modern population.

The Steppe bison has a long history in paleoart. Depictions of it are featured on the walls of such famous cave art sites as Altamira and Lascaux, both dating to around 15-18,000 years ago.

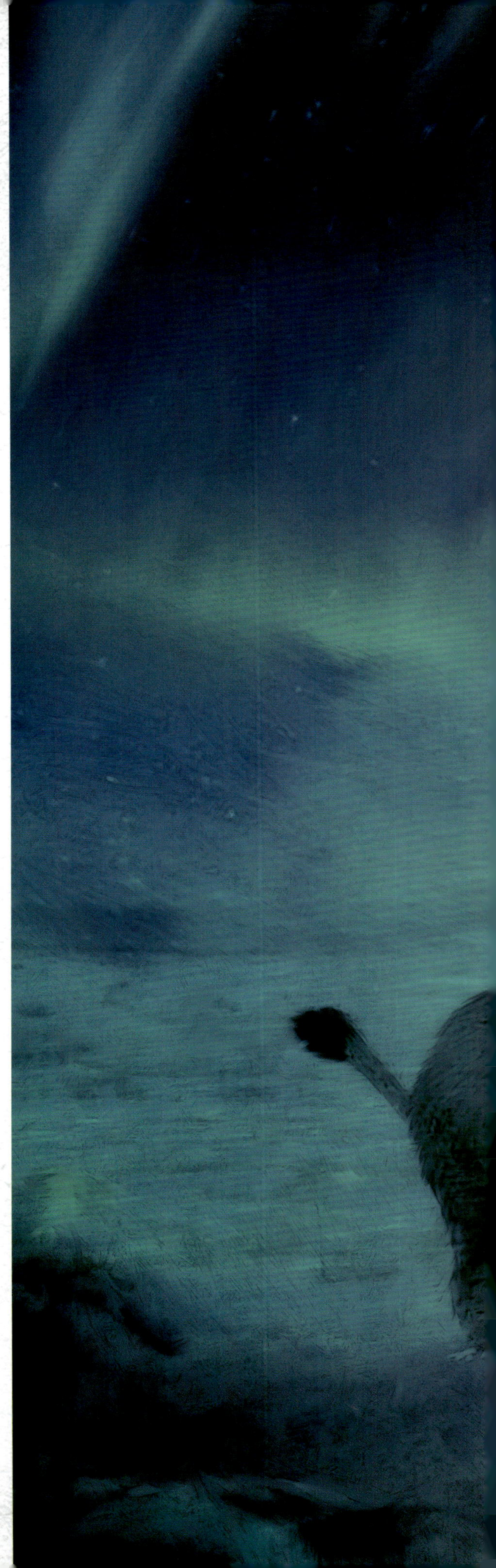

Eternal Elements:
The Death of Blue Babe
Digital, 2014

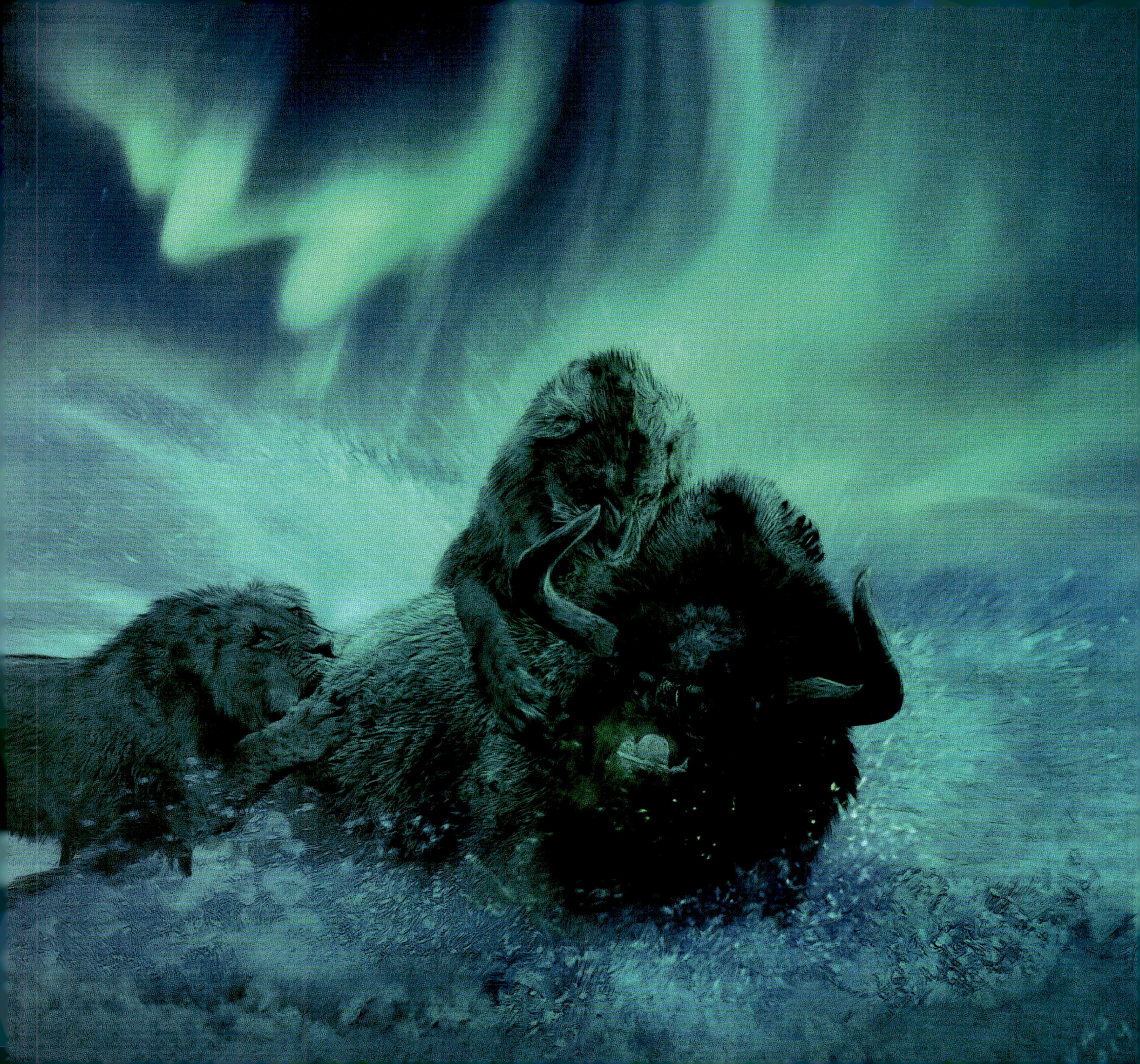

and the last three in particular totally cemented my interest in animals.

What is your fascination with ancient pigs?

I don't have a particular interest in ancient pigs, other than their interactions with big cats as a potential prey species and as a competitor. However, the living [pig] species and their juveniles are a crucial part of my research on the evolution of the external traits of mammals.

While working on your images for the Madagascar volume, to what extent did you use modern, extant species to influence your reconstructions of extinct animals?

Although it might seem as though there is a huge diversity of external traits among living animals, in reality all the variations in coloration and pelage pattern are limited to a few types. I am quite conservative and, as a rule, use variations of these extant external traits in my reconstructions. Of course, it's not possible to say how precise this approach might be, but I think there is a sound logic to it.

How closely have you worked with academics while working on your titles for Indiana University Press?

Quite closely over some aspects, such as the environments and which species to include. I tend to have autonomy over how to render external traits not related to the skeletal structure, although I consider it important to always discuss my approach and the reasoning behind it with my colleagues.

Is your approach to anatomical illustration different to, for instance, one of your big set pieces? Do you do the same amount of preparation work?

Each presents its own challenges. For the anatomical reconstructions, such as drawings of skeletal form or lifelike "portraits", I have relatively limited scope for artistic license: a scientific approach is important. For the big "set pieces", a scientific framework is still there, but I aim to achieve an immersive effect, to which end I apply all artistic tools known to me.

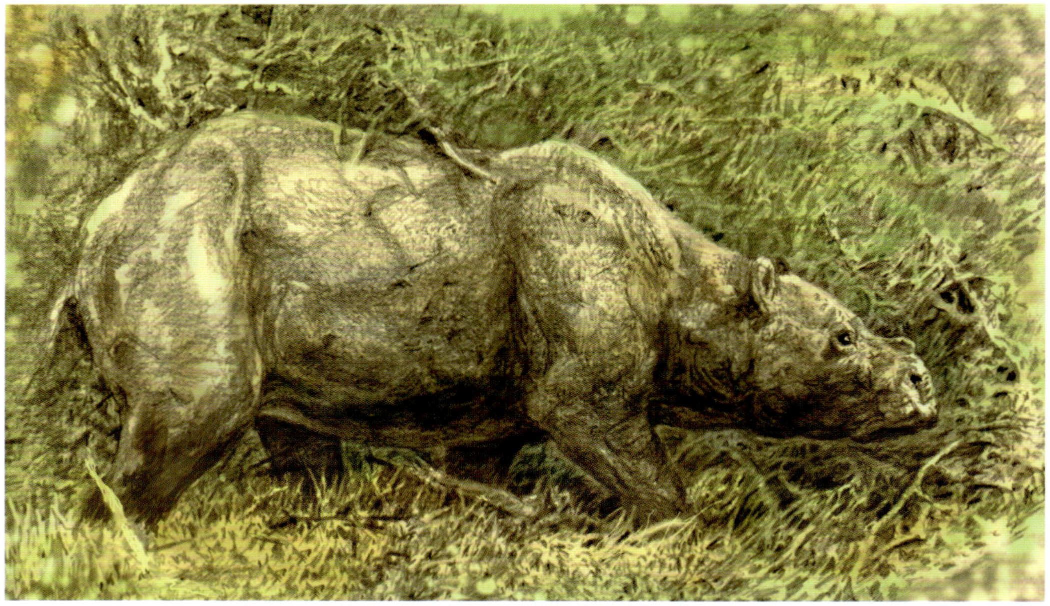

(Above) ***Toxodon***
Mixed Pencils and Digital, 2010

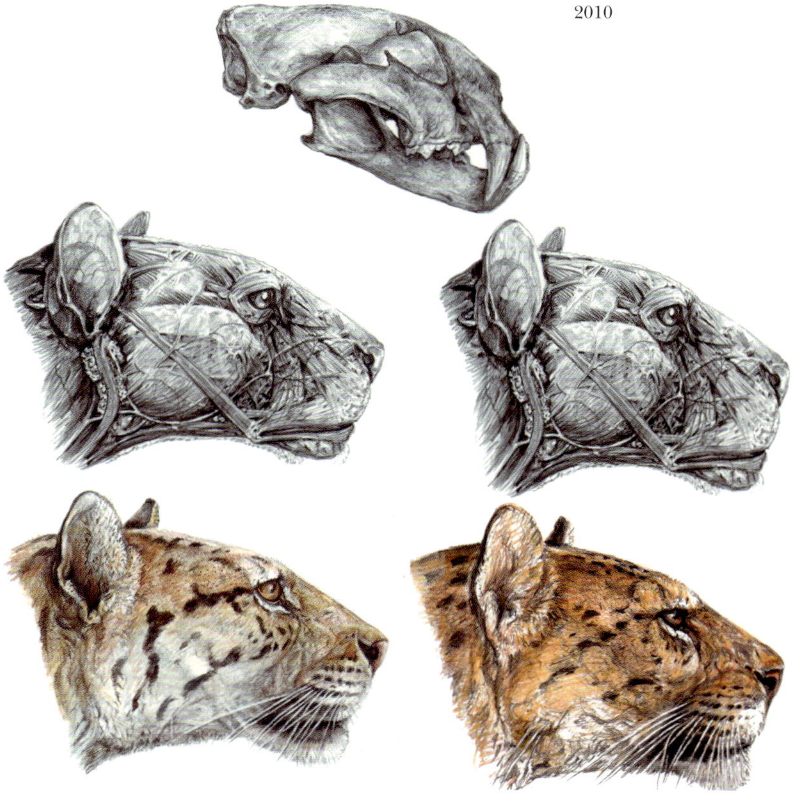

(Left) ***Panthera paleosinensis***
Mixed Pencils and Digital, 2008
Two possible reconstructions of this feline species: the left-hand version models the species on interpretations that it is close to modern lions and leopards; the one on the right is based on a study interpreting the species as a primitive tiger.

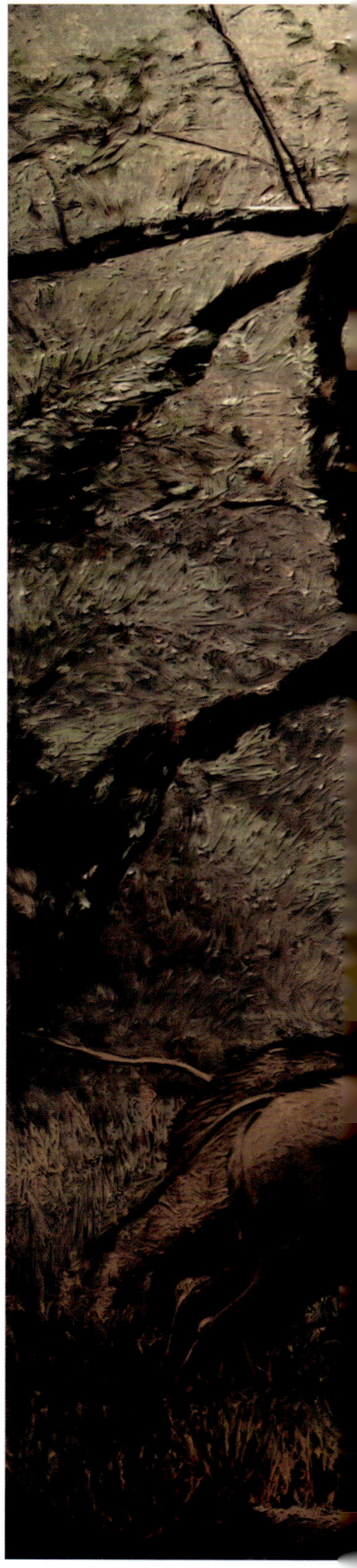

(Right) **Out of Luck**
Digital, 2015
A sabertoothed *Sansanosmilus* got lucky once, when it was able to catch an unattended piglet belonging to a herd of the giant one-horned pig *Kubanochoerus*. Luck was with it a second time when it was able to escape the infuriated boars by climbing on a high log. Then, its luck begins to run away when the pigs start to do what they do best – dig! Gansu, China. Middle Miocene.

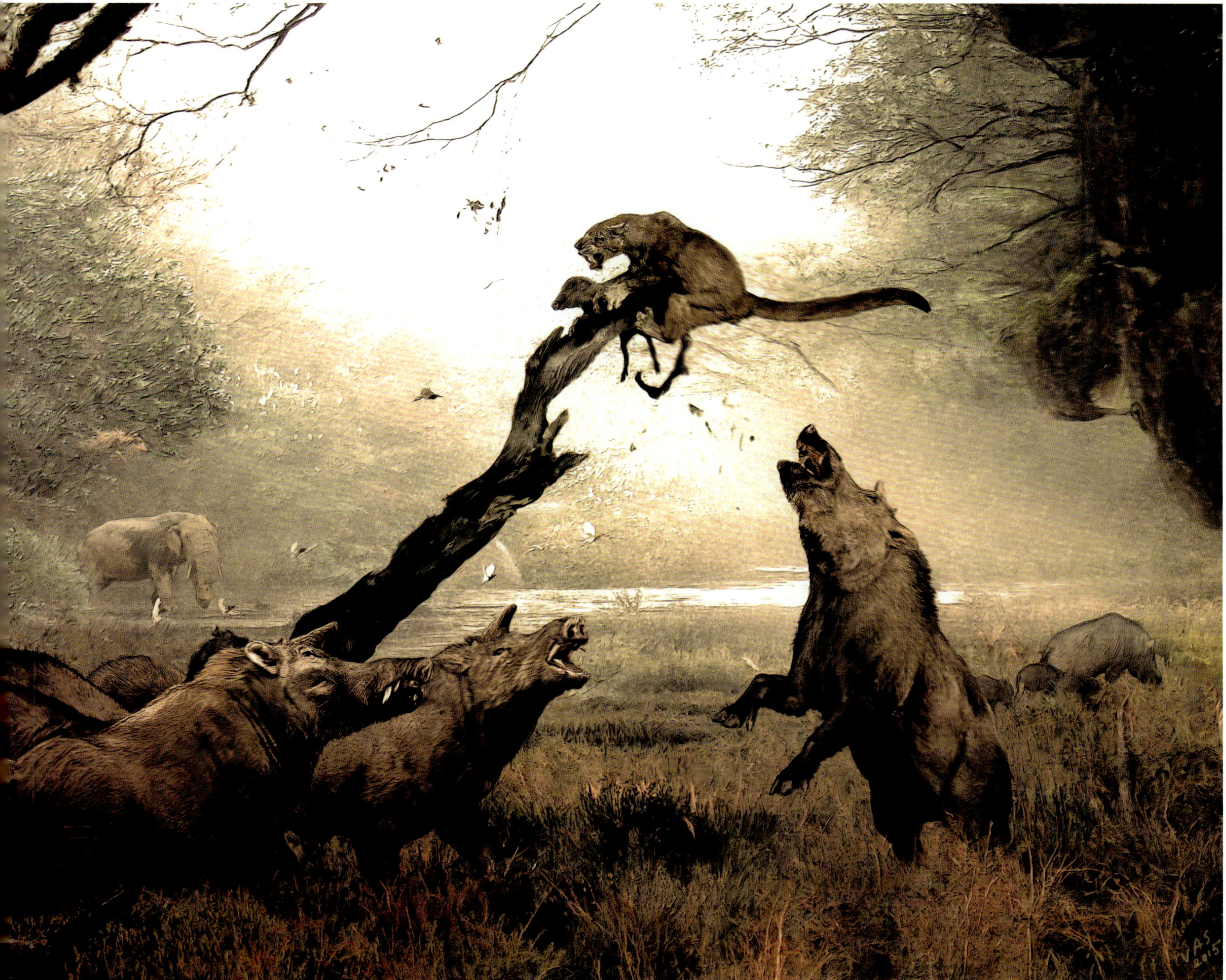

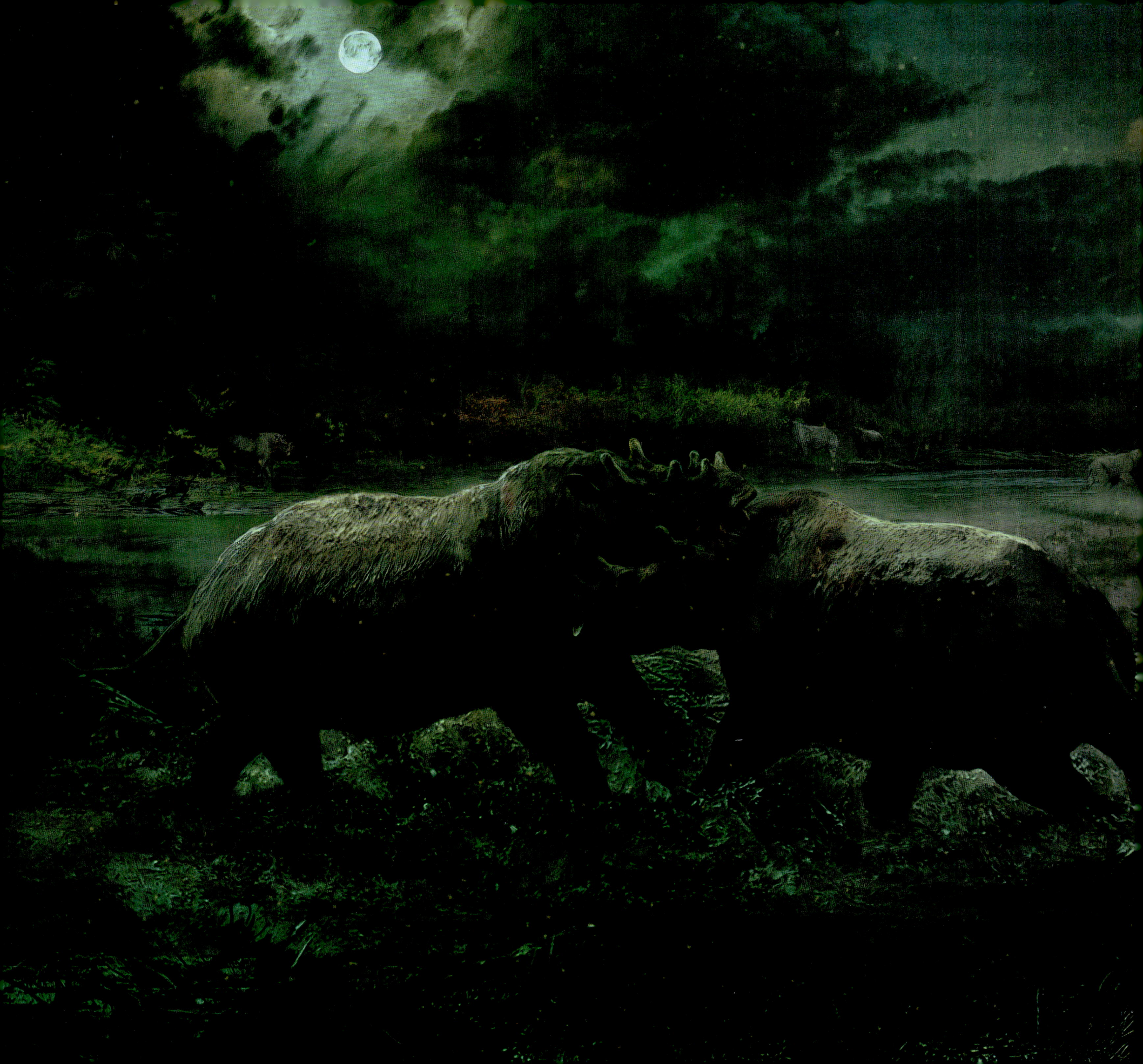

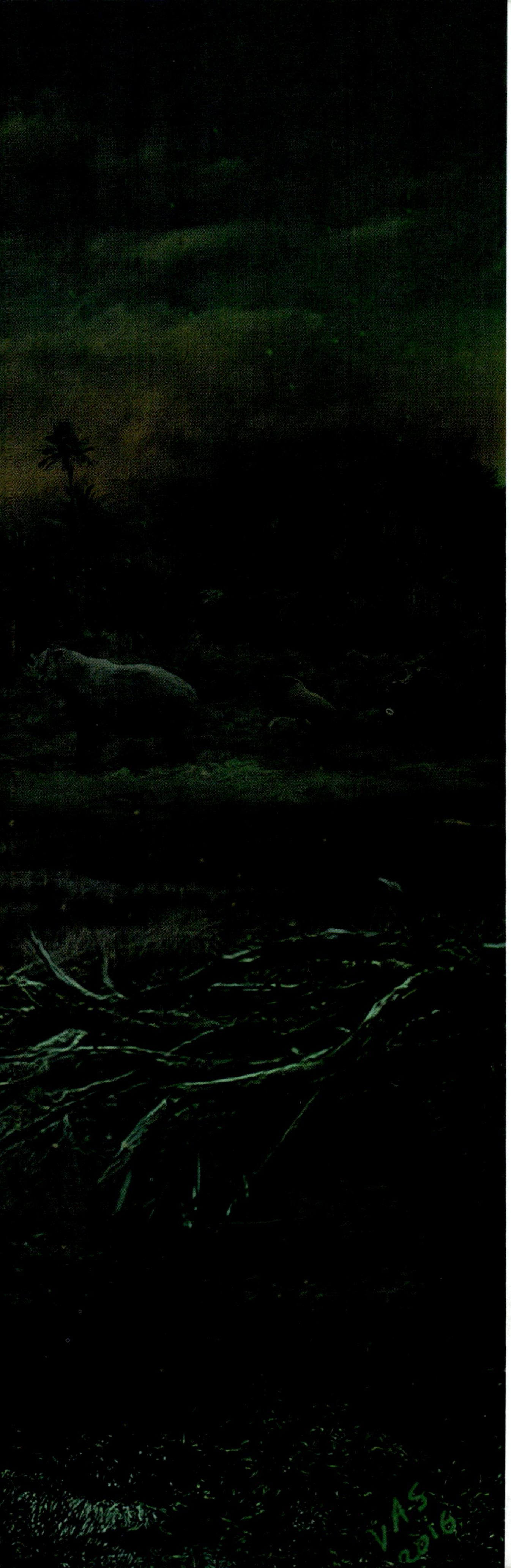

A great deal of your art features big cats in conflict with humans in "recent history". Is that a particular concern of yours?

My intent is to show the real nature of the predator. We should not expect them to be friendly, playful or cuddly – a perception quite widespread in popular culture. You can see this in the way that, when some accident happens in a zoo with a big cat, there are always questions as to, "Why did this happen?" even though this is quite an obvious risk when dealing with predators. These creatures are not our friends; they do not need our love, but rather our respect.

How much research do you do for your historical pieces?

Because of my longstanding interest in the depiction of animals in art, I have a rather good background in ancient and medieval history as well as in art history. But I still do not consider myself a historian, so I still do some digging with regards to some details, even if I usually have at least a general idea in advance about what a given painting will look like.

How did you build your profile as an artist? What sort of impact did social media have?

I grew up in a society where modesty was considered a virtue, so self-promotion is a huge problem for me. What I am trying to do is to attract a following by creating art that speaks not only to science-orientated people, but to a much wider demographic: outdoorsy types, hunters, people interested in archeology, history, literature, etc. Social media is a good way to reach all those people.

(Left) **Primordial Moon**
Digital, 2016
Two male *Uintatherium anceps* do battle during a territorial dispute. Utah, USA. Late Eocene.

(Right) ***Deinotherium***
Mixed Pencils and Digital, 2009
New anatomical reconstruction based on a 2001 study of the facial morphology and feeding behavior of deinotheres.

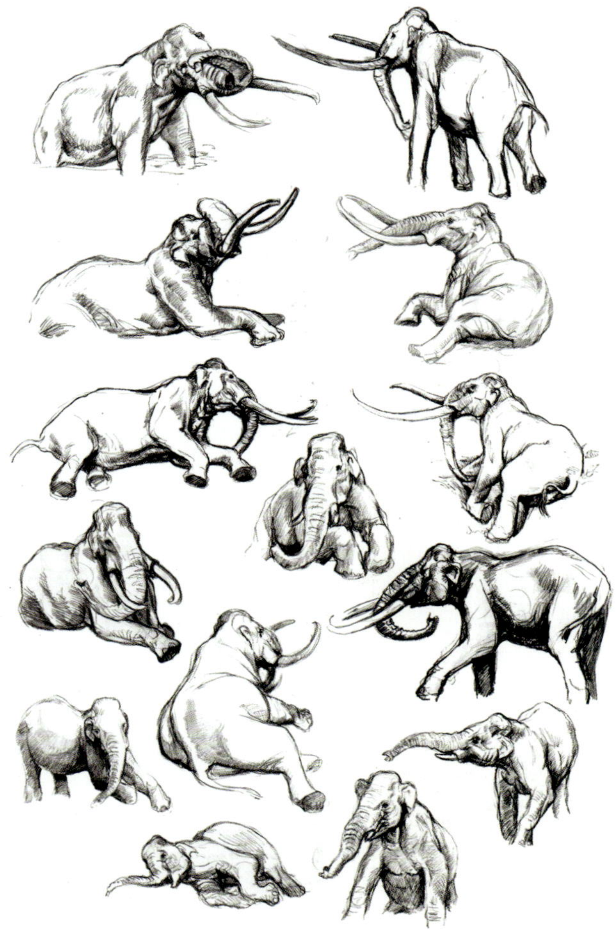

Mammoth Character Sketches
Pencils, 2009

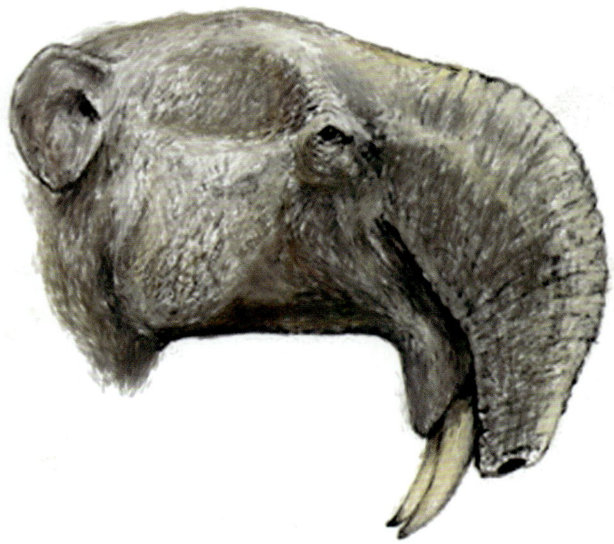

Anatids: a family of birds comprised of ducks, geese, and swans, and their relatives.
Archosauromorphs: an infraorder that broadly includes all reptiles other than lizards, snakes and the order Rhynchocephalia (represented by its sole living representative, the tuatara). The Archosauromorpha include dinosaurs (and, by definition, birds), crocodylians, pterosaurs, and a number of extinct groups.
Azhdarchids: a group of large-to-enormous pterosaurs, predominatly from the Late Cretaceous. They include the largest animals ever to take flight.

Bauplan: another term for 'bodyplan'; a selection of different features shared by the members of a broad group of organisms.

Ceratopsids: a family comprised of the horned dinosaurs of the later Cretaceous. It is broadly split into two subfamilies, the 'short-frilled' Centrosaurinae and 'long-frilled' Chasmosaurinae.
Choristodera: an order of extinct semi-aquatic lizards common throughout the world from 180mya, in the mid-Jurassic (and perhaps earlier) to the early Miocene (approx. 20mya).
Crypsis: the ability of an organism to avoid detection through the use of camouflage and other strategies such as mimicry or nocturnality.

Diapsids: tetrapods recognizable by the two holes (called fenestra) in their skulls; the grouping includes most reptiles, archosaurs and birds. Other groups have lost the high opening (represented by mammals and the extinct 'mammal-like' reptiles), the low opening (including many extinct marine reptiles such as plesiosaurs and ichthyosaurs), or both openings (seen in turtles, tortoises and their relatives).
Deinonychosaurs: a family of small- to medium-sized theropod dinosaurs that lived worldwide during the Cretaceous Period. Famous for the large 'sickle' claw on the second toe, many (if not all) were feathered.

Formation: a geological unit of clearly defined rock strata of a clearly defined age.

Galliformes: an order of birds that includes the likes of chickens, turkeys, quail, partridges, pheasants, and jungle fowl.
Gastroliths: stones found in the stomach of fossil animals. Well-preserved and articulated specimens reveal that the stones were swallowed and stored in the crop or appendix, and used to grind up plant matter rather than process it using teeth.
Gymnosperms: a classification for the group of non-flowering plants often called 'evergreens'; it includes conifers, pines, cycads, gingko, and extinct groups such as the Bennettitales.

K-Pg (or K/Pg): the term for the Cretaceous/Paleogene boundary; previously know as the K/T (Cretaceous/Tertiary) or K-T boundary. It is the geological layer that marks the transition between the Cretaceous Period and the Paleogene Period. It marks the mass extinction event that led to the disappearance of the dinosaurs and numerous other groups.

Maniraptorans: a clade of those theropod dinosaurs most closely related to birds (they are often referred to as 'non-avian' maniraptorans); it includes the Deinonychosauria, Oviraptorosauria, Therizinosauria, and the Avialae (extinct and living birds).
Megafauna: term for an assemblage of the larger animals in an ecosystem.
Melanosome: an organelle found in animal cells; they are responsible for the storage of the pigment melanin, which determines the color of an animal through the light it absorbs.

Ornithischia: a clade of largely herbivorous (but also including a few omnivorous) dinosaurs clearly recognizable by their beaks and distinctive hip structure. The group includes ornithopods, the duck-billed hadrosaurs, horned ceratopsians, armored ankylosaurs and stegosaurs, and the 'dome headed' pachycephalosaurs.
Ornithomimosauria: a clade of Cretaceous dinosaurs that bear a superficial similarity to ostriches, built for speed and possibly omnivorous.
Ornithopod: a clade of mainly herbivorous dinosaurs that includes the medium-to-large Iguanodontia and a number of small genera whose relationship is indeterminate.

Patagium: a membranous flap of skin; it is most closely associated with wing-like structures in the likes of flying squirrels, but also as true wings seen in animals such as bats and pterosaurs.
Phylogeny: the evolutionary relationship between different biological groupings.

Sauropoda: the long-necked, medium-to-giant herbivorous dinosaurs that first evolved in the Late Triassic and came to dominate many Mesozoic ecosystems during the Late Jurassic and Early Cretaceous.
Saurischia: the second group of dinosaurs. Previously thought to consist of the Sauropoda and the Theropoda, new studies have suggested that actually the Theropoda may be more closely aligned with the Ornithischia. The result is a new clade, known as the Ornithoscelida, a division that was originally proposed by Thomas Huxley back in 1870!
Sauropterygia: an assemblage of aquatic reptiles whose earliest members appeared early in the Triassic. The group includes the Plesiosauria and placodonts, and a number of wide and downright bizarre genera.
Squamata: an order of reptiles composed of all lizards and snakes.
Synapsids: a group of animals composed of mammals and those reptile groups closely related to them (informally known as the mammal-like reptiles). *See* Diapsids.

Taphonomy: the study of how an animal died and was subsequently preserved or fossilized.
Tetrapod: the superclass composed of all four-limbed vertebrates. The earliest members were those genera that represent the transition between fish and amphibians.
Theropoda: a group (more officially, a suborder) of saurischian dinosaurs that includes a broad line-up of carnivorous dinosaurs, ranging from the Coelurosauria (tyrannosaurs, birds, deinonychosaurs, and all their relatives) to some of the very earliest known dinosaurs such as *Eoraptor* and the Herrerasauridea.
Thyreophora: a clade comprising the known armored dinosaurs, the Ankylosauria and Stegosauria.
Trilobite: a huge and widespread group of arthropod invertebrates that became extinct at the end of the Permian Period.
Trochanter: a ridge or prominence on the femur.

Eon	Era	Period		Epoch (million years ago)	
Phanerozoic	Cenozoic	Quarternary		Holocene	
				Pleistocene (to 0.01mya)	Late
					Early
		Tertiary	Neogene	Pliocene (to 1.1mya)	Late
					Early
				Miocene (to 5.3mya)	Late
					Middle
					Early
			Paleogene	Oligocene (to 23.7mya)	Late
					Early
				Eocene (to 33.7mya)	Late
					Middle
					Early
				Paleocene (to 54.8mya)	Late
					Early
	Mesozoic	Cretaceous		Late (to 65mya)	
				Early (to 99mya)	
		Jurassic		Late (to 144mya)	
				Middle (to 159mya)	
				Early (to 180mya)	
		Triassic		Late (to 206mya)	
				Middle (to 277mya)	
				Early (to 242mya)	
	Paleozoic	Permian		Late (to 248mya)	
				Early (to 256mya)	
		Pennsylvanian (to 290mya)			
		Mississippian (to 323mya)			
		Devonian		Late (to 354mya)	
				Middle (to 370mya)	
				Early (to 391mya)	
		Silurian		Late (to 417mya)	
				Early (to 423mya)	
		Ordovician		Late (to 443mya)	
				Middle (to 458mya)	
				Early (to 470mya)	
		Cambrian		D (to 490mya)	
				C (to 500mya)	
				B (to 512mya)	
				A (to 520mya)	
Precambrian	Proterozoic	Late (to 543mya)			
		Middle (to 900mya)			
		Early (to 1600mya)			
	Archean	Late (to 2500mya)			
		Middle (to 3000mya)			
		Early (to 3400mya)			

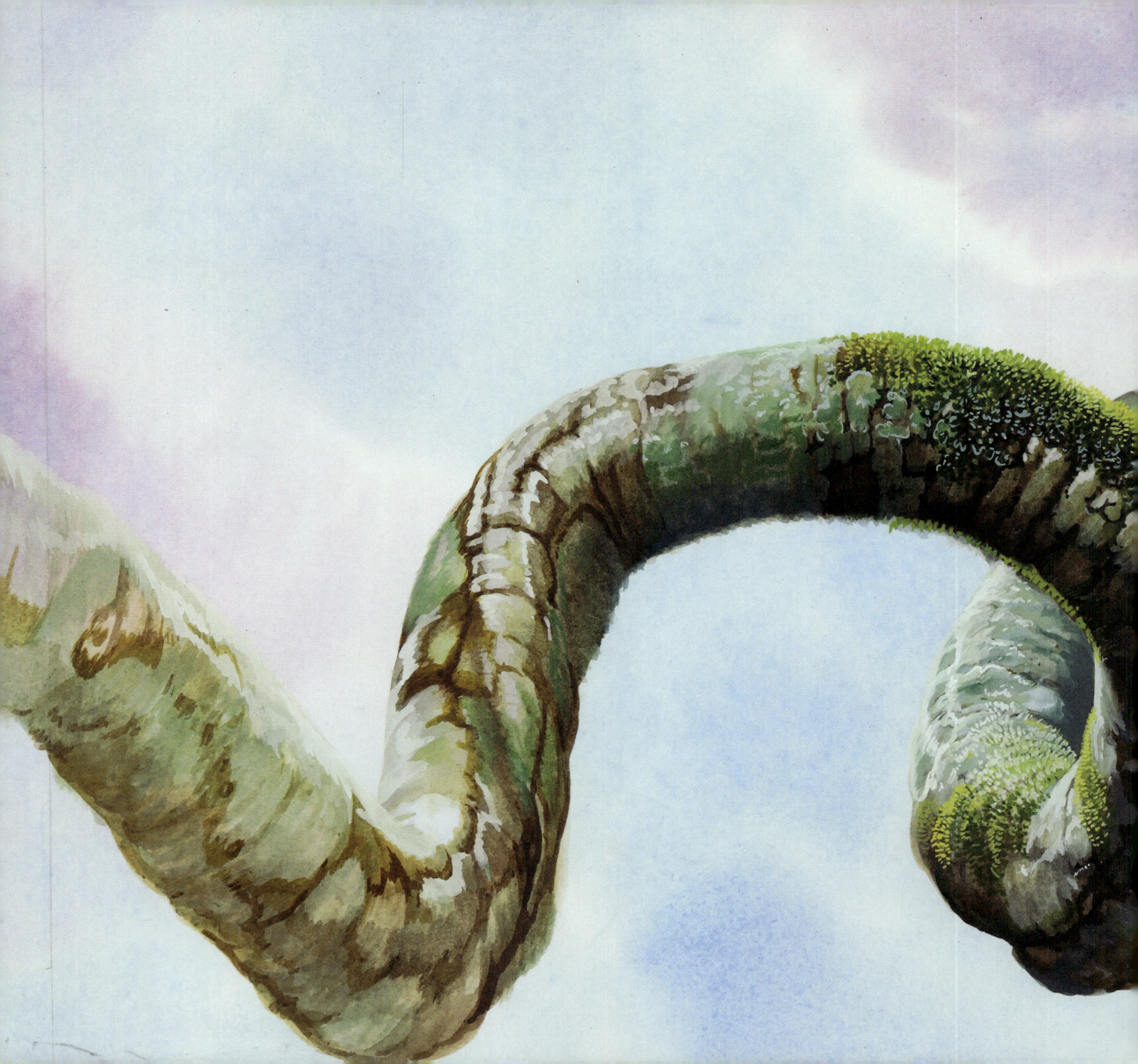